MW00881917

CAN'T GET ENOUGH OF YOU

YVES CHANG

Copyright © 2024 by Yves Chang.

All rights reserved. No part of this book may be used or reproduced in any form whatsoever without written permission except in the case of brief quotations in critical articles or reviews.

This book is a work of fiction. Names, characters, businesses, organizations, places, events and incidents either are the product of the author's imagination or are used fictitiously. Any resemblance to actual persons, living or dead, events, or locales is entirely coincidental.

For those whose love language is bickering.

PLAYLIST

Stuck With U - Ariana Grande, Justin Bieber
Stay Stay Stay (Taylor's Version) - Taylor Swift
From The Start - Laufey
Normal Girl - SZA
Photograph - Ed Sheeran
Soft Spot - keshi
Nonsense - Sabrina Carpenter
Taste - Ari Abdul
Baby I - Ariana Grande
Disillusioned - Daniel Caesar, serpentwithfeet
Joy - PARTYNEXTDOOR
Love Like You - Steven Universe, Rebecca Sugar
Kiss Me - Sixpence None the Richer

CHAPTER 1

HAILEY

MY HOUSE WAS FIRE. I COULD SAY THAT WITH CONFIDENCE, EVEN IF IT MADE ME cringe a little.

It was a house I really appreciated and grew up in. My parents had worked their asses off to finally be able to build their dream house, a large, two-story home with a wraparound porch and a backyard big enough for family barbecues and late-night bonfires.

Every inch of that house held a memory: the time I spilled an entire gallon of paint on the living room floor during a "creative phase," when my dad surprised me with a swing set in the backyard for my tenth birthday, and the dent on the wall by the stairs landing from when my Mom had gotten spooked by my Dad standing there in the dark and threw a toaster at him.

To this day, why he was standing there in the dark and why my Mom was carrying a toaster upstairs was still a mystery to me.

In short, it was more than just a house. It was a home. As cheesy as it sounds, it wasn't just wood and nails. It was us.

So I guess you could say that, all things considered, my house really was fire. Only now, you'd have to add the word 'on' to that sentence, because my house was on fire.

It was like a scene out of a movie. It all happened so fast that I could only fully register it now, standing outside on the dark street, watching my house go up in flames.

One minute, I was asleep, clinging to my pillow and dreaming... well, whatever I usually dreamed about. I was probably drooling, too.

Anyway, one minute, I was lying there, and the next minute, I was being violently shaken awake by my Dad in his white shirt and Superman pajamas, mumbling something about a fire.

At first, I thought I was still in the dream. I mean, how could I not? My dad, dressed like some bedtime superhero, standing over me, all frantic and panicked? I almost laughed, convinced it was one of those weird half-dreams you get when you're half awake.

But then I heard it. The crackling. The thick, choking smell of smoke hit me all at once, and the adrenaline kicked in.

He yanked me out of bed before I could even think, my feet stumbling as we rushed out of the house. I barely had time to grab my phone from my nightstand, let alone think about anything else. The moment I stepped outside, the heat hit me like a slap in the face, and there it was—the house I loved, consumed by flames.

I stood there, dumbstruck, watching the fire eat away at every corner of the place that held my entire life. It was surreal. Like, one second, I was safe and warm in my bed, and the next, everything was burning.

"Are you two alright? Are you hurt anywhere?" my Dad asked, running over to where my Mom and I were huddled together, sitting on the curb like the protagonists at the end of a slasher film.

The scene was perfect, actually. The chaos around us, the wails of the sirens, the flashing red and blue lights cutting through the smoky air. All that was left was for someone to wrap us in a warm blanket like they do in movies, hand us some cocoa, and tell us everything would be fine.

But no one was doing that, because this was reality unfortunately.

"I'm fine," I muttered, even though I wasn't sure that was true. Physically, I guess. Mentally? I didn't know how to process any of it.

"Fine," my mom echoed, but she sounded hollow. Numb, maybe, just like I felt. She looked as if she were in a trance, eyes fixed on what had once been our kitchen window, now shattered and blackened by soot.

I tried to imagine what was running through her head. All the memories she and Dad had made in that house, all the little details they had poured their hearts into, gone in an instant. It was brutal to watch.

"Mama! A fire!" a little kid who I recognized as our neighbor's youngest, pointed at our house which was engulfed in the dancing orange flames, the black smoke billowing in the air.

"Yes, baby, that's a fire! Good job! Yay!" his mom agreed proudly, clapping her hands together at her kid's marvelous intuition.

Well, there was that, I guess. Something good that came out of my house burning down. Yay.

I bit back a laugh, not because it was funny, but because I didn't know how else to react. Maybe I was in shock. Or maybe my brain was just desperate for something light to cling to in the middle of this nightmare.

The kid was still staring at the flames like it was a damn fireworks display. Heck, I wouldn't be surprised if he was gonna come back with some marshmallows from the amazement dancing in his eyes.

His mom, probably trying to make the best out of a terrible situation, gave me a sympathetic look before shuffling him away. But I could still hear the crackle of the fire, still smell the smoke that had seeped into my clothes, my hair, my skin. And with it, the sinking realization that we had nothing left. Everything we had was gone.

I shifted my gaze to my parents. They were both staring at the fire, but the way they did it was different, like they were looking at two separate tragedies.

My dad was pacing back and forth, running a hand through his hair, his shoulders stiff like he was fighting some invisible battle to hold it together. Every now and then, he'd ask the firefighters how things were going, only to be met with the same response or being told to stay back because it was too dangerous.

He'd always been the one with the plan, the fixer, but there was no fixing this. Every few steps, he'd stop and glance back at the flames, his expression stuck somewhere between anger and disbelief. Like he couldn't wrap his head around the fact that our dream home—the one he and my Mom had spent years building and saving for—was now a pile of ash.

Mom, on the other hand, was still. Too still. She sat hunched over, her arms wrapped tightly around her knees, her eyes fixed on the fire but not really seeing it. It was like she had checked out, mentally gone somewhere far away, trying to cope with the fact that her kitchen, her bedroom, her living room, basement—the rooms she had picked every tile and decorative piece for—were reduced to nothing.

I could practically see her replaying all those happy moments, the meals she'd cooked, the way she'd sing karaoke while hitting none of the notes, the flicks we'd watched in our home theater on family movie nights, now gone in the blink of an eye. She wasn't crying, but her silence said everything. Her mouth was set in a thin line, and the way her hands gripped each other, knuckles white, told me she was holding back the flood.

I wanted to say something to comfort them, to tell them we were safe, that we could rebuild. But the words felt hollow in my throat. How do you comfort someone when everything they worked for, every dream they had, was burning right in front of them?

I nudged my mom gently. She looked at me and forced a smile. "What is it, baby?"

I leaned in, hiding my mouth with my hand as I whispered in her ear. "Mom, look. That one firefighter looks like Chris Hemsworth."

She turned so fast I thought she'd hurt her neck. "Where, Hailey? Which one?"

She continued to crane her neck, staring at each of the firefighters one by one, searching for the supposed Thor lookalike that I had just made up. She scanned the line of them, her head moving like a pigeon. I couldn't help but giggle.

Her eyes lit up for a split second as she scanned the line of firefighters, the barest hint of a smile tugging at her lips. "You little brat," she muttered under her breath, swatting at my arm, but it was enough. "Don't do that. I nearly broke my neck."

"I didn't think you would look so desperately." My small laugh turned into a full fit of giggles now as my Mom rolled her eyes in feigned annoyance, a chuckle coming out of her, too.

That tiny spark of normalcy in the middle of the chaos made the overwhelming heaviness just a little lighter.

We sat there, giggling like idiots for a moment, the fire still raging behind us but somehow feeling less suffocating. For a split second, I forgot about the flames, the smoke, the destruction.

It was just me and my mom, laughing over something ridiculous in the middle of what felt like the end of the world.

My dad glanced over at us, eyebrows raised. "What's so funny?"

"Look, Dad has no idea," I whispered to Mom, which only made her laugh even harder. She covered her face, and I leaned into her shoulder as our Dad made his way over to us, the stress from the situation being replaced by confusion.

"What's going on with you two?" We were still giggling when Dad crouched down beside us, his eyes darting back and forth between my mom and me. "You look like you're plotting something, and I'm not sure I'm ready for that right now," he said, a playful smirk tugging at his lips despite the panic still shimmering in his eyes.

"Just sharing a joke," Mom replied, wiping a stray tear from the corner of her eye, the laughter barely masking the heaviness of her heart. "Nothing that needs your superhero intervention."

She nudged me playfully, and I could tell that for just that moment, we had both been reminded that laughter could exist even in tragedy.

My dad shook his head, but even he couldn't hide the smirk tugging at his lips. "You two are something else. Come here."

He pulled us into a tight embrace, his arms wrapping around us like a shield against the chaos surrounding us. At that moment, I felt the warmth of family amidst the icy grip of despair. I closed my eyes, clinging to the comfort of my parents as the fire crackled loudly in the background, a reminder of everything we had lost.

"Just stick together, okay? We'll get through this," Dad murmured, his voice steady but thick with emotion. I nodded, not trusting myself to speak. I wanted to believe him, wanted to hold onto that glimmer of hope, even as the flames consumed our home.

For the first time that night, it felt like maybe, just maybe, things would be okay. We'd lost so much, but we hadn't lost each other. And as long as we had that, we could rebuild.

We could find a way to start over.

CHAPTER 2

CALLUM

FUCK. WHAT TIME WAS IT?

I groaned as my eyes flickered open, the bright light streaming in through the windows immediately feeling like an assault. I rubbed my eyes, trying to shake off the remnants of sleep, but it was like trying to dislodge a stubborn itch.

I felt around for my phone, picking it up and staring at the big white numbers on my lockscreen. 11:32 AM. Great. I had already missed half the day.

I realized as an ache jolted down my back that I wasn't on my soft bed, but rather, laying on a floor next to a bed. A messy ass floor, with boxer shorts and a baseball bat within my reach, and in the corner, I could see some popcorn crumbs, too.

I pushed myself up, wincing as my body protested the sudden movement. My head throbbed like a bass drum, each beat sending waves of nausea crashing through me. "What the hell happened last night?" I muttered to no one, my voice raspy and thick.

I realized immediately that I wasn't in some messy stranger's room, but this was the room of my best buddy, Adam Parker. This was further confirmed by the posters on the wall of... anime girls and whatever else Adam was into.

So, stranger's room? No.

Messy as hell? Yes, unfortunately.

Adam's room always looked like a tornado had passed through, but today, it felt especially chaotic. I ran a hand through my hair, trying to remember bits and pieces of the previous night, but it was like trying to piece together a puzzle with half the pieces missing.

"Look who finally decided to join the living," Adam remarked as he walked into his room, his water bottle in hand. "I thought you'd be passed out on my floor all day, bro. How's your hangover?"

"I feel like shit. And you're such an ass, why would you make me sleep on the floor? I grumbled, looking down at my shirtless body. Why the hell was I shirtless? "Where the hell did my shirt go?"

"It's probably soaking up mud in Sasha's backyard still," Adam teased, his grin wide as he tossed me a wrinkled T-shirt from the pile of clothes on his bed. "Put that on before I start charging you for your night's stay."

I caught the shirt, squinting at the bright graphic on it that read, "I survived Sasha's End of Summer Bash." Great, I thought, another reminder of my shameful state. I slipped it over my head, the fabric feeling like sandpaper against my sensitive skin.

"Seriously, though, what the hell happened last night?" I asked, trying to piece together my fragmented memories. "I remember drinking, and then..." My voice trailed off as I racked my brain for details.

Adam shrugged, taking a long swig from his water bottle. "You were living your best life, dude. You kept doing all the drinking games, challenging everyone to dance-offs, you even made me carry you on my shoulders as you swung your shirt around like some... caveman. Then you ended up face-down on the grass. Thought you'd died. Almost cried, honestly."

"Shut up." I groaned, burying my face in my hands. That's right. Sasha Thompson, the self-proclaimed it girl of our school, had held her big end-of-summer party last night where literally half the town was invited.

I ended up going because why the fuck not, and I guess one thing led to another. "Why do I always let you talk me into these things?"

"Because you love it," he replied, smirking. "And it's not my fault you can't handle your liquor. I had to carry you home like a sack of potatoes. You should be thanking me."

"Thank you? For what, exactly?" I shot back, rolling my eyes. "For letting me wake up on your floor like a damn hobo?"

He chuckled, shaking his head. "You're lucky I even brought you back. I could've left you to fend for yourself at the party. Things got pretty wild."

I nodded, the memories flooding back—loud music, laughter, and the feeling of freedom before everything blurred into a hazy mess. "Wait, did anything crazy happen? Like, any fights?"

Adam's expression shifted slightly, a flicker of serious-ness crossing his face. "There was almost a scuffle between some of the soccer guys and the seniors from Oakridge. Grayson and Ibra were getting heated, and I had to hold them back. You were passed out when it went down."

Damn, I missed it? It was always fun getting into it with those guys from Oakridge, our rival school. And with senior year starting, me being named soccer team captain, I was itching for some good competition. "Good to know I missed the chaos."

"Yeah, you seemed more involved in getting to know the grass of Sasha's backyard, my friend," he said with a laugh. "At least you made an impression. I overheard some girls talking about you when I was getting drinks. They thought you were adorable—face-down and all."

"Great, that's just what I wanted. To be the guy who passed out at a party and is now the subject of girl talk." I rubbed my temples, trying to erase the pounding in my head.

"When are you not the subject of girl talk anyway?" he quipped as he grabbed some hangover relief tablets off his dresser. He tossed the box over to me, and I muttered a small 'thanks' before swallowing one.

"Oh, and Troy Duran was there," Adam said, his tone shifting.

Troy Duran? Oakridge's star player?

"For real?"

"Yeah, he was there. And you know how he gets after a few drinks," Adam said, leaning against the wall. "He was eyeing you like a hawk stalking prey."

"What a weirdo," I groaned, letting my head fall back against the wall. I should've been the one glaring at him after what happened at last season's final match. "What did he want, anyway? And why the hell is Sasha inviting Oakridge people to her parties?"

"She invites everyone, apparently," Adam shrugged. "And I'm not sure what he wanted. Just avoid him if you can. He had his teammates with him, and they were definitely ready to throw down."

"Fuck, I can't wait to just destroy them this year," I muttered, a smirk creeping onto my face. "Can't wait to show them who's boss on the field. They've had it coming ever since that game."

Senior year was beginning in two days, and the anticipation felt electric, a pulsing rhythm in my veins.

This was my last chance to make a mark on the field, to establish my dominance before graduation took me down a different path. The idea of leading the team as captain had me fired up, ready to crush every opponent that stood in our way.

"Bro, you're getting that look in your eyes," Adam said, breaking me from my reverie. "Just remember, it's not all about soccer. We still have a whole year of partying to balance out the training."

"Right, like you're one to talk," I shot back, shaking my head with a grin. "I bet you spent half the night on the sidelines, letting me be the star of the show. What happened to you, man?"

"Dude, I was just trying to keep an eye on you, alright? Someone had to make sure you didn't end up in a ditch somewhere." He rolled his eyes, but I could see the playful glimmer beneath his annoyance.

"Speaking of which, I should probably check in with my mom before she sends out a search party. You know how she gets." I stood, the aches in my body protesting the sudden movement again. My phone buzzed beside me, and I snatched it up to check the screen. Five missed texts from my mom, all varying degrees of panic.

"Shit, she's gonna kill me," I muttered, typing a quick response that I was alive and well, just a little worse for wear. I hit send and tossed my phone back onto the bed, looking at Adam. "How long do you think I can stall before she comes looking for me?"

"Well—" Before Adam finished theorizing, the doorbell rang.

I exchanged a glance with Adam, my heart dropping. "No way it's my mom already," I said, resignation lacing my voice.

Adam raised an eyebrow, the corner of his mouth twitching with amusement. "You sure she doesn't have telepathic powers or something?"

"Adam! Wake Callum up! His mother's here!" Mrs. Parker's voice echoed through the house like a siren, amplifying my headache.

I groaned. "This is why I didn't want to go to that damn party. She's going to have a fit."

Adam chuckled as we made our way downstairs. At the front door, I found my mom, arms crossed, her expression a mix of relief and exasperation.

"Callum! There you are!" she exclaimed, her voice a sharp mix of frustration and concern.

"Hey, Mom," I said, attempting a sheepish smile that probably looked more like a grimace. "I'm fine. Just, uh... spent the night at Adam's."

"Well, obviously!" She huffed. "I was worried sick about you all night! Good thing Mrs Parker here was considerate enough to let me know my son had stayed over instead of partying until dawn like some wild animal," she continued, shooting a pointed look at Adam.

"Sorry, Mrs. Reid," Adam said, raising his hands in mock surrender. "I didn't realize Callum would go full caveman at the party. We were just having fun!"

"Were you, now? Well, I'm sure I'll hear all about it," my mom replied, her tone firm but with a hint of humor beneath her annoyance. She turned back to Mrs Parker, gratitude replacing the features on her face.

"Thanks again, Leanne, for letting him crash here. We'll get out of your hair now," she said, fidgeting sheepishly.

"Don't worry about it, Jade. Now, Callum. You stop stressing your Mom out, okay?" Adam's Mom, who had definitely been in the same shoes as mine right now, said pointedly, glancing over at me with her arms crossed.

"Yes, ma'am..." I mumbled, nudging Adam hard with my elbow when he snickered at my defeated-sounding response.

As the tension in the room eased, my mom let out a heavy sigh, and I knew this was the calm before the storm. She always had a way of packing her lectures with enough concern to make me feel like a total screw-up while still reminding me that she cared.

"Get in the car, Callum," she instructed, her tone leaving no room for negotiation. I shot Adam a look that said, *Help me*, but he just grinned and waved me off.

"Good luck, bro!" he called as I trudged out the door, feeling like I was heading into a lion's den.

I climbed into my mom's car, the familiar smell of vanilla air freshener and her favorite coffee wafting around me. I buckled my seatbelt and braced myself for the inevitable lecture.

"Do you have any idea what time it is?" she began, glancing at me sideways. "You missed breakfast, and you know I was worried sick. You didn't even text or call. What were you thinking?"

"I was just—"

"No. No excuses, Callum," she interrupted, her voice firm yet laced with that motherly concern. "You're turning eighteen soon. You need to start acting like it. You can't just run off to parties and expect everything to be fine when you don't come home."

"I said I'm sorry," I mumbled, staring out the window as the trees flew by. "I didn't mean to worry you."

"Worrying me is exactly what you did. I didn't know if I'd have to call the police to look for you or if you were in trouble somewhere." She paused, taking a deep breath. "I just want you to be safe, Callum. You're getting to the age where these parties can turn dangerous, especially when there's alcohol involved."

"I know, I know," I said, running a hand through my messy hair. "I won't do it again, okay? I promise."

My mom sighed again, shaking her head. "Just be careful next time. You need to keep your priorities straight, especially with school starting soon."

We drove in silence for a few moments, the atmosphere heavy with unspoken words. I knew she meant well, but part of me just wanted her to stop worrying so much. It was exhausting trying to keep her from freaking out.

As we pulled into the driveway, I noticed an unfamiliar car parked there.

Only, it wasn't so unfamiliar. It was familiar enough that I could remember seeing it before, but not who it belonged to. It was a black Porsche SUV, and to my knowledge, no one from my family had a Porsche SUV. So unless they'd decided to give me a birthday surprise four months in advance, I could only assume that we had company.

"Mom, who's that? Do we have a visitor or something?" I questioned as my Mom pulled into the driveway, quickly parking her car next to the unfamiliar-yet-also-somehow familiar one.

"Technically, yeah," she replied vaguely as we began walking up the porch to the front door.

"What? What do you mean by 'technically, yeah'? Who is here—" I froze on the steps to our front door just as it swung open, and there she stood.

She was clad in an oversized sweater and even baggier jeans that looked like they were about to swallow her tiny figure up whole. Her dark, jet-black hair cascaded down her shoulders in waves, and her jade green eyes, which just always managed to infuriate me, gazed down at me, a mix of surprise and curiosity in her gaze.

Hailey Eller.

Why was she looking at me like that when I was walking up to the door of my own house? And wait, why the hell was she coming out of my house in the first place?

My jaw dropped. "You've got to be kidding me."

"Yeah, well, you were out last night, so we didn't get to mention it," my mom replied, her tone shifting slightly. "Hailey and her family moved in. They'll be living here for a while until their house gets fixed."

"What?!" I exclaimed, my mind racing.

"Surprise?" Hailey said, her voice laced with sarcasm as she shifted from one foot to the other, clearly just as surprised to see me. "Nice shirt, by the way."

I looked down at my shirt, my cheeks burning with embarrassment.

Great. Fucking great.

CHAPTER 3

HAILEY

"'I Survived Sasha's End of Summer bash.' Damn, she had t-shirts and everything? Talk about budget," I said as I read the bright red text that was on Callum Reid's shirt.

Callum Reid, aka my school's popular boy who somehow had everyone at his feet, stood before me in that ridiculous shirt, his arms crossed over his chest like he owned the whole damn block.

He wore black jeans that hugged his long, strong legs, and they might've even looked a bit flattering if they weren't covered in grass stains. His tousled, dark brown hair caught the late afternoon sun, and for a moment, I almost forgot the snarky remarks that always tumbled off his tongue like cheap cologne.

Callum and I didn't like each other. At all. It was more like a mutual understanding—him, the popular, carefree jock, and me, the uptight nerd who lived by rules. Our worlds collided like oil and water, each interaction leaving me frustrated and ready to blow.

We first met in freshman year, and it was like fate decided to set the tone for us from day one.

It was the first week of school, and I was navigating the maze of hallways, trying to keep a low profile. I had a tray full of food—pizza, applesauce, and some questionable pudding that looked like it could double as glue—when disaster struck. I turned a corner too quickly, and before I knew it, my tray collided with someone

That someone, of course, had to be Callum Reid.

The pizza, applesauce, and pudding went flying, landing squarely on his shirt. He froze, looking down at the mess that was now splattered across his chest. His mouth opened in shock as if I'd just insulted his ancestors.

"Oh my God, I'm so—" I began, trying to reach for napkins.

But Callum cut me off. "Seriously? First week and you're already trying to assassinate me with pizza?" His tone was sarcastic, but his eyes flashed with irritation.

"It was an accident," I said quickly, feeling my face flush. "I didn't mean to—"

"Sure, didn't mean to," he echoed, shaking the food off his shirt with a grimace. "Just my luck."

From that moment, it was like we were destined to be at odds. Callum had this way of taking every small interaction and twisting it into a reason to mess with me.

Every time we crossed paths, it felt like he had some new snarky remark ready. And it didn't help that he had a fan club around him by sophomore year—people who hung on his every word, laughing at his stupid jokes, which only encouraged him more.

After that first incident, things escalated fast. Anytime we encountered each other, we clashed.

One day in the library, I was quietly reading, and Callum showed up with a group of his friends. They were being loud, messing around with a soccer ball in the study area, of all places. I shot him a death glare, but of course, he didn't care.

"Keep it down, will you? People are actually trying to study here," I snapped, slamming my book shut.

"Oh, sorry," Callum said, not sorry at all. "Didn't realize this was your personal sanctuary, Eller. We'll try to respect the queen's peace."

His friends snickered, and I clenched my teeth, feeling my blood boil. Every time I thought maybe I could just ignore him, he found a way to irritate me all over again. It was like he enjoyed it, seeing how far he could push me before I snapped.

And snap I did. It wasn't long before we started arguing about everything. Locker space? He claimed I was "encroaching" on his side of the hall. Group projects? He'd make some excuse to get paired with me, just to argue over every little detail. Even during gym class, when we were on opposite teams, he'd find a way to turn everything into a competition between us.

By junior year, it had become almost routine. We avoided each other when we could, but whenever we were forced to interact, it was like gasoline meeting fire.

One time, we both showed up at the same science fair. I was presenting my project—an in-depth analysis of the ecosystem in our local pond—when Callum strolled by, barely glancing at my display.

"Wow, Eller, saving the environment one algae sample at a time," he said, hands in his pockets, his signature smirk on full display. "Real cutting-edge stuff."

I rolled my eyes. "I'm sure it's more useful than your 'study' on soccer ball trajectories."

"Hey, soccer saves lives," he shot back with a wink.

I groaned. It was like he lived to push my buttons, and no matter how much I tried to stay calm, he always got under my skin.

We were polar opposites in every way, and the more we interacted, the more it felt like we were destined to argue forever.

So now, standing in front of this house—no, his house, where I was about to spend who-knows-how-many months—I couldn't help but feel like the universe was playing some kind of cruel joke on me.

We'd spent years trading insults, and now we were supposed to coexist under the same roof?

I glanced at Callum, who was still standing there with that infuriating grin, like he was enjoying the situation way too much.

"Seriously," I muttered under my breath. "This is going to be a nightmare."

Callum crossed his arms, still leaning casually against the doorframe, but there was an edge to his voice now. "So, Eller, planning to crash at my place for a while? Can't wait for the endless debates about, what, the quadratic formula?"

I scowled, fists tightening at my sides. "Believe me, I'm just as thrilled about this situation as you are, Reid. And for your information, I was heading out. Don't worry, I won't be in your way."

He snorted, pushing himself off the doorframe and taking a step closer. "Yeah, right. Just don't start organizing the house or making color-coded charts for me and my brothers, alright?"

"Color-coded charts?" I snapped, stepping forward to match his stance. "Please, like you even know how to follow basic instructions."

Callum's smirk vanished, replaced by a narrowed gaze. "Oh, I can follow instructions just fine. What I can't stand is bossy know-it-alls who think they're better than everyone."

I felt my face heat up, not from embarrassment but from pure irritation.

He had this infuriating way of twisting everything I said to make me sound like the bad guy. "I don't think I'm better than everyone, just people who treat life like one big joke."

"Oh, come on, Eller," Callum shot back, his voice rising slightly. "Not everyone wants to spend their life buried in textbooks."

"At least textbooks will get me somewhere," I retorted, crossing my arms. "Unlike endless soccer practice and passing out at parties."

Callum's jaw clenched, and for a moment, I thought he might actually lose his cool.

But before either of us could escalate things further, a voice cut through the tension.

"That's enough, you two."

Mrs. Reid's voice was firm but calm, and she stepped between us like she'd done this before. She had the same dark brown hair as Callum, pulled back into a neat ponytail, and her light blue eyes softened slightly as she glanced between the two of us.

"Callum," she said with a warning tone, turning to him first. "You're not helping."

Callum rolled his eyes but took a step back, shoving his hands into his pockets. "Fine, fine. I was just—"

"And Hailey," Mrs. Reid added, turning to me. "I know this situation is hard for both of you, but let's try to get through this without snapping at each other, okay?"

I took a deep breath, feeling my irritation simmer beneath the surface. I nodded stiffly, though I wasn't entirely sure I could keep that promise. "Okay."

Just then, a small figure came racing out of the house, barreling straight toward Mrs. Reid. "Mom! Mom!"

It was Dalton, the youngest Reid boy. His dark brown hair was a messy tangle, and his light blue eyes were wide with worry as he threw his arms around his mom's waist.

"Dalton, what's wrong?" Mrs. Reid asked, her voice immediately softening as she crouched down to his level, brushing a hand through his unruly hair.

"I woke up and I couldn't find you," Dalton mumbled into her shirt, his voice shaky. "I looked everywhere."

Mrs. Reid bent down to ruffle Dalton's hair, her face softening into a warm smile. "I'm sorry, sweetie. And you were sleeping so peacefully, I didn't want to wake you up."

Dalton clung to her, burying his face in her shoulder. For a second, it was like the whole world paused, and I watched as Mrs. Reid stroked his hair, murmuring soft reassurances. It was strange, seeing this side of Callum's family—so warm, so close. It made my chest tighten with a pang of something I couldn't quite name.

After a moment, Mrs. Reid stood, still holding Dalton close, though his grip on her had loosened now that he knew everything was alright. She turned back to me, her expression gentler than before.

"Hailey, where were you going?" she asked, her voice calm but curious.

I glanced at Callum, who was still watching me with that same irritating expression, and then back to Mrs. Reid. "I was going to Staples," I explained. "I need to buy school supplies. All of mine were... well, they were in the fire."

The reminder of the fire felt like a punch to the gut, but I forced myself to keep my voice steady. Mrs. Reid's face softened with understanding, and she nodded.

Callum's brows furrowed, his confusion evident as he glanced between me and his mom. "Wait, what fire? What are you even talking about?"

Before I could respond, someone else did for me. "Hailey's whole entire house burned down!" Dalton shouted excitedly.

I stifled a laugh at how enthusiastically Dalton was explaining the whole thing, his wide light blue eyes sparkling as if this was the most exciting news he had ever shared. He looked up at Callum, eager to fill him in on every detail. "I heard the fire trucks came, and the house was all, like, 'WHOOSH!' And now she's staying with us!"

Callum blinked, still clearly processing this information. "Uh... what?" His eyes shifted back to me, this time with less irritation and more bewilderment. "Your house... burned down?"

Dalton bounced on his feet. "Yeah! It burned down, so there's nothing left!" His excitement made the whole situation sound like some kind of action movie.

In the few hours since my family and I had arrived here with nothing but the clothes on our backs, I'd already gotten to know Dalton and his older brother Nathan pretty well. Dalton was like a firecracker—bubbly, full of energy, and endlessly curious. He'd followed me around for most of the morning, peppering me with questions about everything from the fire to my favorite ice cream flavor. Nathan, on the other hand, was quieter, more reserved. He mostly stuck to the background, but I caught him watching with those same piercing blue eyes that all the Reid boys seemed to share.

And then, of course, there was Callum, who was... well, a jerk. "Wait, wait," Callum held up a hand as if trying to stop the train of information coming at him. "Your house burned down? That's why you're staying here?"

"Yes, Captain Obvious," I replied with a heavy dose of sarcasm, crossing my arms as I watched him struggle to catch up.

Callum looked over at his mom, who nodded sympathetically. "That's what I was trying to tell you, Callum. The Ellers are going to be staying with us for a while, until things get sorted out."

He blinked, clearly still processing everything. "Right..."

"You know what, Callum, why don't you take Hailey to Staples?" she said, her tone casual but firm. "You're free, aren't you?"

Callum whipped his head around, his expression incredulous. "Who said I was free?"

Mrs. Reid turned her icy blue eyes on him, and the shift in her expression was so subtle but so lethal that I almost felt the air in the front yard get colder. Callum immediately shrank under her gaze, his previous bravado dissolving in a matter of seconds.

"I—I mean, yeah, I'm free," he mumbled, scratching the back of his neck as he looked away, clearly defeated. "I'll take her."

I couldn't help myself. "Damn, Mrs. Reid," I said, feigning an exaggerated shiver. "Even I got scared at that."

Mrs. Reid giggled, her expression immediately softening as she was dragged back inside by Dalton, who was still bubbling with energy. "Come on, Mom! You promised we could finish the LEGO set today!"

"Alright, alright, I'm coming, Dalton," she said, laughing as she followed her youngest son into the house, leaving Callum and me alone on the front porch.

I stood by the door, crossing my arms as I watched Callum glower at the ground. My mind wandered for a moment, thinking about how drastically things had changed in the last 24 hours.

I'd gone from having a place I'd lived my whole life to standing here, in front of a boy who probably wished I didn't exist, waiting to go buy school supplies because everything I owned had literally turned to ash.

The Reid family seemed kind enough, though.

But Callum? Well, he was another story.

I glanced over at him, still brooding silently, and a part of me almost felt bad. Almost. After all, I was barging into his home, disrupting his life. But it wasn't like I'd asked for this, either. None of us had.

Finally, Callum stomped back into the house, muttering something under his breath as he went to grab his keys. A few minutes later, he came back out, jingling the keys in his hand, his face set in a scowl.

"Let's just get this over with," he grumbled, clearly irritated.

I raised an eyebrow, smirking at him. "Uh... you're still wearing that weird shirt."

Callum froze, and his eyes widened as if he'd just realized what he was still dressed in—the wrinkled T-shirt from the party, complete with the obnoxious "I Survived Sasha's End of Summer Bash" slogan in bold red letters, and his dirty, grass-stained jeans from last night's festivities.

A wave of embarrassment washed over his face, and I could see him mentally kicking himself. "Fuck," he muttered, turning red. He looked down at his clothes like they'd betrayed him, his scowl deepening.

I couldn't hold back the laugh that bubbled up in my chest. It wasn't just the fact that he looked ridiculous—it was the way his whole tough-guy attitude crumbled the second he realized what he was wearing.

He shot me a dark look, clearly not amused by my laughter. "I was going to get to it, okay? Just... shut up."

"Right, right," I said, still giggling. "Go get changed, Captain Party."

Callum grumbled something incoherent and stormed back into the house, leaving me standing there with a huge grin on my face. I leaned against the porch railing, shaking my head. As annoying as Callum could be, it was oddly satisfying to see him get flustered.

A few minutes later, Callum emerged from the house again, this time in a plain black T-shirt and a clean pair of jeans. He looked like a completely different person, but the scowl was still firmly in place.

"Happy now?" he grunted, jingling his keys again.

"Much better," I said, giving him a mock thumbs-up. "You don't look like total shit anymore."

He didn't even bother responding, just gestured toward his car. "Come on. Let's go."

CHAPTER 4

CALLUM

Out of all the ways I could've spent my afternoon, chauffeuring Hailey Eller around was at the absolute bottom of my list. If you'd told me a week ago that I'd be spending my time running errands with her, I would've laughed in your face.

But here I was, gripping the steering wheel like it might just save me from the next hour of irritation.

Hailey strolled down the driveway toward my car, her oversized sweater hanging off one shoulder, her dark hair falling in waves down her back. She opened the door, slid into the passenger seat, and glanced around with an appraising look.

"Damn," she said, letting out a low whistle. "This is kinda nice."

I didn't respond, hoping she'd just leave it at that.

But of course, this was Hailey.

"Too bad its owner sucks."

I tightened my grip on the wheel, turning the key in the ignition a little too forcefully. "You know," I muttered, backing out of the driveway, "I don't remember volunteering to be your chauffeur."

"Well, obviously," she replied, her voice dripping with sarcasm. "Your mom totally didn't force you or anything. I could feel the enthusiasm from a mile away."

I scowled at the road, ignoring the fact that she was right. Mom had practically demanded I take her, and that glare... yeah, I wasn't about to argue with that.

I shot her a glare out of the corner of my eye. "You know what, Hailey? You're lucky I didn't leave you standing in that driveway."

She chuckled, but the sound wasn't as biting as usual. "You'd miss me too much."

I let out a low groan, focusing on the road ahead. Of course, she found this whole situation amusing. Meanwhile, I was stuck trying to figure out how I'd ended up here. The universe had a twisted sense of humor.

As the car cruised through the streets, my mind drifted back to the scene at the house. Her house burned down.

It wasn't like I cared—I mean, not in the way people might think. It wasn't my job to feel sorry for her. But the fact that her entire house had gone up in flames was still gnawing at me, even if I hadn't been fully paying attention when Dalton blurted it out.

I glanced at her again, half-expecting her to say something about the fire, to bring it up in her usual sharp tone. But instead, she sat quietly, staring out the window, her face unreadable. I didn't get her sometimes. One minute, she was throwing sarcastic jabs, and the next, she was acting like nothing could touch her.

How does someone's house burn down and they act like it's no big deal?

It wasn't like I was dying to know the details, but I couldn't help but wonder how she was keeping it all together. If my house had burned down, I'd be a wreck. My mom would be a wreck. Hell, our whole family would be scrambling, trying to figure out where to go next.

"So..." I cleared my throat, feeling like I was stepping into dangerous territory. "The fire. That must've been... a lot."

She blinked, her eyes shifting over to me, and for a second, there was something softer there, something that didn't quite match her usual snark. "Yeah," she said, her voice quieter than before. "It was."

I wasn't sure what to say next, so I just nodded, the silence between us feeling heavier now. I wasn't trying to get into some deep conversation about her life falling apart. It wasn't my place, and honestly, I wasn't equipped for it. But there was something weird about seeing her so... unfazed.

Before I could think of anything else to say, she shifted in her seat, her expression softening just a bit more. "I guess it's one of those things, right? You just have to keep moving. What else can you do?"

That surprised me. I didn't expect her to talk about it at all, let alone with any sense of calm. Hailey was usually all sharp edges, sarcasm, and walls. But this? This felt different.

"Yeah," I muttered, unsure of how to respond.

We reached the Staples parking lot, and I pulled into a space near the entrance, killing the engine. For a moment, neither of us moved.

"Thanks for the ride, by the way," Hailey said suddenly, her voice a little softer than usual, though the sarcasm wasn't completely gone.

I glanced over at her, raising an eyebrow. "You seriously thanking me right now?"

She shrugged, unbuckling her seatbelt. "What, I can't be polite once in a while?"

I rolled my eyes. "Sure. And next, you're going to tell me you actually enjoy hanging out with me."

She shot me a look, half-smiling but with that same sharp edge in her tone. "Let's not get crazy, Reid."

Good. That was the Hailey I knew—the one who couldn't resist taking a shot at me no matter the situation. The one who made everything just a little more difficult. I wasn't about to let a burned-down house or a few awkward moments change how I saw her. She was still the same know-it-all who thought she was better than everyone else. And me? I wasn't about to start feeling bad for her, no matter how messed up her situation was.

"Let's get this over with," I grumbled, stepping out of the car. "I've got better things to do than play babysitter."

She snorted, climbing out of the passenger seat and slamming the door behind her. "Right, like what? Practice throwing a ball around? Such important business."

I clenched my teeth, refusing to let her get under my skin. "Better than spending my time organizing highlighters by color."

We walked into Staples, the cool blast of air conditioning hitting me as we passed through the automatic doors. Hailey marched ahead, like she knew exactly what she was here for and had no time to waste.

I stuffed my hands in my pockets and followed behind, glaring at the back of her head. *Great,* I thought. *Another errand with Little Miss Perfect.*

I wasn't about to start feeling sorry for her. I didn't get it, and honestly, I didn't want to. I'd keep my distance, do my part, and then get back to my actual life—the one that didn't involve chauffeuring Hailey Eller around town like some kind of personal assistant.

As we headed deeper into the store, I couldn't help but think: the sooner this was over, the better.

WE HADN'T EVEN BEEN INSIDE STAPLES FOR FIVE MINUTES, AND I COULD ALREADY feel my patience wearing thin.

Hailey was walking down one of the aisles, her eyes scanning the shelves like she was hunting for buried treasure. Meanwhile, I was trailing behind, feeling every second drag like an eternity. My head was still pounding from last night's hangover, my stomach growling in protest because I hadn't eaten a damn thing since waking up, and to top it all off, this place was the last place I wanted to be.

She stopped suddenly, grabbing a pack of mechanical pencils and inspecting them like they were some kind of ancient artifact.

"For the love of God, Hailey, they're pencils," I muttered, rubbing a hand over my face. "Can you just pick one and move on?"

She glanced over her shoulder at me, one eyebrow raised in that infuriating way she always did when she thought I was being unreasonable. "These aren't just pencils, Callum. I need the right ones."

"The right ones?" I echoed, disbelief dripping from my voice. "They're all the same."

She rolled her eyes, turning back to the shelves. "You wouldn't get it."

Of course, I wouldn't. Because apparently, the world of colored pens, fancy notebooks, and ultra-specific pencils was some sacred space that I, the lowly soccer jock, could never hope to understand. I stuffed my hands in my pockets and leaned against the nearest shelf, letting out an audible groan.

More time passed, and we'd been here for at least forty-five minutes already. Maybe an hour. Every time I thought we were close to being done, Hailey found some new section to investigate.

First, it was notebooks. I watched her compare thickness, page count, and God-knows-what-else for what felt like an eternity. Then it was binders. Apparently, there was a whole process to picking the right one. And now we were on pens, and it felt aa if we'd stepped into some never-ending school supply hell.

"Come on, we've been here forever," I grumbled, shifting my weight from one foot to the other. "Can't you just pick the first thing you see and call it a day?"

She didn't even turn around this time, just waved a hand dismissively. "If you're in such a hurry, you can go wait in the car."

I bit back a retort, not because I didn't have one ready, but because I knew it'd only drag this out longer. She was probably enjoying this, too—dragging me around like some kind of personal pack mule, knowing I couldn't ditch her without risking my mom's wrath later.

I shot a glare at the back of her head, wishing she'd just get it over with already. My stomach growled again, louder this time, and I pressed a hand against my abdomen, trying to shut it up.

The worst part was that I was hungover, and I could still feel the remnants of last night's disaster of a party swirling around in my skull. I hadn't had anything to eat since Adam's mom forced me out the door this morning, and it was only getting worse.

Hailey, on the other hand, looked completely unbothered. She hummed quietly to herself as she picked up a pack of colored pens, then put them back, only to pick up another pack and repeat the process.

"How are you even taking this seriously?" I snapped, unable to keep the frustration out of my voice any longer. "They're just pens! Literally no one cares what color you use."

Hailey turned to face me, holding up two nearly identical packs of pens with a look of utter concentration. "This one has smoother ink flow, and this one has finer tips. I care, Callum."

I stared at her, dumbfounded. "Smoother ink flow? What the hell does that even mean?"

She let out a small sigh, shaking her head like she was dealing with a child who just didn't understand. "You wouldn't get it. Some of us actually like being organized."

"Oh, sorry," I shot back, rolling my eyes. "I forgot you're the queen of highlighters and perfectly lined notebook margins."

She ignored me again, turning back to the shelf, still comparing the pens like they were life-altering decisions.

I leaned my head back against the shelf and groaned loudly. I could've been anywhere else right now. I could've been grabbing food, or better yet, recovering from last night in the comfort of my own bed. But instead, I was here, starving, tired, and stuck in what felt like a never-ending shopping spree with Hailey Eller.

"Are we almost done?" I asked, the desperation creeping into my voice now.

"Almost," she replied absently, grabbing yet another item from the shelf and adding it to her basket.

I checked the time on my phone, my frustration bubbling dangerously close to the surface. My stomach growled again—louder this time—and I pressed a hand against it, trying to will it to stop. "I swear to God, Hailey, if I don't get food in the next ten minutes, I'm going to pass out."

Hailey shot me a glance, her lips twitching like she was trying not to laugh. "Wow, you're such a baby when you're hungry."

I glared at her. "Yeah? Well, I wouldn't be if we weren't still here after an hour, looking at the same damn pens."

She rolled her eyes again, clearly unimpressed. "Alright, fine. We're almost done. Just need to check out and we can go. Happy?"

"Ecstatic," I muttered, pushing myself off the shelf and following her to the front of the store. My head was pounding, my stomach was threatening to stage a rebellion, and all I could think about was getting out of here as fast as possible.

At the checkout line, Hailey took her sweet time again, carefully unloading each item from the basket like they were precious treasures that needed to be handled with the utmost care. I stood behind her, tapping my foot impatiently, my arms crossed tightly over my chest.

Finally—finally—the cashier rang up the last item and Hailey paid, packing her bags with the same frustrating attention to detail that had plagued the entire trip.

"See?" she said as we stepped outside, her voice irritatingly chipper. "That wasn't so bad, was it?"

I shot her a look that could've melted steel. "Are you kidding me? We've been in there for a damn hour, Hailey. I'm hungry, I'm hungover, and I'm pretty sure I lost brain cells watching you compare pens for thirty minutes."

She chuckled softly, clearly amused by my suffering. "You're so dramatic, Reid. It wasn't that long."

I narrowed my eyes. "I'm never doing this again. Ever."

She shrugged, swinging the bags in her hands casually. "We'll see."

I stared at her, stunned. "We'll see? What does that even mean?"

She grinned, that same infuriating smirk she always wore when she knew she was winning. "It means we'll see if you can resist the next time your mom gives you that look."

I groaned loudly, walking faster to the car. "There's no way in hell I'm going through this again. You're on your own next time."

She just laughed, clearly not taking me seriously at all, and I could feel my blood pressure rising.

We loaded Hailey's mountain of school supplies into the back of my car, and I couldn't help but let out a long, frustrated sigh.

I'd survived, barely. But now, the hunger gnawing at my stomach had become impossible to ignore. Every second in that damn Staples felt like torture, and I wasn't sure how much longer I could hold out before I passed out or turned into a complete asshole—well, more of one.

I slammed the trunk shut and stalked to the driver's seat, my stomach growling loudly enough that Hailey shot me a sideways glance as she got into the car. I ignored it, turning the key in the ignition with more force than necessary. The second the engine roared to life, I knew exactly what I was going to do.

No more waiting.

No more shopping.

I needed food now.

Without a word, I pulled out of the parking lot and drove in silence, the only sound being the faint hum of the engine and my occasional stomach grumbles. Hailey, for once, was quiet. Maybe she could sense that I was at the end of my rope. Or maybe she just didn't care. Either way, I was grateful for the lack of conversation.

I drove for a few minutes, my eyes scanning the road until I spotted a familiar sign up ahead—a bright neon red one that read Burgers Burgers. The drive-through line was short, and the promise of greasy, glorious food made my mouth water. I could practically taste the burgers already.

I pulled into the line, my fingers tapping impatiently against the steering wheel as we inched forward. Hailey finally broke the silence, glancing at the sign and raising an eyebrow.

"Burgers Burgers?" she asked, her tone somewhere between amused and curious. "Real creative name."

I shot her a look. "Don't care what it's called. They've got food, and I'm about five seconds away from eating the dashboard."

She snorted softly but didn't push further. The line moved up, and soon we were at the speaker. I rolled down my window and leaned out, ready to order enough food to feed an army.

"Welcome to Burgers Burgers! Can I take your order?"

"Yeah," I said, my voice rushed, barely hiding my desperation. "I'll get three double cheeseburgers with bacon, a large order of fries, and—" •

I paused, glancing over at Hailey, feeling weirdly obligated to ask, even though I half-expected her to say something snarky. "You want anything?"

She shook her head slightly. "I already ate at your house, but... I'll take a strawberry shake."

"Right. One strawberry shake," I added, turning back to the speaker.

"That'll be all?"

"Yeah, that's it."

"Your total comes to twenty-two seventy-five. Please pull forward."

I drove up to the window, mentally counting the seconds until I could sink my teeth into one of those burgers. My hunger was practically making me dizzy now, and all I could think about was how good that food was going to taste. The employee leaned out of the window to take my card, but before I could hand it over, Hailey reached across the console.

"I've got it," she said casually, pulling a twenty and some bills from her pocket. "You drove me out here. It's the least I can do."

I blinked, surprised. I hadn't expected her to offer to pay, especially considering how much I'd complained the whole time we were at Staples. For a second, I almost refused out of sheer pride, but my stomach rumbled loudly, reminding me that food was the priority right now. Still, the whole thing caught me off guard.

"You don't have to—" I started.

She waved me off, handing the money to the cashier. "Seriously, it's fine. It's just a burger and a shake."

I frowned, still feeling weird about it. "Thanks, I guess."

She smirked, not even looking at me. "Don't get all emotional on me, Reid. You'll ruin the moment."

I grumbled something under my breath, but I couldn't deny that I appreciated it. Maybe she wasn't completely insufferable. Still, I wasn't about to admit that out loud.

The cashier handed her the change and a receipt, then passed me the bags of food and Hailey's shake. The smell of freshly cooked burgers and salty fries filled the car, and I felt my mouth practically watering on the spot. Without thinking, I grabbed one of the fries from the bag and stuffed it in my mouth, barely tasting it before I shoved another in right after.

"Hungry much?" Hailey asked, raising an eyebrow as she sipped on her strawberry shake.

"Starving," I mumbled around a mouthful of fries, already fishing around for one of the burgers. I drove around the side of the restaurant and parked the car, not even bothering to wait until we got back to the house. The second the engine was off, I tore into one of the wrappers like a wild animal.

I bit into the burger, and the taste hit me like a wave of pure relief. Greasy, cheesy, bacon-y goodness. I groaned audibly, not caring if Hailey was judging me. This was what I needed. This was life.

Hailey leaned back in her seat, watching me with an amused look as she sipped on her shake. "I don't think I've ever seen anyone look that happy eating a burger before."

I didn't even bother looking at her, taking another huge bite. "You don't understand. This is the first real food I've had since last night."

She let out a soft laugh, shaking her head. "You look like you're one step away from proposing to that burger."

I rolled my eyes, stuffing more fries into my mouth. "Maybe I will. It's been more dependable than half the people I know."

Hailey laughed again, the sound surprisingly light. I glanced over at her, still half-expecting her to make some kind of sarcastic comment, but instead, she just took another sip of her shake and looked out the window.

The silence between us stretched out, but for the first time all day, it didn't feel awkward or tense.

Maybe it was the fact that I finally had food in my system, or maybe it was that Hailey wasn't being completely insufferable for once. Either way, I wasn't about to question it.

I was too busy devouring the second burger to care.

CHAPTER 5

HAILEY

THE CAR WAS QUIET EXCEPT FOR THE SOUND OF CALLUM DEVOURING HIS BURGERS. I sat back, sipping my strawberry shake, feeling the cool sweetness soothe my throat. I watched the world pass by outside the window, the low hum of the engine and the smell of grease from Callum's meal filling the air.

I didn't know why I asked what I did next. Maybe it was out of boredom or maybe I just wanted to fill the silence with something other than the sound of him chomping down on food. Either way, the words slipped out before I could think twice.

"So… how was the party last night?"

Callum glanced over at me mid-bite, a fry hanging out of his mouth. He chewed for a second before answering. "Not one of the best ones, to be honest."

I nodded absentmindedly, half-expecting him to leave it at that. But of course, this was Callum, and nothing ever stayed simple with him.

He wiped his mouth on a napkin and gave me a sideways grin. "Why? The little nerd finally wants to go to a party?"

I glared, my grip tightening around my cup. "No way."

He chuckled, clearly enjoying himself. "What, afraid your textbooks will miss you if you leave them alone for a few hours?"

"Ha ha, very funny," I grumbled, rolling my eyes. He always had to go there. Like my love for books was some kind of punchline. "I wouldn't expect someone like you to get it."

"Oh, come on," he said, leaning back in his seat with a lazy grin. "You'd probably show up to a party with a book in your hand. Bet you'd sit in the corner, reading while everyone else has fun."

I opened my mouth to fire back with some retort, but the words got stuck in my throat. Suddenly, out of nowhere, a thought hit me like a punch to the gut.

My books. My book collection.

I gasped, my hand flying up to my mouth as my eyes widened in realization. My heart started to race, and before I knew it, my eyes were filling with tears.

"Oh no… fuck, no."

Callum immediately stopped mid-bite, his eyes narrowing in confusion. "Whoa, what? What did I say?"

I shook my head, barely hearing him, the weight of the realization crashing down on me like a wave. My throat tightened, and the tears I had been holding back since the fire threatened to spill over.

"My books," I whispered, my voice cracking. "My entire book collection… it was in the house. It all… burned."

For a second, Callum just stared at me, his burger halfway to his mouth, like he wasn't sure what to do. I could see the confusion written all over his face, like he was trying to figure out if this was some kind of trick or if I was seriously upset about it.

I blinked, wiping at my eyes with the back of my hand, but it didn't stop the tears from welling up. "I... I've been collecting those books for years," I muttered, my voice thick with emotion. "Some of them were signed. Some of them were gifts. Some of them were special edition... I—damn it, I didn't even think about them until now."

Callum shifted in his seat, his earlier teasing gone. He was watching me now with an expression I couldn't quite place —part concern, part confusion.

"You're... you're crying over books?"

His tone wasn't mocking. It wasn't even annoyed. It was like he genuinely didn't know how to react.

I wiped at my eyes again, feeling a mix of embarrassment and frustration. "Yes, I'm crying over books! You wouldn't get it, Callum. I collected them for years."

He stayed quiet for a moment, chewing slowly like he was processing what I'd just said. I could feel him glancing at me out of the corner of his eye, probably worried he'd crossed some invisible line with his teasing. But this wasn't about him. Not really.

"Shit," I muttered under my breath, leaning forward and pressing my forehead against the dashboard. My books, my prized collection of novels, all the ones I'd spent hours hunting for at second-hand shops and book fairs, were gone. Just like that.

I heard Callum shift awkwardly in his seat beside me, like he wanted to say something but didn't know what. He cleared his throat after a few seconds of silence.

"Uh, look..." he began, his voice hesitant. "I didn't... I mean, I didn't think—"

"Just... don't," I interrupted, my voice shaky. "It's fine. It's not your fault."

We sat in silence after that, the atmosphere suddenly heavy and awkward. I could feel Callum fidgeting next to me, probably wishing he could be anywhere else but here, dealing with me and my emotional breakdown over a bunch of books.

I took a deep breath and leaned back in my seat, forcing myself to calm down.

This wasn't the time to fall apart. I'd cried enough over the house already, and I wasn't about to lose it again.

Not here. Not in front of Callum.

He stayed quiet for once, I was thankful for his silence. I didn't need him trying to comfort me, noe did I think he was gonna comfort me anyway. A much more Callum Reid response would be "Ha! You're really that upset over books? You baby."

The conversation would then turn into me hurling every single curse word I could think of at him. Then I'd probably take that damn burger and smash it into his face. But thankfully, we didn't have to go that far right now.

The car was filled with the smell of burgers and fries, but the scent was now just background noise compared to the sudden ache in my chest. Callum sat there, awkwardly picking at the wrapper of his half-eaten burger, clearly unsure of what to say next.

After a long pause, he finally cleared his throat. "So, uh... how many books are we talking about here?"

I blinked, trying to rein in my emotions long enough to answer. "Over 300."

Callum's eyebrows shot up, and he glanced at me, clearly stunned. "Three hundred? Seriously?"

"Yeah," I muttered, still feeling that ache in my chest. "I was trying to build a collection. I heard once that if you have a thousand books, you can technically be considered a library."

I tried to laugh, but it came out more like a shaky exhale. "I know it's kind of dumb, but... it was just something I liked. Something I was working toward."

Callum stared at me, like he was trying to wrap his head around the concept. "I don't even think I could read 300 books in my entire life," he said, sounding genuinely baffled. "Did you actually read them all?"

I shook my head, biting my lip as the familiar feeling of disappointment settled in. "No. Not all of them." I swallowed hard, blinking away more tears that were threatening to spill over. "I was going to. I had this whole system. A TBR pile and everything."

Callum looked at me like I'd just spoken a foreign language. "A TBR?"

"To be read," I explained, my voice starting to tremble again. "It's, like, a list of books I was planning to read. I had so many I wanted to get through, but..."

But I never would now. Because they were gone.

I couldn't finish the thought. The tears were already burning at the back of my eyes, and I pressed the heels of my palms against them, trying to stop the flood before it started again. I didn't want to cry, not here, not in front of Callum, but it was too late. The reality of it all was sinking in, and I couldn't stop it.

"It's not just the books," I whispered, my voice barely audible. "I lost... everything."

Callum was quiet beside me, and I could feel his discomfort, his confusion, but I couldn't stop myself now. The words kept tumbling out, one after the other, like I was trying to get it all out before the weight of it crushed me.

"All my clothes, all my childhood stuff... photos, gifts, everything I've ever collected. It's all gone." My voice cracked, and I shook my head, my chest tightening with every breath. "I didn't even realize it until now."

I looked out the window, blinking rapidly as the tears spilled over, one by one. I wasn't just crying about the books anymore. It was all of it—the photos of my family, the mementos I'd kept from when I was a kid, the clothes that held memories of important moments in my life.

Even the little things I hadn't thought about until now. They were all gone, reduced to ash and rubble.

For a moment, the only sound in the car was the soft hum of the engine and the distant chatter of the drive-through workers inside Burgers Burgers. Callum didn't say anything, and I didn't expect him to.

What could he even say?

I wiped at my eyes again, frustrated with myself for breaking down like this in front of him, of all people. The last thing I wanted was for Callum Reid to see me as some weak, sobbing mess.

Callum shifted in his seat, looking like he wanted to say something but wasn't sure where to start. His fingers drummed against the steering wheel, and I could see his jaw clenching like he was thinking hard about what to say next.

"Look," he started slowly, clearly uncomfortable. "I... I get it, okay? I mean, no, I don't really get it, but... that's a lot of stuff to lose. Like, a lot."

His voice was quieter than usual, and for once, it didn't have that mocking edge to it. It sounded like he was... actually trying, as clumsy as his words were.

"But, I mean, it's not like..." He trailed off, rubbing the back of his neck awkwardly. "You know, it's not like you lost... people, or anything."

The second the words left his mouth, I could see the regret flash across his face. He immediately winced, probably realizing he'd said the wrong thing.

"Shit, I didn't mean it like—"

"I know what you meant," I muttered, cutting him off before he could dig the hole deeper. "And I'm glad no one got hurt. I am. But losing everything you've worked for, everything you've held onto for years? It still hurts, Callum. A lot."

He was quiet again after that, and I was thankful. I didn't need him trying to fix it. I just needed a minute to pull myself together, to process everything I'd lost.

I stared out the window, my breath shaky as I tried to calm myself down. I didn't want to be here. I didn't want to be sitting in this car, breaking down over things I couldn't get back. But there was nothing I could do about it now.

"Right," Callum muttered after a long pause. "I get it… kind of. I guess."

He didn't sound like he knew what else to say, and for once, I didn't blame him. This wasn't the kind of thing he could tease me out of or brush off with some sarcastic comment. He wasn't equipped for this, and I wasn't in the mood to make it easier for him.

The silence between us stretched out, heavy and awkward, and I leaned my head back against the seat, closing my eyes. I didn't know what I was supposed to do next. I didn't even know how I was supposed to move forward. All I knew was that the weight of everything I'd lost was too much to carry all at once.

"I guess I just wasn't ready for it to hit me," I whispered, almost to myself. "It's all just… gone."

Callum stayed quiet, not moving, not speaking. And for once, I was glad. There wasn't anything he could say to make this better. All I needed was a few minutes to let it sink in.

Callum stayed silent for a few more minutes, his hands gripping the steering wheel as he stared straight ahead. The weight of the conversation seemed to hang between us, and I could feel his discomfort radiating off him in waves. He wasn't used to this—dealing with emotions, handling someone else's breakdown. I didn't blame him, though. It wasn't like I expected him to know what to say.

Finally, with a heavy sigh, he turned the key in the ignition and started the car. The engine hummed to life, and we pulled out of the parking lot, heading back toward his house. The quiet settled back over us like a blanket, and I was left to my own thoughts once again.

I leaned my head against the window, staring at the passing scenery without really seeing it. My mind was still racing, still trying to process everything I'd lost, everything I hadn't realized was gone until now. It was like the fire had burned away not just my belongings, but all the little pieces of my identity I'd spent years collecting.

And just when I thought the conversation was over, Callum broke the silence again.

"So..." he started, his voice gruff, like he was trying to sound casual but wasn't quite pulling it off. "What about your camera?"

I blinked, confused. "My camera?"

"Yeah," Callum grumbled, clearly annoyed at having to explain himself. "Don't you, like, do photography and shit? You know... taking pictures of, I don't know, trees and clouds or whatever?"

I couldn't help it—I chuckled. Photography. I hadn't thought about that in years. It was something I'd picked up in freshman year, back when I was still trying to figure out who I was, what I liked, what I wanted to do. I'd loved it at first, wandering around with my camera, capturing little moments of life that everyone else seemed to miss.

But somewhere along the way, I'd dropped it.

I glanced at him, raising an eyebrow. "You still remember that?"

He shrugged, his eyes still fixed on the road. "I don't know. I just... I thought you were into it. So, did you lose your camera in the fire or what?"

I laughed softly, shaking my head. "Well, yeah. But I stopped doing photography a long time ago. Sophomore year, actually."

"Why?" he asked, sounding genuinely curious for once. "You were always walking around with that thing, snapping pictures of everything."

His words made me smile, but it wasn't a happy memory. "Yeah, well, it wasn't because I didn't like it. I loved photography. It was… the people."

Callum raised an eyebrow, glancing at me. "What people?"

I sighed, resting my head back against the seat. "People at school. They thought it was weird. They'd see me walking around, taking pictures of random stuff, and they'd call me 'photo girl' or make fun of me for it. It wasn't like it hurt my feelings or anything. It was just… fucking annoying. They wouldn't leave me alone."

I glanced over at him pointedly. "And you were one of those people."

His expression flickered, like he wasn't sure if he should deny it or laugh it off. "Wait… I made fun of you for that?"

I nodded, a small smile tugging at the corner of my mouth. "Yup. You and your friends thought it was hilarious."

Callum frowned, his brow furrowing in thought as he tried to remember. "When?"

I let out a small sigh, knowing exactly when it had happened. The memory was still clear in my mind, not because it had hurt me, but because it had been one of those moments that solidified my decision to stop altogether.

It was lunchtime, and the school courtyard was buzzing with the usual chaos—people milling around, laughing, eating, throwing a football back and forth, shouting over each other. I had my camera slung over my shoulder, like I always did. It was something I'd saved up for, a used DSLR I'd found at a second-hand shop.

I loved that camera. It made me feel like I could capture the world, freeze moments in time that everyone else seemed to miss.

I walked around the courtyard, snapping pictures of the way the sunlight hit the trees, the way the shadows danced across the grass, the little details that most people walked right past. It was peaceful, and it made me happy in a way that was hard to explain.

That is, until I heard the voices.

"Hey, check it out, it's photo girl!"

I froze, my grip tightening on the camera as I turned toward the group of guys sitting at one of the picnic tables. Callum was among them, lounging with his friends, a smirk plastered on his face. His soccer buddies were with him, all laughing and nudging each other like they were in on some private joke.

Callum grinned, leaning back in his seat with that infuriating look he always had, like he owned the world. "Probably taking pictures of people's shoes. You know, artsy shit."

His friends erupted into laughter, and I could feel my face heating up with frustration. It wasn't the first time they'd made comments like that, and I knew it wouldn't be the last. But that day? I'd had enough.

I took a deep breath, my fingers tightening around the camera strap as I walked over to their table. I could feel all of them watching me, waiting for me to slink away or get embarrassed, but I wasn't in the mood to give them the satisfaction.

I stopped right in front of Callum, glaring down at him. "At least I'm doing something I care about," I said, my voice steady despite the anger boiling inside me. "You guys just sit here, making fun of people because you have nothing better to do. So, what does that say about you?"

Callum's smirk faltered for a second, and I could see his friends exchange awkward glances, like they hadn't expected me to stand up for myself. One of them muttered something under his breath, and Callum's expression shifted into something closer to annoyance than amusement.

"Relax, Eller," he muttered, sitting up straighter. "We're just messing around."

"Yeah, well, maybe you should find a better hobby," I shot back, turning on my heel and walking away before they could say anything else.

As I walked off, my heart was pounding in my chest, my palms sweaty from the adrenaline. I'd stood up to them, but the moment didn't feel as triumphant as I'd hoped.

The teasing had continued after that, maybe even more than before, and after a while, it just got exhausting.

It wasn't that their words got to me. Not really. I wasn't that fragile. But having to deal with it every day, the constant comments, the whispers, the stares... it was annoying. I'd wanted to take pictures because I loved it, but they'd made it so hard to enjoy.

So, eventually, I'd stopped. I'd put the camera away and decided it wasn't worth it anymore.

"That's why I stopped," I said, my voice quiet as I stared out the window. "Not because I didn't like photography. It was just... too much. People wouldn't leave me alone. 'Photo girl,' 'camera nerd,' whatever. It wasn't that it hurt, it was just... exhausting."

Callum was quiet for a long moment, and I could feel him glancing at me out of the corner of his eye. I could tell he was thinking, probably trying to figure out what to say next. But for once, he didn't have some quick, sarcastic comeback.

He just drove, the hum of the car engine filling the silence between us.

"I didn't know it was like that," he finally muttered, his voice low. "I guess I didn't think about it."

I shrugged, feeling a mix of emotions wash over me. "It's whatever. It's in the past."

Callum didn't say anything after that, and for once, I didn't mind the silence. I didn't expect him to apologize or make things right. It was just part of high school, part of being different in a world where everyone wanted you to fit in.

But as we continued down the road, I couldn't help but wonder if maybe—just maybe—he was starting to see me as something other than the nerd he'd spent years teasing.

Maybe.

CHAPTER 6
HAILEY

THE PAST FEW DAYS HAD BEEN A BLUR OF PAPERWORK, ERRANDS, AND uncomfortable conversations with my parents. Between replacing important documents at various agencies, buying new clothes, and figuring out how to piece our lives back together, I hadn't had much time to think about anything other than survival.

We'd moved into the Reids' house, which, as chaotic as it was, had a certain warmth to it.

My parents were staying in the upstairs guest room, while I'd taken the basement bedroom. To be honest, I was grateful for that. The basement was quiet, private—my own little corner away from the chaos of the upstairs world. I mostly had it to myself, which was a small blessing in the middle of everything falling apart.

The room itself wasn't bad. It had a big window that let in natural light during the day, and the walls were painted a soft gray that made it feel a little more like home. There was a small bathroom down here, too, and a TV mounted on the wall that I'd already claimed as mine.

Honestly, if it weren't for the circumstances that brought me here, I'd probably consider it a pretty sweet setup. My parents, on the other hand, were still adjusting. They were trying their best to keep things normal, but I could see the strain on their faces every time we sat down for dinner.

The Reids had been nothing but welcoming, but it was still weird—sitting around their table like some big dysfunctional family, passing plates of food while everyone pretended that things weren't completely upside down.

Nathan and Dalton were pretty easy to get along with. Nathan kept to himself most of the time, and Dalton was always bubbling with energy, trying to make me laugh or asking me a million questions about anything and everything. How do planes fly? How are clouds made? Where do babies come from? Honestly, I kind of liked the distraction.

Then there was Callum.

After that day in the car, when we'd had that weird, uncomfortable conversation about my books and my photography, Callum had barely spoken to me. Not that I cared. He wasn't exactly someone I was dying to talk to, anyway. It's not like we were friends now just because I had a mini-breakdown in front of him.

But there was something... odd about the way he'd distanced himself. He didn't go out of his way to avoid me, but he also didn't make any effort to talk to me. It was like he was perfectly content to go back to pretending I didn't exist.

And that was fine with me. There were days I wished he didn't exist either, so. I didn't pay much attention to what Callum was doing, anyway. He had his own life, and I had mine —what little of it was left, at least. I'd see him at meals, sitting across from me with his head down, shoveling food into his mouth like he was in a hurry to finish and leave to go to the gym with his bros or practice soccer or whatever the hell it was that Callum Reid did in his spare time.

Occasionally, I'd catch him looking at me, but the second I glanced in his direction, he'd look away as if he would turn to stone when we made eye contact. It was weird, but I wasn't going to waste my time trying to figure it out. I had more important things to worry about than whatever was going on in Callum's head. Still, the meals were a bit... uncomfortable. Every dinner felt like a performance, where we all tried to act normal despite the fact that my entire life had literally gone up in flames.

My parents would make small talk with Mr. and Mrs. Reid, exchanging polite conversation about work, the weather, anything to keep from acknowledging the elephant in the room. Dalton would always chatter away, asking me about school or soccer or whatever random thought popped into his head, while Nathan sat quietly, observing everything but rarely saying a word. And Callum? He was always there, sitting across from me, saying nothing.

After dinner, I usually retreated to the basement, where I could have some time to myself. It wasn't that I didn't appreciate the Reids' hospitality—I really did—but the constant buzz of conversation, the forced smiles, the polite tension... it was exhausting.

I needed the quiet.

I needed space to think, to try to make sense of everything that had happened.

Though there were times when I did feel like some kind of troll that dwelled in their basement and feared the light or something.

I lay on my bed, staring up at the ceiling, listening to the faint sounds of the TV upstairs. My mind kept drifting back to everything we'd lost—our house, my books, all the little pieces of my life that were now just ashes.

My parents were doing their best to be strong, but I could tell they were struggling. My mom tried to keep a brave face, but I'd caught her crying more than once when she thought I wasn't looking. My dad was quieter than usual, his usually upbeat personality muted by the weight of everything we had to rebuild.

And me? I was just… trying to get through each day.

I sighed, rolling over onto my side and glancing at my phone. I had been thinking about calling Nala all day.

My best friend had just gotten back from a vacation in the Dominican Republic, and even though I'd filled her in a little about what had happened via text, it didn't feel real until I could see her in person. She was still on island time, jet-lagged and all, but knowing Nala, that wouldn't stop her from being her usual whirlwind of energy.

I was expecting her to come by the Reids' house today, the day before the first day of senior year. It had been a weird few days, getting used to the fact that I was living with Callum Reid and his family. I was still adjusting, and having Nala here would be like a breath of fresh air. She always had a way of making things feel lighter, even in the heaviest situations.

I was laying on my bed in the basement, scrolling through my phone absentmindedly when I heard a loud knock at the front door upstairs. A smile tugged at my lips. Right on cue.

I made my way up the basement stairs, my footsteps soft on the wooden steps as I moved toward the door. As soon as I opened it, there she was—Nala, standing on the front porch with her dark curls bouncing in all directions, her tan skin a few shades darker from days spent soaking up the sun. Her wide grin was infectious, and before I could even say hello, she barreled into me, wrapping her arms around me in a fierce hug.

"Oh my God, Hailey!" Nala squealed, squeezing me tight. "I missed you so much!"

I hugged her back just as tightly, the familiar warmth of her presence instantly making me feel a little less… lost. "I missed you too, Nala," I murmured, feeling a lump form in my throat despite my best efforts to push it down.

Nala pulled back, holding me by the shoulders as she gave me a once-over. Her brown eyes were filled with concern as she studied my face. "You okay? I mean... how are you really? How are your parents? Fuck, I can't believe it. That's so crazy what happened, girl, like, seriously."

I shrugged, trying to keep my voice light. "You know... we're hanging in there, or trying to at least, given the circumstances."

She gave me a sympathetic look, but didn't push further, instead linking her arm through mine. "Well, I need details, girl. Come on, we need a massive debrief like, right now." Her voice was back to its usual bubbly tone, and I could tell she was trying to lift my spirits. It was one of the many things I loved about her.

I led her down to the basement, the cool air immediately making the room feel like a sanctuary from the chaos upstairs. I hadn't done much to personalize the space yet, but I liked it for what it was—quiet, private, my own little corner of the world.

Nala plopped herself onto the edge of the bed, kicking off her sandals and crossing her legs as she leaned forward, eyes wide with anticipation. "Alright, spill. I can't believe you're living with Callum Reid now. Callum freakin' Reid. Of all people!"

I let out a groan, sitting down beside her. "Trust me, it's as weird as it sounds. It's not like we're suddenly best buds or anything. He's... Callum."

Those words in itself were self-explanatory. In my dictionary, Callum was basically a synonym for asshole, little shit, dickwad... and the list could keep going.

Nala laughed, shaking her head in disbelief. "Seriously, though. I can't wrap my head around it. You've spent the last few years avoiding him like the plague, and now you're living under the same roof. How's that even working?"

I sighed, leaning back on my hands and staring up at the ceiling. "I don't know. We haven't really talked much since... you know, since..."

Her eyebrows shot up. "Since...? Since what? What happened, girl, don't leave me hanging now."

I waved my hand dismissively, not wanting to go into the details. "It was just a conversation we had in his car. I kind of broke down about my books, and he... didn't know what to say. Since then, he's mostly just stayed out of my way."

Nala raised an eyebrow. "Oh, so you had a moment? Like a bonding moment?"

I shot her a glare. "No, it wasn't a bonding moment. It was an awkward as hell moment where he couldn't find it in himself to act like an ass towards me, and now we're both pretending it didn't happen."

She chuckled, leaning back on the bed beside me. "Still, it's weird to think about. You, Callum Reid, under the same roof. Isn't he, like, the last person you'd ever want to live with?"

"Pretty much," I muttered, picking at a loose thread on my shirt. "But I don't have much of a choice, do I?"

Nala was quiet for a moment, her eyes softening as she glanced at me. "I'm really sorry, Hailey. About everything. Seriously. You guys need to sue the hell out of the... gas company or whatever the fuck."

I swallowed the lump in my throat and nodded. "Yeah. I guess. It's been... a lot."

She reached over and squeezed my hand, giving me a small smile. "You're strong, though. So are your parents. You'll get through this. And if you ever need to escape the Reids' house, you know you can always crash at mine."

I smiled back, grateful for her offer. "Thanks, Nala. I might take you up on that."

She sat up suddenly, her eyes lighting up. "Speaking of the Reids... where's Callum, anyway? You know, since you're living together and all." There was a teasing note in her voice, and I could already tell where this was going.

I shrugged, trying to sound as indifferent as possible. "I don't know. Upstairs, maybe? I don't really keep track of him."

Nala let out an exaggerated sigh. "Girl, you are living in prime proximity to one of the most popular guys in school, and you're acting like it's no big deal."

"Because it's not," I said, rolling my eyes. "He's still Callum. Just... more annoying now that I see him more often."

Nala laughed, tossing her curls over her shoulder. "Okay, okay, I'll let it go... for now. But seriously, you've got to keep me posted. If things get... interesting."

I rolled my eyes again, but a small smile tugged at my lips. "Trust me, there's nothing interesting happening."

She grinned mischievously. "We'll see."

I shook my head, but I couldn't help feeling a little lighter with Nala here. Her energy was contagious, and for the first time in days, I didn't feel like I was suffocating under the weight of everything that had happened. It was a nice distraction from the heaviness of the past week, and for a little while, I almost felt like things were normal again.

After we'd spent a while catching up about Nala's trip to the Dominican Republic, the conversation naturally drifted toward the one thing that had been hanging over both our heads —senior year.

Tomorrow was the first day, and while part of me had almost forgotten that in the chaos of the fire and moving in with the Reids, the other part of me felt the weight of it pressing down, making my stomach flip with a mix of excitement and nerves.

Nala, who had been lying back on my bed after kicking her feet and recounting her encounter with the "dreamiest lifeguard ever," sat up suddenly, her eyes wide with anticipation. "Can you believe tomorrow's the first day of senior year?" she asked, practically bouncing with energy. "Like, we're finally seniors!"

I let out a shaky laugh, leaning back against the pillows beside her. "I know. It feels like it took forever to get here, but at the same time... I can't believe it's already happening."

She nodded. "I'm excited, but also... kind of freaking out. I mean, this is it. Our last year of high school. The year that decides, like, everything."

I glanced over at her, feeling the same mix of excitement and anxiety bubbling in my chest. "Yeah. No pressure or anything, right?"

Nala laughed, but I could see the tension behind her eyes. "Exactly. And I've barely started thinking about college apps, and don't even get me started on SAT scores. There's just... so much to do."

I sighed, feeling the weight of her words settle on me. "Tell me about it. I feel like I haven't even had time to think about any of that with everything that's been going on. And now, with the fire and living here... I don't know. It's just a lot."

Nala's expression softened, and she reached over to squeeze my hand. "You'll figure it out, Hailey. We both will. Senior year is going to be our year, okay? We're going to crush it."

I smiled, though the nervousness still lingered. "I hope so. We'll see. I just don't want to mess it up."

"You won't," Nala said confidently. "Besides, this is the year we're supposed to have fun too. You know, make memories, live a little."

"Right," I said with a half-laugh. "You mean, like going to parties and stuff?"

"Exactly!" Nala exclaimed, her eyes lighting up. "Come on, you can't let the whole 'school nerd' thing define you anymore. This is the year we let loose a little, okay? Go to some parties, make some bad decisions—"

I held up a hand, cutting her off with a smirk. "Bad decisions? Really?"

She laughed, nudging me with her elbow. "Okay, maybe not bad decisions, but you get what I mean. Senior year is supposed to be fun too. Not just stress and college apps and worrying about the future."

I smiled, feeling a small sense of relief wash over me. She was right, of course. Senior year was more than just the academic stuff. It was our last chance to make memories, to enjoy high school before we were thrust into the world of adulthood and responsibility. And as terrifying as that sounded, it was also kind of exciting.

"Yeah," I said quietly, nodding. "You're right. I don't want to look back on this year and feel like I missed out on everything because I was too busy worrying."

"Exactly," Nala said, giving me a triumphant smile. "So we're going to make the most of it. Deal?"

I let out a breath and nodded. "Deal."

We sat there for a few moments in comfortable silence, the weight of tomorrow's first day settling over us. It was weird to think about—how this was the last time we'd have a "first day" of high school.

The last time we'd walk into the halls of our school as students. And after that? Everything would change.

"I just hope it's not super awkward," I muttered, more to myself than to Nala.

She glanced over at me, raising an eyebrow. "Awkward? Why would it be awkward?"

I shrugged, staring down at my hands. "You know... with everything that's happened. The fire, moving in here... I'm sure people are going to be talking. And the last thing I want is for everyone to feel sorry for me or treat me like some kind of... charity case."

Nala's eyes softened, and she reached over to squeeze my hand again. "Hey, no one's going to treat you like that. And if they do, I'll shut them up real quick."

I smiled at that, feeling a little less anxious. "Thanks."

She nodded, her expression serious for a moment. "But seriously, Hailey. Don't worry about what other people are going to think. Just focus on yourself. This is your year, okay? You get to decide how it goes."

I nodded, though the nervous flutter in my stomach hadn't completely gone away. "Yeah. I guess you're right."

We sat there for a little longer, talking about the upcoming year, about classes, and how weird it was going to be to see all the underclassmen looking up to us like we were the big kids now. Nala's excitement was infectious, and by the time we wrapped up the conversation, I was feeling a little more optimistic about tomorrow.

"Okay," Nala said, standing up and stretching her arms over her head. "I should probably head home and get ready for tomorrow. Can't be late for the first day of senior year, right?"

I smiled, standing up with her. "Right."

As we walked back upstairs and toward the front door, I felt a weird mix of emotions—nervousness, excitement, and a little bit of sadness for everything that had changed in the past week. But with Nala by my side, it didn't feel quite as overwhelming. Maybe senior year wouldn't be so bad after all.

"See you tomorrow," Nala said, giving me one last hug before heading out the door.

"See you tomorrow," I echoed, watching as she walked down the driveway and out of sight.

As soon as I shut the door, I let out a long breath, already thinking about tomorrow. My nerves were still buzzing, but Nala had managed to make me feel a little more grounded. It was going to be fine. It had to be, right?

But just as I was about to turn and head back to the basement, a deep, husky voice from behind me made me freeze in place.

"You had company?"

I spun around, startled to find Callum standing just a few feet away, fresh out of the shower, his hair still damp and tousled, wearing nothing but a tight tank top and a pair of athletic shorts. His skin glistened slightly, and I could see the faint outline of muscle beneath the fabric. For a second, I was caught off guard, my heart skipping a beat at the sight of him.

Fuck, he's attractive, my stupid hormonal mind whispered before I could shut it up.

I quickly regained my composure, trying not to let my flustered reaction show. He may have looked like he walked straight out of a fitness ad, but this was still Callum. And I wasn't about to give him the satisfaction of knowing he'd caught me off guard.

I raised an eyebrow, folding my arms across my chest. "What is it?"

Callum tilted his head slightly, his blue eyes fixed on me with an intensity that made it hard to look away. "I was thinking," he said slowly, his voice low and deliberate, "maybe we should make some ground rules."

I blinked, caught off guard again. "Ground rules?"

CHAPTER 7

CALLUM

THE KITCHEN FELT QUIET, EXCEPT FOR THE FAINT HUM OF THE REFRIGERATOR AND the ticking of the clock on the wall. I sat back in my chair, crossing my arms over my chest, while Hailey sat across from me, looking equally uncomfortable but determined to act like she wasn't. I figured we might as well set some ground rules and get it over with, though I couldn't deny that part of me found this whole situation... amusing.

"So," I said, breaking the silence, "I've got a few rules to make sure we don't step on each other's toes."

Hailey raised an eyebrow, leaning forward slightly. "Oh, you have rules, do you?"

I ignored the bite in her tone and kept going. "Yeah. First off, no going into each other's rooms. You've got your space in the basement, and I've got mine upstairs. Let's keep it that way."

She gave a small, unimpressed nod, like that was obvious. "Fine. Easy enough. Not like I'd wanna go in your dump of a room anyway."

"It's not a dump, you little shit. And," I continued, "let me know if you're going to have people over. I'm not saying you need my permission or anything like that, but it'd be nice to have a heads-up if someone's going to be here."

Hailey rolled her eyes but didn't argue. "Okay."

I sat back in my chair, feeling like we were getting somewhere. These rules weren't complicated, but they'd make this whole living arrangement a lot easier. I'd just laid out the basics, but I was still waiting for her to push back on something.

"So, what about you?" I asked, my voice casual but with an edge. "Got any rules for me?"

Hailey leaned back in her chair, her green eyes narrowing slightly as she thought for a second. Then, she crossed her arms and looked me dead in the eye. "Yeah. Just one."

I raised an eyebrow, waiting. "Okay. Let's hear it."

"Keep this arrangement a secret," she said, her voice firm. "I don't want anyone knowing I'm living here. The last thing I need is to deal with your fangirls or whatever trying to get to you through me."

For a second, I blinked, surprised by how serious she sounded. Then, I scoffed, leaning forward with a smirk. "Fangirls? Really? That's what you're worried about?"

Hailey's expression stayed flat, though I could see the irritation flicker in her eyes. "Yes, actually. I don't need a bunch of girls thinking they can cozy up to me to get to you. It's not my job to play gatekeeper for your fan club."

I chuckled under my breath, shaking my head. "You know, Eller, I didn't think you'd be the type to care about that kind of thing. Sounds like someone's a little jealous."

Her eyes flashed, and I could tell I'd hit a nerve. "Jealous?" she repeated, her voice incredulous. "Ha. Jealous of what exactly?"

I leaned back in my chair, crossing my arms again, a smirk still tugging at my lips. "You tell me. You're the one making a big deal about it. What's the matter? Afraid someone's going to swoop in and steal your roommate?"

She let out an annoyed laugh, glaring at me. "Please. Like I'd ever be jealous of girls fawning over you. I just don't want the hassle of being involved in your... scene."

"Oh, so that's what it is?" I said, still grinning. "You're just trying to avoid the drama. Sure."

"Exactly," she shot back, her voice dripping with irritation. "I've got enough going on without having to deal with your groupies."

"Hey, it's not my fault if people like me."

She snorted, leaning forward. "Yeah, well, I'm not one of those people. So keep your ego in check, Reid."

I leaned forward too, locking eyes with her, the grin still on my face. "Oh, trust me, Eller. I wasn't worried about you joining the fan club."

Her lips pressed into a thin line, and for a second, I thought she might throw something at me. But instead, she let out a slow breath and straightened up in her chair, clearly trying to regain control of the conversation.

"Look," she said, her voice more measured now. "All I'm asking is that we keep this arrangement between us. The people who need to know, like Nala, already know. But I don't need the rest of the school finding out and making this into something it's not."

I raised an eyebrow, smirking. "Right, 'cause telling your best friend who just left the house doesn't count?"

She shot me a look, her green eyes flashing. "Like you said, Nala's my best friend. She's not going to tell anyone."

I shrugged, not really understanding why she cared so much, but if this was her big rule, then whatever. "Fine. We'll keep it quiet. But if one of my buddies asks, I'm not going to lie about it."

"Deal," she said quickly, as if she was relieved we'd reached some kind of agreement.

We sat there in silence for a moment, the tension still crackling between us. Even with the ground rules established, there was this constant undercurrent whenever we talked—like we were just waiting for the next argument to break out.

I pushed my chair back and stood up, grabbing a glass from the counter and filling it with water. "You got anything else, Eller?"

She stood up too, crossing her arms again. "Nah, we're done. For now."

I took a long sip of water, glancing over at her as she turned to leave the kitchen. "Better make sure Nala keeps that secret, then. Wouldn't want you getting jealous if the other girls start asking questions."

Hailey froze in the doorway, and I could see her fists clench at her sides. She didn't turn around, but I could hear the irritation in her voice as she muttered, "You wish."

I chuckled as she disappeared down the hallway, shaking my head. This was going to be interesting.

I WAS UP EARLIER THAN USUAL, BUT IT WASN'T LIKE I WAS GOING TO SLEEP IN ON the first day of senior year. This was it. The last stretch. And there was something about today that had my adrenaline pumping a little more than usual.

After pulling on my jeans and my favorite gray hoodie, I grabbed my bag and headed downstairs, ready to get the day started. I could already smell breakfast—my mom had probably been up for a while, making sure my brothers didn't starve. Nathan and Dalton were probably still dragging themselves out of bed, as usual.

I had to get to school early to help set up for the club fair. Coach had reminded us yesterday in the team group chat that as part of the soccer team, we were expected to help. To try to get new kids to try out or whatnot.

So, while everyone else was probably still hitting snooze on their alarms, I was gearing up for what would probably be a chaotic morning of hanging up banners and making sure our booth didn't look like total shit. Fun stuff.

As I walked down the hallway, I heard footsteps behind me. I glanced over my shoulder to see Hailey's parents, Mr. and Mrs. Eller, heading out the door for work.

They were both doctors, and from what I gathered, they worked crazy hours. I hadn't seen them much since they'd moved in, mostly because they were always at the hospital. Still, it was weird seeing them in my house. Not that I had a problem with them, but it was... different. Awkward.

Mr. Eller gave me a quick nod, adjusting his tie as he opened the front door. "Morning, Callum."

"Morning," I mumbled, offering him a half-wave.

Mrs. Eller smiled politely as she followed her husband out. "Good luck on your first day of senior year, Callum. Make sure Hailey stays out of trouble, yeah?"

"Thanks, and sure," I replied, althoutgh I didn't even know if Hailey of all people could get in trouble if she tried.

Hailey's parents were nice enough, but it was still strange having them around. The conversations were short, polite, and never really personal. We didn't really know each other, and it showed. I knew Mr Eller and my Dad were friends somehow, but that was it.

I walked into the kitchen to find my mom bustling around, flipping pancakes on the stove while scrambling eggs in another pan. The smell of butter and maple syrup filled the room.

From the living room, I could hear the faint sound of cartoons, probably Dalton watching TV, half-asleep.

"Mornin', Mom," I greeted, grabbing a glass from the cabinet and filling it with water.

She looked over her shoulder and smiled at me. "Morning, sweetie. You're up early."

"Yeah, I've got to get to school to help set up for the club fair," I said, leaning against the counter. "Coach wants the soccer booth to look good."

She raised an eyebrow, clearly amused. "Since when do you care about making things look good?"

I shrugged. "I don't, but Coach does."

Mom chuckled, shaking her head as she flipped another pancake. "Well, don't eat too quickly. I'm making enough for you and your brothers. Nathan should be down soon, and I think Dalton's still waking up on the couch."

I nodded, glancing toward the living room where I could see a tuft of Dalton's messy brown hair poking up from the back of the couch. I could tell he was probably sprawled out, still not fully awake yet.

I was about to sit down at the table when I heard the sound of heavy footsteps on the stairs. Nathan was making his way down, his face scrunched up with a mix of exhaustion and irritation, like he hadn't quite forgiven the world for making him wake up this early.

"Morning, Nathan," Mom called, sliding a stack of pancakes onto a plate.

He grunted something that resembled a "morning" and dropped into the chair across from me, his head practically falling into his arms.

I smirked, leaning back in my chair. "Ready for the first day of middle school, big guy?"

Nathan sighed, running a hand through his thick, dark hair. "As ready as I'll ever be." And that was that. It wasn't that I didn't care about his life, but we didn't exactly have heart-to-heart conversations either. He was at that age where he didn't want advice, and I wasn't the guy to give it, anyway.

Mom was always trying to get us all to connect more, but the truth was, I never felt like I really knew how to talk to Nathan, and Dalton... well, he was still a kid. I wasn't exactly the best at dealing with them, and I think they sensed it.

I was about to dig into my pancakes when Mom asked, "Have you seen Hailey yet this morning?"

I shook my head, chewing on a piece of bacon. "Nope. Probably still sleeping. Or getting ready."

Mom hummed, placing a plate of food in front of Nathan, who finally lifted his head enough to start eating. "Well, when she comes up, let her know there's breakfast for her. I'm sure she's nervous for her first day too."

I raised an eyebrow, swallowing a bite. "Nervous?"

Mom gave me a look, the kind that said I should know better. "Well, considering everything she's been through recently… maybe a little support wouldn't hurt, Callum."

I shrugged. I mean, yeah, the fire sucked. But Hailey was tough, and from what I'd seen, she wasn't looking for anyone to baby her about it. She'd probably snap if I even tried.

Still, I didn't argue. "I guess."

I stuffed the last of my pancakes in my mouth, wiped my hands on a napkin, and stood up. "Alright, I've got to head out," I said to my mom, grabbing my backpack from where I'd left it by the door.

"You're not going to stay for another pancake?" Mom asked.

"Nope, I've got to get to school early for the club fair." I shook my head as I gave sleepy Dalton and quiet Nathan a quick wave. I slung my backpack over my shoulder and was about to head for the door when I heard footsteps coming from the basement. I stopped in my tracks and turned around just in time to see Hailey coming up the stairs, still in her pajamas—a pair of old sweatpants and a baggy t-shirt. Her hair was a mess, and she looked like she had just rolled out of bed.

She blinked at me groggily, then did a double-take when she saw me on my way to the front door. "Uh… where are you going?"

I raised an eyebrow, holding back a smirk. "Uh… to school? Duh?"

Her eyes widened, and she ran a hand through her tangled hair. "Wait! You're not even going to wait for me? We're going to the same damn place!"

I let out a small laugh, shaking my head. "I have to be there early to help set up for the club fair. You're the one still walking around in your PJs."

She scowled at me, clearly not amused. "You could've at least told me. I didn't even know you were leaving."

"Well, now you do," I said, crossing my arms as I leaned against the doorframe. "Hurry up if you want a ride, or you can always catch the bus."

She groaned, throwing her hands up in the air. "Fine, fine! Just give me, like, five minutes."

I watched as she darted back down the stairs, muttering something under her breath that I couldn't make out. The basement door slammed shut behind her, and I sighed, pulling my phone out of my pocket and glancing at the time. I didn't have much of a choice but to wait, but she better actually make it five minutes or we were going to have a problem.

I leaned against the wall near the door leading to the garage, my foot tapping impatiently as I scrolled through messages from the soccer team group chat. A few of the guys were already at school, setting up the booth for the club fair. I was supposed to be there helping, but now I was stuck waiting for Hailey to get her act together.

Of course this would happen.

I could hear her rushing around downstairs, probably throwing clothes all over the place in a mad scramble to get ready. I smirked to myself, imagining her cursing me out under her breath for not giving her more of a heads-up.

Not that I felt bad about it. If she wanted a ride, she could've been up earlier.

After what felt like an eternity (but was probably closer to five minutes), I heard her footsteps pounding up the stairs again. The door to the basement flew open, and Hailey appeared, now dressed in jeans and a hoodie, her hair pulled back into a messy ponytail. She looked a little more put-together, but still flustered.

"Okay, I'm ready now," she said, slightly out of breath. "Let's go."

"About time," I muttered, pushing off the wall and heading for the door to the garage. "You almost missed your chance."

Hailey shot me a glare but didn't say anything as she grabbed her bag and followed me to the car. I could feel her annoyance radiating off her, but I wasn't about to apologize. I was already doing her a favor by giving her a ride in the first place.

"Just so you know," I said as I unlocked the car, "if you're not ready next time, I'm leaving without you."

She rolled her eyes. "Yeah, yeah. Next time I'll make sure to be up at the crack of dawn."

I grinned, opening the driver's side door. "Good plan."

She climbed into the passenger seat and buckled up, and I started the car. The engine roared to life, and I pulled out of the driveway, heading toward school.

"By the way," I said, keeping my eyes on the road, "I'm going to be helping with the club fair after lunch and pretty much until the end of the school day. I'm the soccer captain now, so… yeah, that's part of the deal."

I could feel Hailey glance at me, her eyebrow raised. "Captain, huh? They really trust you with that?"

I smirked, though a part of me knew she wasn't entirely wrong to be surprised. It was still kind of a big deal, even for me. A few weeks ago, I'd gotten an email from Coach Taz. It wasn't the usual "get ready for the season" message; this one was different. He'd straight up told me that he was naming me captain before the season even started.

Usually, Coach waited until we were well into the season to make that call, but this time, he said he believed in me, my skills, and my leadership abilities. He trusted me to lead the team this year, and even though I tried to play it cool, it hit me hard.

"Yeah," I said, shrugging like it was no big deal. "Coach picked me a few weeks ago. Guess he thinks I'm ready."

Hailey let out a short, unimpressed laugh. "Yeah, okay, Captain Reid. If I were the coach, I personally would've made you like, the ball boy or something."

"Yeah, well, good thing you're not the coach, since you don't know shit about soccer anyway," I rolled my eyes. "Anyway, the point is, I'll be at the fair until the end of the school day."

She shifted in her seat, looking thoughtful. "So, what? You're saying I should find my own ride home?"

"Pretty much," I replied, glancing at her. "Unless you want to wait around for me until the very end, which I'm sure you don't."

She shrugged, pulling out her phone. "It's fine. I'll just get Nala to drive me home."

I nodded, figuring that was probably the best option. "Good. 'Cause I'm going to be busy."

The truth was, I wasn't just busy. The club fair wasn't a big deal for most students—it was just an opportunity for all the different clubs and teams to show off what they were about. But for me? It was a chance to set the tone for the year.

Being captain meant more than just playing well on the field. I had to be a leader, someone the other guys could look up to, and today was the first real test of that.

Coach had made it clear when he emailed me that he believed in me, which was why he'd chosen me early. I wasn't expecting it—usually, he waited until the season kicked off to pick a captain—but when I saw that email, I knew I had to step up.

We pulled into the school parking lot, and as I turned off the engine, I glanced over at Hailey. She was sitting there, clutching her stomach a little, her expression tight, like something was bothering her. I raised an eyebrow, about to ask what was going on, but before I could open my mouth, my phone buzzed in my pocket.

I pulled it out to check and saw the messages lighting up in the soccer group chat.

Adam: *Where are you, dude?*
Ibra: *We need you here, like, now.*
Grayson: *The banner looks like crap.*

I cursed under my breath. They were already setting up, and I was supposed to be there to make sure everything looked halfway decent.

"Great," I muttered, shoving my phone back into my pocket. I looked back at Hailey briefly. Whatever was going on with her would have to wait—if it was even something. "I've got to go. See you later."

Without waiting for a response, I grabbed my backpack and dashed out of the car, heading straight for the school entrance.

CHAPTER 8

HAILEY

I WASN'T EVEN HALFWAY TO THE SCHOOL ENTRANCE WHEN MY STOMACH GROWLED loudly enough that I was pretty sure the entire parking lot heard it. I winced, clutching my stomach again. I'd rushed out of the house so quickly that I hadn't even had time to grab breakfast, and now I was paying for it. Hard.

Great, I thought, grumbling to myself as I slung my backpack over my shoulder and headed toward the doors. First day of senior year, and I was about to collapse from hunger before I even made it to my first class.

As soon as I stepped inside, the familiar sounds of the first day filled the air—excited chatter, lockers slamming, the scuffling of shoes against the floor. It was like the building itself was buzzing with the energy of everyone catching up after the summer.

Usually, I'd get that first-day excitement too, but with everything that had happened in the past week, all I could focus on was getting through the day without my stomach embarrassing me in front of the entire school.

I quickly pulled out my phone and sent a text to Nala.

Me: *Where are you? I just got here.*
Nala: *Just parked. Meet you by the cafeteria in five.*

I exhaled in relief. At least I wouldn't have to face the first day alone. Nala and I had been through every first day together after freshman year, so it was tradition at this point to compare schedules, complain about classes, and make vague promises about actually trying this year.

I leaned against a nearby locker, watching the stream of students pour through the doors as I waited for her. A few people I recognized from my classes walked by, waving or nodding, but it all felt so... distant.

My mind was still stuck in the whirlwind of the past week—moving into the Reids' house, the fire, and now, living with Callum freakin' Reid. I couldn't even begin to imagine how today would go, especially since I had no idea who I'd be stuck with in my classes.

A few minutes later, Nala's familiar face appeared through the crowd, her wild curls bouncing as she made her way over to me with her usual smile. She looked fresh and bright, like she hadn't just flown back from the Dominican Republic less than 24 hours ago. Leave it to Nala to somehow always look like she just stepped off a runway, even after a long flight.

"Finally!" she exclaimed, throwing her arms around me in a quick hug. "I thought you were gonna make me survive this madness alone."

I hugged her back, already feeling a little more grounded now that she was here. "You know I wouldn't do that to you. I'm just... starving."

Nala laughed, hooking her arm through mine as we started walking toward the cafeteria. "I'll give you some of my lunch later. You should've had something to eat at home, dummy."

I rolled my eyes, my stomach churning a bit at the thought of having Nala's lunch. Her eating habits were quite unique and... hard to get behind sometimes. "Yeah, I would've if someone had warned me that we were leaving earlier than usual. Stupid Callum."

Nala chuckled as we made our way through the sea of students, navigating the chaos like pros, and found a spot near the cafeteria where it was a little quieter.

I leaned back against the wall, pulling out my phone to check my schedule. "Alright, let's see what kind of hell we're in for this year."

Nala pulled out her phone too, and for the next few minutes, we both scrolled through our schedules, comparing classes and teachers. I frowned as I glanced over my list, noting the lack of familiar names in my classes. I had Mr. Warner for AP Lit, Ms. Yang for Calculus, and a couple of other random electives. I already felt a pang of disappointment.

"So... we don't have any classes together," I said, my voice flat as I looked at Nala.

She groaned, her face scrunching up in frustration. "Are you serious? Not even one?"

I shook my head, feeling the same frustration. "Not even one. I have AP Lit first thing, then Calc, and then that art history class I signed up for last year when I thought I'd actually care about being cultured."

Nala laughed, shaking her head. "Well, at least you can be bored and cultured at the same time."

I sighed, leaning my head back against the wall. "Yeah, great."

She nudged me with her elbow, giving me a playful smile. "Hey, look on the bright side. At least we'll still see each other at lunch, and today's only a half-day, so we have the assembly and then the club fair. We'll survive."

I glanced at her, raising an eyebrow. "You mean I'll survive. You're always thriving."

"Facts," she said with a grin. "But seriously, today's gonna be easy. Half-day, lunch, then assembly, and then we get to walk around and avoid all the annoying people at the club fair. Easy-peasy."

I nodded, feeling a little better now that we'd gone over the schedule. Nala always had a way of making everything feel less overwhelming. I was still nervous, but knowing that we'd at least have lunch and the club fair together made it a little more bearable.

I glanced back down at my phone, scrolling through the rest of my schedule. "Ugh, why don't have any classes together, though? I was really hoping we'd at least have one."

"I know," Nala groaned. "Who am I supposed to share my genius commentary with now? It's not fair."

I chuckled, pushing off the wall as we started making our way toward the main hall. The morning bell would be ringing soon, and we still had a few minutes to catch up before we had to split off to our separate classes.

We hugged quickly before heading off to our separate classes, and as I made my way toward AP Lit, I couldn't help but feel a pang of disappointment that we wouldn't be together for most of the day.

As I walked through the crowded hallways, the familiar nerves of the first day settled in. It was strange, thinking about how this was the last "first day" we'd ever have in high school.

I shoved my phone into my backpack and started walking down the hallway toward my first class, weaving through the sea of students.

As I passed by, I noticed a bunch of clubs were already setting up their booths for the fair later. Posters, banners, tables, and props were being put together as students buzzed around, getting everything ready. The buzz of excitement hung in the air, and it almost made me forget how nervous I was about the first day.

I glanced around at the various booths as I walked, trying to distract myself from the gnawing hunger still twisting my stomach. Robotics, debate team, drama club—they were all getting their displays ready for when the fair opened after the assembly. The whole school would be there, wandering around, checking out what each club had to offer.

As I walked further down the hallway, something caught my eye in the distance—the soccer team's booth. And more specifically, Callum.

He'd ditched the gray hoodie he'd been wearing earlier and was now only in a white t-shirt, his sleeves slightly rolled up as he lifted something heavy—a stack of equipment or some other soccer-related thing.

My eyes involuntarily drifted to the way his back muscles were straining under the thin material of his shirt, every movement making the fabric stretch and cling to him as his arms flexed. I blinked, tearing my eyes away for a second, then shook my head, annoyed with myself for even noticing.

Really, Hailey?

But before I could fully pull my attention away, I saw a girl approach him—a redhead I recognized from the cheerleading squad. She walked up to him with an easy smile, her body language open as she started talking to him. From the looks of it, they were just casually chatting at first, but then she leaned in a little closer.

I couldn't hear what they were saying from this distance, but it wasn't hard to guess what was going on. The way she lightly touched his arm as she spoke, her expression bright— yeah, she was definitely flirting.

And Callum, being Callum, didn't seem to mind. He gave her one of those laid-back, charming smiles that I'd seen him use a hundred times before.

I rolled my eyes and shook my head, quickening my pace as I walked away. It wasn't like it was any of my business, but for some reason, seeing it irked me more than it should have.

Maybe it was just the familiarity of it all—Callum getting attention, girls drawn to him like moths to a flame. That was his world, his scene, and seeing him in his element reminded me of just how different we were.

Whatever, I told myself, pushing the thought of him out of my head as I rounded the corner and headed toward my first class. I had more important things to focus on than whatever Callum was doing with his endless line of admirers.

I finally made it to my first class, slipping through the door just before the final bell rang. AP Lit. Not exactly the most exciting way to start the year, but at least it wasn't calculus first thing in the morning. That would've been a real nightmare.

As soon as I stepped inside, I instinctively gravitated toward the back of the room, finding an empty desk in the last row. I slid into the seat, dropping my bag onto the floor and letting out a quiet sigh.

The classroom was buzzing with conversation, everyone catching up with each other after the summer. I glanced around briefly, noting the familiar faces—some I knew from previous classes, others just from passing in the hallways. None of them were particularly interested in me, though.

I wasn't exactly a social butterfly. Actually, scratch that—I wasn't social at all. Besides Nala, I didn't really have friends. It wasn't like I had some big falling out with anyone, and I wasn't actively avoiding people. It just... worked out that way. Not many people wanted to talk to me, and over time, I'd stopped trying to talk to them.

It wasn't that I was anxious or scared of making friends, either. I wasn't shy, really. If anything, I was more reserved, more focused on my own stuff—my books, my schoolwork, my personal little world. People like Nala could effortlessly make connections, light up a room with their energy, but that wasn't me. I was okay with that, for the most part.

But it did mean that in classes like this, where Nala wasn't around, I found myself... hovering. Kind of like a shadow in the background, quietly observing everything while everyone else was busy with their friends and social circles. I wasn't invisible, but I wasn't really seen either.

I settled into my seat, pulling out my notebook and a pen, pretending to jot something down while the rest of the class slowly filled in.

I could hear snippets of conversation around me—talk about summer trips, internships, gossip about who was dating who.

The usual first-day chatter.

None of it was particularly interesting, and none of it had anything to do with me.

The teacher, Mr. Warner, walked in just as the bell rang, his usual tired expression settling across his face. He gave a halfhearted "good morning" to the class, then immediately launched into an overview of the syllabus, explaining what we'd be covering over the course of the year.

I nodded along, my pen idly tapping against the edge of my notebook, not really absorbing much of what he was saying.

I glanced out the window, my mind wandering. The first day was always like this—everyone catching up, buzzing with energy, and me just... floating. It wasn't bad, exactly. I was used to it by now. And besides, once the actual work started, things would settle down. I was good at that part—the essays, the discussions, the projects.

That was where I felt comfortable.

But still, there was this small part of me, buried deep down, that sometimes wished things were a little different. That I didn't always feel like the outsider, the one sitting at the back, watching while everyone else seemed to be part of something bigger.

I shook the thought away, straightening up in my chair and focusing back on Mr. Warner's lecture. *It's just another year, I told myself.* And as long as I make it through, that's all that matters.

Mr. Warner was mid-sentence, droning on about the importance of literary analysis and the structure of our yearlong projects, when the classroom door suddenly swung open.

I glanced up just in time to see Callum burst in, looking a little winded and clearly in a rush. His white t-shirt was slightly wrinkled from whatever heavy lifting he'd been doing at the club fair setup, and he still had that faintly disheveled, "I just sprinted across the school" look.

"Sorry," Callum said, his voice a little breathless as he ran a hand through his messy brown hair. "I was helping set up for the club fair. Didn't realize I was cutting it this close."

Mr. Warner paused mid-lecture, raising an eyebrow but not looking particularly bothered by the interruption. "That's alright, Mr. Reid. Find a seat and try to keep up."

I blinked, feeling a jolt of surprise run through me. Callum's in this class? I hadn't even considered the possibility. In the years we'd been in school together, we'd managed to avoid most of the same classes, except for the random elective here and there.

Callum scanned the room, clearly looking for a seat, and then his eyes landed on the only empty desk left—right next to mine.

Of course, I thought, trying to keep my expression neutral as he made his way over. He didn't look particularly thrilled about it either, but what choice did he have?

He slid into the seat next to me with a soft sigh, dropping his bag on the floor and flashing me a quick, sheepish grin. Before he could say anything, I leaned over slightly, raising an eyebrow as I whispered, "Long time no see."

Callum glanced at me out of the corner of his eye, his lips twitching into a smirk. "Yeah, it's been, what? All of half an hour?"

"Wish it had been longer," I whispered back, my tone light but sarcastic.

He scowled, shaking his head as he settled into his seat. But then, as Mr. Warner resumed his lecture, I couldn't help but feel a little unsettled. The last thing I needed was to spend an entire semester sitting next to Callum Reid in one of the hardest classes we'd have.

He was distracting enough as it was, and now we were going to be literary analysis partners for the foreseeable future?

Great. Just what I needed.

I shook the thought away, trying to focus on the lecture. At least I could take comfort in the fact that, even though Callum was sitting next to me, it didn't mean we had to interact all the time. We had our ground rules, after all. As long as we stayed out of each other's way, this year would go by just fine.

Or so I hoped.

Class dragged on, with Mr. Warner's monotone voice carrying on about symbolism in literature. I was trying my best to focus, but my stomach had other ideas.

The hunger I'd been feeling since this morning was getting worse, and I could feel it gnawing at me, sharp and persistent. I closed my eyes for a second, trying to ignore it, but it wasn't working.

My stomach growled again—loud enough that I hoped no one around me had heard it.

Damn it. This was not how I wanted to start the first day of senior year—starving, distracted, and sitting next to Callum Reid, of all people.

I shifted uncomfortably in my seat, trying to focus on the lesson, when I heard some rustling coming from Callum's side of the table. I ignored it at first, but then I felt a sharp nudge against my side.

I snapped my eyes open and turned to glare at him, ready to curse him out for elbowing me, when I spotted something unexpected on the desk in front of me.

A sandwich.

I blinked, staring at it for a moment, completely thrown off. What the hell? Where did this come from? I glanced at Callum, my confusion obvious.

"What... what is this?" I whispered, looking at him suspiciously.

He didn't look at me, instead keeping his eyes forward like he was still paying attention to Mr. Warner. "It's a sandwich," he muttered, his voice low enough that only I could hear. "You've been clutching your stomach and groaning for the last half hour, so... eat it."

I blinked again, my brain taking a second to catch up. "You're giving me... your lunch?"

Callum sighed, finally turning his head to give me an exasperated look. "No, I'm giving you a sandwich. I packed more than one. Always do."

I stared at him for a second, still not quite believing it. He wasn't exactly the most generous guy, especially not with me. "I'm not going to eat your lunch," I muttered, pushing the sandwich back toward him. "That's—no."

Callum rolled his eyes, nudging the sandwich back toward me. "I've got another one. Two, actually. I always pack two or three 'cause I'm not an idiot who forgets to eat. Just... take it before your stomach starts a riot."

I hesitated, glancing between him and the sandwich. It wasn't like Callum to do something nice—especially not for me —but I was so hungry that I didn't have the energy to argue.

Still, I narrowed my eyes at him, suspicious. "Why are you even doing this?"

Callum shrugged, looking like he'd rather be anywhere else. "Because you're being annoying with all the stomach growling. Just eat it, Eller."

I let out a small huff, finally giving in. "Fine. But don't think this means anything," I muttered, grabbing the sandwich from the desk.

"Trust me, it doesn't," he replied, his voice dry.

I unwrapped the sandwich, my stomach practically doing somersaults at the prospect of finally eating something. I took a bite, and even though it was just a simple sandwich—turkey and cheese—it felt like the best thing I'd ever tasted. I tried not to make a big deal out of it, though, keeping my face as neutral as possible as I ate.

Out of the corner of my eye, I could see Callum glancing at me occasionally, but he didn't say anything. He just leaned back in his chair, looking as uninterested as ever, like this was no big deal.

I didn't know what to make of it. Callum wasn't being overly nice—he still had that casual, dismissive tone—but the fact that he'd even bothered to give me a sandwich in the first place threw me off. This was Callum. The same Callum who annoyed me on a regular basis. And now, he was... giving me food because I was hungry?

I pushed the thought away, focusing on finishing the sandwich as quickly and discreetly as possible. I wasn't about to overthink it.

Still, as I finished the last bite, I couldn't help but feel a little less irritated by him.

Just a little.

CHAPTER 9
CALLUM

THE BELL RANG, SIGNALING THE END OF CLASS, AND HAILEY STOOD UP immediately, slipping her notebook into her bag and making a beeline for the door without a word. She didn't even glance back, just disappeared into the hallway like she couldn't get away fast enough.

I stayed seated for a moment, watching her leave as I slowly packed up my stuff.

She didn't even say thank you.

Are you serious? I thought, shoving my notebook into my backpack a little harder than necessary. I'd given her my lunch—my sandwich—because she was sitting there basically groaning in pain all class, and she couldn't even bother with a simple "thanks." Not a nod, not a glance. Nothing.

I slung my bag over my shoulder, grumbling to myself as I stood up. "Unbelievable," I muttered under my breath, making my way out of the classroom.

She pissed me off. She always did, but this was a whole new level. I didn't even know why I bothered. It wasn't like I expected her to bow down to me and proclaim her gratefulness or anything, but a little acknowledgment wouldn't have killed her.

I wasn't trying to be nice. It wasn't about that. But she was so… infuriating sometimes, with the way she acted like she didn't need anything from anyone, even when she was clearly struggling. If I didn't know any better, I'd think she was doing it on purpose, just to get under my skin.

I shook my head, pushing my way through the crowd in the hallway as I headed for my next class. Fine. Whatever. If she wanted to act like that, it was her problem. I wasn't going to lose sleep over it.

I pushed my way through the crowded hallway, still grumbling to myself about Hailey. The irritation clung to me like a bad smell, but I tried to shove it out of my mind as I headed to my next class.

First class of the first day of senior year, and already she'd managed to get under my skin.

As I turned the corner and walked into my next class, I immediately spotted two familiar faces: Grayson and Ibra, two of my teammates from the soccer team. They were already sitting near the back, talking and laughing about something, clearly not taking the whole "first day" thing too seriously.

I made my way over, slipping into the seat next to them.

"Hey, finally," Grayson said, glancing over at me with a grin. "Thought you got lost or something."

"Yeah, yeah," I muttered, tossing my bag on the floor and slouching into my chair. "I got stuck in Lit with Warner."

Ibra let out a low whistle, shaking his head. "Warner? Damn, man. That's rough. That dude could put a hyperactive squirrel to sleep."

"Tell me about it," I replied, rubbing the back of my neck. "I nearly passed out halfway through. Would've if it wasn't for—" I stopped short, not wanting to bring up the whole Hailey situation. The last thing I needed was for them to start asking questions.

Grayson raised an eyebrow. "For what?"

I shrugged it off. "For him droning on and on about literary symbolism. You know, the usual."

They both chuckled, clearly not buying the deflection but also not caring enough to push further.

"Anyway, you two ready for this year?" I asked, changing the subject. "It's gonna be our last shot. You know Coach isn't gonna go easy on us."

Grayson leaned back in his chair, crossing his arms. "Man, Coach never goes easy on us. I'm just hoping I can survive the practices without dropping dead."

"Survive?" Ibra echoed, shaking his head. "Bro, I'm trying to thrive. I want us to take the whole league this year."

"Exactly," I said, feeling a spark of competitiveness light up in my chest. "This is our year. We're not just here to survive—we're here to win."

They both nodded, the same intensity I felt flickering in their eyes. We were seniors now. This was our last chance to make a mark on the field, and I was ready to do whatever it took to lead us there. Being captain wasn't just a title—it was a responsibility. And I wasn't about to let Coach, or the rest of the team, down.

But even as we talked strategy and laughed about some of the crazier moments from last season, the frustration from earlier still lingered at the back of my mind. Hailey.

Why couldn't she just—

I shook my head, focusing back on Grayson and Ibra as the teacher walked into the room and started taking roll. This was more important. Soccer. The team. Winning. Everything else could wait.

Grayson and Ibra were still talking about last season's final game, when I spotted someone familiar entering the room. Natalia.

She walked in like she owned the place, her long, red hair cascading over her shoulders, her bright green eyes scanning the room. And then, they landed on me. Her smile curved just slightly as she made her way over.

Natalia and I had this thing—on and off, hot and cold. We never put a label on it, and neither of us seemed too keen on defining whatever it was, but we always found our way back to each other.

Most people at school probably figured we were together, though we weren't exactly consistent enough for that to be true. If I was being honest, I couldn't even remember the last time we had a clear "on" or "off" conversation.

But I was pretty sure, before I'd gotten shitfaced at Sasha's party, we'd hooked up in the bathroom. The memory was fuzzy, at best, thanks to the alcohol, but I distinctly remembered her lips, her perfume, and the way she laughed against my ear as we stumbled into the bathroom.

Now, she slid into the seat next to me, her smile playful as she nudged me with her elbow.

"Hey, stranger," she said, her voice low and teasing. "Didn't think I'd see you in here."

I grinned, leaning back in my chair as I looked over at her. "Yeah, well, we always seem to have at least one class together, don't we?"

"Right," she laughed softly, her eyes sparkling with amusement. "How are you feeling, by the way? After Sasha's? I seem to recall you being... pretty out of it."

I raised an eyebrow, smirking slightly. "Out of it, huh? That's one way to put it."

Her smile widened, and she gave me a knowing look. "So, you don't remember much, then?"

I shrugged, keeping my tone casual. "I remember enough."

That was a complete lie.

Natalia laughed again, the sound soft and warm as she leaned in a little closer, her shoulder brushing against mine. "Well, if you need a refresher... I'm happy to remind you."

Grayson and Ibra exchanged glances, both of them smirking but staying quiet as Natalia and I flirted back and forth.

I could feel the heat of her arm next to mine, her perfume filling the space between us. It was familiar, comfortable, like we'd done this dance a hundred times before.

But even though I was playing along, there was a small part of me that felt... off. Still, I wasn't going to overthink it. Not now, anyway.

"Listen," I said, my voice dropping slightly as I leaned in, "I might've been a little out of it, but I'm pretty sure you and I —"

"Uh-huh," Natalia interrupted, her lips curving into a smirk. "But you're not gonna make me say it, are you?"

I chuckled under my breath, shaking my head. "Wouldn't dream of it."

We both laughed, and the easy banter between us felt like slipping into an old routine. Whatever had happened at the party, we both knew it wasn't the first time—and it probably wouldn't be the last.

As the teacher started droning on about the course syllabus, Natalia shifted in her seat next to me, leaning in just enough so her arm brushed against mine again. She was still smiling, her gaze flicking toward me occasionally, and I could feel the unspoken tension building between us.

Then, under the table, I felt it—her hand lightly grazing my thigh.

The touch was subtle at first, almost like she was testing the waters, but when I didn't pull away, her fingers pressed a little harder, slowly stroking along the fabric of my jeans.

A low groan escaped my throat before I could stop it, the sound quiet enough not to draw attention from anyone else, but Natalia definitely noticed.

She flashed me a playful, knowing smile, her eyes glinting with excitement.

I leaned over slightly, my lips close to her ear, my voice low so no one else could hear. "Meet at my car at lunch?"

She nodded eagerly, her smile widening as she gave my thigh one last teasing squeeze before pulling her hand away. "Can't wait," she whispered back, her voice soft but full of promise.

LUNCH CAME AROUND, AND JUST LIKE WE'D PLANNED, I MET NATALIA BY MY CAR IN the parking lot. We didn't waste any time. The second we got into the backseat, things heated up fast.

I was on top of her, her hands gripping the back of my neck as our lips crashed together, her soft body pressed beneath mine. This wasn't anything new for us—it was what we did.

On again, off again, a constant cycle of makeouts and hookups with no strings attached.

Or, at least, that's what I thought.

Natalia tugged at my shirt, pulling me closer as I kissed her neck, her fingers trailing through my hair. The familiar scent of her perfume filled the car, mixing with the heat of our bodies as we moved against each other. It was like we'd done this a thousand times, and every time, it was the same—intense, but never more than what it was.

I was lost in the moment, focused on the feel of her beneath me, when suddenly she froze. Her lips stopped moving against mine, and I felt her shift under me, her head turning slightly as she looked down at the floor of the car.

"What's this?" she asked, her voice sharp, her hand reaching down to pick something up.

I glanced over my shoulder to see what she was talking about, and my stomach dropped when I saw what she was holding.

A tube of chapstick. But not just any chapstick. It was a girl's, pink and fruity—the same kind Hailey had dropped when I'd given her a ride earlier. I'd noticed it roll onto the floor but hadn't bothered picking it up, figuring it didn't matter.

But now Natalia was holding it up, her eyebrows raised in question. "Whose is this?"

I hesitated for a second, my brain working fast to come up with an answer that wouldn't turn this whole thing into a disaster. "It doesn't matter," I said quickly, shrugging it off like it was no big deal. "Probably just something someone left in here."

Natalia didn't look convinced. Her green eyes narrowed, and she looked at me, clearly trying to piece things together. "It's a girl's," she said, her tone pointed.

I sighed, shifting slightly as I tried to stay cool. "Yeah, so what? You know we're not exclusive, Natalia. It's not like we owe each other explanations."

Her lips pressed into a thin line, and I could see the flash of jealousy in her eyes. She wasn't saying anything, but I could feel the tension rising between us. I knew this was a risk, the whole "on-again, off-again" thing making things messy sometimes, but we'd never had a problem with it before.

"You're right," she said after a moment, her voice tight. "We're not exclusive."

I nodded, relieved that she seemed to be backing off. "Exactly. So don't worry about it."

She looked down at the chapstick again, rolling it between her fingers before tossing it onto the floor with a small huff. "Yeah, okay."

I leaned back in, brushing a strand of her hair behind her ear and pressing a kiss to her jawline, trying to steer things back to where we'd left off. But I could tell the mood had shifted, and even though she wasn't saying it, the jealousy was still there, simmering beneath the surface.

Whatever. We'd deal with it later. For now, we were still playing the same game.

CHAPTER 10

HAILEY

Lunch was the one part of the school day where I could breathe a little. No class to sit through, no awkward small talk with classmates. Just me, Nala, and whatever weird ass food combination she decided to try out that day.

Today was no exception.

I sat down at our usual table in the corner of the cafeteria, setting my tray down and glancing over at Nala. She was already knee-deep in her latest experiment—a pile of chicken nuggets that she was dunking into... was that strawberry yogurt?

I blinked, my stomach churning slightly as I watched her take a bite with zero hesitation, her expression thoughtful as she chewed. "You can't be serious," I said, raising an eyebrow at her.

Nala grinned, holding up one of the nuggets dripping pink like she'd just discovered the secret to the universe. "You have no idea how good this is. Sweet and savory, Hailey. It's such a vibe."

A bad vibe, maybe.

I made a face, shaking my head as I unwrapped my sandwich. "That's not a vibe. That's a stomach ache waiting to happen."

She shrugged, dunking another nugget into the yogurt like she was proving a point. "Your loss. Just wait until I make it onto some food blog. I'll be famous for my culinary genius."

I snorted, taking a bite of my own food. "Famous for making everyone question their life choices, maybe."

Nala laughed, tossing a nugget onto my tray. "Come on, try it. Live a little."

I pushed the nugget away, giving her a look. "There's no way I'm eating that."

"It's your loss," she said again, popping it into her mouth with a grin.

This was just... Nala. She had a habit of discovering the weirdest food combinations and treating them like gourmet meals. A few weeks back, it was dipping fries into pickle juice (which I had outright refused to try), and before that, she'd put peanut butter on her pizza, which was an experience I was still trying to forget.

But she owned it, like she owned everything she did, and I couldn't help but laugh at her ridiculousness.

"So," Nala said, leaning back in her chair, "how's your day been so far? Anything exciting? Or is it just first-day boredom?"

I shrugged, chewing on my sandwich. "Pretty boring, honestly. Classes are fine, but guess who I have AP Lit with?"

Nala raised an eyebrow, intrigued. "Who?"

"Callum," I said flatly, rolling my eyes.

Nala's eyes widened, and she let out a low whistle. "That's going to be fun. Mr. Soccer Star himself. What's he like? Still a pain in the ass?"

I sighed, nodding. "Yeah, pretty much. He showed up late, and now I'm stuck sitting next to him for the rest of the year."

Nala wrinkled her nose. "Yikes. That's rough. Though, let's be honest, he's probably too busy flirting with half the girls in class to even notice you."

I chuckled, shaking my head. "You're not wrong. He already had one of the cheerleaders fawning over him this morning."

"Typical," Nala said, rolling her eyes. "But hey, at least you don't have to deal with him during lunch. This is our time."

"Exactly," I agreed, feeling a little lighter now that I was with Nala, away from the chaos of the rest of the school.

We chatted back and forth, catching up on the first half of the day, but the conversation kept drifting back to Nala's weird food choices. She was already planning out her next culinary experiment—apparently something involving popcorn and orange juice—and I couldn't help but laugh at the ridiculousness of it all.

As Nala continued chatting about her latest summer adventures and all the crazy food she still planned to try, I leaned back in my chair, taking a sip of water as I absentmindedly scanned the cafeteria.

The usual groups were spread out at their tables, same as every year. The debate kids were gathered in the corner, already talking about their next competition.

The drama club was animatedly gesturing and laughing at something I couldn't hear. And then there was the soccer team —Grayson, Ibra, and Callum's best friend, Adam, were all huddled around a table, laughing loudly and being their usual obnoxious selves.

But… no Callum.

I blinked, feeling a weird jolt of confusion run through me. I glanced around, half-expecting him to show up at any moment, but the only thing I saw was a bunch of other students going about their day.

Wait. Why was I looking for him?

I straightened up in my seat, my brows furrowing as I snapped myself out of it. Since when did I care about where Callum Reid was, or whether or not he was sitting with his friends?

I mentally shook myself, trying to shove the thought away. It was weird—so weird—that I'd even let my mind wander in that direction. The last thing I needed was to be worrying about him or what he was doing. He could've been anywhere, and it didn't matter to me in the slightest.

Nope. Not at all.

Nala's voice snapped me out of my daze. "You good? You just spaced out."

I quickly shook my head, forcing a smile. "Yeah, sorry. Just… tired. First-day exhaustion."

She raised an eyebrow but didn't press it. "Mhm. You need to eat more. That's what it is."

I let out a small laugh, grateful she didn't push any further. I shoved Callum and that weird moment out of my mind and turned my attention back to Nala and her ridiculous food experiments.

Whatever Callum was doing, it was none of my business. I didn't care.

I didn't.

Lunch was wrapping up, and I was just about to stand when the loudspeaker crackled to life overhead. "Westview students, please head to the gymnasium for the assembly," the principal's voice boomed through the cafeteria. "After that, we will begin the club fair."

There was a collective groan from the students as everyone started gathering their things. Nala tossed her empty yogurt cup into the trash, looking about as excited for the assembly as I felt.

"Well, I guess it's that time," she said, adjusting her backpack. "You ready for an hour of the principal telling us how amazing this year is going to be?"

I laughed, standing up and slinging my bag over my shoulder. "Oh yeah, can't wait."

The gymnasium was always packed on the first day for the assembly, and it was always the same: the principal giving a long-winded speech about school spirit, how we were seniors now, and all the "opportunities" ahead of us. I wasn't exactly looking forward to it, but at least after that, we'd get to wander around the club fair.

Nala and I headed toward the exit, merging with the stream of students filing out of the cafeteria. As we walked, I felt a bit of that first-day tension start to melt away. The chaos of the morning was behind me, and the afternoon was going to be easy —just a boring assembly and some club booths.

We stepped into the hallway, joining the mass of students heading toward the gym. I glanced around again, making sure not to let my thoughts wander back to a certain soccer captain who wasn't at lunch.

I didn't care. Really.

Nala and I shuffled into the gymnasium, following the steady stream of students filing in for the assembly. The bleachers were already half full by the time we found a spot near the middle, surrounded by a mix of seniors and some unlucky freshmen who'd been herded into the wrong section.

As soon as we sat down, the principal stepped up to the podium, and I had to bite my lip to keep from giggling. Principal Smalls. I'd forgotten just how literal that name was.

He was... well, short. Really short.

And as soon as he appeared behind the podium, some of the freshmen near the front started snickering.

I couldn't help but chuckle, my mind flashing back to our very first day of freshman year. We hadn't known each other at all then, but we'd ended up sitting next to each other in the assembly, just like today. And when Principal Smalls had walked up to the podium that year, both of us had burst out giggling at the exact same time.

That was the moment I knew we'd be friends.

It was such a small, silly thing—laughing at a principal's height—but it bonded us in a way that nothing else could have. By the time the assembly was over that day, we were already talking like we'd known each other for years.

From that point on, Nala and I were inseparable. Every first day after that was marked by the same giggles when Principal Smalls took the stage.

"Remember freshman year?" Nala whispered, her voice soft with nostalgia. "We did the exact same thing."

I nodded, smiling at the memory. "Yeah, and we've been stuck together ever since."

"Damn right," she said with a wink.

Principal Smalls cleared his throat, trying to silence the giggling freshmen at the front, and I quickly turned my attention back to him, though my mind was still buzzing with the warmth of that memory.

The speech was exactly what you'd expect from a first-day assembly—lots of talk about school spirit, about the importance of this year being our last as seniors, and how we should "seize every opportunity" and "make the most of our time." It was the same speech he'd probably been giving for years.

The speech dragged on for what felt like forever, but finally, Principal Smalls wrapped it up with the usual "Go Westview!" cheer, and the room erupted into half-hearted applause. The freshmen looked confused, the seniors looked relieved, and Nala and I exchanged a knowing glance.

"Thank God that's over," I muttered as we stood up.

"I know." Nala turned to me, her eyes lighting up with excitement. "Okay, now it's club fair time. Let's see what we've got this year."

I raised an eyebrow, smirking at her. "You're always way too excited for this. You literally join a different club every year." I couldn't help but chuckle remembering Nala's mishaps in the

Cooking Club where she nearly burned down the school, the Book Club where she never read and made things up at every week's meeting, and the Occult Club that she quit after a day because they tried to do some weird curse on her.

Nala shrugged, completely unbothered by the jab. "Isn't that the point? To try new stuff?" She grinned at me, flipping her curls over her shoulder with a dramatic flair. "Besides, this year, I'm going to find *the* club. The one that speaks to my soul."

I laughed, shaking my head as we made our way toward the booths. "You've said that every year."

"And I'll keep saying it until I find it," she shot back, her eyes scanning the rows of booths with renewed enthusiasm.

We wandered around, checking out a few of the usual suspects—the debate team, robotics club, and a few academic societies that I definitely wasn't interested in. Nala, on the other hand, was bouncing from booth to booth like a kid in a candy store, chatting up the people behind the tables and grabbing every flyer they offered.

Then, we reached the drama club booth.

Nala's eyes widened as she grabbed my arm. "Ooh! Drama club!" She grinned mischievously. "We love gossip and drama. We would totally fit in here."

I snorted, shaking my head as I watched her practically bounce up to the booth. "You're ridiculous."

She ignored me, leaning in toward the students behind the table with a bright, eager smile. "So, what's the scoop? I feel like Hailey and I would be perfect for this club. We love drama. We could totally get involved in all the gossip, right?"

The two students manning the booth—both of them wearing black t-shirts and holding scripts—exchanged an awkward glance. The girl on the left cleared her throat, looking a little unsure of how to respond. "Um... well, we're more focused on, like... theater. You know, acting, improv, that kind of thing. Not... uh, not that kind of drama."

Nala blinked, clearly not expecting that response. "Oh. Right. Yeah, I knew that." She let out a nervous laugh, waving her hand like she hadn't just made a total fool of herself. "I was just joking."

I burst out laughing, covering my mouth to try and hide it, but it was too late. Nala shot me a look, her cheeks flushing slightly. "Shut up, Hailey."

The girl behind the booth tried to smile politely. "You're still welcome to join, though, if you're into theater."

Nala quickly shook her head. "No, no, it's fine. We'll... we'll pass." We walked away from the booth, and I could barely keep myself from laughing as we moved further down the row of clubs. "I can't believe you said that."

Nala groaned, burying her face in her hands. "Okay, that was such a mess. I thought it was like drama, like what's the tea? You know? I don't know what I was thinking."

"You clearly weren't," I teased, grinning at her. "But thanks for the entertainment. That was worth it."

She shook her head, still laughing at herself. "Ugh, let's just pretend that never happened."

After Nala's little drama club fiasco, we wandered further down the rows of booths, the energy of the club fair buzzing all around us.

Nala, despite her embarrassment, was already scanning for her next potential club victim. Meanwhile, I was just along for the ride, figuring I'd stick to my usual routine of not joining anything.

That's when we passed the yearbook club booth.

Nala's eyes lit up again, and she waved excitedly at the guy manning the table. "Lance! Hey!"

Lance, the yearbook club captain, grinned as soon as he saw her. He was tall with a head of blond hair that always looked like it had just been tousled by the wind. "Nala! Long time no see."

They exchanged a quick hug, and I hovered awkwardly beside them, not really knowing what to do with myself. I didn't know Lance all that well—only that he and Nala were friends.

"Are you joining the yearbook club this year, Nala?" Lance asked, his tone light and casual, but there was an obvious note of hope in his voice.

Nala let out a small laugh, already stepping back from the booth. "Oh, Lance, you know me. I'm more of a spontaneous type. Yearbook is too much... planning for my taste."

Lance's face fell slightly, but he covered it with a grin. "Hey, no worries. We're always open to creative minds."

As Nala began to drift away, I glanced down at the sign taped to the front of the table. **Looking for Photographers.**

I paused, something stirring in the back of my mind.

Lance noticed me eyeing the sign and smiled. "Hey, if you're interested, we could really use a photographer. We've got a couple people helping with layout, but we're short on actual photos this year."

I bit my lip, debating with myself. Did I really want to get involved in something like this again? It wasn't like I had any friends in the club, and I wasn't exactly looking to put myself out there more than I already had to.

But... it could be fun. And maybe it wouldn't be so bad to focus on something other than just surviving this year.

I hesitated for a moment, staring at the sign-up sheet on the table.

Nala noticed me looking and perked up, grinning widely. "Oh my God, Lance, you have no idea. Hailey is your girl. She used to be, like, *the* photographer back in freshman and sophomore year. She was amazing."

I blushed, feeling my face heat up. "Nala—" I started to protest, but she wasn't letting me off the hook.

"I'm serious!" she said, turning to Lance. "If you need someone, Hailey's your best bet. She knows her stuff."

Lance's eyes lit up. "Really?" He turned to me, his grin widening. "That's awesome. We've been desperate for photographers this year. Most of the people who signed up are more into the layout side of things, so we're seriously short on photos. We'd love to have you on board."

I hadn't touched my camera in a while, and the thought of diving back into it—especially for something like yearbook—felt a little daunting. But at the same time... maybe it was exactly what I needed.

Nala elbowed me, her grin teasing. "Come on, Hailey. You know you want to."

I rolled my eyes but couldn't help the small smile creeping onto my face. "Fine. I'll think about it."

Before I could second-guess myself, I grabbed the sign-up sheet and scribbled my name down.

Lance looked genuinely thrilled. "Awesome! Hailey... Eller. Welcome aboard, Hailey. We'll have our first meeting later this week. I'll send you all the details."

Nala gave me a satisfied look, like she'd just won some kind of battle. "See? You're gonna kill it."

I shook my head, laughing softly. "Thanks for the hype, Nala. But seriously, no promises. I might be a little rusty."

"Rusty, my ass," Nala teased, linking her arm with mine as we stepped away from the booth. "You're gonna be amazing, and you know it."

I wasn't so sure about that, but for the first time in a long while, I felt a little spark of excitement. Maybe this would be the thing that made this year more bearable.

As we continued down the hallway, passing more booths and the growing crowd of students milling around, I spotted the familiar sight of the cheer team's table up ahead. It was impossible to miss—brightly colored banners, a few pom-poms scattered across the table, and a group of girls all dressed in their cheer uniforms, chatting animatedly with anyone who approached.

And right in the middle of it all was Sasha Thompson, the captain of the cheer team.

Sasha was... well, Sasha. The girl everyone seemed to like, the one who floated effortlessly through high school with a perfect mix of charm, confidence, and actual kindness. She was the type of person who could walk into a room and make everyone feel seen, which was probably why she was so popular.

I'd never had a bad experience with her. In fact, every time we'd crossed paths, she'd been perfectly friendly, always offering a smile or a quick "hey, how's it going?" She was the kind of popular girl who could've easily leaned into being snobby or exclusive, but she didn't. Instead, she managed to be warm and approachable, which just made people like her more.

Honestly? I got it. She deserved her popularity.

As we passed by, I nudged Nala and nodded toward the table. "There's Sasha. Doing her thing."

Nala glanced over and let out a small, amused chuckle. "The queen of Westview High herself."

I grinned. "Pretty much."

Sasha waved at a couple of freshmen who seemed awestruck just to be standing near her. She was like a celebrity around here, and the thing was, I understood why. She wasn't fake, and she wasn't mean.

If anything, she was like the female version of Callum—if Callum wasn't completely insufferable.

Where Callum leaned into being cocky and irritating, Sasha had this natural ability to charm people without making them feel like they were being played. It was weird to think about, but I could almost see why people put her and Callum in the same social tier. They were both good-looking, popular, and captains of their respective teams.

But Sasha? She actually seemed like someone you'd want to be friends with.

Sasha caught my eye and smiled warmly, waving at me like we were old friends. I gave a small, awkward wave back, feeling a little flustered for no reason. "Hailey! Nala!" she called, her voice warm and inviting. "Come here for a second!"

Nala and I exchanged a quick glance before making our way over to the booth, curiosity tugging at us. Sasha leaned against the table, radiating her usual charm as she looked us up and down.

"Damn, girls," Sasha said, her voice dripping with genuine admiration. "You two are looking fabulous today. Senior year glow-up, I see?"

Nala grinned, clearly loving the compliment. "Oh, you know it! And you, Sasha? You look like you stepped straight out of a magazine, as always."

Sasha laughed, brushing off the compliment but clearly appreciating it. "Oh, stop. You're going to make me blush."

I offered a small smile, feeling a little out of place in the conversation. Compliments weren't exactly my thing, but Sasha had a way of making you feel good about yourself, whether you wanted to or not.

"Thanks, though," I said, tugging at the strap of my backpack. "You look great, too."

Sasha's eyes sparkled, and then she gave us both a playful, conspiratorial smile. "So, what do you gorgeous ladies think about coming out for cheer tryouts? We've got them coming up soon, and anyone's welcome. We'd love to have you both."

Nala's face lit up almost immediately. "Wait, really? That actually sounds kinda fun."

I blinked, a little surprised by her enthusiasm. "You want to try out for cheer?"

Nala shrugged, her grin widening. "Why not? Could be an adventure, right?"

Sasha clapped her hands together excitedly. "Exactly! It's a blast, and we're always looking for new people with great energy. You'd totally fit in."

I, on the other hand, wasn't exactly convinced. The idea of trying out for cheer sounded like a nightmare to me—being thrown into a group of loud, coordinated people who expected you to memorize routines and shout about school spirit?

Yeah, no thanks. I'd pass.

"Uh, I think I'll skip on that," I said, shaking my head with a small laugh. "Cheerleading's not really my thing."

Sasha smiled understandingly. "No worries at all, Hailey. It's not for everyone. But Nala, if you're serious, we'd love to see you at tryouts. I think you'd be great."

Nala gave Sasha a thumbs-up. "I'll think about it. Who knows? Maybe you'll see me there!"

Sasha beamed at us both, then turned her attention back to the crowd gathering around the booth. "Well, whatever you decide, you know where to find me if you have any questions. And hey, have an awesome first day!"

"You too, Sasha," Nala said, giving her a wave as we stepped away from the booth.

As we walked further down the hall, Nala nudged me with her elbow, her eyes gleaming with excitement. "Can you imagine me as a cheerleader? I'd literally be unstoppable."

I laughed, shaking my head. "I mean, sure, if you're into that."

"I am into trying new things," Nala replied, grinning. "Come on, it could be fun. Don't knock it 'til you try it!"

I rolled my eyes, but I couldn't help but smile. Nala was always the one willing to jump into something new, no matter how ridiculous it seemed. And honestly? I admired that about her. Even if cheerleading wasn't my thing, it was totally her vibe to try it out.

"Let me know how that goes," I said, laughing softly. "I'll be your number one fan from the sidelines."

"Deal," Nala said, winking at me. "Hey, you know what? I'll be flying through the air and you'll be taking pictures of me for the yearbook. See? It all comes together."

Just as Nala and I were walking away from the cheer booth, talking about the ridiculousness of her potentially joining the squad, someone bumped hard into my shoulder, nearly knocking me off balance.

I stumbled slightly, catching myself before I could drop my bag, and looked up to see who it was.

It was the redhead from earlier. The one I'd seen flirting with Callum at the soccer booth. She didn't even glance back or offer an apology—just strutted away like nothing had happened, her long hair swinging behind her as she disappeared into the crowd.

Nala immediately whirled around, eyes narrowed as she watched the girl walk away. "Bitch," she muttered under her breath. Then, louder, she said, "Who does she think she is, not even saying sorry? I swear, some people around here act like they own the damn place."

I adjusted my bag, still slightly thrown off. "Who was that?"

Nala scoffed. "You don't know? That's Natalia. She's on the cheer squad—always hanging around Callum and his little soccer group. Ugh, I can't stand her."

I blinked. "Natalia?" The name didn't ring any bells.

"Yeah, her," Nala continued, her voice full of disdain. "She thinks she's hot shit because she's always with Callum and playing queen bee or whatever. I had some classes with her last year and she was the definition of insufferable."

I raised an eyebrow, glancing back in the direction Natalia had gone. "I mean... I don't know her, so..."

"You're not missing much," Nala said, crossing her arms as she glared after Natalia. "Trust me. She's one of those girls who thinks she's better than everyone else. You'd think being on the cheer squad would at least make her decent, but nope. She's all attitude."

I shrugged, deciding to brush it off. I didn't know Natalia, and while Nala clearly had strong opinions about her, I wasn't going to get worked up over it. "It's fine. Just a bump."

Nala made a face. "You're too nice. She should've at least said sorry."

I laughed softly, nudging Nala as we kept walking. "Let it go. We've got better things to focus on, like you becoming the next cheerleading superstar."

Nala rolled her eyes but couldn't help grinning. "Okay, okay. But best believe, when I make it on the cheer team, I'm getting you that apology from Natalia."

"I was the one who she bumped into, why are you more mad than I am?" I chuckled.

Nala quickly shifted back into her usual self—hopping from booth to booth like she was on some kind of scavenger hunt. We wandered further down the hall, and soon, she spotted the Cosmetology Club's setup, which had a full station for makeovers and makeup demos. "Oh my God, Hailey, look!" Nala said, grabbing my arm and practically dragging me toward the booth. "This is going to be so fun."

Before I could protest, one of the girls from the club— perfectly polished with a bright red lip and flawless eyeliner— grinned at Nala and gestured to one of the empty chairs. "Want a quick makeover?"

"Hell yes," Nala said, plopping down into the chair with zero hesitation. "Make me look fabulous."

The girl laughed, already pulling out a makeup palette as Nala gave me a wink. "Hailey, come on. You need to get in on this. Free makeover!"

I shook my head, stepping back from the chair. "No thanks. I'm good."

Nala smirked, clearly amused by my hesitation. "You're missing out."

"Yeah, well," I said, crossing my arms, "I'll leave the contouring to you."

As the cosmetology girls started working on Nala, I wandered a little further down the row of booths, glancing around at the various clubs and tables. I didn't plan on signing up for anything else—I was already roped into yearbook photography—but it was still interesting to see the range of hobbies people were into.

Then, I noticed a table that stood out from the rest.

The Occult Club.

Dark banners with mysterious symbols were draped across the booth, and a couple of students wearing all-black clothing were sitting behind the table, flipping through books that looked like they came straight out of some ancient witch's library. Candles were arranged on the table, flickering softly even though we were indoors.

I blinked. Okay, this was… different.

Before I knew it, one of the students—an intense-looking girl with dark eyeliner—locked eyes with me and waved me over. "You look like someone with an open mind," she said, her voice soft but commanding. "Care to learn about the occult? We're doing an exorcism demo later."

I froze, staring at her. "Uh… what?"

"An exorcism," she repeated, dead serious. "We're always looking for volunteers."

I took a step back, quickly waving my hands in front of me, not really in the mood to be exorcised in my high school hallway. "Oh, uh, thanks, but I'm… not really into that. I'll pass, sorry."

The girl raised an eyebrow but shrugged. "Your loss. The spirits will miss your presence."

I couldn't tell if she was messing with me or if she was completely serious, but either way, I hurried back toward Nala, not wanting to get roped into anything involving spirits.

When I got back, Nala was just finishing up her makeover, and she turned to me with a dramatic flourish. "Ta-da! What do you think?"

Her makeup was bold—bright eyeshadow, perfectly winged eyeliner, and a glossy lip. She looked amazing, of course, but Nala always did, with or without the extra glam.

"Wow," I said, smiling. "You look great. But uh, I almost got roped into an exorcism, so there's that."

Nala's eyes widened. "What?!"

I pointed toward the Occult Club booth. "Those guys were trying to recruit me. They wanted me to volunteer for some kind of exorcism demo."

Nala laughed so hard she nearly smudged her lipstick. "Oh my God, Hailey! That's so funny. You honestly should've done it."

"No way," I said, shaking my head. "Who knows what demons they'll pull out of me?"

Just as we started walking away from the booth, still chuckling, we heard it—loud, boyish cheers echoing from the other side of the hall. Nala and I exchanged a glance before heading toward the noise, already knowing who it was before we even saw them.

The soccer team.

Of course, Callum and his group were the center of attention. It wasn't just Callum, though—his whole crew was there, the core four guys who made up the heart of Westview's soccer team.

They called them the "Four Pillars" of the team.

There was Grayson Hart, the forward. Grayson was fast —one of those players who could slip through defenses with ease. He had this laser focus on the field, always looking for the next opening, always ready to take the shot. Off the field, though, he was the joker of the group, the one who kept things light, always pulling pranks or making people laugh.

Then there was Ibra James, the goalie. Tall, solid, and practically a wall when he was in front of the net. If anyone was going to stop a last-minute goal, it was him. He had this intimidating presence that could shake even the best forwards.

But when he wasn't in goal, he was surprisingly easygoing. He was the quiet type, but when he spoke, people listened.

Adam Parker, the defender, was the muscle of the team. He was solid, built like a tank, and he played like one too. There wasn't a single game where he didn't throw himself into tackles or block shots with his entire body. Off the field, Adam was pretty laid-back—a little too laid-back, honestly, like nothing ever phased him.

And then, of course, there was Callum Reid, the striker and the captain of the team. He was the glue that held it all together, both on and off the field.

As much as I hated to admit it, Callum was good—really good. He had a natural talent for scoring, a knack for being in the right place at the right time, and the leadership to make the rest of the team rally around him. He was everything you'd expect a captain to be... except for the fact that he was, well, Callum.

Confident. Cocky. Annoying. And yet, somehow, everyone respected him.

The four of them made up the backbone of the soccer team, the ones who led them to every victory and rallied the rest of the players around them. They were always together, always making their presence known. And, of course, they were the reason the soccer team was such a big deal at Westview.

"Look at them," Nala muttered, shaking her head as we watched the guys pass out flyers. "The whole school practically worships them."

I shrugged. "Yeah, well, they're good. And people like to win."

"Still," Nala said, nudging me. "They could be a little less... loud."

I didn't disagree. Watching Callum and his crew laugh and shout like they owned the place was a little... much. But that was just how they were. They thrived off the attention, off being the center of everything.

I couldn't help but let my gaze drift back to Callum. I noticed Callum had changed out of his regular clothes and into his jersey—number 1. It fit him well, of course. The fabric stretched over his broad shoulders, accentuating his tall frame. He had that athletic build that made him stand out even more, and it wasn't hard to see why so many people were drawn to him.

He was laughing with his friends, completely in his element, like he always was. It was honestly annoying how natural it seemed for him—how easily he commanded attention without even trying. I was about to turn away when, suddenly, he looked up.

Our eyes met.

For a split second, neither of us moved. Then, just as I was about to break the stare, Callum shot me a grin—one of those cocky, knowing grins that made me want to roll my eyes into next week.

Typical.

And that's when I saw it. A small, faint mark on the side of his neck, just below his jawline. A hickey.

Of course. Of course Callum Reid would be walking around with a hickey for everyone to see, like some kind of badge of honor. I shouldn't have been surprised—it was probably from Natalia, or whoever else he'd been messing around with.

My eyes flicked back to his for a second, and his grin widened as if he knew exactly what I'd noticed.

Ugh. Gross.

I didn't give him the satisfaction of reacting. Instead, I just shook my head, turned on my heel, and walked away without a word. "Come on, Nala," I muttered, tugging on her arm. "Let's go."

CHAPTER 11
CALLUM

THE FIRST WEEK OF SENIOR YEAR HAD COME AND GONE, AND IT WAS ALREADY starting to feel like a routine. Not that I was complaining—routine was good.

Especially now, with soccer season right around the corner. I needed to stay focused, keep my head in the game, and get ready for what was going to be a tough season. And honestly, the less drama in my life, the better.

And that included Hailey Eller.

Every morning, she and I drove to school together. We barely said a word to each other, just got in the car, headed to school, and went our separate ways once we arrived. Sure, we had AP Lit together, but even then, we didn't really interact. I'd sit there, half-listening to Mr. Warner drone on about literary symbolism or whatever the hell, and Hailey would be off in her own world, scribbling notes with her specially curated pens like her life depended on it.

We'd leave class, go about our day, and then meet up again at the end of it. Same routine, every day. Drive home, minimal conversation, and then she'd disappear into the basement, while I did my own thing. It was almost like she didn't even exist half the time.

Not that I minded. The arrangement worked for me.

I had enough on my plate without worrying about whatever was going on in Hailey's life. These days, all I could think about was soccer. The season was just around the corner, and as captain, I had to be on top of my game. Coach Taz had picked me for a reason, and I wasn't about to let him—or the team—down.

Every day after school, I'd hit the field or the gym, making sure I was in peak condition. I'd run drills with the guys, work on my form, and get in as many reps as I could. I needed to make sure that when the season started, I was ready to lead the team to victory. The pressure was on, and I wasn't about to slack off.

Soccer was my life, and with senior year here, it was my last shot to make a real mark before everything changed. The thought of leaving this behind after graduation felt strange, like something I wasn't quite ready to process yet. But for now, all I cared about was winning. And that meant cutting out distractions. Though Hailey wasn't a distraction. She was... well, she was just there. In the background, like white noise.

But every once in a while, I'd catch myself thinking about that moment in the car when she had freaked out about her books, or the way she'd looked at me like I was the last person she wanted to talk to in AP Lit.

It was almost... amusing, in a way. I didn't go out of my way to annoy her, but something about her always made me want to push her buttons.

Not that I had the time to do that, either. I had bigger things to focus on. Like getting the team ready for our first game.

This weekend, we had a scrimmage lined up, and I was making sure the guys were on point. Grayson, Ibra, Adam—all of us had been practicing nonstop, getting ready for that first big test of the season. I knew the team was counting on me to lead them, and that weight sat on my shoulders like a constant reminder.

I'd spent the last few days planning strategies with Coach, figuring out who needed to step up where, and pushing the guys to their limits during practice. There wasn't room for mistakes, not now.

Still, in the back of my mind, I couldn't help but wonder how long this routine with Hailey was going to last. We were living under the same roof, driving to school together, but it was like we were existing in two separate worlds.

Though maybe that was for the best.

The scrimmage had gone well. Better than well, actually. The team was sharp, focused, and it felt like everything was starting to click into place. Our passes were tight, our communication on point, and I was already picturing us crushing the competition when the season started.

Afterward, we huddled up on the field, sweaty and exhausted but buzzing with adrenaline. Coach Taz stood in front of us, hands on his hips, his sharp eyes scanning the team like he was mentally evaluating every move we'd made during the scrimmage.

"Good work out there today," Coach said, his voice gruff but approving. "You guys are looking strong. If we keep this up, we're going to be a force to be reckoned with this season."

A murmur of agreement rippled through the group, a few guys clapping each other on the back. I glanced over at Grayson, who was leaning on his knees, still catching his breath, and he shot me a tired but satisfied grin. I nodded back, feeling that same sense of accomplishment. This was what we'd been working toward.

But Coach wasn't done yet.

"Before we get too excited," he continued, his voice turning serious, "we need to talk about the season ahead. You all know what's coming up. Oakridge."

At the mention of Oakridge, the entire mood of the group shifted. The tension in the air thickened, and I felt the familiar burn of bitterness settle in my gut.

Oakridge. Our biggest rivals. We'd had a long history of bad blood with them, but last season's game had taken that rivalry to a whole new level. I clenched my jaw, the memory of that game hitting me hard.

It was the semi-final match, and the stakes couldn't have been higher. Both teams had fought tooth and nail to get there, and everyone knew that whoever won was practically guaranteed the championship. Westview versus Oakridge— classic rivalry, the kind of matchup that drew a crowd from the whole town. The stands had been packed, the energy electric. You could feel the tension before the first whistle even blew.

From the start, Oakridge had played dirty. They were known for being physical, but that game? It was a whole new level. They threw elbows, slid into tackles late, and pushed the line of what the refs would allow. They were relentless, and we weren't backing down either.

But then, things went downhill fast.

First, Grayson took a nasty hit from one of Oakridge's defenders—a shoulder to the ribs that left him gasping for air. The ref didn't even call a foul, despite the fact that it was a blatant shove. Grayson was down for a few minutes, but he managed to get back up and keep playing, even though he was clearly hurting.

Then Ibra, our rock-solid goalie, took a brutal challenge during a corner kick. One of Oakridge's forwards slammed into him mid-air, knocking him off balance and sending him crashing to the ground. Again, no whistle. Ibra was pissed, but he got up and kept going, determined not to let them get the best of him.

And then there was me.

It was late in the second half, and we were tied 1-1. I saw an opening—just enough space to break through Oakridge's defense—and I went for it. I made my move, dribbling past their last defender, and as soon as I got inside the box, I felt it. A hard shove from behind, one of Oakridge's defenders throwing his entire body weight into me. I went down, hard.

The crowd erupted. Everyone thought it was a penalty. Everyone knew it was a penalty.

But the ref? He didn't blow the whistle. No penalty. No free kick. Nothing.

I was furious. We all were. But there was nothing we could do. Oakridge had the game locked down from that point forward, and in the last five minutes, they scored a cheap goal off a lucky deflection.

We lost 2-1. Semi-final gone. Just like that.

The bitter taste of that loss still lingered, even months later. Oakridge hadn't just beaten us—they'd cheated their way to victory. And the worst part? We'd had to stand there, on the field, and watch them celebrate like they'd earned it.

Coach let out a long breath, snapping me back to the present. "I don't need to remind you guys how that game went down last season. We all remember."

There was a collective murmur of agreement, but it wasn't excited—it was angry, determined. That loss had stung in a way that none of us had forgotten.

"They took something from us," Coach continued, his voice low but fierce. "But we're going to take it back this season. I want you all focused. I want you sharp. When we face Oakridge again, we're not going to let them get away with playing dirty. We're going to show them who the better team really is."

The guys nodded, all of us united by that shared anger, that need for redemption. I could feel the fire burning in my chest, that drive to prove ourselves. We weren't going to let Oakridge walk all over us again.

"Keep that loss in the back of your minds," Coach said. "Use it as fuel. Every practice, every game—remember what they did to us. And make sure it never happens again."

I clenched my fists, nodding along with the rest of the team. This season wasn't just about winning—it was about revenge. Oakridge was going to pay for what they did, and we weren't going to stop until we got our redemption.

As we broke the huddle and headed off the field, that bitter memory of last season stuck with me. Oakridge might've gotten the better of us once, but it wasn't going to happen again.

As I made my way off the field, all I could think about was getting out of here and maybe taking a long, cold shower. The tension from Coach's speech about Oakridge still buzzed in the back of my mind, that familiar anger swirling in my gut. That loss had cut deep, and I wasn't about to let it happen again this season.

I grabbed my bag from the locker room and headed toward the parking lot, my muscles aching from the game. I'd pushed myself hard today, but it felt good. That's what we needed if we were going to dominate this year.

As I reached my car, I pulled out my phone and saw a new text waiting for me. I swiped it open and felt a smirk tug at my lips.

Natalia: *Hey. My parents aren't home tonight. Wanna come over?*

It didn't take me long to make up my mind.

I tossed my bag into the back seat, fired up the engine, and peeled out of the parking lot without a second thought.

NATALIA'S BEDROOM WAS DIMLY LIT, THE SOFT GLOW OF HER PHONE SCREEN casting shadows across the room. We were lying side by side, the sheets tangled around us, and the faint hum of her scrolling through Instagram filled the air. I stared at the ceiling, my mind a little foggy from… well, everything.

It was quiet between us. Not uncomfortable, but not exactly cozy either. This was just how it always went. We'd meet up, hook up, and then... this. The lull that came afterward.

I glanced over at her, my eyes trailing lazily down her figure as she scrolled through her phone, seemingly engrossed in whatever was on her feed. I wasn't paying attention, not really. My thoughts had drifted back to soccer, to the season ahead, to anything but what was happening now.

But then, out of the corner of my eye, I caught a glimpse of something on her screen. An advertisement. A photography contest.

I blinked, feeling myself snap back to reality.

The ad was bright, with bold text overlaid on a photograph of a soft, golden sunset. The caption read: **Capture a moment that feels like a warm hug. Winners will be featured in Hermann's magazine and receive a $500 prize.**

Natalia was casually scrolling past it, probably about to move on to the next post, but for some reason, something tugged at me. I wasn't sure why, but the words stuck with me. A moment that felt like a warm hug.

"Wait," I said, reaching out and nudging her arm. "Send me that."

Natalia raised an eyebrow, glancing over at me with mild confusion. "What? Why?"

I shrugged, trying to act nonchalant. "Just... send it to me."

She gave me a look, but didn't argue, tapping the screen a few times before the ad was forwarded to me. "There. Happy?"

"Yeah," I muttered, staring at my phone as the notification came through.

For some weird reason—one I couldn't quite figure out—I wanted to send it to Hailey. I swiped open the message, staring at the contest description for a second. *A moment that feels like a warm hug.*

My thoughts drifted back to that day in the car, the day Hailey had freaked out about her book collection burning in the fire. She'd been trying to hold it together, forcing a smile even though I could tell she was completely shattered. I remembered the way her voice had cracked when she mentioned quitting photography because people started picking on her, calling her "photo girl."

And I remembered how much of an asshole I felt like when she pointed out that I'd been one of the people who did it, too. That conversation had stuck with me more than I wanted to admit. I hadn't thought about it in years—how I'd made fun of her for something as harmless as taking photos around school.

It seemed so stupid now, looking back. And seeing the look on her face when she talked about giving up something she'd clearly loved because of it?

Yeah, it didn't sit right with me.

It hadn't sat right with me since.

Why was I even thinking about her now?

I glanced back at the contest ad on my phone, my thumb hovering over the share button. It wasn't like I owed her anything. We barely talked. We drove to school together, sat in AP Lit together, and then ignored each other the rest of the day at home. But for some reason, the idea of her getting back into photography, of finding something that made her happy again... it felt important.   Like it was a responsibility of mine, almost. Yeah, that's what it was, right? I felt responsible.

I stared at the contest ad on my phone, my thumb hovering over the screen, right above the share button. For some reason, something inside me was telling me to send it to Hailey. But I hesitated.

What was I doing? Why did I care about some photography contest? Why did I care if Hailey saw it? It wasn't my problem, right? She'd quit photography years ago, and it wasn't like we were friends or anything.

I frowned, my finger still hovering over the button.

Stop overthinking it, Callum.

But before I could make a decision, I felt Natalia shift beside me. She turned, pressing herself against my side and resting her chin on my chest. Her fingers lightly trailed over my skin as she looked up at me with a curious expression.

"Everything okay?" she asked, her voice soft, but there was a playful edge to it, like she could sense I was distracted.

"Yeah," I said quickly, locking my phone and setting it face-down on the nightstand. I wrapped an arm around her, trying to focus on the moment. "I'm good."

Natalia didn't seem entirely convinced, but she let it go, shifting herself so that she was closer to me, her lips brushing against my jawline. "Mmm... you sure?"

Before I could answer, she kissed me. Her lips were soft, familiar, and for a moment, I let myself get lost in it. This was easy. This was normal. Something I didn't have to think too hard about. But then she pulled back, her eyes sparkling as she propped herself up on one elbow, giving me a coy smile. "Sooo... homecoming's next week," she said, drawing out the word like she was trying to sound casual.

I raised an eyebrow, feeling a slight sense of where this conversation was going. "Yeah, it is."

Natalia traced a finger down my chest, her tone light but expectant. "Have you, you know... thought about asking anyone?"

I leaned back against the pillow, trying to keep my voice neutral. "Not really. I've mostly been focused on the homecoming season opener for soccer. You know how it is."

As soon as the words left my mouth, I saw the shift in Natalia's expression. It was subtle—just a slight downturn of her lips, a flicker of annoyance in her eyes—but it was there. She wasn't thrilled with my answer, and I knew exactly why.

She'd been hinting at homecoming for the past few days, dropping comments about dresses and parties and who was asking who. It didn't take a genius to figure out that she was expecting me to ask her. But the thing was... I wasn't really thinking about homecoming. I was thinking about soccer, about Oakridge, about everything that had to go right this season. Homecoming was just... background noise. Like everything else was.

Natalia sighed, shifting back slightly. "Right, the soccer game. Of course."

I knew that tone. She wasn't outright mad, but she was definitely annoyed. I tried to brush it off, sitting up a little. "It's a big game," I explained, though I knew she already knew that. "We need to be sharp. After last season, I'm not taking any chances."

Natalia sat up beside me, pulling her knees to her chest and glancing over at me. "Yeah, I get it. It's just... homecoming, you know? Everyone's talking about it. It's kind of a big deal."

I ran a hand through my hair, feeling a twinge of guilt. I knew she wanted more from me—more attention, more commitment—but I wasn't sure I had the energy to give her that right now. Not with everything else on my plate.

"I know," I said, trying to sound more reassuring than I felt. "I'll think about it, okay?"

Natalia didn't look entirely convinced, but she nodded, her expression softening slightly. "Okay. Just... don't forget about it."

I kissed her forehead, hoping that would be enough to smooth things over. "I won't."

But as I lay back down, my thoughts drifted again—to soccer, to the upcoming season opener... and to the ad on my phone that was still sitting there, unsent.

CHAPTER 12
CALLUM

WHEN I GOT HOME LATER THAT NIGHT, THE HOUSE WAS IN FULL WEEKEND MODE. Nathan and Dalton were sprawled out on the couch, watching some animated show with the volume turned up loud enough to drown out any real conversation. The lights in the living room were dim, but the faint glow of the TV lit up their faces as they sat, completely glued to the screen.

In the kitchen, my parents and Mrs. Eller were hanging around the counter, glasses of wine in hand, their laughter filling the air. It was one of those rare moments when everything felt relaxed—no one rushing off to work, no one stressed about school. Just… chilling.

I tossed my keys onto the counter and dropped down onto one of the barstools. My stomach growled, reminding me that I hadn't eaten since before the scrimmage, and I reached for the leftover pasta sitting in a container on the counter.

"Scrimmage go well?" my dad asked, glancing over at me between sips of his wine, jutting his lips out and nodding with satifaction at the taste.

"Yeah," I said, shoveling some pasta onto my plate. "It went well. We're ready for the season opener."

Mom smiled, leaning on the counter. "Good to hear. Just make sure you don't run yourself into the ground before the season even starts."

"I won't," I mumbled through a mouthful of food.

As I started eating, I heard the soft sound of footsteps on the stairs behind me. I didn't think much of it until Hailey stepped into the kitchen, heading toward the fridge.

She was wearing an oversized t-shirt, the fabric hanging loose around her frame, barely reaching mid-thigh. Her hair was pulled up into one of those messy buns that girls do when they're not really trying, but somehow it still looked... good.

I didn't mean to stare, but before I could stop myself, my eyes flicked down. Her bare legs. Her shoulders, which were peeking out from the oversized collar of her shirt. Her collarbone, smooth and exposed. Hell, I even found myself glancing at the back of her neck—the nape of her neck, for fuck's sake.

I quickly looked away, focusing back on my plate, trying to act like I hadn't just checked her out. This was Hailey. The same Hailey I'd barely spoken to in the last week, the same Hailey who was basically just living in my house like a ghost I never saw. I shouldn't be looking at her like that.

But damn if I could help it.

She didn't seem to notice—or if she did, she didn't care. She pulled open the fridge, grabbed something, and then slipped onto the barstool next to me, leaving one seat between us. Neither of us said anything. We didn't acknowledge each other. That was kind of our thing these days—silent roommates.

She started eating, too, quietly digging into whatever she'd grabbed from the fridge. And despite myself, I found my eyes drifting over to her again. The dim kitchen light cast a soft glow over her, and for a second, I found myself fixated on the way her collarbone moved when she breathed, the slight rise and fall of her shoulders.

I forced myself to look down at my plate, my appetite suddenly less important than whatever the hell was going on in my head. I wasn't supposed to be thinking about her like this.

I cleared my throat, shifting uncomfortably in my seat as I tried to focus on eating. The kitchen was still filled with the soft sounds of my parents and Mrs. Eller chatting, but all I could think about was the girl sitting just a barstool away from me.

And how I couldn't stop looking at her.

I tried to keep my head down, focusing on my food, but it was no use. My eyes kept drifting over to Hailey, almost like I had no control over them. It was stupid—I wasn't even into her like that.

She was just... there. But the way her oversized t-shirt hung loosely on her frame, showing more of her skin than I was used to seeing, was definitely throwing me off.

I caught myself staring at her bare thighs again, and before I could snap out of it—

"What are you looking at?"

Hailey's voice cut through the quiet kitchen, and I flinched. My head jerked up, and I found her looking right at me, one eyebrow raised, her fork halfway to her mouth. Shit. I'd been caught.

"I wasn't looking at anything," I said quickly, my voice defensive. I set my fork down, trying to play it off like it was no big deal. "I'm just... eating."

"Uh-huh," she said, her tone dripping with sarcasm. "Sure. Because you were definitely not staring."

"I wasn't staring," I shot back, feeling my face heat up a little. "You're imagining things."

Hailey snorted, clearly not buying it. "Right. Imagining things. Because I just happened to catch you looking at me like I had two heads."

"Stop being dramatic," I grumbled, taking another bite of pasta and avoiding her gaze.

"Dramatic? You're the one who was gawking."

"I wasn't gawking!" I said, my voice rising slightly.

"Oh, so now you admit you were staring?" she shot back, her eyes narrowing at me as she set her fork down.

I groaned, running a hand through my hair. "I wasn't staring. Why do you always have to start something?"

"I'm not starting anything! You're the one who—"

"Kids, please," Mom said, sighing from across the kitchen. She sounded more tired than annoyed, like this wasn't the first time she'd heard us bicker. Which, to be fair, it wasn't. "It's the weekend. Can't you two go one night without arguing?"

Dad chimed in, clearly exasperated. "Yeah, seriously. You're giving me a headache."

Mrs. Eller smiled tightly, trying to keep the peace. "Come on, now. Let's keep things civil."

I glanced at Hailey, who was glaring at me like she was ready to throw her fork across the room. I wasn't in the mood to keep this going, not with everyone watching, but man, she could push my buttons so easily. It was like she knew how to irritate me, and every time she got the chance, she went for it.

"I'm not arguing," I muttered, shoving another bite of pasta into my mouth. "I'm just trying to eat in peace."

"Whatever," Hailey mumbled, rolling her eyes before going back to her food. She didn't look at me again, but I could tell she was still annoyed.

And maybe I was, too.

The kitchen fell back into a tense silence, the clinking of forks on plates and the low hum of conversation between our parents the only sounds left in the room. But despite myself, I could still feel Hailey's presence beside me, the irritation simmering between us like it always did.

I told myself I wasn't going to look at her again.

But I knew better.

Just when the tension between Hailey and me was starting to simmer down, my mom chimed in, clearly trying to change the subject and lighten the mood. "You know what?" she said, turning to the other adults. "Before it starts getting colder, maybe we should get the hot tub up and running again! It's been ages since we used it."

Hailey perked up beside me, looking genuinely surprised. "Wait, you guys have a hot tub?"

I couldn't help but scoff. "Are you dumb or something? It's kind of hard to miss in the backyard."

Hailey shot me a glare, her lips pursing. "Well, excuse me, but I don't exactly spend my time staring at your backyard. I live in the basement, in case you forgot."

I leaned back in my chair, folding my arms across my chest. "Yeah, well, maybe if you came upstairs once in a while, you'd notice the obvious."

"Oh, please," Hailey said, her voice dripping with sarcasm. "The only thing that's hard to miss around here is your ego. It's so damn big, I'm surprised you can fit through doorways."

Mom and Mrs. Eller exchanged glances, clearly trying not to laugh, while Dad just sighed, shaking his head. "Here we go again," he muttered under his breath.

Mrs. Eller, though, tried to keep things diplomatic. "Come on now, you two. Let's keep it light."

But I wasn't done yet. "Yeah? Well, at least I don't hide in the basement all day, acting like I'm too good to be around people."

Hailey shot back immediately. "I'm not hiding. I just prefer not being around you." Her eyes flashed with annoyance, and I could tell she wasn't in the mood to back down.

"Alright, that's enough," my mom said, stepping in before things could escalate further. She gave both of us a pointed look before turning back to the adults. "But really, the hot tub could be nice. We haven't used it in ages, and it's supposed to be warm this weekend.

"Well," Hailey said, leaning back in her chair with a smirk, "maybe I'll take advantage of it. I could use some relaxation after dealing with him all week."

I rolled my eyes. "Whatever, just don't break anything."

She shot me one last glare before turning her attention back to her food, but I couldn't help but notice the small, satisfied smile tugging at her lips. She always had a damn comeback, and honestly, I wasn't sure if I was more annoyed or impressed.

CHAPTER 13

HAILEY

I WAS LYING ON MY BED, SCROLLING MINDLESSLY THROUGH MY PHONE, NOT REALLY paying attention to anything in particular. The house was quiet now, the low murmur of the TV from the living room barely audible through the floor. Dinner had ended, and everyone had gone off to do their own thing. It was kind of nice, being able to retreat to the basement and have my own space.

The basement wasn't exactly luxurious, but it was private, and after the fire… well, privacy was something I appreciated a lot more these days. As I lay there, I heard soft footsteps coming down the stairs. I furrowed my brow, sitting up slightly. A moment later, there was a light knock on my door.

Curious, I got up and opened it, surprised to find Nathan and Dalton standing there, both of them looking up at me with hopeful expressions.

"Hey," I said, leaning against the doorframe. "What's up, you guys?"

Dalton, as always, was the more energetic of the two, his eyes lighting up as he spoke. "We're playing this game on our

Nintendo, and it's three players, so we were wondering if you wanted to join us?"

Nathan, quieter but no less earnest, nodded beside him. "Yeah, we thought it'd be fun if you played with us."

A small smile tugged at my lips. It was hard to say no to those faces, and honestly? I could use the distraction. "Of course," I said, stepping aside and motioning for them to come in. "What game are we playing?"

Dalton grinned, holding up the Nintendo controllers as he followed Nathan into the room. "It's called Overcooked. It's a cooking game."

I chuckled, sitting back on the edge of my bed. "A cooking game? Okay, this I have to see."

They quickly hooked the Nintendo up to the TV in the basement, and soon, we were all settled in on the couch. Nathan and Dalton sat on either side of me, their faces lit up with excitement as they handed me a controller.

"So, how does this work?" I asked, glancing at the screen as the game loaded up, playful music and bright colors filling the TV screen.

Dalton, ever the enthusiastic one, explained. "So like, you're part of a team of chefs, and you have to work together to cook and serve food as fast as possible. It gets crazy, though. Like, really crazy. There's so many customers once you get to higher levels!"

Nathan nodded in agreement, already navigating the menu to set up a three-player game. "Yeah, the kitchens get bigger as you level up. You can unlock new recipes and hire assistants and stuff. It's kinda chaotic, but it's fun."

I raised an eyebrow, intrigued. "Alright, sounds like a challenge. Let's do this."

The game started, and right away, I understood what they meant by "chaotic." The kitchen was a whirlwind of ingredients, orders, and fires—literal fires. The three of us scrambled around the screen, trying to chop vegetables, cook dishes, and serve plates before the time ran out. It was pure chaos, but in the best way possible.

"Hailey! The onions! Chop the onions!" Dalton shouted, his voice a mix of excitement and panic.

"I'm chopping, I'm chopping!" I laughed, trying to keep up with the orders flashing across the screen. "Nathan, we need more plates!"

"On it," Nathan said, his focus intense as he dashed around the virtual kitchen, grabbing dirty plates and washing them.

We ended up playing several rounds of Overcooked, and with each round, the chaos in the virtual kitchen only got more intense. We were loud—shouting instructions at each other, laughing when things went wrong—but it didn't matter. We were in the basement, tucked away from the rest of the house, so there wasn't anyone to tell us to quiet down.

"Dalton, the soup's burning!" I yelled, trying to grab the pot off the stove in time.

Dalton let out a squeal of laughter. "I'm trying, I'm trying! Nathan, help me!"

Nathan, who was usually so quiet, was actually smiling, too. He wasn't as loud as Dalton, but I could hear him chuckling as he scrambled around the kitchen, cleaning dishes and delivering orders like a pro.

When the round ended, we all collapsed back onto the couch, laughing and catching our breath. My cheeks hurt from smiling so much.

"That was insane," I said, breathing exaggeratedly. "I don't think I've ever taken cooking that seriously in my life."

Dalton was still giggling, his eyes bright with excitement. "We did so good, though! We got three stars on that level!"

Nathan, who was usually more reserved, gave a small smile. "Yeah. That was a good round."

As I glanced between the two brothers, I couldn't help but feel a warm sense of contentment settling in my chest. They were so sweet, so full of energy and joy. Spending time with them like this felt... nice. Really nice, actually.

But then, I remembered something. I glanced at the time on my phone, raising an eyebrow. "Hey, wait a second... isn't it a little late? What about your bedtime?"

Dalton covered his mouth and giggled mischievously, leaning in like he was about to tell me a big secret. "It's the weekend, so... there's no bedtime!"

Nathan chuckled softly beside him, nodding in agreement. "Yeah. We can stay up late."

I couldn't help but laugh. "Of course you can." It was hard not to feel a bit of warmth in my chest at their excitement. They were just... so easy to be around.

And that's when the thought hit me. How could these two sweet Reid brothers be so... well, sweet, while the other Reid brother pissed me off to no end?

Dalton and Nathan were kind, funny, and full of this pure, innocent energy that made you want to protect them. They were nothing like their older brother, Callum, who had this uncanny ability to push all my buttons and piss me off without even trying (though right now we were kind of in this weird limbo stage where we acted like the other didn't exist unless it was necessary). To put it simply, I had no idea how these three came from the same family.

But as I looked at Nathan and Dalton, I couldn't help but feel grateful for this moment. I wasn't sure how long I'd be living here, but if these two were part of the deal, then maybe it wouldn't be so bad after all.

The night was still young and so here were, deep into another round of Overcooked, the kitchen on the screen descending into absolute chaos.

Although I didn't want to admit it, something had been nagging at the back of my mind since we started playing. Dalton and Nathan had invited me to join them, which was great—I was having fun, and they were great company.

But even as we continued to play, there was something I couldn't quite figure out.

I paused the game for a moment, biting my lip as I considered whether or not I should even ask the question swirling in my head. It felt kind of personal, but... I was curious. The two boys stared up at me curiously as the chaotic round froze on the screen.

"Hey," I started, my voice hesitant. "I was just wondering... if you guys needed a third player, why didn't you just ask Callum?"

The room went silent.

Nathan and Dalton exchanged an awkward glance, and for the first time since we'd started playing, they both seemed... uncomfortable. The lively energy they'd had just a second ago faded, and they shifted in their seats like they weren't sure how to respond.

I immediately wanted to take the question back.

Dalton was the first to speak, his usual bright tone noticeably quieter. "Uh... I guess we're just not really sure how to talk to Callum."

I blinked, caught off guard by his response. "What do you mean? He's your brother."

Dalton shrugged, looking down at his hands as he fidgeted with the controller. "Yeah, but... I dunno. He just seems so far away sometimes."

Nathan, who had been quiet up until now, nodded in agreement. "He's a lot older than us. He doesn't really talk to us much. It's like... he's always in his own world."

I felt a pang of sympathy for them. They were so young —Dalton especially—and the idea that they didn't feel like they could talk to their own brother hit me harder than I expected.

Dalton glanced up at me, his expression uncertain. "We don't wanna bother him, you know? He always looks busy or... mad about something. We're kinda scared we'll just make him angry."

Nathan nodded again, his face serious. "Yeah. We don't really know how to get close to him."

I stared at the two of them, my heart sinking a little. I'd never really thought about Callum in this way—about how his distance and focus on soccer might affect his brothers. But now that they'd said it, it made sense. Callum was older, wrapped up in his own world of sports and high school drama. To Nathan and Dalton, he probably felt like someone who was out of reach, someone they couldn't connect with.

And that just... sucked.

I didn't know what to say. What could I say? I wasn't exactly Callum's biggest fan myself, but hearing his brothers talk about him like this made me feel bad for them. They clearly looked up to him, but they didn't know how to bridge the gap between them.

"I'm sorry, guys," I said softly, my voice sincere.

Dalton shrugged again, but his eyes were downcast. "Don't be sorry, Hailey. It's not like it's a bad thing. We know Callum still cares for us in his own way and stuff."

Nathan didn't say anything, but the look on his face told me he felt the same way.

I glanced at them, my heart feeling heavier than I expected. Seeing the uncertainty in their faces, the way they tiptoed around the idea of their own brother, it just didn't sit right with me.

They deserved better. And even if I wasn't Callum, I could at least be there for them.

"You know what?" I said, shifting slightly so I could look at both of them. "If you ever need a third person to play with, just know you can always ask me. As long as I'm living here—and even when I move out—I'll be your third player if you need one."

Dalton's face lit up immediately, his eyes wide with excitement. "Really? You mean it?"

I smiled, giving him a nod. "Of course. I'm always up for some Overcooked chaos, now that I know how fun this game is."

Dalton practically bounced in his seat, grinning from ear to ear. "Yes! You're the best, Hailey! Now we'll never lose!"

Nathan, though more reserved, gave me a small, grateful smile, his eyes softening with something like relief. "Thanks, Hailey. That means a lot."

Seeing their reactions made my chest feel warm. These two were good kids, and it was impossible not to want to be there for them. If Callum wasn't going to make the effort, I sure as hell would. And as long as I was under this roof, I'd make sure they never felt like they didn't have someone to hang out with.

CHAPTER 14

CALLUM

THE SMELL OF BACON AND COFFEE HIT ME THE SECOND I STEPPED OUT OF MY room. Hell yeah. This was what mornings were all about.

It was Sunday—the one day of the week where things slowed down around here. Practice was later in the day, so I had time to relax before everything got hectic again.

When I walked into the kitchen, it was... surprisingly lively. Mom and Mrs. Eller were at the table, chatting away like they'd been friends forever. Their husbands, my dad and Mr. Eller, were quieter, but still chiming in occasionally. It was like some weird family brunch that had just become normal since Hailey and her family had moved in.

But what really caught my attention was Dalton and Nathan.

They were seated at the table, too, and... they were actually talking. Like, a lot. More than usual, anyway. Dalton was his usual energetic self, practically bouncing in his seat as he chatted away. But Nathan, who normally kept to himself, was surprisingly engaged in the conversation.

And the weirdest part?

They were both talking to Hailey.

She was sitting next to them, wearing her oversized shirt again but with actual pajamas underneath this time, thank God. The three of them were deep in conversation, laughing about something that had clearly happened last night. It didn't take a genius to figure out that they must've stayed up playing video games after I went to bed.

I grabbed a plate and piled on some eggs and bacon, sliding into my usual seat. I wasn't exactly in the mood for small talk, but it was hard not to notice how different the dynamic felt this morning.

I glanced over at Hailey, who seemed completely comfortable, like she'd always been part of this weird little family setup. I still wasn't sure how I felt about it, but... whatever. If she was keeping my little brothers entertained, I wasn't going to complain.

Mom glanced at me, raising an eyebrow as I dug into my food. "Morning, Callum. Did you sleep well?"

"Yeah," I mumbled through a mouthful of bacon. "You?"

"Pretty well," she replied, smiling. "It's nice to have a quiet Sunday morning."

Mrs. Eller chuckled. "Especially with how busy things have been lately."

I nodded absentmindedly, my focus shifting back to Dalton, Nathan, and Hailey. They were still laughing, and I caught bits and pieces of their conversation.

"Hailey almost set the kitchen on fire," Dalton giggled, clearly exaggerating as he told some story about their Overcooked game. "The soup was burning, and she didn't know what to do!"

"I panicked!" Hailey laughed, holding up her hands in mock surrender. "But I pulled it together!"

Nathan, smiling more than I'd seen him in a while, added, "We got three stars on the level, so it was a success."

Dalton grinned, looking up at Hailey like she was some kind of hero. "We couldn't have done it without you."

I couldn't help but feel a strange tug in my chest. Dalton and Nathan had never looked at me like that. It was like Hailey had slipped into this big sister role with them overnight, and they were already completely smitten with her. It was... weird.

I shoved another forkful of eggs into my mouth, trying to ignore the nagging feeling in the back of my mind.

Whatever. It didn't matter. As long as they were happy, that was all that mattered. Right?

Mom was talking about some weekend plans with Mrs. Eller, while Dad and Mr. Eller added their own thoughts here and there. It wasn't long before the conversation shifted to the upcoming week, and of course, the homecoming game came up.

"So, the big game's next week, right?" Mrs. Eller asked, smiling as she looked over at me.

"Yeah," I said, nodding. "Homecoming game against Oakridge. It's a big deal."

Mom chimed in, her voice full of excitement. "We'll all be there, of course! Wouldn't miss it."

Dad nodded in agreement. "You've been working hard, Callum. We're looking forward to seeing you out there."

Nathan and Dalton, still buzzing from their game night with Hailey, both nodded enthusiastically. "We'll be there!" Dalton said, practically bouncing in his seat. "We're gonna cheer so loud!" He then decided that now would be the perfect time to demonstrate exactly how he planned on cheering for me. "Westview! Westview!"

His enthusiasm drew a few laughs from the table. Even Mrs. Eller smiled warmly. "Of course, we'll all be there."

Everyone chimed in with their support... except for Hailey. She stayed quiet, casually eating her breakfast like she hadn't heard a word. But I noticed. Oh, I noticed.

I couldn't help myself—I shot her a pointed look. "What about you, Hailey? You gonna be there too, or what?"

Hailey froze mid-bite, looking up at me with a slightly caught-off-guard expression. She paused for a second, clearly scrambling for a response before her eyes narrowed slightly. "Uh, obviously, I'll be there. It's my school, too, you know."

"Right," I said, leaning back in my chair with a smirk. "But you didn't sound too excited."

She rolled her eyes, her tone sarcastic as ever. "Yeah, well, I just said I was gonna be there. Don't expect me to be cheering you on."

I raised an eyebrow, crossing my arms over my chest. "Oh? So who will you be cheering for then?"

She shrugged, her lips curling into a teasing smile. "Literally everyone else on the team. Just not you."

That earned a laugh from Dalton, who clearly found the back-and-forth amusing. But me? I wasn't letting that slide. "Right," I said, my voice dripping with sarcasm. "Because cheering for the captain would be way too much for you, huh?"

"Exactly. Can't have your ego inflating more than it already has."

I opened my mouth to fire back, but before I could get a word out, Mom sighed from across the table. "Really? You two can't go one meal without bickering?"

Mrs. Eller chuckled, clearly trying to diffuse the tension. "It's becoming a habit, isn't it?"

Dalton was giggling beside me, clearly entertained by our little argument, but Nathan was a bit more reserved, his eyes darting between us with mild concern. Even Dad shook his head, looking exasperated but not surprised.

I shrugged, grabbing a piece of bacon and shoving it into my mouth. "Hey, she started it."

Hailey crossed her arms, giving me a look that could kill. "Oh, I started it? You're the one who—"

"Enough," Mom said, giving us both a pointed look. "Just get along for five minutes, would you? That's all I'm asking."

Hailey muttered something under her breath, clearly not willing to let it go entirely, but she dropped the argument for now. I, on the other hand, leaned back in my chair, satisfied that I'd at least gotten under her skin a little.

Just when I thought the conversation was winding down and I could finally finish my breakfast in peace, Mr. Eller, Hailey's dad, spoke up.

"Hailey," he said, turning to her with a proud smile. "I heard you're on the yearbook club now, right? So, I guess you'll be snapping pictures at the homecoming game?"

Hailey looked up from her plate, shrugging casually. "Yeah, probably. It's part of the gig."

Mrs. Eller beamed at her daughter. "That's great, sweetie! You'll get to capture all the big moments. Maybe even one of Callum scoring a goal, huh?"

Before Hailey could respond, I leaned back in my chair, smirking as the perfect opportunity presented itself. "Just make sure you don't get too transfixed by me out there," I said, my tone teasing.

Hailey shot me a look that could freeze hell and all its occupants over, her scowl deepening. "Please, like I'd waste good film on you."

"Come on, Hailey. You know you'll be fighting the urge to zoom in."

"The only thing I'll be zooming in on is the back of your head when you miss the goal."

"So you *are* gonna zoom in on me."

"You two..." Mom sighed, shaking her head in disbelief, though there was a hint of amusement in her voice. "I don't know how you manage to argue over everything."

Mrs. Eller chuckled. "It's almost impressive, really."

But Hailey wasn't done yet. She picked up her coffee mug, taking a sip as she glared at me over the rim. "Don't flatter yourself, Reid. I'm more likely to take pictures of the grass than of you."

I smirked, raising an eyebrow. "Guess we'll find out at the game, won't we?"

She didn't respond, just scowled at me before turning back to her food, clearly irritated that I'd gotten the last word in. I bit back a laugh, satisfied that I'd successfully ruffled her feathers yet again.

But as the conversation shifted back to more neutral topics, I couldn't help but feel a small sense of anticipation for the game. Sure, the pressure was on for the season opener, and Oakridge was a tough team to beat, but part of me was curious to see what Hailey would do when she was out there, camera in hand.

I glanced at her from the corner of my eye. She was still glaring at me, but it wasn't the kind of glare that carried any real heat. More like we'd fallen into this pattern of annoying each other, and somehow, it was starting to feel almost... normal.

But then, something else popped into my head—the photography contest. The one I had seen on Natalia's phone last night. The one I'd thought about sending to Hailey but hadn't yet.

I hadn't stopped thinking about it since.

But I hadn't sent it yet. Why? I wasn't sure. Maybe because I didn't want her to think I was being soft. Or maybe because it wasn't really my place to push her into something she'd quit years ago.

Still, as I watched her now, bickering with Dalton about who got the last pancake, the thought gnawed at the back of my mind. I could send it. Just drop it in her messages and forget about it. No big deal.

But every time I thought about pressing send, something stopped me.

I shoved the thought away for now, returning my focus to breakfast. There'd be time to figure it out later. For now, I had bigger things to worry about—like the homecoming game and not letting Oakridge walk all over us again.

But the thought of that photography contest lingered, just out of reach.

I pushed the last of my breakfast around on my plate, my mind still stuck on that damn photography contest. I needed to stop thinking about it.

Finally, I decided to shake it off. I shoved my chair back from the table, the legs scraping against the floor as I stood up. "I'm heading out," I said, tossing my napkin onto the plate. "I'm going over to Adam's."

Mom glanced up from her conversation with Mrs. Eller. "Oh? You boys getting some soccer practice in?"

"Something like that," I mumbled. Truth was, I just needed to clear my head, and hanging out at Adam's place usually did the trick. We'd probably play some FIFA, talk strategy for the homecoming game, and maybe grab something to eat later.

Mrs. Eller smiled at me. "Well, have fun, Callum."

"Yeah, yeah," I muttered, grabbing my keys from the counter.

As I turned to leave, I caught Hailey watching me from across the table. She didn't say anything, but her eyes narrowed slightly, like she knew I had something on my mind. I ignored her, rolling my eyes internally.

"See you guys later," I called over my shoulder as I headed toward the door.

"Have fun!" Dalton chirped, still bouncing in his seat.

As I stepped out of the house and into the fresh air, I let out a breath I hadn't realized I was holding. Maybe some time with Adam would help me forget about everything—about Hailey, about the photography contest, about all the stupid stuff swirling around in my head.

Or maybe I just needed to stop overthinking.

CHAPTER 15
CALLUM

I was sprawled out on Adam's bed, the controller in hand as we went head-to-head in FIFA like we did almost every weekend. Adam's room was just as messy as ever, clothes and random junk scattered across the floor, even more anime posters lining the walls. It was like he lived in a constant state of chaos, but I was used to it by now.

"Bro, you're trash," Adam laughed as he stole the ball from me and sprinted down the virtual field. "You're not even trying!"

"Shut up," I muttered, my thumb jamming down on the buttons as I tried to get the ball back. But he was right—I wasn't really focused. My head was still stuck on other things, even though I'd come here to forget about all that.

Adam shot and scored, throwing his arms up in triumph. "Boom! Another goal. You're slipping, man."

I grumbled under my breath, restarting the game without saying anything. I wasn't in the mood to talk about why my head wasn't in the game, and Adam—thankfully—didn't push it. He knew me well enough to let it slide, at least for now.

As the game loaded back up, Adam grabbed a bottle of water from the floor, taking a swig before turning to me with a smirk. "You ready for the homecoming game next week? I mean, besides getting destroyed by me in FIFA, you think you're actually gonna beat Oakridge this time?"

I shot him a look, my jaw tightening at the mention of Oakridge. "We're not getting destroyed," I said, my tone firm. "We're ready. It's not gonna be like last year."

Adam raised an eyebrow, clearly amused by how serious I sounded. "Chill, bro. I'm just messing with you. But seriously, you've been grinding hard. You think we've got a shot this season?"

I nodded, leaning back against his headboard. "Yeah. We've been putting in the work. Coach is pushing us hard, and the team's looking solid. Oakridge is tough, but we're tougher."

Adam nodded with determination. "Damn right. We're gonna win this thing."

As we kicked off the next FIFA match, my thoughts drifted again, despite my best efforts. I should have been focused on the game, but instead, my mind kept circling back to the same thing: Hailey freakin' Eller.

Damn it, why did I keep thinking about her these days?

"Yo," Adam said, snapping me out of my thoughts. "You good? You're playing like a zombie, man."

I blinked, realizing I'd completely lost track of the game. "Yeah," I muttered, rubbing the back of my neck. "Just got a lot on my mind."

Adam raised an eyebrow, giving me that look like he knew I was full of shit. "Like what?"

I shrugged. "Just soccer stuff. You know, the usual."

Adam didn't push, thankfully, but I could tell he wasn't buying it. We'd been friends long enough for him to know when I wasn't telling the whole story.

"So, bro," Adam started, pausing the game for a second to stretch, "homecoming dance is coming up. You taking anyone?"

I shrugged, focusing on the controller in my hand as I leaned back against the headboard. "Nah."

Adam raised an eyebrow, genuinely surprised. "Damn, really? It's our last homecoming, man. You could literally take anyone you wanted."

I shot him a look, not really interested in the conversation, but Adam being Adam wasn't about to let it go.

"I'm serious, dude," he continued, sitting up and facing me. "You've got options. There's Natalia—your frequent hookup. Or Jessi. And what about Sophia? Brianne? I'm pretty sure half the school would say yes if you asked."

He was right, but none of that mattered to me right now. Natalia was the obvious choice, and Jessi... well, that wasn't anything serious. The idea of asking either of them didn't appeal to me, though. Not anymore.

"Nah," I said again, shaking my head. "I'm not really feeling it."

Adam blinked, clearly confused. "Dude, are you serious? You aren't taking anyone to our last homecoming?"

I sighed, running a hand through my hair. "Yeah, I get that. I just... I don't know, man. It's not really a priority right now. I've got other things to focus on." I glanced at him and grinned slightly. "Like making sure we destroy Oakridge."

Adam laughed, but he still gave me that curious look. "Yeah, yeah, I get it. But you're telling me none of those girls appeal to you right now?"

I hesitated for a second before responding. "Nah. Not really."

Adam looked like he didn't believe me for a second, but then he shrugged. "Well, whatever, man. If that's how you feel."

The truth was, Natalia had been the obvious choice, and we'd hooked up enough times that it would've been a no-brainer. But lately, the idea of showing up to homecoming with her—or anyone, really—felt... off.

Like it was just going through the motions for the sake of it. None of those girls made me want to be at the dance. They didn't make me excited about it, or even interested.

And for some reason, that bothered me.

"Anyway, what about you?" I asked, trying to shift the focus away from me. "You taking anyone?"

Adam grinned, leaning back against the wall, clearly proud of himself. "I'm working on it. Sasha's still single, man. Gotta shoot my shot, you know?"

I snorted. "Yeah, good luck with that."

"Hey, I've got a chance," Adam said, pointing at me with mock seriousness. "I've been playing it cool, biding my time."

"You've been biding your time since, like, freshman year," I shot back with a laugh.

He rolled his eyes but laughed along. "Whatever, bro. You'll see. Slow and steady wins the race."

We got back into the game, but I wasn't really paying attention anymore. Adam kept talking about homecoming, about his "plan" to ask Sasha to the dance, but his voice faded into the background as my mind wandered. The whole conversation had stirred something in me, something I didn't really want to deal with.

How come none of those girls appealed to me? It didn't make sense. Natalia, Jessi, Sophia, Brianne—hell, I could ask any of them, and it'd be easy. No strings attached. No stress. So why wasn't I interested?

I leaned back against the headboard, staring at the screen but not really seeing it.

And then, my mind did that thing I was trying to avoid. It flashed back to Hailey. Hailey in that oversized shirt last night at dinner, her hair up in that messy bun, sitting next to my brothers and laughing like she'd been part of this family forever.

It was casual, nothing special, but the memory was enough to make my stomach twist.

What the hell?

The way her bare legs looked under that shirt, how her collarbone peeked out just a little when she'd shifted in her seat… it had been driving me insane all night. And when I closed my eyes, even for a second, I could feel this heat pooling at the bottom of my stomach, spreading through me like I was some kind of pervert. I clenched my jaw, frustrated with myself. Why was I thinking about Hailey like that? Of all people, why her?

It wasn't like we were friends. We barely tolerated each other. She annoyed the hell out of me, and I went out of my way to irritate her right back. It was how things worked between us— bickering, sarcasm, and nothing more. So why did the thought of her in that damn shirt keep creeping into my mind? Why was it messing with my head like this?

I forced myself to focus on the game, trying to shove the thought of Hailey out of my head. But it was no use. Every time I tried to think about homecoming, or soccer, or anything else, the image of her kept slipping back in.

Adam said something, laughing at a goal he'd just scored, but I barely registered it. All I could think about was how wrong it felt to be thinking about Hailey like this… and how much I couldn't stop.

You've got to be kidding me, I thought to myself, my stomach churning.

The thoughts swirling around in my head were getting unbearable. Hailey. That stupid oversized shirt. The way she'd been on my mind way more than she had any right to be. I needed to shake it off, get rid of this weird tension building up inside me before it got any worse.

I needed to move. Do something—hell, anything—to clear my head.

"Let's go to the gym," I blurted out, dropping my controller onto Adam's bed and sitting up straight.

Adam paused the game, staring at me like I'd just suggested something insane. "The gym? Right now?"

"Yeah," I said, standing up and grabbing my hoodie from the back of his chair. "We're going. Right now."

Adam blinked, clearly still trying to process what I'd just said. "Dude, it's Sunday. We're chilling. Since when do we hit the gym right now? Especially after a scrimmage yesterday? We don't even have practice today."

"I don't care," I muttered, already heading toward his closet to grab his gym bag and some workout clothes. The thought of doing something physical, something that could drown out all the noise in my head, felt like the only solution right now. "I need to get this shit out of my system."

Adam groaned, clearly not thrilled with the idea. "Dude, it's Sunday. The gym can wait. We've got a whole week ahead of us."

But I wasn't listening. I rifled through his clothes, pulling out a pair of his shorts and one of his hoodies. "We're going," I said, tossing the clothes at him. "Get up."

Adam rolled his eyes, standing up slowly. "Fine, but you're acting weird, bro. Did something happen?"

I didn't answer. Instead, I grabbed a t-shirt from his closet, holding it up to make sure it'd fit.

Adam spotted the shirt in my hand and groaned again, louder this time. "You little shit, not that one! That's Essentials! You can't just go around stealing my good stuff."

I ignored him, tucking the shirt under my arm. "Too late. Come on already."

"Unbelievable." Adam grumbled under his breath as he dragged himself off the bed, clearly not thrilled about my sudden burst of energy. But I didn't care. I needed to burn off whatever this was—this frustration, this confusion, this... heat that kept building up every time I thought about Hailey.

We headed out of his room, and I could already feel some of the tension easing up. Hitting the gym would help. It always did.

Adam was still muttering to himself as we walked down the hall. "Can't believe we're doing this… Sunday's supposed to be rest day…"

I chuckled, slinging my bag over my shoulder. "Quit whining, man. You'll thank me later."

He shot me a look. "I better."

CHAPTER 16

CALLUM

THE CLANGING OF WEIGHTS, THE HUM OF TREADMILLS, AND THE FAINT SMELL OF sweat filled the air at the gym. It was busier than I expected for a Sunday, but that didn't matter.

The second we got inside, I hit the weights, and I hit them hard. Adam, on the other hand, looked like he was still trying to figure out how he'd gotten dragged into this.

"Dude," Adam groaned as he wiped sweat from his forehead, already looking winded. "We've been here for, like, an hour. You still going?"

I didn't even bother answering. I was in the middle of another set of deadlifts, and my focus was locked in. The burn in my muscles felt good, like a release of all the tension that had been building up over the past few days. Every time I felt the strain, I pushed harder, like I could physically force all the shit in my head to disappear.

I grunted as I dropped the bar, already moving to set up the next round of weights. My shoulders burned, my legs ached, but I wasn't even close to being done.

Adam, on the other hand, looked like he was about two sets away from collapsing.

"Bro, you're gonna kill yourself. Or me." he panted, sitting down on one of the benches. "If you're gonna go down, just go on your own, spare me. What's gotten into you today?"

I shrugged, grabbing a dumbbell and starting another set of curls. "Just need to get some shit out of my system."

"Yeah, I get that," Adam said, stretching his arms out and yawning. "But you've been going non-stop. What's the deal? Is this about the Oakridge game or something?"

I gritted my teeth, focusing on the weight in my hand. "Something like that."

Truth was, it wasn't just about Oakridge. It wasn't just about soccer. It was everything—the pressure of the season, the constant expectation of being captain, and, of course, the annoying, lingering thoughts about Hailey that I couldn't seem to shake no matter how hard I worked. Adam watched me, leaning back against the wall, watching as I powered through another set, sweat dripping down my face and arms.

"You're insane," he muttered, shaking his head with a grin. "But I guess that's why you're the captain."

I didn't respond. I didn't have the energy for conversation, not when I was in this zone. All I wanted to do was keep lifting, keep pushing, until my body gave out or my mind stopped racing.

Adam, on the other hand, was done. He groaned as he stood up, stretching his sore muscles. "Alright, man, I'm tapping out. You can keep going if you want, but I'm hitting the showers."

"Fine," I said, setting the dumbbell down and moving to the bench press. "I'll meet you after."

Adam gave me a mock salute before heading off toward the locker room, leaving me alone in the weights section. I was glad for the space. The more I worked out, the more I could feel the tension in my chest easing, little by little. Every rep, every lift, was like shedding another layer of whatever was clouding my head.

But as much as I pushed myself, I knew it wasn't enough. Because no matter how many sets I did, no matter how much weight I lifted, I still couldn't get rid of the image of Hailey in my head.

I was halfway through my next set of bench presses, the weight heavy but manageable, when I heard a voice that immediately made my blood boil.

"Well, if it isn't Westview's golden boy."

I froze for a second, the weight suspended in mid-air, before racking the bar with a clank and sitting up. I already knew who it was before I even turned around.

Troy Duran.

Of all the places to run into him. Oakridge's star forward, and a certified pain in my ass. I could feel my blood pressure spike just hearing his voice.

I wiped the sweat off my face and turned to look at him, forcing a grin. "Duran. Didn't know they let clowns into this gym. Thought you'd be too busy practicing those cheap shots you guys are famous for."

Troy laughed, that smug, irritating laugh that always grated on my nerves. "Oh, come on, Reid. We don't need cheap shots to beat you guys. It's just a natural talent thing." He ran a hand through his perfectly styled hair, like he was some kind of damn model.

I rolled my eyes. "Yeah, 'natural talent' and the referees being blind. Must be nice."

He smirked, walking closer, clearly enjoying himself. "Salty much? Can't blame the refs for your team not being able to keep up, can you?"

I stood up, squaring my shoulders as I crossed my arms over my chest. "Last time I checked, we had you scrambling like a headless chicken for most of the game. You wouldn't have scored that last goal if your goalie hadn't practically tackled ours."

Troy waved a dismissive hand. "Details, details. A win's a win, Reid. And this year? We're gonna wipe the floor with you again."

I clenched my jaw, feeling my patience wearing thinner by the second. "Right. Keep telling yourself that. Just don't cry when we take the trophy this time."

"Oh, is that what you're telling your team?" Troy snickered. "Big talk for a guy who hasn't won shit against us. Gotta love that Westview delusion."

I glared at him, my hands clenching into fists at my sides. I wanted to deck him. Really, really wanted to. But I knew better than to let him get to me like that. That's what he wanted, and I wasn't about to give him the satisfaction.

"I'll remember that when you're the one picking grass out of your teeth after we run circles around you," I said, my voice low.

Troy tilted his head, his smirk never faltering. "Looking forward to it, Reid. Just try not to cry when it's over. Again."

He winked at me, a wink of all things, and turned to walk away like he'd already won something, leaving me standing there, fuming.

I took a deep breath, forcing myself to calm down. Troy wasn't worth it. He never was. But damn, if he didn't know how to get under my skin. The game against Oakridge was already weighing on me, but running into him now? That just made it ten times worse.

I shook my head, grabbing the bar again and lowering myself onto the bench for another set. Fine. Let him run his mouth. When game day came, I'd make sure to shut it for him.

I dropped the bar after another set and wiped my face with a towel, breathing hard. Usually, working out helped clear my head, but today? It was only making things worse.

No matter how hard I pushed, the frustration just kept building. Between Troy's bullshit and my own thoughts swirling around in my head, this workout was turning into more stress than it was worth. I ran a hand through my sweaty hair, shaking my head. Enough. I needed to call it quits before I lost my mind.

I headed toward the locker room, hoping a shower would help cool me off. As I stepped inside, I could already hear Adam singing—badly, as usual. He was in one of the stalls, belting out some random pop song so off-tune I bet that if he went on X Factor he'd be booed and kicked off the stage. And make Simon Cowell cry or something.

I shook my head, chuckling to myself. "You sound like a dying cat, bro!" I called out, but Adam didn't even hear me over his own noise. That's what it was. Noise.

I made my way over to my locker, tossing my towel inside and pulling out my phone. As I unlocked it, a text notification popped up from Natalia.

Natalia: What are you up to, hot stuff?
Me: Working out. You know, the usual.
Natalia: Mmm, I like the sound of that. Send me a sexy pic?

I raised an eyebrow, feeling a little smug as I read her message. Alright, if she wanted a pic, I could deliver. Hell, I wasn't exactly in bad shape right now. The workout may have been frustrating, but I couldn't deny that I was looking pretty damn good after all that lifting.

I walked over to the mirror and lifted my shirt, revealing my sweaty abs. The lighting in here wasn't too bad either, so I decided to try out a new angle. I angled the phone lower, flexing my abs a little harder and tilting my phone so my chest looked bigger. The beads of sweat glistened on my skin, and hell yeah, I was feeling it.

I snapped the picture and checked it over. Hah. Not bad. Actually, I looked pretty damn good.

I quickly atttached the picture and typed a little playful message to go along with it.

Me: How's this for a pic?

I hit send, still grinning as I admired my reflection in the mirror. Sure, things with Natalia were casual, but it was nice having someone who was always down for a little fun. And after the morning I'd had, I needed some fun.

A few seconds later, another text popped up.

Natalia: Damn, that's hot. You free later?

I couldn't help but smirk, already feeling a little better than I had earlier.

Me: Maybe.

I typed back to Natalia, still smirking to myself. It was nice having someone around who could always lighten the mood. But as I went to close my messages, I noticed something sitting right above our chat—the post for the photography contest.

Again?

Ugh.

Fuck it.

Whatever. I'd been putting this off for way too long. I wasn't going to sit here and debate it anymore. It was just a contest, and I wasn't trying to be nice or anything. It was just… a good opportunity for her. Right?

I took a screenshot of the contest post, exhaled, and opened up my messages with Hailey. The chat was as dry as a desert—mostly a bunch of old sarcastic quips and reminders about morning rides to school. It wasn't like we ever really texted unless it was absolutely necessary.

But whatever. I wasn't going to overthink it. I hurriedly attached the screenshot, about to send it when—

SHIT.

My thumb slipped, and before I could double-check, I hit send. But as soon as I did, my stomach sank.

Fuck. FUCK.

I didn't send the screenshot of the photography contest. Oh no. I sent... the picture. The picture. The one I just took. Of my sweaty abs. The one I had sent to Natalia.

I just sent that shit to Hailey.

I stared at my phone, frozen, my heart pounding as the realization sank in. "Oh, fuck me," I muttered under my breath.

The message was already sent, sitting there in the chat like some kind of nuclear bomb just waiting to go off. I scrambled, my mind racing with possible solutions. Could I unsend it? No, that wasn't a thing. Maybe she hadn't seen it yet? I could delete it on my end, but that wouldn't help. Maybe I could say it was an accident? I mean, it was.

"Fuck..." I groaned, running my hand through my hair and pacing back and forth in the locker room, my pulse racing.

Adam's off-key singing echoed through the showers, blissfully unaware of the crisis happening on my end.

CHAPTER 17

HAILEY

THE COOL NIGHT AIR FELT NICE AGAINST MY SKIN AS I STOOD IN THE BACKYARD, waiting excitedly by the hot tub. Mr. Reid was fiddling with the last few settings, adjusting the jets or something, while Mrs. Reid and my mom hovered nearby, cheering him on like he was performing some kind of magic trick.

"You got it, honey!" Mrs. Reid clapped, clearly excited for the evening ahead.

My mom grinned, folding her arms as she watched Mr. Reid with amusement. "You're a hero, Keith."

I couldn't help but chuckle. I felt a little… silly, to be honest. Here I was, standing in the backyard, barefoot in a swimsuit, getting ready to hang out in a hot tub with two middle-aged women on a Sunday night.

"Almost there, ladies," Mr. Reid said, straightening up and wiping his hands on a towel. "Just give it a minute."

Mrs. Reid grinned, practically bouncing with excitement. "I can't wait! It's been ages since we've used this thing."

I smiled along with her, though I still felt a little out of place. I mean, here I was, an 18-year-old about to soak in a hot tub with two moms. I felt like I was 30 years too early for this activity.

But then again... why not? A hot tub was a hot tub. And after everything with the house burning down, the constant running around, and the chaos of moving in with the Reids, I'd take whatever peace and quiet I could get.

Mrs. Reid shot me a warm smile. "You excited, Hailey? I bet you could use a little relaxation after all the craziness."

I nodded, feeling my shoulders relax just at the thought of it. "Yeah, there's no way I'd say no to this."

Mr. Reid, with a satisfied nod, stepped back from the tub and wiped his hands. "Alright, it's ready to go. Enjoy, ladies."

The three of us cheered, and even though it felt a little goofy, I couldn't help but laugh. I'd spent so much time stressing lately that I forgot what it felt like to just... have fun.

Even if it was hanging out in a hot tub with two moms.

Mrs. Reid and my mom were already kicking off their sandals and climbing in, and I followed their lead, stepping into the warm water. It felt incredible, like all the tension in my body was melting away the second I sank into the bubbles.

"This is heaven," Mrs. Reid sighed, leaning back against the edge of the tub. "We should do this more often."

My mom nodded in agreement, her eyes closed as she relaxed. "Absolutely. We deserve it."

I smiled to myself, sinking deeper into the water. Yeah, maybe I wasn't exactly living the wild teenage life, but I had to admit—this wasn't so bad.

The warmth of the hot tub was already working its magic, the bubbling water relaxing my muscles as I leaned back and let out a sigh. Mrs. Reid and my mom were on either side of me, equally as content as we soaked in the steamy water. The conversation flowed easily, starting off with casual chatter about school and how I was settling into senior year.

"So, how's it going so far, Hailey?" Mrs. Reid asked, her voice light as she adjusted in her spot. "Everything going good with your classes?"

I shrugged. "Yeah, I guess. I mean, it's school. Nothing too exciting. First week was alright, just went over the syallbus, started some assignments. I joined the yearbook club, as you guys know. Yeah. It's pretty alright."

My mom smiled, her eyes crinkling in that way that told me she was proud of how I was handling everything, even though she didn't say it outright. "You've been doing great, sweetie. Especially with everything that's happened."

I nodded, trying to brush off the compliment. "It's been... an adjustment, but yeah. I'm managing."

Mrs. Reid chimed in again, her eyes sparkling with curiosity. "And what about... relationships, Hailey? Any boys on the radar we should know about?"

I nearly choked on the steam rising from the water. "Boys on the radar?" I echoed, blinking in surprise. That topic had come out of nowhere. "No, no. Nothing like that. Nothing."

Mrs. Reid's eyes sparkled mischievously. "Well, what's your ideal type, then, Hailey? You must've thought about it at some point."

I paused, caught off guard by the question. My ideal type? I'd never really put much thought into it before. It wasn't like I spent hours fantasizing about some dream guy. But if I had to describe someone...

"Hm..." I started, leaning back against the edge of the tub as I thought about it. "I guess... someone who can match my humor? I'd need someone who can keep up with my sarcasm and not take everything so seriously."

Both Mrs. Reid and my mom nodded eagerly, waiting for me to continue. Damn it, when moms wanted to dig, they did it even better than professional miners did.

"And maybe someone a bit taller than me. Nice smile, you know? And... I guess someone who's hardworking. Like, someone who actually cares about what they do and puts effort into it."

Mrs. Reid's eyes went wide, and she gasped dramatically. "Oh my god!" she whispered, covering her mouth with her hand like she'd just discovered a major secret.

I frowned, confused. "What?"

She leaned in closer, her eyes twinkling with excitement. "You know what, Hailey? Your ideal type? You just described Callum to a T."

Excuse me?

I felt like the world stopped for a second. My heart skipped a beat, and I nearly choked on the air around me. "What?!" I sputtered, sitting up straighter in the water. "No way. No, absolutely not."

But Mrs. Reid and my mom were both laughing now, clearly finding the whole thing hilarious.

"Oh, come on," Mrs. Reid teased, a grin on her face. "Taller than you? Nice smile? Hardworking? That's my Callum, through and through."

Through and through? Yeah, no.

"No, no, no, no," I stammered, shaking my head so hard that I thought it might fall off. "That's... not... No way. That's not what I meant. I didn't mean Callum. I was just describing... you know, in general. That's the type of stuff I like in a guy. But there's also a lot of stuff that I don't like in a guy."

Mrs. Reid wiggled her eyebrows playfully. "Sure, sure. If you say so, Hailey."

I shot her a look, feeling like I might spontaneously combust from the awkwardness. "I don't like Callum like that. Seriously. We don't even get along. You know that."

Mrs. Reid giggled, leaning back in the water. "Okay, okay. Just having a little fun. But I still think it's funny to imagine, no?"

My mom, who had been quiet up until now, gave me a knowing smile but didn't say anything. I groaned, sinking further into the water, wanting the conversation to move on immediately.

Callum? My ideal type? No freaking way.

After the whole "Callum is your ideal type" bomb Mrs. Reid dropped, the conversation eventually shifted back to lighter topics. They teased me for a while longer, but I made sure to steer things away from anything that had to do with relationships—or, god forbid, Callum.

I still couldn't believe she'd even said that.

Me? Liking Callum?

It was like saying I enjoyed stepping on Legos barefoot.

But the more I tried to push the thought away, the more it lingered. I shook my head, sinking lower into the warm water. Nope. Not going there. Absolutely not.

"Ah, shoot," my mom said suddenly, looking around. "We forgot the snacks inside."

Mrs. Reid let out a small sigh, sitting up straighter. "We did, didn't we?"

I saw my chance to escape the conversation for a few minutes. "I'll go grab them," I volunteered, wrapping a towel around myself as I stood up. "Be right back."

"Thanks, sweetie," my mom said, and Mrs. Reid smiled, nodding in appreciation.

I stepped out of the hot tub, drying my feet on the rug before heading back into the house. The air inside was cooler, and the sounds of Phineas and Ferb filled the living room as I passed by the couch. Dalton and Nathan were both sprawled out, watching the show intently.

"Hey, Hailey!" Dalton called as I walked by.

"Hey," I said with a small wave, making my way over to the counter where we'd left the bowl of snacks. I grabbed the bowl, but before I could head back outside, I spotted my phone on the counter and decided to check it. You know, just in case I'd missed anything important like a delivery update for the new makeup or clothes I'd ordered.

And there it was—a text from Callum. A photo?

Why the hell was Callum texting me?

Curiosity got the best of me, and I opened the message. What could it possibly be? Maybe it was something about school? Or... maybe—

But the second the photo loaded on my screen, I screamed.

"What the fuck?!"

The phone slipped out of my hand and clattered onto the counter, my eyes wide with shock as I stared at it like it was about to explode.

I had just been sent a picture of Callum's abs.

Sweaty, flexed, and very... there. I immediately realized I was in the middle of the living room, with Dalton and Nathan now staring at me, wide-eyed. I cringed, suddenly remembering that I'd just cursed in front of them.

"Sorry! Sorry!" I said quickly, holding up my hands in apology. "I didn't mean to curse—"

Dalton turned around from the TV, concern written all over his face. "Are you okay, Hailey? What happened?"

Nathan glanced over, looking equally as concerned. "Did something scare you?"

I waved my hands around frantically, trying to regain my composure. "No, no, it's fine! Everything's fine! I just... I, uh... saw a bug. Yeah, a bug. A really... big one."

Dalton's eyes went wide with fear and he glanced around as if I'd just him there was a sniper aiming for him. "A bug?! Where?!"

I groaned inwardly, bending down to retrieve my phone as I tried to keep my heart from exploding. "It's fine! I handled it. No big deal."

Nathan raised an eyebrow, clearly not convinced but too polite to push it.

I stood there frozen, staring at my phone lying face-up on the ground like it was some kind of alien object. My heart was still racing, my mind trying to process what I had just seen. There was no way I'd just imagined it, right? I couldn't have hallucinated something that vivid.

With a deep breath, I crouched down and cautiously lifted my phone, as if something might crawl out from under it. My hands were shaking, but I had to look again. I had to... confirm what I'd seen.

And there it was.

In all its infuriating, sweaty, flexed glory.

Yup. Confirmed.

Callum's abs. Staring back at me from the screen. His smug face peeking just above them, looking like he was so damn pleased with himself. The sweat glistening on his skin, the way his muscles looked like they were practically carved out of stone...

Oh my god.

I felt my face heat up instantly, like my entire body had just been thrown into the sun. My heart pounded so hard I thought I might pass out. What was happening? Why was this happening?

I blinked at the photo, my brain barely keeping up with the flood of emotions surging through me—shock, confusion, and, much to my horror, a tiny flicker of something else.

Wait. NO. Absolutely not.

I squeezed my eyes shut for a second, willing the image to disappear from my brain. But it was too late. I could still see it. Him. His stupid abs. His stupid, perfect abs.

I opened my eyes again, staring at the screen, my mind racing. Why the hell did he send this to me?

Was it a joke? Some kind of weird, messed-up prank? Was he messing with me? Had to be. There was no way he would actually—oh god. Maybe he thought he was texting someone else. Maybe this was meant for Natalia or something, and I'd been the unlucky recipient of the most embarrassing mistake of his life.

That had to be it. Right?

I quickly backed out of the message, my hands still trembling as I tried to calm myself down. My brain was in overdrive, screaming at me to delete the photo, to pretend this never happened, to throw my phone into a lake and run away from civilization.

But I couldn't stop staring at it. Callum Reid. My mortal enemy. And yet, here I was, staring at him like I couldn't look away. Like some kind of magnetic force was pulling me in.

This was a nightmare.

I slammed my phone down onto the counter, maybe a little harder than I meant to. The loud thud echoed in the kitchen, but I didn't care. I needed that thing far, far away from me right now.

No. I wasn't going to look at it again. That picture was definitely meant for someone else. It had to be a mistake. There was no way Callum Reid would send me—me—a picture of his abs on purpose.

But...

My fingers twitched.

Oh my god. No. Don't even think about it.

I pressed my palms flat against the counter, willing myself to ignore the phone that sat there, taunting me. I needed to just grab the snacks and get back outside, back to the hot tub with my mom and Mrs. Reid, back to normal, boring, non-chaotic life.

This was just some stupid mistake, and I didn't need to make it a bigger deal than it was.

But...

What if I just... looked at it one more time?

I groaned internally, feeling my resolve crack as the image of Callum's abs flashed in my mind again. His stupid face. The sweat dripping down his skin. His flexed, taut, torso...

Okay, just one more look. That wouldn't hurt, right? I mean, it's not like anyone would know. And if I confirmed it was an accident, then I could laugh it off later. No big deal.

Slowly, reluctantly, I reached for my phone again, my heart pounding as my fingers hovered over the screen. My brain was screaming at me to stop, to throw the phone into the ocean or something. But... curiosity had its claws in me now, and there was no going back.

Just one more look.

I unlocked the phone, and there it was again. The picture. The stupid, perfect picture. Callum's abs, glistening with sweat, his cocky smirk like he knew exactly what he was doing.

Fuck.

My stomach twisted, and my breath caught in my throat. I couldn't believe I was doing this—looking at Callum Reid like he was some kind of Greek god instead of the insufferable jerk I'd known for years. What was wrong with me?

But... damn. One more look was turning into a very *long* look, and I hated myself for it.

Quickly, I locked my phone again and slammed it down on the counter for the second time, harder this time, as if trying to banish the image from my brain. I squeezed my eyes shut, feeling the heat rise to my cheeks.

Okay, that's enough. That's more than enough.

I needed to get a grip. This was Callum. Callum. The guy who irritated the hell out of me on a daily basis, who I couldn't stand most of the time.

Not someone I should be... admiring. At all.

With a deep breath, I grabbed the snacks and hurried back outside, trying to shove the whole incident to the farthest corner of my mind.

But the image was still there, burned into my brain, refusing to leave me alone.

CHAPTER 18
CALLUM

I GROANED FOR WHAT FELT LIKE THE HUNDREDTH TIME, LEANING MY HEAD BACK against the headrest of my car. I'd been sitting in the garage for half an hour now, staring at my phone like it was going to explode in my hand. My heart was racing, my palms were sweaty, and I couldn't stop replaying the moment I realized what I'd done.

How the hell did I send that to Hailey?

I'd texted her. Multiple times, in fact. I was desperate, telling her to delete the picture, that it wasn't meant for her. But every time I checked, my messages were still unread.

Me: Hey, that wasn't meant for you.
Me: Delete that.
Me: It wasn't for you.
Me: Hello?

I ran a hand through my hair, squeezing my eyes shut as I let out another groan. I couldn't believe I'd done this. I couldn't believe I'd sent that stupid photo to Hailey Eller of all people. The one person I had zero interest in impressing—or, well, I thought I didn't, but this whole thing was making me question everything.

I was just messing around, being stupidly smug, like always. But then, in my rush to send her that contest screenshot... my thumb had slipped, and I hit send before I even realized what I'd done.

The horror that hit me when I saw which photo I had sent was like getting sucker-punched. My stomach dropped so fast I thought I might actually throw up.

And now? Now I was stuck in this nightmare.

I grabbed my phone again, checking one last time. Nothing. Hailey hadn't opened a single message. I tried to picture her reaction when she eventually saw it—the pure shock, maybe even disgust—and it only made me feel worse.

I was on the verge of pacing, but I couldn't exactly do that in my car. So I just sat there, my foot tapping nervously against the floor, my brain racing in circles. What the hell was I supposed to do now? I couldn't exactly walk up to her and say, *Hey, so about that picture I sent you...*

She was probably sitting in the basement right now, either laughing her ass off or planning my murder. Or worse, maybe she'd show the photo to someone else. Maybe she'd use it as blackmail and force me to become her own personal lapdog or something.

No. Hailey wouldn't do that. Right?

I shook my head, clearing my head of the image of me kneeling on some little velvet pillow, leashed on a shock collar in front of Hailey on a throne as I leaned back and groaned again. None of this made any sense. Why did it even bother me so much? It wasn't like I cared what she thought of me.

I mean, sure, it was embarrassing, but I didn't care about her opinion. Right?

I sat in the car for what felt like an eternity, my mind spinning in circles. I knew I couldn't stay here all night. As much as I wanted to avoid this whole situation, I had to face Hailey eventually. The longer I waited, the worse it was going to get.

With a deep breath, I finally yanked the keys from the ignition and stepped out of the car. My stomach twisted with dread as I made my way toward the house, cautiously opening the door and stepping inside. The familiar warmth of the house hit me, but it did nothing to calm my nerves.

Just as I was heading down the hallway, I heard the sound of voices. My mom and Mrs. Eller were coming in from the backyard, towels wrapped around them, their cheeks flushed from the hot tub.

"Oh, hey, Callum!" Mom greeted me cheerfully, her hair still damp from the water. "We just spent some time in the hot tub."

I forced a smile, trying to act normal even though my insides were in knots. "Yeah? That sounds nice."

Mrs. Eller smiled warmly, her towel wrapped snugly around her shoulders. "It was great. You should join us next time."

Chilling in the hot tub with my mom and Hailey's mom didn't seem like the most appealing idea in the world but I just nodded awkwardly, acting like I was paying attention. Though my mind became laser-focused when I heard what she said next.

"Hailey's still out there, though," Mom added casually. "She wanted a few more minutes to relax."

Oh, great. Hailey was still outside. Alone. In the hot tub.

I swallowed hard, my palms suddenly sweaty again. I had to talk to her. I couldn't let this hang over me all night, especially not after the photo fiasco. Maybe if I just got it over with, I'd feel better. Maybe she'd laugh it off, or maybe we'd just pretend it never happened.

Yeah, right.

Still, it was now or never. I couldn't avoid her forever. I mumbled a quick "Thanks" to Mom and Mrs. Eller before cautiously making my way toward the sliding glass door that led to the backyard. As I stepped outside, the cool night air hit me, making the knots in my stomach tighten even more. The backyard was dimly lit, and I could hear the gentle bubbling of the hot tub just a few steps away.

I stepped outside, my heart racing in my chest as I took slow, cautious steps toward the hot tub. The sound of the bubbling water filled the quiet night air, and as I got closer, I spotted Hailey sitting there, her back to me. She hadn't noticed me yet, thankfully, so I had a few seconds to gather myself.

But then my breath caught in my throat.

Shit.

The dim light of the backyard barely illuminated her, but it was enough. Her hair was wet, clinging to her soft skin as she leaned back against the edge of the hot tub. Water droplets shimmered on her bare shoulders, her back smooth and... oh god. I could only see her from behind, but that was enough to mess with my head.

I stood frozen in place for a second, feeling like the world had shifted on its axis. I couldn't even think straight. It was Hailey. The same Hailey I'd been bickering with for years, the same Hailey who pissed me off more often than not. But now, as I stood there, I was suddenly all too aware of the fact that she wasn't just Hailey.

She was... gorgeous.

And that realization hit me like a damn truck.

Fuck. I rubbed my forehead, trying to keep my breathing steady. This was a mistake. A huge mistake. I'd come out here to fix the disaster of the photo I sent, not to have some kind of... crisis over how good Hailey looked in a bikini.

But my eyes kept tracing the lines of her back, the way her skin seemed to glow under the dim lights, the way the water lapped gently at her waist... and I felt like I was coming undone. Like some kind of weird, hormonal mess that I couldn't control.

I knew I had to snap out of it. I was here for a reason. I couldn't stand there like a creep, gawking at her while she had no idea I was there. But, god... it was hard. The sight of her, just sitting there in the water, completely oblivious to the chaos she was causing in my head... it was too much.

I clenched my fists, trying to focus. I had to say something. I had to fix this. But right now, I felt like a complete mess. Taking a deep breath, I forced myself to take a step forward, clearing my throat as quietly as I could.

"Hailey?"

She turned around at the sound of my voice, her eyes widening slightly in surprise as she noticed me standing there. My breath caught again, but this time, it wasn't just because of her back.

Her bikini was a dark maroon, and it clung to her like it was made for her. The way the material hugged her curves, the water glistening on her skin... I was having trouble breathing. My mind went blank, my pulse quickening as I tried to look away and—goddamn it—failed.

Her chest, her waist, everything... it was just—Fuck.

I cleared my throat again, trying to focus. I had to stop staring. I had to say something. But my mind was a mess, and my words felt tangled up in the knot in my chest.

Hailey's eyes flicked to mine, and I could see the shyness there. She shifted slightly in the water, pulling her arms across her chest like she was suddenly self-conscious, her cheeks turning a soft shade of pink. Of course, it wasn't just the fact that she was sitting there in a bikini. I knew the real reason she looked so shy—because of the picture. And now, here we were, in this awkward, tension-filled moment, with me unable to stop staring at her and her trying to avoid eye contact.

For a second, neither of us said anything. The bubbling of the hot tub was the only sound between us, and it felt like an eternity passed before I finally worked up the nerve to speak. "Uh…" I started, my voice rougher than I intended. "I need to explain about earlier. That picture…"

Her eyes widened a little, her lips pressing together as she looked down at the water. "Yeah… I, uh… got it."

I cringed internally, wanting to slam my head into the nearest wall. *Of course she got it. You sent it through text, not a damn carrier piegon.* "It wasn't meant for you," I said quickly, running a hand through my hair. "It was an accident. I didn't mean to send it to you."

She glanced up at me, her cheeks still flushed, and I could tell she was trying to keep it cool. "Yeah, I figured," she said, her voice a little softer than usual. There was still a hint of sarcasm there, but she seemed… off. Shy. Uncomfortable, maybe.

"I sent you the wrong picture," I muttered, rubbing the back of my neck. "It was meant for… uh… someone else."

"Right," she said, nodding quickly. "I assumed that."

The tension between us felt thick, the air heavy with awkwardness. I wasn't used to seeing Hailey like this. She was always so sharp, so quick with her words. But now… she was quiet, shy even, and it was throwing me off balance in ways I couldn't explain. I didn't know what to do with myself.

"I, uh… sent you some messages after," I continued, trying to explain. "Telling you to delete it. But…"

Hailey bit her lip, glancing down at the water again. "Yeah, I didn't check my phone after I saw the… uh, picture." She looked up at me then, and for the first time since I'd stepped outside, she met my eyes directly. "But, like… it's fine. I get it. Honest mistake."

"Right," I said, awkwardly rubbing the back of my neck again. "Well… just delete it, alright?"

She nodded quickly, her eyes flicking away from mine again. "Yeah, I will."

I stood there for another second, unsure of what to do next. My brain was a mess, my body was tense, and all I wanted was to get away from this weird, intense situation. But I couldn't move. Finally, after what felt like an eternity, I muttered, "Well, good. That's that, then," and turned to leave, my heart still pounding in my chest.

I was about to make my great escape when I heard Hailey's voice, soft but steady.

"Callum...?"

I froze, my hand already on the sliding door. Goddamn it. I couldn't just leave now, could I? I turned slightly to look at her. I tried to act like I was irritated—like I usually was with her —but the truth was, I was struggling. Big time.

I turned fully toward her again, my breath catching in my throat. "What?" I asked, my voice sounding more gruff than I intended, trying to hide the fact that every second I spent standing there was making me more uncomfortable. Not because of her, I told myself. Just because of the whole situation.

"Can you, uh... come over here for a second?" she asked quietly. I raised an eyebrow, trying to hold onto the annoyance that was usually so easy with her. But the way she said it, the way she looked up at me with those green eyes of hers, there was something different. Something that made it hard to be irritated.

Still, I sighed, acting like this was the last thing I wanted to do, even though my body was already moving toward her. "Fine," I muttered, taking a few cautious steps closer.

But as I got closer, I couldn't stop myself. My eyes kept flicking to the way the water droplets dotted and trickled over her chest, the dark maroon bikini clinging to her like a second skin. The way her hair was still wet, sticking to her collarbone, her soft, pale skin glistening under the low light. And those green eyes.

God, why did her eyes have to look like that?

Like they could see right through me?

I shook my head, forcing myself to look anywhere else but her, and I cleared my throat. "What's the deal? What do you need?"

She glanced down at the water, her fingers tracing the edge of the tub, and when she looked back up, her voice was even quieter. "I... I don't know how to turn off the hot tub."

I blinked, caught off guard. "What?"

"The hot tub," she repeated, her face flushed with embarrassment. "I don't know how to turn it off. My mom and your mom just left, and I don't want to leave it running all night."

Of course. That's what this is about.

I groaned inwardly, trying to act like it was no big deal. "Seriously? You called me over here for that?"

She nodded, biting her lip slightly. "Yeah. I mean... you live here, so... I figured you'd know."

I sighed again, stepping closer to the tub, even though every fiber of my being was screaming at me not to. Don't get too close. Don't look at her again.

But as I leaned over the edge of the tub to reach for the control panel, I couldn't help it. My eyes betrayed me, flicking down to her chest again, where the water was still clinging to her skin, her chest rising and falling softly. The maroon bikini, the way it hugged her body so perfectly...

Fuck.

I cleared my throat again, shaking my head. "Fine. Here, let me just..."

I leaned over, pressing a few buttons on the panel until the jets stopped bubbling, the water gradually coming to a standstill. I could feel her eyes on me, watching me closely, and I could practically hear my heartbeat pounding in my ears.

"There," I muttered, stepping back slightly, though not enough to make myself feel any better. "All set. It's off."

She smiled at me, and it wasn't her usual sarcastic smile. It was softer, more genuine. "Thanks."

I stood there awkwardly, unsure of what to do next, trying my best not to look at her again, even though my eyes kept wandering back to her face. To her eyes.

To her.

I was just about to finally, finally, make my escape, turning to leave, when Hailey stood up. She rose slowly, the water cascading off her body in shimmering droplets, and it felt like time stopped for a second. My brain short-circuited, and all I could think was holy fucking shit.

Her body...

I had no words. None. It was like seeing something I shouldn't, like a pilgrim getting scandalized over a glimpse of a woman's ankle for the first time. Only, this wasn't just an ankle. This was Hailey. And it wasn't just a glimpse.

The maroon bikini clung to her in ways that made my head spin. The way her wet skin gleamed in the low light, the way her body moved as she stepped out of the hot tub... it was almost too much for me to handle.

I took an intake of air, trying desperately to keep myself from staring, but it was useless. My eyes were glued to her as she reached for a towel, her movements slow and almost hypnotic. The water trickled down her legs, her hips, her stomach, and for a second, I thought I might actually lose my mind.

The rational part of my brain was getting drowned out by the sight of her standing there, her hair dripping down her shoulders, her body still wet as she wrapped the towel around herself. She didn't say anything, and neither did I. The silence between us felt thick, like the tension was a living, breathing thing that had settled in the space between us. I couldn't look away, no matter how hard I tried. It wasn't like before, when we were bickering or making snide comments at each other. This was... different.

And it was messing me up.

She finished wrapping the towel around herself, finally breaking the spell. She didn't look at me, though. Her eyes were focused on the ground, her cheeks pink, like she could feel the intensity in the air, too.

I swallowed hard, forcing myself to look away, but my brain was still stuck on the image of her stepping out of the water. I had to get out of here before I said or did something stupid.

"Uh… let's go inside," I muttered, my voice rougher than I intended.

Hailey nodded, still not meeting my eyes. "Yeah. Okay."

I turned to leave, but my heart was still racing, my thoughts a mess. I didn't know what just happened. I didn't know why it felt like something had shifted between us, like everything was suddenly more intense than before. But I knew one thing for sure—

I was in trouble.

CHAPTER 19

HAILEY

I WASN'T SURE IF I WAS IMAGINING IT, BUT EVER SINCE THAT NIGHT—THE NIGHT Callum accidentally sent me that picture and caught me in the hot tub—he'd been acting… off.

More distant. Ruder than usual.

And that was saying something, considering we didn't exactly have a warm and fuzzy relationship to begin with.

It wasn't like we had ever been best friends or anything close to that. Hell, I don't even think we were friends at all. We just existed around each other, making sarcastic comments, throwing shade when we crossed paths, and trying our best to ignore the fact that we were forced to live under the same roof.

But now? Now it was like he was actively avoiding me. And when he wasn't avoiding me, he was even more of a jerk than usual.

Take yesterday, for example. I was grabbing my usual morning coffee from the kitchen, minding my own business, and when I begrudgingly said a simple, "Good morning," as he walked in, he responded with, "The hell's so good about it?"

Normally, that would've rolled off my back, just another snarky comment to add to the long list of verbal sparring matches between us. But there was something about the way he said it—sharper, more cutting than usual. His eyes didn't even meet mine when he said it, like I was something he couldn't be bothered to deal with.

And then there were the rides to school. Callum had been practically silent the entire time, not even bothering with the usual sarcasm or witty insults. He didn't make a single comment, didn't try to start any banter. He just stared straight ahead, his jaw tight, his knuckles white as they gripped the steering wheel.

When I'd asked him if something was bothering him—because, yeah, I was curious, sue me—he just muttered, "Why would I tell you?" and turned up the volume on the radio to drown me out.

And let's not forget the way he was now when I'd pass him in the hallways at school. Before, we'd have those moments where we'd exchange some half-assed jab or a sarcastic comment. Now? He barely even acknowledged my existence. It was like he'd built a wall between us, and I had no idea why.

At home, it was worse. He was practically a ghost. He'd come in, mumble something to his mom or his brothers, and then disappear to his room without so much as a glance in my direction. When we did cross paths—whether in the kitchen or the living room—he'd make some snide comment and leave before I could even respond.

It was like he was… avoiding me.

Why, though?

Was it because of the photo? Was he embarrassed? Or maybe it was something else. Maybe I'd done something to piss him off more than usual, and now he was taking it out on me by being even colder than before.

But it didn't make sense. None of it made sense.

And the more I thought about it, the more it bugged me. I wasn't used to caring about what Callum Reid thought or did, but now, for some reason, I couldn't stop thinking about it.

"Hailey!"

I blinked, snapping out of my thoughts as I realized Nala had been talking to me. Again. I shook my head, trying to focus. I was in the cafeteria, at our usual lunch table, but my mind had been a million miles away, spiraling around the same thoughts of Callum and his weird, distant behavior.

"Sorry, what?" I asked, turning toward Nala, who was eyeing me with a raised brow.

"You okay?" she asked, shoving another bite of her latest weird food concoction into her mouth—something that involved peanut butter, pickles, and what I assumed was a rice cake. "You were zoning out. Again."

I shrugged, trying to act casual. "Yeah, I'm fine. Just... distracted."

Nala squinted at me like she didn't quite believe me, but she didn't press. "Anyway, I was saying—I officially made the cheer team!" She threw her arms up in mock triumph, grinning from ear to ear. "I'm a Westview cheerleader now, baby!"

I couldn't help but smile at her excitement. "That's awesome! I knew you'd make it."

"Obviously," Nala said with a smirk, tossing her hair dramatically. "I mean, look at me." She gestured to herself, as if she were the most obvious cheer choice in the world. And honestly? She probably was.

I laughed, shaking my head. "You're so humble."

"Right? And *you're* so distracted," Nala shot back, pointing a pickle-covered rice cake at me. "What's going on in that brain of yours? Still thinking about the whole Callum thing?"

I stiffened at the mention of his name. "Uh, no," I lied, probably not very convincingly. "Just... thinking about stuff. School, mostly."

"Mmhmm," Nala said, raising her eyebrow again. But then she seemed to drop it, taking another bite of her strange food combo. "So, what's going on with you today? Anything exciting?"

I nodded, grateful for the subject change. "Actually, yeah. I've got my first yearbook club meeting today."

Nala's eyes lit up. "Ooh, exciting! Ready to flex those photography skills on us again?"

I smiled a little, though it was still hard to shake the weird feelings about getting back into photography after I'd given it up. "Yeah. I mean, I think so. It's been a while, but I'm kind of excited."

"You'll kill it," Nala said confidently, leaning back in her chair. "You're gonna take the best photos this school has ever seen. Just wait."

I couldn't help but laugh at her confidence. "We'll see."

I tried to focus on Nala, on her excitement about making the cheer team and my own nerves about the yearbook club meeting, but my mind kept wandering. Drifting. And before I knew it, my eyes were unconsciously wandering across the cafeteria.

Over to his table.

Callum was sitting with his soccer crew, all of them laughing, talking, probably about the upcoming homecoming game.

It was in two days, after all, and the entire school was buzzing about it. The first game of the season. A big deal, especially since we'd gotten wrecked by Oakridge last year.

I wondered, for a second, if Callum was stressed about it. About being captain. It was a lot of pressure, leading the team, and I couldn't help but think about all the extra practice he'd been doing lately. He probably had the weight of the world on his shoulders right now.

Then, the petty part of me kicked in.

Yeah, I hope you're stressed. You deserve it, prick.

He'd been a complete jerk lately, even more than usual, and maybe a tiny part of me wanted him to feel a little bit of the stress he'd been putting me through. I didn't even know why he was acting like this—distant, cold, even more snappy than before. Maybe it was because of the stupid picture, or maybe it was something else entirely. I didn't know.

And, frankly, I wasn't in the mood to care.

But then... I felt it.

As if he could sense me looking at him, Callum's head snapped up from whatever conversation he was having, his eyes locking onto mine from across the cafeteria.

For a second, neither of us moved. Neither of us blinked. It was like the air between us got sucked out of the room, the noise of the cafeteria fading into the background. All I could feel was the tension between us, thick and heavy, like something was simmering just under the surface.

His blue eyes narrowed slightly, and I could see something there. Was it annoyance? Frustration? Or was it something else? I couldn't tell. But whatever it was, it made my heart race in a way I didn't want to acknowledge.

I glared back at him, refusing to back down, even though I felt like I might burst under the weight of the tension. If he was going to act like this, then fine. I wasn't going to let him get to me.

Finally, after what felt like an eternity, I tore my gaze away, my heart still racing, my chest tight. I tried to focus back on Nala, who was in the middle of describing how tryouts went and her upcoming cheer practice.

Just as I was trying to shake off the tension from my stare-down with Callum, the cafeteria doors flew open with a loud bang. The sound made everyone stop what they were doing and turn their heads.

There, strutting through the doors with a cocky grin on his face, was Adam Parker, Callum's best friend and fellow soccer star. But he wasn't alone. Behind him, a group of band kids were marching in, playing some kind of upbeat, triumphant tune that immediately grabbed everyone's attention.

In Adam's hands was a massive sign, nearly as tall as he was, covered in glitter and decorated with big, bold letters. He held it high above his head, walking with exaggerated swagger as he headed toward the cheerleaders' table. And plastered across the sign, in bright red letters, was a question that had every single person in the cafeteria murmuring and whispering.

SASHA THOMPSON, WILL YOU (please) GO TO HOMECOMING WITH ME?

I raised my eyebrows, not believing what I was seeing. Adam was doing it—an over-the-top, classic high school homecoming proposal. And it was directed at none other than Sasha Thompson, the school's beloved it-girl and captain of the cheerleading team.

"Oh my god. Is this really happening right now?" Nala whispered, her eyes wide with shock and amazement.

Adam reached Sasha's table, the band still playing behind him, and dropped to one knee dramatically. The whole cafeteria erupted in laughter, cheers, and excited chatter at the dramatic display. Adam looked up at Sasha with the cheesiest grin I'd ever seen, holding the sign up even higher.

Sasha, who had been in the middle of chatting with a couple of the other cheerleaders, blinked in surprise as she took in the scene. Her eyes flickered from the sign, to Adam, to the band kids, and back to Adam, clearly caught off guard.

"Sasha Thompson," Adam said, his voice loud and theatrical as he held one hand over his heart. "Will you do me the humble honor of being my date to homecoming? Because, quite frankly, I can't think of anyone else I'd want to dance with more than the queen of Westview High."

The whole cafeteria was watching, waiting. Sasha's cheerleading friends were giggling and nudging her, whispering excitedly, while Adam's soccer bros at Callum's table were whistling and hollering, egging him on.

Sasha blinked again, clearly still processing the whole spectacle. But then, slowly, a wide smile spread across her face. "Oh my god, Adam," she laughed, her cheeks flushing pink. "This is... literally insane."

"So? Is that a yes?" Adam asked, raising an eyebrow as he waggled the sign at her.

Sasha giggled, biting her lip. "Yes! Yes, of course I'll go to homecoming with you."

The cafeteria erupted into applause and cheers, and Adam stood up, sweeping Sasha into a playful hug as the band kids continued to play their tune in the background. Everyone around them was clapping, laughing, and throwing in some teasing remarks, but Sasha looked genuinely happy.

Even Nala was clapping excitedly next to me. "Oh my god, that was amazing. Sasha's so lucky."

I nodded, a small smile tugging at my lips despite myself. It was a pretty bold move. Ridiculous, but bold. As the cafeteria buzzed with applause and laughter, my eyes wandered back to Adam and Sasha. He was still grinning like a kid on Christmas, his arms wrapped around her as he pulled her into a playful hug. His whole face lit up with boyish charm, and Sasha looked equally thrilled, her cheeks pink, her eyes sparkling.

It was like a scene straight out of one of those rom-coms or romance novels I read—the ones with grand gestures, sweeping declarations, and those moments that made your heart flutter. I didn't expect it, but something stirred inside me. A pang of something... unfamiliar. Uncomfortable.

Envy.

I sat there, watching as everyone cheered for them, and for the first time, I felt this strange ache in my chest. It wasn't that I liked Adam, or even wanted that kind of over-the-top attention.

But the way Sasha looked so happy, the way Adam had gone out of his way to make a scene, to do something sweet and ridiculous for her, just to make her smile... it was the kind of thing I'd only ever read about. The kind of thing I'd always convinced myself was just fictional, something that happened to other people, in other stories.

But now that I was seeing it play out right in front of me? It was harder to ignore.

I wished I could experience something like this.

I wished someone would care enough to make a fool of themselves just to make me smile. I wished I could have a moment like that—something sweet and spontaneous, something that made my heart race and my cheeks burn.

But instead, I was sitting here, alone with my thoughts, trying not to let the envy grow too strong.

Nala was still gushing about how cute it was, but her words faded into the background as I watched Adam laugh with his soccer bros, still beaming after his successful homecoming proposal.

For the first time, I realized that maybe I wanted more than what I was letting on. I wanted the kind of romance I'd always read about. The kind that felt impossible and magical and just… real.

THE END OF THE SCHOOL DAY HAD FINALLY ROLLED AROUND, AND WHILE MOST students were already heading out the door, I was making my way down the hall toward the yearbook club's room.

My nerves buzzed as I walked, my camera bag slung over my shoulder. This was it—my first official meeting as the yearbook club photographer.

When I reached the room, I took a deep breath before stepping inside. It wasn't as big as I expected, but it was cozy, with a few tables pushed together, some bulletin boards filled with pictures from previous years, and a whiteboard with doodles and random notes scrawled all over it. The atmosphere was surprisingly relaxed, but I still felt a bit out of place.

Lance, the club captain, was already there, chatting with a couple of other members. When he spotted me, he waved me over, a friendly smile on his face.

"Hailey! Glad you made it," he said as I approached. "Everyone, this is Hailey Eller. She's going to be our photographer this year."

A few heads turned my way, and I gave an awkward smile as I waved. "Hi," I said quietly, feeling that familiar flutter of nerves in my stomach. Meeting new people wasn't exactly my favorite thing in the world, but I was here to do my job.

Lance gestured to the group, introducing each person as we went along. "This is Lisa—she's in charge of layouts. Derek handles the copywriting, and Em is our design expert." They each gave me a small nod or a wave as they were introduced as if this was the opening credits of some sitcom, and I nodded back, waving at each of them, trying to commit everyone's names to memory.

"Hailey's going to be in charge of all our event photos this year," Lance continued, his tone excited. "She's got a great eye, and I'm sure she'll capture some amazing moments for us. We're lucky to have her."

I felt a small warmth in my chest at his confidence. I hadn't taken photos for anything official in a long time, but hearing Lance hype me up made me feel... capable, at least.

"Thanks," I said, a bit sheepish. "I'll do my best."

Lisa, who was sitting at the table with a stack of yearbook pages in front of her, smiled at me. "We're really excited to see what you can do. We always struggle with getting good photos—last year's photographer kind of... dropped the ball."

Derek, sitting next to her, chuckled. "Yeah, last year's pictures were a mess. We could barely use half of them."

"No pressure, though," Em chimed in with a grin. "We're just glad to have someone who actually knows how to use a camera."

I laughed softly, feeling the tension ease a little. "Well, I'll try not to disappoint."

Lance clapped his hands together. "Great! Now that we've got the introductions out of the way, let's talk about what's coming up. We've got the homecoming game in two days, and we'll need photos of that for sure. Hailey, you up for it?"

I nodded, the familiar excitement of photography stirring in me. "Definitely."

"Awesome," Lance said, beaming. "We'll also need pictures at the dance, too, so get ready for that."

The dance. I wasn't sure how I felt about homecoming, but at least I'd have a job to do that would keep me busy. As the meeting went on, I started to get a feel for the other members of the yearbook club.

It was a small group, but there was a clear camaraderie between them that made it feel more relaxed than I expected. They all had their roles, their little quirks, and before long, I found myself fitting into the flow of the conversation.

Lisa, in charge of layouts, was the first to break the ice. She had dark brown hair pulled into a neat ponytail, and her eyes sparkled behind her glasses. She was friendly in a quiet, calming way, and it was clear that she had a meticulous nature about her. She sat beside a stack of yearbook pages with little notes in the margins and Post-its sticking out from nearly every page. "So, Hailey," she started, smiling at me, "what's your favorite thing to take photos of? You know, like outside of school stuff."

I paused, thinking. "Hmm. I'd say candid moments. Like, the kind of pictures where people don't know they're being photographed."

Lisa's smile widened. "I love that. Candid shots really do have a certain magic to them. We definitely need more of that in the yearbook this year."

I felt a little burst of warmth in my chest. This was the kind of thing I'd missed about photography—the way it allowed you to capture life as it happened, unplanned and imperfect. "Yeah, I think that's what makes photos feel more alive."

Next to Lisa was Derek, the copywriter. He had shaggy blonde hair and a habit of twirling a pen between his fingers as he talked. He seemed laid-back but in a "too-cool-for-this" kind of way, like the world could be burning around him, and he'd still be leaning against the wall, unbothered. He was flipping through a notebook filled with handwritten notes, occasionally glancing up at the conversation. "So, what made you decide to join yearbook club?" Derek asked, not unkindly, but with a raised eyebrow like he was genuinely curious.

I shrugged, feeling a little self-conscious. "I guess I missed doing photography, and Lance said they needed someone, so... here I am."

Derek smirked, nodding like he got it. "Nice. We could definitely use someone who actually cares about getting good shots. Last year's photos were... tragic."

Em, the design expert, laughed from across the table. "Understatement of the year." She had short-cropped, bright pink hair and was dressed in an oversized band tee with ripped jeans. Her energy was contagious, and she was constantly sketching little doodles in the margins of her papers. "Half the yearbook last year looked like a bad Facebook album from 2012."

"I'll do my best to avoid that," I said, laughing along.

"Please do," Em replied, grinning at me. "We've got a lot to make up for. But I'm sure you'll be great. Plus, Lance wouldn't shut up about how talented you are, so I'm expecting big things."

I glanced at Lance, who was busy scribbling something down but gave me a thumbs-up when he noticed the attention. "Don't let me down, Eller."

I smiled, feeling more comfortable as the conversation continued. The group had a laid-back vibe, and it wasn't long before I found myself laughing along with their jokes and nodding to their ideas for the yearbook's theme. It felt... good. Like I was part of something again.

Half an hour into the meeting, I was really getting into the groove of things. I'd been talking to Lisa about some ideas for candid shots during the homecoming game when my phone buzzed on the table, the screen lighting up with a message. I glanced down, expecting something from Nala, but my stomach dropped when I saw the name that popped up instead.

Callum.

I hesitated for a second before picking up my phone and unlocking it. A wave of anxiety washed over me as I read the text.

Callum: Where the hell are you?

Oh, shit. I froze, my heart sinking. I'd completely forgotten to tell him that I was staying late for the yearbook club meeting.

I quickly typed back, trying to sound casual even though my fingers were flying across the screen.

Me: I'm at my yearbook club meeting. Don't you have soccer practice today anyway?
Callum: Yeah, but I always send you home before I go to practice. Don't make me mad. You should've told me.

I rolled my eyes at the screen, feeling my frustration bubble up. Don't make me mad?

Who did he think he was, my dad?

The nerve of him.

Me: Sorry, Callum, it slipped my mind.
Callum: Well don't let this stuff slip your mind next time or I'm not giving you rides home anymore.

Now I was really annoyed. I had told him I was joining the yearbook club, and it wasn't like I wanted to have to rely on him for rides. It wasn't like I asked for this situation to begin with.

Me: *It's not like I did it on purpose, I literally forgot.*
Callum: *Yeah, whatever. Just don't literally forget next time.*
Me: *Fine.*

Asshole.

I sent the text and locked my phone, dropping it onto the table with a quiet huff of frustration. I tried to focus back on the conversation with Lisa and the rest of the group, but I couldn't stop the tension from creeping up my neck.

"Everything okay?" Lisa asked, her voice gentle, and I realized she'd been watching me fidget with my phone for the past few minutes.

"Yeah," I muttered, forcing a smile. "Just... stuff."

"Boy drama?" Em piped up from across the table, a knowing smirk on her face.

I forced a laugh. "Something like that."

I tried to focus back on the meeting, but my mind was still stuck on that stupid text exchange. I tapped my fingers against the table, staring down at my phone. *Yeah, I probably should've told him about yearbook club,* I admitted to myself begrudgingly. It would've been the sensible thing to do. It wasn't like I wanted him to worry about where I was.

But in my defense, how the hell was I supposed to tell him? He'd been so distant lately. Cold, even. Every time I'd tried to say something, he either brushed me off, gave me some snide comment, or acted like I was wasting his precious time.

But those texts, I thought, my jaw tightening.

He hadn't just been annoyed, he was downright rude. He acted like I'd committed some grand offense by not telling him where I was going. Like I was supposed to report my every move to him.

The way he'd said, *Don't make me mad*—who did he think he was? The way he tried to control everything like that was infuriating.

I clenched my fists on the table, trying to calm down before I blew my frustration out in front of everyone. I didn't need to give the yearbook club any reason to think I was unhinged on my first day. But seriously, the nerve of that guy…

I didn't know what his deal was, but he'd gone from annoyingly sarcastic to downright insufferable. And now he was trying to act like I had to answer to him? Like I had to check in before I did anything?

No. Absolutely not.

Little shit.

CHAPTER 20

CALLUM

THE SUN WAS SETTING, CASTING AN ORANGE GLOW OVER THE SOCCER FIELD AS practice finally wrapped up. I stood there, hands on my hips, trying to catch my breath, but all I could feel was the lingering frustration gnawing at the back of my mind.

I let out a long breath, running a hand through my damp hair. The field around me was emptying out as the other guys jogged off to the locker rooms, laughing and chatting about practice or the upcoming homecoming game. But I stayed back for a second, trying to let the tension roll off me.

It had started that night. That stupid night at the hot tub, when I saw Hailey like I'd never seen her before. The way she looked, the way she moved, the way her eyes caught mine—it had messed with my head in a way I wasn't ready for. And ever since then, things had been off.

I'd been avoiding her.

fTrying to act like nothing had changed. Trying to bury the fact that, for the first time ever, I'd felt something for her. Something I didn't want to feel.

I hated it. I hated that I felt anything at all. That I was even thinking about her like this.

I kicked the soccer ball in front of me hard, sending it flying across the field, letting out some of the frustration I'd been holding onto all practice.

Coach had noticed I was off today, too. He hadn't said anything, but I could tell by the way he watched me, giving me that look he gave when he knew something was up. He didn't push, though. And thank God for that, because I didn't have it in me to explain why I couldn't get my head in the game lately.

Everything was pissing me off lately. It wasn't just Hailey. It was... everything.

I thought back to the other day at the gym, when Troy Duran, that smug bastard, had run his mouth. Just thinking about him made my blood boil all over again. The way he'd taunted me, trying to get in my head, had stayed with me ever since.

Troy had rubbed it in our faces, like the arrogant prick he was. But this year was going to be different. I was going to make sure of it. With a huff, I grabbed my water bottle and headed off the field toward the locker room, my legs aching from practice but my mind still racing. The tension in my chest hadn't eased at all, and even as I walked, I could feel the frustration building again. I stepped into the locker room and stripped off my practice jersey, tossing it into my bag as I headed for the showers. The hot water would help, I hoped. It usually did.

I turned off the shower, feeling slightly less like I wanted to punch a wall, but not by much. The hot water helped a bit, but my mind was still buzzing. As I towel-dried my hair, I could hear the other guys from the team chatting up a storm in the locker room, their voices bouncing off the walls.

I slipped into my shorts and T-shirt, trying to tune out the noise, but it was impossible. I could hear Grayson and Adam talking about the game on Friday, their voices filled with excitement.

"Coach said we're getting new jerseys soon, right?" Grayson asked, lacing up his shoes.

"Yeah, probably by Friday's game," Adam replied, running a hand through his hair. "He said something about a new sponsor hooking us up. It's about time."

I caught a glimpse of the two of them out of the corner of my eye as I grabbed my gym bag from the bench. They were already dressed, still talking animatedly about the new gear.

"Wonder what they'll look like," Grayson mused. "Hope they're better than the ones we had last year."

"They've gotta be," Ibra chimed in from across the room. "Last year's jerseys were cursed. I bet that's why we lost to Oakridge."

I rolled my eyes, shaking my head and chuckling with the other guys at Ibra's reasoning. Yeah, sure. Blame the jerseys. The loss had been because Oakridge had gotten inside our heads. And more importantly, because we let them.

As I finished packing up my stuff, Adam glanced over at me, his eyes narrowing slightly as he studied my expression.

"Yo, Callum," he called out, his tone half-playful, half-serious. "Why do you look like you've got a stick up your ass, man? You've been off all practice."

I shot him a glare, zipping up my bag with more force than necessary. "I'm fine."

Grayson joined in, raising an eyebrow as he leaned back against the bench. "Fine? Dude, you've been stomping around like you're ready to take someone's head off. What's up?"

Adam chuckled. "Yeah, man. You look like you've been pissed off since practice started. You sure you're not still hung up on what Troy said at the gym?"

I felt my jaw tighten at the mention of Troy, but I wasn't about to get into that right now. "I said I'm fine," I repeated, slinging my bag over my shoulder.

I could feel their eyes on me, like they were waiting for more, but I wasn't in the mood to talk about it. Not here. Not now. Especially not when Hailey was still messing with my head and I couldn't stop thinking about the stupid argument we'd had over text earlier.

"Must be something," Adam chimed in from the corner, his usual calm demeanor replaced with curiosity. "You've been wound tight all week."

I shot them all a look, making it clear that I wasn't in the mood for interrogation. "I said I'm fine. Let it go."

He raised his hands in mock surrender. "Alright, alright. Jeez, man. Just trying to help."

I forced myself to take a breath, trying to ease the tension in my shoulders as I headed for the door. "I'll see you guys at practice tomorrow."

"Yeah, whatever, Captain Stick-Up-His-Ass," Adam called after me, but I could hear the grin in his voice.

I didn't even know why I was doing this. Wandering around the halls after soccer practice like some lost puppy, trying to figure out if Hailey was still at school. It wasn't like I cared what she was doing—or at least, that's what I kept telling myself.

Where was the damn yearbook club room again? I couldn't remember. It wasn't like I'd ever been to that side of the school before. But I kept walking, glancing at the doors as I passed, until I paused outside a room where I could hear voices coming from inside.

I glanced through the glass panel on the door, and sure enough, there she was. Hailey.

She was holding a camera in her hands, a focused, almost happy expression on her face as she adjusted the lens. My stomach tightened. I hadn't seen her look like that in... well, ever. Not when she was around me, at least. She looked... content. And for some reason, that made me uneasy.

I watched as she lifted the camera, aiming it at something—or someone—inside the room. It wasn't until I shifted slightly that I saw who was with her.

Lance.

He was standing nearby, grinning like an idiot, gesturing toward himself as if asking her to take a picture. And she was laughing. *Laughing.*

The uneasiness in my gut twisted into something else, something I didn't want to admit.

It was just the two of them in there. The room was mostly empty, with a few scattered chairs and desks, but there they were—just Lance and Hailey. Alone. And Hailey looked… comfortable. Happy, even.

I felt a tightness in my chest, and my fists clenched at my sides before I could stop them. Why was this bothering me so much? Why did it matter that she was laughing with him, holding that camera, looking more relaxed than she ever had around me?

I told myself it didn't matter. It's just Lance. It's not a big deal. But it felt like a big deal.

I stayed there for a second longer, watching as Hailey snapped a picture of Lance. She laughed again, and I could hear the sound through the door. Light. Easy.

It wasn't the first time I'd heard her laugh, but hearing it now, with someone else, in that setting? It made something stir inside me that I didn't want to acknowledge.

Before I could stop myself, I yanked open the door to the yearbook room and stormed inside. The sound of the door slamming against the wall made both Hailey and Lance jump, and their heads snapped toward me at the same time. Hailey's eyes widened in surprise, and Lance, still standing in the middle of the room, looked downright confused.

I didn't even think. The words just came out.

"It's time to go, Hailey," I said, my voice gruff and a little too harsh. I could feel the tension rolling off me, and I wasn't doing a great job of hiding it.

Hailey blinked, lowering her camera slightly. Lance furrowed his brows, looking between the two of us. "Wait, what? Why is Callum telling you it's time to go?"

The moment the words left his mouth, I froze.

Shit. Right.

That was Hailey's rule, wasn't it?

No one at school knew we lived together. No one knew about her house burning down or that we were stuck under the same roof now. I could feel my brain scrambling for an excuse, my stomach knotting up with the realization that I'd just walked in and said something that made absolutely no sense to anyone but me.

Lance was still staring at me, his eyes filled with confusion, waiting for an explanation. I could feel Hailey's eyes on me, too, though she didn't say anything. She was probably waiting for me to screw up.

I cleared my throat, trying to act casual, even though it was painfully obvious I'd just made everything weird. "Uh... yeah, she, um... has a ride with me today. So we gotta go." I crossed my arms, trying to look like I wasn't lying through my teeth. "I told her I'd drive her home. You know, after school."

Lance's confusion deepened. "But I thought you didn't even talk to each other?"

The corner of my mouth twitched, and I could feel the heat rising in my neck. "We... don't. I mean, we do. Sometimes. Look, it's complicated." I glanced at Hailey, who was glaring at me like I'd just told the least believable lie in the world. Well, kinda had. But I was hoping Lance was either too dumb to question it or didn't care enough.

Lance was still looking between the two of us like he'd just walked into an alternate universe where Hailey and I suddenly gave a shit about each other. "So... you're driving her home? Since when?"

"Since..." I trailed off, trying to come up with something that made sense. "Since today. Yeah. We just... worked it out."

Lance raised an eyebrow, clearly not buying it. But before he could question me any further, Hailey spoke up.

"Callum's just giving me a ride home today," she said, her voice steady but laced with an undertone that I couldn't quite place. "It's no big deal."

Lance blinked at her, then at me, clearly still confused but deciding not to press the issue any further. "Okay..."

I nodded quickly, grabbing onto the lifeline she'd thrown me. "Yeah, no big deal. Let's go." I jerked my head toward the door, hoping she'd follow me before Lance asked any more questions.

Hailey sighed, setting down her camera and grabbing her bag. "Fine. Just give me a second."

Lance watched the whole exchange with a bewildered expression, but I could see the gears turning in his head. He was probably going to ask a million questions later, but right now, I needed to get the hell out of here before I made things worse.

As Hailey moved past me toward the door, I glanced at Lance and gave him an awkward nod. "Catch you later, man."

Lance just stared after us as we left the room, probably more confused than ever. The silence between us was thick as we walked through the hallways toward the parking lot. Hailey didn't say a word, and neither did I. I could feel the tension hanging between us, unspoken but very much there.

I shoved my hands into my pockets, my eyes fixed straight ahead. My head was still buzzing from everything that had just happened in the yearbook room, and I couldn't help but feel like an idiot for barging in the way I did. I'd made it weird—for Hailey, for Lance, and, most of all, for myself.

Why did I do that? Why couldn't I just leave her alone? I had no reason to be pissed, no reason to care about her laughing and taking photos with Lance. But the way I'd acted... it was like something inside me snapped, and I couldn't stop myself from intervening.

Hailey walked beside me, her bag slung over her shoulder, her footsteps quick and quiet. She hadn't looked at me once since we left the yearbook room, and I didn't dare glance in her direction. I could feel the frustration simmering under the surface, but this time, I didn't know if it was directed at her or at myself.

As we stepped out into the cool afternoon air, the parking lot came into view. A few stragglers were still hanging around, but most of the cars had cleared out. The silence between us grew heavier with every step, and I couldn't stand it anymore.

I let out a frustrated breath, my words coming out more gruffly than I intended. "You could've at least texted me back."

"Seriously? That's what you want to talk about right now?"

I clenched my jaw, refusing to look at her. "Yeah. You knew I was waiting for you."

She let out a dry laugh. "You don't exactly make it easy to tell you anything, Callum."

We stood there in the parking lot, staring at each other in silence. The frustration that had been building all day reached a boiling point, but for the life of me, I couldn't figure out why. Why I felt this way. Why she was the one getting under my skin like no one else could.

"Whatever," I muttered, turning away from her and heading toward the car. "Let's just go."

Hailey didn't respond. She just followed behind me, and the silence stretched out again, even thicker than before.

CHAPTER 21

HAILEY

THE AWKWARDNESS BETWEEN CALLUM AND ME HADN'T GOTTEN ANY BETTER BY the next morning. In fact, it felt worse. As I sat next to him in first period, trying to focus on the lesson, the tension between us was practically suffocating.

Neither of us had said a word to each other since yesterday. And now, sitting here beside him, I could feel the awkward energy radiating off him. It wasn't like we were besties before, but this was different. It was like there was this huge, invisible wall between us, and neither of us knew how to tear it down.

I shifted uncomfortably in my seat, glancing at him out of the corner of my eye. He was staring straight ahead, his jaw set, his arms crossed over his chest. He hadn't even glanced at me once, and I was doing my best to pretend I didn't care.

But why did it feel so weird?

And now, on top of that, tomorrow was the homecoming game and the dance.

The dance.

I hadn't even planned on going. Dances weren't really my thing, and I had no interest in spending my night surrounded by couples and slow songs. But then yearbook club happened, and now I was forced to go because I had to take pictures. Part of me wished I could get out of it, but there was no way I could skip it now. Lance had already assigned me to cover the whole event.

Which meant I was now, last minute, going dress shopping with Nala.

Ugh.

I hadn't even picked out a dress yet because I'd spent so much time convincing myself I wasn't going. But now? I had no choice. Nala had insisted we go today after school, and she was probably more excited about it than I was.

I sighed quietly, fiddling with my pen as I stared down at my notes, barely paying attention to what was going on in class. My mind kept drifting to the game tomorrow. The dance. And, more annoyingly, Callum.

I glanced at him again. He was still staring ahead, looking like he was lost in his own world, too. His jaw was clenched, and I could see the tension in his shoulders.

What's his deal?

I turned back to my notebook, trying to push thoughts of Callum aside. I had more important things to focus on—like finding a dress that didn't make me want to die of embarrassment.

The bell rang, signaling the end of first period, and I breathed a quiet sigh of relief. I quickly started gathering my things, stuffing my notebook into my bag, but out of the corner of my eye, I saw Callum stand up.

Wordlessly, without so much as a glance in my direction, he slung his backpack over his shoulder and walked out of the classroom. Again. Just like yesterday.

I watched him go, my chest tightening with an odd mix of frustration and something else I couldn't quite name. It was like he was purposely avoiding me, and I had no idea why. He'd been doing this all week—this silent, cold treatment that left me feeling like I didn't even exist.

I let out a quiet huff as I finished packing my bag. Fine. If he wanted to act like I was invisible, then so be it. I wasn't going to waste my energy trying to figure him out.

Still, I couldn't help but feel a tiny, nagging pang in the back of my mind as I headed for the door.

Why did it even bother me this much?

AFTER SCHOOL, NALA AND I MADE OUR WAY TO THE MALL, READY TO TACKLE THE task of finding a last-minute dress for the homecoming dance. The bright lights and bustling stores were almost a welcome distraction from everything that had been buzzing around in my head all day—mainly, Callum.

I'd made sure to text him this time, letting him know I'd be at the mall with Nala and wouldn't need a ride home. His response had been curt, just a single-word reply: *Okay.*

No thanks, no acknowledgment, just… okay.

Typical Callum. Cold. Distant. It was infuriating. I just wanted to take that okay and shove it so far up his entitled, rude, little ass.

"I can't believe you're actually going to the dance," Nala said, her voice teasing as she flipped through the racks of dresses. "Weren't you the one who swore up and down that you'd never set foot in a dance?"

"Yeah, well, thanks to yearbook, I don't really have a choice," I replied, holding up a sparkly blue dress before immediately putting it back. Too much. Way too much.

We were in the middle of the department store, surrounded by endless racks of dresses—short ones, long ones, frilly ones, glittery ones. I was already overwhelmed by the options, and we'd barely started.

"Honestly, though, I'm just glad you're coming," Nala said, a grin tugging at her lips. "Now we can suffer together."

I rolled my eyes but smiled. "Yeah, yeah. Don't get too excited now."

Nala wandered off to another rack, leaving me to sift through the dresses on my own. As I flipped through a few options, I felt my phone buzz in my pocket, but I ignored it. I'd had enough of Callum's one-word texts for the day.

"So," Nala called out from a nearby rack, "spill. You've been all weird lately, and I know it's not just because of the yearbook."

I hesitated for a second, then sighed. "It's Callum."

Nala peeked around the rack, eyebrows raised. "What did he do this time?"

I bit my lip, debating how much to tell her. I grabbed a dress off the rack—a simple black one that seemed decent enough—and held it up to my body, looking at myself in the mirror. "He's being impossible. He's pissing me off so much these days. I thought we'd gotten like, even a bit civil, but he's acting like an ass now."

Nala nodded sympathetically, holding up a bright red dress to show me. "Well, no surprise there. Honestly? I think he's just being typical Callum. You know how he is."

"Yeah, but this feels... different," I muttered, slipping the black dress over my arm and heading to the dressing room. "Like, before, we used to bicker and argue, but now it's like there's this... I don't know, this wall between us. And it's not just awkward—it's tense."

I slipped into the dressing room, pulling the black dress over my head. It fit snugly, hugging my waist and falling just above my knees. I looked at myself in the mirror, frowning slightly.

It was... fine.

"So, you think it's just him being a jerk?" I called out to Nala from inside the dressing room.

"Honestly?" Nala's voice came through the door, and I could almost hear her grin. "I think he's probably just confused. Guys don't know how to handle emotions, so they either shut down or act like assholes. Or both. Callum sounds like he's doing both."

I stepped out of the dressing room, smoothing the dress down and giving Nala a look. "What do you think?"

Nala eyed me up and down, nodding approvingly. "That one's cute! But we can keep looking if you want."

I turned back to the mirror, frowning at my reflection. "Maybe. I don't know. I just... ugh, this whole Callum thing is stressing me out.."

Nala chuckled, holding up another dress. "Well, the best way to deal with a guy like that is to keep doing your own thing. Let him stew in his own weirdness. Besides, we've got a dance to look forward to, and trust me, he'll be too busy with the homecoming game to bother you."

I sighed, glancing at myself in the mirror again. "I hope so."

After trying on a few more dresses that didn't quite feel right, I spotted something at the far end of the rack—a dark emerald green dress. It stood out immediately. The color was rich and deep, and there was something about it that made me pause.

I pulled it off the rack and held it up. The fabric was soft, with a subtle sheen that caught the light, and the cut was simple but elegant. It was sleeveless, with a fitted bodice that flared out slightly at the waist, giving it a flattering silhouette. Something told me this one was different.

"Hmm," I muttered to myself, eyeing the dress before turning to Nala. "What do you think of this one?"

Nala's eyes lit up the moment she saw it. "Ooh, I love that color! That'll look amazing on you, Hailey. Try it on!"

I nodded, already feeling a little excited. I stepped into the dressing room again, slipping out of the black dress and carefully pulling the green one over my head.

I adjusted the straps and turned to face the mirror.

The dress hugged me in all the right places, the fitted bodice accentuating my waist before flaring out into a soft, flowing skirt that brushed just above my knees. But it wasn't just the fit that caught me off guard—it was the color. The dark emerald green beautifully brought out the jade color in my eyes, making them stand out more than I'd ever noticed before.

I blinked, surprised at how... good I looked.

"Hailey?" Nala called from outside the dressing room. "Let me see!"

I took a deep breath and stepped out, feeling a little self-conscious but curious to hear her reaction.

The moment Nala saw me, her jaw dropped. "Oh my god."

I fidgeted, smoothing the fabric nervously. "Is it okay? I mean, it's not too much, right?"

Nala practically bounced on her toes, grinning from ear to ear. "Too much? Hailey, it's perfect! That dress is gorgeous, and you look amazing. I'm serious, you have to get it."

I glanced at the mirror again, taking in the way the dress fit, the way the color seemed to enhance everything. It wasn't flashy or overly dramatic, but it was... elegant. Subtle. It made me feel confident, in a way I hadn't expected.

A small smile tugged at the corners of my lips. "Yeah... I think I'll get it."

Nala clapped her hands together. "Yes! I knew we'd find something perfect. That dress is gonna turn heads, girl."

I chuckled softly, heading back into the dressing room to change out of it. For once, I felt like I'd found something that wasn't just fine—it was right.

CHAPTER 22
HAILEY

When I got home from the mall, the house was already buzzing with activity. The warm smell of dinner hit me the moment I stepped inside, and I could hear the clatter of dishes and the familiar hum of conversation coming from the kitchen. I glanced at the clock—it was a little later than I expected, but not too late.

I shrugged off my jacket and made my way toward the kitchen, my new dress bag slung over my arm.

As I stepped into the dining area, I saw everyone already seated around the table—Mrs. Reid, Mr. Reid, and my parents. Nathan and Dalton were chattering excitedly between bites of food, clearly in the middle of some animated story. It looked like I'd walked in just as they'd started dinner.

"Hey, Hailey," Mrs. Reid greeted me with a warm smile as she gestured to an empty seat. "You're just in time. We were about to call you."

"Hey," I replied, a little sheepishly. I hadn't expected to come home to a full dinner table, but it was a nice surprise. "Sorry I'm late, I was out shopping with Nala."

"Did you find what you were looking for?" my mom asked, glancing up from her plate. Her eyes lit up a bit, clearly excited about the whole dress shopping thing. I think she was more into the idea of me going to homecoming than I was.

"Yeah, I did," I said, sliding into the empty chair and setting the dress bag down next to me. "Got something last-minute, but it worked out."

Nathan, who was sitting across from me, leaned forward, his face full of curiosity. "What's it look like? Is it, like, super fancy?"

Dalton chimed in, his little eyes wide. "Does it have sparkles on it?"

I chuckled softly. "Maybe a little sparkles. And yeah, it's nice. Maybe I'll show you guys later."

Mrs. Reid smiled at me as she passed a bowl of mashed potatoes across the table. "I'm glad you found something. You're going to have a great time at the dance. I can't believe it's already your last homecoming—the years are flying by, aren't they?"

"Yeah, they really are," I said, though my mind was still buzzing with a different thought. As I reached for the serving spoon, I noticed something—or rather, someone—missing. I glanced around the table again, just to be sure.

"Where's Callum?" I asked casually, not expecting much but still curious.

Mrs. Reid gave me a slight shrug as she took a sip of water. "Oh, he got home earlier but went out again for a bit. I'm sure he'll be back soon."

I blinked. Went out again? That was... strange. I mean, sure, Callum was always doing his own thing, but usually when he came home after practice, he stayed in for the night. So why had he gone back out? And where?

It was weird, but I didn't press the issue. I just nodded and took a bite of food, trying not to let the thought linger too much. It wasn't any of my business where he went, anyway. He could do whatever he wanted.

My parents were discussing work, as usual, and Mrs. Reid was laughing at something my dad said. Nathan and Dalton were now arguing over the correct way to stack Jenga blocks, which made me smile a bit.

It was nice, sitting there with everyone, eating dinner like a big, dysfunctional family. Even if Callum wasn't there, it still felt... homey.

After dinner, I headed downstairs to my room in the basement, feeling relieved to have a moment to myself. I hung up the emerald green dress carefully on the back of my door, making sure it wouldn't get wrinkled. The thought of tomorrow's dance loomed over me, but at least I had one thing checked off the list.

With the dress sorted, I settled at my desk and pulled out my homework. I needed something to take my mind off the weird tension that had been hanging in the air lately—between me and Callum, between everything, really.

The familiar scratch of my pen against paper was comforting, and I let myself get absorbed in the math problems in front of me, blocking out everything else.

For a while, I was able to focus. I worked through one equation after another, and soon, the knot of tension in my chest started to ease. Maybe that was the key—just staying busy. Not thinking about Callum or the weird energy between us.

But of course, just as I was starting to feel calm, my phone buzzed on the desk, pulling me out of my concentration. I glanced at the screen, expecting a text from Nala or maybe a reminder from yearbook club, but when I saw the name that popped up, my heart skipped a beat.

I blinked at the screen, confused. It wasn't a text. It was a call. From Callum. Uh... what?

We'd never called each other before—why would we? We barely talked unless we had to.

Hesitating for a second, I picked up the phone and swiped to answer. "Hello?"

There was a pause, then his voice came through, low and slightly agitated. "I'm in the garage."

I frowned, glancing toward the ceiling as if that would help me understand what he meant. "Okay... and?"

His voice snapped, a little harsher this time. "Come here, damn it."

I blinked, surprised by his tone. What the hell was that about? "What? Why?" I asked, my confusion only growing.

There was another beat of silence before he muttered, "Just... get up here. I'm not waiting all night."

I narrowed my eyes at my phone. The audacity. He calls me out of the blue, gives me zero context, and then demands I come to the garage? Was he serious?

"Callum, if you need something, you could ask, you know? Like a normal person," I shot back, annoyed.

I heard him let out a long, frustrated sigh. "Please. Just come to the garage. I'll explain when you get here."

I stared at my phone for a second, tempted to tell him off. But there was something in his voice—something that didn't quite sound like his usual arrogance. He sounded... off. Like something was bothering him.

With a reluctant sigh, I stood up from my desk, closing my textbooks. "Fine. But this better not be some weird prank or something."

"I'm not pranking you. Just hurry up," he said, and then the line went dead. I stared at my phone, still confused, but I grabbed my hoodie and slipped it on before making my way upstairs. What could he possibly want?

As I headed toward the garage, I couldn't help but wonder what was going on with him. Callum wasn't the type to ask for help, and he definitely wasn't the type to call me out of nowhere. Whatever this was, it had to be serious—or at least something that was really bothering him.

Still, I couldn't shake the feeling that something was off as I pushed open the door to the garage and stepped inside.

When I stepped into the garage, the dim lighting made it hard to see at first. But soon enough, I spotted Callum sitting in his car, the headlights off but the engine running, casting a faint glow through the dashboard.

He didn't look at me, just gestured for me to get inside like this was some kind of normal, everyday thing. I narrowed my eyes at him, standing there for a second. "Are you serious right now?" I muttered under my breath, but reluctantly, I opened the passenger door and climbed in.

As soon as I shut the door, without a word, Callum pulled out of the garage and started driving down the street.

"Wait—hey!" I exclaimed, scrambling for my seatbelt. "You didn't tell me we were going somewhere! What the hell?!"

He didn't answer, his eyes focused on the road, his expression unreadable. I glared at him, feeling my frustration bubble up again. It was one thing to ask me to come to the garage, but now he was just whisking me away to God-knows-where without any explanation?

"Callum!" I snapped, but he still didn't say anything. His hands tightened around the steering wheel, his jaw clenched, and he sped through the quiet streets like this was completely normal behavior.

Okay. What the hell was going on?

My mind started racing, trying to figure out what his deal was, but when he didn't give me anything to work with, my thoughts spiraled out of control. And as the silence stretched on and the streetlights blurred past the windows, my overactive imagination kicked into high gear.

Oh my god.

He was acting weird. Way weirder than usual. And he was being all secretive and cryptic about where we were going. What if... what if Callum was going to kill me?

I swallowed hard, glancing at him from the corner of my eye. He looked calm, way too calm.

Serial killer calm.

That's it. Callum's a secret serial killer. He probably had some kind of double life, and I was the next target. That's why he'd been so cold and distant lately—he'd been planning this.

Oh my god, I'm gonna be on one of those crime documentaries. I could picture it now. I could hear the intro of my documentary playing. *"She was just a normal girl, but little did she know, her quiet classmate... excuse me, classmate slash roommate had a deadly secret..."*

He was probably driving me to some remote spot where no one will hear me scream. This was it. This was how it ended. I was going to be in a documentary, and they'd show montages of pictures of me from yearbook and interview people who would say stuff like, "She was always so nice" or "She kept to herself" while creepy music played in the background. Nala would probably be a wreck.

I clutched the seatbelt tighter, my knuckles turning white. *Okay, Hailey, calm down. You're not in a true crime show. Probably. Callum's annoying, but he's not a murderer. Right?*

But every time I glanced at him, his sharp features illuminated by the passing streetlights, my overactive brain went into full panic mode. He's definitely planning something.

I cleared my throat, trying to sound casual even though my voice came out shaky. "S-So, are you going to tell me where we're going, or should I start preparing my final words now?"

Finally, Callum glanced at me out of the corner of his eye, his expression flat. "Stop being dramatic."

"Dramatic?" I sputtered, my voice rising. "You just kidnapped me without any explanation and I'm the one being dramatic? What the hell, Callum?"

He rolled his eyes but kept driving, not offering me any sort of explanation. His jaw was set, like he was dealing with some internal battle that I wasn't allowed to know about. "Just... relax. You'll see when we get there."

There? To my death? I threw my hands up. "See what? Where are we going? Why are you being all cryptic and weird?"

Still, no answer. He just sped up a little, the night streets whizzing past us, and I could feel my frustration building to a breaking point.

This was it, I thought dramatically. *He's driving me to my doom.* As I sat there, my heart racing and my mind spiraling into the worst-case scenarios, I pulled my phone out of my pocket. Maybe it was time for a little insurance. Just in case this was the last time I'd ever have a chance to say it.

I opened a new message and quickly typed.

Me: *Hey, Mom and Dad. I just wanted to say I love you.*

I hit send before I could overthink it, knowing that they'd probably be confused as hell. I glanced at Callum, who was still driving with that annoying calmness, the streetlights flashing over his face.

Eventually, he took a turn and headed up a winding road, the city lights twinkling in the distance as we climbed higher. My heart pounded even faster as I realized where we were headed. Battery Hill.

The thought only fueled my anxiety.

What was he planning?

As we reached the top, he pulled into a small parking area. My stomach twisted in knots as he parked the car and turned off the engine. Without a word, he unbuckled his seatbelt and stepped out.

"Callum, wait!" I called after him, hesitating for a moment before following.

What were we doing here? If he was going to kill me, this place was way too open. There were families that came here for picnics, couples who enjoyed the view. It wasn't exactly discreet.

I stepped out of the car and stood by the passenger door, watching as Callum walked a few paces away, staring out over the city. The view was breathtaking, the skyline illuminated against the darkening sky, but all I could focus on was the uncertainty of the moment.

"Um, so… what's going on?" I finally asked, crossing my arms defensively.

He turned slightly, glancing back at me, and I could see the tension in his shoulders. "Just come here."

I hesitated for a moment, still unsure of what he was up to, but my curiosity got the better of me. I took a few steps forward, approaching him slowly.

Just as I was about to ask him again what he wanted to talk about, Callum reached into the backseat of his car and pulled out a box. My eyes widened as I caught sight of the familiar logo stamped on the top. It said Nikon in bold letters.

He held it out toward me, and I stared at it, dumbfounded. "What? What is this?" I asked, completely thrown off by his sudden gesture.

"Open it," he replied, his tone a mix of urgency and frustration, as if he was trying to push me past my confusion.

I hesitated for a moment, my fingers brushing over the box before I finally took it from him. As I opened it, I felt my heart skip a beat. Inside lay a beautiful Nikon camera, sleek and professional-looking. It didn't look cheap at all—it looked like something I'd only dreamed of having.

"Callum, I—what?" I stammered, staring at the camera in disbelief. "Why are you giving me this?"

"Just open it," he said again, and I could see a flicker of something in his eyes. Maybe it was vulnerability or regret. I couldn't quite tell.

I carefully pulled the camera out of the box, admiring the craftsmanship. "This is… really nice," I breathed, still trying to process what was happening. "But why are you giving it to me?"

He pulled out his phone and opened it, showing me a post about the photography contest. My heart raced as I recognized the logo at the top. Hermann's Magazine. It was a popular magazine known for featuring indie artists, photographers, and various creative talents. I'd seen their work before and knew that getting featured could lead to significant opportunities.

And the $500 prize? Not too shabby.

"Do you recognize it?" he asked, glancing at me. "They're hosting a contest, and I thought... well, I heard there might be northern lights tonight, and you should take a picture for it."

I blinked, feeling a mix of excitement and confusion wash over me. "Northern lights?"

"Yeah," he said, his expression softening a bit. "I figured it'd be a good opportunity for you to get back into photography."

I was speechless. I hadn't picked up a camera in so long, and now here was Callum, of all people, giving me a chance to pursue something I loved. But at the same time, a knot of doubt twisted in my stomach. "But I haven't done photography in ages. I wouldn't even know where to start."

"Damn it, Hailey," he snapped, his voice suddenly intense. "I feel like shit, okay? I feel like shit knowing that I... I'm one of the reasons you stopped in the first place. So don't stop. Don't just do it for yearbook. Keep doing photography for yourself."

I stared at him, my heart racing as I moved the camera back and forth between my hands, barely being able to believe that it was real. "Why do you care so much?"

"Just stop asking why!" He was raising his voice now, frustration spilling over. "If you like doing something, do it! Don't stop because of some... asshole like me."

I was taken aback by the intensity in his eyes, the way he was staring at me like he was pouring every ounce of sincerity he had into his words. It felt almost vulnerable, and I wasn't sure how to respond.

"I—" I started, but the words caught in my throat.

"Just think about it," he said, his voice softer now, almost pleading. "You have a chance to do and get recognized for something you love. Don't let anything stop you from that. Don't let anyone hold you back from doing stuff you like doing. Especially not me."

I looked down at the camera in my hands, feeling the weight of his words settle in. Maybe he was right. Maybe I didn't have to let the past dictate what I wanted for myself.

"Okay," I said finally, a small smile creeping onto my face despite the confusion swirling in my chest. "I'll think about it."

He nodded, looking a little less tense, but the air was still thick with unspoken words. As I stood there, holding the camera in my hands, I felt a swirl of emotions I couldn't quite pin down. I was still reeling from everything that had just happened. The shock of Callum giving me this incredible camera, a Nikon no less, felt surreal.

I glanced down at the camera again, tracing my fingers over its sleek body. It was nothing like the camera I'd lost in the fire—my old one had been a trusty workhorse, but this? This was something special. I wondered just how much he'd spent on it.

Too much, my brain whispered. It was too nice for someone like me, especially considering I hadn't picked up a camera in ages. But right now, I didn't want to think about that. I didn't want to think about how I had lost everything—my old camera, my memories, my sense of normalcy—when my house burned down.

Instead, I wanted to focus on the moment, on this new opportunity. Taking a deep breath, I started fiddling with the settings, adjusting the aperture and ISO. It had been a while since I'd done this, but some instincts kicked in, and I began setting everything up.

Out of the corner of my eye, I noticed Callum standing a few feet away, looking up at the sky expectantly, his silhouette framed against the darkening backdrop. The city lights sparkled below us, but above, the sky was slowly transitioning to a deeper shade of blue, with hints of orange lingering on the horizon.

I could see the tension easing in his posture, and a small part of me wondered if he was just as nervous as I was. After all, this was uncharted territory for both of us.

"Are you ready for this?" he called over, his voice breaking the comfortable silence between us.

I turned my gaze to him, feeling a mix of excitement and anxiety. "I think so. I just hope I remember how to do this right."

I raised the camera to my eye, squinting slightly as I found the perfect angle to capture the horizon. The city lights twinkled below, and the first hints of stars began to emerge against the deepening sky.

"Can you see anything yet?" Callum asked, shifting his weight as he stepped closer, still glancing up at the sky.

"Not yet," I replied, trying to keep my tone light despite the anticipation building in my chest.

I glanced over at Callum, who was still watching the sky intently. The anticipation of the northern lights had us both on edge, and I felt a wave of excitement wash over me.

"Hey, can you show me that post again?" I asked, hoping to refresh my memory of the contest details. He fished his phone out of his pocket and held it out to me.

I leaned closer, squinting at the screen as I read the prompt: **Capture a moment that feels like a warm hug.**

I blinked, then burst out laughing.

Callum looked baffled. "What? Why are you laughing?"

I shook my head, still chuckling. "Do you not have any sense at all? The prompt is about a warm hug! How are northern lights supposed to be like a warm hug?"

He frowned, crossing his arms over his chest. "Well, aren't they?"

"No! A sunset would be way more fitting for that! Think about it—sunsets are warm and cozy, while nights are cold!" I exclaimed, still giggling at the absurdity of it all.

Callum narrowed his eyes at me, clearly not understanding my reasoning. "Well... some nights are warm!"

"Yeah, but this is definitely not one of those nights," I said, motioning to the chill in the air. "You think this is anything like a warm hug? That makes no sense!"

"It's the fucking northern lights, Hailey!" he replied, a mixture of exasperation and disbelief in his tone. "They're amazing! How is that not a warm hug?"

I couldn't help but laugh harder, the sound ringing out into the night air. Callum rolled his eyes, but I could see the corner of his mouth twitching into a small grin despite his irritation. "You're impossible."

As we continued to bicker, Callum tried to keep up his irritated act, but I could see the cracks forming in his composure. He was trying so hard to stay annoyed, but as my laughter echoed through the night, I noticed his resolve weakening.

His lips twitched again, and before I knew it, he laughed, too—a deep, genuine laugh that I didn't think I'd ever heard from him before.

"Shut up, Hailey," he said between laughs, running a hand through his hair like he couldn't believe I'd gotten him to crack. But there was no real malice in his voice. It was light, almost playful.

I grinned, lifting the camera to my eye. "No way," I said.

And before he could stop me, I snapped a picture.

The moment was perfect. Callum, standing there in the night, a huge smile breaking through his usual tough-guy exterior, his eyes crinkled at the corners as he laughed. Behind him, the northern lights had just begun to paint the sky with faint streaks of color, barely visible but enough to give the scene a magical glow.

"Hey!" Callum snapped, his laughter fading slightly as he realized what I'd just done. "Why'd you take my damn picture?"

I shrugged, lowering the camera and grinning at him. "Because it's my camera, and I can do whatever I want."

He narrowed his eyes at me, clearly trying to look annoyed but failing miserably. "That doesn't mean you can just take pictures of me without asking."

"Sure it does," I shot back, unable to wipe the smile off my face. "Besides, it's a good picture."

"I doubt the judges want to see my face in their contest."

I raised an eyebrow, pretending to think about it. "Maybe not. It's not a bad shot. I'd say your face is at least a solid six out of ten."

"Six?" he repeated, sounding offended. "I'm at least an nine. Maybe a high eight, and that's me being humble."

I burst out laughing again. If that was him being humble I was terrified to find out what he was like when he wasn't being humble. I continued chuckling and soon enough, he joined in, the easy rhythm of our banter flowing naturally now. It was weird how quickly things had shifted. A few days ago, we could barely stand to be in the same room together, and now we were out here laughing under the northern lights.

It wasn't lost on me how rare this moment was—seeing Callum like this, seeing us like this. It was comfortable, in a way that made my chest feel warm. Not the usual kind of warmth I got from teasing him, but something else. Something that made me feel like I was seeing a different side of him, one that wasn't so bad after all.

That was... nice.

Actually, no. It felt more than nice.

It felt... warm. Like a kind of warmth I hadn't realized I'd been missing, like the kind of warmth that sneaks up on you when you least expect it. It was almost like a warm hug.

Maybe, in some strange, unexpected way, this moment— laughing under the northern lights with Callum of all people— was a little like a warm hug.

I glanced at him, standing a few feet away, still gazing up at the sky with that easy smile. He looked more relaxed than

I'd ever seen him, and for a second, the tension between us seemed to dissolve completely.

"Hey," I said quietly, catching his attention.

He looked over at me, raising an eyebrow. "What?"

I hesitated for a moment, then smiled softly. "Thank you. For giving me the camera. It's... really nice."

He shrugged, looking away, but I caught the slight flush of embarrassment on his face. "Well, don't get used to it," he muttered, trying to sound as nonchalant as ever.

CHAPTER 23

CALLUM

THE QUIET HUM OF THE CAR'S ENGINE FILLED THE SPACE BETWEEN US AS WE DROVE back home, the city lights flashing by in a blur outside the windows. Hailey was sitting in the passenger seat, her camera resting in her lap as she scrolled through the photos she'd taken tonight. Every so often, I saw her lips curl into a small smile, and I couldn't help but feel something twist in my chest.

I didn't say anything. I kept my eyes on the road, trying to focus on driving, but my mind was spinning with everything that had happened over the last few hours.

After school today, I'd overheard my mom talking about how there were going to be northern lights tonight. I hadn't paid much attention at first, but something about the conversation stuck with me, nagging at the back of my mind.

Before I knew it, I was in my car, heading to Best Buy.

I hadn't planned on buying Hailey a camera. Hell, I didn't even know why I was doing it. All I knew was that I felt like shit—for everything. For the way I'd been acting the last few days, the way I'd treated her over the years. And maybe I was trying to make up for all of it in one impulsive move.

Why?

Was it because I'd been a total asshole? No—worse than an asshole. A complete and total cunt to her for the last few years? Or was it just because I felt bad? Maybe it didn't matter. Maybe I didn't need a reason.

I just… wanted to do something.

I didn't even think twice when I walked into that store and bought the camera. I picked one out, handed over my card, and left before I could question what the hell I was doing.

And now, here we were. After everything—the ridiculous bickering, the laughter, the northern lights.

But for some reason, seeing her smile as she looked through those pictures made me feel like maybe it hadn't been such a stupid idea after all.

I glanced over at her again, watching as she flipped through the photos, the screen lighting up her face in the darkness of the car. Her hair was still slightly messed from the cold night air, and her expression was soft, almost peaceful.

She looks happy.

That thought shouldn't have hit me the way it did, but it did. I didn't want to admit it, but there was a strange satisfaction in knowing that I'd made her smile tonight. I wasn't used to feeling this way—not with Hailey, not with anyone.

I shifted in my seat, gripping the steering wheel a little tighter as the road stretched out in front of us. I wasn't sure what to say, if I should even say anything at all. The air between us felt lighter than it had in days, but there was still something lingering—something I couldn't quite put my finger on.

Why the hell did I do this?

Tonight, for some reason, I didn't want to be that guy. I didn't want to be the asshole who made her life harder. I just wanted to do something good for once.

Maybe I was overthinking it. Maybe it was as simple as wanting to make up for the past, for all the shitty things I'd said and done.

Or maybe it was more than that.

I wasn't sure. But right now, as we drove through the quiet streets, I didn't need a reason. All I knew was that for the first time in a long time, things felt... different.

Hailey suddenly glanced up from her camera, catching me watching her out of the corner of my eye. "What?" she asked, raising an eyebrow, a small smile tugging at her lips.

I quickly turned my gaze back to the road, shaking my head. "Nothing."

GAME DAY. THE HOMECOMING GAME DAY.

The second I opened my eyes that morning, I could feel the electricity in the air. It buzzed through my veins, waking me up faster than any alarm ever could. Today wasn't just any game —this was the game.

The homecoming soccer match. In most cities, football was the big deal, but here? Soccer was everything. And as captain, it was my job to make sure we crushed it.

I headed downstairs, a bounce in my step, already getting hyped up in my head. The game wasn't until later this afternoon, but it didn't matter. I was ready now. I'd been preparing for this for weeks—hell, for months—and today was finally the day we got to show Oakridge just how much they'd underestimated us.

I made my way into the kitchen, flipping open the fridge and grabbing a water bottle. I was practically bouncing on the balls of my feet, already thinking about the plays we'd run, the goals we'd score.

As I stood there, chugging the water, I couldn't stop myself from shadowing a few moves. I twisted on my heel, flicking my leg out like I was about to take a shot, then pivoted with a quick spin, imagining Oakridge's defenders stumbling over themselves.

Damn, I was so ready for this.

"Jesus Christ," came a voice from behind me.

I spun around mid-move to see Hailey standing there at the edge of the kitchen, her arms crossed and an amused smirk on her face. She raised an eyebrow. "You look like a total freak."

I narrowed my eyes at her, wiping the back of my hand across my mouth. "It's called getting hyped, Hailey. Maybe you should try it sometime. Oh, wait—you don't have anything exciting going on in your life."

She rolled her eyes but didn't respond to the jab. Instead, she stepped into the kitchen, her camera hanging around her neck, the strap resting against her oversized hoodie. My eyes flicked to the camera, and despite myself, I felt a flicker of pride.

The one I bought her.

The sight of it made me feel... good. Like maybe I'd done something right for once. She was actually using it—hadn't just shoved it in a corner or treated it like some weird pity gift. She'd taken it out, slung it around her neck, and today she'd probably be using it to take pictures at the game. My game.

I caught myself before I could get too caught up in that thought, turning back to grab a protein bar from the counter. "Don't you have some yearbook stuff to do today?" I muttered, trying to sound casual.

"Yeah," she said, reaching for an apple from the fruit bowl on the counter. "I'll be at the game, taking pictures. Don't worry, I won't be cheering you on or anything."

"Good," I shot back, ripping the wrapper off my protein bar. "I'd probably play worse if I knew you were cheering for me."

She rolled her eyes again but didn't argue. Instead, she looked down at her camera, adjusting the settings absent-mindedly, and for a moment, there was a comfortable silence between us. No arguing, no tension—just two people standing in a kitchen, doing their own thing.

"Are you ready to go?" I asked, sounding casual.

"Obviously," she replied, as if I'd asked the dumbest question in the world. She held up her camera, letting the strap dangle in front of her. "Got everything I need."

I rolled my eyes. "Yeah, well, before you rush out of here, eat something first."

She blinked, surprised. "What?"

I crossed my arms, leaning against the counter. "You heard me. Eat something. I'm not giving up another sandwich for you today. You almost passed out last time, and I'm not dealing with that again."

She rolled her eyes dramatically but made her way back to the counter. "I wasn't that bad."

I shot her a look. "Hailey, you were clutching your stomach the entire class."

She sighed but grabbed an apple from the fruit bowl and took a bite. "There. Happy now?"

I glanced at the apple, unimpressed. "That's it?"

She narrowed her eyes at me, chewing. "Yeah. Not everyone has the appetite of a titan like you do."

I watched her for a second longer before shrugging. "Your call. But don't come crying to me when you're hungry."

She gave me a half-hearted glare before taking another bite of her apple, clearly not interested in listening to my advice. Typical. But at least she was eating something, which was better than nothing.

We headed to the car, the buzz of excitement for the game building in me again. Today was going to be huge, and I was ready to give it my all. And despite the usual banter between us, I had to admit, it was kind of nice knowing Hailey would be there, capturing the moment.

As soon as I started the car, I connected my phone to the Bluetooth and hit play on my pre-game playlist. The opening beat of "All I Do Is Win" by DJ Khaled blasted through the speakers, and I immediately felt myself getting into the zone. The song was hype as hell—always got me in the right mindset.

But before I could fully lose myself in the music, I heard a loud snort from the passenger seat. I turned my head just in time to catch Hailey giving me a side-eye, her lips curling into a half-smile. "Seriously? This is what you listen to at 8 in the morning?"

"What's wrong with it?" I asked, my voice defensive.

Hailey shook her head, still trying to suppress a laugh. "All I Do Is Win? I mean, it's not a bad song, but… first thing in the morning?"

I shrugged, tapping my fingers along with the beat on the steering wheel. "Yeah, it's my pre-game playlist. Gotta get hyped. Because all I do *is* win, you feel me?"

She gave me a look, somewhere between disbelief and amusement. "You're such a weirdo."

I shot her a glance, raising an eyebrow. "Wow, is the pot calling the kettle black?"

She blinked at me, surprised. "Wait… did you just… use that phrase correctly?"

I smirked. "Yeah. What, you think I'm dumb or something?"

"No, it's just…" She trailed off, shaking her head in disbelief. "Never mind. Not sure you want me to answer that."

I rolled my eyes and kept my focus on the road, but the song continued to thump through the speakers, and I could feel Hailey's curiosity building.

"You know," she said after a beat, "I kinda want to see what else you've got on this 'legendary' pre-game playlist of yours."

I shot her a wary look. "No way."

"Come on," she pressed, grinning. "I want to see what kind of motivational anthems you're listening to at the crack of dawn. Hand over the phone."

I hesitated for a moment. My playlist was personal, okay? I didn't need her judging my music choices, especially when I knew she had no idea what it took to get pumped for a game. But Hailey wasn't letting up, and the glint in her eyes told me she wasn't going to drop it anytime soon.

"Fine," I grumbled, pulling my phone from the dashboard and handing it over.

She took it eagerly, her fingers scrolling through my playlist as if she were about to uncover some kind of deep, dark secret. Her eyes lit up as she read the titles, and I could already see her trying to hold back her laughter. "Oh my god," she muttered, "this is like the bro anthem of all bro anthems."

"Shut up," I snapped, not really mad but kind of regretting handing over my phone. "It works."

"Oh, I'm sure it does," she said, her voice dripping with sarcasm as she scrolled further. "Eye of the Tiger? Really? What are you, Rocky Balboa?"

"It's a classic," I defended. "Gets you in the right mindset."

She snorted again, flipping through a few more songs. "Lose Yourself? Pushin P?"

"It's called getting focused," I shot back. "Unlike you, I actually need to be in the zone to win."

"Right," she said, clearly entertained as she handed the phone back to me. "Well, good luck with that. Maybe you'll get so in the zone that you won't hear me laughing at you from the stands."

I rolled my eyes again, trying to ignore the heat creeping up my neck. "Just make sure you get good pictures. I don't want any blurry shots."

"Oh, don't worry. I'll get a nice, clear one of you tripping over your own feet," she said, smirking.

I clenched my jaw, but deep down, I couldn't help but feel a weird sense of... amusement. As I turned up the volume on the next track, I felt that familiar surge of energy building.

"Eye of the Tiger" started to play, and I couldn't help but smirk at the fact that, yeah, maybe my playlist was a little on the nose, but it worked.

"Oh, hey, you've got a text," she said, her voice casual.

I frowned. "From who?"

She glanced at the screen. "It's from… Natalia."

My body stiffened. "What does it say?"

She raised an eyebrow, clearly enjoying this way too much. "'Hey sexy, you got any time before school? We can—'"

Before she could finish, I lunged, grabbing the phone from her hand so fast she barely had time to react.

"Hey!" she yelped, but I didn't care. My face burned, and I shoved the phone into my pocket, glaring out the windshield like I was about to plow through traffic if I didn't cool off.

For a second, the car was dead silent, the tension thick enough to cut with a knife.

"Oh," Hailey said slowly, her voice dripping with amusement. "That's what we're doing before school, huh?"

"Shut up," I snapped, gripping the steering wheel tighter. "It's not what you think."

The car fell into an awkward silence after that. Hailey turned her attention back to the window, humming a little under her breath as we drove toward school. Meanwhile, I kept my eyes on the road, my hands gripping the steering wheel a little tighter than usual.

That text from Natalia? Normally, I would've been all for it. A quick meet-up before school? No big deal. She knew what it was, and so did I. It wasn't complicated.

But now? Now it felt… weird.

For some reason, the thought of meeting up with her didn't sound all that appealing anymore. The usual excitement, that buzz I got from knowing we'd sneak away for some "fun," wasn't there. Instead, there was just this… weird feeling sitting in my gut.

Natalia was just... Natalia. We weren't serious. We weren't anything. But now, with Hailey sitting right there, her camera around her neck, her stupid teasing still ringing in my ears, it felt... wrong.

CHAPTER 24

HAILEY

"Hey, I've got a yearbook meeting during lunch today."

Nala pouted dramatically. "Ditching me already?"

I laughed. "It's not ditching when I actually have stuff to do. There's a game to cover tonight, remember?"

She sighed. "Fine, fine. I'll sit with Sasha and the cheerleaders. I'll see you at the game, though, right?"

"Yeah, of course," I replied, adjusting the strap of my camera. "And don't worry, I'll make sure to take a few pictures of you."

Nala grinned and wagged her finger at me. "I'd better be the star of that yearbook spread."

I chuckled as I stood. "Yeah, yeah. See you at the game."

Nala waved me off, and I made my way to the yearbook room. The excitement for the game and the homecoming dance was building, and I had a lot on my mind. Balancing photography with interviews tonight was going to be a lot, but it felt good to have something productive to focus on.

When I arrived at the yearbook room, Lance and the others were already seated around the table.

"Hailey! Just in time," Lance called as I stepped inside. He motioned for me to sit down. "We were just talking about tonight's responsibilities."

I slid into a chair, placing my camera on the table. Before we could dive into the details of the meeting, Lisa noticed the camera immediately.

"Whoa, that's a really nice camera, Hailey!" Lisa said, adjusting her glasses to get a better look. "Is it new?"

Derek leaned over, eyes widening. "Damn, it is nice. Way better than the one the school gives us to use."

I felt a small smile creep up on my face as I glanced down at the camera, still not fully believing I had it myself. "Yeah... it was a gift," I admitted, trying to sound casual. "It's way better than the school's one, that's for sure."

"A gift?" Lance raised an eyebrow, clearly intrigued. "Someone must really like you."

I felt my cheeks heat up slightly but shrugged it off. "Something like that."

Lance grinned, adjusting his notepad. "Anyway, we've got a lot to cover tonight. Obviously, we'll need tons of photos— not just of the game but also the cheerleaders, the crowd, and the general atmosphere."

"Got it," I said, patting my camera. "What else?"

"Well," Lance continued, flipping through his notes, "we'll need to interview some students and players during the game and at the dance later. We want this to be a big feature in the yearbook, so we'll need to cover everything."

Derek, who was still twirling his pen absentmindedly, spoke up. "I can handle most of the writing for the spread. Just send me the interviews, and I'll piece everything together— quotes from students, players, maybe even the coach."

Lance nodded. "Yeah, exactly. We'll take turns with the interviews. I can handle a few after the game, but if you get a chance, Hailey, try to grab some quotes from the players too. Especially if they win—it'll make for great content."

I raised an eyebrow, mentally preparing for the long night ahead. "I'll do my best."

Lisa pushed her glasses up her nose. "I'll work on the layout for the spread once we get the photos in. We need to make sure everything looks cohesive."

"And I'll handle some design work for the cover," Em added, not looking up from her sketchpad. "If we get some cool shots from tonight, I can use them in the background."

The conversation flowed easily as we discussed how we'd divide up responsibilities. The game was going to be hectic, but it was the dance that worried me more. I didn't want to be intrusive, shoving my camera in people's faces when they were just trying to enjoy the night. But, we had to get some candid moments for the yearbook.

"Don't worry about the dance," Lance said, as if reading my mind. "We only need a few shots—just enough to capture the vibe."

Lisa nodded in agreement. "Yeah, and make sure to get a couple of candid moments. People laughing, dancing, that sort of thing. It'll add a personal touch."

I scribbled a few notes in my notebook, already trying to strategize how I was going to juggle everything. Photos, interviews, and somehow capturing the spirit of the night—it was going to be a lot, but I felt prepared.

"Alright, I think we're set," Lance said, glancing around the room. "Just make sure you're ready for tonight. It's going to be busy, but we've got a good plan."

We all nodded, packing up our things as the meeting wrapped up. I grabbed my camera, mentally preparing myself for the night ahead. I walked out into the hall, adjusting the strap of my camera. The familiar weight of it around my neck felt grounding, but I couldn't shake the nervous excitement buzzing inside me. The halls were bustling with students, all of them talking excitedly about the upcoming game and the dance tonight. The energy was infectious.

Soon, there would be an announcement over the loudspeakers, calling all the students outside to the bleachers. The homecoming game was about to begin, and I had to admit—I was a little anxious.

I didn't usually care much for sports. If anything, I'd spent most of my time avoiding the entire "jock" culture. But today felt different. Today, Callum was going to play. And for some reason, that thought made me feel... something.

I couldn't help but think about how hard he'd been working over the last few weeks. He was at soccer practice almost every day—both before and after school—and on top of that, he'd been hitting the gym more than ever. It was impossible not to notice how dedicated he was, even if he did act like a cocky jerk most of the time.

And now, here we were, minutes away from the biggest game of the season, and I knew he'd be out there giving it everything he had. I sighed, shaking my head at myself. *Get it together, Hailey.*

Just as I rounded the corner, lost in my own thoughts, I slammed right into someone—hard. The collision knocked the wind out of me, and I stumbled backward, barely managing to keep my balance. I heard a sharp gasp from the other side, followed by an annoyed voice.

"Watch where you're going!" a girl snapped.

I blinked, looking up, my heart sinking when I saw who it was. Natalia. She stood there, glaring at me with one hand on her hip, a pretty brunette at her side who mirrored her disapproving expression.

"I—sorry," I muttered, rubbing my shoulder. My eyes fell to the ground, and that's when I saw it.

My camera.

It had slipped from my hands during the collision and was now lying on the cold, tiled floor.

"Seriously," Natalia scoffed, exchanging a glance with her friend. "You can't just walk around crashing into people like that."

The other girl nodded in agreement. "Yeah, next time watch where you're going."

I bit back the retort I wanted to say and knelt down to pick up my camera. As soon as my fingers wrapped around it, my heart sank. The lens... it was cracked. Shattered, actually. A spiderweb of cracks ran through the glass, distorting everything.

Oh, no. No, no, no, no.

My pulse quickened as I examined the damage. I'd only had the damn thing for a day. Callum had just given it to me. And now it was broken.

"Ugh, whatever," Natalia muttered dismissively, clearly already over the situation. She and her friend brushed past me, walking away without so much as a glance back.

I stood there for a moment, staring down at the camera in disbelief. Of course this would happen. I'd been so careful with it, and now... it was ruined.

My hands shook as I scrambled to think of a solution.

I definitely didn't want Callum finding out. There was no way I could explain this to him without feeling like a total piece of shit. He'd just gotten this for me yesterday, damn it. One of the only nice things he'd done for me.

I took a deep breath, cradling the broken camera to my chest, and hurried back to the yearbook room. When I got there, I saw Lance still sitting at the table, flipping through some papers. He looked up as I entered.

"Hey, Hailey. What's up?" he asked, tilting his head curiously.

I hesitated, gripping the camera behind my back. "Uh... I was thinking... maybe I'll just use the school camera for tonight after all."

Lance raised an eyebrow. "Really? I thought you said the new one was way better."

"Yeah, it is," I replied quickly, forcing a smile. "I just... I think I'd be more comfortable using the school one for now. I don't want to risk anything with mine. You know?"

Lance gave me a weird look but shrugged. "Sure, whatever works for you. I'll grab it for you."

I nodded, trying to keep my voice steady. "Thanks."

As Lance walked over to the storage cabinet to retrieve the school camera, I stood there, feeling the weight of the broken one hidden behind my back. The guilt gnawed at me.

Lance handed me the school camera, his expression still a little puzzled. "Here you go. Are you sure everything's alright?"

"Yeah, totally fine," I replied, forcing another smile as I took the camera from him. "Thanks, Lance."

He nodded, still giving me that curious look, but didn't press further. "Alright."

The school camera was heavy and unfamiliar in my hands as I made my way down the hall, my steps quick. I felt... off. There was this prickling sensation behind my eyes that I was desperately trying to ignore. Ugh, I couldn't let myself cry over this. Not now. Not in the middle of school.

I reached my locker and hastily shoved the broken camera inside, trying not to look at it for too long. But as I closed the door, the reality of the situation hit me like a tidal wave.

It was a gift. Callum gave it to me.

I wasn't supposed to get attached to it, to let it matter this much. But somehow, the camera—this thing that Callum had given me, after everything—felt like more than just a piece of equipment. It felt like... I didn't know.

I leaned against my locker, pressing my palms against the cool metal and taking a deep breath.

CHAPTER 25
CALLUM

I'D BLOWN OFF NATALIA THE ENTIRE DAY. EVERY TIME HER NAME POPPED UP ON my phone, I ignored it. I wasn't in the mood for her flirty texts or her not-so-subtle invitations. Usually, I'd be all over it, but today? Nah. I wasn't feeling it.

Right now, my head was in a different place.

I pushed open the locker room door, greeted by the familiar mix of sweat, body spray, and the echo of loud voices bouncing off the tiled walls.

The guys were already there, hyping each other up for the game, slapping hands and shouting about how we were going to destroy Oakridge tonight. The energy in the room was contagious, but I kept my cool, heading toward my locker to get changed.

Grayson was in the middle of yelling something about how we'd make up for last season's loss, his voice booming through the room. "We're not gonna let those Oakridge assholes do us like they did last time!"

The guys roared in agreement, and I couldn't help but feel that familiar fire start to build inside me.

"Yo, Callum," Adam called, slipping his cleats on. "You ready to tear Oakridge apart?"

I smirked, pulling my hoodie over my head. "Hell yeah. I've been ready."

I could feel the tension in the locker room growing, the excitement building as we all got into game mode. The locker room banter was always the same—guys talking big, trashing Oakridge, reminding each other of last year's loss.

Just as I was tightening my cleats, the door swung open, and Coach Taz walked in, his usual stern expression in place, but there was something else in his eyes today—something like pride.

"Alright, boys," Coach called, clapping his hands to get everyone's attention. The room went quiet almost instantly. "Before we hit the field, I've got something for you all."

We exchanged glances, curious, as Coach reached into a large box he'd carried in and started pulling out... jerseys. Not just any jerseys, though. These were new. Clean. Navy and dark yellow—our school colors, bold and sharp against the fabric.

"New jerseys, just in time for homecoming," Coach said, holding up one for us all to see. The navy blue stood out against the yellow details along the shoulders and sides. It was simple, sleek, and exactly the kind of thing we needed to kick off this game with some extra fire.

The locker room buzzed with excitement as Coach started handing them out, one by one.

"Grayson, number 10," Coach called, tossing one to Grayson, our forward. Grayson grinned, pulling it over his head immediately.

"Ibra, number 1—uh, wait, sorry," Coach paused with a smirk. "Number 12 for you, our goalie."

Ibra grinned, catching his jersey. "Over here."

"Adam, number 7," Coach continued, throwing the jersey to my best friend, our other striker.

The other guys called out their approval as they got their jerseys, and I could feel the energy in the room shift. There was something about wearing those new jerseys—something that made it feel real. We weren't just here to play. We were here to win.

Finally, Coach pulled out the last jersey and looked directly at me. "Callum, number 1. Captain."

I stepped forward and took it from him, my chest swelling with pride as I looked down at the clean, crisp fabric in my hands. Number 1. The weight of the responsibility settled on my shoulders, but instead of feeling heavy, it felt... right. Like this was exactly where I was supposed to be.

"Look sharp out there," Coach said as I slipped the jersey on. It fit perfectly, snug across my shoulders, the navy and yellow popping against my skin. "You boys earned this."

I looked around the room, seeing the same determination in my teammates' eyes that I felt. This wasn't just about the game anymore. This was about redemption, about putting last season behind us and making sure Oakridge never forgot who we were.

Grayson punched my shoulder lightly. "Looking good, Cap."

I grinned, tightening the sleeves of my jersey. "Damn right." The locker room erupted in noise again as the guys hyped each other up, shouting and slapping hands, their new jerseys giving them an extra boost of confidence.

We all stood in a tight circle, jerseys on, ready to tear Oakridge apart. Coach Taz stood in the middle, his voice booming over the noise.

"Alright, boys, let's start this right!" he shouted, clapping his hands together. "On my count." We all put our hands in the middle, forming a huddle, our voices lowering as we focused. The adrenaline was rushing through my veins, my heart pounding in anticipation. This was our game.

"One... two... Westview!" we shouted in unison, our voices ringing out, strong and united.

The sound echoed through the locker room, and for a moment, it felt like we were invincible.

As soon as we broke the huddle, we filed out of the locker room, one by one, heading down the tunnel toward the field. The sound of the assembly outside—the students, the cheerleaders, the crowd—was growing louder and louder, the energy building with every step we took.

I could see the field now, the bright green turf stretching out before us, the bleachers packed with students, teachers, and parents alike. Everyone was out there, the homecoming game drawing the biggest crowd of the year. The sun was starting to set, casting a golden glow over everything, making it feel like the perfect moment.

The crowd was alive with anticipation, Westview students piling onto the bleachers in their navy and yellow colors, waving flags and shouting our school chant.

I spotted the cheerleaders off to the side, led by Sasha, doing some last-minute stretches before they kicked off their routine. Everyone was in position, ready to cheer us on.

As we stepped onto the field, I could feel the weight of everyone's expectations on my shoulders, but it wasn't a bad kind of pressure.

It was the kind of pressure that made me feel alive.

This was what I lived for.

Behind me, the rest of the team filed out onto the field, each of us taking our positions for warm-ups. The noise from the bleachers grew louder, the crowd already getting hyped for the game. Coach Taz stood on the sidelines, his arms crossed, watching us closely as we went through our warm-up drills. I could feel the energy building inside me with every movement, every stretch.

As I jogged across the field, warming up with the rest of the team, I couldn't help myself. My eyes drifted toward the bleachers, scanning the crowd. I told myself I was just looking around, taking it all in—the school spirit, the noise, the excitement in the air.

But deep down, I knew exactly who I was looking for.

Where was she?

It wasn't like I was obsessed or anything. I just... well, I couldn't stop thinking about the look on Hailey's face when I handed her that camera. The way her green eyes had lit up, even though she tried to hide it. I didn't want to admit it, but part of me was hoping to catch her taking pictures with it tonight.

And then, finally, I spotted her.

She was just stepping out of the building with the rest of the yearbook crew. They were walking across the field, heading toward the sidelines to get into position. Hailey had her camera in her hands, but...

It wasn't the camera I'd given her.

What the hell?

I frowned, my attention no longer on the game or the crowd. She wasn't using the camera I'd gone out of my way to get her—the expensive one, the one that I'd hoped would show her that I wasn't a complete asshole. Instead, she had the school camera, the clunky old one we'd used for yearbook projects back in freshman year.

Why wasn't she using mine?

My heart beat a little faster, a weird mixture of confusion and something else—disappointment, maybe? Frustration? I didn't know what I was feeling, but whatever it was, I didn't like it. I told myself it didn't matter. It wasn't a big deal. Who cares what camera she was using?

But the longer I stared, the more irritated I felt. I'd bought that camera because I wanted to make up for being an asshole. Because I'd felt guilty when she told me she quit photography after people, including me, made fun of her.

I thought maybe it would mean something. That it would show her I wasn't as big of a jerk as she thought I was.

My mind was buzzing, and without thinking, I jogged over to where Hailey and the rest of the yearbook crew were setting up by the sidelines. Lance and the others noticed me coming and, after a quick exchange of glances, made themselves scarce.

Good. I didn't need an audience.

Hailey was adjusting the strap of the school camera around her neck when she looked up and saw me standing there, clearly surprised. Before she could say anything, I reached out and grabbed the camera she was holding, inspecting it.

"What is this?" I asked, turning the clunky old thing over in my hands. "Where's the one I got you? You literally had it this morning."

Her face flushed slightly, and I could see her tense up. "It's broken."

"Broken?" I echoed, narrowing my eyes. "What do you mean it's broken?"

She shifted uncomfortably, her fingers fidgeting with the hem of her shirt. "I, uh… dropped it."

I stared at her for a moment, trying to process what she'd just said. She *dropped* it? My chest tightened with frustration. How the hell did she just drop something like that? I mean, I wasn't expecting her to treat it like it was made of glass, but damn, it wasn't cheap.

"You dropped it?" I repeated, a little more agitated now.

"Yeah," she muttered, her voice quiet. "I dropped it, and the lens cracked. It was an accident."

I stood there for a second, running a hand through my hair. Part of me wanted to blow up at her, ask how she could be so careless. But I bit my tongue, taking a deep breath. Getting mad wasn't going to fix the camera. And it wasn't like I could yell at her over an accident, no matter how much it pissed me off.

But… at least it wasn't because she didn't want to use it. That was what really mattered, right?

I sighed, handing the camera back to her. "Let's just go get it fixed on the weekend. I didn't buy it just for it to sit in pieces."

There was a brief silence between us, and I could see her processing what I'd said. She seemed almost relieved, but I wasn't really sure why.

"Okay," she said, giving me a small nod.

I gave her a quick nod in return, still feeling the last bit of frustration simmering inside me. "Just… try not to break it again, damn it."

"I'll do my best," she replied, a hint of sarcasm in her voice, but I could tell she felt bad about it.

As I handed the clunky school camera back to Hailey, the tension in my chest eased slightly, but I couldn't help myself, "You'd better try to get some nice shots of me with this thing."

Hailey rolled her eyes, adjusting the strap on the clunky camera. "In your dreams, Callum."

I chuckled, looking around, and that's when I spotted a group of girls standing nearby, painting their faces with school colors. A mischievous idea hit me, and before I could think it through, I walked up to them.

"Hey, can I borrow this for a sec?" I asked, gesturing toward the tube of face paint.

The girls giggled and handed it over without question, clearly a little too eager. I flashed them a quick smile and headed back toward Hailey. She was busy fiddling with her camera again, completely unaware of what I had planned.

Before she could even look up, I crouched down in front of her and, without giving her a chance to protest, quickly swiped the paint across her cheek, drawing a large number "1."

"Hey!" Hailey yelped, jerking back, her eyes wide in surprise. "What the hell?"

I leaned back, grinning smugly as I admired my work. Ha. She'd just become my own personal cheerleader, and it seemed she noticed that too, as her eyes trailed down to the bold number "1" resting on my jersey.

She blinked, stunned for a second, then narrowed her eyes at me. "You did not just do that."

"Oh, I did," I replied, still smirking. "Now you've got some real school spirit."

She reached up to touch her cheek, her fingers grazing over the big "1" I'd painted. Her mouth opened like she wanted to yell at me, but instead, she just sighed in exasperation.

"You're fucking insufferable," she muttered.

"Yep, but now everyone knows you'll be cheering for number one all night," I shot back, crossing my arms, feeling pretty damn pleased with myself.

"In your dreams, Reid," she said, wiping at her cheek unsuccessfully. "I'm not cheering for you."

"Doesn't matter. You've got my number on your face now," I said with a wink, handing the face paint back to the girls as I jogged off.

As I jogged back toward the field, I could feel Hailey glaring at me from behind, but I didn't care. The game was about to start, and all I could think about was getting that ball in the back of Oakridge's net.

And if Hailey ended up with a few shots of me on the field, well… that was just a bonus.

I jogged back onto the field, feeling the energy in the air. The bleachers were even more packed now, students filling every row. The noise was getting louder, and the Westview crowd was buzzing, faces painted, waving banners, and decked out in navy and yellow. This was it—homecoming. The game we'd been waiting for.

As I looked around, I spotted a small group of kids wearing green and orange on the far side of the bleachers—Oakridge kids. I snorted to myself. Fucking leprechauns. That's exactly what their colors looked like. I couldn't believe anyone thought that combo was intimidating.

The rest of the team was gathered in a loose circle near the center of the field, and I jogged over, still feeling the high from messing with Hailey. I could practically feel her eyes burning into my back from the sidelines, but whatever. She could hate it all she wanted; it was still hilarious.

"Let's go, boys," Grayson said as I reached the group, clapping his hands together. "Time to show Oakridge what we're made of."

"Hell yeah," Adam added, bouncing on his toes. "Let's wipe that smug look off their faces."

Just as we were getting into our own rhythm, the Oakridge team stepped out onto the field. The crowd shifted, some booing while others cheered, but I wasn't really paying attention to the noise. My focus was on the other team.

There they were, in their ugly-ass green and orange jerseys, strutting onto the field like they owned the place. I spotted Troy Duran, leading them with that same arrogant look plastered on his face.

Troy's eyes scanned the field, and when he spotted me, his lips curled into a smirk. He had this face that made me want to punch something.

"Alright, heads in the game," Coach Taz called from the sidelines, his voice sharp. "This is your night. Don't let Oakridge get under your skin."

I forced myself to look away from Troy and focus on my team. The Oakridge squad was strong, but we were stronger. We were ready. And tonight, we were on our turf. There was no way we were letting them take this from us.

"Remember what happened last year," I said, keeping my voice low but firm as I addressed the guys. "We owe them. But play smart. We don't need any dumb fouls or red cards."

The guys nodded, the atmosphere growing more serious. This wasn't just about winning. This was about revenge. We'd been embarrassed last year, and we weren't about to let that happen again.

Grayson cracked his knuckles. "Let's make sure they don't forget who we are."

I nodded, my eyes narrowing as the referee blew the whistle, signaling the start of the game. The roar from the crowd grew louder, echoing through the field, and I could feel the adrenaline pumping through my veins.

This was it.

The game was on.

♦

CHAPTER 26
CALLUM

The whistle blew, and everything else disappeared. The roar of the crowd, the bright lights shining down on the field, the tension in the air—it all faded to the background. It was just me, the ball, and the game.

I tapped the ball forward as we kicked off, sending it to Adam, who was already moving into position. Grayson cut across the field, drawing two Oakridge defenders with him, leaving Adam a lane to push forward. The first few minutes were all about finding the rhythm, getting a feel for how Oakridge was going to play us.

Their defense was strong, just like we knew they would be, but they weren't invincible.

Adam darted past a midfielder and sent the ball right back to me. I took it in stride, keeping my head up as I scanned the field. There was a gap forming on the left side, and I saw Grayson sprinting into space. Without hesitation, I sent the ball flying in his direction, a clean, low pass that slid right between two Oakridge players.

Grayson caught it on his foot, controlling it perfectly before driving it toward the goal. The Oakridge goalie was quick on his feet, though, and Grayson's shot was deflected out of bounds.

"Shit," I muttered under my breath, jogging over for the corner kick.

We took our positions, the Oakridge defenders crowding the box, trying to prevent us from getting any clear shots. Adam signaled, and I knew what he was planning. He always liked to go for the near post on these corners. I moved into position as the ball soared into the box.

It was chaos—bodies flying everywhere, arms and legs tangled up as we all scrambled for the ball. I saw Adam leap, his head connecting perfectly with the ball, sending it toward the goal. The Oakridge goalie dove, but he wasn't fast enough.

The ball hit the back of the net.

Goal!

"1-0!" Adam shouted, his grin wide as he jogged back to our side. I clapped him on the back, adrenaline pumping through my veins.

But Oakridge wasn't going to let that slide.

They pressed us hard for the next few minutes, pushing our defense to the limit. Troy was all over the place, directing their midfielders and trying to find weak spots in our formation. I could feel the tension building as they moved the ball closer and closer to our goal.

"Stay tight!" I yelled to the defense, but Oakridge had already found their opening.

Troy cut past one of our defenders, darting into the box. I sprinted back to try and block him, but he was too quick. He fired a shot at the goal, and Ibra barely missed it as the ball flew past him and into the net. The Oakridge section of the bleachers went wild, waving their green and orange flags as Troy smirked, jogging back to his team.

"1-1," I muttered, frustration gnawing at me. I clenched my fists, but I wasn't going to let this shake me. We had plenty of game left.

The game continued, and the intensity ramped up. Both teams were playing fast, aggressive, not giving each other an inch. The ball flew up and down the field as we tried to outpace them, but Oakridge's defense was holding strong. Every shot we tried to take, they blocked or deflected.

But we weren't giving up. With about ten minutes left in the half, Grayson won a tough battle for the ball in the midfield and sent it flying toward me. I could feel the defenders closing in, but I kept my eyes on the goal.

I took one touch to control the ball, then cut inside, darting between two Oakridge players. The crowd's noise faded into the background as I focused on the goal. I could see the gap. I took a deep breath and let it rip.

The ball soared past the defenders, curving just enough to beat the Oakridge goalie and slam into the back of the net.

"GOAL!" The crowd erupted again, louder than before, the Westview bleachers roaring with cheers.

"2-1!" I pumped my fist, turning back to my teammates as they rushed over to celebrate.

We jogged back to our positions, the energy high as the clock ticked down to the end of the half. Oakridge tried to press again, but our defense held them off, blocking every attempt they made to break through.

Finally, the whistle blew, signaling the end of the first half. We jogged over to the bench to regroup. My legs burned, but it was that good kind of burn—the one that told me we were pushing hard, that we were in control of the game. Oakridge was tough, but we were tougher, and with the scoreboard reading 2-1 in our favor, I felt a surge of confidence.

Coach Taz was already talking strategy, telling us to keep pressing them, not to get lazy. I wiped the sweat from my forehead with the back of my hand, barely listening. My mind drifted for a moment, scanning the bleachers.

That's when I saw them—my parents, Dalton, and Nathan, sitting together and waving. Dalton, in particular, was practically jumping up and down, trying to get my attention. I held up a hand and gave them a nod.

Seeing Dalton and Nathan there made my chest feel tight, like I wanted to make sure I didn't let them down.

As I turned my attention back to the field, my eyes landed on the sidelines, where Hailey was standing with the rest of the yearbook crew. She was fiddling with that old, clunky school camera again, adjusting the strap around her neck as she tried to get the settings just right. I couldn't help but smirk.

Should be using the camera I got her, I thought, but the corner of my mouth quirked up anyway.

She must have sensed me looking because she glanced up from the camera and we made eye contact. I grinned, giving her a quick wink.

She rolled her eyes, of course.

I was about to turn my attention back to Coach Taz when, out of the corner of my eye, I noticed someone walking toward her. My mood shifted instantly, that familiar fire building in my chest as I realized who it was.

"What the hell..." I muttered under my breath, standing up a little straighter on the bench.

Troy strolled over to Hailey with that same cocky swagger he always had, like he thought he owned the place. My jaw clenched.

What was *he* doing talking to her?

Troy leaned in closer to Hailey, that stupid smirk on his face as he continued to talk to her. He was pointing to something —his water bottle—and saying something to her, trying to act all lost like some kid who couldn't find his mom in the middle of a department store.

Without even thinking, I grabbed my own water bottle off the bench, unscrewed the cap, and dumped the entire thing onto the field.

"Whoops, looks like I need more water," I muttered sarcastically.

Adam, who was standing next to me, raised an eyebrow, clearly having seen what I'd just done. "Dude, have you lost your mind? What the hell was that?"

I ignored him, already walking over to where Troy and Hailey were standing. My heart pounded in my chest as I closed the distance between us. Troy glanced up when he saw me approaching, his smirk still firmly in place.

"Hey, what's up, Reid?" Troy greeted me, like we were old buddies or something. I resisted the urge to punch that smug look right off his face.

"What's going on here?" I asked, my voice a little sharper than I intended as I glanced at Hailey.

She blinked, looking between me and Troy, clearly sensing the tension. "Uh, Troy was just asking where to fill up his water bottle," she said, her tone neutral.

I forced a smile, though it probably looked more like a grimace. "Oh, I can show you, Troy," I said, trying to keep my voice casual. "I was just about to refill mine too."

Troy gave me a long look, probably wondering why the hell I was suddenly offering to help. "Alright" he said with a shrug, clearly not sensing the tension rising inside me.

I turned, leading the way toward the school, my grip tightening on the empty water bottle in my hand. Troy followed, probably still thinking we were cool, but inside, I was fuming.

We walked into the hall leading toward the refill station, the noise from the field fading behind us. I kept my grip tight on the empty water bottle, trying to keep my cool, but I could still feel that tight knot in my chest from watching Troy chat up Hailey. I didn't know why it bothered me so much, but it did.

Troy, oblivious to everything, strolled beside me, refilling his water bottle with a casualness that made me grit my teeth. As the water poured into his bottle, he glanced at me, a sly grin curling on his lips.

"So, who was that back there?" he asked, like we were having some kind of casual conversation. "Your little girlfriend or something?"

I turned to him, my heart skipping a beat, my jaw clenching. "What?"

Troy chuckled, still smirking like the asshole he was. "The girl with the camera," he said, nodding toward the field. "Saw she had your jersey number painted on her cheek. And the way you stepped in just now... is she your girl or something?"

I could feel the heat rising in my chest, the tightness returning. I shouldn't have let him get under my skin like that, but something about the way he said it made my blood boil. "So what if she is?" I shot back, my voice sharper than I intended.

Troy's grin widened, clearly amused by my response. "Interesting," he said, raising an eyebrow. What the hell was so interesting about it? "Didn't know you were into photographers. Guess I should've backed off, huh?"

I clenched my fists, resisting the urge to punch that smug look right off his face. "Yeah, maybe you should," I said, stepping closer. "I don't think she's your type, Duran."

He laughed, tossing the water bottle cap into the air and catching it. "Relax, man. I was just asking. No need to get all defensive."

I forced myself to take a deep breath, trying to cool down. I didn't know why I'd said what I did. Hailey wasn't my girlfriend. Hell, I didn't even like her. But the thought of Troy acting like he could just stroll up to her, like she was someone he could mess with... it pissed me off.

Troy gave me a once-over, clearly enjoying the tension he was stirring up. "I didn't mean anything by it," he said with a

shrug, still grinning. "Just figured I'd ask. She seemed...
interesting, that's all."

I narrowed my eyes at him, the irritation bubbling just
below the surface. "You should focus on the game, Duran," I
said, my voice low. "Unless you want to lose."

Troy shrugged again, clearly unbothered. "We'll see,
Reid," he said, capping his bottle and stepping away from the
refill station. "We'll see."

As he walked away, I stood there for a second, gripping
my water bottle so tightly I thought it might crack. I didn't know
what the hell had just happened. All I knew was that I wasn't
going to let Troy get into my head.

Not now. Not tonight.

I took a deep breath, filling my own bottle, and then
turned to follow him back toward the field.

I jogged back to the field, forcing myself to shake off the
exchange with Troy. My heart was still pounding, but I couldn't
let him get in my head. We were still up 2-1, and we had a whole
second half to finish strong. As I rejoined my teammates on the
sideline, I took a deep breath, trying to clear my mind and
refocus.

"Everything good?" Grayson asked, giving me a quick
look. He must have noticed my tension.

"Yeah, fine," I muttered, forcing a smirk. "Just ready to
finish this game."

Coach Taz gathered us in a quick huddle, his voice low
but intense. "Alright, boys, we've got the lead, but don't let up
now. Oakridge is gonna come at us hard. Stay sharp, keep
possession, and don't give them any easy chances. We've got
this."

We nodded, the tension building as we prepared for the
second half. I could feel the adrenaline coursing through me, my
body ready to go, despite the exhaustion creeping in from the
first half.

The whistle blew, and the second half kicked off. Oakridge wasted no time, immediately pressing hard, their midfielders cutting through our defense with a renewed energy. It was clear they weren't going down without a fight.

We fought back, holding our formation, but it wasn't easy. The game was fast and physical, both teams battling for control of the ball. Every time we managed to push forward, Oakridge's defense would close in, cutting off our angles and forcing us to reset.

A few minutes into the second half, Oakridge won a corner kick. I stood at the edge of the box, watching as their players crowded in, jockeying for position. The ball flew into the air, and for a moment, everything slowed down. I saw Troy leap, his head connecting with the ball perfectly.

It sailed past Ibra, hitting the back of the net.

"Goal!" The Oakridge side of the bleachers exploded with cheers as the scoreboard shifted to 2-2.

I cursed under my breath, my hands balling into fists. Troy jogged back toward the center of the field, his smug grin plastered across his face. I could feel the frustration boiling inside me, but I couldn't let it control me. We still had time.

The game resumed, and the pressure only increased. Oakridge was riding high on their momentum, pushing us back, testing our defense at every opportunity. Ibra made a couple of crucial saves, keeping us in the game, but I could feel the weight of the situation pressing down on us.

We were struggling to keep possession, Oakridge's midfielders swarming us every time we touched the ball. It felt like we were on the back foot, and the clock was ticking down. My legs were burning, but I refused to give up.

With less than five minutes left on the clock, we won a free kick just outside the box. It was our chance—maybe our last one. I stepped up to take it, my heart pounding in my chest. The Oakridge wall was set up, their players lined up, watching me closely.

I took a deep breath, my eyes locked on the goal. I could hear the crowd, feel the weight of their expectations pressing down on me. But I blocked it all out. It was just me, the ball, and the net.

I stepped forward and struck the ball cleanly, sending it curling over the wall and toward the top corner of the goal.

The Oakridge goalie leapt, his fingers grazing the ball, but it wasn't enough. The ball slammed into the back of the net, and the Westview side of the bleachers erupted into cheers.

"Goal!" the announcer shouted, his voice barely audible over the roar of the crowd.

"3-2!" I pumped my fist, turning to face my teammates as they rushed over to celebrate.

Grayson clapped me on the back, a wide grin on his face. "That's what I'm talking about, Reid!"

We jogged back to our positions, the adrenaline still pumping through my veins. There were only a couple of minutes left on the clock, and all we had to do was hold them off. I could feel the tension in the air, the anticipation of the crowd as the game drew to its final moments.

Oakridge pressed forward one last time, but our defense held strong. Ibra made another crucial save, and we cleared the ball out of our half, killing the last few seconds.

The whistle blew, and the game was over.

The Westview side of the bleachers erupted into cheers, the sound deafening as we celebrated on the field. I couldn't stop grinning, the weight of the game lifting off my shoulders. We'd done it.

We'd won.

CHAPTER 27
HAILEY

THE FINAL WHISTLE BLEW, AND THE FIELD EXPLODED INTO CHEERS. WESTVIEW had won.

I couldn't help but clap along with the crowd. Even though I wasn't exactly a soccer enthusiast, the energy in the air was infectious, and it felt impossible not to get swept up in the excitement. The boys huddled together near the center of the field, high-fiving and embracing each other, their smiles wide as they celebrated the win.

I stood on the sidelines, adjusting the camera in my hands and snapping a few shots of the players. The way they moved, the pure joy on their faces—it was the kind of thing yearbook material was made of.

As I zoomed in on the team, my gaze drifted toward Callum. He was standing a little apart from the others, catching his breath with that typical cocky grin on his face. His shirt was drenched with sweat, sticking to his broad shoulders and chest, his hair a tousled mess.

He looked up, scanning the crowd, and then his eyes locked onto mine.

For a moment, I froze, my heart suddenly thudding a little harder in my chest.

What... what the hell?

Why did that look make my stomach twist like that?

Callum's grin widened, and before I knew it, he flashed me a wide, boyish smile that made my heart race even more. He looked so... so proud of himself.

And—ugh—he had every right to be. He'd played well. He'd scored the winning goal, after all.

And the way he was grinning now, so carefree, it was almost like a completely different side of him—the side I hadn't seen in a while, maybe not ever.

He held up a peace sign, like he was posing for me or something, his grin never faltering. I could tell he was waiting for me to snap a picture, and for some reason, that smug confidence of his didn't irritate me as much as it should've.

I shook my head, biting back a smile of my own as I lifted the camera.

Fine, I thought, *you win, Reid.*

And he did. Tonight, he really did win. I might not like the guy but there was no denying how much he shone on the field. I pressed the shutter, capturing him mid-smirk, his boyish grin shining through the viewfinder. He gave me a quick nod, clearly pleased with himself, before turning back to his teammates. I lowered the camera, still feeling the faintest trace of warmth in my chest.

What the hell was wrong with me?

Since when did a simple smile from Callum make my heart race like that? I took a deep breath, trying to shake off the weird flutter in my stomach.

Maybe it was just the adrenaline from the game, the excitement in the air. Yeah, that had to be it. Nothing more.

As the team continued celebrating, I snapped a few more pictures of the players, the fans, and the field, but I couldn't stop thinking about that grin. It was annoying. Infuriating, even.

And yet... I couldn't get it out of my head.

THE GAME HAD WRAPPED UP, AND AFTER SNAPPING THE LAST FEW SHOTS, I FOUND myself waiting near the parking lot. The parking lot was bustling with energy—students and parents still buzzing from Westview's win.

People were loading into their cars, and the air was filled with conversations and laughter. I had packed up the yearbook camera and was standing near the Reid family's car, waiting for Callum to show up.

Callum had gone to shower and change after the game, and it seemed like half of the student body was still hanging around, lingering in the post-game high. I spotted Mr. and Mrs. Reid chatting with some other parents nearby, while Dalton and Nathan were practically bouncing on their feet, too excited to stand still.

Dalton spotted me first, running over with his usual boundless energy. "Did you see it? Did you see Callum's goal? It was so cool!" he said, his words tumbling over each other in his excitement.

"I did," I said with a smile, ruffling his hair. "He played really well."

Nathan, quieter as usual but with a smile on his face, nodded in agreement. "Yeah, it was a good game."

Just then, I saw Callum making his way toward us, freshly showered and changed, his hair still damp and pushed back casually. He looked... well, he looked different out of his sweaty soccer gear. He had that same confident air about him, but now he looked more relaxed, still riding the high of the victory.

His parents greeted him with wide smiles, Mr. Reid clapping him on the shoulder while Mrs. Reid pulled him into a quick hug. "That was amazing, Callum! We're so proud of you," she said, her voice filled with pride.

Dalton immediately started bouncing around Callum, going on and on about the game. "Your goal was so awesome, Callum! I knew you were gonna score the second you kicked it!"

Callum chuckled. "Yeah, thanks, little man."

After a few minutes of chatting and congratulations, Mrs. Reid turned to me. "Hailey, sweetie, do you want to ride back with us in the minivan? We've got room."

Before I could respond, Callum cut in. "Nah, Hailey will ride with me."

What?

I blinked, a little surprised by his quick response. Mrs. Reid raised an eyebrow, glancing between the two of us, but didn't press the issue. "Oh, alright then," she said with a smile. "We'll see you two back at the house."

Dalton tugged at Mrs. Reid's hand, still talking excitedly about the game as they made their way to the family minivan. Nathan followed after them, leaving me standing there, a bit dumbfounded by Callum's declaration.

I turned to Callum, crossing my arms. "You didn't ask if I wanted to ride with you."

He shrugged, giving me one of those half-smirks that I was quickly coming to recognize. "Oops, I guess I didn't. Let's go."

Without waiting for a response, he turned and headed toward his car. I let out a huff but followed him, not really in the mood to argue. As we made our way through the parking lot toward Callum's car, I noticed someone else standing by the passenger side of his car. My stomach dropped slightly when I realized who it was—Natalia. Of course, it had to be her.

She was leaning against the door, arms crossed, her bright red hair tumbling over one shoulder as she scrolled through her phone. When she spotted us approaching, her eyes immediately flicked to me, and her perfectly arched brow rose. The tension in the air was almost palpable.

"Oh, hey Callum," she said in a sugary-sweet tone, completely ignoring me at first. Then, her gaze shifted to me, and I could practically feel the judgment radiating from her. "And... Hailey, right?" she added, her tone a little too sharp.

I nodded, unsure of where this was going.

Natalia's eyes darted between Callum and me, and she let out a slow, mocking laugh. "So, why exactly are you going somewhere with Callum in his car?"

Her question hung in the air, the underlying accusation clear as day. I opened my mouth to respond, but before I could say anything, Natalia's expression shifted into one of realization, her eyes widening with a gleam of triumph.

"Ohhhh," she said, dragging the word out as if she had just uncovered some big secret. "So it was *your* chapstick I found that one time in his car, huh?"

I blinked, confused. "What?"

Yeah, I had been missing one of my tubes of chapstick, but what did that have to do with anything? It sounded like she was accusing me of something and I didn't like it. Before I could process it further, Callum stepped forward, his expression hardening.

"Cut it out, Natalia," he said, his voice low and sharp.

Natalia raised her hands in mock surrender, her smirk never faltering. "Oh, I'm just kidding, Callum. No need to get all defensive."

She turned her gaze back to me, her smile still too wide, too fake. "By the way," she said, her tone dripping with sarcasm, "I'm really sorry for bumping into you earlier. Hopefully, that lame camera you dropped wasn't worth too much. It looked pretty... basic."

My heart sank as I realized what she was talking about. She had seen me drop the camera—and not only had she not apologized, but she'd also just outed the truth in front of Callum. I could feel the heat rising in my face, a mix of embarrassment and frustration bubbling up inside me.

Callum turned to me, his eyes narrowing in confusion. "Wait... what?"

Natalia gave us both a little wave, clearly satisfied with the chaos she'd stirred up. "See you later, Callum," she said, her voice sickeningly sweet as she sauntered off into the parking lot.

I stood there, rooted to the spot, feeling completely exposed. My mind was racing, trying to figure out how to explain this to Callum without sounding like an idiot. But the damage was already done.

Callum turned to me, his jaw clenched, his voice low. "What was she talking about, Hailey?"

I opened my mouth, but the words stuck in my throat. I had told him I dropped it because it was easier than admitting that two girls—Natalia included—had knocked into me and caused me to break the camera. I hadn't wanted to make a big deal out of it, but now...

"I... I didn't want to make a fuss," I said quietly, feeling even more embarrassed under his intense gaze. "She and some other girl bumped into me, and I dropped the camera. But I figured... I figured it wasn't worth mentioning."

Callum's eyes darkened, his frustration clear. "Why the hell wouldn't you say something?"

I shrugged, avoiding his gaze. "I don't know, Callum. I didn't think it mattered. It's just a camera."

"It's not just a camera," he snapped, his voice tinged with irritation. "You should've told me what happened."

I stayed quiet, unsure of what to say. Callum let out a frustrated sigh, rubbing the back of his neck. "Whatever," he muttered. "Let's just go."

Without another word, he unlocked the car and climbed into the driver's seat, clearly still irritated. I slid into the passenger seat, my mind swirling with a mix of emotions as I buckled my seatbelt. The silence between us was heavy as Callum started the engine and pulled out of the parking lot, heading toward home.

As the car sped down the darkened streets, I couldn't help but feel a little guilty. But at the same time, I couldn't shake the lingering frustration at how things had gone down. The silence in the car was suffocating. Callum's knuckles were white as he gripped the steering wheel, his jaw set tight as he drove. I didn't know what to say, and honestly, I wasn't sure if I wanted to say anything at all.

But then, out of nowhere, he spoke, his voice low and sharp. "So, what? You're just going to let people walk all over you like that?"

I blinked, turning to look at him, confused. "What did you say?"

"You heard me," he said, his voice a little louder now. "You're just gonna let people like Natalia shove you around and break your stuff without saying a damn thing? You didn't even tell me what happened until she brought it up."

I stared at him, my mind spinning. I hadn't expected him to be this mad. "Why are you so pissed off?" I asked, trying to keep my own irritation in check. "Is it because I wasn't careful enough with the camera? Because it was an accident, Callum."

He let out a frustrated breath, shaking his head. "I'm not mad at you for breaking the camera, Hailey. I'm mad at Natalia."

I frowned, still trying to piece together why this was such a big deal. "Natalia?" I repeated. "Why are you mad at her?"

He shot me a quick glance, his eyes flashing with anger. "Because she's the one who bumped into you and broke the damn camera. She was being careless, and now the gift I gave you is ruined."

I stared at him, the realization slowly sinking in. He wasn't mad at me—he was mad at Natalia. He was mad because his gift, the camera he'd gone out of his way to get for me, had been the casualty of someone else's carelessness.

"I thought you liked Natalia," I muttered, more to myself than to him.

Callum let out a harsh laugh, though there wasn't any humor in it. "I liked being with her."

I rolled my eyes. "Spoken like a true player."

He shot me another glance, his expression hard to read, but I could feel the tension in the air shift. He didn't deny it. Instead, he just kept driving, his jaw clenched again.

I crossed my arms, staring out the window, my frustration growing by the second. Of course he was mad that Natalia had broken something of his. It didn't really matter that the camera was for me—it was about him, as always.

He liked being in control, and this situation had probably made him feel like he'd lost some of that.

But still... something about the way he was reacting felt off. I couldn't quite figure out why, but it almost seemed like he cared more than he was willing to admit. And that... that was strange.

The rest of the drive was quiet, tension hanging between us like a thick fog. I didn't know what else to say, and apparently, neither did he. But as we pulled into the driveway and parked, I couldn't shake the weird feeling that something had shifted.

I unbuckled my seatbelt and opened the car door, stepping out into the cool night air. I was about to head inside, eager to leave the awkward tension hanging in the air, but before I could take a step, I felt a firm grip on my arm.

I froze, turning back to see Callum's hand wrapped around my wrist. His touch wasn't harsh, but it was enough to stop me in my tracks.

"What...?" I started, my voice trailing off, confused.

Callum's eyes were locked on mine, his expression intense—more intense than I'd ever seen it before. There was something simmering just below the surface, something that felt like anger, but also something else I couldn't quite place.

"Next time..." he started, his voice low, barely more than a whisper. "Next time Natalia or anyone else messes with you... you tell me."

I blinked, completely caught off guard. "Why?" I asked, my voice more defensive than I intended.

His jaw clenched, and I could see the frustration building in his eyes. He took a small step closer, his grip on my arm tightening just slightly—not enough to hurt, but enough to make his point clear.

"Just do it, Hailey," he hissed, his voice sharp and cutting through the cool night air. "Got it?"

I stared at him, my heart racing as I tried to figure out what was happening. Why was he so worked up about this? Why did he care so much? He wasn't usually like this—not with me, not with anyone.

But something in his tone, something in the way he was looking at me, made me swallow back my usual snarky response. There was something real behind his words, something that made me hesitate.

"Okay," I said quietly, nodding slowly. "I got it."

CHAPTER 28
CALLUM

I SLAMMED THE DOOR TO MY ROOM, THE SOUND ECHOING IN THE QUIET HOUSE. My whole body was still buzzing from the win earlier—my muscles humming with that post-game adrenaline—but somehow, I couldn't enjoy it. The high from the victory was fading fast, replaced by this boiling frustration that wouldn't go away.

Fucking Natalia.

I yanked open my closet, pulling out the black suit I'd planned to wear for homecoming tonight. The fabric felt smooth under my fingers, but as I started getting dressed, my mind kept circling back to that conversation in the parking lot. Natalia's smug face, her sarcastic ass tone… and Hailey, standing there, taking her shit.

I let out a frustrated sigh, tugging on my tie.

She had no fucking right to treat Hailey like that. I didn't care if it was a joke to her or whatever. It wasn't funny to me. She had no business bumping into her, breaking that camera, and then acting like it was some joke.

I growled under my breath, tugging my tie too tight and nearly choking myself. "Damn it," I muttered, loosening it again. Why hadn't Hailey told me the truth in the first place? Why hadn't she said anything? I could've dealt with it, fixed it, done something. Said something. But no, she had to act like it wasn't a big deal, like it didn't matter. And that pissed me off even more.

I finished buttoning my suit jacket, staring at my reflection in the mirror. I looked fine—more than fine, actually. My hair was still a bit damp, pushed back in a way that looked clean but not too neat. The suit fit me perfectly. I should've felt good. I should've been focused on the fact that tonight was homecoming, that I'd just scored the winning goal in the biggest game of the year.

But instead, I was stuck here, fuming about Natalia and how she'd screwed up the gift I'd gotten for Hailey.

Because it wasn't just about the camera. It wasn't just about Natalia being an asshole.

It was about Hailey.

And I hated that I cared. I hated that I couldn't just shrug it off like I normally would. I hated that seeing her upset did something to me, made me want to fix it, made me want to protect her.

"Fuck," I muttered, running a hand through my hair.

There was a knock on my door, and I glanced up to see my mom poking her head inside.

"Hey, sweetie," she said with a warm smile. "Ahh, you look so handsome! All ready for homecoming?"

I forced a smile, trying to shake off the lingering frustration. "Yeah, I'm ready."

She stepped inside, smoothing down the lapels of my jacket like moms do. "It was such an amazing game today. We're all so proud of you, Callum. I hope you have fun tonight at the dance. You deserve it."

"Thanks, Mom," I said, my voice a little quieter than usual as I patted my suit down.

She gave me a knowing look, her eyes softening. "Is everything alright? You've been a little... distracted."

I hesitated for a moment, wondering if I should tell her what was going through my head. But then I shook it off. "Yeah, I'm good. Just thinking about the game."

She didn't push, just smiled and gave me a quick hug. "Alright. Well, enjoy your night, okay? You've earned it."

I nodded, watching her leave the room before turning back to the mirror. *Just enjoy the night,* I told myself. *It's homecoming. It's not that deep.*

As I reached the bottom of the stairs, I paused, glancing toward the door that led down to the basement—Hailey's new territory. I was just about to knock on the door when I heard the soft creak of it opening.

She stepped out of the basement, and my heart... well, it kind of stopped for a second.

What the hell?

Hailey looked... different. Really fucking different. Her hair was softly curled, bouncing lightly around her shoulders, and there was a hint of makeup on her face—not too much, just enough to make her features pop. But it wasn't the hair or the makeup that got to me. It was the dress.

That dark green dress.

It was the exact same color as her eyes, and it framed her body perfectly. The fabric hugged her curves in all the right places without being too much, and I could feel my throat go dry just looking at her. The way it skimmed her waist, the way it fell just above her knees... it was simple but elegant, and she looked... well, fucking gorgeous.

I blinked, trying to snap out of it, but I couldn't stop staring. For a second, it felt like someone had punched me in the gut. Since when did Hailey look like this?

Her eyes flicked up to meet mine, and I quickly tried to compose myself. I could feel the surprise flicker across my face before I smoothed it out, forcing a casual tone.

"You... uh, you clean up nice," I muttered, doing my best to sound indifferent.

Hailey rolled her eyes, clearly not impressed by my weak attempt at a compliment. "Gee, thanks. Glad I get your approval, Captain."

I swallowed, trying to find something else to say, but my brain was still stuck on how fucking good she looked in that dress. I hadn't expected this—at all. I thought she'd show up in something nice but simple, something that wouldn't grab my attention. But now... I couldn't look away.

"Is this what you're wearing to the dance?" I asked, trying to sound normal, but my voice came out a little more strained than I intended.

"Yeah," she said, giving me a look like I'd asked the dumbest question on earth. "What else would I be wearing?"

I cleared my throat, rubbing the back of my neck. "I don't know. I guess I just didn't expect you to, uh..." My words trailed off, and I had to stop myself from staring at her again.

"Look like a human being?" she finished for me, her tone laced with sarcasm.

"Shut up," I said quickly. "I didn't mean it like that. You just... you look different."

Her eyes narrowed slightly, but there was a faint smirk tugging at her lips. "Different, huh? I'll take that as a compliment, I guess."

We stood there in silence for a second, and I couldn't help but let my eyes flicker down to the dress again. That damn dress. I wasn't used to seeing Hailey like this—so put together, so... stunning.

She raised an eyebrow at me, clearly noticing the way I was looking at her. "Are we going, or are you just gonna keep standing there like an idiot?"

I blinked, snapping out of it. "Right. Yeah. Let's go."

We were just about to head out the door when the inevitable happened.

"Hold on, hold on!" my mom's voice rang out from behind us. I turned around just in time to see both of our moms coming toward us, eyes wide with excitement. "Just look at the two of you! So cute!"

Immediately, Hailey's face turned bright red, and I felt my own cheeks heat up. "No, no, no," I stammered, holding up my hands as if I could somehow stop whatever was happening. "We're not—"

"We're not, like, dates or anything!" Hailey cut in quickly, her voice high-pitched with embarrassment. She looked as mortified as I felt. "This is... we're just... going to the same place!"

But our protests fell on deaf ears. Our moms were already whipping out their phones, practically bouncing with excitement. "Just stand together for a second," Mrs. Eller said, waving us into place. "Come on, just one picture. You both look so nice!"

I shot Hailey a desperate look, and she groaned softly, clearly feeling the same way I did. "Do we really have to do this?" she muttered under her breath.

"Yes, we do," I grumbled back, already resigning myself to the inevitable.

Mrs. Reid giggled, clearly amused by our discomfort. "Oh, stop acting like you want to kill each other for just one second. Smile for the camera!"

I sighed, running a hand through my hair as I reluctantly stepped closer to Hailey. This was ridiculous. The last thing I wanted was a bunch of pictures of us standing awkwardly next to each other, but there was no way we were getting out of this.

"Just... stand still for a second," I muttered to Hailey, trying to keep my voice low. She rolled her eyes but stepped closer, still looking as embarrassed as I felt.

I hesitated for a second, glancing at the camera that my mom was holding up. They wanted us to look like we weren't about to strangle each other, which felt impossible right now. But... fine.

Whatever. If this was what it took to get them off our backs, I'd do it.

Slowly, and a little reluctantly, I placed my hand on Hailey's shoulder. It felt... weird, touching her like this, but I pulled her a little closer, just enough so it would look like we were actually standing together and not at war.

"Smile!" Mrs. Eller called, the excitement in her voice making it clear this was way more fun for them than it was for us.

Hailey let out a sigh but forced a small smile onto her face, her body stiff as she stood next to me. I did the same, though I was pretty sure it looked more like a grimace than a smile. My hand stayed on her shoulder, awkward but steady.

Click. Click. The sound of the camera shutter going off felt like a death sentence.

"See? That wasn't so bad," my mom said, beaming as she checked the pictures on her phone. "You two look so cute together!"

Hailey quickly stepped away from me, muttering under her breath, "I'm so done with this."

"Yeah, me too," I grumbled, lowering my hand from her shoulder.

"Well, don't you two look amazing!" My dad chimed in from behind us, giving me a quick nod of approval. "Be safe tonight, alright? And have fun."

I couldn't help but sigh again as Hailey and I finally escaped, heading out the door and into the night. The tension between us was thick, but there was something about the way her shoulder had felt under my hand that lingered in my mind, even though I tried to shake it off.

As we reached the car, Hailey let out a groan. "That was humiliating."

"Tell me about it," I muttered, unlocking the car and opening the door for her.

She shot me a look as she climbed inside. "I swear, they live to embarrass us."

I couldn't argue with that. Our parents had a knack for making things way more awkward than they needed to be. But now that we were finally alone, headed to homecoming, I couldn't help but feel… a little off balance.

CHAPTER 29
HAILEY

HOMECOMING WAS... SURPRISINGLY NICE.

I hadn't been sure what to expect, especially since I hadn't even planned on going originally. But as soon as Callum and I arrived at the school, we went our separate ways. I didn't have to worry about awkward conversations or lingering tension between us. He went off to hang out with his soccer bros while I drifted toward Nala and the yearbook club.

The gymnasium was decorated way better than I expected. String lights draped across the ceiling, casting a warm glow over the dance floor. Gold and navy streamers were intertwined with twinkling fairy lights, and there were tables set up along the edges of the gym, covered in white linens and small bouquets of flowers.

It was... actually pretty beautiful, in a cheesy high school dance kind of way. It made everything feel more magical, like we were stepping into a different world for just one night.

I had my camera in hand for the first half of the night, snapping pictures for yearbook. There were plenty of moments worth capturing—friends laughing together, couples slow dancing under the lights, groups of kids taking goofy pictures by the photo booth set up in the corner.

At some point, I spotted Callum with his group of friends. He was laughing, his arms draped casually around the shoulders of Adam and Grayson, looking completely in his element. He hadn't even glanced my way since we arrived, which was fine by me. It wasn't like I expected him to stick around or anything. We didn't really... do things together.

But every now and then, I caught myself looking for him in the crowd. I wasn't sure why. Maybe it was because, despite everything, there was still that weird connection between us.

Or maybe it was because of the way he'd looked at me earlier tonight—the way his hand had lingered on my shoulder during those stupid photos.

Ugh. This was seriously so annoying. I wished I could go back to the days where I didn't think of Callum literally 24/7, but now here he was, running laps in my mind like it was his daily workout.

I shook it off before I lost my mind and went back to capturing memories for the yearbook. Once I wrapped up my photo duties, I ditched the camera with Lance and let myself relax. Nala dragged me to the dance floor, and for a while, we just danced and laughed, letting the music take over. It felt good to just have fun, to let loose for once without worrying about anything. The night flew by in a blur of music, laughter, and twinkling lights.

After the dance ended, I noticed a bunch of kids, Callum included, heading to a party at someone's house. Typical. I wasn't in the mood for more loud music or drunken antics, so I didn't bother asking where they were going. Nala and I had our own plans.

"Dairy Queen?" Nala asked as we walked toward the parking lot, still in our dresses, our shoes dangling from our hands.

"Absolutely," I said with a grin.

THE NEAREST DAIRY QUEEN WASN'T TOO FAR FROM THE SCHOOL, SO WE DROVE over and parked ourselves in one of the booths, still in our dresses, looking completely overdressed for an ice cream run. But we didn't care. It felt nice—just sitting there, chatting, and eating Blizzards while the night wound down.

Nala took another big bite of her Oreo Blizzard and then groaned, leaning back against the booth with dramatic flair. "Okay, so verdict on homecoming? It was actually kinda fun. Like, I'm actually shocked."

I laughed, stirring my milkshake with my straw. "You're saying this now after volunteering to go every year?"

"Right?" Nala said, laughing. "I mean, there were some weird moments, but overall... not bad."

Nala took another bite of her Oreo Blizzard, a satisfied smile spreading across her face as she leaned back in her seat. "I swear, Dairy Queen hits different after a school dance. Like, how is this better than all the fancy food they had at the dance?"

I laughed, swirling my straw around in my strawberry milkshake. "I don't know. Maybe because it's not on tiny plates and isn't trying too hard to be fancy."

"True. Those hors d'oeuvres were barely snacks. What were they thinking? I need actual food," Nala said, rolling her eyes. "And don't get me started on the punch. That was just Kool-Aid with some extra sugar thrown in."

I giggled, nodding. "Yeah, I took one sip and immediately regretted it. I think it gave me a headache."

Nala twirled her spoon around dramatically. "If I ever become president, I'm banning gross punch. Like, permanently."

"Oh yeah?" I teased. "That would be at the top of your policies, hm? What else would you change? How about a no-cheesy-slow-dance rule?"

Nala's eyes lit up. "Oh my god, yes! No more awkward slow dances. I swear, there's always that one couple making it way too intense and literally being one step away from having sex on the dance floor. Like, get a room. You know exactly who I'm talking about."

I snorted, knowing exactly who she meant. "Right? Every year, it's the same thing. You'd think they were auditioning for 365 Days or something."

Nala giggled then leaned forward, eyes wide. "You saw saw Sasha and Adam slow dancing, though? It was cute. They were like, in their own little world. You think something's going on there?"

I shrugged, but my lips curved into a grin. "Maybe? You know Sasha better than I do."

"I have my theories," Nala said with a dramatic flair. "I think Adam is just too shy to make a move. But mark my words, something is gonna happen between them before the end of senior year."

I laughed. "I see."

"Also, you and Callum," Nala said, but there was a teasing tone in her voice that made me want to throw my spoon at her. She always knew when something was up, and I could practically hear the gears turning in her head. "You two drove here together, huh?"

"Only because we live in the same house now," I grumbled, taking a big sip of my milkshake. "Don't read into it."

"Uh-huh, sure," she said with a sly grin.

I groaned. "Please stop."

Nala laughed, leaning back in her seat. "Okay, okay. I'll leave it alone… for now. But if anything happens between you two, I demand all the juicy details."

"Nothing's gonna happen," I said quickly, feeling my cheeks warm up. "Trust me."

"If you say so," Nala said, winking at me before she took another bite of her Blizzard. "But hey, you never know.

Sometimes the unexpected happens. And honestly? I think you'd be a cute couple."

I stared at her, utterly appalled. "You did not just say that."

"Oh, I did," she teased, her grin only widening. "Just think about it. You and Callum, Westview's power enemies-to-lovers couple."

I laughed, shaking my head. "You're literally insane."

"I prefer the term *visionary*," Nala said with a wink.

The conversation drifted into the territory of rating everyone's looks—not that it was surprising. After all, homecoming was the one time everyone really tried, you know? Nala twirled her spoon in her Blizzard, her eyes sparkling with excitement.

"Okay, so let's talk about who looked good tonight," she said, leaning in like she was about to spill some top-secret information. "And I mean really good."

I raised an eyebrow, amused. "You're starting with that already? We've barely left the gym."

"Of course I am," she said, not missing a beat. "It's homecoming, Hailey. I mean, if we're not gonna talk about who cleaned up well, then what's even the point?"

I laughed, shaking my head. "Okay, fine. Who's your first contender?"

Nala leaned back in her seat, ticking names off her fingers. "Alright. First off, Grayson Hart? The guy looked *good*. That suit was sharp as hell, and did you see how it fit his shoulders? Ugh."

I rolled my eyes, but couldn't help but laugh. "Yeah, he's... tall, I guess."

"Tall? Girl, that man is a Greek god in the making. But fine, moving on," she said with a dramatic wave of her hand. "What about Derek from yearbook? That shaggy blonde hair cleaned up nicely, didn't it?"

"He did look pretty good tonight," I agreed. "But he's a little too... I don't know, goofy?"

Nala nodded in understanding. "True, true. He's more of the cute-in-a-puppy-dog kind of way."

We shared a laugh, letting the conversation flow, until Nala's eyes lit up with that mischievous glint again. I knew what was coming next before she even opened her mouth.

"And now... let's talk about Callum."

I immediately scoffed, crossing my arms and sinking into my seat. "Please. He was ugly as hell."

Nala gave me a pointed look, and I could feel the judgment radiating off her. "Girl, you don't have to like him, but don't lie to me. Callum was looking fine tonight, and you know it."

I rolled my eyes, refusing to give in. "He was... okay, I guess. But he's still an ass."

"That may be true," Nala admitted, leaning forward and lowering her voice conspiratorially. "But he's an attractive ass. Did you see the way that suit fit him? His arms alone—ugh, I hate him for it. But damn."

I took a long sip of my milkshake, trying to act indifferent. "Whatever. Everyone has arms. He's not that special."

Nala snorted, clearly not buying my attempt at indifference. "Hailey, come on. First of all, not everyone has arms. And second... I get it—you two have this whole 'I hate you' thing going on. But even you have to admit the man can pull off a suit."

I opened my mouth to protest but then closed it, realizing I had no comeback. She had a point—as much as I hated to admit it. He was... good-looking. I guess.

I sighed, giving up the fight for now. "Okay, fine. Maybe he looked decent. But only in, like, a 'I hate his guts but he has nice biceps' kind of way."

Nala burst into laughter, nearly spilling her Blizzard. "See? That wasn't so hard, was it?"

I groaned, covering my face with my hands. "Can we please stop talking about him now? My throat is starting to burn the more we talk about him."

"Fine, fine," Nala said between giggles, waving me off. "But mark my words, Hailey Eller—you won't be able to keep ignoring him forever."

I peeked at her from behind my fingers, giving her a look. "Wanna bet?"

"Oh, I definitely wanna bet," she said, her grin wide. "But for now, let's focus on more important things—like Lance doing the Electric Slide."

I laughed, grateful for the subject change. "That was so embarrassing for him. I almost felt bad."

"Almost," Nala agreed, winking. "But not quite. It was kinda cute, actually."

I was taking a sip of my milkshake and I nearly choked on it. "Wait a minute... Nala, you and Lance?" I asked, raising an eyebrow as I looked at her over the top of my cup. "Is there something going on there that you haven't told me about?"

Nala paused mid-bite, her spoon hovering just inches from her mouth. "What? No! I mean... no." She quickly stuffed the spoon into her mouth, but the guilty look on her face told me everything I needed to know.

I narrowed my eyes, a grin spreading across my face. "Nalaaaaa," I sang, leaning across the table, my voice dripping with accusation.

She groaned, leaning back in her seat. "Okay, fine! I wouldn't hate the idea, alright? Lance is cute, and he's really nice. Plus, he's like... actually funny, not just 'funny because I'm trying too hard.' You know?"

I let out a loud, dramatic gasp. "Oh my god! Nala has a crush on Lance! This is huge."

Nala threw her napkin at me, laughing. "It's not that big of a deal!"

"No, it is! This is major!" I said, practically bouncing in my seat. "Okay, you know what? I'm going to set you guys up. Immediately."

Nala's eyes widened, and she leaned forward quickly, waving her hands in front of her. "Oh my god, Hailey, no. Don't do that. Please."

I crossed my arms, giving her a look. "Why not? You just said you wouldn't hate the idea. You think he's cute, and you guys are basically friends, aren't you? Look at that, you're literally halfway there!"

Nala rolled her eyes but couldn't hide the small smile creeping onto her face. "You're insane."

I wiggled my eyebrows at her. "Maybe. But I'm also right."

She groaned again, but this time it was mixed with a giggle. "Okay, fine. Maybe you can give him a little nudge, but just a little one! Don't make it weird, okay?"

"Oh, I'll make it weird," I teased, bursting into laughter.

Nala's face flushed as she slapped her hand over her face. "I'm gonna regret telling you this, aren't I?"

"Absolutely," I said between fits of giggles. "But you know you love me for it."

We both started giggling uncontrollably, like two little kids with a secret, our laughter echoing through the mostly empty Dairy Queen.

CHAPTER 30
CALLUM

THE BASS OF THE MUSIC WAS THUMPING THROUGH THE FLOOR, VIBRATING IN MY chest, but I wasn't feeling it. Not like I usually did at these kinds of parties. The house was packed—kids everywhere, laughing, dancing, drinking. The whole place was buzzing with that post-homecoming energy, and it was exactly the kind of scene I'd normally be into.

But tonight? I was just... off.

I was at Olivia's house—she was on the volleyball team, popular, and threw the kind of parties that people talked about for weeks. I had barely walked in when some girls were already all over me. It was what I expected, I guess. But even as I lounged on this oversized armchair, with two girls practically sitting in my lap, I couldn't find it in myself to care.

Cassie, one of the girls—a brunette with bright red lipstick and a smile that could probably melt half the guys in this room—leaned in closer, her hand brushing over my chest. "You having a good time, Callum?" she whispered, her lips dangerously close to my ear.

I glanced down at her, forcing a grin. "Yeah, sure," I mumbled, though I wasn't even sure she could hear me over the music.

She took that as encouragement and leaned in further, her lips pressing against mine in a kiss that was... fine. I guess. Cassie was hot—everyone knew that. And under normal circumstances, this would've been exactly what I wanted. Just something casual. No strings, no expectations, just fun.

But as her lips moved against mine, I felt... nothing. Like, absolutely nothing. It was just a kiss. I wasn't into it. At all.

Cassie pulled back after a moment, her eyes searching mine for some kind of reaction, like she expected me to lean in and kiss her again, maybe pull her into my lap and let the night go where it usually did with girls like her. But I just sat there, staring past her, my mind miles away.

She frowned slightly, tilting her head. "You okay?" she asked, her voice barely audible over the music.

I blinked, snapping out of it for a second. "Yeah, I'm good," I lied, managing to sound somewhat convincing. "Just... tired from the game."

Cassie gave me a knowing smile, brushing her hand over my arm. "Well, you were amazing out there today. That goal? Legendary."

I forced another smile, nodding like I appreciated the compliment. But in reality, I wasn't even thinking about the game anymore. Hell, I wasn't thinking of it at all right now.

Cassie leaned in again, clearly not picking up on my lack of enthusiasm. "You wanna head upstairs?" she whispered, her voice low and suggestive.

I hesitated, glancing around the room. The party was in full swing—people were dancing in the living room, playing drinking games in the kitchen, shouting over each other just to be heard. And here I was, sitting in the middle of it all, feeling like I didn't belong.

Cassie was still waiting for an answer, her hand trailing up my arm, but I couldn't do it. I couldn't pretend like I was into this when I wasn't.

"Nah," I said, pulling away slightly. "Not tonight."

Cassie blinked, clearly surprised by my response. She wasn't used to hearing "no," especially not from someone like me. "Oh," she said, her voice tinged with disappointment. "Okay... maybe another time?"

"Yeah, maybe," I mumbled, not really committing to anything.

She smiled, but I could tell she wasn't happy. After a moment, she stood up and walked away, the other girl following shortly after, leaving me sitting there alone on the armchair, feeling even more disconnected than before.

I leaned back, running a hand through my hair and staring up at the ceiling. The music was still pounding, the party still going, but it all felt so distant, like I was watching it happen from a million miles away.

I wasn't sure what was wrong with me. Normally, this was exactly where I wanted to be—at a party, surrounded by people, with girls like Cassie throwing themselves at me. But tonight, none of it mattered.

None of it felt right.

I groaned, rubbing my hands over my face. This was messed up.

A FEW DAYS AFTER HOMECOMING, THINGS HAD PRETTY MUCH SETTLED BACK INTO the same routine. It was the next week now, and Hailey and I had fallen back into our weird, tense... normal. If you could call it that. After the chaos of homecoming, I thought things might stay strange between us, but no. We just slipped back into the usual. Bickering over stupid things, keeping our distance when we weren't stuck together in the car or in class, and avoiding any mention of the hot tub night or the homecoming dance.

Things were… okay, I guess. Comfortable. Or as comfortable as it could be between us.

But something had shifted a little, whether I liked it or not. For starters, I'd ordered Hailey a replacement lens for her camera a couple of days after homecoming. I still hadn't given it to her yet, though. I'd been waiting for the right moment, and honestly, I wasn't sure how she'd react. I wasn't exactly used to buying people expensive stuff without them asking for it.

And then there was Natalia.

I'd stopped talking to her. For the most part, anyway. She'd texted me a few times since homecoming, trying to figure out what I was doing or inviting me to hang out, but I hadn't responded. I didn't know what it was—maybe it was the way she'd treated Hailey after the game, or maybe I was just over it.

Either way, things between us had fizzled out, and I wasn't exactly rushing to reignite anything.

It wasn't like I had time for that, anyway. With soccer practice ramping up, school, and… whatever the hell was going on with me and Hailey, my mind was already too full.

Speaking of Hailey, she'd been using the school's clunky camera ever since she dropped hers, and every time I saw her with it, I felt a little… guilty. I knew it wasn't her fault the camera broke—well, sort of. But I hadn't forgotten how pissed off I was when I found out Natalia had been the one to bump into her.

I hadn't told Hailey about the replacement lens yet. Part of me wasn't even sure why I'd ordered it in the first place. Guilt? Maybe. Or maybe it was just that stupid feeling from before, the one that made me want to fix the fact that I'd been one of the reasons she'd stopped photography in the first place.

Either way, the lens was arriving today, and I had to figure out when to give it to her. Maybe I could do it after soccer practice—get it over with.

I glanced over at her in AP Lit, where she was scribbling something down in her notebook, completely oblivious to the fact that I was even watching her. Not that I was watching her. Just... observing.

She still wore that same neutral expression she always had in class, like she wasn't particularly impressed with anything going on around her. I'd seen her like this so many times before, and yet now, for some reason, I couldn't stop thinking about the way she looked when she was behind the camera. How she looked when she actually seemed... happy.

I shifted in my seat, leaning back as I stared up at the ceiling. It was stupid, this whole thing. I shouldn't be thinking about Hailey this much. But now that I had started, I couldn't seem to stop.

"Reid," Mr. Warner's voice snapped me out of my thoughts, and I looked up, realizing he was calling on me.

"Huh?"

"Do you have any thoughts on the chapter we just discussed?" Mr. Warner raised an eyebrow, clearly unimpressed with my lack of attention.

I cleared my throat, glancing down at my book. "Uh... yeah. I think the author's trying to show how the characters are —"

Before I could even finish, the bell rang, cutting me off. I sighed, grateful for the save, and started gathering my stuff.

As I stood up, I caught Hailey out of the corner of my eye. She was packing up too, shoving her notebook into her bag with that same focused expression. Without thinking, I slung my backpack over my shoulder and took a few steps closer to her.

"Hey," I said, my voice low enough so that no one else would hear.

She glanced up, surprised. "What?"

Why did I even feel the need to tell her about this right now? Ugh, who knows. But I already started the conversation, might as well keep going.

"I, uh… I got something for you," I muttered awkwardly.

Her eyebrow arched, and she looked at me like I'd grown a second head. "For me? Why?"

I rubbed the back of my neck, feeling stupid for some reason. "Just… for your camera. You'll see."

She looked even more confused now, but before she could say anything else, I nodded toward the door. "Let's go. I'll give it to you later."

Without waiting for her response, I started walking, trying to keep my cool. I could feel her eyes on me as we made our way to the door, but I didn't look back.

Yeah, things were mostly back to normal. But something told me they wouldn't stay that way for long.

The school day passed in a blur and the drive home was quiet, as usual. Hailey sat in the passenger seat, her eyes on the window, probably thinking about yearbook stuff or… whatever it was she spent her time thinking about. I didn't bother trying to start a conversation—it wasn't like we ever did much talking outside of our usual bickering, and today wasn't any different.

When we pulled into the driveway, I noticed a small package sitting on the front step. My stomach twisted a little as I realized what it was. The lens. I'd forgotten how soon it would arrive.

Hailey unbuckled her seatbelt and started to open the door when I held up a hand to stop her. "Wait," I said, nodding toward the package on the doorstep. "That's for you."

She paused, glancing at the package and then back at me, clearly confused. "For me? What is it?"

"Just… check it out," I muttered, not really in the mood to explain the whole thing right there in the car.

I got out and walked around to the front, grabbing the package from the doorstep. Hailey followed me, her eyebrows furrowed as I handed it to her.

"What is this?" she asked again, still staring at the small box like it was some kind of mystery.

I rubbed the back of my neck, feeling awkward as hell. "It's a replacement lens... for your camera. The one you dropped. Or I guess the one Natalia made you drop."

Her eyes widened in surprise, and she blinked a few times as if trying to process what I'd just said. "Wait, you... you bought me a new lens?"

I shrugged, trying to play it cool. "Yeah. I mean, it's not like you could keep using that school camera forever, right?"

She stared at the package in her hands, her lips slightly parted in disbelief. "You didn't have to do that," she muttered, her voice quieter now.

"I know," I said, shoving my hands in my pockets. "I wanted to."

She looked up at me then, her green eyes searching mine like she was trying to figure out what my angle was. I wasn't sure what she was expecting—maybe she thought I had some ulterior motive. But really, I just wanted her to have something decent to take pictures with.

I cleared my throat, feeling a little uncomfortable under her gaze. "Anyway, I've got to get back to school for soccer practice," I said, stepping back toward my car. "Enjoy the lens. At least you can actually use the damn thing now."

Hailey opened her mouth to say something, but before she could, I gave her a quick nod and walked away, not giving her a chance to respond. I didn't need a thank you or anything like that.

I just wanted to get out of there before things got even more awkward.

As I got back into the car and pulled out of the driveway, I glanced in the rearview mirror and saw Hailey still standing on the doorstep, staring down at the package like she couldn't believe it.

I wasn't sure why, but seeing her like that—surprised, maybe even a little touched—made me feel... something. I wasn't sure what it was, but it wasn't bad.

I shook it off, focusing on the road ahead as I drove back to school. Practice would help clear my head. It always did.

Practice wasn't anything out of the ordinary that day. Just the usual drills, scrimmages, and the occasional pep talk from Coach Taz. The whole time, though, I couldn't quite get my mind off the look on Hailey's face when I handed her that package.

I mean, it wasn't like I was expecting her to fall over herself with gratitude, but the way she had looked at me—like I'd caught her completely off guard—stuck with me.

"Reid, focus!" Coach Taz barked from the sideline, snapping me out of my thoughts. I muttered an apology and jogged back to my position, forcing myself to concentrate on the scrimmage.

But even as I moved through the familiar motions— passing the ball, taking shots, running the drills—my mind kept drifting back to Hailey and the damn camera lens.

I had no idea why I was so hung up on it. It was just a lens, after all. No big deal. But something about the whole thing felt... different. Like maybe I'd crossed some kind of invisible line between us. And I wasn't sure how to feel about that.

By the time practice ended, I was exhausted. The sun had already started to dip below the horizon, casting long shadows over the field. I grabbed my water bottle and sat down on the bench, wiping the sweat from my forehead as the rest of the team wrapped up.

As I sat there, catching my breath, I couldn't help but wonder what Hailey was thinking right now. Had she opened the package yet? Was she using the new lens?

I didn't know. But part of me hoped she liked it.

CHAPTER 31
HAILEY

THE WEEKEND HAD BEEN PRETTY UNEVENTFUL SO FAR. I'D USED MY CAMERA HERE and there, mostly just taking random shots around the house or when I went for a walk.

It was a nice distraction—especially after everything that had happened with homecoming and the mess with Natalia. Plus, I couldn't lie—it felt good having a real camera in my hands again, even if I didn't want to give Callum too much credit for that.

Callum had played in another soccer game earlier this week, and Westview had (unsurprisingly) won again, which seemed to keep him in a decent mood—at least for the most part. I'd snapped a few shots at that game, too, but I wasn't exactly focused on him while I did it.

Now, though, I was just chilling in my room, scrolling through some reading on my phone, enjoying the peaceful quiet of the house. It was a rare moment where I didn't have to think about anything stressful.

Just me, my book, and—

Suddenly, I heard someone yell from upstairs. It was loud enough to make me jump.

I sat up quickly, straining to hear what was going on. Callum's voice was unmistakable—frustrated, loud, and, well, pissed off. My stomach did a weird flip, and I tossed my phone aside, cautiously getting up and heading upstairs to check it out.

As I reached the top of the basement stairs, I could hear more clearly now. Callum's voice was still raised, and Mrs. Reid was there, her tone softer but trying to calm the situation. The air was tense, and I could feel it even before I saw what was happening.

When I stepped into the living room, I saw Callum standing near the window, his arms crossed and his jaw clenched in that way that told me he was really mad.

His brows were furrowed, and I could practically see the frustration radiating off him as he paced back and forth. Mrs. Reid stood a few feet away, her hands up in a placating gesture.

And there, standing in the middle of the room, looking like he'd just gotten caught doing something bad, was Dalton. He was clutching a pair of safety scissors in one hand, his wide blue eyes darting between Callum and Mrs. Reid, clearly unsure of what to do.

I glanced between them, trying to figure out what the hell had just happened. "What... what's going on?" I asked, my voice cautious as I approached the group.

Callum turned toward me, his face still tight with frustration. "Dalton," he began, his voice low and angry, "decided it would be a good idea to use scissors to draw stick figures on the back of my car."

My eyes widened in shock, and I looked at Dalton, who was still standing there, clutching the scissors like they were a forbidden weapon.

Stick figures?

On the car?

Oh boy.

Dalton, the poor thing, looked like he was about to cry. His little lips were pressed together, and his small hands fidgeted nervously with the scissors. He stared at the floor, unable to meet his older brother's gaze.

"Callum, it's okay," Mrs. Reid said softly, placing a hand on his arm. "He's a kid. It's just the paint. I'm sure we can fix it."

I could understand why he was upset. A car wasn't exactly something you could just draw on and then erase. But still... poor Dalton looked absolutely horrified.

I looked at Dalton again, and my heart kind of broke for him. He was only seven. He probably didn't realize how serious it was. But Callum wasn't exactly the type to let stuff like this slide easily. Not when it came to his precious car, at least.

I cleared my throat, stepping in. "Hey, uh, maybe we should just... calm down a bit?" I suggested, trying to ease the tension. "It's not the end of the world."

Callum shot me a look, still brimming with frustration. "Yeah, easy for you to say. It's not your car."

I rolled my eyes, resisting the urge to snap back. "No, but it's just... paint, Callum. I'm sure Dalton didn't mean to destroy anything. He's just a kid."

Dalton sniffled a little, and I saw Mrs. Reid give him a comforting pat on the back. "That's right, sweetie. It's okay," she said gently. "We can fix it. Maybe next time we'll just use paper for drawing, alright?"

Dalton nodded, still looking like he was on the verge of tears. I glanced back at Callum, who was clearly still struggling to calm down. His fists were clenched at his sides, and he looked like he was trying to keep it together. I understood where he was coming from, but still... it wasn't worth making Dalton cry over.

Mrs. Reid gave a reassuring smile. "I'll take Dalton upstairs to talk, alright? Just... take a breath and try calm down, Callum."

Dalton, still clutching the scissors, followed Mrs. Reid upstairs, his small steps hesitant. I watched as they walked out, leaving me alone with Callum in the now much quieter living room.

I glanced at him, crossing my arms. "So…"

He shot me a glare. "Don't."

I smirked, leaning against the wall. "Look, I get it. I'd be pissed too if someone did that to my stuff. But it's Dalton. He probably didn't know better."

"I know," he grumbled, running his hands through his hair again. "But still…"

I shook my head, letting out a small laugh. "You're seriously this worked up over stick figures? It's not like he keyed 'I hate Callum' on the side or something."

If he did, I would've high-fived the kid.

"Yeah, well…" Callum trailed off, clearly not ready to let it go completely.

I stood there for a second, watching him as he stewed in his frustration. Honestly, it was almost kind of funny seeing him like this—so riled up over something so small. But at the same time, I got it. It was his car, and knowing Callum, he probably cared about that thing almost as much as he cared about soccer.

But still… it was just Dalton. And it was just stick figures. After a moment, I sighed. "Come on. Let's go check the damage. I bet it's not as bad as you think."

Callum grumbled something under his breath but reluctantly followed me outside to the driveway.

When we stepped outside, I followed him to the back of his car, where the damage had supposedly been done.

There, on the back of his beloved car, were three stick figures drawn in jagged, uneven lines. Next to the stick figures was a little circle—a ball, I realized. They weren't Picasso-level masterpieces by any means, but they weren't terrible, either. Just… well, stick figures. Innocent, childlike doodles scratched into the paint.

I tilted my head, studying the drawing. It took me a moment, but something clicked in my brain. I glanced up at

Callum. "Wait... are these supposed to be you, Dalton, and Nathan?"

Callum frowned, staring at the stick figures like he was seeing them for the first time. "What?"

I pointed at the three figures, then at the little ball. "Look. There's three of them. And they're playing soccer. Maybe it's supposed to be you and your brothers."

For a moment, Callum just stared at the drawing, his brow furrowed. I watched as his expression shifted from pure frustration to something else—something softer. He blinked a couple of times, like he was trying to process what I'd just said.

"I guess," he muttered under his breath, running a hand through his hair.

I didn't know what I expected him to say, but the fact that he wasn't immediately pissed anymore caught me off guard. I hesitated for a second, then spoke up, my voice a little quieter this time. "Callum... I think maybe Dalton just wanted to play soccer with you?"

He looked at me, confused. "What?"

I softly traced the childish etchings on his car. "He drew the three of you playing soccer on here. Maybe it's what he wants to do with you guys. Play soccer together."

His gaze softened for a bit before he scoffed, shaking his head. "Well, if he wanted to do that, he could've just asked me. That's no reason to go scratching up my shit."

I sighed, leaning against the car. "Hey. I didn't really think I'd be telling you this, but a while back, when I was hanging out with Dalton and Nathan... they told me some stuff. About how they feel distant from you."

Callum's confusion deepened. "Distant? What are you talking about?"

I bit my lip, trying to figure out the best way to say this without making things worse. "They said... they don't really know how to talk to you. They feel like you're in your own world most of the time, and they don't want to bother you or make you mad. Especially because you're older, and you don't really spend much time with them."

I tried to gauge Callum's reaction to what I said. Would he get mad? Would he deny it? But instead, he just stared at me, clearly shocked. "What? But... they're my brothers. Why wouldn't they just talk to me?"

I gave him a small, sympathetic shrug. "I don't know. I guess they're just... intimidated by you. They think you're too busy or that you might not want to hang out with them."

He was silent for a long moment, his eyes fixed on the stick figures scratched into the back of his car. I could practically see the gears turning in his head, trying to make sense of everything I'd just told him.

When he finally spoke, his voice was quieter than usual. "Well, fuck. I didn't know they felt that way."

"They don't hate you," I softened my tone. "They look up to you, but they don't know how to approach you. You're always busy with soccer or with your friends, and I think they just don't want to feel like a burden."

He shook his head, still staring at the drawings. "I just figured... I don't know. That they were doing their own thing."

I watched him closely, seeing the way his frustration slowly morphed into something else. Guilt, maybe. It was like he was realizing, for the first time, just how much of a gap there was between him and his brothers—and it wasn't one they'd created on their own.

After a long pause, Callum sighed heavily. "Shit," he muttered again, running a hand through his hair.

I gave him a small smile. "Maybe... maybe this is Dalton's way of telling you he wants to hang out more."

Callum didn't say anything for a minute, still staring at the stick figures like they were some kind of mystery he was trying to solve. Then, slowly, he nodded, his shoulders slumping a little as the tension left his body. I straightened up, stepping away from the car. "So... maybe instead of freaking out about the car, you could use this as a chance to, you know, spend some time with them. You're not going to be around forever, Callum. They just want to be close to their big brother."

He glanced at me, his expression softer now, and nodded again. "Yeah," he muttered. "You're right."

"As always."

He huffed out a laugh, but there wasn't any of the usual snark in it. Just a quiet, understanding sort of agreement. We stood there in the driveway, staring at the stick figures that had caused all this drama. Callum wasn't the kind of guy who showed his feelings easily, especially when it came to his family. But now... now it seemed like maybe he was starting to get it.

As Callum and I headed back inside, I felt a strange heaviness hanging between us. It wasn't bad, exactly—just... different. Callum was quieter than usual, his face set in a deep, thoughtful expression. It was like everything I'd said about Dalton and Nathan had hit him harder than I expected.

At the top of the stairs, I noticed Dalton peeking out from behind the banister, his big blue eyes watching us nervously. He looked so small, standing there with his round cheeks and those messy, dark brown curls that made him look even younger than he was. He was clutching something behind his back, but I couldn't see what it was.

Mrs. Reid's voice echoed softly from upstairs, gently encouraging him to come down. "Go on, sweetie. It's okay."

Dalton hesitated for a moment, biting his lip before slowly descending the stairs. His little feet made barely any sound on the steps, and as he got closer, I could see the nervousness in his eyes, his small shoulders hunched as if he was preparing for the worst.

He walked down to where Callum and I were standing, his gaze flicking nervously between the two of us before he stopped in front of his brother.

He looked so guilty, and my heart broke for him a little.

"I'm... I'm sorry, Callum," Dalton said in the smallest, shyest voice I'd ever heard him use. He shifted his weight from one foot to the other, clearly uncomfortable. "I didn't know it was bad. I just saw something like that on someone's car... you know, like stick figures of a family. And I wanted to make those on yours, too."

I blinked, suddenly realizing what he was talking about. Those little stickers people put on the back of their cars, showing their family members as stick figures. I'd seen them a hundred times before.

Dalton sniffled a little, looking down at his feet. "I didn't know it was bad to do with scissors. I didn't mean to mess it up."

I glanced over at Callum, who was standing there, completely still, his expression unreadable.

Dalton hesitated again, then slowly held out his hand. In his small, trembling fingers were a few crumpled dollar bills. "I —I don't know if it's enough," he said shakily. "But it's my savings. I wanted to... to help pay for the car."

I felt something twist in my chest as I looked at those crumpled bills. Dalton's little savings—probably earned from allowance or chores—being offered up to fix something he hadn't even known was wrong. He didn't even look at Callum as he held the money out, his eyes fixed on the floor, his bottom lip quivering like he was holding back tears.

Dalton sniffled again, clearly getting more nervous by the second. "I... I don't know if it's enough," he repeated softly. "But I'm really sorry, Callum."

I glanced at Callum again. At first, he just stared at the crumpled bills in Dalton's hand, completely speechless. I could see the emotions flickering across his face—shock, guilt, something softer, something deeper. His mouth opened slightly, but no words came out.

And then, out of nowhere, I saw it. A single tear slipped down Callum's cheek, and before I could even process what was happening, another one followed. Then another. And another.

Callum was crying.

And not just a little bit. He was crying hard—his shoulders shaking as he tried to hold it in, but it was no use. He looked down at Dalton, still holding out his crumpled bills, and something in him just... broke.

Without a word, Callum dropped to his knees in front of his little brother and pulled him into a tight hug. Dalton let out a surprised squeak, but after a second, he wrapped his small arms around Callum's neck, holding him just as tightly.

I stood there, frozen, completely taken aback. I had never, ever seen Callum like this before. The tough, arrogant jock who never let anything get to him, who acted like the whole world was beneath him... was on his knees, crying, hugging his little brother like he never wanted to let him go.

CHAPTER 32

CALLUM

I couldn't stop staring at the crumpled bills in Dalton's small hands. Six bucks. Maybe. A few dollar bills, some change, all bundled up like it was his life savings, and it probably was.

And he was giving it to me.

To fix the mistake he thought he made.

He'd already apparently been feeling distant from me and probably thought that after all this, it would make things worse. That I'd hate him or something.

My chest tightened painfully, like someone had punched me right in the gut. What the hell was I supposed to say to that? How was I supposed to react when my little brother—my seven-year-old brother—thought he had to give me his entire savings just because of some stupid stick figures on the back of my car?

I swallowed hard, my throat burning. I could feel something building up inside me, something heavy, something that had been there for way too long but was finally breaking free.

Guilt. Regret.

"I... I don't know if it's enough," Dalton's voice was small, shaky. "But I'm really sorry, Callum."

I opened my mouth, but no words came out. I couldn't speak. I couldn't even breathe properly.

All I could do was look at my little brother—standing there, clutching those six dollars like they were the most valuable thing in the world—and feel like the biggest piece of shit on the planet.

He probably thought I was mad at him. He probably thought I hated him for drawing some stick figures. He probably thought he had to pay me for it, like that would somehow make things right.

I felt my eyes burn. I blinked, trying to push it down, but it was no use. A tear slipped down my cheek, and before I knew it, another followed. And then another.

I was crying.

Holy fuck. I was crying.

And I couldn't stop.

I felt my knees go weak, and before I even knew what I was doing, I was on the ground, right in front of him. Dalton let out a small gasp of surprise as I wrapped my arms around him, pulling him into a hug so tight, I wasn't sure I'd ever be able to let go. His little body was warm, trembling slightly in my arms, and I could feel the tears spilling down my face, soaking into his hair. My chest heaved as I tried to get a grip, tried to hold it together, but I couldn't. I couldn't stop the tears, the sobs that were threatening to break out of me.

My brothers were the most precious things in the world to me. I'd cried tears of joy both times I found out my mom had gotten pregnant again. Knowing that in some ways, even though I didn't mean to, I hadn't been the best brother to them, made me like complete and utter shit.

"I'm sorry, Dalton," I choked out, my voice breaking. "I'm sorry... for everything."

Dalton froze for a second, clearly shocked by the whole thing, but after a moment, he wrapped his small arms around my neck and held on tight. "Callum?"

"I'm not mad," I whispered, my throat tight. "I'm not mad at you, okay? You don't have to pay me for anything. You're my little brother. You don't ever have to do that."

He sniffled, his voice barely a whisper. "But I wanted to help you fix it."

I shook my head, still holding onto him like my life depended on it. "It doesn't matter. I'll fix it, Dalton. It's just some stupid paint."

I squeezed him tighter, trying to make sure he understood. "I'm the one who's been wrong. I should've been better. I should've been a better brother to you and Nathan."

Dalton sniffled again, his little voice shaky. "You're not mad at me anymore?"

I pulled back just enough to look at his face, my hands still resting on his small shoulders. His blue eyes were wide and glassy, filled with worry and relief all at the same time.

"No," I said, shaking my head. "I'm not mad. I promise."

He nodded, wiping at his nose with the back of his hand. I could tell he wasn't entirely sure what to make of all this. I mean, it wasn't like I was the emotional type—not around him, not around anyone—but right now, I didn't care. He needed to know that I wasn't mad. That I cared.

I cared more than he'd ever know.

I sat back on my heels, still trying to catch my breath, still trying to process everything that had just happened. I wiped at my face, my tears slowing down but still coming in small waves.

Dalton stood there for a second, his small hand resting on my shoulder, like he was trying to calm me down. I almost laughed. He looked so pensive while trying to act reassuring at the same time.

"It's okay," I told him softly, giving him a small smile. "You can go with Mom."

He nodded slowly, and after a moment, he turned and walked back toward Mom, who had been standing at the top of the stairs, watching the whole thing with wide, tear-filled eyes. She gave me a soft smile, one that was filled with both understanding and sadness, before leading Dalton away.

I stayed there, on my knees in the middle of the room, trying to pull myself together. My heart was still pounding, my chest still tight with all the emotions I hadn't let myself feel in years.

I'd been so focused on soccer, on school, on... me. I hadn't even realized how distant I'd become from my own family. From my own brothers. And it had taken something as simple as a few stick figures to make me realize just how much I'd missed.

I wiped at my eyes again, sniffling as I tried to stand up. My legs were shaky, my mind still spinning, but I managed to get back on my feet.

When I looked up, Hailey was still there, standing a few feet away, her eyes glassy with unshed tears. She was wiping at her eyes, trying to act like she wasn't affected, but I could see it— the way her lip trembled, the way she blinked rapidly to keep the tears from falling.

She was crying, too.

"You okay?" I asked, my voice still thick from crying myself.

Hailey let out a small, shaky laugh, wiping at her cheeks. "Yeah. I'm fine. Just... got something in my eye."

I huffed out a laugh at that, though it came out more like a weak exhale. "Sure."

She gave me a look—one that was part amusement, part something else—and shook her head, sniffling one last time before crossing her arms over her chest. "That was... intense," she admitted softly.

I nodded, feeling the weight of her words. "Yeah. It was."

For a moment, we just stood there, neither of us saying anything. The quiet in the room was heavy but not uncomfortable. I think we both needed a minute to process what had just happened.

I glanced at Hailey again, noticing the way she was still trying to compose herself. I hadn't expected her to cry. I hadn't expected her to feel like this.

But seeing her like that—vulnerable, emotional—it made me realize that maybe I wasn't the only one who cared about my brothers. Hailey did, too.

"Thanks," I said quietly.

Hailey looked up at me, blinking in surprise. "For what?"

"For, uh…" I gestured vaguely, not really knowing how to put it into words. "For telling me what Dalton and Nathan said. I wouldn't have… I don't know. I wouldn't have known otherwise."

She smiled, small but genuine, and shrugged. "I just figured you should know. They're your brothers, Callum. They look up to you, even if they don't always show it."

I nodded again, feeling a weird mixture of guilt and relief wash over me. "Yeah. I guess I've been too focused on my own shit to notice."

Hailey didn't say anything for a moment, just watched me with that same soft look in her eyes. Then, with a sigh, she uncrossed her arms and ran a hand through her hair. "Well, at least now you know. And like I said—you can still make it better."

I swallowed hard, still feeling the lump in my throat from earlier. "Yeah. I will."

CHAPTER 33
HAILEY

It was evening now, and the house had settled into a kind of quiet calm. I was in my room, sitting on my bed with my legs crossed, but my mind wasn't on anything happening here. I was still thinking about what had gone down earlier.

After everything that happened, after seeing Callum break down like that… it was all I could focus on.

It broke my heart.

He probably didn't even know what he was doing wrong. He was just trying to be like one of those people who put those silly family stick figure decals on their cars. And I knew Callum got it, too. I knew he understood, in the end, how much he'd messed up by being distant.

I wiped at my eyes again, still feeling the weight of it. I mean, Dalton was just a kid. He looked up to Callum so much, but he'd been too scared to even approach him, too afraid to bother him. And that… that sucked.

I thought about the way Callum had fallen to his knees, hugging Dalton like he'd never let go. I'd never seen Callum like that before—so raw, so vulnerable. And honestly? I hadn't expected it. He was always so put together, always acting like he had everything under control.

But not today.

Today, he'd let himself break down. And it wasn't just some small, fleeting moment. He'd cried. Like, really cried.

I ran a hand through my hair, sighing heavily as I leaned back against my pillows. The whole thing was still spinning around in my head, and I wasn't sure how to process it. I'd known for a while now that Dalton and Nathan looked up to Callum, but I hadn't realized just how much. And now, seeing how Callum reacted, I knew he felt guilty.

He knew he'd messed up. He'd been so focused on soccer, on school, on everything else that he hadn't noticed his little brothers were watching him from the sidelines, waiting for him to pay attention to them.

My stomach grumbled loudly, pulling me out of my thoughts. I hadn't realized how much time had passed since the whole emotional whirlwind earlier. And as much as I wanted to lie in bed and stew over everything, my body had other plans.

I sighed, sitting up and stretching before heading upstairs to grab a snack. Or maybe supper was ready—if I was lucky.

As I stepped into the kitchen, I paused by the glass door that led out to the backyard. There, in the fading evening light, I saw Callum.

He was out there, dragging the two small goalposts around the yard, positioning them in what looked like a makeshift soccer field. He was concentrating hard, his face set in a determined expression, and for a moment, I just watched him, curious about what he was doing.

He must've felt my eyes on him because he suddenly looked up and caught my gaze through the glass. He stood up straight, wiping his hands on his shorts, and then stepped back inside through the door, shutting it behind him.

I raised an eyebrow as he approached. "What are you doing?"

He brushed a hand through his hair, glancing back at the goalposts. "I'm setting things up so I can play a 2v2 with Dalton and Nathan."

I blinked. "You're... setting up a soccer game with your brothers?"

He shrugged, but there was something different in his tone. "Yeah. I... want to spend some time with them." His voice was quieter, more thoughtful. "I need to, you know? After everything earlier... I realized I haven't really been around for them much."

I stared at him, still processing the fact that Callum— *Callum Reid*—was actively trying to better himself and change his ways. After realizing they felt like he didn't care, here he was, setting up a soccer game just for them.

It was... sweet. In a way I didn't think he was capable of.

He cleared his throat, shifting awkwardly under my gaze. "But, uh... I need a fourth player." He glanced over at me, a slight smirk tugging at the corner of his lips. "Can't exactly play a 2v2 with only three people, can we?"

I raised an eyebrow. "You want *me* to play?"

He nodded. "Yeah. Come on, Hailey. I'm trying to make up for being a shitty brother. I need a fourth player."

I couldn't help but chuckle a little, crossing my arms. "I don't know... Soccer isn't really my thing."

Callum rolled his eyes but there was a hint of amusement in them. "You don't have to be Messi, alright? Just come play. It'll be fun." He paused, his expression softening slightly. "Please. It's important to me... and to them."

That caught me off guard. The way he said it—it wasn't just about needing another player. He was serious. He wanted me to play with them, to help him bridge that gap with his brothers. And after seeing how emotional he got earlier... I knew this was his way of making things right.

I let out a small sigh, pretending to be reluctant. "Alright, fine. But don't expect me to be good at this."

He smirked again, but it was softer this time. "I don't. I expect you to be total shit, actually. But thanks."

That familiar feeling of just wanting to throttle him came back for a second.

Callum and I headed upstairs to gather the troops—or, in this case, his brothers.

As we reached the top of the stairs, we found Dalton already bouncing around the hallway, looking like he was ready to run a marathon. He was wearing an oversized soccer jersey, clearly one of Callum's old ones. The fabric hung off his small frame, but that didn't stop him from jumping around with boundless energy. His eyes lit up the second he saw us.

"Hailey! Callum! Are we playing now?!" he asked, practically vibrating with excitement.

I smiled, amused by his enthusiasm. "Yep, we're playing."

Dalton's grin was contagious as he bounced in place. "I saw Callum setting up the goals through my bedroom window! I knew it was game time!" He puffed out his chest, clearly thrilled to finally be playing with his big brother.

Callum chuckled, reaching out to ruffle Dalton's hair. "Yeah, we're gonna play. But you better be ready, little man, because I'm not going easy on you."

Dalton giggled, swatting Callum's hand away. "Haha, I hope not! Nate and I are gonna beat you guys, just you wait!"

At that, both Callum and I paused. Nathan.

Dalton was already full of energy, but Nathan was more reserved, quieter. And I knew Callum hadn't really had a proper chance to talk to him yet—not after everything I'd told him earlier.

Callum glanced at me, then back down the hallway, where Nathan's room was. I could see the flicker of uncertainty on his face, like he wasn't quite sure how to approach this. I mean, Dalton was easy—he was bubbly and eager to hang out. But Nathan... Nathan was different.

"Wait here a sec," Callum said to Dalton, his voice a little softer now. Dalton, still bouncing on his toes, nodded and stayed behind as Callum and I walked toward Nathan's room.

We stopped outside his door, and I could feel the shift in Callum's mood—the tension in his shoulders, the hesitation in his movements. He wasn't used to this kind of stuff, not with his brothers.

He raised a hand and knocked gently on the door. "Nate?" There was a brief pause, and then we heard the soft shuffle of feet on the other side of the door. Nathan cracked it open slightly, his pale blue eyes peeking out at us from behind the door.

"Hey, buddy," Callum said, his voice more careful than usual. "Hailey, Dalton and I are about to play a little soccer game in the backyard. You wanna join us?"

Nathan hesitated, his eyes flicking between Callum and me. He was always a little more cautious, a little more unsure of himself compared to Dalton. But there was a hint of curiosity in his gaze, like he wanted to say yes but wasn't sure if he should.

Callum rubbed the back of his neck, clearly feeling the awkwardness of the situation. "I know we haven't... I haven't been around a lot. But I'd like it if you came. We need you, man."

I watched as Nathan's eyes widened a little, and I could tell that Callum's words hit home. I could practically see the wheels turning in Nathan's head, trying to decide if he should say yes.

After what felt like forever, Nathan slowly opened the door wider. He wasn't smiling exactly, but there was something softer in his expression, like he was willing to give this a try.

"Okay," Nathan said quietly, nodding.

Callum's relief was palpable, though he tried to play it cool. He gave Nathan a small smile, reaching out to squeeze his shoulder. "Good. Let's go kick some butt."

Nathan gave a small smile in return, and that tiny bit of connection between them was enough to make me feel... well, something. Warmth, maybe. Like I was witnessing something important.

The three of us headed back down the hall, where Dalton was still bouncing around, clearly unable to contain his excitement.

"Nate! There you are!" Dalton asked, his eyes lighting up as he noticed his brother stepping out of his room.

Nathan nodded, and Dalton immediately wrapped an arm around his shoulders, dragging him down the hallway like they were already teammates in the World Cup. "We're totally gonna beat them, Nate! Just wait!" Callum rolled his eyes but there was a small smile tugging at his lips. I could tell that getting Nathan to come out and play had lifted some of the weight off his shoulders. Maybe this was the first step in him finally bridging that gap with his brothers.

As we made our way downstairs and out into the backyard, I couldn't help but feel like this game wasn't just about soccer. It was about something more than that—something bigger.

For Callum, this was his chance to make up for lost time. And for Nathan and Dalton, this was their chance to get closer to their big brother. And for me? Well, I was just happy to be a part of it. Even if I was going to be terrible at soccer.

CHAPTER 34
CALLUM

THE SUN WAS DIPPING LOW ON THE HORIZON, CASTING AN ORANGE GLOW OVER THE backyard. The air was cooling down, but the excitement radiating from Dalton and Nathan was enough to keep things warm. I stood there, glancing over at Hailey as we sorted out the teams. Dalton was already bouncing on his toes, while Nathan hung back a bit, still looking a little unsure but ready to play.

"So, how are we splitting this up?" Hailey asked, pulling her hair back into a loose ponytail. She still looked like she wasn't entirely convinced about playing soccer, but she was here. That counted for something.

Dalton immediately chimed in, his voice loud and clear. "I wanna be on Nathan's team!" He grinned up at Nathan, who gave him a small smile in return. "We're gonna beat you guys!"

I looked at Hailey, raising an eyebrow. "Guess that leaves you with me, Eller."

She crossed her arms, narrowing her eyes playfully. "Ugh, stuck with you? My luck just keeps getting worse, huh?"

I chuckled, shaking my head. "Yeah, yeah. Don't worry, I'll carry us to victory."

She rolled her eyes but smiled a little, and I couldn't help but feel a weird sense of... ease. Like things weren't as tense between us anymore. Maybe it was because of everything that had happened earlier, or maybe it was just this—being outside, doing something that didn't involve snarky comments or avoiding each other. Just a simple game of soccer.

"Well, let's get this started," I said, clapping my hands together. Dalton immediately darted toward one of the tiny goalposts, Nathan trailing behind him, while Hailey and I took our positions on the opposite side.

"Ready?" I called out.

Dalton grinned, raising his fist in the air. "Ready!"

I kicked the ball toward Hailey, who stood a few feet away. She awkwardly kicked it back, and I could tell right away that she wasn't much of a soccer player. Still, I wasn't about to give her a hard time. It was nice of her to join us, even though I could tell she was out of her element.

Dalton and Nathan were quick, especially for their size, darting around us like little lightning bolts. Dalton, in particular, was laughing so loudly I couldn't help but grin. Nathan wasn't as loud, but there was a determination in his eyes that surprised me.

"Come on, Hailey, don't let them get past you!" I called out, nudging the ball toward her.

She let out a groan. "I'm trying!"

The ball flew past her, and Nathan caught up to it, kicking it into our goal with surprising accuracy. Dalton whooped and jumped in the air, giving Nathan a high-five.

"1-0!" Dalton cheered, running circles around Nathan. "We're winning!"

I glanced at Hailey, who was panting slightly. "We gotta pick up the pace, Eller."

She shot me a glare. "Maybe if you didn't keep kicking the ball like it's going through a professional player, I'd stand a chance. I told you I'm not good at this!"

I laughed, shaking my head. "Fine, fine. I'll play easy."

We played for a while, the game becoming a mix of serious play and laughter. Dalton's energy was contagious, and Nathan was starting to open up, even shouting some instructions at Dalton as they worked together. I could feel that tension between me and them starting to ease, little by little.

At one point, Hailey was chasing after the ball, determined to block Dalton from scoring again. She wasn't paying attention to her footing, though, and as she tried to pivot, her foot slipped. I was right behind her, and before I even had time to think, my arms shot out, catching her around the waist just as she was about to hit the ground.

"Whoa, careful there," I muttered, pulling her upright.

Her body was warm against mine, her back pressing into my chest for just a second before she steadied herself. She turned to look up at me, her eyes wide with surprise, her hair falling loose from her ponytail.

For a second, I forgot what I was doing. All I could focus on was the way her waist felt in my hands, the softness of her skin where my fingers brushed against her. I swallowed hard, quickly letting go of her.

Hailey blinked, clearly flustered. "Uh, thanks."

I cleared my throat, stepping back and rubbing the back of my neck. "Yeah."

She turned away quickly, and I couldn't help but notice the slight flush on her cheeks. Maybe it was from the game... or maybe it was something else.

Dalton, oblivious to whatever weird tension had just passed between us, was bouncing up and down. "Hailey almost fell!" he laughed, clearly amused. "But Callum saved her!"

Hailey shot him a playful glare. "Yeah, yeah, laugh it up."

Nathan chuckled softly from the other side of the field, and for the first time since we started, I saw him genuinely smile. It was small, but it was real. And that—well, that felt like a victory in itself.

The game continued, and I found myself loosening up, letting the tension from earlier in the day fade away with every kick of the ball. I went easy on Dalton and Nathan, letting them have their moments. They'd score on us occasionally, and I didn't mind at all. Watching them light up every time they scored was worth it.

But the real entertainment? That came from watching Hailey. Every single time she ended up with the ball, it was like a switch flipped. She'd start dribbling—well, trying to dribble—and the moment Dalton or Nathan got close to her, she'd scream.

And I mean scream.

It wasn't a terrified scream or anything. No, it was more like a combination of frustration and panic, like she had no idea what she was doing but was going to try her best to avoid getting tackled by two little kids. The first time it happened, I couldn't help but burst out laughing.

Dalton and Nathan would dart toward her, and Hailey would shriek, "No! No, no, no!" as she tried to keep the ball out of their reach, flailing around like a fish out of water.

And I couldn't lie—it was hilarious.

"Come on, Hailey!" Dalton shouted, grinning from ear to ear as he chased after her. "You can't run forever!"

"I'm trying!" she yelled, her voice laced with both amusement and panic. She kicked the ball forward, but it went way too far ahead, and Nathan swooped in, easily stealing it from her.

Hailey stopped dead in her tracks, hands on her knees, panting. "I hate this game!"

I grinned, watching as Nathan and Dalton high-fived each other in victory. "You're doing great, Eller," I teased, jogging over to her.

She shot me a glare, still out of breath. "Oh, shut up, Reid. You're letting them score on us!"

I shrugged, still grinning. "Maybe I am, maybe I'm not. But you're not exactly helping our team, you know?"

She groaned, standing up straight again and brushing her hair back from her face. "I'm not cut out for this. I don't know how you guys do it."

After the first game wrapped up, we all stood around catching our breath, with Dalton already bouncing around again like he wasn't the least bit tired. The kid had endless energy—it was honestly impressive.

"Alright," Dalton said, grinning up at me. "Let's play again! But this time, we switch teams!"

I glanced at Hailey, who had finally managed to catch her breath. "What do you think, Eller? Ready for round two?"

She groaned dramatically, throwing her hands in the air. "Do I have a choice?"

Dalton giggled, tugging on her shirt. "Nope! You have to play!"

Hailey sighed but smiled down at him. "Fine. But I'm teaming up with Nathan this time."

Nathan's eyes widened slightly at that, but he gave her a small, shy smile. "Okay."

Dalton clapped his hands, clearly thrilled at the new arrangement. "That means it's me and Callum on one team! And we're totally gonna win."

I smirked, ruffling his hair. "You ready to beat these guys, little man?"

He nodded confidently. "Yep! We're so gonna beat you guys! First to five wins!"

I grinned, glancing over at Hailey and Nathan. "You hear that? First to five. Let's see what you two can do."

Hailey rolled her eyes and Nathan shifted nervously beside her, but I could see the determination in his eyes. He didn't speak up much, but I could tell he was taking this seriously. And I liked that. It was nice seeing him get more fired up about something.

"Alright," I said, clapping my hands together. "Let's get this started."

We set up again, this time with Dalton and me on one side, and Hailey and Nathan on the other. Dalton was buzzing with energy, practically vibrating as he waited for the game to start. Nathan, while quieter, was standing a little taller now, and I could see he was ready to give it his all.

"Ready?" Dalton called out, bouncing on his toes.

Hailey and Nathan nodded, and before I knew it, Dalton had kicked the ball over to me. I caught it with my foot and started dribbling down the makeshift field, already anticipating Dalton's little legs sprinting alongside me.

"Hailey, get it!" Nathan called, surprising me. His voice, usually so quiet, had a bit more volume to it now. I grinned to myself as I saw him take charge.

Hailey groaned and dashed toward me, her eyes narrowed with determination. I was barely holding back laughter at the way she flailed toward the ball like it might attack her. I swerved to the side, passing the ball to Dalton, who immediately kicked it toward the goal.

Hailey screamed again, but this time, Nathan darted in front of her, blocking Dalton's kick with surprising skill. He grinned as he sent the ball flying back toward me, his eyes gleaming with excitement.

"Dang, Nate's got moves!" I called out, impressed.

Nathan ducked his head a little, looking embarrassed but pleased with the compliment.

"Come on, Nathan! Let's go!" Hailey encouraged, her voice bright with energy now.

Nathan took control of the ball, dribbling it down the field with Hailey at his side. I made a move to intercept, but before I could, Nathan passed the ball to Hailey, who screamed again—though this time, it was more out of excitement than panic.

"Get it, Hailey!" Nathan shouted, running alongside her.

Right now, she had the ball. And for once, she wasn't flailing or panicking. No, this time, she was focused, her eyes narrowed as she tried to maneuver past me. Nathan was calling out instructions from behind her, and I could see her trying to figure out what to do next.

I grinned, watching her with amusement. "What's your plan, Eller?" I called out, taking a few steps toward her.

Her jaw was set, her eyes sharp. "You'll see." She kicked the ball forward, her movements a bit more controlled now, and I had to admit—she was starting to get the hang of it.

But I wasn't about to let her score on me. Not without a fight. I moved in, cutting off her path just as she tried to pass me. She let out a soft grunt, trying to keep control of the ball, but I was faster. With a quick flick of my foot, I stole the ball right from under her.

"Too slow," I teased, glancing back at her with a smirk.

But then, in the next instant, I heard her stumble. I whipped my head around just in time to see her foot catch on the uneven grass. She tripped and fell, her body hitting the ground hard.

"Shit!" I dropped the ball immediately and rushed over, my heart racing. She was sitting up, brushing grass off her legs and arms, wincing slightly but not looking too hurt. I bent down beside her, concern creasing my forehead. "You alright?"

She nodded, her face flushed from the fall and the heat of the game. "Yeah, I'm fine," she muttered, trying to wave me off. "Just... got a little too excited, I guess."

I frowned, still not convinced. "You sure? You fell pretty hard."

Hailey met my eyes for a second, and despite her irritation, I could tell she was embarrassed more than anything. "I'm good, Callum. Really."

I hesitated for a moment longer before standing up and offering her my hand. "Come on. Let me help you up."

She looked at my hand for a moment, then sighed and took it, allowing me to pull her to her feet. As soon as she was upright, she brushed more grass and dirt off herself, muttering under her breath.

"I think I'm gonna sit the rest of this one out," she said, wincing as she gingerly touched her knee. "I'm not cut out for this much running."

I watched her for a second, something unreadable passing through my chest. For a moment there, she'd been playing with so much energy, so much determination. Seeing her fall like that... I didn't like it. Not one bit.

"Alright," I said, nodding toward the bench on the side of the yard. "Go take a break. You did good."

She gave me a small, grateful smile before heading over to the bench and sitting down, stretching her legs out in front of her.

Dalton ran over, his eyes wide with concern. "Is Hailey okay?" he asked, his voice filled with worry.

"She's fine," I said, ruffling his hair. "She's just sitting this one out."

Dalton nodded, though he kept glancing over at her to make sure she was really okay. I watched as she leaned back on the bench, her head tilted toward the darkening sky, a soft breeze ruffling her hair. She looked a little tired, a little worn out—but in that moment, she also looked... peaceful.

"Alright," I said, clapping my hands together. "Let's finish this game."

CHAPTER 35
HAILEY

I sat on the bench, stretching my legs out and watching the boys continue the game without me. Callum, Dalton, and Nathan were running around the yard, laughing and shouting, completely absorbed in the moment.

It was strange, seeing them like this. Together. Happy. I wasn't used to seeing this side of Callum—relaxed, almost carefree as he let Dalton score another goal on him. Nathan was more animated, more talkative than I'd ever seen him. And Dalton... well, Dalton was just a ball of energy, as usual, his face glowing with excitement.

Watching them, I felt something shift inside me. It was like I was seeing a different version of Callum—a version that wasn't always brooding or annoyed or distant. He was just... being a big brother. And it made me smile.

Suddenly, an idea sparked in my mind. I shot up from the bench, ignoring the slight ache in my knee from the earlier fall, and hurried inside the house. I practically ran down to the basement and grabbed my camera—the one Callum had gotten me. It was fixed now, with the replacement lens he'd ordered.

I held it in my hands for a moment, feeling the familiar weight of it. I'd been taking photos again, slowly easing back into something I used to love. But right now, I had the perfect opportunity to capture something real—something that actually mattered.

I hurried back outside, camera in hand, and called out to them. "Hey! Boys! Look over here!"

They all stopped in their tracks, turning to look at me. Callum stood there, hands on his hips, his chest rising and falling with each breath. He was sweaty, dirt smeared across his forehead, but there was a smile on his face that made me pause. Nathan and Dalton, both grinning widely, ran over and stood next to Callum, their faces flushed with the excitement of the game.

I raised the camera to my eye, adjusting the lens, the setting sun casting a warm, golden light over them. The sky behind them was painted in soft oranges and purples, a perfect backdrop for this moment.

"Hold still," I said, my voice soft as I focused the camera. "Just… smile."

Dalton immediately struck a goofy pose, throwing his arms around Nathan and Callum. Nathan grinned, his cheeks still flushed from running, and Callum—well, he just stood there, looking at me with that same cocky smile he always had.

I snapped the picture, the sound of the shutter clicking feeling like a release, like I'd captured something important. Something real.

When I lowered the camera, they were all still standing there, looking at me expectantly. I glanced down at the screen and smiled. "Got it," I said, grinning at them. "You guys look like a mess."

Dalton giggled, tugging on Callum's arm. "Can we see it? I wanna see it!"

I walked over and showed them the picture on the camera's screen. It wasn't perfect—it was raw and messy, with them all sweaty and disheveled—but it was real. And to me, it was beautiful.

"This looks awesome!" Dalton exclaimed, his eyes wide with excitement. "We look so cool!"

Callum glanced at the screen, nodding in approval. "Well, look at that, Eller. You actually know how to use that thing."

I rolled my eyes but smiled, tucking a loose strand of hair behind my ear. "Of course I do."

As I looked at the picture again, something stirred inside me. This moment... this messy, chaotic moment... felt like a warm hug. And I felt like I was part of it.

THE YEARBOOK CLUB ROOM WAS BUZZING WITH THE USUAL CHATTER AS EVERYONE gathered around the table, going over the upcoming events. Lisa was scribbling notes furiously, while Derek spun a pen between his fingers, clearly zoning out. Lance stood at the front, pacing back and forth as he talked about our responsibilities for Sports Day.

I groaned internally. Sports Day. Of course. It was that time of year again—the day when every grade competed in a variety of events like track and field, volleyball, tug of war, and a bunch of other exhausting activities.

"We're going to need shots of all the different events, especially the final results," Lance was saying, his voice bright with excitement. "Last year's sports day spread in the yearbook was one of the highlights, and we have to do even better this year."

I sighed, leaning back in my chair. Sports Day was always a big deal at Westview, but it wasn't exactly my favorite. Don't get me wrong, I liked being involved in yearbook, and I didn't mind taking pictures—but running around all day trying to capture people sweating and getting competitive wasn't exactly my idea of fun.

"And don't forget," Lance continued, his enthusiasm barely contained, "each grade has to wear their assigned color shirt. Seniors are red this year. So make sure to get plenty of shots of that."

"Red, huh?" Em, who was sitting beside me, said, glancing at me with a grin. "It'll be easy to spot the seniors then. We'll be running around like a bunch of tomatoes."

I groaned at the thought of having to 'run around.' Great. "Sports Day is so exhausting."

Em laughed, her short, cropped pink hair bouncing as she leaned back in her chair. "Come on, Hailey, where's your school spirit? It's our last ever Sports Day!"

"Exactly," Derek nodded in agreement. "Which means we have to try extra hard to win."

I couldn't ignore the fact that the stakes were higher this year. The winning grade didn't just get bragging rights—they also got a prize. This year, the grade that won Sports Day would get to go on a trip during winter break to a fancy hotel in the mountains of Mammoth Lakes for a few days. And, of course, everyone was hyped up about it.

Lance looked around the room, sensing the mixed reactions. "Look, I know Sports Day isn't everyone's favorite," he said, his tone sympathetic but also shooting a pointed glare in my direction. "But this is our last one. And that trip? It's going to be epic. So let's make the most of it, okay?"

I sighed, crossing my arms. "Yeah, I know. I just wish it wasn't so... sports-focused."

"Uh, Hailey," Derek said, raising an eyebrow, "it's literally called *Sports* Day. What did you expect?"

"Shut up," I chuckled, rolling my eyes. "I just mean, I'm not exactly looking forward to running around all day. The only sport I'm good at is taking pictures."

Lance chuckled, shaking his head. "Well, we'll need lots of photos, so you'll be in your element, Hailey. Just make sure to cover the key moments—the big races, the volleyball matches, tug of war, that kind of stuff."

I nodded, already mentally preparing myself for the day ahead. It was going to be chaotic, with every grade competing for the top spot.

And seniors? We had to win. I wasn't exactly competitive, but the thought of a trip to a mountain hotel during winter break? Yeah, I guess that was pretty appealing.

"Also," Lance added, glancing at me, "you might want to keep an eye on the soccer boys during the events. Callum and his crew usually get pretty intense about Sports Day."

I groaned inwardly at the mention of Callum. Of course, he'd be one of the key players during Sports Day. Over the last few weeks, soccer season had been in full swing, and Callum had been... well, busy. He'd had multiple games, and while there had been some tough losses, Westview's team had mostly been on a winning streak. Sports Day was that time where athletes like him could get their fix of competing and getting all physical without having to worry about the stakes of winning or losing too much.

"Yeah, I'm sure the soccer guys will be front and center," I said, trying to sound disinterested.

"Exactly," Lance said, nodding. "So make sure you get plenty of shots of the action."

I glanced down at my camera, fiddling with the settings. Sports Day. Red shirts. Tug of war. Soccer boys. Great. "I'll be ready," I said, trying to psych myself up for the chaos ahead.

The yearbook meeting was finally winding down, and I couldn't help but let out a small sigh of relief as Lance wrapped things up. "Alright, everyone," Lance said, clapping his hands together, "that's it for today."

The others began packing up their stuff and filing out of the room, chatting about the upcoming events and their plans for the rest of the day. I watched as Lisa and Em exchanged a few words before heading toward the door, and Derek gave me a quick nod as he twirled his pen and sauntered out.

I stayed seated, glancing at Lance, who was busy organizing some papers on his desk. I'd been meaning to talk to him for a while now—ever since that conversation I'd had with Nala about... well, setting them up. Nala hadn't outright said she liked Lance, but there had definitely been some interest.

And as her best friend, I couldn't just let that slide.

This was my chance to get some clarity, and with the room mostly empty now, I figured it was as good a time as any to bring it up. I cleared my throat and stood up, walking over to Lance. "Hey, Lance," I started, trying to sound casual, "can I talk to you for a sec?"

Lance glanced up from his papers, raising an eyebrow. "Yeah, sure. What's up?"

I shifted awkwardly, suddenly realizing I wasn't exactly sure how to start this conversation. "So, um... you and Nala—uh, you guys are friends, right?"

Lance smiled and nodded. "Yeah, Nala's great. Why?"

I bit my lip, trying to figure out how to phrase this without sounding too weird. "Well... you know, she's, like, super awesome and all... and I just thought maybe you two could, you know... hang out more or something?"

Lance blinked, clearly confused. "Hang out more?"

I resisted the urge to facepalm. Why was I so bad at this? "What I mean is... Nala's been talking about you, and I just thought maybe..." I trailed off, feeling a little ridiculous now. How had I even gotten myself into this situation?

Lance looked at me for a moment, and then a small smile tugged at his lips. "Hailey, are you trying to set me up with Nala?"

I cringed inwardly but nodded slowly. "Maybe...?"

He chuckled softly, shaking his head. "Hailey, I appreciate the thought, but... I've actually got a girlfriend."

I froze. "Oh." Well, this was awkward. "You do?"

"Yeah," he said, nodding. "We've been dating for a few months now. I'm surprised it hasn't come up, actually. But, uh, yeah. Sorry."

I blinked a few times, processing this new information. "Wow. Um… no, it's totally fine. I didn't know. I just… thought I'd ask."

Lance grinned, clearly finding the situation a little amusing. "It's all good. I'm flattered, really, but yeah… taken."

I nodded, feeling my cheeks flush slightly. "Right. Got it."

There was a brief, awkward pause before Lance glanced back down at his papers. "But hey, thanks for looking out for your friend. We'll definitely hang out more—just as friends, though."

"Yeah, of course," I said quickly, already feeling like I needed to escape this conversation as soon as possible. "I'll… I'll let her know."

Lance chuckled again, giving me a small wave as I turned to leave. "See you at Sports Day, Hailey."

"Yeah… see you then," I mumbled, hurrying out of the room. I watched Lance push the door open and head out, his footsteps echoing down the hall as he disappeared from sight. I stood there for a moment, still feeling the lingering awkwardness of our conversation. Great. Nala was going to kill me for trying to play matchmaker without all the facts.

Sighing, I adjusted the strap of my camera bag and stepped out of the yearbook room, heading toward the exit. But the moment I walked into the hall, I spotted Callum leaning against the lockers, arms crossed, fresh from soccer practice.

He looked… well, a little pissed.

I walked over to him, raising an eyebrow. "What's up with you? You look like you want to punch something."

Callum grunted in response, his eyes flicking over to me before quickly looking away. "It's nothing."

"Uh-huh." I wasn't convinced. He had that stormy expression on his face again, the one that usually meant something had pissed him off during practice or with the team. "Seriously, what's your problem? Something happen during practice?"

He didn't answer right away, just clenched his jaw like he was trying to keep himself in check. "No," he muttered after a beat, still not looking at me. "Just a long day."

I narrowed my eyes, not buying it for a second. He was clearly irritated about something, but I knew better than to press him when he was like this. Callum had a way of shutting people out when he was in a mood, and right now, he seemed like he was one wrong word away from snapping.

I decided to let it go—for now. "Fine," I said with a sigh, walking alongside him as we headed for the doors. "So... sports day tomorrow. You excited?"

He grunted again, which I assumed meant "no." Typical Callum response.

"Fine, be a grump then," I muttered, stuffing my hands into my pockets as we walked outside. The cool evening air hit my face, and I glanced at Callum again, who seemed lost in his own thoughts.

CHAPTER 36
CALLUM

Later that night, I sat in my room, staring at the ceiling, a knot of irritation tightening in my chest. The glow from my phone dimmed beside me, but I wasn't really paying attention to anything on the screen. My mind kept circling back to what I'd overheard earlier.

Hailey had stayed behind after her little yearbook meeting with Lance. I hadn't thought much of it at first, but as I stood outside the room, waiting for her, I couldn't help but catch the tail end of their conversation.

"I've actually got a girlfriend," Lance had said.

I frowned, replaying those words over and over in my head. Had Hailey just... asked out Lance? And had Lace just rejected her?

I scowled, sitting up on my bed and running a hand through my hair. What the hell was that about? I mean, I didn't care what Hailey did. She could date whoever she wanted. It was none of my business.

But... Lance? Of all people?

I couldn't help but feel a weird surge of irritation at the idea of Hailey asking out some other guy, especially Lance. He wasn't even her type. What the hell did she see in him anyway? He was nice, sure. I guess.

I grabbed my phone and tossed it onto my desk, leaning back against my pillows with a huff. The thought of Hailey dating someone like Lance just didn't sit right with me. Not that I had any say in the matter, obviously. It's not like I was interested in her like that

But still... the idea of her getting rejected? That bugged me. I didn't like thinking about Hailey getting turned down, even though it really wasn't any of my business. And if she had asked Lance out... well, that just meant she was probably feeling embarrassed now.

I sat there, clenching and unclenching my fists, trying to figure out why I was so damn irritated. It wasn't like I had feelings for Hailey. We weren't even close. We barely got along most of the time. So why was I sitting here, stewing over the idea of her getting rejected by Lance?

Maybe it was because I knew Hailey better than most people. I knew she wasn't the type to put herself out there like that, and if she had asked Lance out, that meant she was serious about it.

And now... well, now she'd have to deal with the awkwardness of it all.

I was still lying on my bed, trying to shake off the weird irritation that had settled in my chest after that whole thing with Lance and Hailey when I heard my name being called from downstairs.

"Callum!" My dad's voice boomed through the house. "Come down here, will ya?"

I groaned, rolling out of bed. Whatever it was, it could only mean one thing: I was about to be given some sort of errand. My dad didn't just call me down unless he needed something.

I trudged downstairs and found my dad standing by the counter, flipping through a grocery list. My mom was nearby, setting up some stuff on the table while Dalton and Nathan buzzed around, asking if they could help.

"What's up?" I asked, leaning against the doorframe.

My dad glanced up at me, holding out the list. "We're doing a family BBQ tonight."

I raised an eyebrow. "That's... random."

"Yeah, well, it's gonna get cold soon," he said with a shrug. "Figured we should make the most of the weather while we can. But we're missing a few things—hotdogs, buns, some condiments—so I need you to head to Walmart and pick those up."

I sighed, already knowing there was no way out of this. "Fine. I'll go."

Just as I turned to head back upstairs to grab my keys, I heard footsteps coming from the basement stairs. Hailey came up, her hair slightly mussed and wearing one of those oversized hoodies she seemed to drown in. She looked at us curiously, her gaze shifting between me and my dad.

"What's going on?" she asked, brushing a few strands of hair out of her face.

"Hailey! I was just telling Callum, we're having a family BBQ tonight," my dad said, folding the grocery list and placing it on the countee. "Callum's heading to Walmart to grab some stuff."

Then, as if some cosmic joke had just aligned perfectly, Hailey's dad, who was sipping on a glass of iced tea nearby, chimed in. "You know what, Hailey? Why don't you go with Callum?"

My eyes widened slightly, and I tried not to groan out loud. Of course things would turn out this way. As much as Hailey and I tried to steer clear of each other and keep our interactions to a bare minimum, it was like the universe did everything in its power to shove us in such situations.

Hailey blinked, looking just as surprised as I was. "Wait... what? Why?"

Her dad grinned, oblivious to the silent protest we were both probably trying to telepathically send him. "It's a quick trip, and you can help Callum make sure he doesn't forget anything. Plus, it'll be good to stretch your legs, get out of the house for a bit."

I shot Hailey a look, and she raised her eyebrows at me, clearly not thrilled by the idea. But then, as if resigning to the fact that neither of us were going to win this one, she shrugged. "Fine," she muttered, looking just as exasperated as I felt.

"Great!" my dad said, tossing the car keys in my direction. "Don't take too long, we've got a lot to set up here."

I caught the keys and glanced at Hailey again. This was the last thing I needed after the weird headspace I'd been in all day, but whatever. It was just a quick trip to Walmart. How bad could it be?

"Let's go, then," I muttered, motioning for Hailey to follow me out the door.

Hailey slid into the passenger seat next to me, tugging at the sleeves of her oversized hoodie. I focused on backing out of the driveway, the engine purring softly beneath us as we pulled onto the street.

The silence between us wasn't unusual—we'd gotten used to this quiet routine. But tonight, it felt a little... different. I couldn't shake the weird irritation that had been gnawing at me since I overheard Lance talking to her after the yearbook meeting.

Did she really ask him out? And did Lance actually reject her? I snuck a glance at her while we were stopped at a light, looking for any sign of distress, but Hailey looked... well, normal. She was staring out the window, her chin resting on her hand, seemingly lost in her own thoughts.

I debated bringing it up—asking her about Lance—but decided against it. There was no way to do that without sounding like a complete asshole, and I didn't want to deal with more awkwardness. Not now, anyway.

Instead, we drove in silence, the hum of the engine and the occasional car passing by the only sounds filling the air. As we pulled into the Walmart parking lot and parked, I couldn't help but feel like something about this whole situation was... oddly domestic.

I mean, here we were, heading into Walmart together to buy groceries for a family BBQ. If you didn't know us, you'd think we were just two people who... I don't know, did this all the time. Like it was normal for us to go out shopping together.

The whole thing was almost too... domestic. Like we were a couple, running errands or something. I wasn't used to that feeling. I wasn't used to this at all.

But it wasn't. We weren't close like that.

And yet, as we walked into the store and grabbed a shopping cart, I couldn't shake the weird feeling that this was almost... comfortable.

"So, hotdogs first?" Hailey asked, snapping me out of my thoughts.

"Yeah, and buns," I muttered, pushing the cart forward as we made our way down the aisles.

We wandered through the store, picking up packs of hotdogs, buns, condiments, and whatever else was on my dad's list. I was hyper-aware of Hailey walking next to me, and the more we moved around the store together, the stranger it felt.

At one point, we stopped in the condiment aisle, and Hailey reached for a bottle of ketchup. She glanced at me, raising an eyebrow. "How much ketchup does your family even go through at these things?"

I shrugged, leaning against the cart. "Better to have too much than too little."

She snorted. "Right. Knowing you, you'll probably hog it all for yourself."

I rolled my eyes, but couldn't help the small grin tugging at the corner of my mouth. "I'm not that selfish."

"Sure," she said, tossing the ketchup into the cart.

I pushed the cart toward the frozen section, my mind still circling around that ridiculous idea that Hailey might've asked out Lance and gotten rejected. The more I thought about it, the more I felt like I had to do something—something to, I don't know, help her out or soften the blow, even if she wasn't showing any signs of being upset.

And what did girls usually do after something like that?

Ice cream.

I had no idea if that stereotype was true or not, but I'd seen it in enough movies to make me think it wasn't a bad idea. If Hailey was secretly bummed out about getting rejected, maybe some ice cream would help her get through it. At least, that was my logic. So I stopped in front of the freezer section, looking at the rows of brightly colored cartons of ice cream, trying to figure out what the hell she'd even like. There were way too many flavors. Chocolate, vanilla, strawberry, cookies and cream, mint chip—what did girls even go for when they were down?

I scanned the options, frowning to myself. Should I go with something classic like chocolate, or would she be more into something fancier like Ben & Jerry's with all the chunks of random stuff in it?

As I stood there, overanalyzing the selection like some idiot, I heard footsteps behind me.

"Are you getting something?" Hailey's voice broke through my thoughts, and I glanced over my shoulder to see her standing behind me, one eyebrow raised as she watched me stare at the ice cream aisle like it held the secrets of the universe.

I cleared my throat, quickly trying to think of something nonchalant to say. "Uh, yeah, I was thinking about it."

She stepped closer, looking up at the rows of ice cream cartons with mild curiosity. "What kind of ice cream do you even like?"

I hesitated, not wanting to make this about me. "What do you like?" I asked instead, deflecting the question back at her.

Hailey blinked at me, clearly not expecting that question. "Me?"

"Yeah," I said, trying to sound casual, even though my mind was still on the whole Lance situation. "You eat ice cream, right? What's your favorite?"

She paused, her lips pursed in thought. "I guess... cookies and cream? Or maybe mint chocolate chip. But why are you asking?"

I shrugged, pretending like I wasn't overthinking this. "Just thought I'd grab something."

Hailey gave me a suspicious look, but didn't press further. Instead, she reached out and grabbed a carton of cookies and cream from the freezer, holding it out to me.

"If you're getting something, get this," she said, her tone almost challenging.

I took the carton from her and tossed it into the cart, trying to ignore the fact that I was doing this because I thought she might need a pick-me-up. It wasn't like I could explain my weird logic without sounding like a total idiot.

"Alright, fine," I said, pushing the cart forward again. "Cookies and cream it is."

Hailey just shook her head, still watching me like I was some strange creature she was trying to figure out. But she didn't say anything more, and we continued walking through the store, gathering the last few items on the list.

We'd gotten through most of the list, and now we were in the frozen section, grabbing some meats for the BBQ. Hailey was rifling through the packs of frozen hotdogs and burger patties, picking them up and placing them in the cart with a kind of focus I hadn't expected.

After a minute or two, she kept holding on to one of the frozen packets for too long. Her fingers turned red from the cold, and she winced, shifting it in her hand.

Without really thinking about it, I reached out and grabbed her hand.

"Your hand's cold," I muttered, running my thumb across her fingers as if that would magically warm them up. And for a split second, I didn't think anything of it—just that her hand was, in fact, cold, and I'd been right.

But then it hit me.

We were... holding hands. Like, actually holding hands.

I froze, realizing the weight of what I'd just done. Hailey was staring down at our hands, too, probably just as confused as I was. My heart stuttered for a second, and the realization washed over me like a bucket of ice water.

Before I could stop myself, I pretty much flung her hand away from mine, turning toward the next aisle like I needed to escape.

Behind me, Hailey's indignant voice followed. "Hey! You asshole! What the hell?! Where are you going?"

I kept walking, hoping my face wasn't as red as it felt. What the hell had I just done? Why did I even grab her hand in the first place? It wasn't like I needed to check if her hand was cold—she was holding a freaking packet of frozen meat, of course it was cold.

But my body had acted before my brain could catch up, and now I looked like a total idiot.

"Callum! Hello! Stop walking so fast!"

I didn't look back, just kept walking, silently cursing myself for the stupidest move I'd made in a while.

CHAPTER 37

HAILEY

THE BACKYARD WAS ALIVE WITH THE SMELL OF GRILLING MEAT AND THE QUIET hum of chatter. I was seated at the big outdoor table, watching as the dads worked the BBQ with practiced ease, flipping burgers and hotdogs, making sure everything was cooked to perfection. The late afternoon chill was starting to set in, and I tugged my hoodie tighter around myself as I leaned back in my chair.

Callum stepped outside from the house, now wearing a hoodie of his own, pulling the hood up as he scanned the scene.

His face looked relaxed, which was a bit of a change from his usual scowl. I was still slightly annoyed with him for the whole hand-grabbing incident at Walmart, but I was trying not to think about it too much. He'd panicked, clearly, and I could almost laugh at how awkward the whole thing had been.

But for now, the atmosphere was nice. Almost peaceful.

The kids—Dalton and Nathan—were running around the yard, their laughter filling the space as they kicked a soccer ball back and forth. They were surprisingly energetic after eating most of the snacks that had been put out earlier, and their boundless enthusiasm was kind of contagious.

At the table, the moms were chatting away, laughing about some story Mrs. Reid was telling about a vacation mishap that happened years ago. Mrs. Eller nodded along, adding her own commentary, and they both looked relaxed, happy even. It was kind of nice seeing my mom laugh like that after everything that had happened with the fire.

The whole scene was kind of perfect in a strange way—just the families hanging out, the smell of burgers and hotdogs on the grill, the sounds of kids playing and parents talking, and the chilly breeze reminding us that fall was settling in.

I wrapped my fingers around my glass of lemonade, feeling the condensation cool against my skin. There was something about being outside, surrounded by all of this, that felt... peaceful. It wasn't exactly what I imagined life would be like after moving in with the Reids, but sitting here now, it didn't feel so bad.

Dalton suddenly ran over to Callum, out of breath, and tugged at his sleeve. "Callum! Come play soccer with us!"

Callum rolled his eyes, though I could tell he wasn't really annoyed. He stood up, shaking his head, but there was a small smile tugging at his lips. "Alright, alright. But don't cry when I beat you."

Dalton beamed and ran back toward Nathan, shouting, "Callum's gonna play!"

As Callum headed off to join them, I couldn't help but watch for a second. He seemed more relaxed around his brothers lately, and I knew it had something to do with the conversation we'd had after the whole stick-figure-on-his-car incident. It was like he was trying to make up for lost time with them, and honestly, it was nice to see.

I smiled to myself as I watched the boys kick the soccer ball around, Callum taking it easy on them but still playing with that competitive edge he always had. He'd let Nathan score a goal and then chase after Dalton, who was laughing so hard he could barely kick straight.

Yeah... it was kind of nice.

"Alright, boys, bring it in!" Mr. Reid called from the grill, waving his spatula in the air. "It's time to eat!"

The boys groaned but reluctantly stopped their game, running over to the table with their cheeks flushed and eyes bright from the activity. Callum jogged behind them, shaking his head in mock annoyance, but I could see a smile pulling at the corners of his lips.

As everyone gathered around the big outdoor table, it quickly became clear that seating was a little tight. Nathan and Dalton immediately grabbed the seats closest to their mom and dad, while my parents settled in across from them. That left one spot—directly next to me.

I inwardly groaned, already knowing who was going to end up there. Sure enough, Callum made his way over, plopping down in the seat next to mine with a barely concealed sigh of exasperation.

"Great," I muttered under my breath. "Just what I needed—your charming company."

He shot me a look as he pulled the hood of his hoodie down, ruffling his already-messy hair. "I'm thrilled too, trust me."

I rolled my eyes, reaching for the basket of rolls in the center of the table. The sound of chatter and laughter surrounded us as everyone started piling food onto their plates, but as usual, Callum and I couldn't just sit quietly.

"You'd think you'd be used to it by now," he muttered, grabbing a burger patty with his fork.

"Used to what?" I asked, not really interested but feeling obligated to keep the banter going.

"Me. You're stuck with me for how long now? You've gotta admit, I'm growing on you." He smirked, and I could see that familiar cocky glint in his eyes.

I scoffed, taking a roll and buttering it with unnecessary force. "Yeah, like mold."

Callum laughed under his breath, shaking his head. "You're hilarious."

I bit into the roll, trying to suppress the small smile threatening to form on my lips. "I try."

We sat in an odd kind of silence for a minute— comfortable, but also charged with that same undercurrent of bickering tension that had become our default. It wasn't like we hated each other anymore, but it was easier to pretend we were still at each other's throats than acknowledge… whatever this weird middle ground was. As the food was passed around and plates were filled, I could feel Callum fidgeting next to me, elbowing me slightly as he tried to reach for the ketchup.

I handed it to him without saying anything, and he gave me a quick nod of thanks, our usual back-and-forth falling into an oddly smooth rhythm.

The breeze was cooler now, but the smell of grilled meat and the warmth of laughter kept the chill at bay. I leaned back in my chair, watching as the evening unfolded around the table.

Everyone was relaxed, full from the BBQ, and it wasn't long before the conversation turned from casual talk to deeper reminiscing.

Mr. Reid and my dad were the center of attention, trading stories about their college days, while our moms listened with knowing smiles. I'd heard bits and pieces before about how our dads had been good friends back in the day, but the specifics always seemed to vary.

"So, we met during freshman orientation," Mr. Reid was saying, leaning back in his chair with a grin. "Greg here was the only other guy who showed up to class early. I knew right then we'd be friends."

My dad chuckled. "Yup. We ended up sitting together in nearly every class after that, just because we were always the first ones there."

"Man, we were so eager back then," Mr. Reid added, shaking his head. "Remember all those late-night study sessions? God, those were brutal."

"We got through it," my dad said, smiling. "But then, you know, life happens, and we kind of drifted apart after college. Jobs, families... It's crazy how time flies."

My mom, chimed in at that. "Men are so weird. If I had a best friend who had a kid Hailey's age, I would've made sure our kids became best friends too. Imagine how different things could've been!"

Mrs. Reid laughed and nodded in agreement. "Exactly! If we'd been in charge, Hailey and Callum might have actually been friends instead of at each other's throats all these years."

My mom let out a dramatic sigh. "Ah, missed opportunities."

I glanced at Callum, who was sitting next to me, slouched in his chair, eyes fixed on his plate. He caught my glance and gave me an exaggerated glare, like this whole conversation was my fault.

"Well, we're not that bad," I muttered, crossing my arms, already knowing I was talking out of my ass. "Right?"

Callum snorted. "We literally argue every day."

I rolled my eyes. "Only because *you* always have something annoying to say."

"See? Right now!" He gestured to me with his fork. "This is Exhibit A."

"Oh, hush, you two," Mrs. Reid said with a chuckle. "You're practically professionals at bickering by now."

"We're just giving you all something to talk about," I said dryly, earning a round of laughter from the table.

The conversation continued to roll smoothly from there. Since we already tackled the 'When we were young' chapter, I realized where this was headed—straight into the 'Embarrassing stories about the kids' territory. And, sure enough, Mr. Reid was already grinning like he was gearing up for something.

"Speaking of which," Mr. Reid began, his eyes glinting mischievously, "I've got a great story about Callum from when he was about six or seven..."

Callum groaned, already sinking lower into his chair. "Dad, no."

"Oh, yes," Mr. Reid said with a laugh. "We were at this family picnic one summer, right? And there was a little creek that ran behind the park. All the kids were playing by the water, splashing around, trying to catch frogs or whatever. But Callum? Callum had other plans."

I couldn't help but smirk as I leaned in, knowing this was going to be good. Any opportunity to see Callum squirm or be totally embarrassed was one I welcomed with open arms.

"He decides he's going to 'go fishing,'" Mr. Reid continued, making air quotes with his fingers. "So he finds this long stick, ties some string to it, and starts marching down to the creek like he's some kind of wilderness survivalist."

"Dad, just stop," Callum muttered, covering his face with his hand.

"But here's the best part," Mr. Reid said, laughing. "Instead of, you know, fishing in the water like a normal person, he dips his string into a mud puddle and waits. For hours."

I snorted, trying not to laugh too loudly. "He thought he could fish in a mud puddle?"

"Yup," Mr. Reid said, grinning. "Sat there for hours, getting all muddy and frustrated because 'the fish weren't biting.'"

By now, the whole table was laughing, and Callum's face was a deep shade of red. He muttered something under his breath, still covering his face. "Okay, okay, that's enough about me," Callum said, waving his hand like he was ready to move on. "What about Hailey? Surely there's something embarrassing about her, right?"

My dad perked up, his eyes lighting with mischief. "Oh, do I have a story."

I groaned. "No, no, we don't have to—"

"Oh, we absolutely do," my dad said, cutting me off with a grin. "This was when Hailey was around four or five, I think. We'd gone to the beach for the first time, and she'd been playing in the sand all day. You know, building sandcastles, digging holes, the usual."

I closed my eyes, already dreading where this was going.

"And at one point, she finds this huge, elaborate sandcastle that someone else had made. But instead of admiring it like a normal person, she runs over to it, grabs a handful of sand, and shoves it in her mouth."

The table erupted in laughter, and I buried my face in my hands. "I thought it was cake!" I protested weakly.

"You look like the type of kid to eat sand," Callum teased, amusement glinting in his eyes.

"I was four, okay?" I mumbled, still trying to hide my face. "And what the hell do you mean I look like the type of kid to eat sand?"

As the laughter died down, the table fell back into easy conversation, but I couldn't help but smile to myself. Despite the embarrassment, there was something kind of nice about sitting here, trading stories, laughing at each other's childhood mishaps. Maybe our parents hadn't forced us to be friends growing up, but sitting here now, surrounded by them, it didn't feel so bad.

The conversation around the table carried on, the adults swapping stories about their old college days, laughing and joking like they hadn't just humiliated Callum and me. I was half-listening, half-picking at the food on my plate, when something unexpected happened.

I felt Callum's knee brush against mine under the table.

At first, I thought it was accidental—his legs were long, and the table was kind of cramped. But then... he didn't move it away. He just kept talking, laughing at something his dad said, his focus completely elsewhere, but his knee stayed right there, warm against mine.

I sat up a little straighter, my brain kicking into overdrive. Was this... intentional? No, it couldn't be. Callum was built like a human skyscraper; there probably wasn't enough room for him under the table to not bump into someone. Still, my heart beat a little faster as I glanced at him out of the corner of my eye.

Of course, he wasn't paying any attention to me. Typical.

He was leaned forward slightly, talking to my dad now, his hoodie pulled tight across his broad shoulders. I found myself staring at his arms—those stupid, muscular arms. They were kind of impossible to ignore, especially when they strained against his sleeves like that.

God, he really was huge. I could see the outline of his muscles even through the thick fabric, and I suddenly found myself remembering that stupid ab picture he'd accidentally sent me. My cheeks burned at the memory.

I looked away quickly, grabbing my glass of water and taking a sip in an attempt to cool off. What was wrong with me? This was Callum—the same Callum who made it his daily mission to annoy the hell out of me. The same Callum who had teased me relentlessly over the years, who I'd argued with countless times.

But now... now I was noticing him in a way that I hadn't before. I couldn't stop thinking about the fact that his knee was still touching mine, that his body took up so much space, that—

"Hailey?"

My head snapped up at the sound of my mom's voice. I hadn't even realized I'd spaced out.

"You okay, sweetie?" she asked, giving me a curious look. "You've been a bit quiet."

"Yeah, yeah, I'm fine," I mumbled, giving her a quick smile. "Just... thinking."

Callum shot me a sideways glance, raising an eyebrow, but he didn't say anything. His knee was still against mine, and I wasn't sure if he even noticed, or if I was the only one hyper-aware of it.

The conversation flowed on, and I tried my best to focus, but I kept getting distracted. The adults were laughing again, probably at some other embarrassing story from back in the day, but all I could think about was Callum's stupid knee and the weird fluttering in my stomach that seemed to be growing by the second.

This was ridiculous. I was being ridiculous.

I was just going to have to ignore it—ignore him—and get through this dinner like a normal person. Maybe it would go away if I just pretended it wasn't happening. Right?

CHAPTER 38
CALLUM

THE NIGHT HAD SETTLED IN, COOL AND QUIET, WITH THE LAST REMNANTS OF THE BBQ packed up and the backyard cleared. The adults had already retreated inside to wind down for the night, while Dalton and Nathan had been ushered upstairs by my mom, since there was school tomorrow. I figured I'd head to bed soon, too—after grabbing a seltzer from the fridge, of course.

As I popped the fridge open, the soft click of the door breaking the silence of the kitchen, I glanced outside. The fire pit, which had been cleaned up after dinner, was still sitting unused in the backyard, and next to it… was Hailey.

She was crouched next to it, fiddling with something. I squinted, trying to figure out what she was doing. It looked like she was trying to light the fire pit, but judging by the way she was looking around at it, she had no idea how to make it work.

I hesitated for a second, then grabbed my drink and made my way outside, the cool night air hitting me as I slid open the door. She didn't notice me at first, too focused on whatever she was trying to do with the fire pit, but when I got closer, she finally looked up.

"The hell are you doing?" I asked, stepping toward her.

She huffed, brushing a strand of hair out of her face. "I'm trying to figure out how this thing works, but it's being stubborn."

"You're the only thing being stubborn out here," I bit back a smirk, walking over to her and crouching down a bit. "You're just not doing it right."

She shot me a look. "Oh, thank you, fire pit expert. Mind helping me or you got anything else to say?"

I knelt down next to her and flipped open the gas valve, making sure it was aligned properly. "You've gotta turn this like so, and then push this button." The small igniter clicked, and in seconds, the fire sprang to life, casting a warm, flickering glow across the yard.

Hailey leaned back, staring at the flames as they danced in the pit, her face illuminated by the soft orange light. "Huh. That was... easier than I thought."

I grabbed one of the folding chairs nearby and pulled it up next to her. "You're welcome," I said, sitting down and taking a sip of my seltzer.

She didn't thank me, of course, just gave me a small nod before sitting back herself, watching the fire. It was quiet for a minute, and I wasn't sure why I didn't just head inside after helping her. But for some reason, I stayed.

"Why are you still out here anyway?" I asked, breaking the silence. "It's late."

Hailey shrugged, pulling her knees up to her chest. She was wrapped in some oversized hoodie again, probably one of the thousand she owned. "I don't know. Just... wanted some fresh air, I guess. It's kind of nice out here."

I glanced at her, watching as the firelight reflected in her green eyes. She seemed... calmer than usual, less ready to bite my head off like she normally was.

"Yeah, it's alright," I said, leaning back in my chair. The fire crackled quietly between us, filling the space that neither of us seemed in a rush to fill with words.

It wasn't awkward, though. Strangely enough, it felt kind of... peaceful. The backyard was quiet, the house was still, and the stars were starting to show in the sky above us. I wasn't sure why, but sitting there next to Hailey didn't feel as tense as it usually did.

She let out a small sigh, her breath almost visible in the cool air. "I miss stuff like this," she said softly.

I frowned. "Like what?"

She gestured to the fire, the backyard, the quiet. "Just... moments like this, I guess. Before... everything happened. The fire, moving in with you guys. It's been weird, you know?"

"Yeah. I get it."

Hailey glanced at me, looking almost surprised. She hugged her knees tighter to her chest, resting her chin on them. "It's just... everything changed so fast. One minute I had everything, and the next... I didn't. And now, living here... it's been different."

I didn't know what to say to that, so I just nodded again. It wasn't like I'd ever lost everything I owned in a fire, but I could imagine how that would mess with someone.

We sat there for a while, not saying much, just watching the fire and listening to the crackle of the flames. The tension I always felt around Hailey seemed to ease, and for once, I didn't feel the urge to pick a fight with her.

After a while, I leaned forward, resting my elbows on my knees, staring into the flames. "You know, you could've just asked me for help with the fire pit earlier. I'm not always an ass."

"Sure, you're not."

"Okay, maybe I am most of the time. But still."

She shook her head, a small smile tugging at her lips. "Next time, I'll make sure to come get the fire pit expert right away."

"Good." I leaned back in my chair again, folding my arms over my chest. "Glad you're finally listening."

I glanced over at her. She was staring into the fire, her face lit up by the soft glow, and for a moment, I wondered what she was thinking. I had this weird urge to say something, to break the silence—but not in the usual way. Not with a sarcastic comment or an insult.

I shifted in my chair, sitting up a little. "You know," I started, my voice breaking the quiet, "I wasn't gonna say anything, but... I heard you and Lance earlier."

Hailey blinked, looking over at me. "What?"

I rubbed the back of my neck, feeling a little awkward, but I pushed through. "You know... when you stayed behind to talk to him. I didn't mean to overhear, but I caught the end of it. And look... I just wanna say, don't, like, think lesser of yourself just because he rejected you or whatever."

Hailey just stared at me, her brow furrowing like I'd just spoken to her in a foreign language. "Wait... what?" she said slowly, confusion written all over her face. "What the hell are you talking about?"

I frowned, feeling a little thrown off and frustrated that she was trying to play dumb or whatever. "You know... Lance. I heard him say he had a girlfriend, and I figured you, like... asked him out or something. And got rejected."

Hailey blinked again, and then—before I knew what was happening—she started laughing.

At first, it was just a small giggle, but then it grew into full-blown laughter, her hand going to her mouth as she tried to stifle it. I just sat there, staring at her like an idiot, feeling my face heat up.

"What?" I said, a little annoyed now. "Why are you laughing? What's so funny?"

"You..." she gasped between laughs, wiping her eyes. "You thought I asked out Lance?"

I shifted uncomfortably in my chair, rubbing the back of my neck again. What the hell was going on? Had I misunderstood? "Uh, yeah? Why else would he mention his girlfriend?"

She shook her head, still laughing. "Oh my God, Callum, no. I wasn't asking him out."

I frowned, completely lost now. "Then what were you talking about?"

She let out a long breath, her laughter finally dying down as she sat back in her chair. "I was trying to set him up with Nala."

I blinked. "Wait... what?"

"Yeah," she said, still grinning. "Nala had this little crush on Lance, and I was trying to, you know, test the waters. See if he was single. But then he told me he had a girlfriend, so... obviously, that plan fell apart."

I sat there, stunned for a second, feeling like a complete idiot. I'd been sitting here, thinking she got rejected, that maybe she was upset about it... and she wasn't even talking about herself.

"Oh," I mumbled, scratching the back of my head. "I... I thought..."

"Yeah, I know what you thought," Hailey said, rolling her eyes but still smiling. "And, for the record, I don't need a pep talk about not feeling lesser or whatever. I'm fine."

I stared at her for a moment, feeling more than a little embarrassed now. "Right. Well... good. I guess."

Hailey just shook her head, chuckling softly as she leaned back in her chair again. "God, you're so weird sometimes."

I didn't know what to say to that, so I just sat there, staring into the fire, feeling like an idiot. My brain was still spinning, trying to wrap my head around the fact that I'd gotten the whole thing completely wrong.

I wasn't even sure why I'd cared so much in the first place. I mean, why did it matter to me whether or not Hailey got rejected? Why did I feel the need to say something about it?

Hailey was still grinning like she'd just discovered the best joke of her life, and it was at my expense. I was sitting there, trying to get over the awkwardness of the whole situation, when she opened her mouth again.

"Wait, hold on," she said, raising an eyebrow. "Are you giving me that pep talk you give to all your girlfriends when you decide you don't want something serious?"

I blinked at her. "What?"

She shrugged, that smirk still on her face. "You know, the 'don't feel bad, it's not you, it's me' speech. The same one you probably give to every girl after you've had your fun and are ready to move on."

I scoffed, leaning back in my chair. "I don't know what 'girlfriends' you're talking about."

"Don't lie to yourself," she said, still smirking. "You're like the biggest playboy ever, Callum."

That caught me off guard. "Excuse me?"

"It's not like it's a secret," she said, crossing her arms, clearly enjoying the fact that she had me on the defensive. "I've seen you with plenty of girls. You've got a reputation, you know."

I gritted my teeth. Yeah, sure, I'd been with a few girls—okay, maybe more than a few—but I didn't like the way she was acting like she had me all figured out.

"So what if I've hooked up with a few girls?" I shot back, my voice sharper than I intended. "That doesn't make me a manwhore or playboy or whatever the hell."

Hailey rolled her eyes. "Oh, come on. You're practically the poster boy for 'not interested in anything serious.' I'm just saying, maybe I wasn't the one who needed that pep talk earlier."

I narrowed my eyes at her, feeling a mix of irritation and something else I couldn't quite place. "You don't know anything about my relationships."

She gave me a look, one eyebrow raised, like she didn't need to say anything more. Like she did know. And maybe she did, at least in part. I hadn't exactly been shy about the fact that I wasn't interested in anything long-term with the girls I'd been with. But that didn't mean I was some player who didn't care about anyone.

I stared at her for a second, feeling something simmer beneath the surface—irritation, frustration... and maybe a little bit of guilt. Because the truth was, she wasn't entirely wrong.

I didn't do serious. I didn't let anyone get close enough to make things complicated. But it wasn't because I didn't care—it was because I didn't want to care. It was easier that way. Easier to keep things light, to not get attached, to avoid the mess that came with feelings.

I exhaled through my nose, leaning back in the chair again, staring into the fire. "Look, I don't owe you an explanation, alright?"

Hailey just shrugged, her smirk fading into something more neutral. "Didn't ask for one."

I didn't know what I was expecting from this conversation—maybe some teasing, some back-and-forth like we always did—but this was different. The look on her face, the way she said it... it wasn't just her usual smartass remarks. It felt personal.

"I guess..." Hailey said, her voice steady as she sat up straighter in her chair, "it's just something I don't like about you. How you go through so many girls all the time."

I blinked, my chest tightening a little. "What's that supposed to mean?"

She looked me dead in the eye, her expression serious now, all traces of the smirk gone. "It means... I just don't get how you can go from girl to girl like that. I don't see how you can treat them like... like they don't matter."

Her words hit harder than I wanted to admit. I opened my mouth to say something, to defend myself, but she wasn't done. "Me personally?" she continued, her voice softer now, like she was just stating a fact, not trying to insult me. "I feel like I'd get along so much better with someone who can treat one girl with respect. Someone who actually cares, you know?"

The fire crackled between us, but it was suddenly a lot quieter. I stared at her, feeling something twist uncomfortably in my gut.

Respect.

That word hung in the air between us, heavy and pointed. I'd never really thought of it that way before. I mean, yeah, I hooked up with girls, and yeah, I wasn't looking for anything serious... but I didn't think that meant I was disrespecting them. They knew what they were getting into, right? I never promised anything more than what I could give.

But hearing Hailey say it like that, hearing her flat-out tell me that she didn't like that about me... it felt like someone had poured a bucket of ice-cold water over my head.

For the first time in a long time, I felt... ashamed.

I'd never cared much about what other people thought of me. People talked, I did what I wanted, and that was that.

But this?

This wasn't just some random comment from a classmate or a teammate. This was Hailey—someone who knew me better than most, even if we didn't exactly get along. And the way she was looking at me now, like she was disappointed in me, like she was... judging me—it made something inside me twist.

I shifted in my seat, suddenly uncomfortable, unsure of what to say. I could feel the heat rising in my chest, not from anger, but from... shame.

"I don't treat them badly," I muttered, my voice low. It sounded weak, even to my own ears.

Hailey didn't say anything, just stared at me, her expression still serious.

"I mean... it's not like I promise them anything," I added quickly, feeling the need to defend myself. "They know what it is. I'm not lying to anyone."

She nodded slowly, like she'd heard that line before. "Yeah. Maybe. But still."

"But still... what?" I asked, more frustrated with myself than with her. "What else am I supposed to do?"

"I don't know," she said quietly, leaning back in her chair. "Maybe just... stop treating it all like it's a game."

I bit my lip, feeling the weight of her words press down on me. Stop treating it like a game.

I wanted to argue, to tell her she didn't know what she was talking about, that she didn't know me well enough to make those kinds of judgments... but I couldn't. Because the truth was, she wasn't wrong. I had treated it like a game. I'd made it easy to keep things casual, to avoid getting close to anyone.

But now, sitting here with Hailey, listening to her call me out for it... it made me feel like shit.

She wasn't saying it to be mean. That was the worst part. She wasn't trying to insult me—she was just being honest.

And that honesty hurt more than any of the snarky comments or sarcastic insults we'd thrown at each other over the years. I didn't say anything for a long time, just sat there, staring into the fire, feeling the weight of everything she'd said sink in. I'd never thought of myself as a bad guy. I figured as long as everyone knew the deal, I wasn't doing anything wrong. But now... now I wasn't so sure.

Hailey sighed, running a hand through her hair. "Look, I'm not saying you're a terrible person, okay? I just... I don't get it. I don't get how you can just... not care."

I swallowed, feeling the lump in my throat grow bigger. "I do care."

She gave me a skeptical look. "Do you?"

I clenched my jaw, staring into the fire. "Yeah. I do. I just... I don't know. It's complicated."

The silence stretched on, and eventually, Hailey leaned forward, poking at the fire with a stick. "Anyway," she said softly, breaking the tension. "It's not really my business, I guess."

It really wasn't. It never was. But it was already too late. The damage had been done.

I sat there, feeling like a weight had been dropped on my chest, and for the first time in my life... I didn't like the way I'd been living. Not because of what anyone else thought. But because of how it made me feel.

The weight of Hailey's words was still sitting heavy on my chest, making it hard to think, let alone speak. I stared into the fire, watching the flames flicker and dance, but all I could hear were her questions echoing in my head.

"I just..." I started, my voice low, almost like I wasn't sure I wanted her to hear me. "I don't know. I just wanted to have fun. And it's fun, right? Doing that, messing around with girls who are willing."

I glanced at her out of the corner of my eye, half-expecting her to roll her eyes or say something sarcastic. But she didn't. She just stared at me, her expression serious.

"But is it really fun?" she asked, her voice soft but pointed.

That made me pause. I opened my mouth to respond, to say of course it was fun—because it was fun, right? That's why I kept doing it. Hooking up with girls, keeping things light, avoiding complications... it was fun. That was the whole point.

But... was it, though?

I hesitated, staring into the fire again. "I mean... yeah. Sometimes."

She raised an eyebrow, clearly still unconvinced. "Sometimes?"

I swallowed, feeling that uncomfortable twist in my gut again. "Okay, fine. Maybe... maybe not all the time."

I could feel her eyes on me, watching, waiting for me to say more. And for some reason, I did. I didn't know why—I wasn't exactly the type to open up to people, especially her—but something about the way she was looking at me made it feel... different. Like she wasn't judging me. Just... trying to understand.

"Sometimes..." I started again, my voice quieter now, almost like I didn't want to admit it. "Sometimes I think about what it would be like. To take someone seriously. To have a girlfriend."

Hailey's eyes widened a bit, and I could tell I'd surprised her. "Really?"

I nodded, feeling weirdly exposed. "Yeah. I mean, I don't do it often, but... sometimes I wonder what it'd be like. To have someone who's mine. To go on real dates, to, you know... kiss someone because I want to, not because it's just... there."

I trailed off, feeling like I'd said too much. I could feel Hailey's eyes on me, but I didn't look at her. I couldn't. This wasn't something I'd ever admitted to anyone before, and now that I'd said it out loud, it felt... strange. Vulnerable.

"You think about that?" she asked softly, like she wasn't sure if she believed me.

I nodded again, finally glancing at her. "Yeah. Sometimes. I just... I don't know."

Hailey's expression softened, and for a moment, she looked almost... sympathetic. "Then why don't you have a girlfriend? I mean, you could have anyone. You're Callum Reid."

I snorted at that, shaking my head. "It's not like that."

She tilted her head, looking genuinely confused. "It kind of is. You're popular, good-looking—girls are all over you. So why haven't you... I don't know, picked someone? Why don't you just... try?"

I let out a long breath, staring into the fire again. "I don't know," I muttered, feeling that uncomfortable twist in my gut again. "It's just... easier this way."

"Easier?" she echoed, her voice quiet but curious.

"Yeah," I said, leaning back in my chair and rubbing the back of my neck. "What I'm doing now... it's easier. I don't have to worry about getting close to anyone. I don't have to worry about feelings, or... whatever. I can just... be."

Hailey didn't say anything for a moment, just watched me with that same soft, curious expression. "But you just said you think about it. About having someone. About... being with someone."

I did say that, didn't I? God, I was just so chatty tonight apparently. Who even knew what I was saying anymore. I shrugged, feeling conflicted. "Yeah. I do. But... I guess I just don't know how to make it work. And what I'm doing now... it's just easier. It's less complicated."

Hailey was quiet for a long time, just watching me, and I couldn't tell what she was thinking. Her expression was softer now, less judgmental, more... understanding.

And for some reason, that made me feel worse.

"Callum..." she started, her voice soft. "It's not supposed to be easy. That's the point. Relationships... they're hard, but they're worth it. If you find the right person."

I clenched my jaw, feeling that familiar twist in my gut again. "Yeah, well... I guess I haven't found that person."

She was silent for a moment, her eyes flicking down to the fire, and I could see the wheels turning in her head. She was thinking, processing, probably trying to figure me out.

Hell, I was trying to figure myself out.

"You know," I said, a little sharper than I intended, "you're pretty bold for giving me all this advice when you don't even have a boyfriend yourself."

Hailey blinked, taken aback, and for a second, I felt like an ass. But I couldn't stop. The words just kept coming out, like I was trying to defend myself or shift the focus away from me.

"I mean, you're sitting here, talking about how I should be serious, how relationships are so worth it, but where's your boyfriend, Hailey? Where's this serious relationship you're always talking about?"

For a second, I thought she was going to snap back at me, give me that usual sharp, sarcastic Hailey attitude. But instead, she just... sighed. She looked down at the fire, her expression softening, and when she spoke, her voice was quieter than before.

"Yeah," she said, her tone calm but a little sad. "Maybe I am bold. Maybe I'm giving advice I can't even follow myself."

I frowned, feeling that twist in my gut again. This wasn't the reaction I expected. I'd been ready for her to throw my words right back at me, but instead, she looked... vulnerable. And for some reason, that made me feel like even more of an ass.

"But... you know what?" she continued, still staring into the fire. "We have that in common."

I blinked. "What?"

She shrugged, her gaze still downcast. "Wanting something serious. Wanting something real."

I didn't say anything, just watched her, confused. She wasn't usually like this—this open, this... soft.

Hailey took a deep breath, and when she looked up at me, her green eyes were filled with something I didn't expect to see: sadness.

"You know, this is gonna sound really fucking pathetic of me, but when Adam did that big homecoming proposal to Sasha," she started, her voice quieter now, "I was jealous. Like... really jealous."

"You were jealous of Sasha?" I asked, incredulous.

She nodded, her expression serious. "Yeah. I mean, it was stupid, but... it hit me hard. Because it was the last homecoming we'll ever have. The last time in my life that someone could've asked me to homecoming, and... I had no one."

I didn't say anything, just listened, feeling like there was more she needed to get off her chest.

"I didn't have a date," she continued, her voice a little shaky now. "I don't have a boyfriend. And, honestly? It sucks. It really sucks because I keep seeing people around me, like Lance, or Adam and Sasha, or even you and all your flings... and I just keep thinking, 'Why not me?'"

I swallowed hard, not expecting this turn in the conversation. I didn't think Hailey ever really cared about that kind of stuff. She always seemed so put-together, so focused on school and her future, like she didn't give a damn about dating or relationships. But now, sitting here, listening to her say all this, it hit me that maybe... maybe she wanted those things just as much as I did. Maybe more.

"No one really takes an interest in me," she said, her voice quiet, like she was admitting something she didn't want to. "I've never had anyone ask me out, or do some big gesture like Adam did for Sasha. And I just... I don't know. I guess I'm jealous because it feels like I'm never going to have that."

I stared at her, feeling... guilty. Maybe even a little protective. It wasn't like Hailey to be so vulnerable, and hearing her talk like this made something inside me twist uncomfortably.

I didn't know what to say. I didn't know how to make her feel better or how to fix this. So, I just sat there, the fire crackling between us, feeling like the biggest idiot in the world for snapping at her earlier.

"I didn't know you felt like that," I said quietly, not really sure what else to say.

Hailey shrugged, looking down at her hands. "Yeah, well... it's not exactly like I go around talking about it."

We both went quiet again, the weight of the conversation settling between us. For the first time, I saw Hailey in a different light. She wasn't just the uptight, sarcastic girl I'd spent years bickering with. She was... someone who wanted what I wanted. Someone who felt lonely sometimes, who wanted something real.

"I didn't mean to snap at you," I muttered, feeling like I owed her an apology. "I just..."

She waved me off, giving me a small, tired smile. "It's fine, Callum. I get it. You're right, anyway. I don't have a boyfriend, so maybe I don't know what I'm talking about."

I frowned. "That's not what I meant."

"I know," she said softly, her eyes still on the fire. "But... it's still true."

We sat there in silence, both of us lost in our own thoughts, the fire crackling between us. I didn't know what to say to her, didn't know how to make her feel better. But I wanted to.

I wanted to tell her that she was wrong—that someone would take an interest in her, that she did deserve all those things.

Hailey sighed and shook her head, rubbing her hands over her face like she was trying to erase the conversation we'd just had. "Whatever. This is stupid," she muttered. "I'm being too deep about stuff."

I frowned, feeling a little awkward, but I wasn't sure what to say. The fire was still crackling between us, but the air felt different now. Heavier.

"I mean," I started, trying to lighten the mood a bit, "if you're so worried about it, I know some single guys from the soccer team. I could introduce you to one of them, and you two could... you know, fall in love or something."

Hailey scoffed, her eyes narrowing as she shot me a look. "Seriously?"

I shrugged, trying to play it off like I wasn't being completely ridiculous. "Yeah, I'm sure one of the guys would be into you. You're not bad-looking or anything. If you really want someone to love you, I'm sure one of the single guys on the team will fall for you right back."

She raised an eyebrow, her expression skeptical. "You seriously think someone can just... fall for someone? Just like that?"

I shrugged again. "Why not? It happens, right? People fall for each other all the time."

Hailey stared at me for a second, her green eyes searching my face like she was trying to figure something out. Then, out of nowhere, she leaned forward, her voice quiet but challenging.

"Okay," she said, her gaze intense. "Why don't you fall for me, then?"

I blinked, completely caught off guard. "Huh?"

She didn't break eye contact, her expression dead serious. "Fall for me, Callum. Love me. Can you do that?"

I froze, my brain short-circuiting for a second as her words sunk in.

Love me? Fall for me?

Was she messing with me? She had to be. There was no way she was serious. But the look on her face—the way she was staring at me, completely unflinching—made me question it.

"I... uh..." I stammered, trying to find words but coming up completely empty. "What... what are you talking about?"

Hailey's eyes didn't leave mine, her voice steady. "You said people can just fall for each other, right? So, fall for me. Love me. Show me how easy it is."

My mouth went dry, and for the first time in a long time, I didn't know what to say. She was challenging me, daring me to prove my point. And for some reason, I didn't know how to respond. "I..." I started, my voice weak. "That's not... I didn't mean—"

"Oh, come on," she cut in, her voice sharp but not angry. "You've been with so many girls. You could do it in your sleep, right? So, fall for me."

My heart was pounding in my chest now, and I had no idea why. This wasn't like our usual banter. This felt... different. Heavier. And it was making me feel things I wasn't ready to feel.

"I don't think it works like that," I muttered, shifting uncomfortably in my seat.

Hailey tilted her head, her eyes narrowing. "Why not? You said it was easy, didn't you? So what's the problem?"

The problem was, I didn't know what the hell I was feeling right now. She was throwing me completely off balance, and I didn't like it. I didn't like the way my heart was racing, the way my palms were starting to sweat. I didn't like the way she was looking at me—like she was daring me to do something dangerous.

"I..." I stammered again, completely thrown. "That's not..."

Hailey leaned back, her expression softening slightly, but the intensity in her eyes didn't fade. "Exactly," she said quietly. "It's not that easy, is it?"

I stared at her, feeling like I'd just lost a game I didn't even know I was playing. She wasn't messing with me. She was serious. And that realization hit me harder than I expected.

I didn't know what to say. I didn't know how to respond to her, how to explain why I suddenly felt like I was in over my head.

And the worst part? I wasn't sure why I couldn't just laugh it off. Why I couldn't just brush it aside like I always did.

But there was something about the way she'd said it— love me, fall for me—that stuck with me. Something about the challenge in her voice, the look in her eyes, that made me feel... uncomfortable. Vulnerable.

Hailey let out a long breath, shaking her head slightly. "See? It's not as simple as you think."

I didn't respond. I couldn't. My brain was still trying to catch up with everything she'd just thrown at me.

We sat there in silence for a long time, the fire crackling between us, and for the first time, I felt like I didn't know how to be around her. Like I didn't know how to act, how to talk.

I continued to stare at the fire, my heart still racing from the way Hailey had thrown her words at me. I couldn't stop hearing them. Over and over again.

Love me. Fall for me.

I didn't know why I couldn't let it go. Why it was sticking to me like glue. It was just a challenge, right? Hailey being... well, Hailey.

She probably didn't mean it.

It was just her trying to prove a point.

I watched her stand up, the words still hanging between us like smoke from the fire. She dusted off her hands, looking down at the flickering flames as if she hadn't just thrown a bomb into the conversation.

"Well," Hailey said, her voice a little too casual, "I should probably go to sleep. Sports Day is tomorrow, and I need all the energy I can get."

She started walking away, her footsteps light on the grass, and for a second, I just sat there, frozen. I should've let her go. I should've let her walk away and let the conversation die there.

But something inside me snapped.

Before I even knew what I was doing, I was on my feet. My hand reached out on instinct, fingers curling around her wrist. She froze, turning slightly, and our eyes met. The flickering light from the fire danced across her face, casting shadows on her skin, and for a moment, everything else disappeared.

"What..." she started, her voice softer now, unsure.

"Is that what you want?" I asked, my voice coming out low, but steady.

Her green eyes widened, and she blinked up at me, confusion crossing her face. "W-what?"

I stepped closer, still holding onto her wrist, my grip firm but not tight. "Is that what you want? You want me to fall for you?"

Hailey stared at me, her lips parting slightly, but no words came out. I could feel her pulse quicken under my fingers, and the air between us felt electric, charged with something I didn't fully understand.

"You want me to love you, Hailey Eller?" I asked, my voice dropping even lower, the weight of the question hanging heavily in the air.

Her breath caught in her throat, her eyes locked on mine, and for a moment, neither of us moved. Neither of us said anything.

The fire crackled in the background, but it was like the world had gone completely still, completely quiet, waiting for something.

But whatever it was, it never came.

CHAPTER 39
HAILEY

I DIDN'T SLEEP. NOT A SINGLE SECOND.

I lay there in bed, staring at the ceiling, my heart racing so fast I could practically hear it in my ears. No matter how many times I closed my eyes, no matter how many times I told myself to relax, my mind kept replaying those words over and over again.

"You want me to love you, Hailey Eller?"

What the hell had that been about? Why had he grabbed my wrist like that? Why had he said those things? Why did I say those things?

I let out a long, frustrated groan and turned over, burying my face in my pillow. None of this made sense. I wasn't supposed to feel this way. I wasn't supposed to be lying here, heart thumping like I'd just run a marathon, over Callum Reid, of all people.

But I couldn't shake it. I couldn't shake the way he'd looked at me, the intensity in his eyes, the way his grip had felt on my wrist. It had all been too much, too fast, and I hadn't known how to deal with it.

So I'd done the only thing I could do.

I'd pulled out of his grasp and bolted. Like a complete coward.

I'd practically sprinted back inside, my heart in my throat, not daring to look back. I didn't even stop until I was back in my room, the door shut firmly behind me as if that could somehow shut out the pounding in my chest.

Now, hours later, lying in my bed, exhausted but completely unable to sleep, I couldn't stop thinking about it.

What did he mean by that? Was he serious? Was he just messing with me? Or was it something else entirely?

I squeezed my eyes shut, trying to will the thoughts away, but they just kept coming back. His words, his eyes, the way he'd stood there, holding my wrist like he didn't want to let me go.

It was driving me crazy.

I rolled over again, grabbing my phone from the bedside table and checking the time. 5:30 AM. Ugh. I had to be up soon for Sports Day, and I felt like I'd been hit by a truck. My whole body was heavy with exhaustion, my brain foggy from lack of sleep, and yet… I couldn't stop thinking about him.

Why was I thinking about Callum Reid like this? Why was he stuck in my head like this? It didn't make any sense. We didn't get along. We bickered constantly. We weren't friends. We weren't even close to being friends.

So why did my heart skip a beat when he'd said those words to me last night?

I groaned again, tossing my phone back on the table and rubbing my hands over my face. This was so stupid. I needed to get over it. I needed to get out of my head and focus on Sports Day. There was no point in thinking about something that wasn't even real.

Besides, it wasn't like Callum was going to fall for me. That was ridiculous. He wasn't the kind of guy who just... fell for someone.

I shook my head, trying to clear my thoughts. I had to stop overthinking this. It didn't matter what Callum had said last night. It didn't matter what I'd said, either. We weren't going to fall for each other. That wasn't how this worked. We were two completely different people with completely different lives.

And yet...

I couldn't shake the feeling that something had shifted between us last night. Something I couldn't explain, something I wasn't sure I even wanted to explain.

I took a deep breath, sitting up in bed and running my hands through my hair. I needed to stop thinking about this. I needed to get my mind on something else, anything else. I couldn't let Callum Reid take up any more space in my head.

Not now. Not ever.

I dragged myself out of bed, my body heavy with exhaustion, and made my way to my closet. Today was Sports Day. Great. Just what I needed—a whole day of running around, competing in events, and pretending I hadn't spent the entire night tossing and turning because of Callum freakin' Reid.

I yanked open the closet door, sifting through my clothes until I found what I was looking for: a red hoodie. Since the seniors' assigned color was red this year, it was perfect.

I slipped it over my head, the soft fabric brushing against my skin, along with some comfortable leggings, and glanced at myself in the mirror. My hair was a mess from lack of sleep, and my eyes had those telltale dark circles under them. But I wasn't about to put in any more effort. I had bigger things to worry about than how I looked—like surviving the day without passing out from exhaustion.

I pulled my hair into a messy ponytail, deciding to leave it at that. Sports Day was always a bit of chaos, anyway. I doubted anyone would be paying much attention to how I looked. Besides, I had a job today: to document everyone else's fun, not to join in on the competitive madness.

I grabbed my camera and slung it over my shoulder, feeling its familiar weight. At least I had that to focus on.

Maybe if I kept myself busy with the yearbook duties, I could distract myself from the mess in my head.

Maybe.

I sighed, running a hand over my face. Today was going to be long. And awkward. Especially if I had to see him.

I shook my head, grabbing my phone and shoving it into my pocket. There was no way I was letting Callum get under my skin today. I couldn't afford it—not with all the stuff I had to do.

As I stepped into the kitchen, I spotted my parents at the table, sipping their morning coffee. My mom glanced up from her mug, smiling. "Morning, sweetie. Excited for Sports Day?"

"Thrilled," I muttered, grabbing a quick bite to eat before they could ask me any more questions. I wasn't in the mood for conversation, especially not about the chaos of the day or—God forbid—Callum.

"Callum already left," my dad said, taking a sip from his coffee. "Said he had to help the soccer team set up for the events."

Of course he did. Mr. Soccer Captain, always busy. I fought the urge to roll my eyes and just nodded, keeping my head down. It was better to avoid talking about him at all if I could help it.

After wolfing down my breakfast, I climbed into the passenger seat next to my mom, feeling the weight of exhaustion settle over me like a blanket. My mom glanced over at me as she backed out of the driveway, her brow creasing with concern. "You look really tired, sweetie," she said, her voice gentle. "Everything okay? Did you stay up too late?"

I shifted in my seat, trying to keep my expression neutral. "Uh… yeah, just had a hard time falling asleep, you know how it is."

It wasn't technically a lie. I had stayed up too late. I just wasn't about to tell her it was because I couldn't stop thinking about Callum's stupid words from last night.

My mom gave me a sympathetic smile, but there was a hint of suspicion in her eyes. She could always tell when something was up. "You know, if something's bothering you, you can talk to me. It's not just school stuff, is it?"

I hesitated, looking out the window as we drove. I couldn't tell her. I didn't even know how to explain it to myself, let alone to my mom. How was I supposed to tell her that the reason I looked like I hadn't slept in days was because her best friend's son had said something that had me questioning... everything?

"No, it's just Sports Day," I lied, offering a weak smile. "There's a lot to do. I've got yearbook duties, and... yeah. Just stressed about the usual stuff."

She raised an eyebrow but didn't push further. "Alright, if you say so. But you know I'm here if you ever need to talk. I'm always on your side, honey."

I nodded, grateful she wasn't pushing me. "Thanks, Mom."

The rest of the drive was quiet, but my mind was anything but. I stared out the window, trying to focus on the day ahead, but all I could think about was Callum and what the hell had happened last night. Why did he say that? Why had I even asked him to fall for me in the first place? It was all so confusing.

As we pulled into the school parking lot, my mom gave me a quick kiss on the cheek. "Good luck today, sweetie. Have fun."

"Yeah, thanks," I said, sliding out of the car and adjusting my hoodie. I gave her a quick wave before heading toward the school, trying to shake off the exhaustion and the whirlwind of thoughts that had kept me up all night.

As I walked into the school, adjusting the strap of the camera slung over my shoulder, I quickly spotted Nala standing by the lockers. Of course, she was already dressed head-to-toe in red, as if she were leading the senior pride parade. She even had a red headband on, which matched her bright red sneakers. Typical Nala—always extra, but somehow always making it look effortless.

"There you are! I thought you'd gotten lost or something," she said, bouncing slightly on her toes.

I rolled my eyes. "Please, I'm not that late. I just didn't get as into the senior spirit as you, clearly."

Nala smirked, gesturing to her outfit. "What can I say? I live for these moments. Speaking of, did you sign up for any events?"

I shook my head, adjusting the camera around my neck. "Nope. I'm just here to take pictures and eat all the food."

Nala made a face, crossing her arms over her chest. "Ugh, booooring."

I playfully smacked her arm. "Excuse me? If I didn't take the pictures, who would? Besides, I thought you loved having pictures taken of you."

She grinned, flicking her red headband into place. "Okay, valid. But still. You didn't sign up for any of the events? Not even one?"

I shook my head, adjusting my camera again. "Nope. Just here to document the chaos and maybe grab some snacks."

"Lame," Nala teased, sticking her tongue out. "I signed up for volleyball and the thirty-person musical chairs contest. And let me tell you, it was a tough decision between that and the fifty-person one."

"I didn't even know there were such events," I snorted. "There's a fifty-person musical chairs contest? Why didn't you do that one?"

"Because, Hailey, the fifty-person one has way more rounds, and I value my energy, thank you very much. I'm all for competition, but there's only so much chaotic chair-fighting a girl can handle."

I couldn't help but giggle, imagining Nala in the middle of a musical chairs brawl. I saw the logic, though. Fighting 29 other people would probably be less of a struggle than 49 other people. "Good call, I guess."

Nala grinned, clearly proud of herself. "Exactly. Plus, I'm gonna dominate in volleyball. You should've signed up for that at least."

I raised an eyebrow. "Me? Volleyball? You've seen me play, right? I don't think me flailing around like a baby giraffe is what the seniors need to secure a win."

She laughed. "Fair point. But still, you could've signed up for something. What about the Occult Club's event? I heard it's creepy as hell. Apparently, you have to, like, compete to summon a spirit."

I stared at her, my eyebrows shooting up. "They do that shit on Sports Day?"

"Apparently! I guess they got bored of regular sports," Nala said, grinning. "It's probably just an excuse to mess around with candles and creepy chants. But, you know, points for originality."

I scrunched my nose. "Yeah, I think I'll pass on that one. I'm here for chill vibes, not creepy occult stuff."

"Lame again!" Nala said dramatically, throwing her hands up in mock exasperation. "But fine. If you find something that sparks your interest, you better sign up."

I smiled, feeling a little more at ease now that I was with Nala. She had a way of lightening the mood, and I needed that right now—especially after last night. "Yeah, yeah. If something catches my eye, I'll think about it."

She winked. "That's all I ask."

The energy at the field was electric as everyone filed into the bleachers, buzzing with excitement for the first event of Sports Day: the grade relay race.

It was the biggest event, the one everyone looked forward to every year. Almost everyone from each grade participated, which meant a whole lot of running, cheering, and —if previous years were anything to go by—a few dramatic tumbles on the track.

I made my way to the yearbook club's designated spot on the sidelines, where Lisa and Derek were already setting up. Em was adjusting her camera, and Lance was busy organizing the layout plans for the day's events. I waved to them, positioning myself to get some good shots.

The track was packed with students, each grade lining up around it, getting ready for the big race. Freshmen were at the far end, sophomores next to them, then the juniors, and finally, the seniors. Our class was a sea of red shirts, standing out against the underclassmen's colors. The seniors had the most participants this year, naturally. We all wanted to make our mark before we left Westview behind.

I snapped a few photos of the chaos: some students warming up, others chatting nervously, and then, of course, the soccer boys who were all part of the relay for the seniors. It wasn't a surprise that they'd signed up—they were competitive by nature, especially Callum.

Speak of the devil. I glanced at Callum, who was stretching out near the starting line. His red shirt was snug against his broad shoulders, and I couldn't help but notice how serious he looked. He was definitely in game mode.

"Hey, Hailey! Get a few shots of all the grades, okay?" Lance called over, pointing toward the far side of the track.

"On it," I said, turning my camera toward the freshmen, though my eyes kept wandering back to the seniors.

As I focused on getting more pictures, a small figure suddenly stepped up to the podium near the track. I almost missed him because, well, Principal Smalls being small, yada yada.

He raised the megaphone, and his squeaky voice crackled through the speakers. "Alright, Westview students! Let's get this day started! First up, we have the grade relay race!

Remember, this is a marathon, not a sprint. Teamwork is key. Let's show some school spirit and make this a race to remember!"

The crowd erupted into cheers as the racers got into position. The freshmen were a bundle of nerves, while the seniors—led by the likes of Callum and the other soccer players —looked determined, like they had every intention of showing the younger grades who was boss.

Principal Smalls raised a tiny hand and blew the whistle, officially kicking off the race.

The runners surged forward, and the crowd roared. I lifted my camera, capturing the frenzy as the racers zoomed past, the seniors already taking an early lead.

"Go seniors!" someone in the crowd yelled, and the red-shirted section of the bleachers exploded with cheers.

I shifted my focus from the track to the crowd, snapping pictures of the students cheering, capturing the energy of the day. But every now and then, my lens found its way back to the track, back to the familiar face of Callum Reid, determined as ever.

The race was picking up momentum, and my camera was clicking non-stop as I tried to capture everything. My attention kept bouncing between the runners and the crowd, but it always came back to the track—especially as the senior relay team got closer to Callum's turn. Adam Parker had just grabbed the baton and taken off like a bullet.

I zoomed in on Adam as he sprinted down the track, his face determined and focused. He was fast, no doubt about it, and the seniors were maintaining a strong lead. I snapped a few photos of him mid-stride, the muscles in his legs straining with each powerful step. He was giving it everything he had.

"Go Adam!" someone shouted from the bleachers, and a wave of cheers followed as he neared the end of his stretch.

I lowered my camera for a moment, knowing what was coming next. Callum was up next for the seniors, and even though I'd seen him run during soccer games, something about this race felt different. The intensity was palpable.

Adam neared the handoff point, and I could see Callum in position, his entire body coiled like a spring, ready to take off the second the baton was in his hand.

The moment Adam slapped the baton into Callum's grip, everything changed.

He took off.

And I mean, *really* took off.

The second Callum's feet hit the track, it was like a blur of red and speed. He was so fast. I could barely track him with my camera as he sped forward, his long legs eating up the distance in what felt like no time at all. His focus was razor-sharp, his entire body streamlined as if he were born to run.

I quickly lifted my camera, zooming in on him as best as I could. Click. Click. Click. Each shot showed him mid-sprint, the wind pushing back his dark hair, his red shirt clinging to his body as his muscles flexed with every step. His form was perfect—he made it look so damn easy.

My heart pounded a little as I watched him, completely in his element, focused only on reaching the finish line. The crowd was losing it, people screaming his name as he sped past the juniors and sophomores. He was pulling the seniors even further ahead, creating a gap that seemed almost impossible to close.

"Go, Callum!" someone shouted from the senior section, and the roar of support grew even louder.

I swallowed, feeling that weird flutter in my chest as I kept snapping pictures of him. His speed, his strength, the way he moved—it was all… kind of impressive. I hated to admit it, but there was something captivating about watching Callum when he was like this. Like everything else in the world faded away, and it was just him, the track, and the finish line.

He reached the final stretch and passed the baton off to Grayson Hart, the final runner for the seniors. The crowd erupted again, and I lowered my camera, my heart still racing from just watching him.

"Damn," I muttered under my breath. I didn't even realize I was smiling a little.

Callum jogged off the track, breathing heavily but looking completely unfazed by the fact that he'd just blazed through his part of the race like it was nothing. He glanced over at the bleachers, and for a brief moment, our eyes met.

I quickly turned back to my camera, pretending to adjust the lens, but I could feel my face heating up.

The final stretch of the relay was intense. Grayson Hart, the seniors' last runner, was tearing down the track, his eyes locked on the finish line.

The entire senior section of the bleachers was on their feet, screaming their lungs out, hoping Grayson would maintain the lead that Callum had helped create.

"Seniors, seniors!"

Behind him, the sophomore runner was quickly gaining ground, and the juniors weren't far behind. It was close—closer than anyone expected—but the seniors still had the tiniest lead, just that edge.

I kept my camera trained on Grayson, snapping photos as he pushed forward with everything he had. The crowd's roar was deafening, and I could feel the adrenaline in the air, even from the sidelines.

My heart pounded in time with the cheers.

Grayson crossed the finish line first, and the crowd exploded into cheers and applause. I snapped a few more photos of him as he slowed down, his chest heaving, but a victorious grin on his face. The seniors had won.

"Seniors win!" Principal Smalls' voice crackled over the speakers, barely audible over the cheering students.

I exhaled, lowering my camera as the seniors on the track gathered together, high-fiving and hugging each other.

The seniors in the bleachers were chanting, "Seniors! Seniors!" as if they'd already won the entire Sports Day just from this race. The sophomore runner crossed the line shortly after, securing second place for their grade, and the juniors came in third, looking a bit defeated. Freshmen, predictably, finished last, but they seemed just happy to finish the race without any major incidents.

I zoomed in on the finish line again, snapping a few more photos of the runners as they congratulated each other. The seniors were in full celebration mode now, with some of the soccer boys tackling each other in victory. Callum was at the center of it all, grinning and laughing with his teammates.

I couldn't help but smile a little as I captured the moment. I might've rolled my eyes at the senior pride thing before, but... yeah, I guess it was kind of cool to see them win.

As the runners began to disperse, Callum jogged off the track, looking for a moment like he might head toward the bleachers where the yearbook crew and I were standing. I quickly turned my camera back to the crowd, trying to act like I hadn't just been staring at him.

Because I hadn't.

No way.

"Got some good shots?" Lance asked, coming up behind me and peeking over my shoulder.

"Yeah," I said, nodding. "The relay was definitely worth it. These shots are gonna turn out great."

"Cool. Might need you to send some of those over later for the yearbook layout," he said. "Especially the ones of Callum and the soccer guys. They're probably going to want some pics for the sports section."

I rolled my eyes. "Of course they will."

Lance chuckled. "Hey, they won, didn't they? They deserve the glory."

I watched as Callum and the others walked off the track, still high on their victory. As annoying as he could be, I had to admit he was a part of why we won that race.

Maybe today wouldn't be as boring as I thought.

CHAPTER 40

HAILEY

THE REST OF THE MORNING WAS, IN A WORD, CHAOTIC. AFTER THE BIG RELAY RACE, I figured things might calm down a little, but I was completely wrong. If anything, Sports Day just got crazier from there.

There were so many events happening all over the field and the gym that it was impossible to keep track of them all. Tug of war, the hula hoop race (which I didn't even know was a thing), a ridiculous balloon relay where people had to run with a balloon between their knees without dropping it... And then there was basketball, a three-legged soccer match, because apparently, someone thought playing soccer with your legs tied to someone else's was a good idea.

And, of course, in nearly every single event, there was Callum.

I couldn't escape him if I tried. Every time I turned around, there he was, competing in something like he had all the energy in the world. Tug of war? Yep, there he was at the front of the line, pulling with all his strength. Hula hoop race? Somehow, he was involved in that too, even though I didn't peg him as the hula-hooping type. But nope, he was there, looking surprisingly graceful for someone his size as he twirled the hoop around his hips and sprinted toward the finish line.

I mean, come on. Was this guy in every single event? It felt like no matter where I pointed my camera, Callum was there. I wasn't trying to focus on him, but it was impossible not to when he was everywhere.

By the time the balloon relay came around, I was half-convinced Callum had a clone or something. I stood on the sidelines with my camera, snapping pictures of students awkwardly waddling with balloons between their knees. I spotted Callum on the senior team, of course, holding a balloon between his legs like it was nothing, while the rest of his team struggled to keep theirs from dropping.

I lowered my camera and let out a sigh. As much as I wanted to avoid thinking about him, there he was, constantly in my line of sight. It was like the universe was conspiring against me, making sure I couldn't get through this day without being reminded of him.

And it wasn't just that he was participating in everything —it was how good he was at it all. Whether it was running, shooting hoops, or even balancing a balloon between his knees, Callum somehow made everything look easy. The way he moved, the confidence in his steps, the energy he radiated... it was impossible not to notice.

I clicked the camera a few more times, focusing on the other seniors, but every now and then, I'd catch myself sneaking a glance at Callum. I hated that he was taking up so much of my attention, but it wasn't like I could help it. He was everywhere.

And then, of course, there was basketball. Callum was intense, his movements sharp and precise as he dodged and passed the ball, sinking shots with ease. He might have been known for soccer, but it was clear he was an athlete, through and through. The seniors ended up winning that game, too, which meant more high-fives and celebrations from Callum's group.

Then came the three-legged soccer, where the chaos truly began. Watching people try to play soccer while tethered to their partners was both hilarious and nerve-wracking. Some teams managed to find their rhythm, while others collapsed into a tangled mess of limbs. Callum, naturally, was partnered with Adam Parker, and they somehow made it look almost easy— well, at least compared to everyone else. I captured a few shots of them moving in sync, Callum laughing as they maneuvered around the other players.

It was so frustrating. I wasn't supposed to care. I wasn't supposed to keep noticing him. But how could I not when he was just... there? I groaned internally and forced myself to focus on the task at hand—documenting the day for yearbook, not for my personal entertainment.

"Hailey, you got any good shots of the morning games?" Lance called over, snapping me out of my thoughts.

I cleared my throat, pretending I wasn't hyper-fixated on a certain soccer player. "Yeah, I've got some good ones. I'll send them over later."

Lance grinned. "Awesome. We're definitely gonna need some action shots of Callum and the other guys. The sports section will love it."

"Of course they will," I muttered under my breath, rolling my eyes.

As much as I hated to admit it, I knew Lance was right. The soccer boys were basically the stars of the school, and Callum was the brightest of them all. I just had to keep my head down and get through the rest of the day without losing my mind.

Lunch break had finally arrived, and the entire school flooded into the cafeteria. My legs felt like jelly from all the walking around and snapping pictures, and I was more than ready to sit down for a while. The school had set up some refreshments—nothing fancy, just some sandwiches, fruit, and drinks—and I grabbed a plate before plopping down at an empty table.

I pulled out my phone and shot a quick text to Nala.

Me: *Where are you?*
Nala: *With some girls preparing for the volleyball game. You okay?*
Me: *Yeah, just tired. Might pass out at this table.*
Nala: *Lol, don't die. Come watch us play after the break!*

I promised I'd be there and slipped my phone back into my pocket. For now, I just wanted a moment of peace. I glanced around the cafeteria, watching as everyone milled around, grabbing food and chattering excitedly about the morning's events. The senior section was particularly loud, still buzzing with energy after the relay win. It was nice, seeing everyone so hyped up, but it was also a little overwhelming.

I sighed, taking a sip of my drink. Just as I started to relax, I felt a presence behind me, followed by the sound of chairs scraping against the floor.

"Mind if we sit here?"

I looked up, blinking in surprise as Callum stood in front of me, holding his tray of food. Behind him were Grayson Hart, Ibra James, and Adam Parker, all of them carrying trays and looking around the packed cafeteria.

"Uh…" I glanced around, noticing that, sure enough, all the tables were filled. It looked like every available seat was taken. "I guess?"

Callum didn't wait for a second invitation, plopping down in the seat directly across from me. The others followed suit, Grayson and Adam sliding into the seats beside Callum, and Ibra sitting next to me.

"There were no more tables left," Callum explained, though he didn't really seem apologetic about it. He just dove right into his food, taking a massive bite of his sandwich.

I stared at him for a second, then looked around at the group of guys now surrounding me. Great. Just what I needed—four of the most popular boys in school sitting at my table.

To be honest, it was a little... intimidating.

Grayson Hart, the forward on the soccer team, was tall and lean, with an intense look that screamed "I will destroy you on the field." I'd snapped more than a few photos of him during games, and I knew how seriously he took soccer. He was currently picking through his salad like he didn't trust it.

Ibra James, the goalie, was always cool and collected, and he gave off an air of quiet confidence. He nodded at me in greeting, but mostly kept to himself, sipping on his water. I'd never really spoken to him before, but he had a reputation for being one of the calmest guys on the team—until you tried to score on him, of course.

Then there was Adam Parker, Callum's best friend and partner-in-crime. Adam had this goofy, boy-next-door vibe, always joking around and making everyone laugh. Right now, he was in the middle of some story about a ridiculous prank he'd pulled on one of the juniors, gesturing wildly with his sandwich in hand.

And, of course, Callum was... Callum. Sitting there across from me, shoving food into his mouth like he hadn't eaten in days. His hair was a bit messy from the morning's activities, and his red senior shirt clung to his broad shoulders. I glanced away quickly before I started staring again.

This wasn't awkward at all. Nope. Totally normal.

"So, Hailey," Adam said between bites, drawing my attention back to him. "You're the yearbook photographer, right?"

I nodded slowly. "Uh, yeah. Why?"

"Do you think you got my good side today during the relay?" he asked, grinning. "I need to look my best for the yearbook, obviously."

I couldn't help but smile a little. "Pretty sure I got your 'I'm-about-to-pass-out' side."

Grayson snorted, finally looking up from his salad. "You're not wrong. Bro was dying out there."

"Hey, I was strategically pacing myself," Adam defended, looking mock-offended.

"Right," I said, nodding. "Strategically."

I felt Callum's eyes on me, but I didn't look up. He hadn't said much since sitting down, but I could feel his presence as if it was weighing on the air between us. The table wasn't exactly huge, and with the four of them sitting around me, it was hard not to feel a bit... crowded.

As the lunch conversation swirled around me, I found myself relaxing—just a little. The guys were a lot more easygoing than I expected, and despite the intimidating aura they usually carried around school, they were... well, normal.

Sure, they joked around a lot, but they weren't making fun of me or being condescending. In fact, they actually made an effort to include me in their conversation, which was kind of surprising.

It wasn't long before Grayson turned his attention to me, breaking through my thoughts. "Hey, Hailey," he said, his voice a bit hesitant, as if he wasn't sure how to approach the next topic. "We just wanted to say, um... about all that stuff we used to say. You know, the whole 'photo girl' thing."

I froze, my sandwich halfway to my mouth, and blinked at him.

Grayson rubbed the back of his neck awkwardly. "We didn't really mean anything by it. We were just messing around, but looking back... yeah, it was kind of a dick move. Sorry about that." I stared at him, a little caught off guard by the sudden apology. I wasn't sure what to say.

I had spent years hearing them call me "photo girl" with that weird, mocking edge to their tone, and suddenly... they were apologizing?

It felt kind of surreal.

Grayson cleared his throat, looking a bit uncomfortable. "Yeah... about that. I'm pretty sure I was one of those people who made those dumb comments back then."

I raised an eyebrow, waiting for him to continue.

"Listen," he said, running a hand through his hair. "I don't think any of us realized how annoying that nickname was. We were just messing around, you know? But looking back, it was pretty lame of us. I'm sorry if we made you feel bad."

I wasn't sure how to respond at first. Apologies weren't exactly what I was expecting today, but here we were.

Adam chimed in next, his usual playful tone replaced with something more genuine. "Yeah, same here. I think we all kind of contributed to that 'photo girl' thing, but honestly? It's actually cool that you're into photography. Like, the stuff you do for yearbook now? That's pretty awesome. And... well, we didn't mean to offend you or anything back then."

I looked between the two of them, surprised by how sincere they sounded. Even Ibra, who had been quiet for most of the conversation, nodded in agreement. "Photography's dope. We just didn't get it back then."

I glanced at Callum, wondering if he was going to say anything. He was still eating, but I could tell he was listening to the conversation, his eyes flicking over to me every now and then. He didn't apologize—at least, not outright—but something in the way he was acting made me think he wasn't oblivious to the conversation.

I cleared my throat, feeling a bit awkward but also oddly... relieved. "Thanks, guys. I appreciate that. It's not like I was losing sleep over it or anything, but... yeah, it did kind of suck back then."

"Totally understandable," Adam said with a grin. "But hey, at least now you're the yearbook photographer. That's gotta feel pretty good."

I shrugged, but I couldn't help but smile a little. "It's not bad. I like it."

"See?" Grayson said, nudging Callum. "Told you the whole 'photo girl' thing wasn't as bad as we made it out to be. She's cool with it."

Callum finally looked up, his mouth still full of food. "What?"

Grayson rolled his eyes. "Nothing, man. Just saying Hailey's cool."

Callum grunted, not looking particularly interested in the conversation, but I could see the faintest smirk tugging at the corner of his lips. Typical Callum—never fully letting his guard down, but still paying attention.

I let the conversation flow back into their usual banter, relieved that the awkwardness had faded. Honestly, the guys were a lot friendlier than I'd expected. Maybe it was just the Sports Day energy, or maybe they were all in a good mood after winning the relay and all the other random things they'd participated in all morning, but whatever it was, I wasn't feeling as out of place as I had earlier.

We talked about random stuff for the rest of lunch—Adam cracking jokes, Grayson complaining about how sore his legs were from the relay, and Ibra quietly chiming in with sarcastic one-liners that had me snorting into my drink.

It was... nice, in a way. Not something I'd ever imagined happening, but it wasn't bad.

I stood up, brushing crumbs off my lap. "Well, guess I should get back to work. Gotta regroup with the yearbook team before taking more pictures of you guys being super athletes."

Adam grinned. "Make sure to get my good side again."

I shook my head, but I couldn't help the small smile tugging at my lips. "Yeah, yeah."

CHAPTER 41

CALLUM

I watched as Hailey got up from the table, excusing herself after lunch was over. She slung her camera over her shoulder and gave us a quick wave before heading off to probably take more pictures. I found my eyes following her as she walked away, her hoodie swaying a bit as she disappeared into the crowd.

"Yo, she's actually kinda cool," Grayson said, breaking the silence as soon as Hailey was out of earshot.

I turned my attention back to the guys, who were all smirking at me in that knowing way that only guys who were about to start shit could.

"Yeah," Adam chimed in, grinning like an idiot. "I mean, I always thought she was just the 'quiet nerdy girl,' but she's got some bite, man. I like it."

I rolled my eyes. "She's fine. Let's not make it weird."

Ibra leaned back in his chair, crossing his arms over his chest with a smirk. "Oh, come on, Callum. Don't tell me you're not noticing the same things we are. The girl's kinda cute when she's not glaring at you."

"She glares at him a lot, though," Grayson pointed out, laughing.

"Yeah, but she's got fire," Adam added. "And you love fire. Admit it, dude."

I shot them all a look, trying to steer the conversation away from wherever they were trying to take it. "Don't start, okay? We barely even talk outside of, like, the morning drive to school. That's it."

"Oh, so that's why you kept sneaking glances at her the whole time we were talking just now?" Grayson teased, wiggling his eyebrows.

"I wasn't sneaking any glances," I muttered, feeling my jaw tighten. Had I been? Maybe. But that was only natural when she wss sitting right here, wasn't it? What, was I supposed to just not look at her the entire time?

"Uh-huh," Ibra said, clearly not convinced. "Sure, man. Whatever helps you sleep at night."

I shot him a look, but before I could say anything else, I felt something prickling at the back of my neck. A sense of being watched. I turned slightly and, sure enough, across the cafeteria, I saw her—Natalia.

She was sitting with a few of her friends, but her eyes were locked on me, and the look on her face was... not friendly. More like she was glaring at me like I had personally offended her. I quickly looked away, feeling a bit uncomfortable.

It had been weeks since I'd last hooked up with her— probably the longest it'd ever been between us—and I hadn't reached out to her once.

The thought of it just... didn't appeal to me anymore. Not like it used to. I didn't know why, but every time I even thought about calling her or texting her, I just didn't feel like it. There was no spark, no desire to reach out. Nothing.

We'd both agreed there were no strings attached—it was all just physical fun, period. Once one of us got tired of it, it stopped.

But judging by the way she was staring me down from across the cafeteria, she wasn't too happy about it.

"Yo, Callum," Adam said, snapping me back to the present. "What's with that face? You look like you've seen a ghost."

The ghost of a situationship, maybe. I shook my head, turning my attention back to my friends. "It's nothing. Just... thinking."

Grayson leaned in a little, lowering his voice. "Is it Natalia? She's been throwing daggers at you for the past ten minutes, man."

"Yeah, I noticed," I muttered, running a hand through my hair. "I haven't really talked to her in a while."

Adam whistled. "Damn, how long's it been? You two were always... you know."

"Yeah, well, I'm not really feeling it anymore," I said, shrugging. "It's whatever."

The guys exchanged glances, clearly surprised by my sudden disinterest. "Wow, man. You're not into any of it anymore?" Adam asked, raising an eyebrow. "That's new."

I shrugged again, not really wanting to get into it. "Just got other stuff on my mind, I guess."

Grayson smirked. "Other stuff, huh? Like, say... a certain photo girl?"

I shot him a glare. "Shut up."

He and Adam burst out laughing, while Ibra just shook his head, smirking but staying quiet.

I sighed, feeling more irritated than I wanted to admit. But it wasn't because of the teasing—it was because of the stupid truth of it all. I hadn't been able to get Hailey out of my head. It was messing with me, and I hated it. I didn't want to think about her like that, but every time I saw her... it just happened. She was everywhere, and it was driving me crazy.

And the fact that Natalia was now glaring at me like I owed her something didn't help at all.

Whatever. She could keep glaring and sulking by herself. I already told her what I was looking for with her, I kept it clear, and she'd pissed me the hell off with how she treated Hailey on homcoming, so.

The bell signaling the end of lunch echoed through the hallways, and soon enough, we were all filing into the gymnasium. The next event on the schedule was the girls' volleyball match, and it seemed like half the school had crammed into the bleachers to watch. I spotted a few girls from the volleyball team warming up on the court, their ponytails bouncing as they practiced their serves.

As usual, the guys wasted no time in making their typical comments.

"Yo, check out Brianna over there," Ibra said, nodding toward one of the girls on the court. "She's looking fine as hell."

Grayson snickered. "I've always had a thing for volleyball girls. Something about those shorts, man."

I rolled my eyes, only half-listening as they continued to list off the girls they found hot. Normally, I'd join in on the banter, maybe even throw in a comment or two of my own. But today, I wasn't feeling it. I wasn't as hyped as usual, and for some reason, the idea of ogling the girls felt... stupid. I didn't know why. It just did.

"Callum, what about you?" Adam asked, nudging me with his elbow. "You got a favorite on the court?"

I shrugged. "Nah. Just here to watch the game."

Adam raised an eyebrow, clearly not convinced. "Yeah, right. You're not fooling anyone, bro."

I didn't bother arguing with him. Instead, my gaze drifted across the court, scanning the gymnasium for something —someone—else.

Hailey was standing off to the side, near the edge of the court, adjusting her camera and fiddling with the settings as she prepared to take more photos. Her red hoodie from earlier was gone, and now she was wearing just a simple t-shirt, the senior red still standing out against the crowd.

She was focused, her eyes glued to her camera, oblivious to everything else around her.

Too close, I thought to myself, frowning.

She was practically standing right on the edge of the court, a few feet away from the net. The game hadn't started yet, but I knew how these volleyball matches went. Balls flying everywhere, people diving left and right... it wasn't exactly the safest place to be standing if you didn't want to get knocked over.

I couldn't help the small knot of concern that formed in my stomach. What if she got hit? What if one of the girls accidentally spiked the ball right into her face or something? She didn't look like she was paying attention to anything but her camera, and I could already see a ball going rogue and smacking her straight in the head.

I found myself shifting in my seat, my eyes still locked on her. The guys were still talking around me, making comments about the players, but I was barely listening. My focus was completely on Hailey now.

Suddenly, Adam's voice cut through my thoughts. "Hey, Callum, you good?"

I blinked, turning back to him. "What?"

"You've been staring off into space for the past five minutes, man," Adam said, raising an eyebrow. "What's up? You not feeling the game?"

I glanced back at the court, where the players were finishing up their warm-ups. Then my eyes drifted back to Hailey again, still too damn close to the action for my liking.

"Nothing," I muttered, standing up. "I'll be back."

Adam exchanged a look with Grayson, but they didn't say anything as I made my way down the bleachers and toward the court.

As I got closer to where Hailey was standing, I could see she was completely immersed in what she was doing. Her camera was pressed to her face, and she was snapping photos of the players as they stretched and chatted. She was so focused that she didn't even notice me approaching.

"Hailey," I called out as I stepped up beside her.

She lowered her camera, turning to look at me in surprise. "Wha is it?"

I crossed my arms over my chest, trying to sound casual. "You're standing too close to the court."

She blinked, glancing around like she hadn't even realized where she was. "I am?"

"Yeah," I said, nodding toward the court. "You're gonna get hit if you stay here. Volleyballs fly everywhere. Trust me."

She frowned, glancing at the court again, then back at me. "I'm just trying to get good pictures. This is the best angle."

I raised an eyebrow. "And it's also the best angle to get smacked in the face by a ball."

She let out a small laugh, shaking her head. "I'll be fine."

I rolled my eyes. "Yeah, well, I've seen it happen. One second you're taking pictures, and the next, you're on the ground with a busted nose."

She gave me a skeptical look, but I could see her considering it. "Are you seriously worried about me getting hit by a volleyball?"

"I'm seriously telling you to stand a little farther back," I said, more sternly than I meant to. "Just listen."

She hesitated for a moment, her eyes studying me like she wasn't sure if I was being overprotective or if I actually had a point. But after a few seconds, she sighed and took a step back, moving a little farther from the court.

"Happy now?" she asked, raising an eyebrow.

I shrugged. "Better. Just don't stand too close. I'm telling you, it's dangerous."

She gave me a small, amused smile. "Okay, okay. I'll be careful, Captain Reid."

I ignored the teasing tone in her voice, but a part of me felt oddly relieved that she'd listened to me. I gave her a quick nod before turning to head back to the bleachers. As I walked away, I could still feel her eyes on me, but I didn't look back.

The guys were waiting for me when I got back, smirking like they knew exactly what I'd been doing.

"Making sure your photographer is safe?" Adam teased, winking.

I shot him a look. "Shut up."

But even as I sat back down, my eyes found Hailey again. She was still taking pictures, but now she was standing farther from the court, just like I'd asked.

And for some reason, that small thing—her listening to me—made me feel a little better.

I barely had time to settle back into my seat before a familiar scent hit me—Natalia's perfume. I clenched my jaw, immediately knowing what was coming as she slid into the empty space next to me, way too close for comfort. She leaned in, her shoulder brushing against mine, and I could practically feel the smugness radiating off her.

"So…" she purred, her voice dripping with sarcasm. "You finally replaced me with photo girl over there, huh?"

I shot her a sideways glance, already irritated. "Shut up, Natalia. It's not like that."

She raised an eyebrow, her lips curling into a smirk. "Oh, really? 'Cause it sure looks like it. You've been running after her like a lost puppy lately. I mean, is this what you're into now? The quiet, nerdy types?"

I felt my fists clench at my sides, trying to stay calm. "What I'm into isn't your business."

Her smirk only grew wider, and she leaned in closer, her breath hot against my ear. "I don't know, Callum. It sure looks like it's become everyone's business. People are starting to notice."

I turned my head slightly to glare at her. "What's that supposed to mean?"

Natalia let out a soft, condescending laugh, brushing a strand of her red hair behind her ear. "Oh, you know how people talk. Word gets around. The soccer captain and the yearbook photographer? That's not exactly a match people saw coming."

I groaned, annoyed. "You're blowing things way out of proportion. She's just... someone I know."

"Just someone you know, huh?" Natalia scoffed, crossing her arms over her chest. "So why is it that you're paying more attention to her these days than to me? It's been weeks, Callum. You've barely said two words to me, and now all I see is you hanging around her. What gives?"

I sighed, rubbing the back of my neck, not wanting to get into this here, of all places. "Look, Natalia. It's not... like that. I've just got a lot going on. The team, school, everything. I don't have time for all this drama."

Natalia snorted, clearly not buying my excuse. "Right. 'Cause you used to have all the time in the world for me, and now suddenly, you don't? Please. Don't treat me like I'm stupid, Callum."

I was about to snap back at her, but then she glanced toward the court, where Hailey was still standing, taking pictures. I could already see that gleam in Natalia's eyes, the one that always meant trouble.

"She's not even that cute," Natalia said, her voice dripping with disdain. "I don't know what you see in her, but whatever it is, you're wasting your time."

Something snapped inside me. Where the hell did Natalia get off with just insulting Hailey for no reason? Only I was allowed to do that. I turned sharply to face her, my voice low but firm. "Watch it, Natalia. I'm serious. Don't piss me off."

Natalia blinked, clearly surprised by the intensity in my voice. For a second, she looked like she might back off, but then she rolled her eyes, muttering under her breath.

"Whatever, Callum," she said, standing up abruptly. "Do what you want. But don't come running back to me when you realize you're bored with your little photography project."

Before I could respond, she was already walking away, going back to sit with some of her other friends who had been looking over at us like a bunch of otters. I let out a long breath, feeling my frustration simmering just below the surface.

Natalia's words echoed in my mind, and for the first time, I realized just how deep this whole thing was getting. It wasn't just that people were noticing—I was noticing. And I didn't know how to deal with it.

"Shit," I muttered under my breath, running a hand through my hair.

The gym was buzzing with energy as the girls' volleyball game wrapped up. Cheers and applause filled the space, and I could see some of the girls on the court high-fiving each other as they made their way off the court. The guys' game was up next, and sure enough, Adam and Grayson were already on the sidelines, getting ready for their turn.

I, thankfully, was sitting this one out. Not that I didn't like volleyball, but after being in so many events already, I was ready to just chill for a bit.

That was when I noticed Hailey and Nala walking toward us, making their way through the crowd.

Hailey spotted me, her eyes narrowing a bit, and I could already tell that we were about to start bickering.

"Mind if we sit here?" Hailey asked, her voice teasingly sweet as she pointed to the open spot beside me.

I shrugged. "It's a free country."

Nala plopped down next to Ibra, and Hailey sat beside me, immediately turning to watch the guys warming up on the court. I could feel the tension brewing between us, as usual, and I knew it wouldn't be long before one of us started something.

"You know, you could learn something from them," Hailey said, gesturing toward the players on the court.

I frowned, glancing at her. "What's that supposed to mean?"

She smirked. "Just saying, you could use some finesse. You always go full force with everything, but volleyball? That takes skill. Precision."

"Yeah, right," I muttered. "I could take any of those guys down if I wanted to."

She gave me a sideways glance, raising an eyebrow. "Sure, big shot. Keep telling yourself that."

"Why don't you just shush for once, Eller? You're lucky I'm not playing, or I'd embarrass every guy out there."

She snorted. "Yeah, I'm sure you would, Captain Reid. You're a real volleyball prodigy."

I was about to fire back with another retort when she suddenly nudged me and nodded toward Ibra and Nala, who were sitting on the other side of me.

"Hey, look at them," Hailey whispered, her voice lowering a bit. "They're really hitting it off."

I glanced over and, sure enough, Ibra and Nala were deep in conversation, their heads tilted toward each other as they talked and laughed.

It was kind of surprising, actually. I hadn't seen Ibra like this with a girl in a while, and Nala was grinning, her eyes sparkling as she listened to whatever he was saying.

I rolled my eyes. "Oh, you think you're cupid now?"

She shrugged, leaning back against the bleacher. "Hey, if it works, it works. I think they'd be cute together."

"You really are trying to your bestie up, aren't you?" I teased, crossing my arms over my chest. "You can't help yourself, can you?"

She gave me a playful grin. "I'm just saying, if I see a good match, why not nudge them in the right direction? Plus, Nala deserves someone nice. And Ibra's... nice."

I raised an eyebrow. "Nice? That's all you've got?"

She laughed. "You know what I mean. They're vibing."

I shook my head, amused. "You're really something, Eller. Trying to be a matchmaker now."

"Better than being a manwhore," she shot back, grinning mischievously.

I groaned. "Are we back to that? I thought we moved on."

She just shrugged, her eyes twinkling with mischief. "Some things never change."

I rolled my eyes again, but I couldn't help the small smile tugging at the corner of my mouth. She was impossible, but in a weird way, I was starting to get used to it.

As the guys' volleyball game kicked off, I found myself glancing at Ibra and Nala again. They were still talking, their conversation flowing easily, and I couldn't help but admit that Hailey might have been onto something.

"Alright, fine," I muttered. "Maybe you're not completely delusional about those two."

"See? I knew it." Hailey shot me a smug look. "Hey, maybe watching them will help you pick up a few tips on how to be less of a disaster when it comes to relationships."

I scoffed, but deep down, I knew she wasn't entirely wrong. Maybe I did need to figure my shit out when it came to girls, but I sure as hell wasn't about to admit that to her.

"What, you off photo duty now?" I asked Hailey, watching her as she lazily fiddled with her camera strap.

She rolled her eyes, leaning back against the bleachers. "I'm just taking a break, okay? Is that such a big deal?"

I shrugged, smirking a bit. "I don't know, maybe it's a big deal to someone who's trying to capture all the 'best moments' of the day."

Hailey snorted, giving me a sideways glance. "You're acting like I'm not allowed to sit down for a second. Besides, I've already got a ton of good shots. Don't you worry, soccer boy."

As the guys' volleyball match wrapped up, with the seniors coming in second, Grayson and Adam made their way back to the bleachers, grumbling a bit about the outcome. Of course, they were met with some light teasing.

"Second place, huh? Guess you guys aren't as good as you think," I said, raising an eyebrow.

Adam groaned, wiping sweat from his forehead. "Oh, shut up. At least I'm playing."

Grayson punched him lightly on the arm, laughing. "Yeah, don't get too cocky, Reid. Dodgeball's next. You better bring your A-game."

I rolled my eyes. "Don't worry, I will."

I stretched a bit, standing up as they announced the dodgeball game. Each grade had twenty people, and I was, of course, part of the seniors' team. I looked across the gym and saw the other grades gathering up their players. The tension was already building, especially since dodgeball could get pretty intense.

Then I spotted Natalia, already standing among the seniors, with that glint in her eye that I knew all too well. She was definitely planning something.

My gut twisted slightly, but I pushed it aside. I wasn't about to let her throw me off.

Mr Hayes, the teacher in charge of overseeing the dodgeball game, was just about to blow his whistle when Natalia raised her hand dramatically, her voice echoing through the gym. "Wait! Mr Hayes, the seniors only have 19 players!"

I frowned, glancing around at our team. She was right. We were one player short.

Natalia's lips curled into a smile, and she turned her gaze right toward Hailey, still sitting next to me. "How about Hailey Eller joins us? Come on, photo girl, we need you."

I froze, my gaze snapping to Hailey. She looked just as shocked as I felt, her eyes wide as she stared at Natalia from across the gym.

Shit. Natalia was definitely up to something.

CHAPTER 42

HAILEY

My heart was pounding in my ears as I handed my camera to Nala. "Here. Keep this safe for me," I muttered, trying to steady my breathing.

Nala raised an eyebrow, taking the camera carefully. "Are you sure about this? You could just say no."

I glanced down at the gym floor, where Natalia stood, smirking like the devil herself. I straightened my shoulders, determination hardening in my chest. "Yeah, I'm sure."

Nala gave me a look, but she didn't push it. "Alright, but be careful. And if you survive this, I'll help you get Natalia back."

I snorted, rolling my eyes. "If I survive? Thanks for the pep talk."

She grinned and waved as I turned to face the stairs leading down to the gym floor. My stomach twisted with nerves, but there was no way I was backing down now. Not with Natalia watching, waiting for me to chicken out.

I carefully made my way down the bleacher stairs, feeling like everyone's eyes were on me. Callum was standing by the edge of the court, his arms crossed over his chest, and when he saw me, his expression softened — just for a second. He stepped closer as I reached the bottom of the stairs.

"You sure you're good?" he asked, his voice low.

"I'm fine," I replied, though my heart was still racing. I gave him a small nod. "Let's just... do this."

Callum didn't look convinced, but he stepped aside, letting me join the team on the floor. The rest of the seniors were gathering up, ready for the dodgeball game to start, but I couldn't shake the knot in my stomach. Natalia stood a few feet away, tossing a ball up and down in her hands, her eyes glinting with mischief.

Just focus, Hailey, I told myself. *Don't let her get to you.*

The whistle blew, and the game was on.

Immediately, balls started flying everywhere. I ducked out of the way as one zoomed past my head, narrowly missing me. I scrambled backward, trying to find some cover behind one of the taller players, but I wasn't fast enough.

WHAM.

A ball hit the ground right beside me, and I jumped, turning to see Natalia standing there, her arm still raised from the throw.

I blinked in confusion. What the hell?

I glanced around. We were on the same damn team. Why was she throwing at me?

Natalia smirked, shrugging her shoulders as if to say, *Oops*, like she hadn't done that shit on purpose.

What the actual fuck? I thought, dodging another ball as I backed away from her.

I shook my head, focusing back on the game. Maybe it was just a mistake. A misfire. But as the game continued, it became harder to ignore the fact that every time I dodged a ball, Natalia seemed to be the one throwing it in my direction.

And she wasn't missing.

I ducked again, feeling the rush of air as another ball whizzed past my shoulder. My blood boiled, frustration building with every throw. I managed to grab a ball of my own and threw it toward the other team, but my aim was shaky, and it didn't hit anyone.

"Hailey! Watch out!" Callum's voice cut through the noise just as another ball came flying toward me. I jumped out of the way, barely avoiding it, and when I looked up, I saw Natalia smirking at me again.

That was it. I was done.

She's trying to get me out. We were literally on the same team, and she was deliberately throwing at me.

"What the hell is your problem?" I snapped, stepping closer to her, but before I could say anything else, I had to dodge another ball from the opposing team.

Natalia just shrugged, her smile widening. "Whoops. Guess my aim's just off."

Yeah, right.

I gritted my teeth, focusing on staying in the game, but the more I dodged, the more I realized this wasn't just about the dodgeball game. Natalia was trying to send a message. She was still pissed about... what? The fact that Callum and I had been around each other more lately? The fact that I was staying at his house?

Get over it, I thought bitterly, ducking behind another player just as Natalia lobbed another ball my way. But there was only so much dodging I could do.

As I crouched down, trying to stay out of the line of fire, I glanced over at Callum. He was locked in his own game, focused on the other team, but every once in a while, I caught him looking my way.

I wasn't sure if it was to make sure I was still in the game or if he was noticing Natalia's little "accidents" too, but either way, it pissed me off even more.

I dodged one more throw, and before I could even process what was happening, another ball came flying toward me.

I threw dodgeballs at people from the other grades, ducking and weaving to avoid the incoming ones from the opposite side. But the thing that made it almost impossible to concentrate was the fact that I had to keep an eye on the balls coming from behind me. The ones Natalia was throwing.

What kind of teammate literally aims at their own team?

Either she didn't know the rules at all or she was trying to hurt me. And I was putting my money towards the latter.

I grit my teeth, dodging another one of her throws. This was beyond ridiculous. If she wanted me out so bad, why not just come out and say it? The other team didn't even have to try anymore — Natalia was doing their job for them.

Just as I thought I was out of her line of fire for a second, I felt it.

SMACK.

A ball hit me square in the back of the head, so hard that I stumbled forward, clutching my skull. Pain exploded at the back of my head, and for a second, everything around me blurred. I could hear someone shouting, but it sounded muffled, like I was underwater.

"Hailey's out!" Natalia's shrill voice rang through the gym, loud and triumphant. "She's out!"

I blinked, trying to clear my vision, but my heart was racing. My hands trembled as I reached for my head, the sting from the hit spreading through my skull. I could feel the heat rising in my cheeks, and anger bubbled in my chest.

Before I could even think of what to say, before I could turn around and give Natalia a piece of my mind, someone grabbed my arm — firmly.

I looked up at him, blinking through the haze of pain. "Callum—"

But he wasn't listening. He was staring past me, his jaw clenched, his eyes dark with fury.

"Natalia!" His voice rang out across the gym, booming in a way I had never heard before. The sound of it made my stomach flip, and from the shocked looks on some of the other players' faces, I wasn't the only one caught off guard by it.

"What the hell do you think you're doing?" Callum barked, his grip tightening on my arm.

Natalia froze, her smirk fading slightly as she met Callum's glare. She raised her hands in mock innocence, batting her lashes. "What? I was just playing the game."

"Playing the game?" Callum's voice was ice. "You're supposed to be on our team, not aiming for your own fucking players."

Natalia crossed her arms, rolling her eyes. "It was just a mistake. I didn't mean to—"

But before she could finish her sentence, Callum cut her off. "You meant to do it, and we both know it."

I stared up at him, wide-eyed, as the tension in the gym thickened. Callum was fuming — like, absolutely livid. I'd seen him mad before, but this... this was different.

His whole body was tense, his fists clenched, and his eyes burned with something I couldn't quite place. It was a mix of anger and protectiveness, and it was all directed at Natalia.

For a split second, I saw a flicker of something in Natalia's expression—maybe guilt, or fear—but it quickly vanished, replaced by her usual arrogance.

"Whatever," she muttered, turning her back on us. "She's out. Get over it."

I expected Callum to say more, to keep yelling, but instead, he turned back to me, his hand still gripping my arm. "Come on," he said quietly, his voice tight with barely-contained frustration.

Before I could protest, he was dragging me out of the gym, his hand firm around my wrist as we pushed through the gym doors and into the hallway.

"Callum, what—" I tried to speak, but the words got caught in my throat. The adrenaline from the hit and the tension with Natalia had my head spinning.

He didn't stop until we were outside the gym, in the empty hallway. Finally, he let go of my arm, running a hand through his hair as he paced in front of me.

I stood there, still trying to process everything that just happened. My head throbbed, both from the dodgeball and from the sheer intensity of the moment. I swallowed hard, the words finally coming out in a rush.

"What the hell was that?" I asked, my voice shaky but strong. "Why did you scream at her like that?"

Callum stopped pacing, turning to face me. His expression was still stormy, his jaw clenched. "Because she was out of line. She had no right to do that to you."

I blinked, my heart still racing. "But—"

"No, Hailey," he interrupted, his voice firm. "She knew exactly what she was doing. She's been doing this since the moment she called you down to play."

I opened my mouth to argue, but… he was right. Natalia had been targeting me. But Callum's reaction, the way he screamed at her, the way he dragged me out of there—it was like something snapped inside him.

"Look," I said, trying to calm myself down. "I appreciate you standing up for me, but you didn't have to scream at her like that. I'm not some damsel in distress, Callum. I can handle myself."

Callum's shoulders slumped slightly, some of the tension leaving his body as he let out a long breath. "I know," he said quietly. "I just… I couldn't stand seeing her do that to you. She crossed a line."

I stared at him, unsure of what to say. His anger wasn't just about Natalia hitting me with a dodgeball. It was deeper than that.

But I wasn't sure I wanted to dig into it. Not now.

I glanced back toward the gym doors, feeling a surge of frustration bubbling up again. "Well, I'm not going back in there," I muttered, rubbing the back of my head. "She'll probably throw another ball at me just for fun. Or a chair if she's feeling extra pissed off."

Callum's expression softened slightly, his eyes flicking to where I was rubbing my head. "Does it hurt?" he asked, his voice softer now, but still carrying a tense edge.

Before I could answer, he stepped closer, his hand reaching up. I froze as his fingers gently brushed against the back of my head, cradling it like he was worried I'd break.

I blinked up at him, caught off guard by the sudden tenderness in his touch. "No," I mumbled, my voice barely a whisper. "It doesn't hurt."

He didn't seem convinced, his eyes searching my face as his thumb lightly grazed the spot where the ball had hit me. "Are you sure?"

I nodded, my throat dry. "Yeah... I'm sure."

He stayed there for a moment, his hand still cupping the back of my head, and I felt my heart thudding in my chest—faster than it should've been.

His touch was warm, and despite the tension from earlier, I felt a strange sense of calm wash over me. Like for a second, nothing else mattered. Not Natalia, not the dodgeball game, not even the fact that we were supposed to be mortal enemies. It was just... us. Standing there in the empty hallway.

I swallowed hard, trying to make sense of the moment. "Callum, I'm fine. Really."

He blinked, as if snapping out of whatever trance he'd been in, and slowly let his hand drop from my head. The warmth from his touch lingered, and I had to fight the urge to reach up and touch the spot myself.

"Alright," he said, his voice gruff again, like he was trying to shake off the softness from earlier. "But if it starts hurting more or anything, tell me."

I gave him a small nod, still feeling a little out of sorts from the whole thing. My head didn't hurt that badly anymore, but the way he was looking at me—like he genuinely cared—was throwing me off balance.

"Thanks," I muttered, not sure what else to say.

He shoved his hands into his pockets, taking a step back and glancing around the hallway, like he didn't know what to do with himself. "Yeah. Sure."

The silence stretched between us, awkward and heavy, but neither of us seemed to know how to break it. Callum looked like he wanted to say something more, but instead, he just ran a hand through his hair and let out a long breath.

The doors to the gym burst open behind us, and I barely had time to register the footsteps rushing toward us before I saw Nala, Ibra, Adam, and Grayson charging over.

"Yo, Callum! What the hell happened, man?" Adam called out, jogging up beside us. The teasing lilt in his voice told me he didn't think it was anything serious, but one look at Callum's face probably told him otherwise.

Callum's eyes hardened again, and with a brief nod to me, he turned toward the guys. "We're leaving," he muttered, brushing past them. The guys exchanged glances, and then, in typical fashion, they started teasing him relentlessly.

"What, you had to play hero and save Hailey from dodgeball?" Grayson smirked, elbowing Callum in the side. "That's cute, man. Didn't know you had it in you."

"Yeah, totally swoon-worthy," Adam added, snickering.

"Shut up," Callum growled, but his lips quirked up slightly as he walked off with them. They continued ribbing him as they all headed back inside, leaving me standing there with Nala, who looked like she was ready to throw down.

"I swear to god, if that nasty bitch ever touches you again, I'm gonna rip her hair out," Nala snapped, her eyes flashing with fury. She was practically vibrating with anger, her hands clenched into fists at her sides. "I'm gonna do more than I..."

"Nala, what did you do?" I asked, narrowing my eyes suspiciously.

She crossed her arms, huffing and staring in the direction of the gym, like she was trying to direct all her negatiive energy at Natalia. "I threw a ball at her face."

I blinked, taken aback. "What? But... you weren't even playing!"

She shrugged, completely unfazed. "Who cares? That cow deserved it after what she did to you."

I couldn't help it—I laughed, despite everything that had just happened. "You're ridiculous, you know that?"

Nala grinned, the tension easing slightly as she wrapped her arms around me, pulling me into a tight hug. "Yeah, well, that's what best friends are for."

I hugged her back, my earlier frustration melting away in the comfort of her embrace. "Thanks, Nala," I whispered, feeling a lump form in my throat. As much as I wanted to play it cool, her fierce protectiveness meant the world to me.

Nala pulled back, her expression softening. "No one messes with my best friend, okay? You deserve better than that bullshit."

"I know," I mumbled, my chest feeling a little lighter. "Thanks for always having my back."

"Always," Nala said, squeezing my hand before stepping back, her grin returning as she returned my camera to me. I nodded, taking a deep breath to steady myself. The hit to the back of my head still stung a little, but Nala's words and

Callum's unexpected protectiveness were enough to make me feel like maybe... things would be okay.

As we turned to walk away, I couldn't help but glance at Callum's retreating figure. He was surrounded by his friends, laughing and joking, but something about him looked a little... different.

I wasn't sure if it was the way he'd stormed to my defense, or the way he'd cradled my head so gently in his hands, but something in my chest felt off-balance, like the ground had shifted beneath me.

And I wasn't sure if I liked it or not.

CHAPTER 43
HAILEY

THE CAFETERIA WAS UNUSUALLY QUIET FOR THE FIRST TIME ALL DAY, AND NALA and I took full advantage of the peace, sitting down with popsicles in hand.

I needed the break after everything that had happened during dodgeball. We sat back, enjoying the cool, sugary treat, when Nala—true to form—came up with her latest weird-ass food combo.

She dipped her popsicle into a cup of ranch dressing.

I stared at her, horrified but also morbidly curious. "Nala, seriously? Ranch? With a popsicle? Girl, I'm seriously concerned for you."

"Don't knock it until you try it!" she sang, dipping it again and licking off the mixture. "It's weird, but it's got that sweet and tangy thing going on. Trust me, you're missing out."

"Yeah, well, I'll pass," I muttered, making a face as I took another bite of my normal popsicle. "You know, one of these days, you're going to make yourself sick with these weird combinations."

Nala just shrugged, clearly unfazed by my warning. She had a stomach of steel, apparently. As I shook my head, something else caught my attention. A sudden rush of movement from the girls around the cafeteria. They were getting up, leaving their seats, and practically sprinting toward the doors. I raised an eyebrow, watching them as they fled in droves.

"What's going on now?" I asked, confused. "Why are they all leaving so fast?"

Nala popped the rest of her popsicle in her mouth, sucking on it as she leaned back in her chair. "Oh, it's probably the final event of the day. The fan favorite."

"Fan favorite?" I echoed, curiosity piqued.

She nodded, grinning. "Yeah, Capture the Flag. Everyone loves that one. It's boys only, and trust me, you'll see why all the girls are flocking to the field."

I arched an eyebrow, finishing off my popsicle before tossing the stick into the trash. "Alright, let's check it out."

We stood and made our way out of the cafeteria, following the trail of excited girls toward the field. The moment we stepped outside, I could see what Nala was talking about. The bleachers were already packed with students, mostly girls, and a few boys who were probably just there to watch the chaos unfold.

I glanced toward the field, my eyes widening a little as I took in the scene. It was absolute boy mania.

The guys were getting ready, but that wasn't what had everyone's attention. No, it was the fact that almost all of them were shirtless, their shirts tied around their heads like makeshift headbands.

Apparently, Capture the Flag was the one event where they got to get physical—tackling, shoving, and basically roughhousing to their heart's content.

And judging by the reactions from the bleachers, it wasn't just the competition that had everyone so excited.

"Okay, I get it now," I muttered under my breath, finding an empty spot in the stands with Nala.

The boys were already on the field, most of them shirtless with their shirts tied around their heads like makeshift headbands. They were stretching, shoving each other playfully, and... well, I could see why this was a fan favorite.

It was a sea of muscle, bare skin, and adrenaline-fueled testosterone. And yeah, I'll admit it—there was a certain appeal to seeing guys tackle and roughhouse like they were in a wrestling match. It was primal, competitive... and apparently a hit with the crowd.

Nala nudged me, waggling her eyebrows. "Told you. Boy mania. This is what people live for on sports day."

I rolled my eyes, though my heart had started to race a little faster. "It's just guys running around. Big deal."

"Uh-huh. Sure." Nala leaned back in her seat, clearly entertained by my reaction. "I saw your face. You were definitely looking."

"I was not," I muttered, folding my arms over my chest.

I definitely was.

"Sure, sure," she teased, her smirk growing wider. "Come on, who's caught your eye?"

I glared at her, trying to brush it off, but... then I saw him. Callum. And suddenly, my heart wasn't just racing. It was sprinting.

He was shirtless, too, just like the others, and his skin gleamed in the afternoon sun, muscles rippling with every stretch and movement.

He wasn't just built—he was... god, I hated myself for thinking it, but he was perfectly built. His broad shoulders, toned arms, the sharp cut of his abs. It all came together in this infuriatingly perfect package that made my brain short-circuit.

"Oh, fuck," I whispered to myself.

"Hmm?" Nala leaned in, smirking like the devil herself. "Who are we eyeing, Hailey?"

"No one!" I hissed, desperately trying to tear my gaze away from Callum. But it was too late. I couldn't stop looking.

Why the hell does he have to look like that? My traitorous brain supplied images of that stupid ab picture he sent me weeks ago, and now it felt like I was seeing it in high-definition.

"Sure, sure," Nala said again, but this time her voice was knowing, like she had me figured out. "You're totally not checking out a certain shirtless soccer captain, huh?"

I shot her a look. "Can you not?"

But before Nala could tease me any further, the whistle blew, signaling the start of the game. The field erupted in shouts and cheers as the boys took off, charging toward the center of the field, tackling and shoving as they fought for the flag.

Despite myself, my eyes kept drifting back to Callum. He was in the thick of it, effortlessly dodging players and bulldozing through anyone who got in his way. His shirt was still tied around his head, but his face was serious, determined, like he was in the zone.

And the way his muscles flexed with every movement, the sheer power behind his steps…

I swallowed hard.

Nala was right. It really was boy mania. And god help me, I was right there with the rest of them, watching it unfold.

She nudged me again, breaking me out of my daze. "Uh, shouldn't you be capturing pics for the yearbook?" she asked, popping her gum as if she hadn't just made my internal freak-out worse.

I blinked, my heart skipping a beat. "R-right." My voice came out shaky, and I internally cursed myself. Pull it together, Hailey. Focus.

But focusing was easier said than done.

The cheers and shouts of the crowd barely registered as I positioned my camera, but instead of snapping the first shot, I just stood there.

I couldn't stop watching Callum.

Every move he made was confident, purposeful, and... yeah, a little too mesmerizing for my own good. My fingers trembled on the camera as I finally lifted it to my eye, trying to pretend I was just doing my job.

Click.

The camera caught a moment of the game, but my lens was focused on him—his serious expression, the way his jaw clenched as he dodged a tackle. Even through the lens, the intensity of it all hit me.

Nala leaned back, sighing contentedly. "It's wild, right? How sports bring out the animal in them. Look at them go. Honestly, it's like watching a bunch of action figures come to life."

She wasn't wrong. The field was pure chaos—guys throwing themselves at each other, chasing after the flag like their lives depended on it. Callum was in the middle of it all, focused, and aggressive in a way that was... different. It was like seeing a whole new side of him, one that was serious and unstoppable.

"You're getting some good shots, right?" Nala asked, leaning over to peek at my camera screen. I quickly flipped it off before she could see what—or rather who—I'd been zoomed in on.

"Yeah, totally. Got some good action shots," I mumbled, trying to play it cool.

But it was clear Nala wasn't buying it. Her knowing smile widened as she casually popped a piece of gum in her mouth.

"You know," she began, drawing out her words, "there's nothing wrong with a little eye candy now and then. Just saying."

I glared at her, though I could feel my cheeks heating up. "Nala, I'm working here. Can you please not?"

"Whatever you say, girl," she teased, turning her attention back to the game. But I knew better. She'd be back to teasing me about Callum before the day was over.

I tried to refocus on the game, but my attention kept drifting back to Callum. He was in the thick of it, going full beast mode on the field. Every time he tackled a junior or darted past someone trying to grab the flag, I couldn't help but notice the way his muscles flexed with every movement. He was covered in a thin sheen of sweat, his skin gleaming under the sunlight. Each drop rolled down his chest, catching the light, and—dammit.

I swallowed hard, the heat rising in my face as I watched him plow through another player like it was nothing. He wasn't just playing; he was dominating. There was something wild, almost primal, in the way he moved, as if the game were a battlefield and he was some kind of warrior in it. The other guys didn't stand a chance, and it wasn't just his skill—it was the way he carried himself. Confident, unstoppable, and yeah, a little dangerous.

I couldn't tear my eyes away from him. And I hated myself for it. I was no better than all the other girls in the bleachers right now, ogling the guys like they were some kind of spectacle. It felt ridiculous, objectifying, and yet…

I was doing it anyway.

Damn it.

My face burned as I glanced down, pretending to adjust my camera, but my mind was still racing. This wasn't supposed to happen. Callum was supposed to be the one person who annoyed me more than anything, the guy who I swore I couldn't stand. So why the hell was my heart pounding like this?

I risked another glance at the field, just as Callum charged toward the opposing team's flag. His eyes were sharp, focused, and determined, and for a split second, I forgot how to breathe. His body collided with another player, a junior, sending him sprawling to the ground like it was nothing.

The roar of the crowd intensified as the final whistle blew, signaling the end of the game. Callum stood in the middle of the field, flag in hand, his chest still rising and falling with every breath. The juniors were scattered around the field, defeated, and the seniors erupted in cheers, high-fiving and embracing each other in victory.

I blinked, trying to pull myself out of the daze I'd fallen into. Right. Sports Day. The seniors had won.

I glanced over at Nala, who was grinning like an idiot. "Looks like your soccer captain came through, huh?"

"Shut up," I mumbled. "He's not 'mine.'"

The PA system crackled to life, and the voice of none other than Principal Smalls boomed over the speakers, his excitement clear. "Seniors, congratulations! You have won Sports Day!"

The bleachers erupted again, and I couldn't help but join in the clapping, though my heart still hadn't slowed down from earlier. I tried to focus on Principal Smalls, who continued, his voice full of pride for the senior class. "As promised, your prize for this year's Sports Day victory is..."

A drumroll sounded over the speakers, and Nala gave me an eager look, her eyes sparkling with excitement.

"A trip during winter break to a luxury hotel in the mountains for a few days of rest, relaxation, and fun!" Principal Smalls announced, and the crowd went wild.

Nala grabbed my arm, shaking it in excitement. "Oh my god, Hailey, we're going to the mountains! Can you imagine how awesome it's going to be?"

I couldn't help but smile at her enthusiasm. It did sound pretty incredible.

The stands were still buzzing with excitement as the crowd slowly started to disperse, the adrenaline from the Capture the Flag game lingering in the air. Callum and the other seniors had claimed victory, and Sports Day officially wrapped up with cheers echoing through the field. I stretched my legs, feeling a mix of exhaustion and relief.

Nala, still brimming with energy, nudged me with her elbow. "So, Halloween's coming up in a few weeks," she said, her voice lilting with excitement. "Sasha's having a big party again this year. Doesn't that sound like fun?"

I made a face, pulling my bag over my shoulder as we made our way out of the bleachers. "Fun is one way to describe it, I guess…"

"Exactly!" Nala said, as if that was the selling point. "Plus, I heard this year she's going all out—costume contest, decorations, the works. Come on, don't you wanna try coming this time? It'll be epic, and you know everyone's going to be there."

I hesitated. Normally, parties weren't my scene. I'd skipped every one of Sasha's parties so far, and Callum would definitely be there, which only made things more complicated. The idea of being around him, with all those people, in a costume no less? It made me nervous just thinking about it.

"I don't know…" I trailed off. "Maybe."

Nala gave me a look, sensing my reluctance. "Maybe? Come on, Hailey! It's Halloween. You gotta live a little! Plus, you can go all nerdy and creative with a costume. You'd kill it."

I bit my lip, the thought of a costume distracting me for a moment before I glanced down at the camera hanging around my neck. "I'll think about it," I said quickly. "But I still have to hand this off to Lance for yearbook stuff. I'll be right back, okay?"

Nala raised an eyebrow, clearly amused but letting it slide. "Alright, I'll wait by the bleachers. Don't take too long, though. We've got some planning to do."

As I turned to leave, I couldn't shake the feeling that this Halloween was going to be different.

Whether I wanted it to be or not.

CHAPTER 44

CALLUM

I LAY SPRAWLED ON MY BED, STARING UP AT THE CEILING, STILL FEELING THE DULL ache in my muscles from yesterday's Sports Day.

What the hell had possessed me to sign up for so many damn events? I wasn't sure, but my body was paying for it now. But at least we won. Not that there was any other option. The seniors were stacked this year, and with the season we'd been having in soccer, I couldn't afford to let up on anything.

Soccer season was winding down, and we were in a good spot. Our track record so far was solid, but there were still a few more matches ahead—key ones—that would determine whether or not we made it to division champions.

No pressure or anything.

I rolled my shoulders, trying to loosen up the tightness there. It was all I could think about lately. The team, the plays, our chances. Coach had been on my case more than usual, but I got it. This was my year to prove I had what it took, not just as a player but as a leader.

Still, a break would've been nice. But of course, I had to go all out yesterday. Dodgeball, Capture the Flag, the relay, even the damn hula hoop race. My hips were definitely reminding me of that brilliant decision.

With a groan, I pushed myself up and rubbed my face. Saturday morning. Nothing on the schedule today except... well, maybe some extra practice. Couldn't hurt to keep sharp, right? I wasn't the kind of guy who could sit still for long anyway.

I threw on a t-shirt and some sweatpants before heading downstairs, my body protesting with every step. The soreness lingered, but I'd push through it. I always did.

As I reached the bottom of the stairs, something caught my attention—whistling. Soft, casual, like whoever it was didn't have a care in the world. I stepped quietly into the kitchen and peeked around the corner.

Hailey was standing by the counter, humming some random tune and focused on whatever she was mixing in a bowl. She didn't even notice I was there. I stood there for a second, just watching her, half-amused.

Then she turned around, and the second she spotted me, her eyes went wide. "AHH!" She jumped back, nearly knocking over the bowl, her scream loud enough to wake the whole house.

I grinned, leaning against the doorway. "Geez, calm down, Eller. It's just me."

She glared at me, her face flushed. "What the hell, Callum? Don't sneak up on people like that!"

I couldn't help but laugh at her reaction. "Didn't think you'd be so jumpy. What are you even doing?"

"Baking," she said, as if it were the most obvious thing in the world.

I raised an eyebrow. "Baking? At ten in the morning? On a Saturday?"

She crossed her arms, clearly not in the mood for my teasing. "Sorry, didn't know there was a specific time when you're allowed to bake."

I chuckled, stepping further into the kitchen. "Fair point. So, what are you making?"

"Breakfast pastries," she said, turning back to the counter and resuming whatever she'd been doing. "I saw a video of it on TikTok last night and figured I'd try it."

I shook my head, still smiling. "I see."

She shot me a look over her shoulder. "What? You think I can't bake?"

"Never said that," I said, holding up my hands in surrender. "Just didn't take you for the 'impulsive TikTok baker' type."

"There's a lot you don't know about me, Callum," she muttered, going back to her bowl, though I caught the small smile tugging at the corners of her lips.

I leaned against the counter, watching her work for a second. "You know, if those pastries are good, I'm claiming first dibs."

She rolled her eyes but didn't argue further. "We'll see about that."

I collapsed onto the couch, letting out a heavy sigh as I sank into the cushions. My muscles were still sore from yesterday, but at least I had the day to recover. With nothing better to do, I grabbed the remote and flipped on the TV, finding an old World Cup replay to zone out to.

As I settled in, something black caught my eye, sitting on the far end of the couch. I reached over and picked it up, inspecting it.

"What's this?" I asked, holding it up.

Hailey glanced over from the kitchen, her hands still sticky from whatever pastry creation she was whipping up. "Oh, that's my Kindle."

"Your what?" I raised an eyebrow, looking at the sleek black device and turning it over. It looked a little like an iPad, thin, sleek, and black, with a soft screen.

She rolled her eyes like I was the dumbest person alive. "My Kindle. I read books on it. You know, since I lost my whole book collection in the fire, that's where I read now."

"Oh." I paused, the realization hitting me. I'd heard of stuff like this before. I think. "Interesting, I guess."

She turned back to her baking, clearly not interested in explaining further, but I was still curious. I tapped the screen and it flickered on, lighting up with what seemed like... a book?

I started scrolling through the text, curious to see what she'd been reading lately. But as I got further into it, my eyes widened. The book wasn't just... normal.

It was full of... well, sex.

What the hell was this stuff? Hailey was just reading about some woman getting bent over backwards on her kitchen counter on a Saturday morning?

"Oh, shit," I muttered under my breath, scanning a particularly detailed scene.

Hailey caught my expression and looked over. "What are you doing?"

"Uh..." I shot her a look, half-grinning, half-shocked. "Should you be reading this?"

Her face turned beet red as she realized what I was talking about. "HEY! Don't read what's on there!" She abandoned her pastry dough and bolted over, looking absolutely horrified.

"Damn, relax," I teased, still holding the Kindle up as I scrolled a little further. "You're gonna wake up the whole damn block with all this yelling. Besides, I had no idea you were into... this kind of stuff."

Her face somehow turned an even deeper shade of red as I read out loud, "'His hands roamed over her body, igniting a fire down in her—'"

"Callum!" she shrieked, her face even redder now as she tried to wrench the Kindle out of my hands.

But I wasn't about to make it easy for her. I held it up higher, still grinning as she made a desperate grab for it. "Seriously, Hailey, I didn't take you for the type to read such filth. You dirty girl."

She groaned, clearly mortified. "Give it back! You're such an ass!"

In her effort to get the Kindle, she lost her balance and tripped, falling straight into me. The sudden weight knocked us both back onto the couch, her landing on top of me, and I barely caught her in time before she crashed into my face.

For a second, everything went still.

She was right there, her face just inches from mine, her body pressed against me. We both froze, staring at each other, the playful energy suddenly replaced with something heavier, more charged. My heart sped up, and I could see her eyes widen, her breath coming in short bursts as she processed what had just happened.

Neither of us said anything, and the only sound in the room was the low hum of the TV in the background.

My head spun, and for a second, I couldn't think straight. Hailey on top of me, and everything seemed to slow down. I could feel the weight of her body against mine, and there was this soft, sweet scent—blueberries.

It was on her fingertips, or maybe... her lips? I couldn't tell. My heart was pounding in my chest, faster than it should have been, and I couldn't help but wonder why.

I forced a grin, trying to play it cool even though my pulse was racing. "You know... if you wanted to get on top of me, you could've just asked."

Her eyes narrowed, and I could tell she was irritated— more than usual. Without missing a beat, she shoved off me, her face a shade of pink that wasn't just from embarrassment. "You're impossible," she muttered, snatching her Kindle back like it was a lifeline.

I sat up, still grinning, though my heart was pounding in a way I wasn't sure how to deal with. "Alright, alright. Just saying."

She snatched the Kindle from my hands, glaring at me like I'd committed some unspeakable crime. "And don't ever read my Kindle again."

"No promises," I teased, though there was something about the way my chest tightened when she looked at me like that.

I leaned forward and examined the tray of pastries. They were golden brown and looked perfect from the outside, but as I peered closer, I could see that they were berry-filled—blueberry, from the looks of it. The smell was sweet, and my stomach rumbled in anticipation.

Hailey stood there, arms crossed, watching me with a raised eyebrow. "Well, go on. If you want to try one, try it already," she said, a little too eager.

"Be patient, damn it," I muttered, reaching out and picking one up. It was warm in my hand, and I turned it over, examining it like it might have some hidden secret. I glanced over at her, smirking. "These aren't poisoned, right?"

She rolled her eyes, the impatience clear in her voice. "You know what? Don't even eat it anymore. Give it back."

"Whoa, whoa, calm down," I said, raising a hand in surrender. "I'm just messing with you." I took a deep breath and bit into the pastry.

And immediately regretted it.

It was... terrible.

Horrible, in fact. The pastry was doughy, like it hadn't cooked all the way through, and the berry filling was way too sour—like she'd forgotten sugar altogether. I fought the urge to spit it out, my brain screaming at me to stop chewing. But Hailey was watching, her eyes on me like a hawk.

I swallowed, forcing it down, and gave her a tight-lipped smile. "Not bad."

Her eyes narrowed suspiciously. "Really?"

"Yeah," I said, trying not to grimace. "It's... different. You know, unique."

Hailey didn't look convinced. "Callum, if you hate it, just say so."

I shook my head, attempting—and nearly gagging—at another bite. "Nah, it's fine, really."

But the second the dough hit my tongue again, I nearly gagged. It was the worst thing I'd ever tasted. It tasted like depression, loneliness, and broken dreams. But no way was I going to crush her.

She crossed her arms, still watching me closely. "You're such a bad liar."

I forced another bite, chewing slowly, trying not to grimace. My taste buds were screaming at me to stop, and my stomach churned in protest.

These tasted like broken dreams and lost hope—like someone had taken every ounce of sweetness life had to offer and replaced it with despair. But there was no way in hell I was going to admit that to Hailey.

"No, really," I managed, swallowing the vile dough as quickly as I could. "They're... good."

Hailey tilted her head, giving me a look that said she wasn't buying it. Her arms were still crossed, and she seemed to be waiting for me to crack. My eyes watered slightly from the sour filling, but I held my ground, smiling through the pain.

She raised an eyebrow. "You sure? Because it kind of looks like you're suffering."

I waved her off, fighting to keep the pastry down. "No, no. It's just, uh—different. You know, a unique flavor."

Dalton, who had been mumbling who knows what under his breath as he walked down the stairs half-asleep, was now fully alert thanks to the prospect of food, and he shuffled over to the counter with wide eyes.

"Ooh, did you bake that, Hailey? I want one too!" he said, sounding way too excited for what was about to happen. I tried to warn him, to stop him from making the same mistake, but my mouth was still full of Hailey's… creation, and all I could do was make a muffled noise of protest.

"Here, Dalton," Hailey said, smiling warmly as she handed him one of the pastries. "Tell me what you think."

No. Don't do it, kid. I silently screamed, but there was nothing I could do. Dalton was already clutching the pastry in his small hands, completely unaware of the culinary nightmare he was about to dive into. He took a big, excited bite, his face lighting up with anticipation.

And then it happened.

His eyes widened in shock as he chewed. For a moment, he looked like he couldn't understand what had just hit his taste buds. But then, slowly, tears began to fill his eyes as the horror of the situation sank in.

He swallowed—barely—and stared at the half-eaten pastry in his hand, his expression one of pure betrayal. "What… is this?" he croaked, his voice trembling.

He looked genuinely heartbroken, like the pastry had just ruined his faith in all things good. I gave him a sympathetic look, still unable to speak with my own mouth full of the same torturous concoction.

Hailey's face fell, her confidence clearly shaken. "Wait, is it really that bad?"

I swallowed the last of it, barely keeping it down, and forced a grin. "No, no, he's just… being dramatic."

Dalton glared at me, wiping at his eyes like the betrayal had personally wounded him. "I'm not being dramatic! It tastes like… like… I don't even know what it tastes like, but it's bad!"

Hailey's shoulders slumped, and she reached for one of the pastries herself, as if needing proof. "It can't be that bad. I followed the recipe…"

I watched in horror as she took a bite, and the second it touched her tongue, her face scrunched up in disgust. She spat it out almost immediately, covering her mouth with her hand. "Oh my god!"

Dalton looked up at her, eyes still wet. "See? I told you."

I sighed, finally free from the pressure of pretending. "Okay, fine," I admitted, laughing. "Yeah, they're awful."

Hailey shook her head, looking at the tray of pastries with disbelief. "I don't understand. The video made it look so easy. What the hell did I do wrong?"

Dalton, still licking his lips like he was trying to get rid of the taste, pointed accusingly at the pastries. "You poisoned us. I trusted you, Hailey."

"I didn't poison anyone!" Hailey said, exasperated as my little brother started limping to the couch. I didn't know the taste of it had been so bad that it affected his range of motion, but I wasn't surprised. She turned to me, eyes narrowing. "And you— you were going to let me believe these were good? You should've just told me they were terrible!"

I raised my hands in defense. "Look, I've had worse. At least you tried, right?"

"That's not comforting," she muttered, glaring at me as she tossed the rest of the pastry in the trash. "I'm never baking again."

Dalton nodded fervently. "Good idea."

I stared at Hailey, still trying to process what I'd just tasted. God, the taste of that shit would probably be on my tongue for the next week or two. "What the hell did you even do to these?"

She hesitated for a moment, clearly embarrassed, then mumbled, "I told you, I followed the recipe! Mostly... I mean, I kind of ran out of flour halfway through, so I just replaced the rest with baking powder."

I almost choked on my own spit. "You did *what*?! You used that much baking powder?!"

Hailey winced. "It didn't seem like that much…"

I stared at her, completely dumbfounded. "That explains why it tastes like I'm chewing on chalk mixed with floor cleaner. Holy shit."

She shot me a look, half-defensive and half-ashamed. "Okay, well, I didn't know it would turn out like this. I thought it'd be fine! They're both white powder."

"So is cocaine, Hailey," I muttered, still feeling the aftertaste lingering on my tongue.

We started bickering back and forth, my irritation rising but also mixing with a weird sense of amusement. It was such a Hailey thing to do—trying to make something nice but somehow turning it into a kitchen disaster. I shook my head, giving in, and walked over to the sink with her to help wash up the dishes, figuring I might as well make myself useful. As irritated as I was, there was something oddly fun about this whole mess.

"Seriously, Hailey," I said, handing her a plate. "Next time, just ask someone before you go rogue in the kitchen. Or, I don't know. Google some shit you're not sure of. Replacing flour with baking powder is crazy work."

She rolled her eyes, though I could tell she was trying to hide her embarrassment. "Noted. No more improvising with baking powder."

Just then, I heard the sound of footsteps coming into the kitchen, and I glanced up to see my mom walk in, humming to herself. She spotted the tray of pastries on the counter, her face lighting up.

"Ooh, pastries!" she said with enthusiasm, heading straight for the tray. "Don't mind if I do!"

Dalton, who was still recovering on the couch, shot up in panic. "Mom, no!"

But it was too late. She picked one up and took a bite before anyone could stop her. I watched in horror as she chewed, her expression shifting from casual curiosity to pure regret. Her jaw seemed to tremble slightly, and her eyes widened in shock.

For a moment, it looked like she might spit it out, but she swallowed with great difficulty, her face contorting like she'd just eaten a lemon wrapped in sawdust.

"Oh, wow…" she managed, her voice shaky. "That's… strong."

Dalton groaned, dropping his head into his hands. "I tried to warn you."

I couldn't help it—I burst out laughing. My mom tried to keep her composure, but even she looked like she was struggling to stay polite and trying not to gag at the same time. Hailey, red-faced and mortified, tried to apologize, but I was already grinning, shaking my head.

Only Hailey Eller could pull off some shit like this.

CHAPTER 45

HAILEY

I SAT DOWN AT OUR USUAL SPOT IN THE CAFETERIA, MY TRAY CLATTERING A LITTLE too loudly as I plopped into the seat across from Nala. I couldn't hold back the excitement buzzing through me, and I leaned forward, grinning.

"Girl. Guess. What?" I said, practically bouncing in my seat.

Nala, midway through chewing her crab legs and egg salad sandwich, raised an eyebrow. "What?"

"BookishCon is coming to our city this weekend!" I blurted out, unable to contain my enthusiasm any longer.

Nala's eyes widened, and she swallowed quickly, her expression lighting up. "No way! You mean that huge book convention where all those authors show up and there are special editions of everything?"

I nodded eagerly. "Yes! A bunch of famous authors are gonna be there. I've been dying to rebuild my collection since the fire, and this is the perfect chance. Plus, I might even get to meet my favorite author."

"Girl, we should definitely go!" Nala said, her excitement matching mine.

I grinned even wider. "Say less. I already bought us two passes."

Nala's jaw dropped in mock disbelief, but she quickly turned it into a smile. "You legend. This is gonna be so much fun!"

I nodded, imagining all the bookish treasures we were about to discover. A weekend spent among book lovers, snagging rare editions, getting autographs, and basking in the glory of my favorite authors—it was perfect. The kind of escape I'd been needing since everything turned upside down after the fire.

This was gonna be so much fun.

NEVER MIND.

I stared down at my phone, reading the message that had just come in from Nala.

Nala: I'm so sorry, Hailey. My grandma collapsed, and we're rushing to the hospital. I can't go to BookishCon today...

Of course Nala couldn't come. This was serious. Her grandmother was in the hospital, and suddenly, all the excitement I'd been feeling was replaced by worry for her.

Without a second thought, I texted back.

Me: Oh my god, Nala, I'm so sorry. Don't worry about it. Take care of your grandma, okay? Call me if you need anything.

I sighed, staring at the BookishCon passes on my dresser.

Well, I could always go by myself, right? It wasn't like I needed Nala to enjoy the convention, though it would've been more fun with her around. But this was my chance to replenish my collection, maybe even get some special edition books or meet my favorite author. I couldn't pass that up.

I got dressed quickly, throwing on my favorite oversized sweater and jeans, and grabbed my backpack. I slung it over my shoulder and headed upstairs, the sound of voices reaching me as I climbed.

In the kitchen, my mom and Callum's mom were chatting over coffee, laughing about something. They noticed me as I stepped into the room.

"Oh, where are you going, Hailey?" my mom asked, a smile still on her face.

"BookishCon," I said, trying to keep my voice upbeat. "But... Nala can't come now. Her grandma collapsed, and she had to go to the hospital."

Both of them gave me sympathetic looks. "Oh, honey, I'm sorry," Mrs. Reid said. "But you're not going alone, are you?"

I shrugged, not really wanting to get into it. "I mean, I could. It's just a book convention."

"No, no, you can't go by yourself," my mom insisted, exchanging a glance with Callum's mom. "That's not safe."

Before I could protest, Mrs. Reid cupped her hands around her mouth and called out, "Callum! Get down here!"

"Wait, no, I'm fine!" I said quickly, my voice a little panicked. "I don't need—"

But it was too late. Callum's heavy footsteps could already be heard coming down the stairs, and I could feel a wave of frustration rising in me. The last thing I needed was to drag him along to something like this.

"What?" Callum asked as he appeared on the stairs, looking slightly annoyed as he ruffled his hair. He was dressed in a tank top and sweats, clearly not expecting to go anywhere today.

"Hailey's going to a book convention," Mrs. Reid said, with a casual wave of her hand. "Nala can't go, so you're going with her."

Callum's eyes flicked to me, eyebrows raised. "Wait, what?"

"No, really, it's fine—" I tried to jump in, but Mrs. Reid waved me off.

"You can't go alone, Hailey. Callum, you're going with her. End of story," she said firmly.

Callum blinked, clearly not thrilled, but didn't argue with the moms. He let out a small sigh, glancing at me with a mix of reluctance and resignation. "No way am I going to a damn book convention," he muttered.

I groaned internally, rubbing my forehead. "You really don't have to."

But it was already decided. Callum's mom shot him a look that said he didn't have a choice, and after a long pause, he just shrugged. "Alright, fine. Let me grab my jacket."

As he disappeared back upstairs, I stood there, feeling a mix of frustration and awkwardness.

This wasn't how I'd planned today at all.

CHAPTER 46

CALLUM

I PULLED INTO THE PARKING LOT OF THE CONVENTION CENTER AND KILLED THE engine, glancing at the towering building ahead.

BookishCon. Not exactly my idea of a Saturday well spent, but here I was. I rubbed the back of my neck, already feeling out of place. I'd just thrown on a jacket over my tank top and sweats, not bothering with much else because, let's be honest, this wasn't exactly a Callum Reid event.

I glanced over at Hailey as she unbuckled her seatbelt. She was all bundled up in her oversized sweater and jeans, looking cute in a way that was kind of… irritating. She had that excited look in her eyes, like a kid about to walk into a candy store. I grumbled under my breath, "Let's get this over with."

Hailey shot me a look, clearly not in the mood for my attitude, and handed me one of the convention passes. "Try not to look so miserable," she muttered as she got out of the car.

I rolled my eyes but followed her out, adjusting my jacket against the crisp October air. I'd barely shut the car door when she added, "You're lucky you're even coming. Some people would kill to be here."

"Yeah, lucky me," I muttered sarcastically as we headed toward the entrance. "Maybe those people should've just killed me, honestly."

We bickered the entire way inside, her throwing jabs about how I didn't appreciate books, and me shooting back about how I could've been sleeping in today. It was the usual banter, nothing too serious, but I was already counting down the hours until I could leave.

But then, as soon as we stepped into the exhibition hall, everything changed.

Hailey gasped, stopping dead in her tracks. Her eyes went wide, and her mouth dropped open. "Oh. My. God."

I followed her gaze and felt my own eyes widen a little, though for completely different reasons. The hall was packed, rows upon rows of tables lined with books, trinkets, and merchandise.

Authors sat behind stacks of their novels, signing copies for eager fans. There were booths everywhere—small shops selling rare editions, handmade bookmarks, literary-themed candles, and more. It was a sea of books and people, buzzing with excitement.

"Holy…" I muttered, but Hailey didn't even hear me.

She was practically vibrating with excitement, her eyes darting from table to table like she didn't know where to go first. "This is amazing," she whispered, more to herself than to me.

I watched her for a moment, taking in how genuinely happy she looked. It was a side of Hailey I hadn't seen often— but here, surrounded by books and the stuff she loved, she was practically glowing.

"Alright, alright, let's do this," I grumbled, trying to shake off the weird feeling of being out of my element. But it was hard not to be affected by her enthusiasm, even if I was still clueless about what half of this stuff was.

Hailey didn't even acknowledge me, already halfway toward the first booth. I sighed and followed her into the chaos.

Hailey was like a kid in a candy store—only this was a candy store filled with books, and she was determined to check out every. Single. One.

As soon as we stepped deeper into the exhibition hall, she latched onto my arm and started chatting my ear off, pointing out different books, authors, and random facts about genres I didn't even know existed.

"Oh my god, look at that!" she squealed, pointing to a table stacked with fantasy novels, their covers adorned with shimmering dragons and dark forests. "I've heard this series is incredible, but it's been out of print for ages! And over there, they have first editions of The Shadow Grove Chronicles—super rare."

I just nodded. To be fair, I had no idea what she was talking about half the time, and the other half, I was trying not to zone out completely. The sheer amount of books and people made it feel like we were wading through a maze.

Hailey didn't seem to notice—or care—that I was barely keeping up with her excitement. She just kept going, babbling on and on as we passed by literally every single table. "Oh, that one's a debut author! I've heard amazing things. And this table—wait, is that a signed edition of Into the Wildlands? That's impossible to find!"

I grunted in response, glancing down at her every now and then as she talked. She was completely in her element, moving from booth to booth like she had a checklist of things to see and was determined not to miss a single one. Her eyes sparkled with every new discovery, and she'd go off on tangents about the world-building in one series or the character development in another.

Meanwhile, I just nodded along, muttering an occasional "uh-huh" or "cool," trying to stay on autopilot.

"...And I swear, the way she weaves the themes of loss and redemption into the narrative is just—it's breathtaking," Hailey said, clutching a book to her chest as she marveled at yet another table. "I've never read anything like it."

"Sounds... deep," I offered, glancing around for the nearest exit, but there was no escaping this. We still had rows upon rows of tables left, and Hailey wasn't slowing down anytime soon.

But even with all the nonstop talking, I couldn't help but notice how much she was glowing.

It was like seeing a completely different side of her—the quiet, bookish girl who kept to herself was now a walking encyclopedia of literary knowledge. And even though I wasn't into any of it, I couldn't really be annoyed by how happy she seemed.

She was completely absorbed in the moment, rattling off facts and stories like it was second nature.

This was Hailey.

A girl who loved books, photography, and wasn't ashamed of being seen as a nerd or whatever. She didn't try to hide it, didn't care that she was diving headfirst into every table, clutching books like they were treasure. She was in her element here, and for the first time, I realized just how much this world meant to her.

I couldn't help but smile as I watched her ramble on, pointing out book covers or author names like they were celebrity sightings. There was something genuine about it—about her. No pretense, no hiding behind walls. Just Hailey, doing what she loved without a care in the world.

She didn't even notice me staring, too wrapped up in her excitement to realize I'd gone quiet. And weirdly, I didn't mind the constant chatter, not when it came with that kind of smile.

"So, yeah, I've been waiting forever to get my hands on this edition," she said, hugging a book to her chest, still buzzing with excitement.

We made our way toward the center of the exhibition hall, and just as I was about to check the time, Hailey suddenly froze. Her entire body went rigid, and her eyes widened like she'd just spotted a unicorn.

"Oh my god," she whispered, barely audible.

I stopped, confused, and glanced around. "What? What's going on?"

She didn't answer me. Instead, she kept staring, like she was in a trance.

"Hailey," I said a little louder, starting to get impatient. "What?"

"Oh my god," she repeated, this time louder.

I frowned and followed her gaze. All I saw was a table with a long-ass line of people waiting, most of them clutching books and looking just as eager as Hailey. "Seriously, what is it?"

She turned to me, her jaw practically on the floor, eyes wide with disbelief. "It's her."

"Her?" I repeated, still not following.

"It's Delilah Cadman," she whispered, almost reverently, like she'd just spotted some kind of literary deity.

I blinked. "And that's…?"

"Delilah Cadman," she said again, like I should know exactly who that was. "She's my favorite author. She's here! She has special editions of her book Blush and she's signing them!"

Her voice got more and more excited as she spoke, her eyes glued to the table where the line snaked around. I looked again, noticing the sign behind the table: Delilah Cadman, Author of Blush—Book Signing & Special Editions. Hailey's jaw was still dropped, her whole body frozen in awe.

"Wow," I said, not really sure what else to say. To her, this was clearly a huge deal. "That's… cool?"

"Cool?!" she gasped, turning to me with wild eyes. "It's more than cool! This is *the* Delilah Cadman! I can't believe she's actually here."

I watched her for a moment, amused by how starstruck she looked. It was like her world had just tilted on its axis, and all she could do was stand there, stunned.

I raised an eyebrow and smirked, my mind flashing back to that spicy book I'd seen on her Kindle. "Wait... is she the one who wrote that smut book I saw on your Kindle that one time?"

Hailey's eyes widened slightly, but she didn't miss a beat. "Yes! She's the one," she said, her voice brimming with excitement, though her cheeks tinted a bit pink. "Oh my god, I need to get a signature from her."

But as she looked back at the long line of people waiting to meet Delilah Cadman, her face fell. Her excitement deflated a little as reality set in. She took a step back, shaking her head. "You know what... never mind."

I frowned, confused. "What do you mean never mind?"

She pointed toward the long line of fans, all clutching books and chattering excitedly. "Look at that line. It's insane. It'll take forever."

"So? Do you not wanna wait?" I asked, narrowing my eyes as I tried to figure out why she was suddenly backing out.

She let out a small sigh, looking a bit guilty. "It's not that... I just don't wanna make you wait. I can tell how much you're hating every second of this," she said, giving me a weak smile. "This really isn't your thing."

I groaned, rubbing the back of my neck as I looked at her. She was trying to act like it wasn't a big deal, but I could see how badly she wanted this. And yeah, I wasn't exactly loving the whole book convention experience, but seeing her excited... that was something else.

I gave her a hard look. "Don't you remember what I told you before?"

Hailey blinked, her brow furrowing in confusion. "What are you talking about?"

I sighed, shaking my head with a small smile. "That night we went up to see the northern lights. The night I gave you the camera. I told you, 'Don't let anyone hold you back from doing stuff you like doing.' Remember?"

Her eyes widened as the memory hit her, and I could see the realization dawning in her expression. She bit her lip, glancing from me to the line and back again.

"Callum, you really don't have to—"

"Yeah, yeah," I interrupted, rolling my eyes but grinning. "I know this isn't my scene, but this is your thing. And if getting a signature from your favorite author is that important to you, then you should do it. I'm not gonna let you back out just because the line's long."

She looked at me for a long moment, as if trying to decide whether I was serious. I met her gaze, and eventually, she smiled—like, really smiled.

"Thanks," she whispered, and I could tell it meant more to her than she was saying.

"Yeah, yeah. Now go get in line before I change my mind," I said with a mock groan.

She laughed and turned to head toward the line, a new bounce in her step as she made her way over. I watched her go, feeling strangely good about the whole thing.

WE'D BEEN STANDING IN LINE FOR ABOUT HALF AN HOUR, AND I WAS TRYING MY best not to zone out. The convention hall was buzzing around us, but Hailey was practically bouncing with excitement the closer we got to the front.

She kept clutching the convention pass in her hand, her eyes darting between the line and the table ahead, where her favorite author was signing books.

When we finally reached the front, Hailey was almost vibrating with energy. She stepped up to the table, her face lit up like it was Christmas morning. I stood just behind her, trying to stay out of the way as she eagerly bought the special edition of

Blush—the book that started all this—and placed it on the table for Delilah Cadman to sign.

Delilah, sitting behind a neat stack of books, looked up with a warm smile. She had that kind of calm, authorly presence, like she was in her element surrounded by her stories and her fans.

Hailey practically held her breath as Delilah took the book and began signing it with a graceful flourish. "Thank you so much," Hailey gushed, unable to contain herself. "I've been waiting forever for this. I absolutely love your work."

Delilah chuckled softly, her smile never faltering as she handed the signed book back. "I'm so glad to hear that. Always wonderful to meet a fan." Then she glanced up at me, her eyes twinkling with amusement. "Is this your boyfriend with you today?"

I felt my heart skip a beat as Hailey froze, her excitement suddenly mixing with embarrassment. Her face flushed a deep red, and she quickly shook her head, stammering. "Oh, no! He's not—um, we're not—he's just a friend."

Delilah raised an eyebrow, clearly not convinced, but she smiled knowingly. "Ah, I see. Well, it's always nice to have someone to share these moments with, isn't it?"

I scratched the back of my neck awkwardly, trying to play it off. "Yeah, I'm just the tagalong today."

Hailey shot me a look, still flustered, but I could see the faintest hint of a smile tugging at the corner of her lips. She quickly grabbed her newly signed book, clutching it to her chest like it was the most precious thing in the world. "Thank you again," she said to Delilah, her voice soft and full of gratitude.

Delilah just smiled, giving us both a little nod as we stepped aside, making room for the next person in line.

As we moved away, Hailey's face was still pink, but she was practically glowing with happiness. I couldn't help but smile at her. Despite the awkwardness, it was worth it just to see her so happy.

"Guess that went well," I teased, nudging her shoulder lightly.

She laughed. "Yeah. Even if she did think you were my boyfriend," she added with a playful glare.

"Hey, can you blame her?" I shot back, smirking.

She rolled her eyes but laughed again, her mood too good to be ruined by anything.

"So what? We're in 'friend' territory now?" I asked, raising an eyebrow. "I heard you call me your friend back there."

Hailey scoffed, hugging her book tighter to her chest as she gave me a mock glare. "You wish," she shot back, rolling her eyes, though there was a faint smile tugging at her lips.

I chuckled, nudging her lightly with my shoulder. "Hey, you're the one who said it. I'm just going off the facts."

She shook her head, but the laughter was bubbling just beneath the surface. "Yeah, well, don't get too comfortable with that title. I could revoke it at any moment."

I grinned, enjoying how easy it felt to tease her now. "So what do I have to do to keep it, then?"

"Try not to be an ass for, like, a solid day," she said, raising an eyebrow in challenge. "Think you can manage that?"

I pretended to think it over, then shrugged. "No promises. But I guess I could try."

Hailey laughed again, and the tension from earlier had completely melted away. We might bicker all the time, but for a moment, it felt like we really were... well, something like friends.

CHAPTER 47

HAILEY

AFTER THE CONVENTION, CALLUM AND I MADE A PIT STOP AT A NEARBY SUBWAY. I was still buzzing from the excitement of meeting Delilah Cadman and getting my special edition signed, clutching the book in my lap like it was a treasure.

Callum, on the other hand, looked like he was more focused on one thing—food.

We stepped up to the counter, and I ordered a simple 6-inch sub, feeling like that was more than enough for me. Callum, though, went all out and ordered two footlongs. My eyes widened in shock as I turned to look at him, wondering how he planned to eat both of those.

When we sat down at the table, I unwrapped my sub and glanced over at him as he tore into the first one with zero hesitation.

I could barely even finish a 6-inch, and here he was going at it like it was nothing. "How can you eat two footlongs?" I asked, shaking my head in disbelief. "I can barely finish this one."

Callum paused for just a second, smirking as he chewed. "Oh, so 6 inches is too much for you?" he teased, his eyes glinting with mischief.

I nearly choked on my sandwich, but I quickly recovered, narrowing my eyes at him. "Don't worry," I fired back smoothly, "that won't be a problem for you."

His grin widened, and he leaned back in his seat, clearly enjoying this a little too much. I rolled my eyes but couldn't help the small smile that tugged at my lips. Typical Callum—always ready to turn any conversation into an opportunity to tease me. But even as I poked at my sub, I realized I didn't mind as much as I used to.

Callum finished one of his footlongs and was halfway through the second before he glanced up at me, his expression thoughtful. "So, what's the big deal with all this?" he asked, nodding toward the signed book I still had resting on the table. "Why do you get so hyped about this kind of stuff? Like, books and whatnot?"

I paused, wiping my hands on a napkin, trying to figure out how to explain it. "Well... I guess it's because I'm kind of a hopeless romantic," I admitted, feeling a bit embarrassed saying it out loud. "I love the way stories can pull you into a different world. There's beauty in the fictional world, in the characters, their journeys. It's like you get to live a hundred different lives, feel a million emotions, and you can escape into a place where things—no matter how hard—usually turn out okay in the end."

Callum raised an eyebrow, still chewing on his sub, but he didn't interrupt, so I continued.

"It's not just about the romance," I added quickly, "though that's part of it. It's about how stories can capture the beauty of things, the way words can create something that feels real even when it's not. I think... it ties into why I like photography too. I love being able to capture those moments of beauty in the real world. The little details—the light, the colors, the emotions—that make life special."

I realized I was rambling, but it felt good to explain something I was so passionate about. "In a way, it's like books capture the beauty of the imaginary world, and photography captures the beauty of the real one."

Callum leaned back, wiping his mouth, and then grinned that cocky grin of his. "So, since you keep taking pictures of me, does that mean I'm the beauty of the real world?"

I shot him a glare and immediately fired back, "No, you represent the evil in this world."

Callum groaned dramatically, throwing his head back. "Always with the insults, Eller. I'm starting to think you actually enjoy bullying me."

I snorted. "Well, maybe I do. Someone has to keep you grounded."

He shook his head but smiled, still chewing on his sandwich, the banter flowing between us easily now. It felt different, more relaxed than before.

I finished the last bite of my sub, feeling pretty content, but Callum was still going strong on his second footlong. I leaned back in my chair, feeling like the tables had turned a bit. "You got to ask me all these questions," I said, crossing my arms and smirking. "Now it's your turn."

He raised an eyebrow, mid-bite, and gave me a look like he knew exactly where this was going.

"So, why do you like soccer so much?" I asked, leaning forward slightly, because yes, I was actually kinda interested in hearing about this. "You never really talk about why you're so into it."

Callum paused, chewing thoughtfully for a moment before swallowing. "Huh. I don't think anyone's really asked me that before." He leaned back in his seat, his expression shifting from his usual cocky grin to something more serious. "I guess it started when I was a kid. My dad used to take me to these local games, nothing professional, just rec leagues. He'd always get really into it, and I kinda caught that energy, you know?"

I nodded, listening closely. It wasn't often that Callum talked about personal stuff like this.

"When I was, like, five or six, my parents signed me up for my first team. I didn't really know what I was doing back then, just chasing the ball around, but I remember the first time I actually scored a goal." He smiled, a genuine one this time. "That feeling, man... it was like nothing else. Everyone cheering, my teammates lifting me up—it made me feel like I was part of something bigger."

He glanced over at me, as if checking to see if I was still following. "And I think that's what kept me going. Soccer isn't just a sport; it's like... it's everything in one. It's strategy, it's teamwork, it's pushing yourself physically and mentally. Every game is different. You never know how it's gonna go, but you have to give everything you've got, no matter what.

"It's that rush, that adrenaline. When I'm out on the field, everything else just fades. It's just me, the ball, and the game. And as captain, I get to lead the team, which is a whole other challenge, but it's a good one. I like knowing that they count on me, that I have to be at my best so they can be too."

I didn't interrupt, just letting him talk, and it was kind of amazing to hear him explain it all. I'd realized it for a while, but now more than ever, it was hitting me: there was more to Callum than just being the soccer guy or the popular jock. There was real passion and drive behind everything he did.

"I guess I just love the way it makes me feel," he added, shrugging as if he'd just unloaded something huge. "Like I'm really doing something with purpose, you know?"

I nodded, finally speaking. "I get that. It's like how I feel about books and photography, I guess."

Callum smiled slightly. "Yeah, exactly. Everyone's got their thing."

There was a moment of quiet between us, not awkward but reflective, like we were both seeing each other a little differently now.

Callum chuckled as he looked back, still in that reflective mood. "You know, my first ever kiddie soccer team was called FC Chicken Nuggets."

I was in the middle of taking a sip from my drink when I nearly spit it out, choking on laughter. "What?!"

He shrugged, completely nonchalant. "Yeah. FC Chicken Nuggets. What, is there a problem with that?"

I covered my mouth, still laughing as I wiped away a tear from my eye. "I'm sorry, that's just—what kind of name is that?"

"Hey, it was legit," he said, smirking at me. "We even had custom jerseys. Bright yellow, with a chicken nugget logo on the front. It was a big deal, okay?"

"Oh my god," I gasped, still trying to catch my breath. "That's adorable. And ridiculous."

"Ridiculously awesome," he corrected, leaning back with a proud grin. "I'm telling you, we were fierce on the field. Nobody messed with us."

I laughed, shaking my head. "Yeah, I'm sure you were a real terror."

He shot me a playful glare. "Careful, Eller, I might have to bring the FC Chicken Nuggets spirit back and show you how it's done."

I rolled my eyes but couldn't stop smiling. "I'd love to see that."

We continued teasing each other, trading snarky comments back and forth, when an older couple walked by our table. The woman smiled warmly at us as they passed. "You two are such a cute couple," she said sweetly.

I froze for a second, my face heating up. I could feel Callum pause next to me too, though he played it off a second later, smirking. "Thanks," he said casually, and the couple continued on their way.

As soon as they were out of earshot, I groaned. "Oh my god, not again."

Callum grinned, raising an eyebrow. "It's the second time we've been mistaken for a couple today. Must be a sign."

I rolled my eyes, feeling my face still burning. "Yeah, no thanks."

"Hey, just saying," he teased, nudging me lightly. "People seem to think we look good together."

"People are delusional," I shot back, but there was a warmth behind the banter that felt strangely comfortable.

We headed out of Subway and back toward Callum's car, the air cool and crisp, a reminder that fall was in full swing. As we walked, Callum glanced over at me, hands stuffed in his jacket pockets.

"So, are you going to Sasha's Halloween party next Friday?" he asked, opening the car door and sliding into the driver's seat.

I hesitated for a second before nodding. "I was thinking about it."

"Damn, really?" Callum gave me a mock-shocked look as he started the car. "Little Hailey's finally going to her first high school party? What's the world coming to?"

I rolled my eyes. "Very funny."

He smirked, shifting into reverse to back out of the parking spot. "So, what're you gonna dress up as? A minion from Despicable Me or something?"

I shot him a deadpan look. "No. Nala and I were planning to go as Joker and Harley Quinn."

Callum visibly tensed for just a second. "Oh."

I raised an eyebrow. "Oh?"

He cleared his throat, glancing at me briefly before pulling out of the lot. "Yeah, okay. Cool."

I frowned, feeling a little confused by the sudden shift in his tone. "Is something wrong with that?"

He shook his head quickly, though his expression was a little harder to read now. "No, nothing's wrong. Just... surprised, I guess."

I stared at him for a second, waiting for him to say more, but he didn't. He just focused on the road, his face neutral but maybe a little more tense than before.

I leaned back in my seat, my arms crossed, feeling like I missed something. "Okay," I mumbled, glancing out the window as the city passed by.

The rest of the drive was quiet, and I couldn't help but wonder what that was all about.

CHAPTER 48
CALLUM

LATER THAT NIGHT, I SANK INTO BED, FEELING THE WEIGHT OF THE DAY SETTLE into my muscles. I was still a little tired from the convention and hauling myself through endless book booths, but it wasn't just the physical exhaustion that was gnawing at me.

My mind kept drifting back to that conversation in the car—Hailey and Nala planning to go as Joker and Harley Quinn for Sasha's party.

For some reason, it stuck with me. It shouldn't have. But there I was, lying in bed, staring at my phone. After a moment of hesitation, I unlocked it and found myself typing **"Harley Quinn costume"** into the search bar.

I hit enter, and instantly, a flood of images popped up— Harley's signature look from the movies: the tight, ripped shorts, the fishnet stockings, her shirt that read "Daddy's Little Monster." Her hair in those cute pigtails, dyed pink and blue.

I took a deep breath, scrolling through the pictures. I don't even know why I was doing this, but all I could think about was Hailey. Hailey, dressed like that. And once the image formed in my mind, it was impossible to shake.

Those tight shorts. Her hair pulled into those playful pigtails. The way the outfit hugged her body.

"Fuuuuck," I muttered under my breath, dropping my phone onto my chest. This was not good. Why was I even thinking about her like this? I should've just brushed it off, made some dumb joke and moved on, but now the thought of Hailey in that costume was stuck in my head, and it wasn't going anywhere.

I stared up at the ceiling, my phone still resting on my chest, trying to push the images out of my mind. But it wasn't working.

The more I tried not to think about it, the more vivid it became. Hailey, in those tight shorts, her hair in those playful pigtails… that alone was enough to mess with my head.

But then I thought about the shirt. The one that said "Daddy's Little Monster," clinging to her in all the right places. I swallowed hard, feeling a heat rise in my chest.

If I had to actually see her in that? Holy shit.

Holy fucking shit.

I could already picture it: her walking into Sasha's party, that confident, slightly mischievous look she gets when she's having fun. The way the shirt would fit snugly, drawing attention to—

I groaned, rolling onto my side, squeezing my eyes shut. This was so bad. I shouldn't be thinking about her like this, but it was impossible to stop.

Damn it, Callum, I thought, my heart still racing. I didn't know what was worse—the fact that I couldn't stop imagining it, or the fact that part of me wanted to see her like that.

Just as I was trying to shake the thoughts of Hailey out of my head, my phone buzzed on my chest.

I grabbed it, relieved for the distraction, and saw it was a text from the group chat I had with Ibra, Adam, and Grayson.

The guys were always up to something, and tonight was no different.

Grayson: *Yo, what are we doing for Halloween?*
Adam: *We could do something classic, like vampires. I'm not wearing fake teeth though.*
Ibra: *Nah, man, too much work. What about something easy, like…
cowboys?*
Grayson: *I am not wearing a hat.*
Me: *What about just going as a group of prisoners? Easy, simple, and we can make it look good.*
Ibra: *I'm down. We could mess with it, maybe add some fake tattoos or whatever.*
Adam: *Alright, I'm in. I can throw together something for that.*
Grayson: *Cool. Prisoners it is then.*

I smirked, shaking my head. A bunch of prisoners. Classic, easy, and not much thought required. Definitely more my speed. At least I wasn't gonna have to put much effort into a costume this year, unlike some people.

As I stared at the ceiling, a new thought hit me, and my stomach dropped. What if Hailey dresses up as the Joker instead?

She hadn't exactly clarified which one of them—her or Nala—was going to be the Joker or Harley Quinn. I had just assumed… but what if I was wrong? The idea of Hailey showing up as the Joker, with all that makeup and green hair, made me feel… uneasy.

No, no, that couldn't happen. Hailey had to be Harley Quinn. It just made sense, right? But I wasn't about to leave this to chance.

Not when I'd already spent way too much time imagining her in those tight shorts and pigtails.

If she showed up in a purple suit and clown makeup instead, it would totally ruin my… well, my expectations.

I groaned, already feeling the stress of the situation. There was only one solution. I'd have to talk to Nala tomorrow. Convince her to be the Joker, make sure everything went the way it was supposed to. I wasn't about to let this go wrong.

I made up my mind, determined. Tomorrow, I'd talk to Nala and set things straight.

THE NEXT DAY, I FELT LIKE A COMPLETE IDIOT. OR MAYBE A PERVERT. MAYBE both. Honestly, I hadn't figured it out yet.

What the hell was I even thinking? I mean, I couldn't just walk up to Nala and say, *"Hey, can you be the Joker so I can see Hailey in fishnets?"*

There was no universe where that didn't sound messed up. But I was already in too deep. I had convinced myself last night that I had to do something, and now there was no backing out.

I spotted Nala at her locker, casually putting her stuff in, completely unaware of the internal crisis I was going through. I clenched my jaw, wiped my sweaty palms on my jeans, and decided to bite the bullet.

As I walked over, every step felt heavier, like my body was trying to stop me from making a huge mistake. But I couldn't turn back now. I stopped a few feet away, cleared my throat, and plastered on a casual grin.

"Hey, Nala."

She glanced over at me, smiling brightly. "Oh, hey, Callum! What's up?"

I felt a knot tighten in my stomach. Here we go.

"Uh... so, I wanted to ask you something about the Halloween party. Sasha's," I said, my voice sounding way too forced. This was already off to a bad start.

Nala raised an eyebrow, intrigued. "Yeah? What is it?"

I took a deep breath. I had to play this cool. "You and Hailey are going as Joker and Harley Quinn, right?"

She nodded, closing her locker and leaning against it. "Yep! It's gonna be epic. Why? Are you planning on dressing up as Batman or something?"

I laughed awkwardly. "No, no Batman for me. I was just... curious. Like, uh... which one of you is going as the Joker?"

Nala squinted at me, clearly sensing something weird in my question. "I haven't decided yet. I mean, I could be Joker, but Hailey could pull it off too. Why?"

Crap. This was the moment. I had to think fast. "I was just thinking..." I hesitated, trying to come up with something that didn't make me sound like a complete creep. "You'd make a badass Joker. You know, with your personality and all. I think you'd really sell it."

Nala tilted her head, still eyeing me with a mix of curiosity and suspicion. "Huh. You really think so?"

I nodded, maybe too eagerly. "Yeah! Totally. I mean, Hailey would make a great Harley. You guys would be the perfect pair."

She crossed her arms, smirking. "Okay, Callum. What's the deal? Why do you care so much about who's who?"

My mouth went dry. I was not prepared for follow-up questions.

I could feel my brain short-circuiting as I tried to come up with something, anything, to explain why I was suddenly so interested in their costumes. "Uh... well, it's just, you know... um... it's all about the vibe, right?"

Nala raised an eyebrow, clearly unimpressed.

I swallowed, scrambling. "I mean, you've got that chaotic energy, the kind that totally fits the Joker's whole thing. And Hailey's, uh... she's got that Harley Quinn vibe. You know, the quirky, but, like, charming kind of thing." I nodded, as if that would somehow make my terrible excuse sound more convincing.

Nala stared at me for a long moment, her smirk widening, and I could tell she wasn't buying a single word. "Uh-huh. So, you just want to make sure the 'vibes' are right?" She even threw in air quotes, mocking me a little.

"Exactly," I said, trying to keep my voice steady. "Gotta get the vibes right."

Nala burst out laughing, shaking her head. "Oh my god, Callum, you're terrible at lying."

I felt my face heat up, but I forced a grin that probably made my face look like I was fucking constipated or something. "What? No, I'm serious."

She was still laughing. "Sure, sure. I'll think about it, okay? I'm not making any promises, but if it's that important to you for some mysterious reason, I'll consider being Joker."

I let out a breath I didn't realize I was holding. "Thanks. You'd definitely rock it."

Nala winked at me, clearly still amused by the whole thing. "You're welcome, but this better not be about some weird crush or something."

I quickly shook my head, forcing out a laugh. "Crush? Nah, no way."

She just gave me a knowing look before turning back to her locker. "Uh-huh. We'll see."

As I walked away, I couldn't shake the feeling that I'd just made things a whole lot more complicated.

CHAPTER 49
HAILEY

THE BRIGHT LIGHTS OF SEPHORA WERE BUZZING AROUND ME AS NALA AND I wandered through the aisles, swatching makeup and testing perfumes.

Halloween was coming up fast, and we'd decided to come here for some last-minute touches for our costumes. Nala was knee-deep in the lipsticks section, holding up different shades and muttering to herself.

"You think this red's too much?" she asked, turning to me with a bold red lipstick in her hand.

I shrugged. "Depends. You want to go for intense or more subtle?"

"Intense," she said, grinning. "Always intense."

I laughed, turning back to the display in front of me, idly picking through makeup I didn't really need. I was still thinking about how we were going to pull off our Joker and Harley Quinn costumes. Then Nala, in her usual casual way, dropped a bomb on me.

"By the way," she said, completely nonchalant, "I was thinking about it, and I think you should be Harley Quinn."

I blinked, turning to her with a confused look. "What?"

"Yeah, you should be Harley," she repeated, like it was no big deal. "I'll be Joker. I've got the attitude for it."

I stared at her, my brain trying to process. "Wait, I thought you were going to be Harley."

She waved it off. "Nah. You'd be a way better Harley. It suits you more. Plus, the Joker costume is easier for me. Just face paint and a suit, really. I'll probably switch out the bottoms for a skirt or something. But you'd kill it as Harley. Harley Hailey. Wait, no… Hailey Quinn! Oh my god, it's perfect."

"Is it, though?" I frowned, not sure how to respond. The idea of dressing up as Harley Quinn felt… intimidating. Or Hailey Quinn apparently.

The costume was bold, sexy even, and I wasn't sure I could pull that off. "I don't know," I said, hesitating. "I don't really think I'm the Harley Quinn type."

Nala raised an eyebrow, clearly not buying it. "Why not? You've got that whole 'don't mess with me but secretly sweet' vibe. Plus, you'd look amazing in the costume."

I gave her a doubtful look. "I don't know if I can pull off fishnets and pigtails."

She laughed. "You don't have to! There's so many versions of Harley. You can do the fun, quirky look instead of the super sexy one if you want. But trust me, you'll rock it."

I bit my lip, still unsure, but Nala wasn't letting this go. She grabbed a red and blue eyeshadow palette and held it up in front of me, grinning like the Cheshire Cat. "Come on, Hailey. It'll be fun. You need to step out of your comfort zone a little."

I stared at her for a long moment, the idea slowly sinking in. Maybe she was right. Maybe I did need to stop playing it safe all the time.

And besides, it was just a costume. Just for one night. "Alright," I finally said, giving in. "I'll be Harley Quinn."

Nala's grin widened, and she tossed the eyeshadow into her shopping basket. "Knew you'd come around. This is gonna be awesome."

We finished up at Sephora, and after loading our bags into the car, Nala suggested grabbing some milk tea before heading back. It was a good call—we were both craving something sweet after all that shopping.

But, of course, Nala being Nala, she accidentally asked the cashier for "booby" instead of boba. The second she realized what she'd said, her eyes widened, and we both burst into laughter. We'd been snickering about it the entire car ride home, my stomach hurting from how much I'd laughed.

When we finally pulled up in front of the house, I unbuckled my seatbelt, still giggling. As I reached for the door handle, Nala leaned over, a wicked grin on her face. "Hey, before you go, tell Callum I say 'you're welcome.'"

I blinked, confused. "What? For what?"

Her grin widened, but she just shrugged casually. "You'll figure it out."

"What are you talking about?" I asked, my brow furrowing, but she just waved me off.

"Don't worry about it! I'll see you later," she said, her voice sing-song as she shooed me out of the car.

I frowned, still puzzled, but I figured it was just Nala being weird. I shrugged it off, grabbed my bags, and got out of the car, waving as she drove off. The autumn breeze hit me, and I headed toward the front door, my mind still stuck on Nala's cryptic message.

But then I froze.

Standing on the doorstep was a familiar figure with striking red hair. My stomach sank when I realized who it was. Natalia.

She turned around at the sound of my footsteps, her eyes narrowing in confusion when she saw me. "Hailey?" she asked, her tone incredulous. "What are you doing here?"

I stood there for a second, caught off guard. Natalia didn't know I lived here now. Hell, she probably thought I was just some weirdo showing up at Callum's house.

Only, that wasn't exactly me. That was her.

"Uh, I'm just..." I trailed off, trying to think of something—anything—that didn't sound ridiculous.

But before I could come up with an excuse, the door swung open, and there stood Callum, looking equally surprised to see the two of us standing there.

He glanced between us, his eyebrows raised. "What's going on?" he asked, clearly confused.

Natalia folded her arms, glancing at me like I was an intruder, like I was the one who'd just randomly showed up at Callum's doorstep. "Yeah, Hailey. What's going on? What are you doing here?"

I looked at Callum, waiting to see what he'd do. I wasn't sure if he'd explain things—maybe tell Natalia that I lived here now or explain why she was here.

But instead, he did something I wasn't expecting at all.

Without a word, Callum reached out, gently grabbed Natalia's arm, and pulled her inside. Before I could process it, the door closed with a soft thud, leaving me standing there on the doorstep.

I blinked, staring at the door in disbelief.

What just happened?

For a moment, I stood frozen, the confusion and awkwardness swirling in my chest. Had he seriously just... left me out here? I glanced around, hoping maybe this was some kind of misunderstanding, but no. I was alone, standing there like an idiot. I glanced down at my bags and the newly acquired makeup I was excited to try out. I'd been in a good mood not even five minutes ago, and now I felt ridiculous.

It wasn't like I wanted to be involved in whatever was going on between Callum and Natalia, but still... being shut out like that? It stung more than I wanted to admit.

My chest tightened, and I clenched my fists around the handles of the bags.

What the hell was I supposed to do now? Knock on the door? Go around back and sneak in like I didn't exist? A mix of frustration and embarrassment bubbled up inside me.

I let out a slow breath, my throat tight as I turned away from the door. Maybe this was a sign that I didn't belong here in this weird, tangled-up mess between Callum and Natalia.

I was just Hailey—nerdy, awkward Hailey. And maybe I wasn't supposed to be part of whatever was going on in that house right now.

With a lump in my throat, I picked up my bags and started to walk around the side of the house, heading for the back entrance.

I took the long way around, slipping through the side gate and heading to the back door, trying to keep my footsteps quiet. My emotions were all tangled up—anger, embarrassment, and a deep sense of confusion. I wasn't even sure why I was this upset. It wasn't like Callum owed me anything, and yet… being shut out like that stung way more than I was prepared for.

I shouldn't be feeling this much, right? It wasn't a big deal. It shouldn't have been. But as I opened the back door and quietly stepped inside, that tight knot of frustration only grew.

I moved through the kitchen, trying to make my way downstairs as quickly as possible. I just needed to get to my room and cool off. But before I could make it down the steps, I saw Callum standing in the hallway.

He opened his mouth to say something, probably to explain or—hell, I didn't even know—but I didn't give him the chance.

Without even thinking, I harshly shoved past him, not caring if I was being rude. I just needed to get away from him, away from everything. He called my name, but I didn't turn around. I headed straight for the basement, my steps down the stairs quick and heavy.

I slammed the door behind me once I reached my room, the sound echoing in the small space. My heart was still pounding, my emotions too raw to deal with. I didn't know if I was more angry at him or at myself for feeling this way.

All I knew was that I didn't want to face any of it right now. I didn't wanna fucking face him.

I flinched when I heard the banging on the door. My heart skipped a beat as I realized it was Callum. Of course, it was. "Hailey, open up!" His voice was muffled but tense, frustration clear in every word.

I clenched my fists, determined to ignore him. I wasn't ready to deal with him, not now, not when I felt like this. I stared at the floor, hoping he'd give up.

But then his voice came again, louder, more demanding. "Open the door!"

I snapped, shouting back before I could stop myself. "Go away! It was in our rules to not go into each other's rooms, wasn't it?"

There was a moment of silence, just long enough for me to hope he'd finally leave. But then he banged on the door again, harder this time.

"Fuck the rules!" he shouted, his voice raw and insistent. "I need to talk to you!"

I squeezed my eyes shut, my emotions a whirlwind. The anger, the confusion, the embarrassment—it was all bubbling to the surface. Part of me wanted to open the door and demand answers, to confront him for making me feel like this. But another part of me just wanted to be left alone. I didn't trust myself to face him right now, not with everything so raw and unfiltered.

"Just... go away, Callum," I muttered, my voice quieter now but just as stubborn.

But I knew he wouldn't.

I started unpacking my bags, my back turned to the door, trying to focus on anything except the fact that Callum was standing just on the other side. I figured he'd get tired and leave eventually, but instead, his voice came through the door, softer now, but no less intense.

"I was just explaining to Natalia," he began, almost like he was pleading with me to listen. "I told her to never come here again. To stay away from you. I said if she even comes close to you, she'd regret it."

I paused for a second, my fingers still gripping a makeup palette, trying to make sense of what he was saying. I shook my head, continuing to unpack. "Yeah, right," I muttered under my breath. "Why should I believe that?"

"I'm serious," he said, his tone sounding desperate now. "I don't want her anywhere near you."

I set the palette down and turned toward the door, still not opening it. "Why are you trying so hard to convince me?" I asked, my voice sharper than I intended. "Why should I care what goes on between you and Natalia?"

There was a pause on the other side, and I could hear Callum shift. His voice came quieter, almost hesitant. "Because… I care. And it's not like that between her and I anymore, okay? It hasn't been for a while."

I swallowed, my heart pounding in my chest. "*You* care?" I repeated, my voice softer now, but still holding onto the remnants of my frustration. "And why do you care so much about what I think?"

"I don't know!" he blurted out, sounding frustrated with himself. "I just… I can't stand the thought of you being pissed off at me for something that's not even like that. Natalia doesn't matter. I just told her to fuck off, that's it."

The intensity of his words hit me like a punch to the gut, and I felt my throat tighten. With his voice on the other side of the door, all the feelings I'd been trying to bury—confusion, frustration, and something else I didn't want to name—were rising to the surface.

I didn't know what to say.

I didn't know how to feel about any of this.

"I don't know what you want from me, Callum," I whispered, feeling the weight of everything pressing down on me.

He let out a long breath, his voice quiet but filled with something raw and real. "I just want you to open the door. Please. Let's talk."

The room felt smaller now, the air heavy as I stood frozen, his words echoing through the door. I didn't know what to do with them—what to do with any of this.

I clenched my fists at my sides, staring at the door like it could somehow give me answers. I could hear him shifting outside, waiting for something—anything—from me. But I couldn't. I couldn't open that door.

"I can't," I finally said, my voice tight. "I can't open the door."

"Why not?" Callum's voice came back, rough around the edges, like he was trying to keep it together. "What are you so afraid of, Hailey?"

"Afraid?" I scoffed, more at myself than him, because maybe that was exactly it. "I'm not afraid. I just don't want to deal with this. I don't want to deal with you right now."

"Bullshit," he shot back, his voice raising. "You're mad. You're pissed because of Natalia. And you know what? I get it. I shouldn't have left you outside, alright? But you won't even listen—"

"Why shut me out?!" I fired back, stepping closer to the door, my chest heaving. "Why close the damn door on me like I didn't even matter?"

There was silence on the other side, but I could hear his breathing—quick, uneven. Then, in a low, tense voice, he said, "Don't say that. You do matter, Hailey. More than you realize."

My heart lurched at that, but instead of softening, it made me angrier. Why was he saying all this now? Why did he have to confuse everything?

"You don't get to say that," I said, my voice shaky but loud, as the tension between us reached its breaking point. "You don't get to make me feel like this. I don't even know what you want from me!"

"I want you to stop pretending like you don't care!" he shouted, his voice cracking with frustration. "You're pissed at me because you do care, and you know it!"

The words hit me like a punch. My hands shook at my sides, the feelings too big to contain anymore. I felt like I was teetering on the edge of something I couldn't control.

"And what about you?" I yelled back. "Why do you care so much about what I think? You act like I'm just some annoying houseguest, then turn around and pull this shit! What the hell do you want, Callum?!"

"I don't know!" he shouted, his voice raw and breaking. "I don't fucking know, alright? I just know that I can't stand this —this thing between us—this whatever it is. You drive me crazy, Hailey!"

I was breathing hard now, my emotions crashing over me in waves. I wanted to deny it, to push all of this away, but there was no escaping it.

"*You* drive *me* crazy," I shot back, my voice almost shaking now. "I don't understand you! One minute you're a jerk, the next you're…"

"What?" he challenged, his voice lower now, but no less intense. "What am I, Hailey? Tell me."

I swallowed hard, my throat tight. The truth was right there, but I wasn't ready to say it.

"I don't know," I whispered, my anger giving way to something even scarier. "I don't know what you are to me anymore."

For a long moment, there was silence, heavy and charged. Then he said, his voice softer but still filled with frustration, "Then open the door. Let's figure it out."

I bit my lip, torn between the pounding in my chest and the anger still burning under my skin. But I couldn't move. I was paralyzed by the fear of what would happen if I opened that door—and what would happen if I didn't.

"I can't," I said, my voice barely above a whisper now.

"Fine," Callum muttered, his voice cold again. "Then stay in there. Just don't act like you don't care when you clearly do."

And with that, I heard him walk away, leaving me standing alone in the deafening silence.

CHAPTER 50

CALLUM

I STORMED INTO MY ROOM, SLAMMING THE DOOR BEHIND ME SO HARD THE WALLS shook. My chest was heaving, my fists clenched. I was beyond pissed. I saw both our parents downstairs, their concerned looks obvious—they'd definitely heard the argument. But I didn't care. I couldn't care right now.

Fucking Natalia.

She showed up out of nowhere and messed everything up. I had yanked her inside because the last thing I needed was Hailey or anyone else seeing that mess play out on the front porch. I'd told Natalia, pretty harshly, to fuck off, to stay away from Hailey, to stop showing up uninvited.

By the time I'd opened the door to send her off, Hailey had already gone around the back.

She didn't see what really happened. She didn't know how I'd handled it—how much I wanted to make sure Natalia stayed out of our lives for good.

I sat down hard on the edge of my bed, running a hand through my hair, feeling the anger burn in my chest. Hailey had no idea why I'd pulled Natalia inside.

I didn't want to expose that Hailey and I were living together, didn't want anyone knowing the personal stuff going on in our lives. And yeah, maybe I didn't want Hailey to see how mean I was to Natalia. I knew she'd think I was a jerk.

But fuck. She misunderstood everything.

She thought I was shutting her out, that I didn't care. I'd hurt her, and now, no matter what I said, she didn't believe me. My mind raced through the argument, the way her voice broke when she said she hated how it made her feel. She cared. She actually fucking cared about me, more than she was willing to admit. And I'd ruined it.

It was my fault.

Why did I have to be so damn stupid?

I slammed my fist into my mattress, frustration boiling over. "Fuck!"

I sat on the edge of my bed, my head in my hands, breathing hard. Panic was twisting in my gut, something I hadn't felt in a long time.

Hailey probably hated me. That thought kept circling around in my mind, and no matter how hard I tried to push it away, it wouldn't leave.

But here's the thing—I was used to Hailey hating me. That's how it had always been. Since freshman year, we had traded insults and gotten under each other's skin. It had been part of our weird, messed-up dynamic.

But now? Now it felt different. Now I was panicking about it. Because I didn't want her to hate me. I really didn't. And that realization hit me like a truck, making my chest tighten with a frustration I didn't know what to do with.

She was Hailey—nerdy, reclusive Hailey. The girl who drove me crazy, who always knew how to push my buttons, who could get under my skin without even trying.

And yet, here I was, spiraling because I couldn't stand the idea of her actually hating me now. Not after everything. Not after... whatever this was between us had started shifting.

I was so pissed. At the situation, at Natalia for showing up and making everything worse, but mostly at myself.

THE NEXT MORNING, THE AWKWARDNESS HUNG THICK IN THE AIR AS I MADE MY way downstairs. I was still half-asleep, hoping that maybe today wouldn't feel as messed up as yesterday. But as soon as I sat down at the table, the unease settled right back in.

I glanced around. "Where's Hailey?" I asked, trying to sound casual.

Mrs. Eller gave me a tight smile, not quite meeting my eyes. "Oh, she already ate."

I blinked. "Already?"

Mr. Eller chimed in, looking between his coffee and me. "Yeah, she was up pretty early."

I didn't have to ask why. It was obvious. She'd eaten early to avoid me. I could feel my stomach twist with that familiar frustration, but I just nodded and sat down, grabbing some toast and eggs. I picked at the food more than I ate it, my thoughts running in circles about everything that had happened.

No Hailey. No chance to talk to her or fix this. Just me, sitting in awkward silence with her parents, who probably knew something was up but weren't saying anything.

I finished my breakfast in record time, the quiet eating away at me. And then, without much thought, I retreated to my room. I shut the door behind me, sinking onto my bed, feeling that same frustration bubble back up.

Ugh.

Nothing was going right. Not with Hailey. Not with anything.

I tried again at lunch, hoping maybe this time I'd catch Hailey, but when I asked her parents, the answer was the same.

"She already ate," her mom said again, giving me a sympathetic look.

Of course, she did. Avoiding me again. My frustration grew, bubbling under the surface. This was getting ridiculous. I wanted to talk to her, clear the air, but it felt like every time I tried, she was one step ahead, making sure I never got the chance.

I was about to head back to my room when the doorbell rang. I sighed, figuring it was probably some delivery or something. But when I opened the door, I found Nala standing there with a big smile on her face.

"Hey, Callum! I'm here to get ready with Hailey for Sasha's Halloween party tonight," she said, holding up a bag filled with what I assumed was makeup and costume stuff.

"Shit, yeah, that's tonight," I muttered to myself, suddenly realizing I'd completely forgotten about the party. My mind had been too wrapped up in everything else.

As Nala stood there, it hit me. Wasn't one of our house rules to let the other person know before bringing someone over? I hadn't even thought about it, but then again, I had broken a rule myself last night by going down to Hailey's room. We weren't supposed to invade each other's space, and I'd done exactly that.

I sighed, figuring it wasn't worth bringing up now. "Come on in," I said, stepping aside to let Nala in.

She smiled and walked past me, heading straight for the basement. "Thanks! See you later!"

I stood there for a moment, watching her disappear down the stairs. I couldn't help but feel a twinge of something— maybe guilt, maybe frustration.

I dragged myself back up to my room, sinking onto my bed like some kind of sad, pathetic idiot. The day had felt like one long, frustrating blur, and with Hailey avoiding me at every turn, I couldn't shake the feeling that everything was falling apart. I just lay there, staring at the ceiling, feeling sorry for myself while the sun began to set outside.

I knew I should get up, should probably start getting ready for Sasha's stupid Halloween party. The guys were all planning to go, and it wasn't like I could just bail. With a groan, I sat up and spotted the Spirit Halloween bag sitting in the corner of my room—the prisoner outfit I'd picked up with Grayson, Adam, and Ibra the other day.

I pulled it out and threw it on, but as I looked at myself in the mirror, all I felt was… well, like shit.

The orange outfit hung on me like some cheap costume, but that wasn't the real problem. The real problem was this mess with Hailey. I couldn't stop thinking about how we'd left things, and now, even getting dressed for a party felt wrong.

I rubbed my face, trying to shake off the heaviness in my chest, but it didn't go away. It was all I could think about—the argument, the hurt in her voice, the way I kept screwing this up.

This wasn't how today was supposed to go. But now, here I was, standing in a damn prisoner costume, feeling more trapped by my own feelings than by anything else.

CHAPTER 51
HAILEY

I STOOD IN FRONT OF THE MIRROR, ADJUSTING MY PIGTAILS FOR WHAT FELT LIKE THE hundredth time, the strands dyed pink and blue (with temporary spray-on hair dye) just like Harley Quinn's.

I couldn't shake the self-conscious feeling as I stared at my reflection, my mind racing through everything that had happened between me and Callum. It had been a mess, and now, as I stood here getting ready for Sasha's Halloween party, I still couldn't stop thinking about it.

Nala, already half-dressed in her Joker costume—complete with a tight purple suit, a short skirt, and a bright green wig—was sitting on the bed, cursing out Natalia for the tenth time as we recounted what happened. "I swear, if I see her, I'm gonna lose it," Nala muttered, smoothing out her skirt with a fierce look on her face. "What the hell was she even doing here?"

I rolled my eyes, tugging on the hem of my fishnet tights. "I don't know. Showed up uninvited, I guess. She's literally a nightmare."

Nala snorted. "A nightmare with zero boundaries. You should've shoved her out the door."

I laughed despite myself, shaking my head. "Trust me, I wanted to." But the thought of seeing Callum pull her inside still stung. That frustration bubbled up again, but I pushed it down. I didn't want to dwell on it right now.

Tonight was supposed to be fun—just me and Nala, living our best life as Joker and Harley Quinn.

"Hey, are you sure about this?" I asked, glancing at her. "You look way more like Joker than I look like Harley. I feel ridiculous."

Nala stood up, pulling her green wig into place with a playful smirk. She looked fierce, completely owning the Joker look. "You look gorgeous," she said, giving me a once-over. "Trust me, Hailey, you're killing it. You've got the Harley Quinn thing down. Sexy, bold, and badass."

I shifted a little, still feeling unsure as I looked at my reflection. The red and blue shorts, the fishnets, the shirt that said "Daddy's Little Monster"—it all felt a bit much for me. But the way Nala said it made me feel a little better. I managed a small smile. "Thanks. You really think so?"

Nala nodded confidently. "One hundred percent. I bet Callum's gonna lose his mind when he sees you."

I groaned, shaking my head. "Can we not talk about him right now?"

"Alright, alright," Nala said, hands up in mock surrender. "But you'll see."

We laughed, and the tension eased as I grabbed my camera from the dresser. I felt a little better with it in my hands, like I always did when I was behind the lens. "Let's take some pictures before we head out," I said.

Nala put on her best Joker face, and I snapped a few shots, smiling as I did. I turned the camera toward myself, taking a couple of us together, trying to capture the carefree moment before we had to face whatever awkwardness was waiting for us at the party.

As I lowered the camera, catching my breath from all the laughing and picture-taking, Nala gave me a long, thoughtful look. She had that expression she always wore when she was about to ask something serious—like she was reading me, seeing past all the surface-level stuff and straight into my head. I sighed, knowing what was coming before she even said it.

"Hailey, come sit," Nala said, her voice softer now, but firm. She patted the spot next to her on the bed, her Joker grin replaced with something more sincere. "We need to talk."

I frowned, already feeling the tension creeping back into my chest. "About what?"

"You know what," Nala said, crossing her legs and turning to face me fully. "About Callum. About everything that's going on between you two."

I groaned, dropping onto the bed next to her but refusing to meet her gaze. "Do we have to?"

"Yes, we do," she said firmly, nudging my shoulder. "I get it, you don't want to deal with this, but you've been avoiding your feelings for too long. It's time to sit down and confront them. Once and for all."

I swallowed hard, feeling the weight of her words sink in. She was right. I had been running from how I felt—from the frustration, the confusion, the anger, and... whatever else it was between me and Callum. I didn't know how to make sense of it, didn't know how to untangle everything that had built up between us over the years.

"I don't know how to," I admitted quietly, my voice barely above a whisper. "I don't even know what I'm feeling half the time." Nala didn't say anything right away. She just gave me time, letting the silence hang between us until I felt ready to speak again.

"I mean, I should hate him, right?" I started, picking at the edge of my fishnets nervously. "We've never gotten along.

We're always at each other's throats. I've spent years thinking he was the most irritating person I'd ever met. But now..." I trailed off, my stomach twisting. "Now I don't even know."

Nala nodded, listening intently. "Go on."

I stared at the floor, trying to sort through the mess in my head. "It's like... he drives me insane, but it's not the same anymore. It's not just about him being annoying or us arguing. It's... it's like there's something else underneath all that. And I hate that I'm even feeling this way."

"Why do you hate it?" Nala asked gently.

"Because I don't want to care," I admitted, my voice cracking slightly. "I don't want to care about what he thinks or what he does. But I do. I care so much that it hurts sometimes, and I hate that I can't just ignore it. When he shut the door on me with Natalia, I felt... I don't know. Betrayed? Angry? Like he picked her over me, even though it doesn't make sense because why should I care?"

Nala's hand rested on my arm, grounding me as I let out the torrent of feelings I'd been bottling up for so long.

"And the worst part," I continued, feeling the emotion rise in my throat, "is that I don't know what I want from him. I don't know if I want him to apologize, or explain, or... something else. But I hate feeling this way. I hate feeling like I don't understand my own emotions when it comes to him."

Nala was quiet for a moment, taking in everything I'd said. Then she gave my arm a gentle squeeze. "It sounds like you've already figured out a lot more than you realize."

I looked at her, confused. "What do you mean?"

"You're not mad because you hate him," Nala said softly. "You're mad because you care about him. And caring about someone... that's a lot scarier than hating them. It means you're letting them in. It means they can hurt you."

Her words hit me like a brick, and I felt my chest tighten. She was right. The anger, the frustration—it wasn't just because Callum was irritating. It was because he had gotten under my skin in a way that no one else had. I cared about him, even when I didn't want to.

"I don't know what to do with that," I whispered, my voice trembling. "I don't know how to deal with it."

"You don't have to know everything right away," Nala said gently. "But you can't keep pretending you don't care. Not to yourself, and definitely not to him."

I swallowed hard, the truth of her words settling into the pit of my stomach. "What if he doesn't feel the same way?"

"Then you deal with that when the time comes," Nala said, smiling softly. "But judging by the way he looks at you, I don't think you need to worry about that."

No matter how hard I tried to stay present, flashes of that conversation kept popping up, like my brain was on a loop, replaying his words over and over.

"You matter, Hailey. More than you realize."

That one had hit hard. When he'd said that, it had shaken something in me. I didn't know if it was the way his voice had cracked, or the intensity in his eyes, but it felt different from the usual Callum who loved to get under my skin.

For once, he wasn't teasing or being sarcastic—he'd been serious. I hated how much those words stuck with me. How they made me feel seen in a way I wasn't sure I was ready for.

"Now, enough of this emotional stuff," Nala said suddenly, brightening the mood. "Let's take a few more pictures before we ruin our makeup by crying or something."

I laughed, wiping at the corner of my eyes. "Deal."

I picked up my camera again and snapped a few more shots, trying to focus on the moment. But even as we posed and joked around, my mind kept drifting back to Callum and everything that had been left unsaid between us.

We grabbed our things and headed up the basement stairs, laughing about how much makeup we'd used, feeling lighter after the conversation. Nala was still fixing her wig, adjusting the green strands so they sat perfectly, while I focused on not tripping over my boots. But as soon as we reached the top step, I nearly walked straight into someone.

Someone tall. And irritated.

It took me a second to realize it was Callum, standing there in the hallway, arms crossed over his chest, his expression set in that familiar frustrated scowl.

And… he was very, very orange.

Was he the Lorax or something?

Oh, no, he was a prisoner. Could've fooled me.

CHAPTER 52

CALLUM

I WAS ADJUSTING THE COLLAR OF THE DAMN ORANGE PRISONER JUMPSUIT FOR WHAT felt like the hundredth time, trying to make it look less like I'd been stuffed into it at the last minute.

It wasn't working. The jumpsuit was scratchy, too bright, and definitely not as cool as I'd hoped it'd be.

Just as I thought about ditching it entirely, I heard clattering coming from the basement stairs. I straightened up, trying to play it cool, like I wasn't just internally groaning about the outfit, but then Hailey and Nala came up the stairs, laughing about something. I tried to act nonchalant, like I didn't care, but the moment I saw her—Hailey—I felt my stomach drop. My mind went completely blank, and for a second, I thought I might actually pass out.

She was dressed up as Harley Quinn.

Holy fuck. Holy *fucking* fuck. I don't know what I'd been expecting, but this? This was something else. Hailey, in those tight shorts, the fishnets, the pigtails dyed pink and blue... She looked better than I could've ever imagined. Way better than I had pictured that night when I'd stupidly searched for Harley Quinn costumes. She was standing there, looking a little shy, but absolutely gorgeous.

I could barely keep it together.

Nala, the little devil, caught the look on my face and winked at me, smirking as she slipped past. "Gotta use the bathroom," she muttered, leaving me and Hailey alone in the hallway.

I stood there, frozen, my heart hammering in my chest. I was sure I was going to pass out. Hailey glanced up at me, her lips parting like she was about to say something, but all I could think was how unfair it was that she looked this good.

"Uh…" I managed, completely lost for words.

We stood there in this awkward silence, the air between us still tense from the argument the night before. I could feel the weight of it settling on my chest, making it hard to even breathe right.

Hailey looked at me for a split second before averting her eyes, clearly unsure of what to say, and I was no better. My throat was dry, my mind racing, but not with anything useful. It was just—her.

And that damn costume. Fuck, I couldn't focus on anything else.

My heart was still pounding like crazy, and I couldn't stop my eyes from trailing over the details. She looked incredible, better than I could've ever imagined. But we weren't talking. And we couldn't just pretend like last night didn't happen. The tension was thick, and the last thing I needed was another argument. Still, it felt like I was going to explode if I didn't say something.

I cleared my throat, but no words came. Hailey shifted slightly, as if waiting for me to break the silence, but I just couldn't figure out where to start.

It wasn't like I could say, *Hey, sorry I was an asshole last night, but also, you look insanely hot right now, and I can't handle it.*

"I—" I started, but then stopped, frustrated with myself for not knowing what the hell to say. The argument was still there, lingering, but the sight of her like this was messing with me too much. I couldn't concentrate.

Damn it. I couldn't handle it any longer.

"I... uh, you look—" I stopped again, feeling like an idiot.

She frowned, probably wondering why I was being so weird, and all I wanted to do was fix everything, say the right thing, but my brain wasn't working. I felt trapped between what I should say and the fact that she was standing right in front of me looking like every damn thought I'd been trying to bury.

"Forget it," I muttered, shaking my head.

I glanced down at myself, suddenly hyper-aware of how ridiculous I must've looked. The orange prisoner jumpsuit didn't fit right at all. The thing was practically hanging off of me, making me look like I was drowning in fabric. I must've grabbed the wrong size at the store, because this wasn't it. And here I was, standing in front of Hailey, looking like total shit while she looked... well, like that.

Frustration flared in my chest again, but this time it wasn't just about the argument or the tension. It was about the fact that I looked like an idiot. I couldn't handle standing here next to her looking like I'd walked straight out of a bad prison-themed gag reel.

I tugged at the jumpsuit, trying to think of a way to salvage it. Anything would be better than this. That's when an idea hit me.

Without thinking too hard about it, I grabbed the bottom half of the jumpsuit and ripped it up the sides. The fabric tore with a satisfying sound, and suddenly, the pants were jagged and tattered at the edges. It wasn't perfect, but at least it looked more like something intentionally messy instead of a kid wearing his dad's clothes.

As I looked down, part of my abdomen was now exposed, and the jumpsuit didn't feel quite so suffocating. I took a deep breath, trying to shake off the embarrassment that had been gnawing at me. I glanced back at Hailey, half expecting her to laugh, but instead, she just stared at me for a second, her eyes flicking briefly to the exposed skin.

"Better, right?" I said, trying to sound casual even though my heart was still pounding in my chest. "Had to make it work somehow."

Hailey blinked, and for the first time, I saw the tiniest flicker of a smile tugging at the corner of her lips. But the tension was still there, hanging between us like an invisible wall.

"Yeah," she said quietly, her eyes meeting mine for a moment before she looked away again. "It's... better." But even though the costume wasn't quite as ridiculous anymore, I still felt like a mess. The jumpsuit might've been fixed, but nothing between us had been.

I glanced around, realizing that we were still alone. The hallway felt quieter, the tension between us palpable, but for once, there was no one around to interrupt. At least, not yet.

My eyes flicked back to Hailey, and I could feel something rising in my chest—something I couldn't quite keep down anymore.

I wanted to make this clear for her, for both of us. I wanted to lay it all out, say whatever the hell I'd been trying to push back for weeks now.

The argument, all the frustration—it all came from something deeper, something I wasn't ready to admit until now.

I stepped forward, closing some of the space between us. My heart raced, and my words were on the tip of my tongue. I wanted to say it. Needed to say it.

But before I could even finish the thought, a small, excited voice cut through the air.

"Hey, guys! Look at us!"

I froze, my head snapping to the side just in time to see Dalton and Nathan clamoring down the stairs, their little costumes bouncing as they hurried into the hallway. They looked adorable, with Dalton in some kind of dinosaur suit and Nathan as a mini superhero.

Their excitement shattered the moment between me and Hailey, and I felt my shoulders sag a little with disappointment, even as they ran up to us with big grins on their faces.

"Look! Roar!" Dalton cheered, striking a ridiculously cute pose in his dinosaur suit.

I forced a smile, trying to switch gears. "Yeah, you guys look great," I said, glancing at Hailey, who was watching the whole thing with an amused look. She had stepped back, the tension between us dissolving into the chaos of the kids' excitement.

Nathan beamed up at Hailey. "What do you think of our costumes?"

"They're awesome," Hailey said, her voice a little softer, but with a genuine smile.

"I know! We're gonna go trick-or-treating and I'm gonna get so much candy, I juat know it," Dalton beamed.

I stood there, feeling the moment slip away, frustrated but also realizing that maybe this wasn't the right time. Not with the kids running around, not with the party looming. But damn, it was hard to shake the feeling that I'd missed my chance—again.

Of course, Nala chose that exact moment to pop out of nowhere, her voice bright and full of energy. "Okay, guys! Let's go! The party's not gonna wait!"

I could practically feel the moment slipping away from me, and the frustration built up again. I'd had the chance. We'd been alone, and I was this close to making things clear—to saying what needed to be said—but it was gone now. Wasted.

CHAPTER 53

HAILEY

The car ride to Sasha's place was quiet—at least between me and Callum. The air was still thick with everything unsaid between us, and I could feel the awkwardness pressing down on me. I kept my eyes on the road ahead, trying to focus on anything but the tension sitting between us in the front seats.

Luckily, Nala was sitting in the back, completely unbothered. She was singing loudly and dramatically to whatever was playing on the radio, her voice cutting through the silence and making the awkwardness a little more bearable. I glanced back at her, and despite everything, I couldn't help but smile.

"Come on, guys!" she called out between verses, nudging me playfully. "You can't be this tense before a party! You're supposed to have fun!"

I forced a laugh, but I couldn't ignore the tight knot in my stomach. This was my first real high school party. I'd never been to one of Sasha's infamous parties—or any party, really. The thought of walking into a place filled with so many people I barely knew made me more nervous than I wanted to admit.

When we finally pulled up to Sasha's house, my jaw almost dropped.

I knew her family had money, but seeing it in person was a whole different story. The place was huge, practically glowing with all the lights strung up outside, and there were already a ton of cars parked along the street. Music was thumping from inside, the low bass echoing out into the night.

Nala hopped out of the car first, looking completely at ease, but I hesitated for a moment before getting out. I glanced at Callum, who was quietly shutting the door and adjusting his jumpsuit. He caught me looking but didn't say anything.

I took a deep breath, trying to calm the nerves bubbling in my chest. This was just a party. A party with a lot of people, sure, but I could handle it.

I followed Nala and Callum up the driveway, my stomach doing nervous flips the whole way. As we got closer, the music thumped louder, and the hum of voices and laughter spilled out into the night.

Callum walked ahead, his hands stuffed in his pockets, looking like he'd been to a million of these parties. To be fair, he probably had. Nala, on the other hand, was practically glowing with excitement, clearly ready to dive headfirst into the chaos.

When we stepped inside, I froze.

The house was packed—people everywhere, talking, laughing, dancing. The music was even louder now, the bass vibrating through the floor. There were lights strung up, casting a warm glow over the entire place, and the energy was electric. Everyone was in costume, some more extravagant than others, and it felt like I'd just walked into some kind of wild, crowded dream.

My breath caught in my throat. Oh my god. There were so many people. My head spun as I tried to take it all in, feeling like I was being swallowed up by the crowd.

Nala must've noticed my deer-in-the-headlights expression because she immediately turned to me, her hand resting on my shoulder. "Don't worry, girl," she said with a reassuring smile. "I got you. You're gonna be fine."

I nodded, though I wasn't so sure. "There are so many people here," I muttered, my voice almost lost in the noise.

Nala just laughed. "It's a party, girl! This is what it's all about! Just stick with me, and you'll have fun. Promise."

I could see now why everyone talked about her parties. The place was decked out from top to bottom, every inch decorated for Halloween.

Cobwebs stretched across doorways, fake spiders dangled from the ceiling, and eerie orange and purple lights bathed everything in a spooky glow. There were carved pumpkins lining the walls, some with flickering candles inside, others grinning with sharp teeth. The whole place had this energy that was hard to ignore.

People were scattered everywhere—some in intense conversations, others dancing in the living room where the music was loudest, and even more spilling out onto the back patio. Everyone seemed so... alive, like this was the highlight of their month.

I had to admit, as overwhelming as it was, there was something about it that made sense. I could understand now why Sasha's parties were such a big deal. It was like stepping into a different world, one where everything was more intense, more exciting, more fun.

Nala bumped me with her shoulder, grinning as she took in the decorations. "Now do you get it? This is why everyone talks about Sasha's parties. She goes all out."

I nodded, feeling the slightest bit more at ease as we walked through the crowd. "Yeah... I can see that now."

Nala gave me a knowing smile. "Don't worry, you'll settle in. Let's grab some drinks, loosen up a bit, and then we'll have some real fun."

I still wasn't completely sure about it, but seeing the effort Sasha put into this—the decorations, the vibe, the sheer excitement in the air—it was hard not to be impressed. Maybe this wouldn't be so bad after all.

I couldn't help but notice Callum still hovering awkwardly around us. He kept glancing around, but I could tell he wasn't fully engaged. It was like he was there, but not really there. The tension from earlier hadn't disappeared, and it was making things feel weird. I tried to ignore it, but every time I caught his eye, it brought back all the unresolved stuff between us.

Before I could dwell on it too much, something else caught my attention—a group of guys standing near the kitchen, dressed in matching prisoner costumes. I squinted, realizing who they were.

The... prison gang.

Grayson, Adam, and Ibra had also gone all out for their prisoner look. Some of them had fake tattoos, others had handcuffs dangling from their belts. They were clearly leaning into the whole "rough and tough" theme, and they seemed to be enjoying every second of it.

Grayson caught sight of Callum first and waved him over with a grin. "Hey, Reid! About time you showed up!"

I glanced at Callum, who looked relieved to see his crew. He gave me and Nala a quick look before heading over to them, his mood seeming to lighten up a little as he joined their group.

For a second, I watched them interact—joking around, roughhousing a bit, and showing off their costumes. It was almost like watching Callum slip into a different version of himself, one that wasn't weighed down by whatever was between us.

Nala leaned in with a smirk. "Looks like they went all out, huh?"

"Yeah," I muttered, still watching as Callum and his friends laughed about something. "They really did.

After dancing for a bit with Nala, I was starting to loosen up. The initial nerves that had gripped me when we first arrived were finally fading, and the music, the crowd, and even the decorations were beginning to feel more like fun than overwhelming.

Nala twirled me around, laughing as we stumbled slightly, our costumes swishing under the flashing party lights.

"See?" Nala teased, grinning. "Told you this would be fun!"

I couldn't help but smile. Maybe she was right. Maybe I'd been overthinking everything. We eventually made our way toward the kitchen to grab something to drink, feeling more at ease. Just as we reached the counter, we heard a familiar, shrill voice.

"Ahh! Hey, girlies!"

I turned to see Sasha, dressed as Tinker Bell, practically floating over to us. Her costume was spot-on, with shimmering wings and a glittering green dress that sparkled under the lights. She looked radiant, as always—Sasha had this way of being effortlessly charming.

Sasha's eyes landed on me, and her expression lit up even more. "Oh, wow, Hailey! I've never seen you at one of my parties before!" She beamed at me, looking genuinely pleased to see me here. "They're always open invite, so I thought maybe you just didn't know about them, or…"

She trailed off, waiting for me to fill in the blanks. The truth was, it wasn't that I didn't know about her parties—it was that I'd never wanted to come. I'd always been more comfortable staying out of the social spotlight. But standing here, looking at Sasha's eager face, I couldn't exactly say that.

"Yeah, I guess I never really got around to it before," I said with a shrug, keeping it vague.

Sasha waved her hands dramatically. "Well, I'm so glad you came tonight! You and Nala look amazing! I mean, Joker and Harley? You're killing it!"

Nala winked, clearly loving the attention. "Thanks, Sasha! You're looking pretty fierce as Tinker Bell yourself."

Sasha grinned, her wings fluttering slightly. "I try, I try." Then she turned back to me. "But seriously, Hailey, it's so awesome to have you here. I've always wondered why you didn't come before. You know, you're welcome anytime."

I nodded, smiling awkwardly. Sasha was being her usual sweet self, and it made me feel a little guilty for avoiding her parties all these years. But tonight? Tonight I was here, and maybe that was enough.

Sasha leaned in, her eyes sparkling with excitement as she grinned at us. "Alright, girlies, now for the fun part—boy chat!"

Nala and I exchanged amused looks, but Sasha didn't waste any time diving in. "So, I'm totally locked in with Adam," she announced, a satisfied smile spreading across her face.

I wasn't surprised. Adam was one of the more laid-back guys on the soccer team, and knowing Sasha, they probably balanced each other out perfectly. Nala chimed in, her voice playful. "I've got my sights set on Ibra."

I raised an eyebrow, unable to stop the grin that spread across my face. "I knew it! Ever since Sports Day, I've had a feeling you were vibing with him."

Nala laughed, flipping her hair over her shoulder. "Well, you know, the man's got some serious game, on and off the field."

Sasha giggled and then turned her attention to me, her eyes lighting up with curiosity. "Ooh, ooh! What about you, Hailey? Who's caught your eye?"

I froze for a second, not expecting to be pulled into this conversation. My heart skipped a beat, the image of Callum flashing through my mind for a split second. But I quickly forced myself to laugh, trying to keep it casual. "Oh, no one, really," I said, brushing it off as best as I could.

Sasha narrowed her eyes playfully, clearly not convinced. "Come on, Hailey. You're at a party with a bunch of cute guys, and you're telling me none of them have your attention?"

I shrugged, trying to deflect. "I'm just here for the good company."

Nala, being Nala, gave me a knowing look, one that told me she wasn't buying it for a second. And suddenly, I felt that familiar tension creep back in—tension that had nothing to do with the party and everything to do with a certain someone.

But she didn't push it further.

The party continued and before I noticed, it had shifted gears. After wandering around and watching some of the drinking games from the sidelines, I felt a little out of place but was doing my best to enjoy the chaos. The laughter, the music, the thumping energy—it was all fun to watch, but I didn't really know how to jump in. That was, until Nala and Sasha roped me into Spin the Bottle.

We gathered in one of the hallways, sitting in a circle on the floor almost like we were about to summon something. I glanced around at the group, feeling my nerves fluttering again. It was me, Nala, Sasha, the four boys—Callum, Grayson, Adam, and Ibra—and Cassie, another cheerleader who'd been giving Callum those I'm-so-into-you looks for the last few minutes. Her eyes kept flicking to him like she was hoping he'd notice.

The bottle was in the middle, an empty glass one that Sasha had grabbed off a shelf somewhere. We all sat cross-legged, some of us leaning against the wall, others more relaxed. I wasn't as relaxed.

I'd had a few sips of something earlier, but not enough to feel bold. My experience with drinking was mostly confined to Nala and me having a couple of low-key nights in her basement, so I was definitely not ready for this.

Sasha was already grinning, clearly in her element. She clapped her hands together. "Alright, here's the deal. Whoever the bottle lands on, you have to kiss them. If you don't want to, you take a shot out of this." She held up a bottle filled with something dark, probably whiskey or rum. "We'll go until it's empty, got it?"

Everyone nodded or murmured in agreement, but I could feel my heart beating faster. Kiss someone? I wasn't sure I was ready for that. Not in front of this group.

"Come on, Hailey, it's just for fun," Nala whispered beside me, nudging me with her shoulder. "And you just have to drink that if you don't wanna kiss anyone. It's nothing strong, I checked it earlier."

"Okay," I smiled nervously, nodding but still feeling uneasy.

Sasha, being the fearless leader, decided to go first. She leaned forward, grabbed the bottle, and gave it a hard spin. We all watched as it whirled around, the glass catching the light. My stomach did a nervous flip as it slowed down, finally landing on... Adam. The group erupted in playful cheers and teasing laughter.

"Shit's rigged!" Grayson called out, pointing at the bottle dramatically.

Sasha grinned, completely unbothered. "Oh, please. Like I need a rigged bottle to kiss my man." She crawled forward with a confident smirk, closing the distance between her and Adam before pressing a quick, playful kiss to his lips.

Adam grinned as the group whooped and hollered, and Sasha leaned back, wiping the lipstick off the corner of her mouth with a playful flourish.

"Alright, alright, your turn, Adam," she said, handing him the bottle.

Adam grabbed it, still smiling from the teasing. He gave the bottle a spin, and again, the glass whirled around as everyone leaned in, waiting to see who'd be next. My nerves spiked again, and I found myself holding my breath, hoping it wouldn't land on me.

It slowed down, the clinking sound of the glass echoing in the hall as the bottle spun once... twice... then finally stopped.

On Callum.

I felt a jolt go through me as everyone's attention shifted to him. Adam's grin widened as he looked between Callum and the bottle. "Well, well, looks like it's your lucky day, man."

Callum, who had been sitting quietly, shrugged, his usual smirk tugging at the corners of his mouth. "Let's get this over with," he muttered, crawling forward to Adam. The room filled with laughter as the two quickly shared the briefest, most reluctant kiss on the cheek, followed by exaggerated groans of mock disgust.

"Disappointing," Sasha teased, shaking her head. "I was expecting more commitment."

Grayson laughed, "Yeah, Callum, you gotta bring the heat next time!"

Callum smirked, rolling his eyes as he grabbed the bottle for his turn to spin. And as the bottle began its next spin, I couldn't help but feel a knot forming in my stomach.

Callum spun the bottle, and we all watched as it slowed down, the tension building. I kept my eyes on it, feeling that nervous flutter in my stomach, until it finally landed on... Cassie.

The room went quiet for a split second, and Cassie immediately perked up, her eyes practically lighting up. She shot Callum a confident, flirty look, clearly expecting him to follow the rules of the game. But Callum, without missing a beat, reached for the bottle of liquor.

He uncapped it, poured himself a shot, and downed it, avoiding eye contact with Cassie the entire time.

"Okay, rude," Cassie muttered, her tone playful but with a hint of annoyance.

I tried not to react, but I couldn't help the strange mix of relief and confusion bubbling up inside me. Callum didn't want to kiss her.

Why? He'd kissed girls before, probably tons of them, so why was he avoiding it this time?

Cassie, trying to brush it off, grabbed the bottle and spun it again, putting on a dramatic show as if Callum's rejection hadn't fazed her at all. We all watched as the bottle spun, whirling around and around until it finally slowed and pointed toward... Ibra.

A grin spread across Cassie's face, and she wasted no time crawling forward to kiss him. I watched as she pressed her lips to his, and it was then that I felt Nala tense up beside me. I glanced at her, seeing the tightness in her jaw, the way her posture stiffened as she watched Cassie and Ibra.

Cassie leaned back with a satisfied smile, clearly pleased with herself, and the group laughed and teased, but Nala didn't join in. I could feel her frustration even though she didn't say anything, and it made me shift uncomfortably.

Ibra took the bottle, his usual confidence showing in the way he gave it a firm spin. Everyone leaned in a little, watching as it whirled around, slowing as the neck of the bottle pointed... directly at Nala.

I felt her stiffen beside me, but Ibra grinned, clearly unbothered by the fact that she had been a bit tense since Cassie's kiss. He didn't hesitate. Crawling forward, he closed the distance between them with a playful swagger that only made the others laugh and cheer even louder.

Nala, still trying to shake off her frustration, gave him a half-hearted glare, but before she could say anything, Ibra cupped her face and pulled her into a hard kiss on the lips.

The circle erupted into cheers, whistles, and laughter, the noise echoing down the hallway. Nala's face turned a deep shade of red as everyone whooped around us, but she didn't pull away. If anything, she leaned into the kiss a little, and when Ibra finally let go, her eyes were wide, her lips slightly parted in surprise.

"Okay, okay, calm down, people," she said, her voice a little shaky, trying to act like she wasn't flustered. But I could see her cheeks burning with embarrassment—or was it something else?

She sat back, adjusting her costume as the group continued to tease her, but she quickly grabbed the bottle and gave it a hard spin, clearly ready to shift the attention. The bottle spun and spun, slowing down as I watched it intently.

And then, it stopped.

On me.

I blinked, surprised, as the others turned their attention to us, their teasing grins widening. Nala, still flushed from her kiss with Ibra, shot me a mischievous look. "Well, well, Hailey," she said with a playful smirk. "Guess it's our turn."

I couldn't help but laugh, a mix of nerves and amusement bubbling up inside me.

Nala leaned in, crawling forward with exaggerated flair, making everyone laugh again. She wasn't about to back down from the moment, and neither was I. As she reached me, she gave me a wink before pulling me into a quick, playful kiss.

The kiss was light, more fun than anything else, but the group cheered like it was the most intense kiss they'd ever seen. We both broke apart, laughing as the others clapped and whistled, Sasha in particular giggling loudly.

"Look at you two!" Sasha teased. "Totally killing it."

I couldn't help but feel a little more relaxed now, the initial tension of the game easing as the laughter and playful energy around us took over. The teasing, the kisses—it all felt like part of the fun now, and I was starting to enjoy the chaos.

I could feel my heart pounding as I reached for the bottle, knowing it was my turn. My fingers trembled slightly as I grabbed it, and I could feel everyone's eyes on me—waiting, watching. I'd been doing okay so far, but now that it was my turn to spin, the nerves came rushing back.

I gave the bottle a good spin, watching it whirl around, the glass catching the light as it twirled. The anticipation in the circle grew as the bottle began to slow down. Everyone leaned forward, their eyes glued to where it would land. My heart raced faster with every passing second.

The bottle slowed, turning one last time before it stopped.

On Grayson.

My breath hitched as I stared at the bottle pointing right at him. Grayson, who had been lounging back against the wall, raised an eyebrow with a playful smile. He didn't seem to mind, but I froze, unsure of what to do.

The group went quiet for a second, waiting for me to make a move. But all I could feel was the weight of the moment pressing down on me. I wasn't ready for this—for kissing Grayson in front of everyone, especially not with Callum sitting right there.

I hesitated, and the silence stretched longer.

Suddenly, Callum's voice cut through the tension, sharp and impatient. "Keep it going already," he snapped, his tone cold. I glanced at him, startled by how irritated he sounded. He was sitting there, arms crossed, glaring at me like I was taking too long.

His words stung, even though I knew I shouldn't care. But something about the way he said it made the knot in my stomach tighten. I didn't know what I was expecting—maybe for him to say nothing, maybe for him to not even care—but the irritation in his voice made me feel small.

I looked back at Grayson, who was still waiting, his expression more amused than anything. Everyone else was watching me, their curiosity piqued by my hesitation.

I took a deep breath, my mind racing. I could kiss him. It was just a game, after all. But the thought of it made my stomach flip in ways I couldn't explain. Maybe it was Callum's reaction. Maybe it was the weird tension in the air. I didn't know.

Instead of leaning in, I reached for the bottle of liquor sitting in the middle of the circle. "I'm taking a shot," I muttered, forcing a small smile to cover my nerves.

The group erupted into playful groans and laughter. "Come on, Hailey!" Nala teased, nudging me with her elbow. "It's just Grayson!"

I shrugged, trying to play it off. "I guess I'm just not feeling it," I said, avoiding Callum's gaze as I poured myself a shot.

The others teased me good-naturedly as I downed the drink, the burn of the alcohol hitting my throat harder than I expected. I coughed a little, making everyone laugh, but at least it gave me an excuse to avoid looking at anyone—especially Callum. As the group moved on, I sat back, feeling a mix of relief and embarrassment wash over me.

My heart was still pounding, and even though I'd avoided the kiss, I couldn't shake the strange tension lingering in the air. Callum's words echoed in my head, sharper than they had any right to be.

I could feel it—the heat of Callum's glare from across the circle, even as the game moved on without me. Everyone else was laughing and teasing each other, but I couldn't shake the uncomfortable knot in my stomach.

His eyes were on me, sharp and unrelenting, like he was silently judging me for what just happened.

It was too much. I needed to get out of there.

"Excuse me for a second," I muttered, my voice barely cutting through the noise. No one really paid attention except Nala, who gave me a quick glance of concern, but I waved it off.

I stood up and slipped out of the circle, weaving through the crowded hallway until I found a quieter part of the house.

I leaned against the wall, taking in a deep breath, trying to calm the whirlwind of emotions inside me. I was still buzzing from the shot, the alcohol warm in my chest, but that wasn't what had me so rattled.

It was everything that happened in the last few minutes —the tension with Callum, his snide remark, the way I froze when I could've just kissed Grayson and moved on.

I ran my fingers through my hair, still feeling the lingering frustration twist in my gut. I couldn't understand why I hesitated. Grayson's great, he's nice, and it wasn't like anyone would've thought twice about it.

But deep down, I knew it wasn't about Grayson.

It was about Callum.

I leaned my head back against the wall, closing my eyes as I tried to sort through it all. Callum didn't kiss Cassie either. He could've. He should've, right? Everyone expected him to. And yet, he took a shot instead. Why?

Was it because... of me?

The thought made my heart race in a way I wasn't ready to deal with. Maybe I was overthinking it. Maybe he just didn't want to kiss Cassie for his own reasons.

But something about the way he glared at me after I took that shot made me question everything. The tension between us had been growing for a while now, and I wasn't sure where it was headed—or how I felt about it.

"Hey."

I froze, my eyes snapping open at the sound of his voice.

I turned around to see him standing a few feet away, leaning against the doorway with that same brooding expression on his face. His arms were crossed, and there was something in his eyes that I couldn't quite read. Frustration? Curiosity? It was hard to tell.

"Why'd you walk off?" he asked, his voice low, but there was a strange softness to it, like he wasn't entirely pissed, just... confused.

I shrugged, trying to play it cool even though my heart was pounding. "Just needed some air. Is that a problem?"

He raised an eyebrow, pushing himself off the doorframe as he took a step closer. "Seemed like you were trying to avoid something."

I frowned, folding my arms across my chest, trying to match his stance. "What do you care, Callum?"

He didn't answer right away. Instead, he stood there, staring at me with that same intensity, like he was trying to figure me out. The tension between us was thick, unspoken, and it was starting to suffocate me. But I couldn't bring myself to look away.

"I care because you could've kissed Grayson," he finally said, his voice quieter, but still sharp. "But you didn't. Why?"

I felt my chest tighten at his words, his question hanging in the air like a challenge. I didn't know how to answer, because the truth was I didn't even fully understand it myself.

"Why didn't you kiss Cassie?" I shot back, my voice more defensive than I intended. "It's the same thing, right?"

He stiffened at that, his jaw tightening. "That's not the same."

"Isn't it?" I asked, my frustration bubbling to the surface. "You took a shot, too. So why are you coming after me for doing the same thing?"

Callum took another step forward, closing the distance between us until I had nowhere else to go. My back pressed against the wall, and my heart raced as his presence filled the space between us. His eyes locked onto mine, and I could feel the intensity rolling off him in waves.

"Because I didn't want to kiss Cassie," he muttered, his voice low, rough around the edges.

I stared up at him, unable to move, my breath catching in my throat. He was so close now, too close, and I could feel the heat from his body as he leaned in, his hands resting on the wall on either side of me, trapping me in.

"There was only one damn person in that circle I wanted the bottle to land on when I spun it," he said, his voice dropping even lower. His eyes bore into mine, and for a second, I couldn't breathe.

"Do you wanna guess who it is?"

CHAPTER 54
HAILEY

THE AIR BETWEEN US FELT IMPOSSIBLY THICK, CHARGED WITH SOMETHING I couldn't ignore anymore. Callum's eyes were burning into mine, and my heart raced so fast I was sure he could hear it. Every word he said hung heavy in the space between us, and I could feel the tension rising, swirling around us like a storm.

"Fuck, Hailey," he muttered, his voice raw and full of frustration. "It was you."

His words hit me like a jolt of electricity, and I could feel my entire body freeze as I waited for him to continue, my breath caught in my throat.

"I wanted the bottle to land on you," he said, his voice low and rough, like he was admitting something he had been holding back for too long. "I wanted it to land on you so I could kiss you so damn hard your lips turn sore."

The words sent a shiver through me, and for a moment, I couldn't think, couldn't move. All I could do was stare up at him, my back pressed against the wall as his presence overwhelmed me.

He wanted to kiss me. Me. Not Cassie. Not anyone else. And the way he said it, the way he was looking at me—it wasn't just about the kiss. It was more than that. It was everything we'd been avoiding, everything we hadn't said.

Callum leaned in closer, his hands braced on either side of me, his breath hot against my skin. I could feel the tension rolling off him, the frustration, the desire. He wanted to do it. I could see it in his eyes, feel it in the way his body was so close to mine, like he was barely holding himself back.

And in that moment, something inside me snapped. I didn't want to hold back anymore either.

"Then do it," I whispered, my voice shaky but firm.

For a second, I thought he would. I thought he'd just close the gap and finally kiss me the way we both seemed to want. But he paused, his eyes flickering with something deeper—something that wasn't just about the kiss.

"If I do," he said, his voice tight, strained, "there's no going back. You know that, right?"

His words hung in the air, heavy and thick with meaning. He wasn't talking about just a kiss anymore. He was talking about everything—the boundaries we'd built between us, the rules we'd set to keep each other at a distance. He was warning me that if we crossed this line, if we let this happen, it would change everything.

"I'll keep breaking our rules," he continued, his voice low and intense. "I'll keep crossing our boundaries. I'll keep wanting you. Pining for you."

His face was so close to mine now, his eyes dark and filled with something that made my heart pound even harder.

"Is that what you want?" he asked, his voice barely above a whisper now. "You want me to fall for you, Hailey Eller?"

I swallowed hard, my throat tight, my mind racing. I didn't know what to say, didn't know how to process everything he was laying in front of me.

For so long, we'd been at each other's throats, pushing each other away, pretending like the tension between us didn't mean anything. But now, standing here, I couldn't pretend anymore.

This wasn't just about a stupid game or a kiss anymore. It was about everything we'd been hiding from, everything we hadn't wanted to admit. Everything that had been there that none of us wanted to address... the feelings we'd been denying for so long were now standing right in front of us, impossible to ignore.

I thought about Callum—the way he frustrated me, the way he could get under my skin like no one else, but also the way he could make me feel seen in a way that terrified me. I thought about the arguments, the moments we'd almost crossed the line, the way my heart had been racing ever since this tension started growing between us.

And as I stood there, staring up at him, feeling his presence, his intensity, I realized something. Maybe I'd already fallen for him.

I took a deep breath, feeling the weight of everything, but instead of running from it this time, I finally let myself lean into it.

I stared at him for a long time, feeling the weight of the moment press down on me. But then, slowly, I nodded.

I couldn't pretend anymore.

I couldn't deny the pull between us or the way my heart felt like it was about to explode in my chest. The moment I nodded, something inside Callum snapped.

He crashed into me, his lips slamming against mine with a force that took my breath away. There was no hesitation, no holding back.

His hands gripped my waist, pushing me hard against the wall as he kissed me like he'd been holding this in for far too long. And maybe he had.

The kiss was rough, desperate, like we'd both been waiting for this moment without even realizing it. His body pressed against mine, the heat between us undeniable, and I couldn't think, couldn't breathe—everything was just him.

His hands, his lips, the way he was so close, so overwhelming. My heart pounded in my chest, and I felt my knees weaken as I kissed him back just as fiercely, my hands tangling in his hair, pulling him closer.

Every part of me was on fire.

I could feel the frustration, the tension, the longing in every movement, in the way his lips moved against mine, in the way his hands gripped me like he never wanted to let go. And I didn't want him to.

Callum's groans rumbled against my lips, his cursing barely muffled as he kissed me harder, deeper. His hands moved urgently, gripping my waist, pulling me closer until there was no space left between us. It was overwhelming, the intensity of it all —the way he was practically devouring me, as if we'd both been waiting for this moment without realizing just how badly we needed it.

A small whimper escaped me, and I felt his grip tighten for a second. His lips slowed, just barely, as if he'd heard that sound and realized he needed to dial it back. One of his hands moved up to cup my face, his thumb brushing my cheek as he continued kissing me, but this time, with a little more control.

Still just as passionate, still making my heart race, but softer. His lips pressed against mine, more deliberate now, like he was savoring every second. And I let myself melt into it, into him, losing myself in the feel of his hands on me, the warmth of his body so close.

Callum pulled away, panting heavily, his forehead resting against mine as we both caught our breath. His eyes were dark, still filled with that intensity that had been building between us.

"We need to get the fuck out of here, Hailey. Now," he muttered, his voice low and rough. "I want you to myself."

My heart was still racing, and the pull to leave with him was strong. But I hesitated, thinking about Nala. She had been so excited for this party, and I couldn't just disappear without making sure she was okay. "What about Nala?" I asked, my voice soft. "I want to check on her first."

Callum groaned, clearly not thrilled with the idea. He leaned back, rubbing the back of his neck in frustration before meeting my gaze again. "Fine," he grumbled, his voice thick with reluctance. "Go check on Nala, but come straight back here. You come straight back to me. Got it?"

I nodded, my heart still pounding, knowing I would go back to him—knowing I couldn't stay away even if I tried.

CHAPTER 55

CALLUM

I LEANED BACK AGAINST THE WALL, MY HEART STILL POUNDING IN MY CHEST, frustration bubbling beneath the surface. Hailey had gone to check on Nala, and now I was standing here, waiting like an idiot.

But, holy shit—I kissed her.

I fucking kissed Hailey. And she kissed me back.

And it wasn't just any kiss. No, it was the kind of kiss that knocked the wind out of you, the kind of kiss that left you dizzy, wanting more.

My fingers itched, still feeling the warmth of her skin, the way she'd melted into me when I pushed her against the wall. I couldn't stop replaying it in my head—the taste of her, sweet and addictive, the way she'd whimpered, her breath catching just enough to make me lose control.

And the way she moved? God, the way she moved against me drove me in-fucking-sane.

I ran a hand through my hair, trying to calm myself down, but it wasn't working. Everything about that kiss, everything about her, was still running through my mind, and the more I thought about it, the more it consumed me. I'd spent so long denying what I felt for her, pretending like the tension between us was just some passing annoyance, but now? Now I couldn't un-feel it.

The way she sounded, those little whimpers, the way her lips had trembled under mine—it was all I could think about. And I wanted more. So much more.

"Where the hell is she?" I muttered to myself, pacing back and forth, my patience running thin. I'd been standing there, waiting, with all that tension building up inside me. Every second that passed made me more restless, more desperate to see her again. The way she'd tasted, the way she'd moved—it was all driving me crazy, and I needed more.

Finally, I heard footsteps, and I looked up to see Hailey jogging back toward me, her breath coming in short bursts. "Nala's gonna catch a ride with Ibra," she started, still a little out of breath.

But before she could finish, something snapped inside me. I didn't let her say another word.

I grabbed her by the arm, pulling her into the nearest bedroom. The door slammed shut behind us, and I locked it without even thinking. All I could focus on was her—how much I wanted her. My lips crashed into hers again, more urgent, more possessive than before. I couldn't hold back anymore, and it felt like the second our lips touched, everything else in the world fell away.

She gasped for air, but I didn't stop. I couldn't. I kissed her like a man starved, like I'd been waiting for this for so damn long. And maybe I had. My hands tangled in her hair, pulling her closer as I backed her up toward the bed, the heat between us building until it felt like we were both about to combust.

Her hands found my chest, gripping the fabric of my shirt as if she needed to hold onto something—anything—while the intensity between us grew. I groaned against her lips, pressing harder, deepening the kiss. She whimpered softly, her breath hitching as we stumbled backward, and before I knew it, we were falling onto the bed, her body beneath mine.

We were lost in each other, everything else forgotten. The feel of her under me, the way she moved against me—it was overwhelming, intoxicating.

I kissed her harder, my hands roaming over her body, and every touch, every gasp, made me want more. I felt her fingers dig into my shoulders, pulling me closer as we both gave in to the tension that had been building between us for so long.

The world outside the bedroom didn't exist. It was just us, the heat between us, the way our bodies fit together perfectly. I could barely breathe, but I didn't care.

I didn't want to stop.

I didn't want this to end.

I could feel it—the way my body responded to hers, the way my breath grew heavier, my pants tighter with every kiss, every touch.

It was like I was losing myself in her, in the heat between us. My hands slid down her sides, feeling the soft curve of her waist, my lips still pressed to hers, kissing her like I couldn't get enough.

"Fuck, Hailey," I groaned, my voice low, almost desperate. Every part of me wanted her. She was all I could think about, all I could feel.

I was completely hypnotized by her—by the way she tasted, the way she moved beneath me, the way her breath hitched every time I kissed her harder.

But then, just as I was about to lean in even closer, Hailey suddenly pressed her hands to my chest, pushing me back.

"W-wait. Callum," she stammered, her voice shaky.

I froze, my mind still racing, my body still on fire. Her hands stayed against my chest, keeping me at a distance, and for a second, I couldn't move. I was panting, my heart pounding in my chest as I tried to figure out what just happened.

I looked down at her, my mind hazy, trying to focus. "Hailey...?" I said softly, my voice rough with need. But I could see it in her eyes—uncertainty, hesitation.

I forced myself to stop, to pull back, even though every part of me was screaming not to.

I stayed where I was, feeling her hands pressed against my chest, the weight of the moment suddenly shifting. My breath was still heavy, and my heart was racing, but I could see the hesitation in her eyes, the way her chest rose and fell as she struggled to catch her breath.

"What's wrong?" I asked, my voice quieter now, trying to pull myself back from the edge.

She swallowed hard, her fingers still trembling slightly as she kept me at arm's length. "I... I don't know," she stammered, her voice soft, almost fragile. "This is... it's just a lot."

I blinked, the haze in my mind starting to clear. Of course it was a lot. It wasn't just the kiss or how fast things were escalating—it was everything.

Everything that had been building between us, everything we hadn't dealt with. The argument, the tension, the way we'd both been hiding from our feelings. And now here we were, tangled up in something we weren't ready to confront.

I leaned back a little more, giving her some space, even though every part of me wanted to pull her back to me. But this wasn't just about me—it was about us. And if she wasn't ready, I had to respect that.

"Okay," I said, my voice softer now. "We can slow down. Just say so." I looked into her eyes, seeing the mix of emotions there—desire, confusion, maybe even a little fear. I wasn't about to push her, no matter how much I wanted her. Not like this.

We sat there on the bed, both of us panting, the adrenaline still coursing through my veins. The air between us was thick, but the intensity from before had faded into something else—something quieter, heavier. I could feel her sitting next to me, her body still close, but the tension had shifted.

Neither of us spoke for a moment, both of us trying to catch our breath and process everything that had just happened.

Hailey shifted slightly, her hand resting in her lap, but I could feel her eyes on me. She wasn't looking away this time. I glanced over, and there was something in her expression, something that told me she wasn't just sitting there waiting for the tension to pass.

She wanted answers.

"Callum," she started, her voice quiet, but there was a firmness in it that hadn't been there before. "I need to know."

I frowned, trying to meet her gaze, but she quickly looked away again, her hands fiddling with the hem of her shirt. "How do you feel about me?" she asked, her voice soft, almost vulnerable.

That question hung between us like a weight. I didn't know how to answer—not because I didn't know what I felt, but because putting it into words felt like a risk. We'd spent years hiding behind insults and arguments, and now she wanted me to strip all of that away and say it straight up.

I ran a hand through my hair, trying to find the right words, but they felt too small for what I was feeling. "I don't wanna say I 'like' you," I muttered, my voice rough. "Because it's more than that."

She looked up at me, her eyes searching my face, and I could feel my heart start to race again—not because of the physical tension between us, but because of what I was about to admit.

"Every second of the day," I continued, my voice low, "I'm thinking of you. Even when I don't want to. Even when you drive me crazy. You're always in my head."

I paused, trying to gauge her reaction, but she was just listening, her eyes wide, her lips parted slightly as if she was waiting for me to say more.

"It's not just about wanting you, Hailey," I said, leaning in a little closer. "It's more than that. You make me feel like I'm losing my mind half the time, but I still can't get you out of my head."

She stayed silent, her eyes locked on mine, and I felt the weight of everything I hadn't said before crashing down on me. The way she made me feel was more intense than anything I'd ever experienced, and now that I was saying it out loud, it felt even more real.

"You're everywhere," I said quietly, almost like a confession. "I don't know how to shut it off."

For a long moment, neither of us spoke. I watched her process my words, her expression shifting as she tried to make sense of it all. And for the first time, I felt exposed—like I'd laid everything out on the table, and I was waiting for her to react.

Finally, Hailey took a deep breath, her hands still fiddling with her shirt as she looked down at her lap. "I didn't know," she whispered, her voice barely audible.

"I didn't want you to know," I admitted, my chest tightening. "I didn't want you to think... I don't know. I didn't want it to change things."

I leaned in, my voice quieter but more intense, like every word was charged with everything I'd been holding back for so long. "Hailey, you're not just some passing thought. You're not just someone I argue with or try to avoid. You're more than that. So much more."

Her breath hitched, and I could see her eyes widen slightly as I moved closer, but she didn't pull away. I kept going, needing her to understand, needing her to feel what I was feeling. "I wake up thinking about you. I see something, hear something, and it reminds me of you. Even when we're not together, you're still there—always there."

I reached out, my hand brushing against her cheek, and she looked up at me, her eyes searching mine, trying to figure out if what I was saying was real.

"And I don't know how to turn it off," I continued, my voice softer now but still firm. "I don't want to turn it off. You've been in my head for so long, I don't even know what it's like without you anymore."

Hailey's lips parted slightly, her breath shallow as she listened. I could see the conflict in her eyes—the way she wanted to believe me but was still hesitant.

But I wasn't done.

"I don't just like you, Hailey. It's more than that. I feel like I need you, like without you, everything else just feels… off." I could feel my heart racing, the vulnerability of what I was saying sinking in. "You don't just make me crazy—you make me feel something real. And I don't want to let that go."

There was a long pause, the weight of my words settling in between us, and I could feel the tension shift again—less about uncertainty and more about everything that was building between us.

"Do you get it now?" I whispered, my hand still gently holding her face. "It's not just some game or stupid attraction. You're… everything to me."

Hailey's breath was shaky, and I could see the impact of my words hitting her. She was quiet, processing, but I could see the change in her eyes—the way she was finally starting to believe me.

"Callum…" Hailey whispered softly, her voice barely more than a breath. The way she said my name sent a shiver down my spine, and I couldn't hold back any longer.

I leaned in again, capturing her lips in a slow, tender kiss. This time, it wasn't rushed or desperate like before. It was softer, more deliberate, like we were taking the time to finally feel every moment. My hands slid up to her face, cupping her cheeks as I kissed her gently, savoring the way her lips moved against mine.

She kissed me back, her hands sliding up to my chest, fingers gripping my shirt as I slowly leaned into her. I could feel the warmth of her body against mine as we melted together, the world outside this room completely forgotten.

Without breaking the kiss, we fell back down onto the bed, my body following hers as we sank into the mattress. I hovered over her, one hand braced against the bed, the other still holding her face, keeping her close as we kissed—slow, tender, but filled with something deeper.

Something so hot and suffocating that had been building between us for far too long.

She whimpered softly against my lips, and I could feel my heart race at the sound. I pulled back just enough to look into her eyes, our breaths mingling in the small space between us. My voice was low, rough, filled with everything I hadn't said before.

"Mine, Hailey," I muttered, my hand slipping into her hair, gently tugging. "You're mine. Got it?"

She stared up at me, her eyes wide, filled with a mix of emotions—desire, confusion, vulnerability. But she didn't say anything, just nodded slightly, and that was all I needed.

"No one else," I whispered, leaning down to kiss her again, my lips brushing against hers before trailing down to her jaw, her neck. "Only you."

I could feel her body tense beneath me as my hand tangled in her hair, pulling it back just enough to expose the smooth skin of her neck.

I pressed my lips to the curve of her throat, kissing her softly at first, my breath warm against her skin. I could feel her pulse racing under my lips, and the sound of her soft gasps only made me want more. I moved lower, kissing her neck, and then I began to nip at her skin, teasing her with soft bites.

Each time my teeth grazed her, she shuddered, her hands clutching at my back, pulling me closer. I could feel the way her body reacted to every touch, every kiss, and it only fueled the fire burning inside me.

I sucked at the sensitive spot just beneath her ear, and she let out a soft moan, her fingers tightening in my shirt. Her neck arched as I continued, biting gently and then soothing the marks with my lips.

The way she was responding to me, the way her body moved beneath mine—it was intoxicating. I was completely lost in her, in the feel of her skin, the taste of her.

"You're mine," I whispered again, my voice rough with need as I pulled back just enough to look into her eyes. I wanted her to know it, to feel it in every kiss, every touch. "Only mine."

She whimpered again, her lips parting as she struggled to catch her breath, and I could see the way her eyes fluttered closed as I kissed her neck again, biting gently, sucking at her skin until her body trembled beneath me.

I wanted her to remember this moment—remember the way I made her feel, the way we fit together so perfectly. I wanted her to know that she was mine, and nothing was going to change that.

As I pulled back, I couldn't help but grin at the sight of the small mark I'd left on her neck. The skin was already darkening, a perfect reminder of this moment, and I rubbed my thumb over it, feeling a strange sense of satisfaction settle over me.

Hailey's eyes snapped open, and she looked at me with wide, startled eyes. "Callum!" she gasped, her hand flying up to touch the hickey. She looked somewhere between shocked and amused, her fingers brushing over the mark like she couldn't believe I'd actually done it.

I chuckled, the grin still plastered on my face, when she suddenly slapped me—playfully, of course—across the chest. "What the hell?" she muttered, her tone a mix of disbelief and teasing.

I shrugged, still feeling that smug satisfaction from marking her, and leaned in a little closer, smirking down at her. "You're always free to return the favor," I teased, raising an eyebrow and cocking my head to the side, baring my neck for her.

Her face flushed, her lips parting slightly as she looked at me, caught between amusement and something else entirely. She bit her lip, probably debating whether she should smack me again or take me up on my offer. Either way, I could tell the moment had shifted into something playful, lighter.

But the mark on her neck? That was all mine.

She was all mine.

CHAPTER 56
CALLUM

AFTER THE HALLOWEEN PARTY, THINGS GOT CHAOTIC. SOCCER BLEW UP, AND I didn't even have time to process what was happening with Hailey.

Three game days in a row? Who the hell scheduled that?

By the time the final whistle blew on the last game, I was dead on my feet, barely holding it together from the exhaustion.

And through all of it—through the non-stop practices, the late nights prepping for matches, and those god-awful recovery sessions—I couldn't stop thinking about Hailey.

But the insane schedule didn't leave us any room to talk, to figure out what the hell was going on between us after that kiss. Every day flew by, and it felt like we were in this weird limbo, where nothing was said but everything was felt.

In the shadowed corners of the hallways at school, we'd find each other. It wasn't much—just a stolen moment, a quick hug or kiss when no one was watching. But those small moments kept me grounded, kept me going. I'd catch her eye, and she'd give me this small smile, like she knew exactly what was running through my mind.

But at home? We had to play it cool. Act like everything was perfectly normal. The last thing we wanted was to make anything awkward around the house, especially with our parents there, completely unaware of the undercurrent between us.

So, we'd sit across the dinner table, talking casually like we hadn't been sneaking kisses between classes. Or in my car. Or in the garage just before we stepped into the house. Or in the corner of the parking lot where no one could see. Or literally anywhere. It was maddening, but we couldn't afford to let anyone notice.

Tonight, though, was different. A quiet, chill Thursday night. I was finally back home, laying in bed, the chaos of soccer behind me for a few days. My body was sore from the non-stop action, but my mind?

It was entirely focused on Hailey. I couldn't stop thinking about her, about how everything had shifted between us after that kiss. The way she felt, the way she looked at me when we were alone—it was all-consuming.

I found myself grinning like an idiot, thinking about her. Even now, when we weren't together, she had this way of creeping into my thoughts, making me feel like a teenager with a crush all over again. But this was different. This was deeper. More real. And it wasn't just some fleeting thing. It was her.

As I lay in bed, grinning like an idiot, an idea hit me. It was late—everyone in the house was asleep, and for the first time in days, I didn't have to worry about a game or practice tomorrow. It was just me, my restless thoughts, and the fact that I hadn't gotten to spend real time with Hailey since... everything.

Without thinking too much, I grabbed my phone and shot her a quick text.

Me: *Are you awake?*

I stared at the screen, waiting for those little dots to pop up, half-expecting her to be asleep already. But then, the dots appeared, and her response came through.

Hailey: *Yeah. Why?*

My heart sped up, and I could feel that familiar excitement creeping in. The kind I'd only been feeling when I was around her lately.

Me: *Can I come down to the basement?*

It felt like I was crossing some kind of line, but at the same time, I didn't care. I wanted to see her. Needed to.

A moment later, her reply came through, and I could almost hear the hesitation in her words.

Hailey: *Yes, but give me 5 minutes to clean my room first.*

I chuckled softly to myself, shaking my head as I sat up in bed. Of course she wanted to clean up first. Typical Hailey. But damn, the idea of sneaking downstairs to see her in the middle of the night? My pulse was already racing.

Me: *Okay.*

Five minutes felt like forever, but when they were up, I jumped out of bed, my excitement getting the better of me. I quietly slipped out of my room, making sure not to make any noise as I sneaked down the hall.

The house was dead silent, just the soft hum of the fridge in the kitchen. I made a quick pit stop to grab a few snacks— chips, a couple of granola bars, whatever I could find that wouldn't make too much noise—and then headed down to the basement.

My heart was pounding the whole way down, thumping hard in my chest as I approached Hailey's room. This felt like sneaking around in the best way, like I was about to do something completely ridiculous and exciting.

When I reached the basement, the dim light from under her bedroom door caught my eye, and then I saw her. She was peeking out of the door, her eyes wide and cute as she waited for me. It was such a small thing, but damn, it made my heart race even more.

I stopped just outside her door, grinning as I raised the snacks in my hand. "Can I come in? I brought snacks," I said, my voice low but teasing.

Hailey's face softened into a smile, and I could see the hint of a blush creeping up her cheeks. She opened the door a little wider, her eyes sparkling with that mix of nervous excitement that was quickly becoming my favorite look on her.

"Fine," she whispered, stepping aside to let me in. "But only because of the snacks."

Hailey stepped aside, letting me into her room, and the second I stepped in, I couldn't help but stare at her. She was just wearing a simple tank top and some plaid pajama pants, nothing fancy, but somehow she looked so effortlessly gorgeous that it knocked the breath right out of me.

It was like she didn't even have to try, and it still drove me crazy. She was really the only person who could consistently drive me crazy.

I walked over to her bed, setting the snacks down on her nightstand before sitting on the edge. She reached for one of the bags, starting to open it, but before she could even get it unwrapped, I couldn't resist anymore.

I slid my arms around her waist and pulled her toward me, catching her completely off guard. She let out a quiet gasp as I tugged her into the bed with me, her back against my chest as I settled in, wrapping her up in my arms.

"Careful now," I whispered, my breath warm against her ear. "We have to be quiet, or we'll wake everyone up."

Hailey's breath hitched, and I could feel her relax against me, her body melting into mine as I held her close. There was something about this—about sneaking around, being together like this, with no one else knowing—that made the whole thing feel electric. Like we were getting away with something that was ours and ours alone.

She turned her head slightly, her hair brushing against my cheek, and I couldn't stop the small smile that spread across my face. This was perfect—just her and me, cuddled up in her bed, the rest of the world fading away. I tightened my arms around her, pulling her even closer, feeling the warmth of her body pressed against mine.

"I can't believe we're actually doing this," Hailey whispered, her voice soft but filled with a quiet excitement.

I chuckled softly, nuzzling my face into her hair. "Yeah, well, I wasn't gonna let you get away with sneaking down here without me."

She laughed quietly, the sound muffled as she leaned back into me, her head resting against my shoulder. We lay there like that, tangled together in the dim light of her room, the snacks completely forgotten as the thrill of sneaking around took over. There was something so intimate about being here with her like this, knowing that no one else could know—at least, not yet.

My hand slid up her waist, fingers brushing against the soft fabric of her tank top as I held her close, and I could feel her shiver slightly in response. I pressed a soft kiss to her temple, unable to help myself, and I could feel her smile against me.

"This is kind of fun," Hailey whispered, her voice barely audible as if she was afraid speaking too loud would break the moment.

"It is," I agreed, my lips brushing against her skin again. "Sneaking around with you like this? Best part of my night."

She turned her head to look at me, her eyes shining with that same excitement, and for a moment, everything else faded away. It was just us, here in her room, with no one else to interrupt. And for once, I wasn't thinking about soccer or school or anything else. Just her.

We stayed there, wrapped up in each other, the warmth of her body pressed against mine as the silence settled comfortably around us. I could feel her breathing slow down, her head resting against my shoulder, and I couldn't help but smile.

After a few minutes, I broke the silence, my voice quiet but steady. "So, how was your day?"

Hailey let out a soft laugh, her fingers absentmindedly tracing patterns on my arm. "Nothing too exciting. Had a pop quiz in Calc, though."

I groaned dramatically, making her giggle. "Pop quizzes should be illegal. Did you ace it?"

"Obviously," she teased, turning her head just enough to glance up at me with a small smirk. "What kind of question is that?"

I chuckled, brushing a strand of hair away from her face. "You're too much of a nerd to fail a pop quiz. I should've known."

Hailey nudged me with her elbow, playfully swatting at me. "You say 'nerd' like it's a bad thing. I happen to like being a nerd, thank you very much."

"I never said it was a bad thing," I said, grinning as I kissed the top of her head. "I like that you're a nerd. Means you can help me study for finals."

She rolled her eyes, but I could feel the smile tugging at her lips. "Yeah, because that's the reason you like me."

"Okay, fair point," I admitted, chuckling again. "But seriously, how's everything else? How's Nala? I haven't seen her much lately."

"She's good. Busy, but good. She's been spending a lot of time with Ibra lately, which is… interesting." Hailey's voice took on a teasing edge as she mentioned Nala and Ibra. I could practically see her smirking as she spoke.

I raised an eyebrow, intrigued. "Oh? So is there something going on there, hm?"

"Maybe," Hailey said, her tone playful. "But I'm not gonna spill all her secrets. You'll just have to wait and see. Or get Ibra to tell you."

I sighed dramatically. "Fine, I'll just sit here in suspense, wondering what's happening in everyone else's love lives."

Hailey giggled softly, turning her head slightly to look up at me. "What about your love life, Callum?"

I smirked, tightening my arms around her waist. "I think it's going pretty well, actually."

She blushed, biting her lip, but then, of course, she had to ruin the moment with a playful jab. "Except for the part where you suck at texting."

"I do not suck at texting, what?" I protested, laughing. "I'm just... selective about when I text back."

Hailey scoffed, turning around in my arms so she was facing me more directly. "Selective? Callum, you take like, hours to respond sometimes."

I raised my hands in mock surrender, grinning down at her. "Okay, okay, maybe I'm not the best at it, but I make up for it with my in-person charm, right?"

She rolled her eyes again, but there was a fondness there, and I could see her trying not to laugh. "You're lucky you're cute."

"I'll take it," I said, laughing as I pulled her back into my chest, holding her close again.

We stayed like that, just talking about random, sweet things—our classes, how our friends were doing, plans for the weekend. And every once in a while, we'd bicker like we always did, but this time it was light, playful, filled with teasing rather than frustration. It felt good. Easy. Like we were slipping into a rhythm that neither of us had fully realized we needed.

"Okay, but seriously," she said after a bit, poking me in the side. "You should at least try to be better about texting. It's basic communication skills."

"I'll work on it," I said with a smirk, squeezing her lightly. "But only because you asked so nicely."

I glanced down at her neck, noticing something I'd left there last time was now gone. The hickey. Faded, barely visible anymore. A grin spread across my face as an idea popped into my head.

"Should I leave another one?" I teased, leaning down a little closer to her neck.

Hailey's eyes went wide, and she sat up quickly, swatting me playfully. "No way!" she said, laughing but also sounding a bit exasperated. "Do you know how hard I had to work to hide that every day?"

I couldn't stop laughing. "Okay, okay, no more hickeys," I said, though the temptation to tease her about it wasn't going away any time soon. "But you have to admit, it was a good one."

She just groaned, shaking her head as if she couldn't believe I was still talking about it. "You're impossible."

"And yet, here we are," I said, smirking as I wrapped my arms around her waist again, pulling her back into the bed.

I leaned in and kissed her again—soft at first, but then it deepened, the warmth between us growing. Her lips were addictive, the way they moved against mine, soft and tender, but quickly turning more intense. I could feel her body relax into mine, and the heat between us built as my hands slid down to her waist, pulling her even closer.

Everything about this moment—the quiet thrill of sneaking around, the way her body fit perfectly against mine—was driving me wild.

The more we kissed, the more I could feel my control slipping. I was getting lost in her—lost in the feel of her lips, the soft gasps she made between kisses.

It was like I couldn't stop, didn't want to. My heart was racing, and I could feel myself getting harder with every second that passed, my body reacting to hers in ways I couldn't ignore.

My grip on her tightened, my hands roaming down her back, and I shifted slightly, trying to adjust, but damn—there was no hiding it. I was rock hard now, and the way she was pressed against me wasn't helping. Every touch, every movement, just made it worse.

I kissed her deeper, harder, my breath coming in short, ragged bursts as I struggled to keep myself in check. But it was impossible. Everything about this—about her—was turning me on so much, and I could feel myself losing control.

I pulled back slightly, my breathing heavy, my forehead resting against hers. I could feel my heart pounding, my body practically screaming for more, but I had to check in with her. This was a line we hadn't crossed before, and I wasn't going to push her into something if she wasn't ready.

"Hailey…" I whispered, my voice low, rough with everything I was holding back. "Should we stop?"

I looked into her eyes, searching for any hint of hesitation. I wanted her so badly—more than just the kissing, more than just the touch. Everything about her was driving me insane, and my body ached to feel her even closer, to lose myself completely in her.

But I wasn't going to push her. I wasn't going to do anything she didn't want.

My thumb brushed against her cheek as I waited for her response, my breath shallow, my whole body on edge. The way she was looking at me, the way her lips were still parted slightly, made it harder to hold back. I wanted to kiss her again, to pull her closer, to do so much more.

But I needed her to say it. To make the call.

Hailey's eyes softened, and I could see the nervousness flicker across her face as she pulled back slightly. For a second, I thought she might want to stop completely, and my heart raced, waiting for her to say something.

"I'm just... I'm nervous," she whispered, her voice barely audible. "I've never done anything like this with a boy before."

I stayed still, watching her closely, trying to understand what she meant. Then she took a deep breath, her eyes meeting mine, and she admitted quietly, "I'm still a... virgin."

Hearing her say that made my heart warm, and all the tension in my body shifted. I could see how much it took for her to tell me that, and I felt protective of her in that moment, more than anything else.

I gently cupped her face, brushing a thumb across her cheek. "Hey, don't worry about that," I said softly, my voice steady. "We won't do anything you're not ready for. I promise."

Her eyes searched mine, and I could tell she was still a little unsure, but I wanted her to know that she had control over this. Over us. "All you have to do is say the word," I continued. "If you want to stop, we stop. If you're not ready, we'll wait. It's all up to you."

Her shoulders seemed to relax a little, and she gave me a small nod. I kissed her softly, gently, hoping to reassure her that I meant it—that I would never push her into anything she wasn't comfortable with.

"We don't have to rush anything," I murmured against her lips. "We'll go at your pace, Hailey. I'm not going anywhere."

And I meant it.

CHAPTER 57
HAILEY

THE WEATHER OUTSIDE HAD TAKEN A TURN, THE AIR CRISP AND BITING, THE NIGHTS darker and colder. But my nights? They'd only gotten warmer. Every night, without fail, Callum would sneak downstairs to my room, slipping quietly into the basement like we were both in on some thrilling secret. It was becoming our thing—something that was just for us.

He'd push the door open, his eyes lighting up the second he saw me, and we'd settle into bed together. Sometimes we'd talk for hours, whispering about random things—soccer, school, or whatever nonsense was on our minds.

Other times, we wouldn't talk much at all. Instead, we'd just melt into each other, lips pressed together, our bodies tangled up, and our hearts racing.

The feel of him next to me was becoming my new normal, the warmth of his body chasing away the chill of the outside world. We'd make out until our lips were practically numb, the heat between us growing every night, but no matter how intense it got, Callum always stopped when I needed him to. He never pushed, never crossed the line. He was careful with me, always respectful of my boundaries.

And as much as we'd bickered in the past—hell, we still did—it felt different now. The teasing, the playful jabs... they were lighter, warmer, like we were both in on the joke. But it was more than that.

It was the way he held me, the way he kissed me, the way he made me feel safe and cared for, even when we were sneaking around like this.

It felt so good. Too good, sometimes.

Every night, after we'd spent hours wrapped up in each other, he'd eventually pull himself away, sneaking back upstairs before anyone could notice. And every night, I'd lay there, heart racing, a part of me aching for more but also so content with what we had.

I GIGGLED TO MYSELF AS I SNAPPED A FEW MORE SHOTS OF THE SKI CLUB members. Their ridiculous costumes—giant snowflakes, reindeer onesies, and oversized ski jackets—made the whole scene even more hilarious.

The posters they were holding weren't much better—bold, glittery letters that read **SIGN UP FOR THE SKI TRIP TODAY!**

It was hard not to laugh at how over-the-top they were being, but honestly, it was perfect for the yearbook. I could already imagine how these photos would brighten up the winter section.

"Alright, guys, one more! Give me your best 'we're ready to shred the slopes' pose!" I called out, holding back another laugh.

They all struck exaggerated poses, some throwing up peace signs, others pretending to ski down an imaginary mountain. I quickly captured the shot and lowered my camera, still grinning.

"Thanks, guys!" I waved as they started to break up, some of them dramatically wiping sweat from their foreheads like they'd just finished an intense photoshoot.

Shaking my head in amusement, I headed back toward the yearbook club room. As I walked through the halls, camera in hand, I couldn't help but feel a little rush of excitement. Winter break was just around the corner, and with it, our senior trip to Mammoth Lakes—the prize we won on Sports Day.

The thought of it sent a little thrill through me. A few days at a hotel in the snowy mountains, away from school, away from the stress of classes and assignments. It felt like the perfect getaway, a chance to unwind and just have fun with everyone before the chaos of senior year really ramped up.

I opened the door to the yearbook club room and stepped inside, still smiling as I thought about the trip. The room was quiet, the other members having already left for lunch, but I liked it that way. It gave me time to focus, to work through the photos I'd just taken and organize them for the upcoming yearbook pages.

I dropped my camera bag onto the table and sat down, flipping through the photos I'd just taken on the screen. Each one was funnier than the last, the ski club really going all out with their costumes. I'd have to remind Lance to feature these prominently. They deserved their own page.

Mammoth Lakes, though... I couldn't stop thinking about it. It wasn't just the idea of going on a trip. It was the fact that it was with everyone—the whole senior class. The chance to make some real memories before everything changed after graduation.

And, if I was honest, it was also a chance to spend more time with Callum.

I hadn't had a lot of time to think about that lately—everything between us had been so crazy and unexpected.

Sneaking around at night, him sneaking into my room, us cuddling and making out until we were both breathless. It was a lot, but in the best way. I couldn't help but wonder what the trip would be like with him around.

Would we get any time alone? Or would we have to pretend like nothing was happening between us?

The idea made my stomach flip.

I had just started reviewing the photos on my camera when the door to the yearbook club room swung open, startling me. Before I could even process what was happening, Callum burst in, his eyes scanning the room to make sure it was empty.

I opened my mouth to ask what he was doing here, but before I could get a word out, he crossed the room in a few quick strides, leaned down, and pressed his lips to mine.

The kiss was quick but firm, silencing whatever question I'd been about to ask. My heart jumped into my throat, and I barely had time to react before he pulled back, a smirk playing on his lips. He didn't say anything, just plopped down in the seat next to me like this was a totally normal thing to do.

"What—" I started, still a little dazed, but Callum just shrugged, looking way too relaxed for someone who'd just barged in and kissed me in the middle of an empty room.

"I figured I'd take a break," he said, kicking back in the chair. "Besides, I wanted to see you." He shot me a look that made my stomach flip, but I tried to focus.

"You could've knocked," I teased, trying to regain some semblance of control over the situation. "What if Lance had been in here?"

"Lance wasn't here," he said simply, like that explained everything. "I checked, didn't I?"

I shook my head, a small laugh escaping me as I leaned back in my chair. Callum always knew how to make an entrance. But behind his casual demeanor, I could tell something was on his mind.

Soccer had been eating up most of his time lately, and I knew the end of the season was weighing on him.

"How's everything going with soccer?" I asked, turning to face him.

Callum sighed, running a hand through his hair. "It's been… a lot. We're coming up on the final game, and it's against Oakridge again."

I raised an eyebrow. Oakridge? Again?

"That's gotta be intense," I said, understanding why he might be feeling the pressure. Oakridge was one of their toughest competitors, and the rivalry between the two schools had been brewing all season.

He nodded, his jaw tightening slightly. "Yeah, I mean, we've beaten them already, but it's always close. This one's for everything—the division title, the whole season. It's all on the line."

I could hear the weight of it in his voice, and I reached out, placing my hand on his arm. "You'll crush it. You always do."

Callum met my gaze, a soft smile tugging at the corner of his lips. "Thanks. I'll try not to get too distracted." He winked, his hand brushing against mine.

Callum's hand wrapped around mine, and I felt a rush of warmth shoot through me. He glanced at me, a soft but determined look in his eyes.

"Hey," he said quietly, his thumb brushing over my knuckles. "After school tomorrow… let's go somewhere. A proper date."

I blinked, surprised. A date? We hadn't really talked about it before—not officially, at least. Everything between us had been stolen moments, secret kisses, but never a real date.

"We haven't been able to go to one yet," he continued, a small smile tugging at his lips. "But practice is canceled today because of the snow, and Coach Taz didn't book the indoor field at the sports complex. So, I've actually got time."

My heart skipped a beat. A date. Just the two of us. No sneaking around, no hiding. I smiled back at him, excitement bubbling up inside me. "A date sounds perfect."

Callum's smirk deepened as he leaned in, kissing me again, quick but soft, before pulling back with that same playful grin. "You're such a cutie," he teased, his voice low enough that it made my heart race.

Before I could say anything, he grabbed the strings of my hoodie, pulling them tight and trapping my head inside the hood. My vision was blocked, and all I could hear was his chuckle as he did it.

"Callum!" I squealed, playfully smacking him on the arm as I struggled to free myself. "Hey! What are you doing?"

He just laughed, clearly enjoying himself as he pat my head. "Keeping you bundled up. It's cold right now."

I couldn't help but laugh, too, even as I tried to push his hands away and loosen the strings. "You're ridiculous!"

But honestly?

I loved it.

CHAPTER 58

HAILEY

THE YEARBOOK CLUB MEETING FELT LIKE IT WAS DRAGGING ON FOR HOURS, EVEN though I knew it had only been about thirty minutes. I tapped my fingers lightly on the table, glancing at the clock every few seconds, silently willing the hands to move faster.

We'd already covered everything we needed to—photo layouts, section assignments, upcoming deadlines—but Lance was in full-on editor mode, making sure every little detail was discussed to the point of exhaustion.

But I wasn't focused on the yearbook today. My mind was somewhere else—specifically on the fact that Callum and I had a date after school.

Our first real date. And I couldn't wait.

I shifted in my seat, trying to keep the excitement from bubbling over. My leg bounced under the table as I pretended to pay attention to the conversation happening around me, but all I could think about was how Callum had asked me to go out with him. A real date, no sneaking around, no interruptions. Just us.

I glanced at the clock again. Another fifteen minutes? Ugh, this was torture.

Lance finally closed his binder, signaling the end of the meeting, and I was out of my chair before he even finished his sentence. "Alright, everyone, make sure to get your photos in by the end of the week—"

"Got it!" I chirped, grabbing my camera and bag, not even bothering to wait for any follow-up instructions. I offered a quick wave to the rest of the team, flashing a smile as I bolted for the door.

"Someone's in a hurry," Lance called after me, sounding amused, but I didn't stop to explain.

I practically sprinted down the hall, the sound of my footsteps echoing in the mostly empty corridor. It was that perfect time of the day—just after the final bell, when most people had either already left or were heading to their lockers, the school quieting down.

I turned the corner, practically bouncing on my feet with anticipation. I still couldn't believe we were going on a date. I saw him standing by the lockers, leaning casually against the wall, and my stomach did a little flip. He looked up just as I approached, and that familiar, cocky smirk spread across his face when he saw me.

"There you are," he said, pushing off the wall and walking toward me. "I was starting to think you ditched me for yearbook duties."

I rolled my eyes, but the grin on my face betrayed me. "Yeah, right. I've been counting down the minutes until this meeting was over."

Callum chuckled, his hand brushing against mine as we started walking toward the school exit. "Well, you're free now. Ready to get out of here?"

"Absolutely." I glanced up at him, my heart doing that fluttery thing it always seemed to do when we were together. "Where are we going, anyway?"

He shrugged, a mischievous glint in his eye. "It's a surprise."

I raised an eyebrow. "Oh, is that so?"

"Yep," he said, his smirk growing. "But don't worry. You'll love it."

I slid into the passenger seat of his car, and before I even had my seatbelt on, Callum had already started.

"You're slow," he teased, glancing over at me with a smirk as he started the car. "I've been waiting here for like ten years."

I rolled my eyes, reaching for the seatbelt with a dramatic sigh. "Oh, please. I had to get out of a yearbook meeting. You should be grateful I even showed up."

He chuckled, shifting the car into gear. "Yeah, yeah. You say that like you don't want to be here."

"I don't want to be here," I shot back, turning in my seat to face him with a smirk. "I'm only here because I heard there'd be free food."

"At least you're here. That's good enough for me," he quipped, his grin growing as he glanced over at me again.

I couldn't help but laugh at how easy it was to fall into this banter with him. We bickered, but it was light, playful, and it made me forget about the nerves I'd felt earlier. He had a way of making everything feel natural, like we'd been doing this for years.

"So, where are we actually going?" I asked, leaning back in my seat as we drove through town.

He just smirked, keeping his eyes on the road. "Like I said, it's a surprise."

When Callum pulled up in front of a cozy-looking café with a sign that read "Play & Sip: Board Games & Coffee," I blinked, surprised. I glanced at him, my eyebrow raised as I took in the vibe of the place—warm lighting, shelves packed with board games, and a few people sitting at tables, deep into what looked like a heated match of Scrabble.

"Wait, a board game café?" I asked, turning to him with a smirk. "Who knew a meathead like you was into places like this?"

Callum shot me a sideways grin, clearly pleased with himself. "What, you thought all I cared about was soccer and the gym?"

I shrugged, leaning back in my seat. "Well, I didn't think this would be your idea of a date."

He chuckled, turning off the engine. "I figured it was right up your nerd alley."

I snorted, giving him a playful glare as we got out of the car. "Nerd alley, huh? I'll have you know, I dominate at board games."

Callum raised an eyebrow as we walked inside, his eyes gleaming with challenge. "Is that so? We'll see about that."

The café had a relaxed, inviting atmosphere. The walls were lined with shelves full of board games, everything from classics like Monopoly to more obscure strategy games I'd never even heard of. The tables were scattered with people, some laughing over their games, others deep in concentration.

We found a spot near the back, and after scanning the game shelves, I grabbed a few options, excited to show him just how much of a "nerd" I could be.

As we settled into our seats, Callum leaned forward, a mischievous look on his face. "So, what game are we playing first?"

I tapped the stack of games in front of us, a grin spreading across my face. "Oh, we're starting with Catan. I hope you're ready."

He smirked, leaning back in his chair with that casual confidence he always carried. "Bring it on."

We spent the next hour going back and forth over the game, our playful banter filling the air as I managed to build my settlements while Callum, surprisingly, caught on faster than I'd expected. It didn't take long for me to realize that even though I had the board game experience, Callum's competitive nature meant he was in it to win.

"You're taking this too seriously," I teased, laughing as he furrowed his brow, calculating his next move.

"I play to win," he said, his grin betraying the seriousness of his tone.

"Yeah, well, so do I," I shot back, playfully nudging his arm as I placed another settlement on the board.

We kept at it, the game getting more intense with each move. But in between the banter and the teasing, there were these little moments—his hand brushing against mine, the way his eyes would linger on me a second too long, making my heart race. It wasn't just about the game. It was about us.

As the game came to a close, and I narrowly managed to win (much to Callum's dismay), I leaned back in my chair, feeling more relaxed than I had in days. "Told you," I said, giving him a triumphant grin.

He sighed dramatically, leaning back and running a hand through his hair. "Okay, fine, you win this round. But next time, I'm not going easy on you."

"Next time?" I teased, raising an eyebrow. "You already planning a second date?"

Callum grinned, his eyes locking on mine. "Depends. You gonna let me win next time?"

I rolled my eyes, laughing as I grabbed a handful of the café's complimentary snacks. "Not a chance."

He chuckled, but there was a softness in his gaze that made my heart flutter. This whole date—this whole thing between us—it felt so natural. Easy, even with all the teasing.

As we packed up the game and sat back, sipping on our drinks, Callum leaned forward, his expression a little more serious now. "You having a good time?"

I smiled at him, my heart warming at the question. "Yeah, I really am."

And I meant it.

Callum's playful grin softened as he suddenly reached out and grabbed my hand, his fingers threading through mine. The warmth of his touch was immediate, sending a small, unexpected shiver through me. I looked up at him, surprised by the sudden gesture, but what caught me off guard even more was the way he was looking at me.

His usual teasing smirk was gone, replaced by something quieter, more genuine. There was a tenderness in his eyes that I hadn't seen before, and for a moment, it felt like the entire café faded into the background. It was just him and me, sitting there, holding hands, his thumb gently brushing against my skin.

Neither of us spoke for a few seconds. It was like we didn't need to. The air between us had shifted, and in that moment, I realized just how much this was starting to mean to him. To me.

"You know..." he started, his voice softer than usual, "I'm really glad we're doing this."

I blinked, my heart skipping a beat as I squeezed his hand a little tighter. "Me too," I whispered, feeling the words stick in my throat for a second before I finally let them out.

Callum's grip on my hand tightened slightly, and I could see the shift in his expression. The lighthearted banter we'd been sharing seemed to fade, replaced by something more serious. He took a deep breath, like he was trying to find the right words.

"I really wanted to talk about something," he said, his voice soft but steady. "About us. You know... our label."

My heart skipped a beat, and I felt a small knot of uncertainty form in my stomach. A label? I hadn't really thought about it in those terms. We'd been sneaking around, sharing kisses and moments together, but we'd never really defined what we were. And now, here we were.

I hesitated, biting my lip. "Uh... well, I guess we're technically boyfriend and girlfriend, right? But..." I trailed off, glancing down at our intertwined hands, my mind racing. "We haven't really made it official. You haven't asked me yet, so—"

Before I could finish, Callum's hand tightened around mine, and he cut me off, his voice firm and sure.

"Be my girlfriend, Hailey. Be mine."

I looked up at him, my heart pounding. There was no hesitation in his eyes, no teasing smirk. Just the raw, honest truth of how he felt. And in that moment, everything else seemed to melt away. It wasn't just about sneaking around or stolen moments anymore. It was about us. About something real.

A small smile tugged at my lips, and I nodded, my voice barely above a whisper. "Okay. I'm yours."

Callum's face lit up with a smirk, and he leaned back in his chair, looking way too pleased with himself. "Ha. That was easy."

I scoffed, rolling my eyes. "Never mind, I take it back."

His eyes widened, and he leaned forward, clearly panicking. "Hey! You can't take it back! You're my girlfriend now, you just said so!"

I crossed my arms, pretending to be unimpressed. "Yeah, well, maybe I changed my mind."

Callum groaned dramatically, reaching for my hand again. "No, no, no. You're not getting out of this. You agreed. You're stuck with me now."

I raised an eyebrow, giving him a playful glare. "We'll see about that."

We both fell into a playful back-and-forth, teasing each other, but there was no denying the warmth between us. Even through the bickering, it felt right. As much as we loved to get on each other's nerves, that truth made my heart race in the best way possible.

CHAPTER 59

CALLUM

I slouched back on Grayson's worn-out couch, pretending to listen to the conversation between Adam, but my mind was elsewhere. Grayson's little brother, Josiah, was in the kitchen, focused on something in a comic book, occasionally glancing over at us but mostly lost in his own world.

The four of us were just chilling—hanging out, shooting the shit like we always did. But lately, something felt different. Or maybe it was just me. I couldn't help but feel a little restless, glancing at my phone every couple of minutes like a damn fool.

Not that I expected anything, really. Hailey and I had already texted earlier. But ever since we started dating, it was like I couldn't stop thinking about her. Couldn't stop wanting to hear from her.

I wasn't being subtle about it either. For the past few weeks, I'd been checking my phone nonstop, barely even glancing at any other girl that wasn't Hailey. Hell, I'd even gone as far as blocking every random girl that tried to message me, just to make sure there was no chance of anyone getting in the way.

And I felt fucking good about it.

But still, something I didn't feel fucking good about was that not one of them—not one of these guys who called themselves my friends—had said a damn word about it.

Adam was sprawled out in the armchair, tossing a soccer ball between his hands, while Ibra and Grayson were discussing some upcoming video game release like nothing was out of the ordinary.

But I could tell they knew something was up. I mean, how could they not notice? I'd been acting weird for weeks, constantly on my phone, zoning out mid-conversation, and I hadn't so much as glanced at another girl since Hailey came into the picture.

It was driving me crazy. Here I was, clearly acting like a guy head over heels for someone, and these idiots were just ignoring it? I almost felt like a child sitting in the middle of the room, waiting for someone to acknowledge that something had changed.

Hellooo? I thought. *Aren't you guys supposed to be my closest friends?*

Grayson tossed a half-empty water bottle onto the coffee table and leaned back, stretching. "Man, I'm starving. We should order pizza or something."

Adam nodded. "Yeah, I could go for that. What about you, Callum?"

"Huh?" I blinked, pulling myself out of my thoughts. "Uh, yeah, sure. Pizza sounds good."

Grayson shot me a look, eyebrow raised. "You've been in your head a lot lately, man."

Finally, a crack in the armor. I straightened up a bit, wondering if this was the moment they'd start grilling me about Hailey. But Grayson didn't push. He just shrugged and grabbed his phone to order pizza.

What the hell was going on? Why weren't they asking me about it? It was like they were purposely avoiding the subject, which made no sense. These guys had been my closest friends for years. We teased each other about everything—from girls to soccer to the dumbest inside jokes we could think of. So why were they tiptoeing around this? Was I not being obvious enough?

I glanced at my phone again, tempted to send Hailey a text just to have something to do with my hands. But then I stopped, feeling stupid. This wasn't like me at all. I wasn't the kind of guy to get all wrapped up in a relationship—at least, I hadn't been until her.

And maybe that was it. Maybe they were waiting for me to bring it up because they knew this was different. They knew that I hadn't acted this way over a girl before, and maybe they were giving me space to figure it out. Or maybe they were just oblivious.

Either way, it was starting to get under my skin.

"So," I said, finally breaking the silence, "none of you are gonna ask me what's up?"

Adam looked up, tossing the soccer ball from one hand to the other. "What do you mean?"

"I mean," I said, waving my phone a little, "I've been glued to my phone for weeks. You guys really haven't noticed?"

Ibra chuckled. "We've noticed. We were just waiting for you to say something."

Grayson shrugged, a grin tugging at the corner of his mouth. "Didn't take him long. He's whipped as hell."

I rolled my eyes, but I couldn't help the small smile that crept onto my face. "I'm not whipped. I'm just... I'm with Hailey now. We're, you know, together."

Adam raised an eyebrow. "Hailey Eller? As in, 'we argue all the time and can't stand each other' Hailey?"

"Yeah," I said, feeling the heat rise in my face a little. "That Hailey."

They all exchanged looks, and then Grayson let out a low whistle. "Damn, man. Definitely didn't see that coming."

Ibra laughed, shaking his head. "Total surprise."

I leaned forward, the words spilling out before I could stop them. "I mean, she's amazing. I like her, like, really like her. She's not like anyone else, you know? I thought she was just this quiet, nerdy girl, but she's got so much fire, and she keeps me on my toes. And, I don't know, man... being around her just makes everything better."

The more I talked, the more animated I got, my hands gesturing as I tried to explain what it was about Hailey that had me all twisted up in knots. "And the thing is, she gets me. She's funny, too, in this dry, sarcastic way that just... I don't know, it makes me feel like we're in on the same joke, you know?"

The guys just stared at me, and then, all at once, they burst out laughing.

"What?!" I snapped, confused.

Grayson leaned back, arms crossed, grinning from ear to ear. "We knew it. We knew you were just waiting for the chance to start bragging about her."

Adam nodded, barely containing his laughter. "Seriously, man. We could see it all over your face the second we walked in. You've been dying to gush about her."

I blinked, completely caught off guard. "Wait, what? Is that why none of you asked? You were waiting for me to just... explode?"

Ibra smirked, shrugging. "Pretty much."

I gaped at them, feeling half-offended. "You little shits. I thought you didn't notice. I've been waiting for you guys to say something!"

Adam chuckled. "Nah, man, we noticed. We just figured we'd let you come to us when you were ready."

I rolled my eyes, but I couldn't help the smile tugging at my lips. "You guys are the worst. But, okay, fine. I'll admit it— I'm crazy about her."

"Yeah, we can tell," Ibra said, still grinning. "You've been glued to your phone every time we hang out."

"Okay, fair point," I muttered, leaning back into the couch, feeling a mix of relief and exasperation. At least now they knew—and of course, now that they knew, the teasing would never stop.

As we continued lounging around Grayson's place, I watched Josiah walk past, carrying a thick book. He didn't say anything, just gave us a quick glance before heading back upstairs. It was hard not to notice how much he reminded me of Nathan.

Quiet, reclusive, always lost in his own world.

Grayson caught my eye and shrugged. "Jo's an introvert. Total bookworm. I barely get a word out of him half the time."

I sighed, smiling to myself. "Yeah, I know someone like that," I muttered, thinking about Hailey. Her love for books, the way she could get so wrapped up in her own little world—it made me feel soft inside.

Before I could get too caught up in my thoughts, a pillow came flying out of nowhere, smacking me right in the face. I sputtered, blinking in shock as I looked over at Adam, who had the audacity to look proud of himself.

"We get it!" Adam laughed, throwing his hands up in mock surrender. "You're dating! You're about to make every damn thing about her!"

I picked up the pillow and chucked it right back at him, smirking as it hit him square in the chest. "Says you! You should brag about Sasha, too, you asshole!"

Adam glared, and just as he was about to retaliate, Ibra grabbed a pillow and whacked me across the shoulder. "You know what, you're make me sick with all this Hailey talk, too."

"Oh, yeah?" I shot back, grabbing another pillow and swinging it at him. "You literally have a thing with Hailey's best friend, you hypocrite!"

Before I knew it, Grayson—who had been quietly minding his own business—grabbed a pillow and started hitting all of us, his voice loud and dramatic. "Screw all of you! I'm still fucking single!"

That was it. Chaos erupted in the room. Pillows were flying left and right, with no one holding back. Grayson was going full-on berserk, attacking anything that moved, while Adam and Ibra tried to double-team me, but I held my own, swinging pillows like a madman.

"Callum, you better shut up about Hailey before I suffocate you with this!" Adam shouted, trying to land a hit.

I dodged, laughing as I smacked him in the back. "Not happening! You guys are just jealous I've got the best girl!"

Ibra laughed, lunging at me with a pillow in both hands. "Jealous? I don't need to be! Nala's way more fun!"

Grayson, still shouting about being single, swung wildly at all of us, missing most of his shots but determined to cause as much havoc as possible. "Y'all suck! I need a girlfriend so I can brag too!"

We all devolved into laughter, pillows still flying, like a bunch of idiots who had forgotten how to act like adults. The room was filled with noise—shouts, laughter, the sound of pillows smacking against bodies—and for a moment, it felt like we were kids again, just fooling around and not caring about anything else.

THAT NIGHT, WHEN I WALKED UP THE DRIVEWAY, THE SNOW WAS STARTING TO come down harder, blanketing everything in white. It wasn't too bad yet, but I could feel the cold bite in the air, and I knew it was going to get worse as the night went on. Shoving my hands deeper into my pockets, I unlocked the front door and stepped inside, shaking off the chill.

The house was quiet, almost too quiet, and when I kicked off my shoes, I noticed the faint sound of something coming from the kitchen. I glanced around, expecting to hear my brothers fighting over video games or my parents chatting, but... nothing.

"Hello?" I called out, heading toward the kitchen.

That's when I saw her. Hailey, standing by the stove, focused on whatever it was she was cooking. She looked up when I walked in, offering a small smile.

"Oh, hey," she said, stirring something in a pot. "Where've you been?"

"Grayson's," I replied, grinning as I stepped closer. "Where is everyone?"

Hailey wiped her hands on a dish towel, turning slightly toward me. "Your parents and the boys went to a birthday party. My parents are working late at the hospital."

I raised an eyebrow, a grin spreading across my face as the realization hit me. "Oh. So... we have the house to ourselves, huh?"

Her eyes flickered with amusement, but before she could say anything, I wrapped my arms around her from behind, hugging her tight and resting my chin on her shoulder.

She smelled faintly of whatever she was cooking—something warm and savory—and just being close to her made me feel better after a long day.

But then, I saw what was happening on the stove, and a wave of panic surged through me. "Wait, are you cooking again?"

I pulled back, my eyes wide with suspicion, remembering the last time Hailey tried her hand at baking. The thought of tasting anything that involved baking powder in place of flour was enough to make me flinch.

Hailey laughed, nudging me playfully with her elbow. "Calm down, I followed the recipe this time."

I raised an eyebrow, still skeptical. "Are you sure?"

"Yes," she insisted, turning off the burner and giving me a mock-serious look. "I'm learning, okay? I want to be able to cook well before Thanksgiving next week."

"Alright, alright," I muttered, wrapping my arms around her waist again, but still eyeing the pot warily. "Just... no baking powder, right?"

"No baking powder," she laughed, rolling her eyes. "I promise."

I relaxed, resting my chin on her shoulder again. "Okay, as long as you're not trying to poison me."

We stood there for a moment, just wrapped up in each other. It was nice, being in the quiet house with just her. It felt... different. But in a good way. Then, I remembered something.

"Oh, I told the guys about us," I said casually, kissing her on the cheek.

She turned her head slightly, surprised. "You did?"

"Yeah," I replied, chuckling at the memory. "I figured it was time to come clean. They were teasing me like hell about it."

Hailey laughed softly, leaning into me a bit. "Of course they were. How'd they take it?"

"They're happy for us," I said, squeezing her waist. "Well, happy and a little sick of me talking about you."

She blushed slightly. "Did they really say that?"

"Yep. All of them," I said with a grin. "Grayson was especially dramatic about it, though. You'd think I'd been talking about you non-stop."

"Well, who could blame you?" she teased, glancing back at me with a playful smirk.

"Fair point," I admitted, smirking back. " How about you? Have you told Nala yet?"

Hailey shrugged. "Not yet, but I'm going to. I want to. I've just been trying to figure out how to bring it up."

"She'll be happy for you. For us."

"I hope so," Hailey said quietly, her eyes focused on the stove. "But yeah, I'll tell her. Soon."

I couldn't help myself. Standing there with Hailey wrapped up in my arms, her back pressed against me, the soft scent of her filling the air—it was impossible to resist. Her oversized shirt hung loosely off her shoulder, exposing her bare skin, and the way it draped over her made her look effortlessly beautiful. My fingers gently brushed her hair aside, revealing more of her neck and shoulder.

I leaned in, pressing my lips to the soft skin at the nape of her neck, mumbling something incoherent as I kissed her. The warmth of her skin beneath my lips sent a shiver down my spine, and I felt her relax in my arms.

"You're making it really hard to focus on cooking," she murmured, but there was a smile in her voice.

"Good," I whispered against her shoulder, my lips trailing lower. "I'm not interested in food right now anyway."

I could feel her pulse quicken under my lips as I continued to kiss her skin, my hands sliding around her waist, holding her close. Everything about this—about her—was intoxicating. The way her body fit so perfectly against mine, the way she smelled, the way her skin tasted—it was driving me crazy.

"Callum…" she whispered, her voice catching slightly, but she didn't pull away.

I pressed one last kiss against Hailey's bare shoulder, savoring the warmth of her skin, before pulling back slightly and asking, "So, what are you even making over here?"

She turned her head, her lips curving into a small smile. "Alfredo pasta," she said, stirring the pot of sauce in front of her. "I'm trying it out for the first time."

I raised an eyebrow, peeking over her shoulder at the sauce. "You sure it's edible this time?"

She rolled her eyes playfully, grabbing a spoon and dipping it into the sauce. "I think so," she said, bringing the spoon to her lips and tasting the sauce. I watched her face as she thought it over, then saw a flicker of uncertainty cross her features.

"I'm not sure how it tastes," she admitted, frowning slightly. Then she took another spoonful, turned around, and held it up toward me. "Here, taste it."

I smirked, leaning in like I was about to take the spoon from her. But instead of tasting the sauce like she expected, I closed the distance between us and kissed her, my lips pressing firmly against hers.

She gasped, her eyes widening for a moment before they fluttered shut as I deepened the kiss, pushing my tongue into her mouth.

The kiss was hot, heavy, the kind that made my heart pound and sent heat rushing through my veins. My hands slid up her waist, gripping her hips as I pulled her closer, feeling the soft fabric of her oversized shirt beneath my fingers. Hailey let out a soft sound against my mouth, her body melting into mine as we kissed like we couldn't get enough of each other.

I could taste a hint of the Alfredo sauce on her lips, but it was the sweetness of her that overwhelmed my senses, making it impossible to focus on anything else.

The way she moved against me, her hands sliding up my chest, the little noises she made in the back of her throat—it was driving me insane.

Finally, after what felt like forever but still wasn't long enough, I pulled back, both of us breathing hard. I brushed my thumb across her bottom lip, grinning down at her.

"Mmm," I said, my voice low and teasing. "Tastes delicious."

Hailey blushed, biting her lip as she stared up at me, a little breathless from the kiss. "That's not fair," she murmured, her voice soft but full of warmth.

I just shrugged, smirking as I leaned down to kiss her again, this time softer, more teasing. "Who said I play fair?"

She laughed, shaking her head as she rested her forehead against my chest, still holding the spoon in her hand. "You're impossible, you know that?"

"Maybe," I admitted, my hands still holding her waist, not wanting to let go. "But you like it."

Hailey didn't argue. Instead, she lifted the spoon again, this time actually offering it to me. "Come on, taste it for real," she said, her eyes sparkling with amusement.

I finally took the spoon from her, tasting the Alfredo sauce she'd been working on. "Okay," I said, licking my lips and giving her a thoughtful look. "Not bad. Could use a little more garlic, though."

Hailey smirked, nudging me with her elbow. "See? I'm learning."

"You're getting there," I said, teasing but proud. I leaned down to kiss her again, because honestly, there was no stopping me now. "But I'd still rather taste you."

Hailey's breath caught as I kissed her again, my hands gripping her waist tighter, pulling her closer until I couldn't stand it anymore.

In one swift motion, I lifted her up and placed her on the counter, her legs brushing against mine as I stepped between them. She gasped softly, her fingers digging into my shoulders as I pressed myself against her, my lips trailing from her mouth to her neck, my mind hazy with the need to feel her closer.

I pulled back just enough to look at her, my breath heavy as I mumbled, "I'm about to lose it, Hailey."

Her wide eyes locked onto mine, and I could see the way her chest rose and fell with each breath. The sight of her sitting there, looking so damn gorgeous in her oversized shirt, her hair tousled, and her lips swollen from our kisses, was enough to make my head spin. She looked perfect. She was perfect.

"We're home alone, and you're standing here cooking, looking like that..." I muttered, my voice rough as I traced my fingers up her thighs. "Do you even know what you're doing to me?"

Her lips parted, but no words came out, just a soft, shaky breath. I pressed my forehead against hers, my hands gripping her hips, trying to keep myself grounded because, God, I was so close to losing all control.

Just as I leaned in to kiss Hailey again, the sound of our phones blaring shattered the moment. Both of us froze, the loud, insistent tone cutting through the heated air between us. I sighed, stepping back a little as Hailey reached for her phone first, glancing down at the screen.

"It's a weather alert," she muttered, her brow furrowing as she read the message. I picked up my phone, too, seeing the same thing.

SEVERE SNOWFALL EXPECTED. DO NOT DRIVE. STAY INDOORS.

I looked out the window, noticing how much heavier the snow was coming down now. It had been getting worse since I got home, but I hadn't realized it was this bad. I let out a low whistle. "Damn. Looks like we're snowed in."

Hailey nodded, still looking at her phone. "I should check on my parents. Make sure they're okay."

"Yeah, I should call mine too," I said, stepping away to grab my phone. As much as I didn't want to leave her side, the sudden reality of the situation hit me—if the snow was this bad, we'd better make sure everyone was safe.

I dialed my mom's number first, pacing a bit while it rang. After a few rings, she picked up. "Hey, Mom. Are you guys okay? The snow's getting pretty bad," I said.

"Oh, we're fine, sweetie," my mom answered, her voice calm. "We're staying at the party for a little longer and then heading to a friend's house nearby. We'll be safe for the night."

I exhaled in relief. "Good. Just wanted to check."

"How's everything at home?" she asked.

I glanced over at Hailey, who was on the phone with her parents, looking just as relieved as I felt. "It's good. Just me and Hailey here."

My mom laughed softly. "Alright, well, stay warm and don't do anything too crazy, okay?"

I could hear the teasing in her voice and rolled my eyes, though a smile crept onto my face. "Yeah, yeah, don't worry about us. Just be safe."

We hung up, and I looked back over at Hailey, who had just finished her call. She turned toward me, biting her lip as she set her phone down on the counter.

"They're okay," she said. "They'll be staying at the hospital. They've got everything covered."

I nodded, a sense of relief washing over me. But then, as the reality of the situation settled in, I glanced out the window again, watching the snow continue to fall thick and fast. No one was going anywhere tonight.

Slowly, I turned back to Hailey, and I could see the same realization dawning in her eyes.

"Holy shit," I murmured, stepping closer to her. "We're... we're gonna be alone. Tonight. Like, really alone."

Her eyes widened, and for a moment, neither of us said anything. The tension that had been building between us earlier came rushing back, stronger than before. The air felt thicker, heavier, as we both processed what this meant.

We were snowed in together. No parents, no siblings. Just the two of us. Alone.

CHAPTER 60

CALLUM

It had been a few hours since we both called our parents, confirming they were safe and not planning on coming back anytime soon.

The snow outside was relentless, piling higher by the minute, and the quiet house felt even more isolated now. We were huddled in the living room, some random movie playing in the background, but honestly? I couldn't focus. Not with Hailey sitting right next to me, her body warm and close, her presence doing things to me I couldn't ignore.

I shifted in my seat, trying to watch the screen, but my thoughts kept drifting.

We were alone. Not just for a little while, but for the entire night. And that thought... well, it was driving me crazy. I stole a glance at Hailey, who seemed to be a little more absorbed in the movie than I was, but I could tell she wasn't entirely relaxed either. There was a tension in the air, something unspoken but heavy between us.

I cleared my throat, my heart racing a bit. "Hey," I said quietly.

She turned to me, her eyes soft and questioning. "Yeah?"

I hesitated for a moment, wondering if this was a stupid idea. But then again, we'd been tiptoeing around each other, and I wanted to spend more time with her... in a different way. "Do you wanna... go up to my room?"

Her eyes widened slightly, a mix of curiosity and nerves flashing across her face. "Your room?"

"Yeah," I said quickly, trying to reassure her. "I promise I won't try or do anything you don't want. I just... I've been down to your room so many times. You haven't seen mine yet, so I thought, you know... while no one's home, I could show you."

Hailey bit her lip, clearly thinking it over. I could see the hesitation in her eyes, the way she was processing the idea. But there was also a hint of curiosity, a part of her that seemed intrigued by the offer.

"Okay," she said finally, her voice soft but steady. "Let's go."

My heart leapt as I got up, offering her a hand. She took it, her fingers slipping into mine, and I led her through the hallway and up the stairs. The house was quiet, save for the muffled sound of the movie still playing downstairs, and each step we took felt heavier, more loaded with meaning.

When we reached the door to my room, I paused for a second before opening it. This was different from sneaking down to her basement room in the middle of the night. This felt more intimate, more... real. I wasn't sure why, but it mattered. A lot.

I opened the door and stepped aside, letting her walk in first. Hailey looked around, her eyes scanning the room as she took everything in. It wasn't much—just my bed, a desk cluttered with stuff, some posters on the wall, and a few trophies from soccer over the years.

"Well," I said, trying to break the tension with a grin, "this is it. Welcome to my humble abode."

She turned to me, a small smile on her lips. "It's... nice. Very 'you.'"

I chuckled, closing the door behind me as I leaned against it. "Yeah, well, I figured it was time to let you in on the mystery that is my room."

Hailey walked over to my desk, picking up one of the soccer trophies, her fingers brushing the engraved plate. "You've got a lot of these," she commented softly.

I shrugged, feeling a little self-conscious. "Yeah, I guess. I've been playing soccer for as long as I can remember."

I gestured for Hailey to follow me as I took her on a little tour of my room. It wasn't like there was anything groundbreaking here, but there were a few things that meant something to me, and I wanted her to see that part of my life.

"So," I said, pointing toward my desk, "this is where I do absolutely no homework." Hailey laughed, rolling her eyes as I continued. "But I spend a lot of time here messing around with soccer videos, trying to improve my game."

I walked over to the bookshelf in the corner, picking up a small soccer ball that was more for decoration than anything else. "This was my first-ever ball, from when I was a kid. My parents have been forcing soccer on me since I could walk."

Hailey smiled, her eyes softening. "And look how far it's taken you."

I grinned, feeling a little proud, but I wasn't done yet. "Oh, and this..." I rummaged through the closet for a second, digging through a pile of old clothes and random stuff until I found it. Holding up a tiny, faded soccer jersey with a yellow chicken nugget on the front, I turned back to Hailey, the grin on my face widening.

"This," I said, with mock-seriousness, "is my prized possession. My very first soccer jersey. From the legendary FC Chicken Nuggets."

She covered her mouth, still giggling. "Oh my God, you were being serious about FC Chicken Nuggets? I thought it was just you messing with me!"

I shrugged, smirking. "I was serious. Clearly."

Hailey couldn't stop laughing, and her laughter was contagious. I couldn't help but join in, feeling lighter than I had in days. Seeing her like this, laughing in my room, sharing these little pieces of my life—it felt good. Like we were getting closer, letting each other in.

After a minute, I tossed the tiny jersey back into the closet, shaking my head. "Yeah, I've had that thing forever. My mom keeps trying to throw it out, but I can't let it go."

Hailey's laughter finally died down, but she was still smiling. "You really were destined for soccer greatness, huh?"

"Obviously," I said, grinning as I flopped back onto the bed. "And FC Chicken Nuggets was just the beginning."

She sat down beside me, her fingers tracing the edge of my desk as she looked around again. "I like it here," she said softly, her voice almost shy. "Your room, I mean."

I looked at her, my heart warming at her words. "I'm glad you do," I said quietly, the playful teasing fading into something softer. "I wanted you to see it. To be here."

As Hailey wandered around my room, her eyes landed on something on my desk. She reached out and picked it up, her expression shifting into one of curiosity.

"What's this?" she asked, holding up a small printed photo. I froze for a second, realizing exactly what she'd found—a picture of her from the night of our first date at the board game café. She looked so pretty that night, her smile lighting up the room, and I couldn't help myself. I had printed the photo and kept it on my desk, not for anyone else to see, just for me.

I rubbed the back of my neck, feeling a bit embarrassed as I stepped closer to her. "Oh, uh… yeah, that's from the café, when we made things official."

Hailey raised an eyebrow, her lips curving into a soft smile. "You printed it out?"

I shrugged, trying to play it cool, but there was no denying the warmth spreading across my face. "Yeah… You just looked so pretty that night, and it made my heart feel warm. I wanted to have it by me. Something to look at."

Her cheeks flushed slightly, and for a moment, neither of us said anything. She glanced back down at the photo, her fingers tracing the edges of the picture as she smiled softly. "You're such a sap," she teased, but there was something tender in her voice.

I shrugged again, stepping closer and wrapping my arms around her from behind. "Maybe. But you're the reason for that."

She tilted her head back slightly, looking up at me with that smile of hers, the one that always made me feel like the luckiest guy in the world.

Hailey took a slow step toward me, her eyes locked on mine, and I could see something swirling in them—something deep, something that made my heart start to race. She stopped right in front of me, still holding that picture, and her lips parted slightly as if she was trying to find the right words.

"You're so… agh," she finally muttered, her brow furrowing as if she couldn't quite express what she was feeling.

I blinked, tilting my head. "Agh? What does that mean?" I asked, half-amused, half-confused.

Hailey let out a frustrated little laugh, shaking her head as she stared up at me. "It means you're just… You're so—ugh, I don't even know. You're sweet, and thoughtful, and you drive me crazy, but in the best way possible. And now I can't even think straight around you."

I couldn't help but smile, my heart swelling at her words. "I think I'll take that as a compliment."

She rolled her eyes, but the smile on her face didn't fade. Then, without warning, Hailey took another step forward, closing the gap between us. Her hands reached up, resting lightly on my chest as she looked up at me, her eyes full of something that made my breath catch in my throat.

And then, she did something that caught me completely off guard—she leaned up on her toes and kissed me.

Her lips pressed against mine, soft and sure, and for a split second, I was stunned. But the shock didn't last long. I wrapped my arms around her, pulling her closer as I kissed her back, letting the warmth of the moment wash over me.

The kiss deepened, slow and tender, and I could feel everything in that one simple touch. All the teasing, the bickering, the tension—it all melted away, leaving just us. Just Hailey and me, standing in the middle of my room, sharing something that felt more real than anything else.

As we continued to kiss, I slowly pulled Hailey down with me, guiding us toward the bed. My legs hit the edge of the mattress, and I sat down, still holding her close, our lips never parting. She moved with me instinctively, sliding onto my lap, her legs wrapping around my waist. The sensation of her pressed so close to me, her warmth and softness, was driving me wild.

My hands roamed up and down her back, feeling the gentle curve of her spine beneath her oversized shirt. Her fingers tangled in my hair, and a soft sigh escaped her lips as the kiss deepened, our breaths becoming more ragged. I could feel her heartbeat against my chest, matching the rapid rhythm of my own.

The way she fit perfectly in my arms, the way she tasted, the way her body melted into mine—it was everything I didn't know I needed. I held her tighter, my hands slipping under her shirt slightly as I caressed the small of her back, pulling her even closer.

The heat between us was building fast, every touch, every kiss sending my mind spinning. Hailey's legs were wrapped around me, her fingers tangled in my hair, and all I could think about was how badly I wanted her.

Every part of me was screaming to keep going, but there was also this small, rational voice in the back of my head, warning me that we were treading into dangerous territory.

I pulled back for just a second, breathing hard, my forehead resting against hers. "Fuck," I whispered, running my hands down her sides, feeling the curve of her hips under my fingertips. "This is... dangerous."

Hailey blinked, her breath coming in soft, uneven pants, her lips still parted from our kiss. "Dangerous?" she echoed, her voice a little breathless.

I nodded, leaning in to press a kiss to her jaw, trailing my lips down her neck as I tried to catch my own breath. "Yeah... We're home alone, and... this." My hands gripped her waist tighter, feeling the tension coiling in my chest. "You're in my arms, we're in my room, and we're kissing... If we keep going like this..."

I trailed off, not finishing the sentence because it was already clear where this could lead. The feel of her so close, her warmth against me, was making it hard to think straight.

The line between control and giving in was getting blurrier by the second, and I wasn't sure how much longer I could hold on.

She looked into my eyes, and for a moment, there was this understanding between us, an unspoken agreement about how fast things were moving.

I could see the conflict in her gaze—there was the same desire I felt, but also hesitation.

"I... I know," she whispered, her voice soft but sure. "But I trust you."

Those three words hit me like a punch in the gut. She trusted me. That meant everything.

I pulled her closer, kissing her softly on the lips this time, slow and tender. "We can stop anytime, Hailey. You know that, right?"

She nodded, her arms still wrapped around my neck. "I know. But I don't want to stop... not yet."

The moment she said it, something inside me surged. My entire body reacted, heat pooling low in my gut, my desire for her spiking to an all-time high. She was right there, so close, so trusting, and I could feel how much she wanted this, too.

I leaned in, my breath coming out rough as I whispered against her lips, "Just say stop. The moment you say it, I'll stop. But if you don't..." I paused, brushing my lips over hers, feeling her tremble under my touch. "I'll keep going. Is that okay?"

Hailey's eyes met mine, wide and filled with a mix of anticipation and nervousness. She nodded, her voice shaky but resolute. "That's okay."

The second those words left her lips, I couldn't hold back any longer. In one swift motion, I turned, guiding her down onto the bed, placing her beneath me. She let out a small gasp, her body shifting as she settled onto the mattress, and I climbed over her, my hands on either side of her head, caging her in.

I looked down at her, her flushed face, the way her chest rose and fell with quick, uneven breaths, her eyes locked on mine with a mix of desire and vulnerability.

God, she was beautiful. And she was mine.

Without wasting another second, I leaned down and captured her lips in a kiss, but this time it was different. It was hungrier, more intense.

I devoured her, my mouth moving against hers with a need that was impossible to ignore. Her lips parted under mine, and I deepened the kiss, my tongue sliding into her mouth, tasting her, exploring every inch of her. She let out a soft whimper, her fingers gripping the fabric of my shirt as she kissed me back just as fervently.

The kiss was hot, consuming, and everything about it made my heart race faster. My hands moved down her body, tracing her sides, feeling the way her body responded to every touch, every kiss. The way she tasted, the way she moved beneath me, the way her breath hitched every time I pressed harder against her—it was all driving me wild.

I broke the kiss for a moment, just to catch my breath, but even then, I couldn't stop myself. My lips trailed down her jawline, down to her neck, sucking and nipping at the delicate skin there. Hailey's head tilted back, giving me more access, and I took full advantage, my mouth leaving a path of kisses down her throat.

Her fingers dug into my shoulders, and I could feel the tension building between us. Every touch, every kiss, every whispered breath—it was all leading to something more. Something bigger. And I wanted it. I wanted her.

As my hands moved under Hailey's shirt, I paused for a second, searching her eyes for any hesitation, any sign that I should stop. But she nodded, wordlessly giving me permission, and that was all I needed. In one swift motion, I lifted her shirt over her head, tossing it aside, leaving her in just her shorts and a bra.

The dim light from the window cast shadows across her body, highlighting the soft curves of her skin, the way her chest rose and fell with each breath. I stared down at her, my own breath catching in my throat as I took it all in.

"Holy… fuck," I muttered, the words slipping out before I could stop them. I couldn't help it. She was stunning, more beautiful than I had ever imagined, and the sight of her lying beneath me like this—her body bare, her skin flushed—it was everything.

I swallowed hard, my hands moving to her waist, feeling the warmth of her skin beneath my fingertips as I leaned down, pressing my lips to the soft skin of her chest.

Her skin was warm, her pulse racing beneath my lips as I kissed her there, right above her heart. I could hear her breath hitch, could feel her body arch slightly under my touch, and it only made me want more.

I kissed my way across her chest, taking my time, savoring every inch of her. God, this was like every fantasy I'd ever had coming to life, but better. So much better.

Because it wasn't just about the physical—though that was a huge part of it—it was about her. About being with Hailey like this, seeing her, touching her, knowing she wanted this as much as I did.

Her hands slid into my hair, tugging lightly as she let out a soft moan, her body pressing closer to mine. I could feel her trembling beneath me, could hear the way her breath came in short, shallow bursts, and it made my heart race even faster.

"You're so beautiful," I whispered against her skin, my voice rough with desire. "So fucking beautiful."

Her only response was a soft whimper, her fingers tightening in my hair as I continued to kiss her, my hands roaming up and down her sides. I couldn't get enough of her— the way she felt, the way she responded to my touch—it was intoxicating.

I leaned back slightly, my eyes tracing the line of her bra before my fingers found the clasp at the back. I hesitated for a moment, giving her one last look, silently asking if she was okay with this.

Hailey met my gaze, her eyes dark with want, and she nodded again, her lips parting as she whispered, "Yes."

With that, I unclipped her bra, the fabric loosening under my hands. I slipped the straps off her shoulders, taking my time as I pulled it away and tossed it to the side.

CHAPTER 61

HAILEY

CALLUM'S EYES WERE LOCKED ON ME, AND THE INTENSITY OF HIS GAZE SENT A shiver down my spine. My upper half was bare, my skin exposed, and the way he looked at me—like I was the most beautiful thing he had ever seen—made my heart race. There was something animalistic in his stare, something raw and hungry that both thrilled and terrified me.

I swallowed hard, nerves bubbling up inside me. I'd never been this vulnerable with anyone before, never let someone see me like this. My body felt warm, my skin tingling under the weight of his gaze, and I wasn't sure if I wanted to cover myself up or pull him closer. Maybe both.

The air between us felt charged, electric, and despite the nervous flutter in my chest, there was a sense of excitement coursing through me. I had no idea what was going to happen next, but the anticipation of it—the way he was looking at me, the way my body reacted to him—was overwhelming in the best possible way.

Callum reached out, his fingers grazing my skin softly, almost reverently, as if he was afraid to touch me too hard. The warmth of his hand made me gasp, and I felt my body arch toward him, instinctively craving more of his touch.

"Are you okay?" he asked, his voice low and rough, but there was concern there, too.

I nodded, my breath catching in my throat. "Yeah... I'm okay."

But I wasn't sure how to explain what I was feeling—this strange mixture of nerves and excitement. I was nervous because everything was so new, so intense. But at the same time, I was excited because it was him.

His hand continued to trace the curve of my waist, his fingers brushing along my ribs before he leaned down, pressing a gentle kiss to my shoulder.

My breath hitched, and I felt myself trembling slightly under his touch, but not from fear. It was like my body was waking up in ways it hadn't before, every nerve on high alert, sensitive to every little movement he made.

Callum's lips moved lower, kissing his way down my chest, and I could feel his breath hot against my skin. My heart was pounding so loudly I was sure he could hear it, and the closer he got, the more my stomach fluttered with nerves and excitement.

I could feel his hesitation, too, like he was holding back, making sure he wasn't pushing me too far too fast. And that made me love him even more. He was being careful, making sure I was comfortable, even though I could tell how much he wanted this.

I let out a shaky breath, my hands sliding into his hair, tugging lightly as I pulled him closer. "Callum," I whispered, barely able to get the words out, "I'm okay. Just... keep going."

His eyes flicked up to meet mine, and for a moment, we just looked at each other, the room filled with nothing but the sound of our breathing and the soft hum of electricity between us.

Then Callum's mouth moved lower, and when I felt his lips on my breast, I gasped, my whole body tensing and arching into him. The sensation was overwhelming, and I had to bite my lip to keep from crying out.

Oh my god. His tongue circled slowly, teasing, sending waves of heat through me, while his lips devoured me, pulling me deeper into a state of complete surrender.

I had never felt anything like this in my entire life. It was as if every nerve in my body had been set on fire, every touch from him making me more sensitive, more aware of just how much I wanted him. I could barely breathe, every inhale coming out ragged as his hand moved to my other breast, massaging it gently, his fingers rolling over my skin in a way that made my head spin.

"Fuck..." I whispered, my voice trembling with a mix of pleasure and disbelief. I had never imagined anything could feel this intense, this all-consuming. My entire body was humming, completely focused on the way his mouth and hands were exploring me.

He switched from one breast to the other, his tongue flicking over my skin, and I let out a low moan, my fingers tangling in his hair, pulling him closer. The way he was taking his time, savoring every moment, only made the heat between us build faster, and I could feel my body responding to every little thing he did.

"Callum..." I gasped again, his name slipping from my lips before I could stop it. It was like I couldn't control myself anymore, my body and mind completely taken over by the way he was touching me, the way he was making me feel.

His hand continued to knead my breast, and when he pinched my nipple softly, a shock of pleasure shot through me, making me let out a sharp whimper. I wasn't sure how much more of this I could take, every part of me aching for him, wanting more, needing more.

I felt like I was floating, like the world around us didn't exist. It was just him, his hands, his mouth, his heat—and the way I was losing myself in every second of it. My entire body was trembling, and I could feel myself growing wetter, my thighs instinctively squeezing together as I fought to keep some semblance of control.

"Oh," I breathed out, my voice barely more than a whisper. "Callum, please..."

He looked up at me, his eyes dark and filled with desire, and I knew he could feel how much I wanted him.

Callum's mouth shifted to my other breast, and when his lips closed around it, his teeth grazed my nipple in a way that sent a sharp jolt of pleasure coursing through my entire body. My back arched off the bed as I gasped, the sensation so intense that it was almost too much, but in the best way possible.

"Fuuuuck," I whimpered, my hands gripping his hair tighter as I tried to ground myself. "Oh my god..."

His tongue swirled around the hardened peak, teasing it as his hand continued to massage the other, and every movement of his mouth sent another wave of heat rushing through me. It was a wild mixture of pleasure and tension, and I could feel myself losing control, my body reacting to him in ways I didn't even know it could.

He bit down lightly again, just enough to make me gasp, and I felt like I was unraveling under his touch. Every part of me was on fire, and the way he was taking his time, savoring every inch of me, only made the feeling stronger.

My breath came out in short, shaky bursts, and I could barely think straight.

I couldn't take it anymore. My hands, almost instinctively, moved to Callum's shirt, clawing at the fabric, needing to feel his skin beneath my fingers.

He got the message and, with a quick pull, lifted the shirt over his head, tossing it aside. My breath hitched as his abs were revealed—each muscle perfectly defined, every line and curve of his body making my head spin.

Holy shit.

His skin was warm under my hands as I tentatively reached out, but before I could do much, Callum grabbed my wrists, pulling my hands firmly against his chest. He dragged them slowly across the hard muscles of his upper body, making me feel every inch of him.

"You like that?" he asked, his voice low and full of heat.

I nodded, completely speechless as I stared up at him. My fingers traced the ridges of his abs, marveling at how perfect his body was, how every part of him seemed to be sculpted out of pure strength. His muscles tensed under my touch, and I felt a rush of heat as I realized how much he enjoyed me touching him.

My hands drifted lower, tracing the sharp lines of his V-line, my fingers trembling slightly as they traveled downward. I could feel my heartbeat pounding in my chest as my eyes followed the path of my hands, moving from his perfectly toned abs to his waist... and then, lower.

And that's when I saw it.

My hands landed on the waistband of his sweatpants, and my gaze dropped down to the unmistakable imprint pressing against the fabric. My eyes widened, and my breath caught in my throat as I realized just how hard he was.

And just how big.

Oh. *Oh.*

My mind reeled as I tried to process what I was seeing. I knew he was turned on, but the sheer size of the bulge straining against his sweatpants made my pulse race faster than it ever had before. I swallowed hard, my fingers instinctively tightening around the waistband as my eyes flicked up to meet his, and I could see the hunger in his gaze.

He wasn't just turned on—he was ready.

A nervous shiver ran down my spine as my hands lingered on his waist, but there was excitement there too. I could feel the heat radiating from his body, the tension between us growing thicker with every passing second.

Callum watched me closely, his lips curving into a teasing smirk as he saw where my eyes had landed. "What's wrong, Hailey?" he asked, his voice low and full of amusement. "Something catch your attention?"

I swallowed again, feeling my cheeks flush as I tried to gather my thoughts. "I... I just..."

He chuckled softly, leaning in closer, his breath hot against my ear. "Don't worry," he whispered, his hands sliding down to rest on my hips. "We'll take it slow. You tell me when to stop. Always."

His reassurance sent a wave of comfort through me, but the heat between us didn't dissipate. If anything, it grew stronger. My fingers brushed against the hard ridge pressing against his sweatpants, and a low groan escaped his lips, making my heart stutter in my chest.

I had never been this close to anyone like this before, and it was overwhelming in the best way. Every part of me was trembling with nerves and excitement, and all I could think about was how much I wanted him, how much I wanted to keep going.

Callum's lips crashed down on me again, his mouth exploring my skin with a hunger that left me breathless. He kissed every inch of my body—my neck, my shoulders, my chest—his hands roaming as if he couldn't get enough.

I was overwhelmed, struggling to keep up with the intensity, my mind spinning as every nerve in my body came alive under his touch.

His lips left a trail of fire across my skin, and I gasped, arching into him as he moved lower. My breath hitched, and my hands tangled in his hair, pulling him closer even though I could barely handle how good it felt.

His hands slid down to my hips, his fingers tracing the waistband of my shorts, teasing me with the idea of what was coming next.

I could feel his hesitation, the way he was moving slowly, making sure I was okay with every step we were taking. But the anticipation was killing me, and I didn't want him to stop. Not now.

With careful, deliberate movements, he hooked his fingers into the waistband of my shorts, tugging them down slowly. I lifted my hips to help him, feeling my pulse race as the fabric slid down my legs.

Callum stared down at me, his eyes dark with desire as he took in the sight of me lying beneath him, now only in my panties. I could see the tension in his body, the way his jaw clenched as he cursed under his breath. His gaze was heavy, heated, and the intensity of it made me shiver.

"Oh my fucking god..." he muttered, his voice rough with barely contained restraint. His hands gripped my hips gently, and then he leaned down, pressing soft, lingering kisses against my lower stomach.

I gasped, my body arching involuntarily as his lips trailed lower, sending electric waves of pleasure coursing through me. The warmth of his breath against my skin, the way his lips teased and tasted me—it was all too much. Every kiss made the tension in my body coil tighter, the need for him growing stronger with every second.

When his mouth moved to my thigh, I felt my heart practically leap into my throat. My legs trembled as his lips grazed the sensitive skin there, and I bit my lip to keep from crying out.

The heat between my legs was unbearable now, and I couldn't help the soft whimper that escaped my lips as I tried to hold on, to keep some semblance of control.

But I was losing it. Fast.

I could barely take it anymore. The way he touched me, the way he kissed me—it was driving me to the edge, and I wasn't sure how much longer I could hold on.

"Callum..." I breathed, my voice shaking, my hands gripping the bed sheets tightly as I struggled to keep up with the whirlwind of sensations he was sending through me. I wanted more. I needed more.

Callum's eyes locked on mine as his fingers dipped under the waistband of my panties, hooking beneath the fabric. My breath hitched, and my heart pounded so loudly in my ears that I could barely hear anything else.

Slowly, teasingly, he pulled them down, the cool air hitting my skin and making me shiver.

My body tensed, every nerve lit up as he continued to remove the last barrier between us. His gaze never left mine, and the intensity in his eyes made me feel like I was about to combust under his touch. The way he looked at me was both thrilling and terrifying in the best way.

My panties slipped off completely, and I was left completely bare beneath him. Vulnerable. But instead of fear, all I felt was anticipation, heat coursing through me, and the overwhelming need for him to keep going.

Callum tossed my panties aside, his eyes dark and filled with hunger as he stared down at me, and I could barely breathe from the tension building between us.

Every moment, every second of this was like a dream come to life, and I couldn't stop trembling with the excitement and nerves swirling inside me.

He leaned down again, his lips hovering just above mine, his breath warm against my skin. "You're so fucking beautiful," he whispered, his voice rough with desire.

Callum pulled back slightly, his breath coming out in short, uneven bursts as he hovered over me. His eyes were filled with a mix of desire and concern, and I could see him trying to keep control, trying to make sure he wasn't rushing anything.

"You..." he began, his voice low and a little shaky. "You're a virgin, right?"

I nodded, feeling the nervous flutter in my chest return, but at the same time, there was this steady warmth beneath it. I trusted him. I wanted this. But the anticipation was making my heart race faster.

Callum exhaled slowly, his hand gently cupping my cheek for a moment as he whispered, "Okay. I'll take it slow, then. I don't want this to hurt for you."

There was something so tender in his words, something that made me feel even more safe and cared for. Despite the tension, the heat between us, I knew he wasn't going to push me into anything I wasn't ready for. And that made all the difference.

His lips brushed mine softly, and then he began to kiss his way down again, tracing the curves of my body, taking his time. His mouth moved over my stomach, my hips, kissing the sensitive skin there, teasing me with feather-light touches. I gasped softly, my body trembling under his attention, the anticipation building with every kiss.

He teased the skin around my most sensitive spot, his fingers brushing lightly against my inner thigh, making me shiver. The teasing touches were driving me crazy, every part of me aching for more.

I bit my lip, trying to keep my breathing steady, but it was impossible. The heat between us was suffocating, my body screaming for more, and I wasn't sure how much longer I could take the slow build-up.

Then, finally, I felt his finger slide gently along my slick entrance, teasing me with the promise of what was coming next. My heart stuttered in my chest as I felt him push just the tip of his finger inside, the sensation so foreign, so intense, that I couldn't stop the soft moan that escaped my lips.

"Callum..." I whispered, my voice shaky, filled with both nerves and desire.

He leaned down, kissing me again softly, reassuringly. "It's okay," he whispered against my lips. "I've got you."

And then, slowly, carefully, he pushed his finger in deeper.

The feeling was strange at first, a slight pressure that made me gasp, but it wasn't painful. It was more... intense. My body was trembling beneath him, and I could feel my legs instinctively parting, my hips arching slightly toward him as I adjusted to the new sensation.

He moved his finger inside me, slow and deliberate, giving me time to get used to it. The way he watched me, the way his eyes stayed locked on mine, made me feel safe, even as my body reacted to every little movement he made.

My breath came out in short, ragged bursts, and I could feel my body growing warmer, more sensitive with every passing second.

"You okay?" he asked, his voice soft but rough with desire.

I nodded, biting my lip as I tried to steady my breathing. "Y-yeah... I'm okay," I whispered.

He smiled slightly, his fingers moving inside me again, and I gasped as a wave of pleasure washed over me. It was unlike anything I'd ever felt before, this mix of tension and release, and I could feel myself getting lost in it, lost in him.

I could feel myself starting to unravel, and I couldn't hold back the groans and moans that escaped my lips, filling the quiet room with the sounds of my pleasure.

I hadn't done this to myself much, hadn't really explored these feelings the way I was feeling them now with him. But Callum... oh my god, it was like he knew exactly what to do to make my body sing, to make me melt completely beneath him.

The rhythm of his finger quickened, moving in and out with a steady, deliberate pace, and I could feel the heat between my legs growing, the pleasure rising in waves.

My breath came out in short, ragged bursts, and I could barely keep up with the sensations flooding through me. Every nerve in my body was on fire, and I felt myself teetering on the edge of something bigger than I could handle.

Just when I thought it couldn't get more intense, I felt him gently, carefully add another finger. The stretch was sudden, and I gasped sharply at the feeling of his thick fingers filling me. It was a new kind of pleasure, one that made my toes curl and my back arch off the bed.

"Fuck…" I groaned, my voice trembling as I clutched the sheets, my body quivering with the effort to contain the pleasure. I felt like I was going to pass out from how good it felt, like my mind couldn't keep up with the way my body was reacting.

He began moving his fingers faster now, in and out, in and out, the pace quickening as his thumb gently brushed against a spot that made me cry out. My moans grew louder, uncontrollable, the pleasure building so high I thought I might break apart from it.

"Callum…" I gasped, his name slipping from my lips in a desperate moan.

I couldn't handle how much pleasure was coursing through me, how my body was reacting to every single movement he made.

It was too much, but I didn't want it to stop.

My legs trembled as the pressure inside me built higher and higher, my breath coming out in ragged bursts as I felt myself getting closer to something I'd never experienced before.

Callum's pace quickened, and the intensity of his movements had me on the brink of something I could barely comprehend. My body was trembling, my breath ragged as I moaned loudly, the pleasure almost too much to handle. His fingers worked expertly inside me, hitting spots I didn't even know existed, making my mind go blank from the sheer intensity.

Then, with a low, guttural voice, he leaned in close to my ear, his breath hot against my skin. "You're so fucking wet for me, Hailey... You love the way I'm making you feel, don't you? You're gonna come all over my fingers, aren't you?"

His words sent a shockwave through me, and before I could even respond, he hit a certain spot deep inside me—one that made me lose all control. The pleasure was overwhelming, consuming me completely, and I felt the tension snap.

"Callum!" I cried out, my body arching off the bed as I came undone on his hand. Waves of ecstasy rippled through me, and I could barely catch my breath as the intensity of the orgasm washed over me, leaving me gasping and shaking beneath him.

He didn't stop, his fingers working me through the orgasm, drawing out every last bit of pleasure until I was trembling and breathless. Then, slowly, he pulled his fingers out of me, his gaze dark and full of desire as he brought them to his mouth.

Without breaking eye contact, Callum licked his fingers, tasting me with a smirk playing on his lips. "God, you taste so fucking good," he murmured, his voice thick with lust.

I could barely respond, my body still buzzing from the release, my mind spinning from everything that had just happened. All I could do was stare up at him, completely undone, completely his.

In one swift motion, he kicked off his sweatpants, leaving him in nothing but his boxers. I couldn't help but stare—his arousal was impossible to ignore, the bulge in his boxers straining against the fabric. My heart pounded in my chest as I realized how close we were to crossing the line we'd been tiptoeing around for so long.

He leaned over me, his face hovering just above mine, his eyes searching my face for any sign of hesitation. "Hailey," he whispered, his voice low and almost desperate, "I fucking want you. I need... I need to be inside you."

My breath caught in my throat, and I could feel my pulse racing. The weight of his words hit me, and all the nerves and anticipation that had been building for so long reached a boiling point.

"Will you let me?" he asked, his voice almost a plea, his fingers gently brushing my cheek. "Will you let me take your virginity?"

The air between us was thick with tension, with desire, and I felt my body trembling with the weight of the decision. But as I looked up at him, at the need and care in his eyes, I knew my answer.

I was so fucking turned on, my body still buzzing from everything he'd done to me. I wanted this, wanted him, more than I'd ever wanted anything before.

"Y-yes," I mumbled, my voice shaky but sure. "Yes, Callum."

The second the words left my lips, his eyes darkened even more, filled with a new kind of hunger, and I knew there was no going back.

Callum straddled my waist, his body tense with anticipation as he reached over to the nightstand and grabbed a condom. The sound of the wrapper tearing open sent another wave of nervous excitement through me, and I couldn't tear my eyes away from him.

He held it out to me, a teasing smile on his lips. "Put it on me, Hailey," he said, his voice low and full of heat.

I froze for a moment, my breath catching in my throat as I took the condom from him, my hands trembling slightly. I'd never done this before, never even been in a situation like this, and the reality of what was about to happen hit me all at once. But there was also this thrill, this rush of excitement that made me want to do everything right.

I took a shaky breath as my fingers hooked into the waistband of his boxers. Slowly, I pulled them down, my heart pounding in my chest. And then his length sprang free—hard, thick, and dripping.

My eyes widened as I stared at him, completely overwhelmed by the sight. "What the fuck?" I blurted out, unable to keep the words from slipping out. "How is that… gonna fit?!"

Callum chuckled softly, his fingers gently brushing my cheek as he reassured me. "It's fine," he murmured, his voice soothing. "I'll take it slow. I promise."

Once the condom was on, Callum shifted, his body hovering over mine as he positioned himself. He reached over to the bedside table again, grabbing a bottle of lube. "This will help," he said softly, squeezing a generous amount into his hand before slicking it over himself.

I nodded, my breath coming in shaky gasps as I tried to calm the nervous flutter in my stomach. I wanted this—I wanted him—and the look of care in his eyes only made me more sure of that.

Callum leaned down, pressing a soft kiss to my forehead, then my lips, his voice a low whisper. "If anything hurts, or if you need me to stop, you tell me, okay? Just say stop and I'll stop."

"I will," I whispered back, my hands finding their way to his shoulders, gripping him tightly as I braced myself for what was to come.

He positioned himself at my entrance, his tip teasing against me as my breath hitched in anticipation.

Slowly, ever so slowly, he began to push in, the pressure of him entering me making my body tense. The stretch was unfamiliar, intense but not painful, and I gasped, my fingers digging into his skin as I adjusted to the sensation.

Callum groaned softly, his voice thick with restraint as he moved carefully, barely an inch inside me. "You okay?" he asked, his voice tender, his gaze searching mine for any sign of discomfort.

I nodded, exhaling shakily. "Yeah... I'm okay," I managed to say, though my heart was racing, and every nerve in my body felt like it was on fire.

He pressed forward a little more, his movements slow and deliberate, giving me time to adjust. The stretch deepened, and I felt the burn of something entirely new—intense, yes, but also incredible. I moaned softly, my body trembling beneath him as he filled me bit by bit.

"You're doing so good," Callum murmured, his voice husky with need. He kissed me again, his lips tender against mine as he held still, letting me get used to the sensation of him inside me.

The fullness was overwhelming, the pressure a mixture of discomfort and pleasure, but I could feel my body relaxing, adjusting to him as the seconds passed. I could sense his restraint, the way he was holding back for my sake, and it only made me trust him more.

"Can I move a little?" he whispered, his breath warm against my ear.

I nodded, biting my lip as I whispered, "Yeah... move."

With that, Callum began to move, gently pulling back before pushing in again, his rhythm slow and careful. The sensation was strange but thrilling—each movement sending waves of heat through me, the friction between us making my entire body tingle.

I gasped softly, my fingers clinging to him as he found a slow, steady rhythm.

It wasn't painful—it was intense, yes—but the way he was taking his time, making sure I was comfortable, made it feel good in a way I hadn't expected.

Callum's breath came in ragged bursts as he moved inside me, his muscles taut with restraint. "Fuck, Hailey," he groaned, his voice strained. "You feel so fucking good."

I moaned in response, my body arching beneath him as I adjusted to the feeling, the pleasure starting to overshadow the nerves. His movements were slow but deliberate, each thrust sending sparks of pleasure through me as I grew more comfortable with the sensation.

"Callum..." I gasped, his name slipping from my lips as I tightened my grip on his shoulders. My body was responding to him in ways I hadn't imagined—waves of heat spreading from my core, every inch of me sensitive to his touch.

He kept his pace slow, his eyes locked on mine as he moved inside me, the intimacy of the moment making my heart race even faster. "You're so fucking beautiful," he whispered, his voice filled with awe as he kissed me again, his lips soft against mine.

I felt myself relaxing further, my body starting to crave more as I adjusted to the rhythm of his movements. "A little faster," I whispered, my voice trembling with a mix of nerves and desire. "Please."

Callum groaned softly, his pace picking up just a little, his hips moving with a bit more urgency. The sensation of him moving faster, deeper, sent a jolt of pleasure through me, and I gasped, my body arching into him as I held on tight.

"Fuck... Hailey," he breathed, his voice thick with lust as he continued to move inside me, his eyes locked on mine. The connection between us was palpable, every thrust bringing us closer together, the pleasure building with each passing second.

My breaths came out in ragged gasps, the intensity of the moment almost too much to handle, but I didn't want it to stop. "Callum... don't stop," I whispered, my voice barely audible over the sound of our breathing.

"I won't," he promised, his lips brushing against mine as he continued to move, his body pressing against mine, filling me completely. "I've got you."

His thrusts grew faster, more rhythmic, each movement making my body tighten and quiver under him. The pressure inside me was coiling again, this time with a delicious burn that I had never felt before. I was so full, the sensation so overwhelming that it was hard to keep up, but at the same time, I didn't want it to stop.

Callum's hands dug into my skin as he pulled me closer to him, his body pressing deeper against mine. His breaths came out in ragged gasps now, the same as mine, both of us lost in the moment. I could feel his need, his desperation, the way his body was moving with an urgency that matched the tension inside me.

The faster he went, the harder it became to control the sounds escaping from me. Soft whimpers turned into full-on moans, and I didn't care how loud I was anymore. The pleasure was too intense, the way he was filling me, moving inside me, bringing me closer and closer.

We were both a mess now—whimpering, moaning, and groaning as the intensity of it all took over. I could feel him trembling, his body shaking against mine, and I was right there with him, my legs wrapped around his waist, pulling him closer.

"Callum," I moaned, my voice barely a whisper as my nails dug into his back, the tension inside me growing unbearable. Every thrust, every movement sent me spiraling further, and I didn't know how much more I could take.

"Goddamn," Callum groaned, his voice thick with raw desire, his hips working faster now, deeper. "You're squeezing me so fucking tight."

His words sent a surge of heat through my body, and I whimpered, my legs trembling around him as I clung to him, feeling every inch of him inside me. The tension was unbearable, coiling tighter and tighter inside me with each thrust, each movement pushing me closer to the edge.

"I'm about to fucking come," he gasped, his breath ragged, his body trembling with the effort of holding back. "Oh my god..."

He started moving faster—so much faster—his hips slamming against mine, the sound of our wet flesh filling the room, echoing in my ears and driving me absolutely wild. I could barely think, barely breathe, lost in the overwhelming pleasure of it all. My entire body was trembling, every nerve on fire, every sensation heightened as the tension inside me built to a fever pitch.

Callum was groaning, his grip on my waist tightening as he thrust into me with a desperation that matched the fire burning inside me. His movements were frantic, erratic, as if he couldn't control himself anymore. The pace was almost brutal now, but I loved it—every single second of it.

The wet sound of him moving in and out of me was driving me insane, and I could feel myself getting closer, teetering on the edge of release. My breath came out in short, desperate gasps, my moans turning into cries as I felt my body begin to spiral out of control.

"Oh, Callum..." I gasped, my voice trembling as I felt the pressure inside me building to its peak. I was so close, so unbelievably close.

Then, with a deep, guttural grunt, Callum's body tensed. He thrust into me one last time before pulling out, his muscles trembling as he ripped the condom off and tossed it aside. His hand moved down to his length, stroking himself roughly as he hovered over me, his chest heaving with every breath.

"Fuck... Hailey..." he groaned, his voice low and strained as he worked himself, his eyes dark with lust.

I could feel the heat radiating off him, could see the tension in his body as he edged closer to his release. And then, with a sharp, broken grunt, he came, his release painting my stomach in hot, thick spurts. His body shuddered above me, every muscle tight with the force of his orgasm, his hand still moving as he milked every last drop.

The sight of him coming, the intensity of it, was enough to push me over the edge. The pleasure I had been holding back surged through me all at once, and I cried out, my body convulsing as my own orgasm hit me like a tidal wave.

I could feel myself tightening, pulsing, every inch of me trembling as I came hard, my hips bucking against him as the pleasure tore through me. My moans filled the room, loud and unrestrained as I rode out the waves of ecstasy, my entire body shaking with the intensity of it all.

I collapsed back against the bed, completely spent, my chest heaving as I tried to catch my breath. Callum fell beside me, his body still trembling slightly from the aftershocks of his release. We lay there for a moment, panting, our bodies slick with sweat, the weight of what just happened slowly settling in.

I could feel his warmth beside me, his hand resting gently on my waist as we both came down from the high, the room still filled with the sounds of our labored breathing.

"Fuck..." Callum muttered, his voice low and rough, a soft chuckle escaping his lips. "That was..."

I didn't have the words either. All I could do was lie there, completely spent and completely in awe of what had just happened.

Callum quickly jumped off the bed, his legs a little wobbly as he rushed to the bathroom.

A moment later, he returned, towels in hand, and knelt down beside me, his usual cocky grin back in place. "Alright, hold still," he said, dabbing at my stomach with a towel, wiping me off with surprisingly gentle care.

As he worked, our usual banter picked up right where we left off. He smirked down at me, shaking his head dramatically. "You really had to come that much, huh? Now I'm gonna need new sheets. Thanks for that."

My face flushed instantly, the embarrassment hitting me hard as I covered my face with my hands. "Oh my God, Callum."

He chuckled, clearly enjoying my reaction as he continued to clean me up. "I'm just saying, Eller. Couldn't control yourself, could you?"

I peeked at him through my fingers, trying to hide my embarrassment. "You started it," I muttered, feeling flustered as his teasing got to me.

Callum just grinned wider, leaning down to press a playful kiss to my forehead. "Yeah, yeah. Whatever helps you sleep at night."

Despite his teasing, there was a warmth between us now, something more comfortable and familiar, and it was hard not to feel like everything had changed but also stayed the same.

Callum carefully wiped away the last of his release from my skin, the warm towel soothing as he worked. Once he was done, he slipped his boxers back on, still moving with that casual confidence, like we hadn't just crossed every boundary imaginable.

He went to his closet and grabbed a shirt, one of his oversized tees, then turned back to me with a soft smile. "Here," he said, holding the shirt out. "Sit up."

I slowly pushed myself upright, still feeling a little dazed from everything, and he slipped the shirt over my head, pulling it down gently until it covered me. The fabric was soft and smelled like him, making me feel safe and warm.

"There," he said, satisfied, stepping back and admiring his work. "Much better."

CHAPTER 62
CALLUM

I pulled Hailey against me, wrapping my arm around her as she snuggled into my chest. Her soft breathing was soothing, her body warm against mine, and I couldn't help but feel a surge of pride.

Fuck, that was… incredible.

Better than I could've ever imagined. My mind was still buzzing from it all, and my body was humming with a kind of satisfaction I hadn't felt before.

The way her body had clenched around me, so tight, so warm—it was enough to drive me insane. Every thrust, every movement had been pure bliss. And the way she came around me, her body trembling and gripping me like that, it nearly sent me over the edge harder than I'd ever been before.

I came so fucking hard… I nearly saw stars. Hell, I think I did for a second. I'd never experienced anything like it in my life.

And the crazy part? I was still hard. As fuck. Even after all that, my body was still aching for more, still wanting her. The heat between us, the tension, it was something I'd never felt with anyone else, and it was almost impossible to believe we'd just crossed that line.

But I knew it was her first time. I didn't want to push her, didn't want to overwhelm her. It was already a lot, and the last thing I wanted was to do too much, more than what she could handle right now. I had to remind myself to be patient, to take things slow even though every part of me was still on fire with need.

We lay there in silence for a while, just cuddling. Hailey's head rested against my chest, and I couldn't stop the soft smile that tugged at my lips.

I gently traced circles on her back, feeling her breathing slow as she started to relax. Everything felt calm, but I could still feel the lingering heat between us, the memory of what had just happened, and it made my heart pound a little faster.

I shifted slightly, pulling her closer, and finally broke the silence. "How was your first time?" I asked softly, my voice a little hesitant. I wanted to make sure she was okay, that I hadn't done anything to make her uncomfortable. "I hope I didn't hurt you too much."

Hailey looked up at me, her cheeks flushed, and I could tell she was still processing everything, just like I was. There was this nervousness in her eyes, but also something deeper—like she had enjoyed it, even if it had been a little overwhelming.

She shook her head, smiling softly. "No, you didn't hurt me... not really." She bit her lip, like she was trying to find the right words. "It was a lot, but I'm okay."

Hearing that made a wave of relief wash over me. I'd been so worried about hurting her, especially since I couldn't thrust fully inside her.

God, that was hard. Not going all the way when every part of me wanted to just sink deeper into her, to give her all of me. But I knew she wasn't ready yet. Her body was still adjusting, still hurting a little, and I didn't want to push her beyond what she could handle.

"I'm glad," I murmured, pressing a kiss to her forehead. "It was hard... not thrusting all the way, only halfway. But I knew you were still hurting and adjusting."

She blushed, and I couldn't help but grin a little at how cute she looked when she did that. Hailey always tried to play it cool, but moments like this, when she was vulnerable, made me fall for her even more.

"Don't worry, though," I said with a smirk, my fingers brushing her cheek. "We'll practice a lot, until you can take all of me."

Her face turned an even deeper shade of red, and she quickly buried her face in my chest, groaning in embarrassment. "Oh my God, Callum," she muttered against my skin, her voice muffled.

I chuckled, enjoying the way she reacted. "What? I'm just being honest," I teased, my hand running through her hair as I spoke. "You'll get used to it. We'll take our time, but I know you'll be able to take all of me soon."

Hailey squirmed a little in my arms, clearly flustered, but I could tell she liked the idea of it, even if she was too shy to admit it. The thought of her getting used to me, of us growing closer and more comfortable with each other, made my chest tighten with something I couldn't quite explain.

It wasn't just about the physical stuff, though that was definitely a part of it. It was about being with her, about sharing this kind of intimacy with someone I genuinely cared about. I hadn't felt this way before, and it was new, but in a good way. It made me want to keep her close, to keep exploring whatever this was between us.

"So..." I said softly, my fingers tracing patterns on her back. "Do you feel okay? I mean, really okay?"

I couldn't help but smile to myself. Everything about this moment felt perfect. But then, I noticed something change in her. The way her expression shifted, how her eyes dropped from mine, her body tensing slightly against me.

"What's wrong?" I asked, frowning as I tilted her chin up gently to look at me. Her gaze flickered away, and I could tell something was on her mind, something bothering her.

She shook her head, letting out a small sigh. "Never mind, it's stupid."

I wasn't about to let that slide. "Even if it is," I said softly, brushing a strand of her hair behind her ear, "I want to know. Tell me, Hailey."

She hesitated for a second, her fingers fidgeting with the edge of my shirt, and then finally, she sighed again. "It's just... it was my first time, you know? But..." She trailed off, biting her lip nervously, avoiding eye contact with me.

I waited, watching her carefully, feeling the tension rise in her as she continued. Then, after a pause, she added quietly, "This must be like, your hundredth time, right?"

Her words hit me like a punch to the gut, and I blinked in surprise. It wasn't the question itself that startled me—it was the vulnerability behind it, the way she said it with that little flicker of doubt in her eyes.

I stared at her for a second, trying to wrap my head around where this was coming from. "Hailey..." I started, but she shook her head, cutting me off before I could say anything more.

"I know, I know," she muttered, her voice a little shaky. "It's dumb. I shouldn't even be thinking about it. It's just..." She let out another breath, her hands still fidgeting nervously. "I'm nervous now. What if I'm just... just another girl you've been with? Like, you've done this so many times before, and this was my first, but to you, it's no big deal, and I'm..." She trailed off, the words getting caught in her throat. "I'm anxious that I'm just another girl you fucked, Callum."

Hearing that... it hurt. Not because she was wrong to feel that way, but because I hadn't even considered that this would be on her mind.

Of course, she'd be worried about that. I had a reputation—hell, I'd been with girls before, and I wasn't exactly known for sticking around. But this, with Hailey? It was different. She was different.

I blinked, startled, trying to find the right words. "Hailey," I said softly, turning her face gently toward mine, making sure she saw that I was serious, that I wasn't brushing this off. "I get why you'd think that, okay? I do. But... you're not just some other girl I fucked."

She looked up at me, her eyes still filled with that uncertainty, and it made my chest tighten. I hated that she was feeling this way, that I had somehow made her think she wasn't important, that she wasn't special to me.

"Yeah, I've been with other girls," I admitted, trying to be as honest as possible. "But none of that... none of them were like this. None of them were like you."

Her gaze softened a little, but I could still see the worry lingering in her eyes. I squeezed her hand gently, wanting her to understand, to really hear me.

"This wasn't just about sex, Hailey. It wasn't just some random hookup to me," I continued, my voice firm but gentle. "I care about you. More than I've ever cared about anyone before, and I don't take this lightly. You're not just another girl to me. You're... you're everything."

Her breath hitched slightly, and I could see her trying to process my words, her eyes flicking back and forth between mine as if she was searching for something—any sign that I wasn't being sincere.

I sighed softly, leaning down to press a kiss to her forehead. "I've been with other people, yeah. But I've never felt the way I feel with you. You're the only one that matters to me, Hailey. And I know I have a shitty reputation, but I don't want you to ever think you're just some girl I'm messing around with. You're so much more than that."

She stayed quiet for a second, her eyes still wide, but I could feel the tension slowly easing out of her body as my words sank in. I knew I had to work to prove that to her, to show her that she wasn't just another girl, but I meant every word.

Finally, she nodded slowly, biting her lip again. "I guess I just got... insecure for a minute," she admitted softly, her voice almost a whisper. "This was a big deal for me."

"I know," I murmured, stroking her cheek gently. "And it's a big deal for me, too. I'm not going anywhere, Hailey. I'll prove it to you. I'll prove to you that you're the only girl that matters to me."

Hailey blinked, her lips parting in surprise as she waited for me to continue.

"You know, what, I've already blocked every other girl I was ever acquainted with," I added casually.

She stared at me, her eyes widening as she processed what I just said. Then, out of nowhere, she burst out laughing. "You did *what?*"

I grinned, leaning back a little, feeling proud of myself for the ridiculous but effective move I'd made. "Yeah," I said, nodding. "I blocked every girl in school, even the ones from other schools that liked me."

Her laughter filled the room, and I couldn't help but smile wider. "Oh my God, Callum, that's so..."

"I'm serious!" I shot back. "You think I'm messing around? I'm telling you, I blocked them all. Even some of my friends' moms who I used to follow on Instagram. You know, just to be safe."

Hailey was practically doubled over now, her laughter contagious. She tried to cover her face, shaking her head like she couldn't believe I was saying all of this. "You blocked your friends' moms?!"

"Yeah," I said, keeping a straight face even though I knew how ridiculous it sounded. "I'm dedicated. I want you to know I'm not playing around here. No distractions. No other girls. Just you."

She wiped at her eyes, still giggling, her cheeks flushed from the laughter. "That's crazy. You didn't have to do all that."

"Maybe," I admitted, smirking at her, "but I'll do anything to prove to you that I'm not the manwhore I used to be."

Her eyes sparkled with amusement as she looked up at me, and for a second, I saw the tension in her ease. I wanted her to laugh, to relax, but I also wanted her to understand how much she meant to me. I wasn't that same guy anymore—the one who flirted with girls for fun, who didn't care about the consequences. Hailey changed all of that.

"I'll be your manwhore," I added, raising an eyebrow playfully. "Only yours."

She looked up at me, shaking her head like she still couldn't believe what she was hearing. "You're ridiculous," she muttered, though I could tell by the soft smile on her face that she was touched by the gesture, no matter how over-the-top it seemed.

"Maybe," I agreed, leaning down to kiss her softly, "but I mean it, Hailey. You're the only one I care about."

She sighed, her smile lingering as she kissed me back. "I believe you," she whispered, her voice softer now.

I leaned down, capturing Hailey's lips in another soft kiss, feeling the warmth and tenderness that seemed to flow between us with every touch.

One kiss wasn't enough, though, and I found myself kissing her again. And again. Each one was softer than the last, but filled with this intensity I couldn't quite explain. It was like I couldn't get enough of her, like I needed to keep reassuring myself that she was here with me.

My lips trailed down to her collarbone, where I spotted the faint marks I had left earlier—darkened spots that were a physical reminder of what we'd shared.

The sight of them made something primal and possessive stir inside me. Those hickeys were mine. Hailey was mine. It was an overwhelming thought, but one that settled in my chest with a kind of satisfaction that was hard to describe.

I kissed the marks softly, letting my lips linger there for a moment, and I felt her shiver slightly beneath me. The way her body responded to my touch, how easily she melted into me, sent a rush of warmth through me, and I couldn't help but hold her closer, tighter.

"Let's fall asleep like this," I murmured, my voice low as I pressed my forehead against hers, my arms wrapping securely around her waist.

She hummed in approval, her body relaxing into mine as she snuggled closer. The sound was so soft, so content, and it made my heart swell in ways I wasn't used to.

As we lay there, tangled together, I could feel every breath she took, every soft rise and fall of her chest. Her scent was all around me, her skin warm against mine, and I felt this overwhelming sense of peace. Like this was exactly where I was supposed to be.

"AHHHHHHH!" The piercing scream jolted me awake, my heart racing as I blinked in confusion, trying to figure out what the hell was going on.

"What? What happened?" I mumbled, my voice thick with sleep, but the fog of confusion disappeared the second I spotted Dalton standing in the doorway, his eyes wide in shock, his face pale as a sheet.

My heart dropped. Oh. Fuck.

I glanced down. Hailey was still in my arms, curled up against my chest, wearing nothing but my t-shirt. And me? I was only in my boxers, clothes scattered haphazardly across the room from the night before.

Oh. Fuck. Fuck, fuck, fuck.

"Dalton, I can explain—" I started, my voice coming out panicked and rushed, but before I could even finish, I heard my mom's voice, echoing from the hallway.

"What's wrong, honey? Why are you screaming?" she called out, her footsteps growing louder as she approached.

My eyes went wide, and I felt my stomach drop even further. Oh, shit. This was bad. Really fucking bad.

My mom stepped into the doorway, her face filled with concern, but that quickly turned into something else—shock, disbelief—when she spotted the scene in my room. Her eyes landed on Hailey, still half-asleep in my bed, and then on me, and then on the mess of clothes scattered all over the floor.

"Callum," my mom breathed, her voice tight with surprise and a bit of... well, horror. "What... what is going on in here?"

I scrambled to sit up, my mind racing, trying to come up with something, anything, to explain this away. "Mom, I—uh, it's not what it looks like," I stammered, but it absolutely was what it looked like. I mean, how else could I explain waking up with Hailey in my bed, the two of us barely dressed, clothes everywhere?

Before I could even get another word out, I heard the last voice I wanted to hear in this moment.

"Is everything okay? What's going on?" Mrs. Eller's voice echoed down the hallway, growing closer with every word.

My heart practically stopped in my chest, my mind going into full-on panic mode. I couldn't let Hailey's mom walk in here. No way. Not like this. Oh God, please no.

But it was too late. By the time I scrambled to grab the blanket and pull it over Hailey, who was still just waking up, Hailey's mom was already in the doorway. And the look on her face when she saw the two of us in bed together?

I thought I might pass out.

Her eyes widened in shock, her mouth dropping open as she took in the scene—me, shirtless and in my boxers, and Hailey wrapped in my shirt, the sheets tangled around us, clothes strewn all over the room like a bomb had gone off.

"Oh my God," she gasped, covering her mouth with her hand. "What... what is this?"

"Mom!" Hailey yelped, finally snapping awake and sitting up in bed, her face flushed a deep red as she tried to pull the blanket over herself. "I can explain!"

But could we? Could anyone explain this?

Panic surged through me as I shot up, grabbing for my clothes, but my brain wasn't working fast enough to handle the chaos of the situation. Dalton was still standing in the doorway, frozen like a statue, his eyes huge and staring at me in disbelief.

"Dalton, get out!" I snapped, waving him away, but he was too stunned to move.

I heard my mom mutter under her breath, "Oh, Lord," before she crossed her arms and narrowed her eyes at me. "Callum Reid, you better explain this right now."

"I—uh," I stammered, pulling my jeans from the floor and yanking them on, my hands trembling. "It's not... we didn't... I mean, we just fell asleep, okay?"

"Just fell asleep?" Mrs. Eller echoed, her eyes narrowing as she looked at me and then at Hailey. "Do you think we're that stupid, Callum?"

Hailey buried her face in her hands, mortified, as she tried to piece together an explanation. "We didn't... I mean, we... it wasn't..."

Mrs. Eller's voice sharpened. "This is not appropriate!"

"I know! I know!" I practically shouted, feeling like I was digging myself deeper into a hole I couldn't get out of.

"Callum, Hailey," Mrs Eller, her tone sharp and unyielding. "I expect you both downstairs and decent in five minutes. We need to talk!"

I swallowed hard, my stomach twisting in knots as she turned on her heel and left, leaving me standing there in the middle of the room. Hailey was already scrambling to get dressed, her face still flushed with embarrassment, and I was pretty sure I was paler than a ghost.

"Fuck..." I muttered under my breath, running a hand through my hair.

This was so bad. So, so bad.

CHAPTER 63

CALLUM

HAILEY AND I WALKED DOWNSTAIRS SLOWLY, THE WEIGHT OF WHAT WAS WAITING for us making each step feel like it was leading to the gallows. My mind raced as I tried to think of what to say, but the more I thought, the more I came up with nothing. By the time we reached the kitchen, I was running on pure nerves.

The moment we stepped in, my heart sank further. There they were—my mom, my dad, and Hailey's mom—all sitting around the kitchen table, staring at us like we were criminals caught in the act. My dad had his arms crossed, his face unreadable but stern. My mom, on the other hand, looked a mix of shocked and disappointed, while Hailey's mom… she looked like she was ready to kill us both on the spot.

The tension in the room was so thick you could cut it with a knife. We stood there awkwardly by the entrance, neither of us daring to speak, just waiting for one of the parents to start. I could feel Hailey standing close beside me, her body tense, her face flushed with embarrassment.

"Sit," my mom said finally, her voice tight.

We both shuffled to the table and sat down, but the silence dragged on, every second making my heart pound louder in my ears.

My dad was the first to break the silence, his voice low and firm. "So… does anyone want to explain what exactly was going on upstairs?"

I opened my mouth, but no words came out. I glanced over at Hailey, who was staring down at her lap, clearly mortified. It was like we were kids being caught sneaking cookies from the jar, only a hundred times worse.

Mrs. Eller, folded her arms, narrowing her eyes at us both. "This is completely inappropriate. I don't know what either of you were thinking, but this… this is unacceptable."

"We're sorry," Hailey mumbled, her voice barely above a whisper.

"We are," I quickly added, feeling like my throat was tightening. "We didn't… I mean, we weren't trying to…"

My mom cut in, her face still pale. "You two can't just sneak around like this. Especially not under our roof." She paused, looking at both of us in turn. "What were you thinking?"

I swallowed hard, not sure what to say. It wasn't like we planned for this to happen. It just… happened. But I knew there was no way I could explain that in a way that would make this any better.

"We didn't mean for it to happen like that," I said quietly, knowing how lame it sounded.

Mrs. Eller's gaze narrowed further. "Callum, Hailey—if this relationship is serious, you need to treat it with respect. What you did this morning doesn't show that."

I swallowed hard, feeling like I was in over my head, but I couldn't back out now. I needed to make them understand. I needed to make them see that this wasn't just some reckless, meaningless thing.

"I really love Hailey," I said, trying to keep my voice steady. I could feel everyone's eyes on me, but I didn't look away from Mrs. Eller. "What happened last night... it was a mutual decision. We didn't mean for it to happen the way it did, but it wasn't something we regret." I glanced at Hailey, who gave me a small, encouraging nod, even though her face was still bright red.

"We're a happy couple," I continued, my heart pounding in my chest. "I know this probably seems sudden, and I know it wasn't how we should've gone about it, but I really care about her. And I hope... I hope you guys can support us."

The room was dead silent.

Everyone was staring at me, processing what I'd just said, and the weight of their judgment felt like it was crushing me. I held my breath, waiting for someone to respond, but then I heard a voice that sent my heart plummeting into my stomach.

"Excuse me?"

I froze. That voice—deep, groggy, and confused—was the one I had been dreading the most. My head snapped toward the doorway, and there, standing with a cup of coffee in his hand and a confused frown on his face, was Mr. Eller.

Hailey's dad.

He blinked at the room, clearly trying to make sense of the tense atmosphere. He was still in his pajamas, his hair a little disheveled from sleep, and I could tell he hadn't been expecting to walk into this kind of situation first thing in the morning. "What's going on?" Mr. Eller asked, his eyes flicking between all of us before landing on me. "What's this about?"

The air in the room seemed to freeze, and I suddenly felt like I was sinking into quicksand.

Oh God, this was the worst possible moment for *him* to walk in.

My mouth went dry.

I couldn't speak.

Hailey's mom cleared her throat, glancing at her husband, and Hailey shifted nervously beside me. I could feel her tension radiating off her.

"Well, Mr. Eller," my mom started, her voice a little shaky, "it seems that Callum and Hailey... have been dating."

Mr. Eller's eyes narrowed slightly as he looked at me, his confusion turning into something more serious. "Dating?"

I nodded, swallowing hard. "Yeah, sir. We've been seeing each other for a while now."

His gaze moved to Hailey, who was biting her lip and looking like she wanted to crawl into a hole and disappear. "Is this true, Hailey?"

She nodded, her voice small. "Yeah, Dad. We've been together... for a while."

Mr. Eller's face tightened, his frown deepening as he processed this new information. "And what was that about last night?" he asked, his tone sharpening as he looked directly at me.

I stammered, trying to find the right words. "It wasn't... we didn't..."

Mr. Eller's eyes zeroed in on me, his face unreadable but his tone sharp as a knife. "Did you and my daughter sleep with each other last night?" His voice was calm, too calm, and it only made the tension in the room thicker. "While we were all out because of the snowstorm?"

I felt a chill run down my spine as his words hung in the air, and my heart pounded so loudly I thought everyone could hear it. My throat went dry, and I could feel the weight of everyone's eyes on me, especially Hailey's dad's piercing gaze.

I swallowed hard, trying to find my voice, but the knot in my stomach made it impossible to speak. What could I even say?

I couldn't lie—not with everything that had already happened—but admitting it outright? That was something else entirely.

"I..." My voice cracked, and I quickly cleared my throat, feeling my palms grow sweaty. "I promise, it wasn't like... like that."

Mr. Eller raised an eyebrow, clearly unimpressed with my weak attempt at explaining myself. "So you didn't sleep with her?"

I could feel Hailey's mom and my own parents holding their breath, waiting for me to answer. My gut twisted, and I realized that no matter how I said it, this conversation wasn't going to end well.

"We did... spend the night together," I admitted, my voice quieter now, but I forced myself to keep going. "But... it wasn't just some random thing. We really care about each other."

I wasn't sure if that was helping or making things worse, but I needed to be honest. I wasn't going to disrespect Hailey or her family by lying. I just hoped they would understand.

"So, Callum," Mr. Eller said slowly, his eyes narrowing as he crossed his arms. "You knew our family was vulnerable. We came to yours for help because our house burned down, and you decided to take that opportunity—us being under your roof —to seduce my daughter?"

My stomach dropped. Seduce? That wasn't what this was. My mind raced as I tried to figure out how to respond, but before I could say anything, Hailey shot up from her seat, her face flushed with frustration.

"Dad, no! It's not like that!" she snapped, her voice louder than I'd ever heard it. "It wasn't some... some scheme or plan. We didn't even mean for it to happen like that! It just did."

Mr. Eller's eyes flicked from Hailey to me, still glaring. "You expect me to believe that, Hailey? You're telling me that, while we were out dealing with a snowstorm and trying to keep everything together, this *just* happened?"

"Dad!" Hailey's voice was firm, her hands clenched at her sides. "Okay, it didn't just happen. We're in a relationship, okay? Callum and I are."

I watched them argue, feeling like I was drowning in the middle of a storm I couldn't control. My brain was spinning, and my mouth was dry as sandpaper. It wasn't supposed to go like this. Not at all.

But then something in me snapped.

I shot up from my chair, interrupting Hailey and her dad mid-argument, my heart still racing but my mind strangely clear. If there was ever a moment to just say everything I'd been holding back, this was it.

"Mr. Eller!" I called out, my voice louder than I intended, but it silenced the room.

Everyone turned to look at me, including Hailey, who looked like she was bracing herself for whatever was about to come out of my mouth.

"I know what this looks like," I started, my hands gesturing wildly. "And I know you probably think I'm some... player or some guy who's just taking advantage of the situation. But that's not it, okay? That's not it at all."

Mr. Eller raised an eyebrow, clearly unimpressed, but I wasn't backing down now. "I'm in love with Hailey. Like, really in love with her," I continued, feeling my chest tighten. "I know I've got a reputation, and yeah, I've made mistakes, but this? This isn't one of those mistakes. This is different. She's different."

Hailey's mouth fell open slightly, her cheeks turning pink as I kept going. I was on a roll now, and there was no stopping it.

"I wake up thinking about her. I go to sleep thinking about her. And in between, all I'm thinking about is how to not screw this up," I said, waving my arms for emphasis. "She's the only one who makes me feel like I want to be better. She's the only one who makes me feel like I'm not... I don't know, just some jock who only cares about soccer."

I could see Hailey's dad staring at me, his face still hard, but he was listening now. The room had gone completely quiet. Even my mom and dad were sitting there, wide-eyed, probably shocked that I was even capable of talking like this.

"And yeah," I added, running a hand through my hair, "maybe we didn't handle this in the best way. Maybe we should've told you guys earlier, or been more upfront. But I promise you, it wasn't some plan to take advantage of the situation. I love her. I'm crazy about her. I'd do anything for her."

I paused, catching my breath, feeling like I'd just run a marathon. "And, uh... I know that probably sounds dramatic," I admitted, "but it's the truth. I'm not the same guy I was before. Not with her. So... yeah. That's... that's where I'm at."

The room was quiet after my little outburst, and I could feel my face heating up from the intensity of what I'd just said. The parents, all of them, just stared at me, stunned.

I shifted awkwardly, rubbing the back of my neck, suddenly feeling a bit flustered. Did I go overboard?

"Oh," was all Hailey's mom managed to say, her expression softening as the shock settled. My mom and dad exchanged a look, both of them looking slightly dazed.

Then, after what felt like an eternity, my dad cleared his throat. "Well... I guess there's nothing wrong with you two dating," he said slowly, his tone more reasonable now. "But—" he shot me a look, "there need to be some boundaries."

I blinked, the tension in my shoulders loosening slightly. "Boundaries?" I asked, still trying to gauge how bad the damage was.

"Yes," he continued, glancing at Hailey's mom and dad, as if they were all in agreement. "You still live in the same house. That's not going to change for the time being, but that means you can't just be... doing stuff whenever you're home alone."

I nodded quickly, trying to look as responsible as I could. "Of course. We get it."

Hailey's mom sighed, rubbing her temples as if this whole ordeal had given her a headache. "We're just trying to make sure you two are careful, okay? This... sneaking around can't happen again."

"Understood," I said, glancing at Hailey, who gave me a small, relieved nod. It felt like we'd just survived a hurricane, and the worst of it was passing.

But as much as the situation seemed to be calming down, Hailey's dad still didn't look convinced. He hadn't said much after my big declaration, but there was something in his eyes—a tension that hadn't quite eased. He didn't seem angry anymore, but... he wasn't exactly thrilled either. His arms were still crossed, his gaze heavy on both me and Hailey, like he was waiting for something.

"Well, I hope you're serious about this," he muttered finally, his tone cool. "But don't think I'm just going to let this go easily."

I swallowed hard, meeting his gaze. "I understand, sir."

There was still an uneasy silence, but I could tell things were settling—at least for now.

CHAPTER 64

HAILEY

THE LAST FEW DAYS HAD BEEN... AWKWARD. NO, SCRATCH THAT. THEY'D BEEN extremely awkward. Ever since the big blow-up with our parents, it felt like we were under constant surveillance. My mom and Callum's parents were watching us like hawks now, as if they were just waiting for us to make another mistake. I couldn't even sneak a glance at Callum without feeling the weight of someone's gaze on us.

It was exhausting.

At breakfast, lunch, or even in passing, there was always this unspoken tension in the air, a constant reminder that we weren't just under the same roof—we were being watched. I couldn't stand it.

Callum had been trying to play it cool, but even he looked like he was getting fed up with the whole situation. He'd been way more careful, keeping his distance whenever we were around our parents, which only added to the awkwardness.

It wasn't just that, though. Things between us felt... different. The fallout from that morning had left us both shaken, and we hadn't really had a chance to talk it all out. And I missed him. Not just in the sneaky, late-night sense of him sneaking down to my room, but I missed being able to just be with him. It felt like we were suddenly under a spotlight, and neither of us knew how to move forward without tripping over each other.

The whole thing made me feel anxious. I found myself walking on eggshells around the house, trying to keep things casual while also feeling like I needed to look over my shoulder constantly.

It didn't help that every time Callum looked at me, I could tell he was frustrated too. I knew him well enough to see it in his eyes, in the way his jaw clenched when his parents made some passing comment about "boundaries" or "responsibility."

I sighed as I walked through the hallway toward my room. It was late, and everyone had already gone to bed, but I could feel the weight of the last few days bearing down on me. What were we supposed to do now? Just act like nothing had changed? Like we weren't secretly together, sneaking around behind the very people who'd helped us after the fire?

I leaned against the door to my room, lost in thought. We couldn't go back to how things were. But with the way things were now, it didn't feel like we could move forward either.

Just as I was about to settle in, I heard a soft knock on my door. I froze, my heart skipping a beat. I didn't even have to look to know who it was.

"Hailey," Callum whispered through the door. "Are you up?" I opened the door just enough to see Callum standing there, looking as mischievous as ever. I frowned, glancing down the hallway, half-expecting one of our parents to pop out of nowhere.

"What are you doing?" I whispered, my heart racing. "They're gonna kill us if they find out you're down here."

Callum smirked, leaning against the doorframe like nothing could faze him. "I'm fine with being a sacrifice."

I rolled my eyes, though I couldn't help the smile tugging at the corners of my lips. "You're ridiculous."

He stepped closer, closing the gap between us. "I just missed you. A lot."

That hit me right in the chest. The past few days had been awkward and tense, but hearing him say he missed me—it made everything else melt away for a moment. I sighed, stepping back to let him inside.

"Fine," I muttered, trying to sound annoyed, even though I wasn't. "But if we get caught, it's on you."

Callum grinned, slipping into my room. "Deal."

As soon as the door clicked shut, Callum wasted no time. He gently pushed me toward the bed, his strong hands firm but playful, and I let out a surprised laugh as I stumbled backward onto the mattress. Before I could say anything, he collapsed next to me, wrapping his arms around me and pulling me into his chest, his warmth surrounding me like a blanket.

I could feel his heart beating steadily beneath me as he let out a long, content sigh.

"I miss this," he mumbled, his lips brushing my hair as he held me close. "I know we sneak moments together when we can—on the way to school, in the halls between classes—but it's never enough. It's never enough for me."

I smiled softly, my head resting against his chest as I listened to his heartbeat, steady and comforting. His warmth was intoxicating, and the way his arms fit around me made me feel like everything was right in the world, even if just for a little while.

He had a point. It wasn't enough. We had to be so careful around our parents, and even at school, we couldn't act like a normal couple. Every moment we could steal together felt like gold, but then there were all the stolen glances, the secret touches, the rush of excitement every time he brushed past me in the hall. That thrill was still there, but the frustration of not being able to fully be together was overwhelming.

I giggled softly, the sound filling the quiet basement. "Yeah, it's been... interesting, sneaking around."

"Interesting?" Callum's voice was playful, but there was an edge to it. "I don't want 'interesting,' Hailey. I want you. All the time."

My heart fluttered at that, and I nuzzled closer, feeling the intensity behind his words. His grip tightened around me, and I could feel the weight of his frustration—the same frustration I felt too. I wanted the same thing.

"I told Nala about us the other day," I said after a moment, shifting in his arms to look up at him.

Callum raised an eyebrow, curiosity flickering in his eyes. "Oh yeah? What did she say?"

I couldn't help but laugh at the memory. "She was... well, let's just say she was shocked. And then she screamed. Loudly. Right in the middle of the cafeteria."

Callum chuckled, shaking his head. "I can't say I'm surprised. How did you break it to her?"

I shrugged, trying to keep a straight face. "I just told her casually, you know? Like, 'Oh hey, Nala, by the way, I'm dating Callum Reid.'"

"And she screamed."

"Like a banshee," I confirmed, grinning. "She kept asking me a million questions after that. Like, 'How? When? Why?' It was a lot."

Callum groaned, rubbing his forehead. "I can imagine."

"Yeah, but after she got over the shock, she was really happy for me. She even teased me, saying I'm probably the only girl in the school who could actually make you settle down."

He snorted, giving me a playful nudge. "She's not wrong."

I rolled my eyes, poking him in the ribs. "I'm serious! She kept going on about how you're the 'biggest flirt' and how it's weird seeing you all... I don't know, domesticated?"

"Domesticated?" Callum laughed, the sound rumbling in his chest. "Like I'm some wild animal or something?"

I grinned, snuggling deeper into his embrace. "Well, you kind of were. Now you're like a puppy—sweet and cuddly."

Callum groaned again, but I could hear the amusement in his voice as he shifted slightly in the bed so I'd be more comfortable. "I'm still a badass. Don't forget that."

"Uh-huh," I teased. "Whatever you say, puppy."

He growled playfully, pinning me back against the bed, his face hovering just above mine. His eyes sparkled with mischief as he grinned. "I'll show you a puppy," he murmured before leaning down and nipping at my neck, sending a shiver down my spine.

I squealed, squirming beneath him as his playful bites turned into soft kisses. "Callum, stop!" I laughed, trying to push him off, but he just laughed and held me tighter.

"I missed this, Hailey," he said again, his voice softer now as he buried his face in my neck. "I really did."

I smiled, my fingers brushing through his hair as I let out a content sigh. "I missed this too."

Callum shifted beside me, his arm still draped over my waist as we lay tangled on my bed. He let out a soft sigh. "The final game of the season's coming up soon," he said, his voice low and thoughtful. "I'm hoping I can count on my number one fan to be there?"

I looked up at him, blinking innocently. "Hmm, I'm not sure who that is," I teased, trying to keep a straight face.

Callum chuckled, his fingers tracing lazy patterns on my arm. "Really? You've got no idea? After all this time, and you don't know who my number one fan is?"

I shrugged, biting back a smile. "Nope. No clue. You should probably find her though—sounds important."

He shook his head, grinning as he tugged me closer. "You're impossible."

I laughed, settling back into his embrace. "So... what are your plans after high school? Have you heard back from any of your college applications yet?"

Callum was quiet for a moment, and I felt his hand stop its gentle movement against my arm. "I haven't heard back from the apps yet," he said slowly, as if choosing his words carefully. "But... I do have offers from some schools. For soccer, I mean."

I froze, blinking in surprise as I pulled back slightly to look up at him. "What the hell? Why are you only telling me this now?"

Callum raised an eyebrow, his expression amused. "I thought it would be common knowledge that I'd get offers."

I gave him a playful shove. "It's also common knowledge that being humble doesn't come easy to you."

He laughed, his grip on me tightening slightly. "Fair enough."

I studied him for a moment, my curiosity piqued. There was something in his voice—something deeper than just casual conversation. "So... what's your plan, then?" I asked, tilting my head. "Do you want to play college soccer? Go pro?"

Callum hesitated for a second before letting out a long breath. "Yeah," he admitted softly, his gaze drifting to the ceiling. "I want to make it. Up there, you know? On the world stage. I want to be the next Messi."

"More like the next *Messy*." I teased, trying to suppress my giggles.

Callum narrowed his eyes at me, but the corner of his mouth twitched upward. "Oh, you think you're so funny, huh?"

I grinned, unable to resist. "I mean, you've got the 'Messy' part down, at least."

Before I could say another word, Callum lunged at me, his hands finding my sides as he started tickling me mercilessly. I squealed, trying to squirm away, but he held me in place, his fingers digging into my ribs as I dissolved into a fit of laughter.

"Take it back!" he demanded, grinning wickedly.

"Never!" I gasped between laughs, my body shaking as I tried to wriggle free. "Callum, stop!"

"Not until you admit I'm not Messy!" he teased, his fingers relentless as they continued their assault.

I could barely breathe, my laughter uncontrollable. "Okay, okay!" I cried, kicking my legs helplessly. "You're not Messy! You're... you're perfect!"

He paused, looking down at me with a satisfied smirk. "That's more like it."

I lay there, breathless and still giggling, as he finally stopped tickling me. My heart was pounding, but the warmth between us had spread like a cozy blanket.

He looked down at me, still grinning. "See? I can be serious," he said, his voice softening slightly. "I really do want to make it big. And I will. You'll see."

I gazed up at him, my smile lingering as I reached up to brush a strand of hair out of his face. "I believe you, Callum," I said quietly. "You've got this."

Callum's grin softened into something more tender, his eyes locking with mine. "Thanks, Hailey," he murmured, leaning down to press a kiss to my forehead. "Means a lot coming from you."

I felt my heart flutter in my chest, warmth spreading through me as I settled back into his arms. "You're welcome," I whispered, feeling content in the moment.

Before I could even process what he'd just said, Callum leaned down and kissed me. Hard. His lips crashed into mine with an intensity that took my breath away. My heart pounded as I melted into the kiss, my hands instinctively reaching up to grab onto his shirt, holding him close.

It was one of those kisses that made the whole world disappear, where everything else faded into the background and all I could focus on was him—his lips, his warmth, the way his body pressed against mine. He kissed me like he'd been holding back, like he needed this just as much as I did.

When he finally pulled back, both of us were breathless.
I blinked up at him, my mind still reeling from the kiss. "What...
was that for?" I asked, my voice barely a whisper.

Callum grinned, his thumb brushing gently across my
cheek. "For being my number one fan," he murmured, his voice
low and playful.

We started kissing again, and before I even realized what
was happening, I was straddling Callum's waist. His hands
roamed up and down my back, settling at my waist, gripping me
firmly as his lips moved against mine with a kind of desperate
intensity that sent shivers down my spine. My fingers tangled in
his hair, pulling him closer, needing him closer.

His hands slid up under my shirt, his touch leaving a
trail of heat on my skin, and I couldn't help but let out a soft
gasp. The sound seemed to spur him on, and he groaned,
deepening the kiss as his hands explored the curve of my waist,
pulling me tighter against him.

As I shifted in Callum's lap, I felt him growing harder
beneath me, pressing against me through his pants. The
realization sent a rush of heat through me, my breath hitching as
the intensity of the moment deepened. His hands tightened on
my waist, pulling me even closer as we kissed, the heat between
us becoming almost unbearable.

Every movement, every touch was electric, and the
feeling of him beneath me—growing harder with each second—
made my heart race even more. It was overwhelming, this mix of
desire and closeness, the way we seemed to fit together so
perfectly.

Callum groaned softly, his lips leaving mine as he buried
his face against my neck, his breath hot against my skin.
"Hailey..." he murmured, his voice thick with need. I could feel
his hands tremble slightly as they moved over my waist, his
touch both firm and careful.

I swallowed, my own body trembling with the intensity
of it all, but I didn't want to stop. Not yet.

Callum suddenly pulled back, his chest heaving as he broke the kiss, his face flushed but his expression serious. "No," he said, almost like he was convincing himself as much as me.

I blinked at him, still breathless, trying to understand what he was saying. "What?" I asked, confused.

He shook his head, his hands still resting on my waist but no longer roaming. "We can't. I promised."

"Promised?" I repeated, my brow furrowing as I tried to keep up. "What are you talking about?"

Callum let out a deep breath, sitting up slightly and rubbing the back of his neck. "I promised our parents that we'd be responsible. That we wouldn't just... do stuff like this. Sneaking around and shit.."

The realization hit me, and my heart softened a little. He was right. He had promised, and sneaking down here was already breaking that promise. I could see the guilt flickering across his face, the conflict in his eyes.

"I want to prove to your parents," he continued, his voice quieter now, more vulnerable. "Especially your dad. I want him to know that I'm not just some reckless guy who's going to take advantage of you. I want him to know I'm good for you."

I couldn't help but smile at the way he said it, trying so hard to be serious and responsible. He had that determined look in his eye, the same one he had when he was trying to win a soccer game or when he was hell-bent on proving something. It was kind of adorable.

"You think you're good for me?" I teased, tilting my head playfully.

Callum pouted, his lips curving downward in the most exaggerated way. "What, you don't think I am?"

I laughed softly, running my fingers through his hair. "Well... you can be bad sometimes. But I guess... you're a good boy most of the time."

Callum's eyes widened slightly, and I could feel the shift in the air as his expression changed from playful to something else. He stared at me for a second, like he was processing what I'd just said, and then his voice dropped to a low, almost pleading tone.

"Say that again."

I raised an eyebrow, surprised by his sudden request. "What?"

"Call me a good boy again," he whispered, his eyes locking onto mine with a mix of intensity and curiosity.

I blinked, caught off guard by how serious he seemed. The way he was looking at me, like he needed to hear those words—it sent a shiver down my spine.

"Callum..." I began, but he leaned in closer, his grip on my waist tightening just a little.

"Please," he murmured, his voice almost a whisper now. "Call me a good boy again."

My heart fluttered at the way he was looking at me, so full of vulnerability, like this moment meant something more to him than I realized. I could feel the heat rising between us again, but it was different now—softer, more intense.

I bit my lip, leaning down slightly so my lips were just inches from his ear. "You're a good boy, Callum," I whispered, my voice soft but teasing.

He let out a shaky breath, his hands gripping me tighter as he closed his eyes, like the words were more than just playful banter to him. His reaction surprised me, but I couldn't help but feel a strange sense of satisfaction at how much he seemed to enjoy it.

"Again," he whispered, his voice rough with need.

I smiled, brushing my lips against his ear. "You're my good boy, Callum."

He groaned softly, and I could feel his body tense beneath me.

The way he reacted to those simple words was unlike anything I'd seen from him before, and it made my heart race. He was always so confident, so in control, but now... now he was looking at me like I had the power, like I was the one in control.

And it was intoxicating.

"Say it one more time," he pleaded, his voice barely audible as his breath quickened.

I smirked, pressing a soft kiss to his cheek. "You're a good boy."

He exhaled shakily, his eyes fluttering open as he looked up at me, his expression soft and filled with something I couldn't quite place. Vulnerability. Trust. Desire.

"You're killing me," he muttered, his lips curling into a half-smile.

I shifted slightly, feeling the hard pressure of Callum's erection poking against my butt, unmistakable and insistent. His body was tense beneath mine, and I couldn't help the small smirk that formed on my lips.

"You feel a little excited," I teased softly, my voice barely above a whisper.

Callum growled, the sound deep and rough in his throat, sending a shiver down my spine. His hands tightened on my waist, as though he was holding himself back, but I could feel how much he wanted me. "Hailey..." His voice came out strained, a mix of desperation and frustration.

I leaned closer, my breath brushing his ear as I whispered, "What's wrong? Having trouble being a good boy?"

He groaned, his body trembling beneath mine. "Stop," he whispered, but his grip on me tightened. His eyes fluttered shut for a moment, his jaw clenched as if he was fighting a losing battle with himself. "You have to stop..."

But then, almost immediately, he let out a broken sigh, his voice full of pleading. "But... also... don't stop."

The conflict in his voice made my heart race. He was torn, wanting me so badly but trying to be responsible, to keep his word. But every brush of my hips against him, every teasing word I whispered, was pushing him closer to the edge.

I shifted again, feeling his hardness throbbing against me. His breath hitched, and he growled low in his throat. "Hailey, please..." He groaned, his voice thick with desire. "You're driving me insane."

I could feel his hands shaking slightly as he gripped my waist, his body tense and coiled like a spring, ready to snap at any moment.

It was intoxicating, the way he was so torn between wanting to stop and needing to go further.

I could feel the heat between us intensifying, his hardness pressing even more insistently against me, and I couldn't help but move, slowly grinding against him.

Callum's reaction was instant—his entire body tensed beneath me, and his hands tightened on my hips, his fingers digging into my skin as if he was holding on for dear life.

"Hailey..." His voice came out as more of a groan, rough and strained, like he was fighting a losing battle against his own desire.

He covered his face with one hand, trying to suppress the sounds coming from deep in his chest, but I could feel his body responding to every movement I made. Every slow, deliberate grind of my hips sent a ripple of tension through him. His breaths were coming out in sharp gasps now, the frustration and pleasure mixing into something intense, something primal.

"Hailey... fuck..." he muttered from behind his hands, his voice shaking with need. His entire body was trembling beneath me, as though he was trying to resist but couldn't.

The way he was struggling with himself only made me bolder, and I leaned down, my lips brushing his ear as I whispered, "Callum... you feel so good."

He let out a low, tortured groan, his body arching slightly as I continued to move against him. I could feel him throbbing beneath me, his erection straining against his pants, and the sensation of him so hard, so desperate for me, sent a wave of heat coursing through my own body.

His other hand came up to cover his face completely now, trying to hide how much he was struggling. "Please," he groaned, his voice muffled behind his hands. "I can't... fuck, I can't take it."

I didn't stop. If anything, I moved slower, more deliberately, grinding down against him as I felt his body twitch beneath me. His hands slid down from his face to grip my hips harder, like he was trying to anchor himself, but I could feel how close he was to snapping.

I bit my lip, watching him as his head fell back against the pillows, his face flushed, his eyes squeezed shut. He was doing everything he could to suppress the groans threatening to escape, but the way his body was trembling beneath mine told me everything I needed to know.

I leaned down again, pressing my lips to his neck, feeling the rapid pulse beneath his skin. "You like this, don't you?" I whispered, my voice teasing but soft.

"Fuck, Hailey, yes," he groaned, his voice breaking slightly. His hands were gripping my hips so tightly now that I was sure there would be marks later, but I didn't care. The way his body was responding to me, the way he was losing control, was enough to drive me wild.

He shifted beneath me, his body rising off the bed slightly as he pushed his hips up, grinding harder against me. I could feel him pulsing beneath me, his erection straining painfully against his pants, and I knew he was close—so close to losing the last bit of control he had left.

I leaned down, my lips brushing his ear again. "You're such a good boy, Callum," I whispered, knowing exactly how much it affected him.

That was it. Callum's entire body shuddered, his hands flying up to cover his face again as he tried, and failed, to suppress the sound. His hips jerked beneath me, and I could feel the raw need in every movement he made.

"Hailey..." he gasped, his voice strained.

My eyes widened as I felt him tense under me, the realization hitting me all at once. I stopped moving, frozen in place as I stared down at him, my heart racing in confusion.

"Callum," I whispered, my voice shaky. "Did you just...?"

His face was flushed a deep red now, and he looked both embarrassed and frustrated, like he couldn't believe what had just happened either.

"I—" He stammered, running his clean hand through his hair, clearly flustered. "I couldn't... fuck, Hailey, I couldn't help it. You were driving me crazy, and I just—"

He cut himself off, his eyes flicking between me and... down there, as if he wasn't quite sure how to explain what had just happened.

I stared at him, my mouth slightly open, my mind racing. Callum, the guy who always had control, who always kept it together, had just... lost it.

Completely.

And it was because of me.

I had made him come—right there, in his shorts, just from grinding against him.

"I... wow," I muttered, still in shock, trying to process it.

Callum let out a shaky laugh, wiping his hand on a nearby towel, his face still red with embarrassment. "Yeah, no kidding," he muttered, his voice still breathless. "That's never happened before."

I couldn't help but feel a strange mix of pride and disbelief. I had been teasing him, sure, but I hadn't expected that.

The fact that I could affect him so much, drive him to that point, made my heart race even faster.

"You're dangerous," he whispered, his voice rough as his hand slid down to cup the side of my face. "And I can't get enough of you."

CHAPTER 65
CALLUM

THANKSGIVING NIGHT HAD A BUZZ OF ENERGY, THE KIND THAT MADE EVERYTHING feel warm despite the chill outside. The Reid/Eller household was busy, with everyone scurrying around to get the dinner ready. The dining table was already set with plates and silverware, and the air smelled like freshly baked pies and mashed potatoes.

I tugged at the collar of my shirt as I walked through the living room, feeling the slight tension in my chest. It wasn't just because of Thanksgiving—though, that was always a bit chaotic —but because of Hailey's dad. Mr. Eller had been distant since everything went down between Hailey and me. I understood why, but it still didn't make things easier.

As I passed by the window, I caught sight of Mr. Eller outside, tending to the turkey in the cold. The wind bit at the air, but there he was, bundled up in a jacket, focused on getting the turkey just right.

I paused for a second, watching him, before I made up my mind. This was my chance.

I stepped outside, the cold air immediately hitting my face. I zipped up my jacket and made my way over to him, my heart pounding a little harder with every step. This wasn't going to be easy, but I needed to do it. I couldn't keep tiptoeing around this tension with Mr. Eller.

I wanted—no, needed—his respect.

Not just because of the awkwardness, but because I knew how much he meant to Hailey. If I couldn't make things right with him, I'd never truly feel comfortable.

Mr. Eller didn't notice me at first, his focus still on the turkey, so I cleared my throat softly to get his attention.

"Mr. Eller?"

He glanced up, his eyes narrowing slightly when he saw me. He didn't say anything, just gave me a slight nod of acknowledgment before going back to the turkey.

For a second I wondered whether he imagined chopping me up and tossing me in some hot oil, as well. But I shook away those thoughts. I was here to have a serious conversation with my girlfriend's dad and that's what I planned on doing, not running away.

I rubbed the back of my neck, already feeling the weight of the conversation before it even began. I took a deep breath, trying to gather my thoughts. "I, uh… I wanted to talk to you. If that's okay."

He paused for a moment, then straightened up, wiping his hands on a towel before turning to face me fully. His expression was unreadable, but I could tell he wasn't exactly thrilled to see me.

"About what?" he asked, his voice gruff.

I swallowed hard, knowing I had to be careful with what I said next. "About Hailey. And… us."

Mr. Eller's gaze hardened a little, but he didn't interrupt, so I continued.

"I know… I know things got off to a rough start. And I know you probably don't trust me right now," I admitted, my voice steady despite the nerves eating at me. "But I care about Hailey. A lot. And I want to make things right with you."

He didn't say anything, just crossed his arms over his chest, waiting for me to continue.

"I'll do anything," I said, my voice firmer now. "I want to earn your respect, sir. I know how important you are to Hailey, and I want you to know that I'm serious about her. I'm not just some... reckless kid who's going to screw things up."

Mr. Eller's brow furrowed slightly, his eyes narrowing as he studied me. "Why should I believe that?"

I exhaled, already expecting the question. "Because I love her," I said simply. "I know we've made some mistakes, but I'm willing to do whatever it takes to prove to you that I'm serious about her. I want to be the kind of guy you'd trust with her."

He let out a sharp breath, his eyes never leaving mine. The silence stretched between us, heavy and cold like the wind biting at my cheeks. I stood there, feeling the weight of his judgment, but I didn't back down. I wasn't going to walk away from this.

"I know I messed up," I added quietly. "I know it doesn't look good, what happened between us. But I'm here, standing in front of you, because I want to make things right. Not just for me, but for Hailey. She deserves that."

Mr. Eller sighed, his expression softening just a fraction. He uncrossed his arms, glancing down at the ground before looking back at me. "It's not that I don't believe you care about Hailey," he said slowly. "I can see that... I guess. But caring about someone isn't enough, Callum. It's about responsibility. It's about proving that you're ready to be the kind of man she needs."

I nodded, taking his words in. "I know. And I want to be that. I'm not perfect, but I'm willing to do whatever it takes to show you that I'm serious about her. I'll prove it to you."

He studied me for a long moment, the cold wind whipping around us as we stood there. Finally, he sighed, his shoulders relaxing just a bit. "I don't know if you're the right one for my daughter," he admitted, his voice rough. "But... I can see you're trying. That means something."

I felt a wave of relief wash over me, though I knew this was just the beginning. I wasn't going to win him over with one conversation, but at least he was willing to listen.

"I'll keep proving it to you," I said, my voice sincere. "I just want you to know that I'm not going anywhere."

Mr. Eller nodded slowly, still looking me over like he wasn't completely convinced, but at least I had made some progress.

"Just don't let me down, Callum," he said, his voice low. "For Hailey's sake."

"I won't," I promised, meaning every word.

We stood there for a moment longer, the tension between us easing just slightly, but the weight of his expectations still hung in the air. It was a start, but I knew I had a long way to go.

"Need any help with the turkey?" I asked, trying to ease the heaviness.

Mr. Eller looked at me, then down at the turkey. He let out a small chuckle, though it was more tired than anything. "Sure. Why not?"

I stepped up next to Mr. Eller, grabbing a pair of tongs from the table and helping him turn the turkey. The cold wind nipped at my face, but the heat from the grill kept the worst of it at bay. It was a quiet moment, but not uncomfortable. I could feel Mr. Eller watching me out of the corner of his eye, and I knew he wasn't just checking to see if I could handle the turkey.

As I worked, I noticed him fold his arms again, leaning slightly against the side of the house. His expression was calmer now, but there was still a sharp edge to his voice when he finally spoke again.

"Look, Callum," he started, glancing at me with a hardened gaze, "I appreciate what you said, and I can see you're trying. But let's get one thing straight."

I nodded, bracing myself for whatever was coming next.

"If you ever hurt Hailey," he continued, his tone low and serious, "I'm not going to give you a second chance. I don't care how much you say you care about her or how much you've tried to prove yourself."

I swallowed hard, feeling the weight of his words hit me like a brick. He wasn't pulling any punches. "You hurt her," Mr. Eller said, his eyes locking onto mine with a deadly seriousness, "and it'll be you getting thrown into a boiling hot vat of oil. Do you understand?"

I knew it. He *had* been imagining on doing that to me. But only if I ever hurt Hailey.

And that was something I'd never do.

The intensity in his voice was clear—this wasn't a joke or a casual warning. This was a father's protective instinct, and he wanted to make sure I understood the consequences.

I met his gaze and nodded, my throat dry. "I understand, sir." I meant it, too. I wasn't just saying it to ease the tension. Hurting Hailey wasn't something I ever wanted to do, but hearing her dad put it so bluntly reminded me just how high the stakes were.

Mr. Eller studied me for a long moment, then gave a short nod, satisfied with my answer. "Good. Just remember that."

We went back to working on the turkey, the silence between us a little less tense now. As we finished up, I couldn't help but feel like I'd just passed some kind of test. A tough test, but one I needed to pass.

"Thanks for the help," Mr. Eller said after a while, his voice less stern.

"No problem," I replied, wiping my hands on a towel. "And… thanks for giving me a chance."

He gave me a small, almost imperceptible nod.
It wasn't full acceptance, but it was a start.

DINNER WAS FINALLY KICKING OFF, AND THE LONG DINING TABLE WAS A SIGHT TO behold. Plates stacked high with all the classic Thanksgiving staples—turkey, mashed potatoes, cranberry sauce, stuffing— were lined up neatly, but what really caught my eye was Hailey's Alfredo pasta. I hadn't expected her to actually make it, but there it was, golden and creamy, looking like it came straight out of a professional kitchen.

I glanced over at her, sitting across the table, and caught her shy smile as she noticed me eyeing the dish. She looked nervous, but proud. It was her first Thanksgiving contribution, and from the looks of it, she nailed it.

The room was filled with the warm chatter of both our families, the clinking of plates and silverware as people settled in around the table. My parents were in a good mood, laughing about something with Hailey's mom, and even Mr. Eller seemed to have relaxed a bit since our conversation earlier. For the first time in a while, it felt like the tension had eased.

As everyone sat down, my mom cleared her throat, calling attention to the head of the table. "Before we dig in," she said, smiling at everyone, "I think it's only right that we take a moment to say what we're thankful for."

There was a general murmur of agreement, and she looked around before landing on Dalton, who was practically vibrating in his chair with excitement. "Dalton," she said, giving him an encouraging nod. "Why don't you say a few words for us?"

Dalton's eyes lit up like Christmas lights. He sat up straighter, puffing out his chest as if he'd just been asked to deliver the State of the Union. "Yes! I got this!" he said, his little voice filled with determination.

I leaned back in my chair, stifling a grin. My little brother, always ready for the spotlight.

Dalton stood up on his chair, clearing his throat dramatically before launching into his speech. "Okay, everybody! First of all, I'm thankful for the food—because it looks really, really good. Like, especially the mashed potatoes. And the turkey. And the... uh, everything!" He waved his hands around, clearly impressed with the spread.

There was a ripple of laughter around the table, but Dalton wasn't done. "I'm also thankful for... uh, video games! And Nintendo! Because without them, I'd be really bored a lot!" He beamed proudly, as if this were the most profound thing anyone had ever said during a Thanksgiving dinner.

I rolled my eyes, but I couldn't help but chuckle. That was Dalton for you.

But then, he surprised us all. "And... I'm thankful for my family," Dalton continued, his voice a little softer now, more serious. "Because even though we fight sometimes, and Nathan doesn't always want to play with me... I still love him. And Callum..." He looked over at me, his big brown eyes wide with admiration. "Even though Callum is really busy with soccer and stuff, ... I'm thankful for him, too. 'Cause he's still my big brother."

I felt something tighten in my chest, and I had to look down at my plate for a second to keep from showing just how much that hit me. Dalton was always a little ball of energy, always jumping around and causing chaos, but hearing him say that—it meant more than I could explain.

"And I'm thankful for Mom and Dad," Dalton continued, turning to my parents, who were both smiling warmly at him. "Because they take care of us and make sure we always have food and a house to live in. And I'm thankful for Mrs. Eller and Mr. Eller, too, because they're really nice, and it's fun having them around." He glanced at Hailey's parents with a grin.

"And last but not least," Dalton finished, puffing out his chest again, "I'm thankful for Hailey... because she's like my big sister. And she made Alfredo which looks really, really good!" He pointed at her dish, his eyes wide with excitement.

The whole table erupted in laughter, and even Hailey blushed, shaking her head but smiling. I couldn't help but laugh, too. Leave it to Dalton to make the cutest damn speech ever.

"Great job, Dalton," my dad said, clapping his hands together once. "That was a good speech, buddy."

"Yeah, that was awesome," I added, giving him a thumbs-up. Dalton beamed, clearly proud of himself as he sat back down, finally ready to dig into the meal.

The room settled into a comfortable rhythm after that, with everyone passing plates and bowls around, filling their plates with turkey, stuffing, and, of course, Hailey's Alfredo. It was a full table, full of food, laughter, and conversation, and for the first time in a while, everything felt... right.

I looked over at Hailey, who was happily dishing out some Alfredo for her mom. She glanced at me, catching my eye, and gave me a small smile, one that made my heart do that weird flip thing it always did when she looked at me like that.

As I helped myself to some turkey, I couldn't help but feel thankful, too. Not just for the food, or the soccer season, or even Dalton's goofy little speech. But for this—this moment. For Hailey. For our families. For the way things were slowly starting to fall into place.

"Hey, Callum," Hailey whispered across the table, snapping me out of my thoughts.

"Yeah?" I asked, raising an eyebrow.

"Don't forget to try the Alfredo," she said, her tone teasing. "Dalton's counting on you."

I grinned, nodding as I scooped a generous portion onto my plate, then placing some on Hailey's plate as well. "Wouldn't dream of it," I said, winking at her.

Just as I was about to take another bite of her Alfredo, I heard a snicker from beside me. I looked over to see Dalton, who was grinning like a mischievous little gremlin.

"Ewwww," he teased, dragging out the word in the most obnoxious way possible. "You two are smiling at each other like lovebirds!"

I nearly choked on my bite, and Hailey's face immediately flushed red. I could feel my own cheeks heat up as I glared at Dalton, who was still snickering like he'd just won some kind of sibling lottery.

"Shut up, Dalton," I muttered, trying to play it cool, but my little brother was having none of it.

"No way!" Dalton continued, giggling uncontrollably now. "Look at you two! You're all, 'Oh Hailey, I loooove you!'" He made kissy noises, pressing his hands together and mimicking what was clearly supposed to be me swooning over Hailey.

I groaned, feeling a mix of embarrassment and amusement rise in my chest. "Dalton, seriously, you're embarrassing yourself," I shot back, giving him a look. But he wasn't deterred in the slightest.

"And Hailey's all like, 'Oh, Callum, you're soooo amazing!'" Dalton continued, this time batting his eyelashes dramatically, his voice going up in an exaggerated high-pitched tone. "Let's get married and live happily ever after!"

Hailey's face was practically glowing red now, and she tried to cover her laugh with a hand. "Dalton, stop!" she said, her voice full of a mixture of embarrassment and laughter. "You're being ridiculous!"

But Dalton wasn't going to stop.

Oh, no.

He was having way too much fun.

"Wait! Wait! I got more!" Dalton said, bouncing in his seat as if he were about to deliver the punchline of a lifetime. "Then Callum's like, 'No, Hailey, you're the beautiful one! Let's kiss and hold hands forever!'" He clasped his hands together dramatically and made a loud, exaggerated smooching sound, which was enough to send the rest of the table into fits of laughter.

Even Nathan, who was usually the quieter one, cracked a smile at Dalton's antics. My parents were chuckling, and even Hailey's parents were grinning at the scene unfolding before them.

I groaned, trying to fight the embarrassment creeping up my neck. "Alright, Dalton. That's enough."

But he wasn't finished yet. "Oh, but it's soooo romantic!" Dalton said, batting his eyelashes at me and Hailey. "You guys are, like, total lovebirds!"

At this point, Hailey buried her face in her hands, laughing uncontrollably despite her best efforts to stay composed. I couldn't help but crack a smile, shaking my head at my little brother's ridiculousness.

"Okay, Dalton," I said, rolling my eyes but grinning despite myself. "You made your point."

Dalton finally sat back in his chair, looking very proud of himself for having roasted us so thoroughly. "Just saying," he added with a shrug, still grinning. "You two are gross."

I threw a napkin at him, but it only made him laugh harder.

CHAPTER 66

HAILEY

I SAT IN THE PASSENGER SEAT, WATCHING THE WORLD BLUR BY AS NALA AND I drove toward the indoor sports complex. The final soccer game of the season was today—Westview versus Oakridge. A rematch.

Whoever won this one would take home the division championship trophy, and I knew Callum had been thinking about this game nonstop for weeks. My heart raced just thinking about it.

Nala glanced over at me, her hands steady on the steering wheel. "Girl, you look like you're about to pop. Relax."

I laughed softly, shaking my head. "I'm just... I don't know. I want them to win. Callum's been so focused on this game."

"Uh-huh." Nala gave me a side-eye, a sly smile playing on her lips. "Sure, it's all about the game. Totally not about you wanting to see your man show off and be the big soccer hero."

I shot her a playful glare. "It's not like that!"

Nala raised an eyebrow, smirking. "Sure, it's not. But admit it—you wouldn't mind if he scored the winning goal and then ran over to you, did that slow-motion dramatic soccer slide, and kissed you in front of everyone."

I couldn't help but burst out laughing at the mental image. "Oh my god, stop. That's so cheesy."

"Cheesy or not, I see that look in your eyes," Nala teased. "You're imagining it right now, aren't you?"

"Maybe," I admitted, still giggling. "But seriously, this game means a lot to him. I just want them to win."

Nala nodded, but her smile softened. "I get it, girl. Ibra's been talking about it, too. He's all 'we're gonna crush them' and 'this is our year.'" She laughed, imitating his deeper voice, and I couldn't help but smile wider. "But listen, I'm happy for you, Hailey."

Her tone was more sincere now, and it made me pause. I glanced over at her. "Happy for me?"

"Yeah," Nala said, keeping her eyes on the road but with a knowing grin. "You really, really look happy these days. Happier than I've seen you in... well, forever. And I know it's because of Callum."

I felt my cheeks heat up, but I didn't deny it. It was the truth, after all. I did feel a lot happier these days, and as much as I didn't want to admit it, most of it was because of the handsome, irritating, irritatingly handsome soccer captain I lived with. And who happened to be my boyfriend. "Yeah... I really am happy."

Nala side-eyed me again, clearly fishing for more details. "Okay, spill. What is it about him that's got you looking like you're glowing 24/7? Is he that good in—"

"—Nala!" I interrupted, my face probably turning tomato red. "It's not... ugh, stop!"

She cackled, delighted by my reaction. "I'm just saying! You two are all over each other. I need the tea."

I rolled my eyes, trying to hide my smile. "It's not just that. I mean, yeah, he's great, but it's more about how he makes me feel. He's always... I don't know, I feel like I can be myself with him, you know? Like, I don't have to hide anything. And he's really supportive—he's been so good to me, Nala. Like, genuinely."

Nala nodded, her teasing grin softening into something more serious. "That's how it should be, girl. I'm really happy for you. Callum's lucky to have you, but I guess he's not too bad of a catch either."

I laughed at her semi-grudging admission. "Yeah, he's alright, I guess."

"Alriiiiight," Nala teased. "Girl, he's like... soccer captain, broad shoulders, total hottie. Don't act like you didn't score a damn good deal."

I rolled my eyes but couldn't help the grin spreading across my face. "Okay, fine. Yeah, he's amazing. But what about you and Ibra, huh? When are you gonna admit you're totally in love?"

Nala gave a loud, exaggerated sigh. "Ugh, fine. I'll say it. Ibra's..." She shot me a mischievous grin. "He's great. I didn't think we'd actually hit it off like we did, but he's kind of the best."

"Uh-huh, sure. I see how you two are, always all cute together," I teased, nudging her.

"Don't even," she shot back, laughing. "You and Callum are way worse. Every time I see you two, it's like a rom-com in real life. It's honestly disgusting."

I grinned, feeling that familiar flutter in my chest whenever I thought about Callum. "Well, we're happy. That's all that matters."

"You really are," Nala said, her voice softer again. "You deserve it, Hails. After everything... I'm glad you found someone who makes you happy."

I felt my heart swell with warmth. "Thanks, Nala."

"Now," she said, shifting back into her playful tone. "Let's get to this game and watch our boys win. And maybe afterward, you'll get that dramatic, slow-motion kiss after all."

I laughed, shaking my head. "I swear, you watch too many movies."

"Maybe, but don't act like you wouldn't love it," she teased, pulling into the parking lot of the sports complex.

She was right. I would love that, actually.

We stepped out of the car and headed toward the entrance of the sports complex, the cold air nipping at my cheeks. Inside, it was a completely different world. The energy was electric, the crowd buzzing with excitement. One side of the bleachers was packed with Westview students decked out in navy and yellow, waving banners and shouting cheers. On the opposite side were the Oakridge kids, wearing their bold orange and green, already looking like they were ready for a battle.

"Wow, this place is packed. I'm hyped already," Nala said, her eyes wide as she took in the scene. "This is going to be intense."

"Yeah," I agreed, feeling my own excitement—and nerves—bubble up. The championship trophy was on the line, and both teams were hungry for it. Especially Westview.

Nala nudged me. "Alright, I'm gonna go join the cheer squad. You know, gotta get the crowd fired up for our boys. You good?"

I nodded. "Yeah, I'm good. I'm going to regroup with the yearbook club, get some good shots of the game."

"Cool. We'll meet up afterward, alright?"

"Yup," I said with a grin, and with that, Nala disappeared into the crowd, heading toward the section where the cheerleaders were gathering. I took a deep breath and scanned the bleachers for my yearbook crew.

As I weaved through the Westview side of the complex, I could feel the buzz of excitement pulsing through the air. The game hadn't even started yet, but people were already on edge, shouting to friends and waving their school flags. I spotted a few familiar faces from my classes, everyone hyped for the big rematch against Oakridge.

"Hailey!" I heard a voice call, and I turned to see Lance, waving me over. He was standing with a few other members by the side, our usual spot during these games.

"Hey!" I called back, making my way over to them.

"Glad you made it," Lance said as I joined them. "You ready to capture the chaos of what's about to go down?"

I laughed. "Oh, absolutely. It's going to be wild."

"No kidding," Lisa chimed in. "Last time we played Oakridge, it was brutal. This one's going to be even more intense."

"Yup," I agreed, glancing over at the Oakridge side. Their kids were already chanting, the sound of their drumline filling the air with a sense of impending showdown. "We better be ready."

Lance grinned. "Oh, we're ready. Just make sure to get the good shots—especially when Callum scores the winning goal. You know, for documentation purposes."

I rolled my eyes but smiled. "Right, documentation purposes. Got it."

The rest of the team chuckled, and I settled in with them, adjusting my camera and making sure everything was set. I could feel the excitement building up inside me again. This was going to be a big game, and it was all about to unfold right in front of us.

As I glanced back at the field, I spotted the Westview boys emerging from the locker room, Callum leading the way, looking intense and focused.

My heart did a little flip, and I couldn't help but smile to myself. Today was huge for him—and for the entire team. I knew how much this game meant to them.

I zoomed in with my camera, catching a candid shot of him as he walked onto the field with that determined look in his eye.

God, he was handsome.

And he was all mine.

As Callum scanned the crowd, his eyes landed on me again. I couldn't resist the mischievous grin spreading across my face. Today was special, and I had prepared something for him—something to show just how much I was rooting for him.

With one quick motion, I unzipped my jacket, slowly revealing what was underneath: his old Westview jersey, the one I'd awkwardly asked his mom for a few days ago.

It was a little oversized, but I didn't care.

This was for him.

I watched as Callum's expression shifted. He froze for a second, his intense game face completely wiped away as he took in the sight. His eyes widened, and then—just like that—a huge smile spread across his face, full of pride and something softer. The way he looked at me in that moment... it made my heart skip.

He stared at me for a moment, his eyes lit up with joy, and then he mouthed three simple words: *I love you.*

My heart skipped a beat, pounding so hard I could barely breathe. The intensity of it hit me all at once—his smile, the way his eyes softened as they focused on me. I wasn't even sure how I was still standing.

I bit my lip, unable to contain the giddy feeling bubbling up inside me, and mouthed back, *I love you too.*

CHAPTER 67

CALLUM

I SAT ON THE FLOOR OF MY ROOM, STARING AT THE MESS OF CLOTHES AND RANDOM stuff I was supposed to be packing for the senior trip. Winter break had just started, and in a couple of days, we'd be heading up to Mammoth Lakes to spend a few days at some hotel in the snowy mountains. It was supposed to be a reward for winning Sports Day, but right now, all I could think about was the framed pictures on my desk.

The first one was a shot Hailey had taken of me and the boys, all of us grinning like idiots, holding the division championship trophy.

We'd won.

We actually pulled it off. The game had been tight—Oakridge wasn't playing around—but in the second half, we managed to take back the lead and keep it. I couldn't stop replaying those moments in my head: the adrenaline, the roar of the crowd, the rush of relief when the final whistle blew.

I shifted my gaze to the other photo, the one Lance had taken not too long after we'd secured the win. It was of me lifting

Hailey up and kissing her on the field. The entire crowd had been watching, but in that moment, it was just her and me. I could still feel the warmth of her in my arms, the way her smile lit up the whole world.

I grinned to myself, running my thumb over the edge of the frame. That was one hell of a moment.

Still, the game wasn't without its weird feelings. Oakridge had been weaker this time. Troy Duran, their captain, and their best player, had torn his ACL a few days before the game, and as much as I didn't like the guy, I had to give him credit. He was a damn good player. That was part of the reason why he pissed me off so much in the first place, and I knew the game could've turned out a bit different if he'd been on the field. It felt strange winning against them knowing that.

I'd sent him a short, blunt text after the game.

Me: Hey. Heard about the ACL. That sucks. Hope you recover soon.

He hadn't responded, but I hadn't expected him to. It wasn't like we were friends or anything. But it felt right to say something. I hated losing, but I could respect a good player when I saw one.

I sighed, refocusing on the task at hand. Packing. The senior trip was supposed to be fun, but all I could think about was spending time with Hailey, uninterrupted, in the mountains. I wasn't sure what was going to happen up there, but the idea of getting away with her, even for just a few days, was enough to make me feel like a kid on Christmas Eve.

I threw some clothes into my duffel bag—sweaters, jeans, a few t-shirts—but my mind was somewhere else. I glanced back at the pictures again, that same stupid grin creeping up on me. God, I was such a sap. But Hailey had that effect on me.

I couldn't help but think about how far we'd come. A few months ago, I couldn't stand her—thought she was a total know-it-all. And now? Now I was sitting here, packing for a trip and wondering how I could possibly love someone this much.

I stood up and stretched, glancing out the window. The snow was coming down hard again, covering everything in a thick blanket of white.

It reminded me of that night of the snowstorm, the night I first snuck Hailey into my room and we made this space feel so fucking hot despite the cold outside. Things had been a whirlwind since then, and honestly, I wouldn't trade any of it for the world.

I zipped up my duffel bag, still lost in thought. The trip to Mammoth Lakes was going to be incredible. A few days away from everything, just me, Hailey, and our friends. I could already picture us on the slopes, or warming up by a fire, or maybe even sneaking away for some alone time...

A knock at the door interrupted my thoughts, and I looked up. My mom poked her head in, raising an eyebrow at the half-packed bag on the floor.

"Still not done packing, Callum?"

I laughed sheepishly. "Yeah, I'm working on it."

She smiled, stepping into the room. "I saw the pictures Hailey took. They turned out beautifully."

"Yeah, they did," I agreed, glancing at the framed photo again. "She's amazing."

My mom's smile softened, and she gave me a knowing look. "I'm glad you found someone who makes you happy."

"Me too," I said, my voice a little quieter. "She really does." As I finished packing, my mom lingered at the doorway, that familiar look of concern mixed with amusement on her face. I slung my duffel bag over my shoulder, ready to head downstairs, when she cleared her throat, and I turned back to face her.

"Callum," she started, folding her arms, "I know you two are going to be there for a few days..."

"Four days," I corrected, raising an eyebrow.

She nodded, giving me a pointed look. "Four days. But please, be responsible."

I opened my mouth to respond, but she held up her hand, cutting me off. "I'm not saying you need to stay away from her completely, I know that's... well, that's inevitable," she said, rolling her eyes with a sigh. "But I just want you to be smart about it. You're still young, and the Ellers still live with us. So, please, just... be careful."

I nodded slowly, understanding exactly what she was getting at. "Mom," I said, scratching the back of my neck, "I promise, I'll be careful. We'll be careful."

She raised an eyebrow, still not entirely convinced. "You'd better be. I trust you, Callum, but don't push those boundaries. You've got plenty of time to enjoy your relationship without rushing into things."

I nodded again, feeling a little embarrassed but grateful for the reminder. "Yeah, I get it. We'll be responsible. Promise."

My mom's expression softened, and she smiled. "I know you will. Just... have fun, but don't lose your head, okay?"

I grinned. "I'll keep my head right where it is, don't worry."

"Good," she said, patting my shoulder as she turned to leave. "Now go finish packing and make sure you've got everything."

I watched her leave, feeling a mix of relief and nerves. She wasn't wrong to remind me—this trip was going to be amazing, but I knew we had to be careful. Four days alone, in the mountains, at a hotel with Hailey... yeah, there'd definitely be some moments. But I couldn't let myself get carried away.

With a sigh, I zipped up my bag, making sure I had everything. Responsibility wasn't just about us; it was about proving to everyone—especially Hailey's parents—that I could be trusted with her.

I glanced at the picture on my desk again, a small smile tugging at my lips. Yeah, I could be responsible... but it didn't mean I wasn't counting down the minutes until we were in those mountains together.

I headed downstairs to grab a seltzer or something, and as I turned the corner, I saw Hailey sitting with Nathan at the kitchen table. They were chatting, both of them smiling, and I couldn't help but pause for a second. She got along so well with my brothers. It was nice seeing them together like that—like she'd always been a part of the family.

I leaned against the doorframe, watching for a moment before stepping in. "What's going on in here?" I asked, my voice playful.

Nathan looked up, his face turning a little red, and Hailey grinned at me, a mischievous glint in her eyes. "Oh, nothing," she said. "Just telling Nathan here how to approach girls."

I raised an eyebrow, a smirk tugging at my lips. "Oh, really? Does someone have a crush?"

Nathan's blush deepened, and he shot me a look like he wished the floor would swallow him whole. "Shut up," he muttered, but there was a hint of a smile there.

Hailey laughed softly, patting Nathan's arm. "Don't worry, you've got this," she reassured him. "Just be yourself."

I chuckled, moving to sit across from them. "Well, I'm glad to know my girlfriend is out here giving advice on dating. But hey, little man, if you ever need real advice, you know where to find me." I winked, teasing him.

Nathan rolled his eyes. "Yeah, no thanks."

Hailey nudged me, her smile warm. "He's got it covered. Besides, your 'real' advice might just get him into trouble."

I grinned, leaning in closer to Hailey. "What, you don't think my dating advice would work?"

She raised an eyebrow. "I'm just saying, your approach was a little… unconventional."

I laughed, leaning back in my chair. "Hey, it worked, didn't it? You're sitting here with me now."

Nathan groaned, standing up from the table. "Alright, I'm out of here. You two are gross."

Hailey and I burst into laughter as he walked out of the room, shaking his head. When the door swung shut behind him, I turned to Hailey, still grinning. "You know, I like that he talks to you about stuff like that."

She smiled back, shrugging. "He's a good kid. It's easy to get along with him."

I reached for her hand across the table, giving it a gentle squeeze. "Yeah, well, he's lucky to have you giving him pointers."

Hailey blushed slightly but squeezed my hand back. "He'll figure it out."

I smiled, content, knowing she fit so perfectly into my life—into my family.

Just as I got up, about to wrap my arms around Hailey, I heard someone clear their throat. I froze and turned toward the living room, my heart sinking a little when I spotted Hailey's dad sitting there, book in hand, glancing over at us.

The soft lamp next to him shadowed his face and made him look some always-watching overlord or something. He must've been reading the whole time, and I hadn't even noticed.

I quickly stepped back, rubbing the back of my neck, feeling a bit embarrassed. "Uh, hey, Mr. Eller," I muttered, trying to sound casual. But inside, I was cringing.

Hailey's dad just raised an eyebrow, giving me that classic dad look that said *I'm watching you and could still throw you into a vat of hot oil if you acted up.* He didn't say anything, just nodded slightly before returning his attention to his book.

Hailey shot me an amused glance, clearly finding the whole thing hilarious. I mouthed oops to her, and she stifled a giggle, shaking her head. It was like we were constantly walking on eggshells with her parents these days.

And with her dad? Yeah, I definitely still had to tread carefully there.

Still, I couldn't help but grin at her, even though my face was burning. It was all part of the awkward fun, I guess.

THE DAY OF THE TRIP HAD FINALLY ARRIVED, AND I WAS PUMPED, THOUGH THE early morning was hitting me harder than I expected. I woke up to the sound of my alarm blaring, and after stumbling around for a bit, I managed to get dressed and head downstairs with my bags. Everything was packed and ready to go, but when I saw Hailey lugging her stuff into the hallway, my jaw nearly dropped.

I stared at the mountain of bags and let out an incredulous laugh. "Hailey, what the hell?" I groaned, walking over to where she was finishing zipping up the last of them. "We're going for four days, not moving across the country."

She shot me an innocent look, then nodded toward her backpack. "I have clothes in this one, and…" she hesitated for a second, then sheepishly pointed at a different bag. "That one is full of books."

I blinked at her, processing the sheer number of bags. "You brought a backpack full of books?"

She straightened up, looking at me like it was the most normal thing in the world. "Well, yeah. It's a four-hour drive, and then we're in the mountains for four days. I need options!"

I couldn't help but laugh in disbelief. "Are you serious? Why didn't you just bring your little Kindle or something? That thing is, like, the size of my phone."

Hailey paused, narrowing her eyes as if she was actually considering it for a moment. Then she said, "You know what? You're right. The books can stay." She hoisted the giant backpack over her shoulder and started walking downstairs, the books inside thudding heavily with each step.

Her collection had grown a lot recently, mostly because I kept buying her more every time we went out together. I knew I had no one but myself to blame for this growing collection. Every time we'd go somewhere, I'd spot her eyes lighting up at a bookstore window, and next thing I knew, I was grabbing a new book for her. I liked that she smiled every time we walked out of the bookstore with one, so it was all worth it, even though I worried that one day I'd go down to her room and she'd just be missing in all the novels she'd started to hoard down there.

She arrived back at the top of the basement stairs with one less backpack in tow, just as our parents, still yawning and bleary-eyed, came shuffling into the hallway to see us off.

Hailey's dad rubbed his eyes and blinked at the sight of all Hailey's stuff. "Are you kids moving out, or going on a trip?"

Hailey's mom stifled a yawn, giving Hailey an amused glance. "A little overpacked, aren't we?"

"I just wanted to be prepared!" Hailey defended herself, her smile a little sheepish.

I groaned dramatically, making sure Hailey heard me. "Prepared to open a library in Mammoth Lakes."

Hailey bumped me with her elbow, but she was laughing. Our parents chuckled, still half-asleep, as they helped us carry some of the bags outside to where the car was parked.

Mom hugged me tightly, "Be safe, okay? And remember what we talked about." She gave me that motherly look, the one that said she trusted me but still wanted me to be cautious.

"Yeah, yeah," I said, hugging her back. "We'll be fine."

Hailey's parents gave her a tight hug, too, with her dad offering one last stern glance my way. "Be responsible, Callum."

"I will, Mr. Eller," I promised, nodding seriously.

After a few more goodbyes and hugs, we finally made our way outside. The snow had started falling gently again, blanketing everything in a soft, white layer. I loaded all of Hailey's bags into the trunk, making space where I could, while she zipped up her jacket and adjusted her beanie.

Damn it, she looked so cute. I couldn't help but pet her soft head, to which she let out a giggle.

I shut the trunk, leaning against the car for a second. "Alright," I said, looking up at her. "You ready for this?" She smiled, her eyes bright with excitement. "Let's go." We pulled into the school parking lot, and it was packed with buses and students, all buzzing with excitement as they loaded their bags and prepared for the trip to Mammoth Lakes. Hailey and I hopped out of the car, stretching as we took in the chaotic scene.

As soon as we spotted our group—Grayson, Ibra, Adam, Nala, and Sasha—Hailey immediately whipped out her camera. "Okay, everyone, gather around! We need a picture before we get on the bus," she called out.

She had that determined glint in her eye, and no one was going to say no to Hailey when she was in photography mode.

"Fine," Grayson muttered, pretending to be annoyed, but he was already moving into place.

"Get in here, G," I teased. "You're not escaping this."

He shot me a look. "Yeah, yeah. At least let me make it a cool seventh wheel pose."

Everyone laughed, gathering together while Hailey adjusted the camera. Nala and Sasha stood in front, while Grayson, Adam, Ibra, and I made up the back row. Hailey quickly set the timer, then dashed into the group, squeezing in next to me.

The camera clicked, and Hailey smiled brightly as she glanced at the shot. "Perfect!"

"Can we get on the bus now, Miss Photographer?" I teased, throwing an arm around her shoulder.

She rolled her eyes but nodded, and we all started loading our bags into the bus. Once we were settled, I slid into the seat next to Hailey, satisfied with how smoothly everything was going.

But just as I got comfortable, I noticed Hailey pulling out her Kindle. I couldn't help but frown, nudging her playfully. "Hey, you're already blowing me off?"

She looked up at me, a mischievous smile on her face. "I thought you'd be happy I left the giant backpack of books behind."

I raised an eyebrow. "Yeah, but now you've got your Kindle. What am I supposed to do for the next few hours?"

She tilted her head, clearly enjoying teasing me. "Oh, I don't know. I'm sure you'll survive. It's just a bus ride, Callum."

I sighed dramatically, leaning back in my seat. "You're lucky I like you. Otherwise, I'd toss that thing out the window."

She giggled, her eyes sparkling. "Well, I guess I'll keep you entertained later."

I smirked, leaning in a little closer. "Yeah, you better."

Before we could continue, Nala turned around from the seat in front of us. "You two better not be starting your weird banter again. We've got four hours on this bus, and I'm not in the mood."

Sasha nodded in agreement, adding, "Seriously, keep the flirting to a minimum, guys."

Ibra chimed in. "Good luck with that. Callum can't go five minutes without some kind of comment."

I shot him a look, though I couldn't deny it. "You're all just jealous."

Grayson, sitting a few seats over, groaned. "Jealous? Dude, I'm seventh-wheeling. This is a nightmare."

Hailey laughed, pulling me closer to her as she leaned her head on my shoulder. "Come on, Grayson, you know we love having you around."

"Sure," he muttered, but he cracked a smile. "As long as you don't make me take any more pictures."

The banter continued for a bit, filling the bus with laughter as everyone settled in for the long ride ahead. I snuck a glance at Hailey, who was trying to focus on her Kindle again, and grinned.

We had four days in the mountains together, and I was planning on making every moment count.

As the bus rolled on, I leaned against Hailey's shoulder, trying to get comfortable for the long trip ahead. My eyes drifted toward the screen of her Kindle, and though I wasn't exactly paying full attention,

I found myself absentmindedly reading a few words here and there. But honestly? I wasn't really focusing on the book at all. It was more about just being next to her, the warmth of her shoulder against mine, and the peacefulness of the moment.

She didn't say anything, but I noticed her eyes flicker toward me for a second, a tiny smile tugging at her lips before she turned back to her Kindle. I let my hand rest casually on her knee, not thinking too much about it, just enjoying the quiet, the bus humming around us, and the steady rhythm of her breathing.

I read another line or two off her Kindle, something about a knight and a dangerous quest or whatever. I didn't care about the story, but it was just... nice being here like this.

"I can feel you reading over my shoulder, you know," Hailey murmured, breaking the silence between us.

I smirked, turning my head slightly to meet her gaze. "It's not my fault. You're not exactly giving me much else to do."

She chuckled softly, nudging me playfully with her elbow. "You're such a baby. Want me to read it out loud to you?"

"Nah," I replied, smiling. "I'm just enjoying the view."

Her cheeks flushed a little, but she didn't say anything, letting her eyes drift back to her Kindle while I stayed there, close, soaking it all in.

CHAPTER 68

HAILEY

THE BUS RUMBLED TO A STOP, AND I LOOKED OUT THE WINDOW, SPOTTING THE hotel's giant sign glowing against the evening sky.

We'd finally arrived at Mammoth Lakes.

The tall, snow-covered mountains loomed in the distance, and the hotel itself was like something out of a holiday postcard—rustic wood accents, icicles hanging from the roof, and a cozy glow coming from the windows.

Everyone was already starting to stir, excitement buzzing through the bus as people gathered their stuff, chattering about what room they'd get, the views, and just generally how epic the trip was going to be.

But Callum? He was still fast asleep on my shoulder, his breath slow and steady, completely oblivious to the fact that we'd made it.

I glanced down at him, smiling softly. His head was nestled into the crook of my neck, his hair a bit messy from the ride. It was kind of adorable, actually, seeing him like this— totally relaxed, no snark, no teasing, just… peaceful. But, unfortunately for him, there was no way I was going to let him stay asleep when we'd just arrived at the coolest place ever.

"Callum," I whispered, nudging him gently with my shoulder. He didn't move. I tried again, this time a bit louder. "Callum, wake up. We're here."

Nothing.

I sighed and poked his cheek. "Callum!"

Finally, he stirred, blinking groggily as he lifted his head from my shoulder. He squinted around, clearly trying to get his bearings. "Huh? What? We here already?"

I snorted. "Yeah, Sleeping Beauty, we're here. Get your stuff. You drooled a little, by the way."

His eyes widened in horror as his hand shot up to wipe his mouth. "No, I didn't," he said, rubbing his cheek.

"Totally did," I teased, grabbing my bag and sliding out of the seat.

"Rude," he muttered, still groggy as he stretched, following me out of the bus.

Outside, everyone was gathering their stuff, the cold air hitting us in sharp contrast to the warmth inside the bus. I pulled my jacket tighter around me, the snow crunching under my boots as we stepped off the bus. Callum was still rubbing his face, blinking like he was trying to wake up completely.

"I didn't drool," he grumbled, catching up to me.

"I'm just messing with you," I said, laughing. "But you did fall asleep on me for like two hours."

He gave me a lopsided grin. "Guess your shoulder's more comfortable than I thought."

Our teacher chaperone, Mr. Bowers, stood at the entrance of the hotel, holding a clipboard with room assignments. He waved us over as the last of the students filed out of the buses.

"Alright, everyone, listen up!" Mr. Bowers called out, his voice echoing in the cold air. "I'm going to read out your room assignments, so pay attention. Once you've got your assignment, head inside and get your room keys from the front desk. No switching rooms, alright? This is final."

Everyone groaned a bit, but we all knew there wasn't much room to argue. It wasn't like we were going to swap rooms anyway—at least, I wasn't. If anything, the boys would probably try to switch if they got stuck with someone they didn't like.

"Let's get this over with," I muttered, shifting on my feet as Mr. Bowers started reading off the list.

Nala bounced up next to me, practically vibrating with excitement. "You think we're on the same floor as the boys?"

I smirked. "Probably. You and Ibra might as well be joined at the hip at this point."

She blushed, nudging me playfully. "Oh, please. Look who's talking. You and Callum have been attached since we left Westview."

Before I could reply, Mr. Bowers finally called our names. "Hailey Eller and Nala Johnson, room 312."

I grinned at Nala. "Well, look at that."

Nala high-fived me. "Hell yeah! This is gonna be so fun."

Mr. Bowers continued down the list, and I waited for Callum's name. I knew he was nervous about who he'd end up with. His friends were fine, but if he got stuck with some random guy, he'd probably complain for the rest of the trip.

"Adam Parker and Callum Reid, room 310."

Callum sighed in relief next to me, throwing a fist in the air. "Yes! My boy Adam. Crisis averted."

Adam, who was standing nearby, nodded in approval. "I mean, obviously. They couldn't stick me with Grayson. We'd kill each other."

Grayson, overhearing, grinned from across the group. "As if, dude. I'd be the best roommate ever. I'd serenade you to sleep every night."

"Serenade with what? The sound of your loud ass snoring?" Adam shot back. "Dude, I swear, you sound like a pig getting slaughtered when you sleep sometimes."

"Exactly. Soothing as hell, isn't it?" Grayson replied with a smirk.

We all started heading inside, shuffling toward the front desk to grab our keys. The lobby was just as cozy as the outside of the hotel, all warm wood tones, soft lighting, and a massive stone fireplace crackling in the center of the room. A Christmas tree was already up in the corner, twinkling with lights, and the smell of hot chocolate wafted through the air. It felt like we'd stepped into a winter wonderland.

"So, first night here," Nala said as we grabbed our keys from the front desk. "We going to explore the hotel, or are you guys all just gonna huddle in your rooms?"

Adam tossed his key into the air and caught it. "I vote for exploring. It'd be a waste if we didn't check out the place before we crash."

Sasha chimed in, "There's supposed to be a hot tub, right? We should totally hit that up."

Grayson groaned. "You guys are gonna make me the seventh wheel again, aren't you?"

Everyone burst out laughing, and Adam threw his arm around him. "Don't worry, Grayson. I'm sure you can find someone at the hot tub to flirt with."

"I'm holding you to that," he said, pointing a finger at him dramatically.

NALA AND I UNLOCKED THE DOOR TO OUR ROOM AND STEPPED INSIDE, TAKING IN the cozy, rustic vibe. There were two twin beds, each covered in thick, soft blankets, and a big window that overlooked the snowy mountains outside.

The soft hum of the heater made the room feel warm and inviting, a stark contrast to the cold air that awaited us outside. I dropped my bag onto the bed nearest the window and sighed, relieved to finally be here.

"Ah, I love it!" Nala exclaimed, flopping down on her bed. "This is gonna be so much fun, Hailey."

I smiled, pulling off my coat and tossing it onto the chair by the desk. "Yeah, it's gonna be amazing. This place is so gorgeous, too. It literally looks like it came out of a Hallmark movie."

Nala chuckled. "You're so right."

After we unpacked a few essentials and got our things organized, we decided to head down to the lobby to meet up with the others. Nala was already messaging Ibra, but we knew it'd take the guys a while to settle in, so we had some time to kill. As soon as we stepped into the lobby, we spotted Sasha lounging on one of the couches near the fireplace. She waved us over, flashing her signature bright smile.

"Hey, girls! You all settled in?" she asked as we approached.

"Yep! Our room's so cute, it looks like it came out of Pinterest or something," Nala said, glancing at the towering Christmas tree in the corner. "What about you?"

"My room's cute too, but I'm bored!" Sasha groaned dramatically, tossing her head back. "My roommate's still asleep! I have nothing to do, so I figured I'd chill down here. But now that you two are here, we should all go do something! What do you say?"

I looked at Nala, who raised an eyebrow, clearly interested. "What do you have in mind?" I asked, curious.

Sasha grinned mischievously. "Well, there's a snowboarding area right outside the hotel. It's not too intense, just a practice slope. We could go try it out!"

My stomach flipped. Snowboarding? Uh-oh.

Nala, on the other hand, was already on board, clapping her hands together in excitement. "That sounds awesome! Let's do it!"

I hesitated, giving them both a wary look. "I mean... I've never snowboarded before. It can't be that hard, right?"

Sasha smirked. "Come on, Hailey, how bad can it be? We'll take it slow."

"Famous last words," I muttered under my breath, but I shrugged, figuring why not? "Alright, fine. Let's go. But don't laugh at me if I fall."

Sasha laughed, grabbing our arms and pulling us toward the door. "Deal. But only if you don't laugh at me either."

The cold hit us as soon as we stepped outside, our boots crunching in the snow. The practice slope wasn't too far from the hotel, and the sounds of people laughing, cheering, and the occasional whoosh of a snowboard sliding down filled the air. A few instructors were standing by, handing out equipment and offering tips to the brave souls who attempted to conquer the slope.

We strapped into the snowboards after a brief lesson from one of the instructors. He made it sound so easy—just lean forward a bit, keep your balance, and let gravity do the work.

Simple, right?

Wrong.

So, so, wrong.

The first few seconds of me on the snowboard felt like slow-motion chaos. As soon as I tried to glide forward, I immediately started wobbling, my arms flailing like some kind of broken windmill.

"Hailey, you've got this!" Nala called, already gliding smoothly down the slope with a grin on her face. Show-off.

"Yeah, it's easy!" Sasha added, already halfway down the hill.

Easy for them. I was barely holding it together. But just when I thought I might have a chance at making it down the hill without embarrassing myself, my snowboard caught on something—maybe a tiny bump in the snow—and the next thing I knew, I was face-first in a pile of snow, my board awkwardly stuck in the air behind me.

"Oof! Hailey, you okay?" Nala called out, snickering.

I pushed myself up, coughing snow out of my mouth, and glared at them. "I'm fine! I meant to do that."

Sasha burst out laughing, but she glided over and offered me a hand. "Come on, it wasn't that bad. Just try again. We're all learning."

"Yeah, we're all learning. Except for you and Nala who are apparently already pros at this," I muttered, accepting her hand and getting back up.

The second attempt wasn't any better. I managed to stay upright for all of ten seconds before I wobbled again, this time crashing onto my butt. The impact sent a shock through me, and I groaned loudly, sprawled out on the slope like a starfish.

Sasha slid by, spraying snow into the air as she stopped. "That was… better?"

"I'm killing it," I said flatly, shaking my head and trying to brush snow off my jacket. "Totally killing it."

Nala was laughing so hard she nearly fell herself. "Okay, okay, one more try! You've got this!"

I narrowed my eyes at her but nodded. "Alright, third time's the charm."

I got back into position, focusing as hard as I could. I leaned forward, feeling the board begin to glide, my arms steady this time. I was doing it—actually snowboarding! For about five seconds. Then I wobbled again, and instead of falling straight down, I veered off to the side, crashing into a pile of snow near the edge of the slope.

I heard Sasha and Nala cracking up behind me. "Hailey, you okay?" Sasha called, trying not to laugh.

I groaned, lying in the snow, my dignity long gone. "This is impossible. I was not built for snowboarding."

Nala skidded over, laughing as she crouched next to me. "You're getting better! You didn't fall as fast that time!"

I lifted my head to look at her. "You're not helping."

She grinned, offering me a hand. "Come on, let's go again."

I grabbed her hand, but as I got up, I smirked. "You know what? No more snowboarding for me. I'm clearly not cut out for this."

Sasha came over, clearly still amused. "Are you sure? Third time was kind of the charm!"

"Third time just gave me bruises," I quipped. "But I'll cheer you guys on from the sidelines."

Nala and Sasha exchanged a glance before laughing, nodding in agreement. "Alright, Hailey, you can be our personal cheerleader," Nala said.

"Thank you," I said dramatically, brushing more snow off of me. "I'll be the best cheerleader you've ever had."

I spent the rest of the afternoon laughing at their snowboarding attempts (Sasha ate it a few times too, thank God), but eventually, we were all too cold to keep going. We decided to head back to the hotel, snow-covered and sore, but in high spirits.

CHAPTER 69
CALLUM

I LAY BACK IN BED, STARING AT THE SOCCER MATCH ON THE TV. ADAM WAS sprawled out on the other bed, flipping through channels absentmindedly. We'd landed on a match on one of the sports channels, and while usually, I'd be fully invested, my mind was somewhere else.

"Man, I'm still wiped from the drive," Adam muttered, stretching out and letting out a yawn.

"Same," I said, though it was only partly true. Sure, the drive had been long, but it wasn't the road trip that was making me restless. It was something—or rather, someone—else entirely. I glanced at my phone, checking the time. Hailey hadn't texted since she and Nala went off. And, well... I kinda missed her. Finally, I let out a groan and sat up. "I'm going to find my girlfriend."

Adam smirked without looking away from the TV. "Can't stay away for five minutes, can you?"

"Not when she's as cute as Hailey," I shot back, tossing my hoodie over my head.

Adam chuckled. "Simp."

I flipped him off with a grin as I slipped on my shoes and headed for the door. "Enjoy your solitude, bro. Maybe you and the TV will hit it off."

"Don't get lost in the snow!" Adam called after me, but I was already out the door, my mind on Hailey. I took the elevator down to the lobby, scanning the area as soon as the doors opened. There they were—Hailey, Nala, and Sasha, coming in through the entrance, snow covering their boots and hats. Though Hailey looked a bit more covered than them. She almost looked like a human snowman.

I grinned, heading over. "What have you three been up to?" I asked, pulling my hood over my head.

Nala gave me a wide smile. "We went snowboarding. Hailey's a natural—at eating snow."

Sasha burst out laughing, and even Hailey cracked a smile, though she looked a little sheepish. "It was... not my best moment," she admitted, her cheeks red from the cold.

"Snowboarding, huh? I'm sure you were great," I teased, glancing at her as I pulled her closer to me.

Nala winked at Hailey and grinned. "Well, we'll leave you two lovebirds alone. Callum, take care of her—she's been through a lot out there."

Hailey rolled her eyes, but I could see her cheeks flush even more. Nala and Sasha waved goodbye and headed toward the elevators, leaving us alone in the lobby.

I turned to Hailey, still holding her close. "Come on," I said, gently pulling her toward the big fireplace in the center of the room. The warm glow of the flames was inviting, and I could tell she needed it after being out in the cold. "Let's warm you up. You look like you could use it."

Hailey smiled gratefully, letting me lead her to the fireplace. We sat down on the big, plush chairs nearby, the warmth from the fire slowly thawing her cold hands and face. I draped my arm over her shoulder, pulling her in close.

"So," I started, smirking, "tell me what happened. I need to hear how my girlfriend became a snowboard—sorry, snow-*eating* pro."

Hailey groaned and covered her face with her hands. "Oh, my God, Callum, it was so embarrassing."

I raised an eyebrow. "Really? It couldn't have been that bad."

She peeked at me through her fingers, her eyes wide. "It was worse than bad. It was awful. I fell every five seconds. And I don't mean cute little stumbles, I mean full-on faceplants into the snow. Repeatedly."

I couldn't help but laugh. "Yeah?"

"Yes!" she cried, laughing despite herself. "It was like I was cursed. Every time I thought I had it, I was down again. I think I swallowed half the snow on that slope."

I shook my head, trying to stifle my amusement, but it was too damn funny. "And here I was, thinking you'd be some kind of hidden snowboarding prodigy."

"Ha. Ha." Hailey rolled her eyes but was smiling. "Nala and Sasha were basically pros compared to me. I'm pretty sure they only invited me so they could have someone to laugh at."

"Doubt it," I said, squeezing her shoulders. "You're just too cute when you're falling on your face."

She shoved me playfully. "Thanks for the support."

I grinned and leaned in to kiss her temple. "Anytime."

We sat there for a few moments in comfortable silence, the fire crackling in front of us as Hailey snuggled closer. I could feel her relax in my arms, her body warming up from the chill outside.

"So... snowboarding isn't your thing," I teased gently. "Anything else on the agenda for tomorrow?"

She sighed, resting her head on my shoulder. "I don't know. Maybe I'll stick to something less likely to land me in a snowbank."

I chuckled. "Smart plan."

For a moment, we just sat there, watching the flames flicker in the fireplace. I glanced down at her, feeling a sense of calm wash over me. Being here with Hailey like this, just the two of us in this warm, quiet space... it was perfect.

Hailey pulled back and gave me a playful glare, her eyes narrowing as she crossed her arms. "You wanna go grab lunch in the dining hall?" she asked.

I couldn't resist. "Hmm," I said, pretending to think it over. "I mean, I'm in the mood to eat something else, though..."

Her eyes widened, and she slapped my chest playfully. "Seriously, Callum?!"

I chuckled, catching her hand before she could slap me again. "What?" I asked, feigning innocence. "I just meant dessert. You've got such a dirty mind, Hailey."

She rolled her eyes, though she was smiling. "Yeah, right. Sure, that's what you meant."

I pulled her closer, grinning as I leaned down to kiss her quickly on the cheek. "Hey, you can't blame me for being honest."

"You're impossible," she said again, but I could see the way her eyes sparkled. "Come on, let's go. I'm starving."

I groaned playfully as she stood up, grabbing her jacket. "Alright, alright. But I'm still holding you to that dessert later."

She shook her head, grabbing my hand and pulling me toward the dining hall. "You've got a one-track mind, you know that?"

"And you love it," I teased.

She shot me a look over her shoulder. "Debatable."

THE NEXT FEW DAYS FLEW BY IN A BLUR OF LAUGHTER, SNOW, AND MEMORIES. OUR group spent every day out in the cold, but none of us seemed to mind. We built snow forts, had ridiculous snowball fights, and even organized a makeshift soccer game on the icy field behind the hotel.

The game wasn't serious—it was more slipping, falling, and laughing than actual goals—but it was fun as hell. Even Hailey got in on the action, her cheeks flushed red as she tried to dribble the ball across the ice, nearly face-planting more times than I could count.

But, of course, she was never without her camera. Every time I looked up, she was there, the lens of the camera I'd gotten her capturing the chaos, the fun, and the candid moments. Whether it was the snow-covered field, Grayson making a fool of himself trying to tackle Ibra, or Nala sneaking a snowball into Adam's face, Hailey was behind the scenes, snapping away with that quiet smile of hers. It became a running joke—if Hailey wasn't playing, she was taking pictures. And she took a lot of pictures.

As the days passed, the snow piled up, and the nights grew colder, but the laughter didn't stop. We hit the slopes, attempted snowboarding again (this time Hailey had a little more success, but not much), and ate way too much at the dining hall.

Now, it was the last night of our trip. We were all crammed into the hotel's jacuzzi, the steam rising into the crisp winter air. The sound of the bubbling water mixed with the occasional bursts of laughter from the gang as we lounged in the warmth, letting the last remnants of the trip settle in.

I glanced around at the crew—Grayson, Adam, Ibra, Nala, Sasha—and, of course, Hailey, who was leaning back against me, her wet hair sprawled across my shoulder. We were all exhausted, but it was that kind of tired where you're so happy that the exhaustion feels good. Like every ache and bruise from the snowball fights and soccer games had been earned.

"Best. Trip. Ever," Sasha declared, stretching her arms out dramatically as she let out a satisfied sigh. "I'm never leaving this jacuzzi."

"Same," Grayson muttered, sinking lower into the water until only his head was visible. "Let's just live here. We'll all drop out of school and become jacuzzi bums."

I snorted. "Good luck explaining that one to your parents."

Grayson gave me a lazy grin. "Worth it."

The water sloshed as Adam moved to stretch his legs out. "I don't know about you guys, but I'm ready to sleep for a week straight."

"Same," I groaned. As fun as the trip was, all thse back-to-back days of activity made me feel like I'd gone on a bender or something. "My ribs are still sore from the snow tackle."

"Still can't believe Hailey got a goal on you," Ibra teased, earning a glare from me and a playful laugh from Hailey. It had barely been a goal. Hailey slipped on the ice and I was so worried the ball whizzed past me.

"She was lucky," I muttered.

"Skill, Callum. It's called skill," Hailey said softly, her voice teasing but warm. I could feel the heat of her body against mine under the water, and damn if it didn't feel perfect.

"Yeah, yeah," I mumbled, pressing a quick kiss to her temple. "Only you could call falling on your ass a 'skill.'"

The conversation drifted in and out as we soaked in the warmth, the laughter settling into a comfortable hum. Hailey sat up a little, looking out at the snowy landscape through the glass windows, and I knew she was itching to grab her camera again, even though it wasn't exactly jacuzzi-proof.

"You know," I said, resting my chin on her shoulder, "you took more pictures on this trip than anyone else in the world probably has in their entire life."

She turned and grinned at me. "I'm the yearbook photographer, Reid. I'm just doing my job."

"And doing it really well," I teased, pulling her a little closer. "But maybe you could take a break from being behind the lens for tonight. You know, enjoy the view instead."

Hailey shook her head, her eyes twinkling with amusement. "By the view, you mean you?" she asked, raising an eyebrow.

I couldn't help but chuckle. "Hey, your words, not mine," I teased, grinning at her like I had all the time in the world. She gave me a playful shove, and I leaned back, enjoying how easily we fell into our usual banter, no matter what. There was something so natural about being with Hailey, like every sarcastic comment or teasing remark was part of some unspoken language we both knew.

Before I could say anything else, Lance strolled in, water dripping off his swim trunks as he waved us down. "Yo, just a heads-up! They're giving out some special food in the dining hall since it's our last night," he called out. "I think they mentioned something about a chocolate fountain and those mini cheese-cakes. Just saying."

Immediately, I heard the rustling of everyone getting out of the jacuzzi. Grayson was the first to bolt, dragging a very unenthusiastic Ibra with him. "Come on, dude! Chocolate fountain! I need to see this shit!"

Sasha and Nala exchanged a glance before standing up and heading out, too, and within seconds, the jacuzzi was almost empty. Everyone else was rushing toward the dining hall, leaving me and Hailey alone in the bubbling water.

I turned my head, watching as the others disappeared around the corner. I looked back at Hailey, still lounging in the water next to me. The soft steam curled up into the night air, and her skin was flushed from the heat, a few tendrils of her hair damp and sticking to her neck. I couldn't help but smile at how comfortable she looked, sitting there like she belonged in this moment.

"They can rush all they want," I said, shrugging, "but I think I'm good right here."

Hailey tilted her head, her eyes questioning me. "You don't want to go with them?"

I shook my head slowly. "Nah, I think I'd rather stay and enjoy the jacuzzi a bit more." I flashed her a teasing grin. "Especially if you'll stay with me."

She rolled her eyes but didn't make a move to get out. That was all the confirmation I needed.

"Come on," I murmured, my voice soft but full of intent. "Come up here." I patted my lap, keeping my eyes locked on hers. "Sit on my lap."

Her eyes widened slightly, and for a second, I thought she might hesitate. But then she gave me this look—this mix of playful challenge and curiosity that made my heart pound. Slowly, she moved through the water, the ripples parting around her as she made her way toward me.

Without a word, Hailey straddled my lap, her legs brushing against mine as she settled into place.

The warmth of the water pressed between us, and for a moment, the only sound was the bubbling of the jacuzzi and the distant chatter from the dining hall. I wrapped my arms around her waist, pulling her closer until our bodies were pressed together.

Her skin felt warm and soft against mine, and her face was so close I could see the way her lips curved into the faintest smile. "Comfortable?" I asked, raising an eyebrow as I held her gaze.

She let out a small laugh, her hands resting lightly on my shoulders. "More than comfortable."

I leaned in a little, brushing my lips against her temple as I whispered, "Good. Because I'm not letting you go anytime soon."

The soft giggle that escaped her lips made my chest tighten in a way I couldn't quite explain. It was just the two of us now, alone in the heat of the jacuzzi, and everything about this moment felt perfect. I tightened my grip on her waist, feeling her body relax against mine.

Her head rested on my shoulder, and for a few seconds, neither of us said anything. We just let the world fall away, content in the quiet, private bubble we'd created for ourselves.

Her fingers traced lazy circles on the back of my neck, sending shivers down my spine despite the heat of the water. I couldn't help but sigh, the tension from the past few days melting away. Being with Hailey always felt like that—like a weight I didn't even know I was carrying had been lifted.

"You know," I started, my voice low and quiet, "we've done a lot of cool stuff this trip. But this... this right here? This might be my favorite part."

I could feel her smile against my skin as she nuzzled closer. "Sitting in a jacuzzi, avoiding chocolate fountains and mini cheesecakes?"

I chuckled, shaking my head slightly. "No, smartass. Just... being with you. Without everyone else around. It's nice."

She pulled back just enough to meet my gaze, her eyes searching mine for a second before she gave me a soft, genuine smile. "Yeah," she whispered. "It is."

I could feel the heat rising between us—not just from the jacuzzi but from the way Hailey fit so perfectly on my lap. It was one of those rare moments where we were completely alone, without the usual chaos of school, friends, or family. Just us.

I watched her, the way her damp hair framed her face, the soft blush on her cheeks, and the way her eyes sparkled under the dim lights. God, she was beautiful. I'd thought it before, sure, but there was something about this moment that made it hit me even harder.

"Now that we're alone," I started, my voice low and quiet, "I can finally say what's been on my mind."

She tilted her head slightly, her lips quirking up in that curious way of hers. "And what's that?"

I smirked, leaning in just enough to close the space between us, my hands resting lightly on her waist. "That you look way too fucking hot in this bikini," I whispered, my voice coming out rougher than I'd expected. Her eyes widened a bit, and I could see the blush deepen on her cheeks.

I chuckled, running my fingers gently along her waist, my thumbs brushing against her damp skin. "The last time I saw you in the hot tub at my place," I continued, my voice dropping even lower, "I thought you looked so fucking hot then too. But now…" I paused, my eyes locking onto hers, "now you're mine."

"You're mine too, you know," she whispered, her voice barely audible over the bubbling water.

I grinned, brushing a strand of hair out of her face as I held her close. "Yeah. I know."

I couldn't resist anymore. Slowly, deliberately, I leaned in and pressed a soft kiss to her shoulder, letting my lips linger against her skin. She shivered a bit, and I couldn't help but grin, knowing I was the reason for that reaction. My hands slid up to her back, holding her steady as I kissed along her collarbone, taking my time. Her skin was warm and slightly slick from the water, and every touch sent a rush of heat through me.

Hailey's breath hitched, and she shifted slightly on my lap, her fingers gripping my shoulders. I could feel her heart racing just as fast as mine, and that only spurred me on.

"You have no idea how crazy you make me," I murmured against her skin, my voice barely above a whisper. "Just looking at you…"

She let out a soft, almost nervous laugh, her hands moving to my hair, threading through the damp strands. "Callum…"

I pulled back for a moment, just enough to look her in the eye. Her cheeks were flushed, her lips parted, and there was something vulnerable but electric in the way she gazed at me. The tension between us was almost unbearable, but it wasn't just about desire—it was about the fact that she was mine, and I was hers.

"I mean it, Hailey," I said, my voice more serious now. "You're… everything."

Her breath caught in her throat, and I could see the way my words hit her, making her eyes soften. She didn't say anything for a second, but she didn't need to. The way she looked at me, the way she held onto me—it was enough.

I leaned back in, kissing her again, this time on her neck, right where her pulse beat the fastest. Her hands tightened in my hair, and I could feel the way her body responded to every kiss, every touch. It was like the rest of the world didn't exist—just the two of us, lost in the heat and the quiet intimacy of this moment.

I kissed my way up to her jawline, then finally back to her lips, claiming them in a kiss that was soft but full of everything I felt for her. It wasn't about rushing—it was about being here, with her, like this.

As Hailey shifted on my lap, straddling me and facing me head-on, I felt like the air had been sucked out of my lungs. Her body pressed against mine, her damp skin brushing against my chest, and I couldn't think straight. My hands instinctively moved from her shoulders down to her waist, gripping her tighter as I pulled her even closer.

Our kiss deepened, growing more intense with each passing second. The soft sounds she made, the way her fingers tangled in my hair—it was driving me insane.

Every brush of her lips against mine sent a jolt through me, and I groaned softly into her mouth, my heart pounding in my chest.

"Hailey," I whispered, my voice strained as I pulled back for just a second, resting my forehead against hers. Her breath was hot on my lips, her eyes half-closed as she gazed at me, and I felt my control slipping more and more with each passing moment.

"Oh, god," I muttered, my hands sliding down to grip her hips as she shifted again on my lap. "You're making it so fucking hard to stay responsible."

She let out a soft laugh, but it was shaky, like she was feeling just as overwhelmed as I was. Her fingers brushed against my neck, tracing the skin there, and it took everything in me not to completely lose it.

"I know," she whispered, her voice barely audible over the bubbling water of the jacuzzi. "But..."

I swallowed hard, trying to steady my breathing, trying to hold on to the last bit of control I had. But with the way she was looking at me, the way her body pressed against mine, it was getting harder and harder to remember why we had to hold back.

"We're alone," I whispered, my voice rough as I pressed a kiss to her jawline, trailing down to her neck. She tilted her head slightly, giving me better access, and I groaned softly against her skin. "No one's around..."

She gasped softly as I kissed her neck, her hands tightening in my hair. "Callum..."

Hearing her say my name like that, with so much need, only made me want her more. My hands slid down from her hips, brushing against her thighs, feeling the warmth of her skin beneath my fingers. Every inch of her was driving me crazy, and I was barely hanging on.

As Hailey leaned forward on my shoulder, her breath coming out in short, quick pants, I could feel her body trembling against mine.

My hand rested against the fabric of her bikini, my fingers lightly pressing as I massaged the spot between her legs. I felt her shiver, her grip tightening on my shoulders, and I couldn't help but lean closer, my lips brushing the shell of her ear. "You like that?" I whispered, my voice low and thick with tension.

She nodded, her face buried in my neck, her breaths coming faster now. The heat between us was overwhelming, and I could feel my own pulse racing as I tried to stay in control. It was hard—every little sound she made, every small movement of her body, was testing my limits. Her response, soft and breathless, sent a jolt through me, and I kept my movements slow, deliberate. I wanted to savor this moment, to feel every bit of the connection between us without rushing. Her fingers curled into my hair as she shifted slightly, pressing closer to me, and I could feel her heartbeat racing just as fast as mine. I groaned softly, feeling the tension build as her soft gasps filled the quiet space.

The soft sounds she made sent a thrill through me, and it was all I could do to hold on to my self-control. I didn't want to push her too far, but damn it, the way she was trembling against me, her body melting into mine, made it so hard to pull back. I could feel her pulse through her skin, her heat mixing with the warmth of the bubbling water.

"Callum," she whispered, her voice breathless, almost unsure, but there was something else behind it—something that made me want to kiss her all over again.

I kissed her shoulder softly, trying to ground myself in the moment, my heart racing. "We can stop whenever you want," I murmured against her skin. "Just say the word."

She didn't say anything, just shifted a little in my lap, her body pressing closer as if she didn't want any space between us. That was all the answer I needed. My hand continued to move in slow, teasing circles, feeling the way she responded to my touch, the way her voice sounded and her body tensed in all the right ways.

Hailey's breath hitched as she whispered, "I don't want to stop." Her words were barely audible, but they echoed in my mind, pushing my restraint to its limits.

I swallowed hard, feeling the weight of her words, her trust, and her desire. I shifted my hand, gently pushing the fabric of her panties aside, and then, slowly, I let my finger slip inside her. Her body tensed, her soft gasp filling the air between us as I touched her in a way I hadn't before.

Her fingers dug into my shoulders, and I felt her lean forward, pressing her forehead against mine as if grounding herself. We were so close, so wrapped up in each other that nothing else seemed to exist. Every breath, every heartbeat, every tiny movement felt magnified.

"Hailey," I whispered, my voice strained, struggling to maintain control. "You're everything."

She responded with a soft whimper, her hips shifting just slightly, encouraging me. The connection between us was electric, a current that hummed in the air, pulling us closer and closer. As I continued to move my hand, I could feel Hailey's body responding to me, her soft moans filling the air between us.

Each sound she made sent a rush of heat through me, fueling the desire that was building between us. I leaned in closer, catching her moans with my mouth, kissing her deeply as I lost myself in the moment. Her warmth enveloped me, and I relished the feeling of her soft skin against my fingers. It was intoxicating—the way she surrendered to me, the way her body reacted to every movement. I added another finger, stretching her gently as I quickened my pace, wanting to draw out every moment of pleasure for her.

"Callum…" she breathed, her voice a mixture of urgency and pleasure. The way my name rolled off her tongue sent jolts of electricity through me, amplifying the need coursing through my veins.

"Just let go," I murmured against her, my lips brushing against hers as I kept my movements steady and controlled. "I've got you."

With every thrust, I felt her body quiver beneath me, each wave of pleasure washing over her more intensely. She gasped against my mouth, her back arching slightly as her hands tangled in my hair. I could feel her muscles tightening around me, and it only spurred me on further. The tension in the room was thick with desire as I continued to thrust my fingers in and out of her, matching the rhythm of our kisses.

"Faster," she breathed, and the urgency in her voice drove me wild. I obliged, quickening my pace, pushing her closer to the edge. The sounds she made were music to my ears, a symphony of need and trust that only made me want to dive deeper into this moment.

"Callum..." she whispered again, but this time it was a plea, an invitation to go further. I leaned in, capturing her moans with my mouth, kissing her harder as I pushed her further over the edge.

"Come for me, Hailey," I urged, my voice thick with need. "I want to feel you."

She let out a cry that sent a thrill through me, her body tensing as I found that sweet spot inside her. The sound of her pleasure drove me wild, and I could feel her walls fluttering around my fingers, drawing me in closer as I coaxed her to the brink.

"I'm—oh my god, Callum!" she cried out, her voice breaking, and in that moment, I felt her let go completely. Her body quaked beneath me, the intensity of her release washing over her like a tidal wave. I held her close, feeling the rush of warmth enveloping us both as she came undone in my arms, the moment stretching into something beyond words.

The room was filled with the sound of our breaths, the soft splashes of water from the jacuzzi, and the deepening intimacy between us. I was lost in her, in this moment that felt like it could last forever.

As she slowly came down from the high, I brushed my thumb gently over her cheek, my heart swelling with affection and pride. "You're incredible," I whispered, kissing her softly, wanting her to know how much she meant to me, how much I cherished this moment we had shared together.

Her eyes sparkled with a mix of happiness and vulnerability, and I couldn't help but feel a sense of awe at the connection we had forged. I wanted her to know that what we shared was more than just physical—it was emotional, it was real.

"Did you really just do that?" she asked, a teasing smile creeping onto her lips, but I could see the softness in her gaze, the warmth that radiated between us.

"Maybe," I replied, unable to hide the smirk that tugged at my lips. "But it was all for you, Hailey. Every second of it."

She chuckled softly, shaking her head as she leaned in to press her forehead against mine. "You're insatiable," she teased, her breath warm against my skin.

"Only when it comes to you," I confessed, my voice low and sincere. "You drive me crazy... in the best way."

CHAPTER 70
HAILEY

It was finally happening. After months of living with the Reids, my parents and I were moving out. It felt surreal, like the end of an era. The snow had melted, the air had that fresh spring smell, and everything was starting to bloom again. It was a season of change, and we were part of it.

We ended up snagging a house just down the street from the Reids. Same neighborhood, same cul-de-sac, but it was still strange. For so long, we'd been under the same roof, part of the chaotic but comforting rhythm of their household. Now, we were going to be... separate. It was bittersweet, but I couldn't deny the excitement bubbling up inside me.

I looked around the basement, which had been my refuge for months. It was where I'd slept, studied, laughed, cried, and, well... shared a lot of moments with Callum.

I was packing up the last of my books—of course, Callum had added a whole new collection to my shelves—and trying to sort through the clutter. The boxes were piling up, a strange mix of relief and sadness swirling in my chest.

Callum and Nathan were actually helping, or at least trying to. Nathan was sorting through some random knick-knacks, tossing them into a box without much thought.

Callum, though... he was hovering. Half helping, half watching me with that look of longing he'd been giving me since he found out I'd be moving out. It made my heart race, even though I'd gotten used to it by now. Then there was Dalton. He was sitting cross-legged on the floor, arms crossed, pouting like a kid who just lost his favorite toy. He hadn't said much since I told him we were moving, but I could tell he wasn't happy about it. He kept stealing glances at me, his lower lip jutting out in that adorable way that made me want to ruffle his hair.

"Dalton, you wanna help pack this box?" I asked, trying to coax him out of his funk.

He shook his head, frowning. "I don't want you to leave."

My heart sank a little. "We're not leaving-leaving," I said gently, walking over and sitting next to him. "We'll still be right down the street. You can come over whenever you want. It's not like I'm disappearing."

He looked up at me, his big eyes filled with a kind of sadness I wasn't ready for. "But it won't be the same."

I sighed, giving him a small smile as I nudged him with my shoulder. "No, it won't. But change isn't always bad. You'll still see me all the time. Besides, you're gonna have your whole house back. No more sharing the basement."

Callum, who had been folding some of my clothes and tossing them into a suitcase, smirked. "He's not worried about that. He's just gonna miss beating you at Mario Kart."

I rolled my eyes, laughing. "Please, I was letting him win."

Dalton huffed. "No, you weren't."

Callum snorted, shaking his head as he crossed the room to stand behind me. "We'll see about that. When you come over, we'll have a rematch."

I tilted my head back to look up at him, and he gave me that lopsided grin that always made my heart skip. I could see the faintest hint of tension in his eyes, though. As much as we joked, this change was big for us too. No more sneaking into the basement at night. No more stolen moments when no one was watching. It was going to be different.

Nathan, who had been quiet for most of the packing, suddenly spoke up. "It's gonna be weird not having you here, Hailey." He was crouched down by a box, looking a little unsure of himself. "It's been kinda... nice."

I smiled at him, touched by the sincerity in his voice. "I'm gonna miss you guys too. But like I said, I'm not far. We'll still hang out. I promise."

Nathan nodded, but I could see that same unease lingering in his expression. We had all grown closer over the past few months, especially after the awkwardness of Callum and me being caught together. It hadn't been easy, but we'd figured it out, and now it felt like a family.

"Besides," Callum chimed in, his voice low, "you'll be seeing a lot of Hailey, trust me."

Nathan rolled his eyes at Callum's not-so-subtle comment, but Dalton still wasn't convinced. He stood up, walking over to me with a determined look. "You better come over all the time," he said seriously. "Like, every day."

I grinned, ruffling his hair. "Deal."

As Dalton finally joined in, helping to pack up some of the last boxes, I glanced over at Callum. He was watching me, his gaze soft but intense, like he was feeling all the same things I was. The end of this chapter was hitting him too, but I knew we'd be okay.

As we finished packing up the last box, I straightened up, dusting off my hands and giving the boys a little smile. I could feel a mix of emotions buzzing inside me—excitement, nostalgia, and a tinge of sadness—but I was determined to end this day on a good note.

"Hey, before we wrap things up, I've got something for you guys," I said, pulling out a small wrapped item from one of the boxes I'd set aside. The three of them—Callum, Nathan, and Dalton—looked at me curiously.

Callum raised an eyebrow, smirking as he glanced at the package. "A gift, huh? What is it, another one of your books?"

I rolled my eyes but smiled, feeling a little flutter of nerves as I handed it to him. "No, it's not a book, you jerk. Just open it."

Nathan crowded closer, curious, while Dalton stood on his tiptoes, eager to see what was inside. Callum carefully unwrapped the gift, and as the paper fell away, a framed picture of the three of them—Callum, Nathan, and Dalton—from that day when we all played soccer together was revealed.

For a second, they all just stared at it, taken aback. It was a candid shot, one I had managed to snap when none of them were paying attention. They were all grinning, looking a little winded, but there was something warm and genuine about the photo. It perfectly captured the fun and closeness of that day.

Nathan was the first to speak, his eyes widening a little as he took in the picture. "Whoa... I didn't even know you had this."

Callum's smirk softened, and I could see the faintest hint of emotion in his eyes as he looked down at the photo. "This is... really nice, Hailey."

Dalton, however, crossed his arms, frowning as he leaned in closer. "I don't like it," he announced, turning his chin up with a small pout.

I blinked, a little surprised. "What? Why not?"

Dalton huffed as he answered, as if it was the most obvious answer in the world. "Because you're not in it. It's just us. You should be in the picture too."

His words caught me off guard, and I felt a soft warmth spread through my chest. I hadn't even thought about that—how I wasn't in the photo. I had wanted to capture a moment of the three of them together, but Dalton's words reminded me that I had become part of their little family too, in some way.

I smiled, kneeling down in front of him and giving his shoulder a gentle squeeze. "You're right, Dalton. I should be in it. But I'll tell you what—we can fix that right now."

Just as I said that, my mom came downstairs, probably checking in on how the packing was going. She smiled when she saw us all gathered in the basement. "Everything going okay down here?"

"Yeah," I said, standing up. "Actually, perfect timing. Can you do me a favor, Mom?"

She raised an eyebrow. "Sure, what do you need?"

I walked over to her, holding out my camera. "Could you take a picture of me with these three? Dalton says the one I gave them isn't good enough because I'm not in it."

My mom chuckled, her eyes softening as she took the camera from me. "Of course."

I turned back to the boys, grinning. "Alright, you heard Dalton. Let's make this a better picture."

Dalton beamed, quickly jumping up and standing beside Nathan. Callum moved to stand behind me, his hand resting lightly on my shoulder. I could feel the warmth of him at my back, that familiar, comforting presence that always made me feel safe. Nathan, smiling a little shyly, positioned himself next to me, and Dalton tugged at my arm until I was crouching beside him.

"Alright," my mom said, holding up the camera as she prepared to snap the picture. "Everyone smile!"

I felt a surge of warmth as I looked around at the boys—my boys, in a way—and smiled wide, genuinely happy despite the strange sadness of the day. My mom snapped a few photos, and then she lowered the camera, giving us a thumbs-up.

"Perfect!" she said, handing the camera back to me.

I looked at the new picture, a smile tugging at my lips. It was better than the first one—complete, in a way. We were all in it together, and the bond we'd built over the past few months was clear in each of our faces.

"There," I said, turning the phone to show Dalton. "Now we've got a better one."

Dalton nodded with approval. "That's more like it."

Nathan smiled too, nodding in agreement, while Callum leaned down, whispering softly in my ear, "Now it's perfect."

I blushed, nudging him playfully. "Yeah, yeah. Let's just get these boxes upstairs before I get all sentimental."

As we carried the boxes out to the moving truck, something caught my eye—the flag on the Reids' porch. It was new, fluttering proudly in the breeze, its deep purple color stark against the bright spring sky. I squinted at it, and then it hit me. It was a University of Clarketon flag.

I stopped in my tracks for a second, staring at it. University of Clarketon. The school Callum had committed to for soccer. It had only been a few weeks since he made his decision, but seeing that flag made it all feel so much more real. Clarketon was all the way in Illinois, thousands of miles from here. From me.

Callum had told me about the offer over winter break, but we hadn't really talked about what it would mean for us— what it would mean when he left.

I knew it was a huge opportunity for him, and I was genuinely proud, but the thought of him being so far away gnawed at me. I felt a weird lump in my throat, the reality of it sinking in all over again.

"You alright?" Callum's voice broke into my thoughts. He was standing next to me, holding a box, his brow furrowed as he followed my gaze to the flag.

I forced a small smile, nodding as I picked up another box. "Yeah… just saw the flag."

He glanced at it, then back at me, his lips curving into a small, proud grin. "Mom put it up this morning. She's really leaning into the whole school spirit thing."

I chuckled softly, but my heart wasn't in it. I could feel the weight of the flag's meaning pressing on me—the reminder that soon, Callum would be gone, off chasing his dream while I stayed here. We'd be separated by more than just a few houses or a hallway. It was Illinois, and we were in California. A whole country apart.

Callum must've noticed the shift in my mood because he set the box down on the truck's edge and stepped closer, his voice soft. "You're thinking about it, huh?"

I bit my lip, trying to act casual, but there was no point in hiding it from him. "It's just… Illinois is really far, you know?"

He nodded, his expression serious as he slid an arm around my waist, pulling me close. "Yeah, I know."

We stood there for a moment, the sounds of the others moving boxes around us, but everything felt distant—just me, him, and that damn flag fluttering in the background. The weight of the future hung between us.

He pressed a kiss to the top of my head, his voice low and reassuring. "And I'm not going anywhere without making sure we're good, Hailey. We'll figure it out, I promise."

AFTER EVERYTHING THAT HAD HAPPENED OVER THE PAST SEVERAL MONTHS, IT WAS hard to believe that my family finally had a new house—one we could actually call home again.

I stood by the entrance, watching as that familiar minivan pulled into our street, and my heart skipped a beat when I saw the familiar faces of the Reids walking up the driveway. Dalton and Nathan were first to bound inside, their eyes wide with excitement as they took in the space.

"Whoa, this place is so nice!" Dalton exclaimed, spinning around to take in the high ceilings and the open living room. Nathan nodded in agreement, still a bit shy but clearly impressed.

I smiled at them, feeling a little flutter of warmth at seeing how happy they were for us. Then Callum stepped in, his presence immediately commanding my attention. He had that relaxed, confident grin on his face, the one that never failed to make my heart race a little faster.

"Not bad, Eller," he teased as he approached, his eyes sweeping the room before landing on me. "Pretty fancy."

I laughed, shaking my head. "Thanks, Reid. I'm glad it meets your high standards."

He stepped closer, pulling a small box from his jacket pocket. "Here," he said, his voice softer now. "Just a little something for the new house."

I raised an eyebrow, curious, but before I could even reach for the box, Callum leaned down and kissed me—soft and fond, the kind of kiss that said more than words could. His lips were warm, and for a moment, everything else faded into the background.

It was mid-April now, six months since Callum and I had started dating, and somehow, we'd made it through everything —our initial bickering, the fire, the tension with our families, and all the challenges that came with blending our lives. And here we were, standing in my new home, surrounded by people who mattered, feeling... happy.

It was just him and me, like it had been for the last six months.

I still couldn't believe it sometimes—that we had gone from snarky banter and barely tolerating each other to this. To being in love. Real love, the kind that made everything feel... brighter.

I pulled back, smiling up at him as I took the small box from his hand. "You didn't have to get us anything," I said, even though I couldn't help but be touched by the gesture.

Callum shrugged, smirking. "I know. But you deserve nice things."

I rolled my eyes but couldn't suppress the smile spreading across my face. "You're such a sap sometimes, you know that?"

"Only for you." He winked, and I felt my cheeks warm as I opened the box to find a set of elegant, engraved pens—simple, yet thoughtful. Of course he'd know exactly what would make me smile.

"Ha! Where'd you get these?" I chuckled, holding up the pens to the light so I could see what was engraved on them. **H+C 4EVA.**

If this was anyone else, I would've cringed. But he was my boyfriend so he was allowed to be cringey. He chuckled as he absentmindedly brushed some hair out of my face. "Staples. I finally understand why you spent so much time there looking for the right damn pens. It took me a while to find ones that I thought you'd like."

"Thank you," I said, leaning into him for another quick kiss. "I love it. I'll use them to write my breakup letter to you."

"You're not funny," he deadpanned, though a small smirk played at his lips nonetheless.

Nathan and Dalton, who had been busy inspecting the new kitchen, called out to us. "Hailey, this place is awesome! You have so much space now!" Nathan said, clearly impressed as he peeked into one of the side rooms.

"I know, right? You guys can come over and hang out anytime," I replied, grinning at how excited they seemed.

"Hey, don't go offering my brothers unlimited access to your house," Callum joked, draping his arm over my shoulders. "I might get a little jealous."

"You're gonna get jealous of your 7 and 12 year old little brothers?"

"Yes. Got a problem?"

I shot him a look, but it was playful, my heart feeling lighter than it had in months.

"So," Callum murmured in my ear, his voice low. "How does it feel? Having your own place again?"

I took a deep breath, glancing around the room. My parents were laughing with Callum's parents, and Dalton and Nathan were already talking about how they could turn one of the rooms into a "gaming dungeon" whenever they came over. The house was filled with warmth, laughter, and life.

"It feels... good," I said, turning back to him with a smile. "It feels like we're finally getting our lives back."

He nodded, brushing a strand of hair away from my face. "You deserve this, Hailey. You and your family. After everything that's happened... you deserve to be happy."

I leaned into him, resting my head against his chest. "I am happy," I whispered. "I really am."

Callum and I were still wrapped up in our little world when I heard my mom's teasing voice break through the moment.

"Oh, come on! You two see each other almost every day and still act like that?" she called out, grinning from the kitchen as she set down a dish of lasagna on the counter.

I felt my face heat up as I pulled back from Callum, only to see both sets of parents smiling at us with amusement.

"Exactly," Callum's mom chimed in, crossing her arms as she leaned against the counter, raising an eyebrow at us. "What are you, newlyweds?"

Dalton, never one to miss a chance to tease, piped up from the living room. "Yeah! You guys are so gross!" he said, scrunching his face up in mock disgust.

Callum rolled his eyes and tightened his arm around my waist, pulling me closer. "Jealous much, Dalton?"

"Pffft, yeah right," Dalton replied, but his grin betrayed him. Nathan stood nearby, smirking but staying quiet—he was used to this routine by now.

I couldn't help but laugh, feeling slightly embarrassed but also kind of happy. It was nice to see everyone so lighthearted after everything that had happened. Even my dad, who had been a little tense about our relationship at first, was chuckling at the banter.

"All right, all right, break it up, lovebirds," Mr. Reid joked as he waved us over. "It's dinner time, and I'm not waiting for you two to finish making eyes at each other."

We all gathered around the long dining table that was now filled with dishes, each one more delicious-looking than the last. There was lasagna, roasted chicken, mashed potatoes, and a few different salads. My mom had gone all out, as usual, making sure the housewarming dinner would be one to remember.

Everyone began passing dishes around, filling their plates and chatting about random things—work, school, life in general. The atmosphere was warm and relaxed, the house filled with the sounds of laughter and the clinking of silverware against plates.

"Okay," my dad said, leaning back in his chair after a few minutes. "I think it's time for a toast."

He lifted his glass of wine, and everyone else followed suit, raising their glasses high.

"To new beginnings," he said, looking around the table at all of us. "And to family—old and new."

I smiled, feeling a swell of emotion as I glanced around at the people I loved most. Even though things had been hard, and there had been moments where I didn't know if we'd ever get to a place of peace again, we were here. Together.

"To new beginnings," everyone echoed, clinking glasses as we all shared a warm, collective smile.

I took a deep breath, my heart pounding in my chest, before deciding to speak up. "Actually, uh… speaking of new beginnings," I started, and all eyes turned to me. "I've been wanting to share something with everyone."

The room fell quiet, and I could feel the tension rise slightly as curiosity flickered across everyone's faces. Callum, sitting beside me, looked at me with a raised eyebrow, intrigued.

"I... got into NYU," I announced, my voice a little shaky. "For photography."

There was a brief moment of stunned silence, and then it hit—the excitement, the surprise.

"What?!" Callum blurted out, his eyes wide with disbelief. "NYU? That's amazing, Hailey!"

My parents were already smiling proudly, and Mrs. Reid's hand flew to her mouth in surprise while Mr. Reid grinned broadly. Dalton and Nathan looked equally shocked, exchanging glances before cheering.

"Oh my gosh, congratulations, Hailey!" Callum's mom exclaimed, getting up to give me a warm hug. "That's incredible!"

"Wow, NYU!" Callum's dad added, nodding in approval. "You must be so proud."

My heart swelled as the compliments poured in, and Callum, clearly thrilled, pulled me into a tight hug, pressing a kiss on my lips right in front of everyone. He pulled back just enough to beam at me. "You're amazing. I'm so proud of you," he whispered before leaning in to kiss me again, this time more tenderly.

His eyes sparkled with genuine pride, and I couldn't help but smile back at him, feeling all the warmth of the moment. "Hey," he said as he pulled away slightly, "we'll be a little closer now! Illinois and New York are much closer than California."

I could see the wheels turning in his head as he thought about how much easier it might be to visit each other when we were both on the East Coast. The idea lit up his face like he'd just been handed the best news ever.

"Callum... don't get ahead of yourself," his mom warned, her tone teasing but laced with seriousness.

"Yeah, let's keep things realistic, okay?" Mr. Reid added, shooting him a playful yet pointed glance. "You guys still need to be responsible."

Callum groaned dramatically but smiled at his parents, his arm still draped around my shoulders. "I know, I know," he said, nodding. "But hey, it's not as bad as California and Illinois, right? We'll make it work."

"You will," Mrs. Reid said, giving him a knowing look before turning back to me. "Hailey, we're so proud of you. NYU is an incredible opportunity."

"Thanks," I replied, my cheeks warming from all the attention. "I'm really excited, even though it's a little nerve-wracking."

"You'll be amazing," Callum said softly, squeezing my hand under the table.

As the conversation continued and the evening wore on, I found myself just sitting back and taking it all in—the warmth of the room, the laughter of my family and Callum's, the way Callum's hand found mine under the table and squeezed gently every so often.

I wouldn't trade it for anything.

EPILOGUE

HAILEY

6 YEARS LATER. SIX YEARS LATER, AND HERE I WAS, STANDING IN THE BUSTLING stadium, the sounds of the crowd roaring around me as I held our son, Matthew, on my hip.

He was squirming with excitement, his tiny fists waving in the air as he babbled incoherently, completely enthralled by the energy of the game. Callum was out on the field, playing for FC Riverford, the pro soccer team he'd joined after graduating. It still felt surreal sometimes—watching him out there, in front of thousands of cheering fans, wearing that familiar jersey with his name on the back.

We had made it. After everything—the long-distance relationship, the late-night calls, the flights back and forth between New York and Clarketon, balancing my life at NYU and his soccer career—we were finally here.

Together. Living in the same city. It hadn't been easy, but as I glanced down at Matthew, his wide eyes fixed on the game, and then back up at Callum dominating the field, I knew every sacrifice had been worth it.

Callum had gone off to Illinois to play soccer for Clarketon, and I had gone to New York to pursue my dream of becoming a photographer.

The time apart had been brutal, especially in the beginning. We'd gone from seeing each other every day in high school to being thousands of miles away from each other. But we made it work. Callum would drive over to New York every chance he got, and I'd visit him in Illinois whenever I had a break from school.

We texted constantly, FaceTimed late into the night, and leaned on each other in ways I never thought possible.

Those years were tough, but they made us stronger. Every goodbye made the hellos that much sweeter. By the time Callum graduated and was scouted by FC Riverford, I had already started building a career as a sports photographer, capturing moments from every corner of the field. It wasn't lost on me that our lives had merged in ways neither of us expected. I spent years documenting athletes in action, as well as doing some side gigs shooting some models for romance book covers, and now I got to run down my path with Callum—my Callum—right there in the spotlight.

After Callum signed with FC Riverford, we moved to Atlanta, where the team was based. It was a big move, but we were ready. By then, I had built up a solid portfolio, and the opportunities to work as a photographer for other sports teams and events were everywhere. Plus, being in the same city as Callum meant we could finally put down roots and start the next chapter of our lives—together, as a family.

And then came Matthew.

I smiled down at him as he let out another excited squeal, pointing in the vague direction of the field. He had his father's wide, curious eyes, and the same energy that made me wonder if he was going to be a little soccer player himself someday.

Becoming parents had been the biggest adventure yet. Matthew had been a surprise, but a good one. He was everything we didn't know we needed—this tiny, beautiful reminder of how far we'd come, of everything we'd built.

Callum had taken to fatherhood like it was second nature. Sure, there were sleepless nights and moments where we both felt like we had no idea what we were doing, but we figured it out.

Together. Watching Callum with Matthew was like seeing him in a whole new light. The same dedication and focus he put into soccer, he now poured into being a dad. And even though his schedule was hectic—training, traveling, games—he always made time for us. For me. For Matthew.

The game was nearing the end now, and I could feel the tension in the crowd as the clock ticked down. FC Riverford was up by one, and Callum was in his element, leading the charge as usual. FC Riverford was playing their hearts out, but the opposing team, Camden United, was relentless, pushing them to their limits.

The fans around me were on their feet, cheering wildly as the ball moved across the field, but all I could focus on was Callum—his determination, his confidence, the way he made everything look effortless.

Callum's teammate sent a perfect pass down the field, and Callum, in his signature way, anticipated it perfectly. He darted forward, weaving through Camden's defenders like they were standing still. The stadium held its breath as he lined up the shot.

Time seemed to slow down as his foot connected with the ball, sending it soaring toward the goal. The keeper dove, arms outstretched, but it was too late. The ball sailed into the back of the net with a satisfying *thud*.

The stadium erupted.

I let out a cheer, my voice lost in the deafening roar of the crowd. Matthew clapped his tiny hands, his face lighting up as the final whistle blew and Riverford secured the win. "Ya! Da!" He cried out in excitement. The stadium erupted into cheers, and I couldn't help but join in, bouncing Matthew on my hip as I shouted along with the crowd.

I smiled down at him, pressing a soft kiss to his messy brown hair. "That's right, baby. Daddy won today."

It had been quite a journey since those early days when Callum was just a determined kid on the field, working tirelessly to make a name for himself and I was the hotheaded recluse he lived with. But we'd come so far. We made it. Together.

As the team celebrated on the field, Callum's eyes found mine. He gave me that familiar smirk, the one that made my heart race even after all these years. He jogged over to the edge of the field, grinning like the boy I'd fallen in love with all those years ago in high school. I could see the exhaustion in his eyes, but also the pure joy of the win.

"Hey, you two," he called out as he reached us, reaching up to ruffle Matthew's hair. Matthew squealed in delight, reaching out for his dad, and I passed him down into Callum's waiting arms.

"You killed it out there," I said, beaming.

Callum held Matthew close, planting a kiss on his head before looking up at me. "Wouldn't have done it without my biggest fans."

I rolled my eyes playfully. "You know we're always here. Every game."

"And I love you for it," he said softly, his voice full of warmth.

We stood there for a moment, the noise of the crowd fading into the background as we soaked in this little piece of happiness. It hadn't always been easy, and there had been times when the distance felt like it would tear us apart. But standing here, with Callum holding our son and the future laid out in front of us, I knew we had made it. Our journey was just beginning.

"Come on," Callum said, shifting Matthew in his arms. "Let's go celebrate."

We pulled into the parking garage beneath our building, and as we made our way up to our penthouse, I couldn't help but let out a sigh of relief. It had been a long day, and as much as I loved watching Callum play, there was nothing quite like coming home.

The elevator doors slid open, and we stepped into the spacious living room of our place—a luxury penthouse that still felt surreal sometimes. Floor-to-ceiling windows stretched across one wall, giving us a stunning view of the city skyline. The warm glow of the city lights always made the place feel cozy, despite its modern elegance.

Callum set Matthew down on the floor, where he immediately started crawling toward his favorite pile of toys in the corner. Callum stretched, letting out a tired groan as he kicked off his shoes.

"So, I was thinking," he said, turning toward me with a grin. "Why don't we order our usual food to celebrate?"

I smiled, already knowing what he meant. Our "usual" had become a bit of a tradition after each of his wins. We'd order in from this amazing Italian place down the street—pizza, pasta, the works. It was indulgent and exactly what we needed after a long day.

"I like the way you think," I said, collapsing onto the couch with a laugh. "But you're getting the dessert this time. I want that tiramisu."

Callum chuckled, pulling out his phone to place the order. "You got it. Tiramisu coming right up."

As he tapped away at his phone, I remembered something I'd been meaning to tell him. "Oh! Guess what I got in the mail today."

He glanced up, one eyebrow raised in curiosity. "What?"

"Nala and Ibra's wedding invitation," I said, grinning. "It's official—they're getting married in June."

Callum's face lit up, a smile tugging at his lips. "Finally! I was wondering when they'd set the date."

"I know, right? It's been forever," I said, shaking my head. "But it's perfect timing. I can't wait to see Nala walk down the aisle."

Callum laughed, sitting down next to me on the couch. "And I can't wait to see Ibra sweat through his tux. You know he's going to be a nervous wreck."

I grinned, leaning back against the cushions. "Oh, absolutely. But they're so good together. I'm happy for them."

Callum slipped his arm around me, pulling me close. "Feels like everyone's settling down, huh?"

"Yeah," I murmured, resting my head on his shoulder. "But we've got our own adventure going on. We're doing okay."

He pressed a kiss to the top of my head. "More than okay. We're killing it."

I smiled, snuggling into him as Matthew let out a happy squeal from across the room, banging one of his toys on the floor.

"Yeah," I whispered, feeling the warmth of our little family settle over me. "We really are."

It was crazy to think how much had changed over the years. Nala and Ibra had started dating not long after graduation, and now here they were, tying the knot. I couldn't help but feel a little nostalgic as I thought about how far we'd all come—from high school seniors navigating the chaos of life, to adults with careers, relationships, and, in my case, a family.

Then there was Nathan and Dalton. They weren't little anymore. Nathan had just started college, pursuing something tech-related that made perfect sense for his quiet, thoughtful personality. He was thriving—still introverted, but he'd found his group of friends and seemed happier than ever.

Dalton, on the other hand, was in high school now, and just like his older brother, he was a social butterfly. He was all about sports, not soccer like Callum, but hockey. Callum and Dalton bonded over their respective games, and Dalton always looked up to Callum's success.

It was sweet to see how much they'd grown—both as individuals and in their relationship with Callum.

We still made time to visit San Alfonso every now and then. It was a bit nostalgic, coming back to where everything started—where we fell in love. It was comforting to see how much things had changed, but also how some things remained the same.

Nathan and Dalton, though... God, they had both shot up like weeds.

They were tall and lanky now, just like Callum had been at their age. Nathan's voice had deepened, and Dalton had lost most of that boyish roundness in his face. Every time we visited, they were either talking about sports or teasing each other, and it was like watching a younger version of Callum.

They both had this quiet determination in them, something that made me think they'd do big things one day.

Callum glanced at me, noticing I had drifted off in thought. "You thinking about something?" he asked, his voice light.

I smiled softly. "Yeah, just... everyone. Our friends, family, hell, your brothers. It's crazy how much they've grown."

He chuckled, leaning back against the couch. "But I'm your favorite Reid, right?"

I shook my head with a smirk, pointing to Matthew, who was playing happily on the floor with his toys. "Nope. Matthew's my favorite Reid."

Callum raised his hands in surrender, laughing. "Fair enough." He leaned over to plant a kiss on my cheek. "Can't argue with that."

Just as Callum leaned in to steal another kiss, we heard a little whimper from across the room. Matthew, who had been happily playing with his toys moments ago, was now looking at us with wide eyes, his lower lip trembling in that way that always signaled he was feeling left out. "Uh-oh, looks like someone's not too happy," I said, glancing over at Matthew as his small whimper turned into a more persistent fuss. He reached out, clearly wanting to be part of whatever was happening.

Callum chuckled, pulling back and shaking his head. "Guess we're in trouble."

I stood up, making my way over to Matthew, who immediately stretched his arms up toward me, his little face crumpled with a mix of frustration and longing. I couldn't help but smile as I scooped him up, his tiny hands clinging to my shirt as I brought him over to the couch.

"Come here, little guy," I cooed, kissing the top of his head as I sat back down next to Callum. "You're part of this family too."

Matthew nestled into my arms, still a bit fussy but calming down quickly now that he was close to us. I snuggled him between Callum and me, letting him rest against both of us. Callum reached over, gently stroking the top of Matthew's head, his smile softening.

"There we go," Callum said, leaning down to kiss Matthew's chubby cheek. "Now it's a family cuddle."

Matthew let out a contented little hum, his tiny fingers grabbing onto Callum's shirt, and I couldn't help but grin at how adorable the two of them looked together.

"All better now?" I asked, leaning in to kiss Matthew's forehead.

He babbled something in response, his big eyes looking up at both of us as if to say he was perfectly fine now that he had our full attention.

The three of us stayed there on the couch, wrapped up in each other, and for a moment, everything felt perfectly still. Just us, in our little bubble of happiness.

CALLUM

I STEPPED OUT OF THE BATHROOM, FEELING THE WARMTH OF THE SHOWER STILL clinging to my skin. My hair was damp, and I rubbed a towel over it as I walked into the bedroom.

The apartment was quiet now, the noise of the day having settled into the peaceful hum of nighttime. Hailey had just put Matthew to bed, and for the first time in what felt like hours, the house felt still. Calm.

I glanced over to see Hailey sitting on the edge of the bed, stretching out her arms, probably unwinding after a long day of chasing around our little tornado of a son. She looked tired, but there was a quiet peace in her movements, like she was savoring the quiet moment as much as I was.

"Matthew finally asleep?" I asked, tossing the towel onto a chair in the corner of the room.

Hailey smiled softly. "Out like a light. Poor thing was wiped after all that excitement at your game."

I smiled, crossing the room and sitting down beside her. The bed dipped slightly under my weight as I reached out, gently tucking a loose strand of hair behind her ear. "Sounds like his dad isn't the only one who had a long day."

She let out a small, tired laugh, leaning her head against my shoulder. "You're not wrong. But it's a good tired."

I wrapped my arm around her, pulling her closer as we both sat there in the quiet. The city lights outside cast a soft glow into the room, making the space feel warm and intimate. After a full day of everything—parenting, soccer, and the general chaos that had become our everyday life—this moment of quiet was exactly what I needed.

"I still can't believe we've got a kid," I murmured, leaning down to kiss the top of her head. Hailey was everything I loved and more, and I didn't think I was capable of loving someone more than her until our little boy came barreling into our lives. In a way, Hailey had shown and given me a love I didn't even know I was capable of. She taught me patience, strength, and a gentleness that softened parts of me I hadn't realized were still rough around the edges.

Having Matthew only deepened that feeling, and sometimes, like right now, I found myself wondering how I'd gotten this lucky.

Hailey chuckled softly, her fingers lightly tracing patterns on my leg. "Sometimes it feels like we blinked and ended up here, huh?"

I nodded, my hand sliding down to rest on hers. "Yeah. From high school to this... it's wild." I paused, glancing at her. "You ever miss the old days? Just you and me, no responsibilities?"

She smiled up at me, her eyes sparkling in the soft light. "Of course I do sometimes. But this?" She gestured around the room, then toward the door where Matthew was sleeping in the next room. "This is so much better."

I felt my chest tighten, not with anxiety, but with the overwhelming sense of love I had for this woman. For our life. She was right—this was better. There had been plenty of wild, carefree days back in high school, but this?

This was what made it all worth it.

"Yeah," I murmured, leaning in to kiss her softly. "It is."

We kissed slowly, no rush, no urgency—just the two of us, soaking in the rare moment of stillness. After a long day of running around, there was something grounding about this quiet intimacy, about having her here, just the two of us, like we were stealing a moment for ourselves.

When we finally pulled apart, Hailey rested her forehead against mine, her breath warm against my skin. "So, what's the plan now? Popcorn and a movie?" she asked, her voice laced with that familiar teasing tone.

I grinned. "That sounds perfect." Then I kissed her again, because I could. Because after everything we'd been through, every challenge and joy, this—these quiet moments together—was the real prize.

As Hailey slipped off the bed, she gave me one last playful look before heading out of the room. "I'll make some popcorn," she said, smiling as she disappeared down the hallway, leaving me alone in the soft glow of the bedroom.

I leaned back against the pillows, running a hand through my damp hair, feeling a sense of peace settle over me. The quiet hum of the apartment, the faint sound of Hailey moving around in the kitchen, it all felt like home. Real, solid, undeniable home. I stretched out, sinking into the bed as my mind drifted back to her.

I smiled to myself, thinking about how far we'd come. I couldn't help but laugh a little when I thought about how things used to be between us.

Hailey had been the only person in high school who could piss me off so much with just one sarcastic comment or a well-placed eye roll. I'd get so riled up whenever we were around each other, like she knew exactly which buttons to push. And, of course, I'd push hers right back. It was this constant battle of wills.

But now?

Now, my heart beats for her. Everything that used to irritate me, every little quirk and sharp remark—it's what l love most about her. She's the only person who ever challenged me, pushed me, made me see the world differently. And somehow, through all the chaos and bickering, I fell in love with her.

And she gave me the greatest gift I could have ever imagined: Matthew.

I glanced toward the door, picturing Matthew fast asleep in his crib, and my heart swelled. I still couldn't believe it sometimes—that I was a dad. That we had this perfect little boy who had completely turned our lives upside down in the best way possible.

Hailey had given me more than I ever thought I'd deserve. She was my equal, my partner, the mother of my son. I loved her with a depth I couldn't have imagined back when we were teenagers, always at each other's throats. She had become my home, my peace, my everything.

And Matthew… he was this perfect little reflection of us, with Hailey's bright eyes and my unruly hair. Every time I looked at him, I saw the life we'd built, the future we had ahead of us. I couldn't imagine loving anyone or anything more than I loved them.

I sighed contentedly, letting the weight of those feelings settle over me as I closed my eyes for a moment. The world outside was loud and chaotic, but here, in this quiet space with Hailey and Matthew, I had everything I'd ever need.

A few minutes later, I heard Hailey's footsteps as she returned, the smell of fresh popcorn wafting into the room. I opened my eyes just as she appeared, holding a big bowl of popcorn with a cheeky smile on her face.

"Ready for our movie night?" she asked, sliding back onto the bed beside me.

I wrapped my arm around her, pulling her close. "Always," I said, kissing her temple as the warmth of her presence wrapped around me like a blanket.

Her and Matthew. They were everything—my whole world, my whole heart. And as we settled in to watch the movie, her head resting on my shoulder, I knew I was exactly where I was meant to be.

As Hailey sank into the bed next to me, the soft glow of the TV screen flickered in front of us. She settled against my side, pulling the blanket up over both of us, her head resting comfortably on my shoulder.

She pressed play, and the movie started—a familiar one we'd seen a dozen times before. But as the opening credits rolled, I found myself completely distracted, not by the film, but by her.

The way she fit against me, her warmth, her presence—it was everything I never realized I needed until I had it. I glanced down at her, watching as she absentmindedly popped a piece of popcorn into her mouth, her attention on the movie, but relaxed, content.

The soft curve of her smile, the way her hair fell messily around her face—it all made my chest feel too tight, like I was brimming with more love than I knew what to do with. I wasn't even paying attention to the movie. My thoughts were a million miles away, running through everything we'd been through, everything we had built.

From high school to here. From bickering to falling in love. From being two stubborn kids to raising a family. Matthew was already the center of our world, but... there was something more now. A thought that had been creeping into my mind more and more recently.

I glanced down at her again, my heart pounding a little faster with the question that had been rattling around in my head for weeks.

"Hey," I said softly, my voice cutting through the soft sound of the movie.

She looked up at me, her eyes curious. "Hmm?"

I hesitated for a second, suddenly feeling a little nervous. This wasn't something we'd talked about seriously yet, but the more I thought about it, the more it felt like the right time to bring it up. I cleared my throat, running a hand through my hair as I shifted slightly in the bed. "What do you think of... giving Matthew a sibling?" I asked, my voice low but steady.

The words hung in the air for a moment, and I watched her eyes widen slightly in surprise. She blinked, sitting up a little straighter as she processed what I'd just said. Her lips parted as if she was about to speak, but no words came out at first. I could tell she was caught off guard.

"A sibling?" she repeated, her voice soft, like she was testing the idea.

I nodded, my heart pounding a little harder now that the question was out there. "Yeah... I mean, I know we've got our hands full with Matthew right now, but... I don't know. I've been thinking about it a lot lately. How amazing it would be to have another one. To give Matthew a little brother or sister."

She stared at me for a moment, her eyes searching mine as if trying to figure out if I was serious. Then, slowly, a soft smile tugged at the corners of her lips.

"You've been thinking about this?" she asked, her tone playful but laced with warmth.

I shrugged, a little sheepish. "Yeah, more than I realized. I love being a dad, Hailey. And Matthew... he's the best thing that's ever happened to us. I just... I can't stop thinking about how amazing it would be to have another. To grow our family even more."

Her smile widened, and she shifted, sitting up fully now so she could look at me properly. I could see the emotions swirling in her eyes—surprise, affection, maybe even a little excitement. She tucked a strand of hair behind her ear, leaning back against the pillows as she considered the idea.

"I can't lie," she said after a moment, her voice thoughtful. "I've thought about it too. I mean, it's crossed my mind every now and then. Especially when I see Matthew with other kids... but I didn't know you were thinking about it seriously."

I reached out, gently taking her hand in mine, my thumb brushing over her knuckles. "I didn't want to push you or rush into anything. It's up to you at the end of the day," I said softly. "But I love this life we've built, and I love our little family. I can't help but imagine what it would be like to grow it. To give Matthew a sibling he can play with, grow up with. And I know we'd be great at it, Hailey. We've done this before, and we'd do it even better a second time."

She looked down at our hands, a soft laugh escaping her lips. "You really have been thinking about this."

"Yeah," I admitted, squeezing her hand gently. "More than you know."

There was a long pause, the movie completely forgotten in the background as she looked back up at me. Her eyes were soft, her expression thoughtful as she weighed the idea. I could see her considering it, imagining what life would be like with another little one running around.

"I love being a mom," she said quietly, her voice barely above a whisper. "And Matthew... he's everything. I guess the idea of giving him a sibling—someone to grow up with, to be there for him—it's kind of amazing."

My heart soared at her words, and I felt a flicker of hope light up inside me. "So... what do you think?"

She bit her lip, smiling up at me with that familiar spark in her eyes. "I think... it sounds kind of perfect."

I grinned, pulling her closer into my arms, kissing the top of her head. "You sure?"

She laughed, wrapping her arms around my waist as she snuggled against my chest. "Yeah. I'm sure. Let's give Matthew a sibling."

Without another word, I reached over and grabbed the bowl of popcorn from her lap, setting it down on the nightstand with a soft clink.

I leaned in, hovering over her, my knees sinking into the mattress on either side of her as I moved closer. Her breath hitched slightly, and I couldn't help but smirk as I looked down at her. "Let's get to work, then," I murmured, my voice low and teasing.

She laughed softly, a blush creeping up her cheeks as I leaned down further, my lips brushing against her neck. Her skin was warm, and I could feel her body tense slightly beneath me, anticipation humming between us like a live wire.

I pressed a kiss just below her ear, feeling the shiver that ran through her at the contact.

"Callum…" she whispered, her voice barely audible, but I could hear the desire there, the way she was already melting into the moment.

I smirked against her skin, my hands sliding up her sides as I kissed her again, this time slower, letting the weight of everything we'd just talked about sink in.Her fingers tangled in my hair, tugging lightly as I kissed her neck, trailing my lips down to her collarbone, taking my time.

We both got lost in the sheets, in each other, the world outside fading into nothing as I kissed and loved her again, and again, and again.

ACKNOWLEDGMENTS

First of all, thank you so much to YOU for picking up my first ever book! Writing has been a passion of mine since I was first young, and eventually publushing a book had always been a dream of mine. I'm so glad this dream has finally come true, and it's all thanks to you guys, the best best readers in the whole world!

I've been writing on a platform called Episode for almost 4 years as of 2024 when this book is being published, so if you're here as a reader from my Episode stories, thank you for taking a chance on exploring more of my writing!

And if you're a new reader and want to see more of my stories, go check out my stories on Episode, under the profile "Yves" ;) I have one completed story called Bad Influence and an ongoing one called Play Dirty.

To the ones who were there with me throughout the

entire writing process and listened to me bounce plot ideas of them for hours on end, my best friends ever, AC, Katherine, thank you for putting up with me for so long and for telling me which parts of the books were really good and which ones I had to delete because they were total hot garbage. It's not only this book, but none of my other stories would've come to fruition without your help and support.

Thank you also to Mari who so kindly edited this book and for catching all the little mistakes I definitely wouldn't have. Thank you so much as well to Ned for designing the stunning cover.

Shoutout to my Mom, as well, who, although has basically no sense when it came to writing (sorry Mom), did whatever she could to support me anyway! Though I didn't take your suggestion to add a talking dog to this story for comedic relief purposes, the way you kept assuring me to keep going and gave me courage when I felt like I was lacking means the absolute world to me. You'll forever be my best friend and my biggest supporter.

To every reader who's followed my journey—whether you've been here since my Episode days or are just finding me now—thank you. Thank you for your enthusiasm, your feedback, your encouragement, and for sharing my stories with others. Every single comment, every message, and every ounce of support you've shown me over the years has meant the absolute world to me.

You've been my motivation when I needed it most, and I hope this story has given you even a fraction of the joy you've given me. It's such a beloved project of mine and I'm so glad I finaly get to share it with you all!

Again thank you so much for reading Can't Get Enough of You! If you hadn't noticed, there were many characters introduced in this story so we may or might not be quite done with this universe yet... I'm so excited to see where the next step of our journey takes us, and I hope to see you there as well!

- Love, Yves

ABOUT THE AUTHOR

Yves Chang is a hopeless romantic who lives in Vancouver, BC (Oh Canada!). She first started writing in elementary school and eventually published her first stories on the Episode app under the name "Yves." When she's not writing, she's pretending to write or crushing on her fictional book/manga/manhwa boyfriends.

She also finds it weird that she's writing about herself in third-person. She says you can check out her social media for more updates on her upcoming stories and ongoing Episode stories!

Instagram:
https://www.instagram.com/episode.yves/
https://www.instagram.com/yvesauthor/

BONUS CHAPTER

CALLUM

WE WERE CROUCHED BEHIND THE COUCH, BARELY CONTAINING OUR EXCITEMENT as we waited for Dalton to come home. It was his 8th birthday, and we had planned the perfect surprise.

The living room was decked out in his favorite superhero decorations—Spider-Man balloons, banners, and streamers hanging from every possible corner. The cake sat proudly on the coffee table, covered in bright red and blue frosting, complete with an edible Spider-Man figurine on top. The whole place looked like a mini superhero convention, and I knew Dalton was going to lose his mind when he walked in.

"Is everything ready?" Hailey whispered next to me, her voice filled with anticipation as she peeked over the edge of the couch. She was holding one of those party poppers, her eyes bright with excitement.

"Yeah," I whispered back, grinning. "He's going to freak out."

Hailey's parents were hiding near the kitchen, their heads poking out just slightly, while Nathan was trying not to fidget too much beside me. He had been bouncing off the walls all day, excited to surprise our little brother. I couldn't help but chuckle at the sight of him, barely able to stay still for more than a second.

"Shh, he's coming!" Nathan whispered loudly, and I shot him a look, pressing a finger to my lips to signal for silence.

The door creaked open, and we all froze, holding our breath as we heard Dalton's voice from the hallway.

"I'm telling you, Mom, I nailed that last piece! Miss Turner said I'm improving a lot!" Dalton's voice was full of enthusiasm as he walked in with my mom and dad trailing closely behind him, also in on the surprise. "I'm gonna be the next Mo... what was his name? Mo-chart?"

I could hear his little footsteps getting closer, and my heart raced with anticipation. We waited for the right moment, the tension building as he made his way into the living room, still rambling about how well his piano lessons were going and that he was going to be the next "Mo-chart."

And then, just as he stepped in front of the couch, we all jumped out.

"SURPRISE!" we yelled in unison, party poppers going off, balloons bouncing into the air.

Dalton's wide eyes darted around the room, from the decorations to the cake to all of us grinning at him. He was completely overwhelmed, his little body shaking as he looked up at Mom and Dad, then at me.

"Surprise, Dalton! It's your birthday, look!" Mom said softly, softly poking Dalton's shoulder. The little guy was still frozen, like he couldn't believe what he was seeing.

And then, he started to cry.

At first, it was just a sniffle, but then the tears came in full force. He covered his face with his hands, trying to hide it, but it was too late. He was crying, full of emotion, and before I knew it, my throat was tightening too.

"Oh, buddy..." I stood up, crossing the room in a couple of steps and kneeling down in front of him. "Hey, why are you crying? It's okay. It's your birthday, remember? You really thought we wouldn't do anything to celebrate your big day?"

But his crying didn't stop. His face was red, tears streaming down his cheeks, but they weren't tears of sadness. They were the kind of tears that made everyone around him feel it too. One by one, everyone else in the room started tearing up too.

Hailey was the first. I glanced at her, and sure enough, she had tears welling up in her eyes as she watched Dalton. My mom was already dabbing at her eyes with a tissue, and even Dad looked like he was holding back some tears.

Hailey's parents were trying not to break down, but I could see the emotion hitting them too.

Dalton sniffled again and looked up at me with the biggest, most grateful eyes I'd ever seen. "I— I love it, you guys. I love it so much."

I wrapped my arms around him, pulling him into a tight hug. "Happy birthday, buddy."

The whole room felt like one big, emotional wave. Everyone joined in, giving Dalton hugs, whispering birthday wishes in his ear as he cried and smiled at the same time. It wasn't just about the surprise—it was about how much we all loved him, and he felt it, deeply.

"Alright," Hailey said, her voice a little shaky as she wiped away a tear. "Let's get this birthday party started, huh?"

Dalton nodded, still sniffling but beaming now. The tears had dried up, but the feeling in the room lingered—warm, full of love, and shared joy.

We all gathered around the cake, lighting the candles as Dalton stood in front of it, his eyes shining with excitement now. He took a deep breath and blew out all the candles, everyone cheering him on.

The party continued in full swing after Dalton's emotional surprise. The energy in the room had shifted from the overwhelming tears to sheer joy and excitement. Everyone was now in high spirits, and the living room was filled with the sound of laughter and games.

After cake and presents, we decided it was time to get the party games started. Dalton was blindfolded, spinning around a few times before attempting to stick a paper web on the giant Spider-Man poster taped to the wall. Everyone cheered him on as he tried to find his way.

"You're close! Just a little to the left!" Hailey called out, her camera in hand as she snapped pictures of the little guy tripping over his own feet, clutching the paper web in his hands.

I stood back, watching Hailey capture all the little details —the smiles, the laughter, Dalton's concentrated expression as he tried to pin the web in the right place. She was in her element, moving around the room effortlessly, her camera clicking away.

After a few more games, including a messy (but hilarious) round of balloon popping, I found myself standing next to Hailey, who was adjusting her camera's settings.

"Hey, can you do me a favor?" I asked, leaning in so only she could hear. "Take a photo of Dalton for me? Just one where he's smiling, you know, like the big, cheesy grin he gets."

She looked up at me and nodded, her smile softening. "Of course."

Dalton was sitting on the floor, surrounded by presents and torn wrapping paper, his face lit up with pure happiness. He let out a particularly loud squeal when he reached the present the Ellers got for him, which were these really cool Nike shoes.

"Hey, Dalton!" I called his name, and he looked up, his face bright with excitement. Hailey knelt down, raising her camera to capture the moment.

"Dalton, smile!" Hailey said, her voice light and encouraging.

Without hesitation, Dalton broke into the biggest grin, his eyes squinting with joy as he flashed that toothy smile. Hailey clicked the shutter, capturing the image of my little brother in a moment of pure happiness. She glanced at the screen and smiled, clearly satisfied with the shot.

"Got it," she said, standing back up. "Ugh, he's adorable."

I glanced at the camera screen, seeing the photo of Dalton beaming at us, his joy practically radiating from the image. "Yeah, he is."

The room was buzzing with activity, and I felt a warmth settle in my chest as I looked around at everyone—my parents, Hailey's parents, Nathan laughing at one of Dalton's jokes, and, of course, Hailey by my side.

Dalton bounced back from his surprise tears, and now, he was the center of attention, surrounded by everyone who loved him.

Hailey kept taking photos, capturing every little smile and burst of laughter. It was moments like this that reminded me how lucky we were—surrounded by family, by people who cared.

At some point, Dalton ran over, grabbing my hand and pulling me toward the pile of Spider-Man-themed presents still waiting to be opened. "Come on, Callum! Let's open the rest! I wanna open your gift, too!"

I chuckled, glancing back at Hailey, who had her camera ready again. "Alright, buddy, let's do it."

HAILEY

THE CONVEYOR SUSHI PLACE WAS A WHIRLWIND OF ENERGY AND COLOR. PLATES whizzed by us at every second, each one topped with different kinds of sushi, sashimi, and things I could hardly identify.

Summer and the end of high school had arrived even faster than we anticipated. In a few weeks, Callum and I were both leaving for university, so we made it our mission to explore and do literally the most random shit on dates, just so we could experience everything with each other while we still had time. We'd done it all, basically, Go-Karting, laser tag, Korean BBQ, axe-throwing, a rage room, fortune-telling... yeah, it got a little wild, and I did have to draw the line when he suggested skydiving.

Because hell no.

That's why now, Callum and I sat across each other at this place effectively named Sushi Sushi (I wondered whether it was ownded by the same creative geniuses who named Burgers Burgers), our eyes fixed on the little conveyor belt as if it were the most fascinating thing in the world.

Callum's jaw dropped as he pointed at a particularly loaded plate with slices of salmon, tuna, and even a little dollop of wasabi on the side. "Look at that one! That's, like... a buffet on one plate," he said, reaching out and then hesitating, his hand hovering over it. "Wait, do I... just take it? Are we allowed?"

"Honestly, I have no idea," I admitted, stifling a laugh as I shrugged. "But people are doing it, so I guess we're good?"

He shrugged, going for it with a triumphant grin. "If I get in trouble, I'm blaming you," he teased, piling a couple of plates in front of him before digging in.

I'd seen Callum eat before, but never in a setting like this, where he could grab plate after plate without moving an inch. The result was as hilarious as it was impressive.

Every few seconds, his eyes would light up as something else passed by. "Hailey, look! That looks so fucking good." He grabbed a plate of unagi, barely finishing his previous bite before he was on to the next.

"Callum, slow down," I laughed, watching as he started stacking his empty plates higher and higher in a colorful tower. "You're going to run out of space."

"Nah," he said with a mischievous glint in his eye, grabbing yet another plate of tuna rolls. "I'm just getting started. Besides, we have to try everything, right?"

"Everything?" I raised an eyebrow, giggling as he shoved another piece into his mouth, looking far too pleased with himself. "We're going to get kicked out if you keep going at this rate."

"Then at least we'll go out full," he said, his voice muffled with sushi as he offered me a piece from his plate. "Come on, live a little."

I took it, laughing as I tried to keep up with him, but it was a losing battle. Callum was in his element, and before I knew it, he had a pile of plates in front of him, all stacked to impressive heights.

Meanwhile, I was barely halfway through my second plate, watching as he devoured one piece after another, like he'd been starved his whole life.

Amid the chaos, I could see a little kid eyeing the growing stack in front of Callum with something between awe and horror.

"I think we're intimidating the kid next to us," I whispered, nodding towards the kid who was nudging his mom and pointing. "You're gonna be in his nightmares now."

Callum grinned, leaning in conspiratorially. "I like to make an impression." He leaned over and whispered, "But also... I'm still starving. So, excuse me." And, as if to emphasize his words, he reached out and grabbed another plate, looking far too pleased with himself.

We kept going like that, laughing and sampling whatever caught our eye, often without knowing exactly what it was. At one point, I accidentally grabbed a plate of pickled octopus and nearly choked on my green tea as I chewed it, making Callum howl with laughter.

"This place is basically made for you," I said, nudging him as he polished off yet another plate. "All-you-can-eat without even getting up? It's a dream come true."

He grinned, piling his latest empty plate on top of the tower. "Oh, it definitely is. Just what I need before Clarketon tries to kill me with early-morning practice schedules. And I don't even have to feel guilty about going back for seconds. Or thirds. Or sixths, apparently."

As the initial chaos started to calm and we settled into a comfortable rhythm, I noticed Callum glancing at me, his face softening in a way that made my stomach flutter. He reached into his pocket, a subtle shift in his demeanor.

"Hey," he said, looking a bit more serious, "I've actually got something for you."

I blinked, surprised. "For me?"

He nodded, pulling out a small, neatly wrapped package and setting it in front of me. I looked at him, curious but touched, my hands already reaching to unwrap it. Beneath the paper, I found a small silver keychain—a simple design with a tiny heart charm and a miniature key attached.

"A keychain?" I asked, tilting my head as I held it up, a smile tugging at my lips.

"Not just any keychain," he said, his voice softening as he watched my reaction. "It's... a promise. You know, we met living together, we fell in love living together. This keychain is kind of my way of saying... I want us to share a home again one day."

My heart skipped a beat, and I stared at him, feeling the weight of his words settle between us. He took my hand, his thumb tracing gentle circles over my knuckles as he continued.

"One day, when we're both done with all the college and distance stuff... I want that keychain to hold the key to our own place. The first key on it will be the one to our home. Together."

A lump formed in my throat, and I could feel my eyes starting to well up with tears. "Callum..."

He smiled, squeezing my hand. "I know it's a lot, but I wanted you to have something to remind you that no matter how far we go... I'll be right there, waiting for the day we can build something together. For real."

I couldn't hold back the tears anymore. They slipped down my cheeks as I looked at him, overcome with the depth of what he was saying, of what he wanted for us.

"You're such a sap," I whispered, my voice thick with emotion as I wiped at my eyes, laughing a little even as I cried. "But... I love it. I love you."

He chuckled, his hand moving to wipe away my tears with his thumb. "Good. Because you're stuck with me. Even if you go all the way to New York, you're still mine, Hailey."

I squeezed his hand, smiling through my tears. "And you're mine," I whispered. "Even if you're off in Illinois, eating up all the food you can find."

"Hey, if they've got a place like this in Illinois, I'll be living my best life," he teased, making me laugh again as he reached over and pulled my hand into his.

Callum held my hand a little tighter, his thumb grazing over my knuckles as he looked at me, that playful spark in his eyes softening into something deeper. He took a breath, a smile tugging at the corners of his mouth. "One day," he murmured, giving my hand a squeeze, "I'm gonna put a ring on this finger."

I choked, nearly dropping the keychain as I stared at him. "Hey now," I managed to sputter, my cheeks flushing as I laughed, trying to process the unexpected shift from heartfelt to... engagement-level serious.

He smirked, clearly enjoying the reaction he'd stirred up. "What? I'm serious. You're stuck with me, Hailey," he said, watching me like he was memorizing every reaction. "You think I'd give you a gift like that and not have plans to make it official someday?"

"Oh my god," I groaned, hiding my face in my hands, half-laughing, half-panicking at how real this suddenly felt. "You just—you can't just say that stuff so casually, Callum."

"Why not?" he shrugged, his smile widening as he pried my hands away from my face, pulling me a little closer. "I already know it. I'm gonna marry you. And you're gonna be the mother of my kids, too."

I stared at him, my heart pounding, my voice barely a whisper as I repeated, "Mother of your kids?"

He nodded, looking all too pleased with himself as he leaned back, arms crossed like he was announcing our life plan. "Yep. Enough for a whole soccer team. We'll have the best players around, all with your brain and my moves," he added, waggling his eyebrows.

I gawked at him, laughing despite the surprise. "A whole soccer team? You do realize how many kids that is, right?" I quipped, arching an eyebrow as I tried to play it cool. "Won't you feel bad for my poor vagina if I have to give birth to an entire team?"

It was Callum's turn to choke, his face going bright red as he let out a strangled laugh, eyes wide as if he hadn't expected me to go there. "Well—I mean... yeah, when you put it that way..." he stammered, scratching the back of his head, clearly flustered now. He shook his head, laughing as he rubbed a hand over his face. "Okay, maybe not that many," he conceded, still chuckling, "but a couple of little Callums and Haileys running around doesn't sound too bad, right?"

I giggled, playfully nudging him. "How about we start with, I don't know, one kid? And see how that goes before you start filling out a roster."

Callum leaned in close, grinning down at me. "Fine, fine. One kid. But I'm warning you, you're gonna love them so much, you'll be begging me for a second right away."

"Oh, is that so?" I shot back, narrowing my eyes at him as I shook my head, fighting back a laugh. "I think you're forgetting who'll be doing the actual carrying and delivering here, Mr. Team Captain."

He chuckled, lifting his hands in mock surrender. "Okay, okay, fair point. But you'd still be the best mom," he added, his voice softening, that playful glint replaced with genuine warmth.

"Honestly, I can't imagine doing this whole life thing with anyone else but you."

I felt my heart melt, my gaze meeting his as I soaked in the sincerity of his words. "Me neither. Even though you are kinda cringey sometimes," I whispered, leaning into him, our faces close enough that I could see every little fleck of color in his eyes. "But... I kinda love it."

He grinned, wrapping an arm around my shoulders as he pulled me close. "Good. Because you're stuck with me."

I was. God, I really was.

And there was nowhere else I'd rather be.

Made in the USA
Columbia, SC
05 December 2024

48531098R00416